For more information contact: http://www.saheiden.com/

Book Cover by Getcovers

Interior Images and covers by Etheric Tales

Printed Edges by Painted Wings Publishing

ISBN: (paperback) 979-8-9882709-7-3

ISBN: (hardcover) 979-8-9882709-8-0

THE LUMEN LEGACY SERIES

S.A. HEIDEN

CONTENTS

THE ARCHER'S AMULET

THE ARCHER'S ALCHEMY

THE ARCHER'S ALLEGIANCE

S.A. HEIDEN
THE LUMEN LEGACY SERIES
THE
ARCHER'S
AMULET

*To my husband, Kevin,
who always helps me find my way.*

ONE

The cream-colored envelope shook in her hands; the embossed design on the wedding announcement looked both beautiful and ruinous. Lucy refused to cry. The truth behind the announcement was the one thing she could not accept.

"Oh, Lucy!" her mother exclaimed as she walked through the great wooden door into the room from behind her. "You found the announcements! Aren't they beautiful? I just sent them over to Lord Sloan for his approval." She hastily picked them up to inspect them closer, a smile beneath her red painted lips — her mother was always perfectly poised.

"*His* approval," Lucy mused, disgust lacing her tone. Her hands tensed, threatening to crumple the parchment in anger. Keeping her thoughts to herself was more difficult now than ever before, but of course, as a female in Denora, it was what was expected.

"Of course, dear," her mother replied, placing the announcements down and smoothing the wool blanket upon her bed. "Your wedding will be the largest in Denora this year. Your father wants everything to go as planned, no errors." She looked at Lucy, a bright smile filling her face, hazel eyes alight with excitement.

Lucy couldn't seem to lift her gaze from the wedding announcement. *Her* wedding announcement. Her heart pounded within her chest as she tore through her mind, trying to uncover one final chance to stop all of this from happening before her last desperate gamble forced her into action. The previous weeks of desperately trying to get her father's attention accomplished nothing, and now the proof was in the writing. She would be married to Laurent Sloan, Lord of the Northern Territory, whether she liked it or not.

Her mother, Anita, walked gracefully across the room, her long pale blue dress swaying perfectly in her stride. Madame Baum never had a hair out of place or a dull jewel on her neck. She was the picture perfect Denoran wife: service to the husband first, beauty and appearance second, and nothing after that. It was everything Lucy loathed.

Anita put her hands around her daughter's shoulders and walked her to a nearby stool, perching Lucy in front of a mirror and vanity. She lifted her hands gracefully, and the neatly laid out hairpins rose with them. This was her mother's favorite way to use her magic: to create intricate and beautiful hair designs that displayed elegance and prestige. Her fingers fluttered swiftly as she manipulated Lucy's hair with ease, pinning her hair into an elegant braid. Anita preferred to use her magic to help with common daily tasks. Lucy chose to use her magic only when necessary.

Despite Lucy not using this area of the room, the maids kept it clean. The Baum family was not royalty, but the status of their family due to her father's business made them wealthy enough to indulge in the finer things. They had a beautiful estate on the outskirts of the Capital, far enough away to have privacy yet, the space and ability to entertain. The location was advantageous to her father, allowing him to complete his business transactions with the Central Dukes and the Southern Lord.

Lucy hesitantly looked at her mother in the mirror's reflection, but she may as well have been looking at herself: long, dark curly hair, a small pointed nose, and hazel eyes. The biggest difference between the two was Lucy's freckles — she spent more time out in the sun than her mother and had a face full of freckles to prove it. Some said it made Lucy seem immature, but Lucy scoffed at the idea that something like the appreciation of nature would cause her intelligence to suffer.

"I thought Father said he was going to talk to me about the proposal when he returned from his trip?" Lucy said to her mother in a near whisper.

There was nothing more that Lucy wanted more than to be honest with her mother, and finding the courage to do so was not as easy as she had wished. She couldn't fathom the thought that they had the announcements done without her approval.

Lord Sloan had asked Lucy's father for her hand in marriage, but at no point had anyone asked for her consent. She was a full grown Fae, yet still not allowed to make her own decisions. Her eyes darted around the room, trying to find something to focus on in order to keep the tears at bay. The brass mirror frame. The dark brown brick walls. The pale white curtains, blowing in the wind.

"He left it up to me, honey," Anita replied, cheerfully oblivious to Lucy's emotional turmoil. "They are beautiful, and I think Lord Sloan will love them." She continued to fluff Lucy's hair and lay each dark brown piece into an ornate braid, attempting to tame her voluminous curls. "Just imagine, Lucy. In less than a year's time, you will be known as Lady Lucella Sloan! You will fit so perfectly within the Northern Territory. They will all love you!"

Her mother spoke with excitement, but Lucy's stomach roiled at the thought. She closed her eyes tightly to hide a grimace. She wouldn't allow this to happen to herself. She wouldn't allow her father to send her off to marry a stranger. "Why didn't he wait to talk to me? Doesn't he care about what I think at all?"

"Lucella," she scolded. "Of course your father cares about you. My goodness, at one point, you two were thicker than thieves. You must try to see his side of this." She combed Lucy's hair gently as she spoke, slowing her movements. "He just wants what's best for you.

What is better than the Lady of the Northern Territory? The most you could do here is to find a pleasant lad who could work for your father. Becoming Lady Sloan will open so many doors for you. Imagine the parties you will throw!"

"Excuse me, Mother," Lucy said, turning to face her mother with a smile plastered to her lips. "I think I'll take some time to freshen up before dinner."

"Of course, dear," her mother replied with a sincere smile. Her beauty made Lucy's heart ache, knowing that what she was about to do would hurt her mother. Unfortunately, her time was up, and she was left with no other choice.

Lucy stealthily moved down the dimly lit hall as fast as she could, using her Fae speed and hearing to help her navigate. Her father's office was at the end of the long hallway on the far side of the property, and dodging the manor staff would be a challenge. At the moment, the room was vacant of any potential interruptions to her plans, so there was no time like the present. The room held the precise items Lucy needed to have a successful journey. She needed her bow and quiver, her father's amulet, and to leave as quickly as she had come.

Lucy stopped at the end of a hallway and listened, checking to see if anyone was going to cross her path. In the distance, she heard her two younger brothers playing in the foyer, but if she moved swiftly, they would not notice her presence.

Her father and four older brothers were on their way to the city for a business meeting with the dukes, discussing the next big purchase from the Kingdom. The generational business, held by the Baum males in Lucy's family, was her father's greatest pride. Corvus made sure to respond to every beck and call from any royalty because that meant there was more coin in the coffers. There was always a royal to speak to and more specialty bows to be made. It was to be expected when they were the lead in the industry for over 3,000 years.

The Baum family made bows, quivers and arrows for all the wealthy families in Denora, and had single-handedly provided these custom combat weapons for the entire Denoran army. No battalion in all the realm had sturdier, more powerful, or more accurate archers — and that was all thanks to the unique lumber that only Lucy's family had access to. The most current order of custom bows for Duke Renfro's three sons would bring the Baum Bowyer's a fair amount of money. Lucy hoped that his involvement with the Duke would keep him busy enough to not notice her brief absence.

Duke Renfro was in command of the military for Denora. He had a reputation of immediately enforcing decrees made by the King, even without giving proper notice. For Corvus Baum, having Renfro on his side was sure to reward him one day — beyond the conventional orders of custom weaponry. He was an authority you did not cross, and it paid to stay in his good favor.

Currently, the Baum Bowyers held business in the Central Territory of Denora, where King Tralont's castle sat in the Capital, as well as in the warmer Southern Territory with Lord Isaacs. Only the Northern Territory was hesitant to ally with the Baum Bowyers.

Once, all of Denora was one unified land, but the Addaxe Wars changed the landscape of the realm. Since then, the Northern Territory was as cold to the rest of the realm as the mountains it housed. Lucy pulled her cloak closer to her body at the thought. She quickened her pace in the hallway, the threat of living the rest of her life in the freezing tundra urging her forward.

There were once rumors that Lord Sloan had an arsenal of weapons stockpiled in a hidden reserve in the Leithe Mountains. He was a very secretive man and preferred to be left out of any Denoran politics that didn't affect the North. However, Duke Renfro was insistent on getting Lord Sloan into an alliance with the rest of the territories. By banding with the Baum Bowyers, it would be the perfect opportunity to align the Northern Territory with the rest of Denora.

What better way to merge with the north than to sell off your only daughter, Lucy thought to herself bitterly as she traversed the winding hallways of the manor over to her father's offices.

Her great-grandfather originated the business and kept the family's wealth and status at an all-time high throughout tumultuous periods in the Kingdom since the Addaxe Wars. The business was now her father's primary focus, along with sharing those successes with the rest of the males in her family. Keyword being *male*. Corvus Baum was strong in the ways of Denoran tradition and took every step he felt necessary to keep the company thriving. Though, each year, her father made more and more decisions that she simply could not understand.

His study sat at the end of the narrow hall, providing the most privacy and a separate entrance that led to the outside courtyard near the back of the house. It had an exterior access so her father could hold his business meetings with his most trusted advisors without disturbing the rest of his large family. Lucy had been hoping to use that for a stealthy escape, though with her current appearance, she wasn't sure if she would be as quiet as she had hoped.

It was important to keep up the human facade when she entered the mortal realm of Joterra, so she had a few sets of clothing tucked in a satchel for the trips that she made with her older brother, Wes. She had changed out of her floor-length gown and instead donned a pair of thick, black leggings and a forest green shirt. The clothes were so fitted, they would be deemed entirely inappropriate in her realm, though it didn't help that Lucy was naturally curvaceous in the places that mattered most to males. The delicate belt she wore secured the garments around her slim waist, accentuating her figure even more.

She had exchanged her thin leather-soled shoes for a pair of sturdy boots that laced above the ankle — the kind mortals wore as they traveled through the forests of Joterra. The boots always struck Lucy as too big and cumbersome for walking around in the woods, but clearly humans were less concerned about what they would find in their own woods than what Lucy could potentially run into within the forests that lined the territories of Denora.

In the mortal realm, the biggest scare was always the humans, followed by beasts called bears and mountain lions; although Lucy had yet to meet one of them. Most forests were quiet, with deer traveling with their young, bugs and birds in the air, and an overabundance of rabbits. She never understood why there were always so many rabbits.

Here in Denora, the wooded areas were far more dangerous. In the Leithe Grove, a few miles out of town passing into the Northern Territory, six-legged cat-like creatures, called calynx, roamed the base of the mountains and were larger than a mortal's elephant. In the Nilban Woods near the Baum Estate, the wolven hunt in packs of up to fifty, their eyesight sharper than any creature known, and their nose for blood, which could rival a shark. Luckily, they were nocturnal creatures that prowled in the dark; most Fae could avoid them as long as they steered clear of the woods after dusk.

It was pertinent to walk with a quiet finesse to avoid any attention that could end your life when you roamed these woods. That was the main reason she brought her bow and quiver stocked full of arrows with her when she traveled.

Her bow was made from the special lumber only found in The Elderwood, and stained with a beautiful deep brown finish to blend in with her surroundings when she took it into the woods for practice. The unique material allowed for the bow to be both flexible yet sturdy, lightweight but accurate. Each piece of wood from The Elderwood's forests was imbued with magic, which allowed them to create unparalleled weaponry that promised expert precision. To honor The Elderwood, Lucy carved delicate flowers and leaves in the limbs of her bow. Even the leather quiver and pointed arrows were handmade by Lucy. She would never leave home without them.

However, today there was one more thing she would have to take with her, and Corvus had the one-of-a-kind heirloom safely tucked away in his office.

When she finally arrived at his study, she put a hand on the large wooden door, feeling the humming vibrations of the magic within it. She put her ear close to hear, ensuring that the room was empty. A powerful spell kept his quarters secure from trespassers, and only those who were granted permission could enter without triggering the alarm. The spell included those with Baum ancestry, so the magic recognized her immediately, disarming the spell. She quickly opened the door to the study and slunk inside, quietly closing it behind her.

It was dark and musty, the scent of sawdust and wood lacquer with a hint of tobacco assaulted her senses. She tiptoed the best she could over to the oversized desk built to fit her father's colossal frame: a present from Duke Renfro himself. Hopefully, she could find the amulet quickly and begin her journey.

"It'll only be a second, Gus," her father's second-in-command, Jasper, said from the outside entrance to the office. Lucy's heart jumped in surprise. If she was found in here without her father's permission, there would be terrible consequences. She couldn't afford a mistake this significant, and Jasper would be sure to tell her father of her unexpected presence in his office. He was loyal to her father, but in Lucy's mind there was something about him that felt untrustworthy.

Lucy darted to the shadows and crouched beside a large cabinet in the corner of the room, praying that she would remain out of sight until Jasper left the room. She pulled her long legs close to her body in an effort to make her tall frame less visible, staying as still as possible as the wooden floor creaked beneath her. A sheen of sweat peppered her brow; her curls stuck to her forehead and freckled cheeks.

"I just need my ledger for the meeting, then we can finish," he called over his shoulder toward the open door that supplied the only light in the room. If he had come mere minutes later, he would have seen a light on within the study and known someone was there. He rearranged the papers on his desk on the other side of the study for a moment more and then left the room, securing the door behind him.

Lucy let out a sigh of relief. Maybe she was crazy for trying to pull this off, but what other choice did she truly have? She pushed the unruly hair out of her face and tucked it back into her braid, getting it out of the way so she could attend to the task at hand.

She lifted her hands close to her lips and whispered the old Fae language. A bright ball of light illuminated within her hands and her hazel eyes twinkled with delight. She kept her hands cupped, holding the light and using it to scope around the study, searching desperately for the amulet, trying to keep the glow to a minimum in an effort to not be noticed from the outside.

Her father's amulet was the only key she would be able to get her hands on if she wanted to pass through the gateways to other realms. Most keys were rare, and losing one would come with dire consequences, but Lucy knew she could get in and out of Joterra with no problems. By the time she returned with the lumber for the Duke's bows, her father would finally see her worth in the bowyer industry.

Seeing her ability to travel alone and create such beautiful bows would force him to agree that she was ready to take on a significant role in the family business. He would recognize her worth and refuse to send her away; he would have to call off the arrangement to Lord Sloan. *He'd have to,* she tried to convince herself.

She lifted the orb of light higher, allowing it to hover close to her while she used both hands to search. Most Fae her age could do simple magic, allowing them to accomplish most daily tasks with greater efficiency. Every Fae in Denora was given an opportunity at the appropriate education; whether it was in a schoolhouse or with private tutors.

Lucy grudgingly learned the ways of magic but preferred to put in the hard work, using her hands to create things of substance. Although she had to admit, finding light when there was none was some of the most useful magic she had learned in her courses. She kept up with the tutoring her father had arranged for her until she completed the basics. She appreciated simple spells that could assist her when necessary, but beyond that, she declined further lessons.

Sitting around in a dimly lit room memorizing ancient Fae spells was not how Lucy preferred to spend her time. Besides, Denora's approach to "preparing women for marriage" was less than enticing.

Her sewing course was in place to teach young women to create beautiful gowns, but Lucy used that knowledge to patch holes in her pants when she tore them in the woods. The skill also came in handy when lacing her leather quivers together.

Cooking class was to teach the women how to prepare a pheasant properly. Lucy used it to learn the anatomical parts of the animals so she would know where to aim her arrows when she went hunting.

Her father had no idea of Lucy's true intent while taking these classes, but then again, he also paid very little attention to her, and she used that to her advantage.

Lucy felt a rush of adrenaline as she took in the details of her father's office, her fingers grazing the surface of the furniture. The focal point of the room was his enormous fireplace. The lingering smoky aroma settled deep within the plush seating area. Separating that area with the rest of the space was larger furniture, which cast a deep shadow on the far wall. The display cases against the wall held an array of oils and stains in various colors used for finishing the bows. They left a pungent smell of wood lacquer in the air. A number of cabinets in the center of the room held ledgers and paperwork that Jasper usually oversaw. Jasper's desk was against the wall closest to the outside entrance.

Her father's desk and large wing-backed chair commanded attention at the far end of the room. The dark wood desk held five drawers; two on each side and one across the top. If someone was hiding something, they wouldn't put it in such an obvious place, but Lucy needed to cover all of her bases.

She first opened the drawer on her bottom left. It was filled with documents which she had little interest in scrutinizing. The drawer above that was heavy, but once she pulled it open, she found an assortment of objects within it: a compass, a pouch of candy, blank notepads, and a small red box. Lucy cast her orb of light into her father's lantern upon his desk, then reached for the small velvet wrapped box. The container fit squarely in her palm. She held it close to her ear and shook it gently.

Clunk, clunk, clunk. The heavy item within the box rattled back and forth, making Lucy's heart skip a beat. Could this be what she was looking for? Her hands fumbled as she lifted the lid.

Her eyes set directly on the small silver talisman engraved with her family's insignia hanging from an elegant metal chain. It was about the size of a river rock and easily concealed within the palm of her hand.

This was it. This was the amulet she needed; the key to pass through the gateways into the other realms. More specifically, the only key that would allow passage into The Elderwood.

There was no way to tell with any certainty how prepared it was for travel. It may not have been charged since the last time it was used, but there was no time to waste. She placed the amulet in her bag, removed her bow and quiver from her father's armory, and grabbed her cloak. Who knew what time her father would be back? She needed to get to Abe, and fast.

TWO

A loud crack came from behind Lucy— something was following her through the Nilban Woods. She paused as she pulled her hood down to better hear her surroundings. Her long braid hung down her back, hidden beneath the deep red cloak that kept her warm during the cool night. She had never walked these woods alone before, and night was quickly falling, naturally masking the creatures Lucy knew to be lurking in the shadows.

The air was thick with the scent of damp earth, pine sap, and decaying leaves. She couldn't shake the feeling of being watched, and the weight of her heavy satchel seemed to grow with each movement she made.

As she trudged forward, she could feel the cool air seeping into her bones. The outdoors didn't normally frighten Lucy, but the woods felt as though they were closing in on her; the shadows growing more menacing with every step she took. This would not stop Lucy; she was determined to keep going.

This visit was crucial if she was ever going to convince her father that she was worthy of the title of lead artisan in the family business. Her genuine talent for woodworking was something so deeply ingrained within her, and she could not conceive how her father could just ignore it. Lucy's skill at creating bows outshined her brothers, even with her being 100 years younger. Her bows were exquisite and deadly accurate; a combination that made the royals fall to their knees, begging for more.

Corvus held fast to the idea that one day Lucy would put aside her *hobby* and announce to the world, "I am done with woodworking. Please marry me off to some stranger". But that day would never happen, which was why her father made the decision for her.

If she didn't prove her true worth to her father, his arrangement would go into effect and she would be married. *But why Lord Sloan?* She groaned internally. He was more than 500 years her senior and had overly traditional views. His reputation as Lord in the North was as chilling as the snowcapped mountains where he resided. He was known for being cold and calculating, though beyond the rumors and gossip, no one really had a first-hand account to share.

Unfortunately for Lucy, her father didn't consider Sloan's icy persona in his arrangement, instead focusing on how the merger could aid *him*. Marrying Laurent would be the end of Lucy's personal interests and opinions. She would be a silent figurehead of the Northern Territory. All marriages in Denora were final until death. In Lucy's mind, this arrangement was equivalent to a death bond — irrevocable and unwanted.

Lucy was past the ideal age deemed "desirable" for marriage. She was able to stave off previous arrangements by keeping herself useful to her father creating bow designs.

Corvus once entertained the ideas that Lucy shared with him, but as the years progressed, his focus changed course. It was her idea to carve the Baum Bowyer's sigil in each of the bows, reminding each archer who lifted the weapon that it was a masterpiece unlike any other. Her father jumped at the idea, arrogantly flaunting the promotion of his business. Yet, as time passed, he only wanted her oldest brothers, Hugh and Gregory, to share any business ideas. Once they left, his attention turned to Wes, and has stayed there ever since.

Her mother, Anita, thought nothing of Lucy's involvement with woodworking, thinking it was a phase that would pass. However, now that the youngest Baum males had come of age to hold more responsibility within the business, there was no room left for Lucy. There was nothing else that could prevent the next predetermined steps as an adult female Fae, and her father had made it clear that by her next birthday, she would be married.

Anita never had any opinions about familial decisions, and that's precisely the way her father preferred it. It wasn't that her mother was brainless, she simply held the role of "Denoran Housewife" and followed it definitively. Lucy would sooner self combust than keep her thoughts to herself. But then again, that was a large part of the reason this arrangement existed — Corvus knew that Lucy would be a difficult person to marry off because of her fiery spirit. Lord Sloan accepted the offer because of her foretold beauty, not compatibility; and her father encouraged it due to money, not love.

The mere thought made Lucy cringe. There was nothing wrong with marriage if it was for genuine love, though that happened so infrequently where she lived. Lucy wanted someone who could be her equal. Unfortunately, the majority of marriages in Denora were for power and posturing — not love.

She couldn't marry him. She wouldn't.

This trip would finally prove that Lucy was more valuable to the family than an arranged marriage. Therefore, that was her focus: a successful round trip.The few tasks at hand would be easy for her to accomplish in the next 24 hours. She would need to travel quickly through these woods, get through the portal, head over to Abe's property where the human man kept the entrance to The Elderwood protected, grab supplies and head back home again. With Lucy having the amulet, no one could come after her once she got through the first portal, so time was on her side... if she could make it past step one.

Every crack and rustle in the underbrush made Lucy jump, but she forced herself to keep moving forward. An occasional spiderweb clung to her face, and she swiftly swept it away, shivering at the thought of the creatures crawling upon her.

She was looking forward to seeing Abe and to fulfilling her promise to him. Lucy hadn't seen Abe in months, since her father told her she could no longer go on company trips to The Elderwood. Instead, he ordered that she prepare for her betrothal. It destroyed her.

When she was younger, she was allowed to visit the mortal realm with her family any time the business called for it. Normally, the trips were with her father and older brothers, though Tristan usually chose to stay home instead. While Corvus and her brothers conducted business with Abe's father, Lucy and Abe would run off into the woods and play in his tree house. Lucy smiled at the thought, the memories of her youth feeling so far away.

The first time she met Abe, he was just 10 years old, and she was a young Fae. They slunk off into the woods and hid in Abe's tree fort he had made with his father. They had created it with pieces of wood and old blankets for a touch of comfort. The tree house perched high up in the branches of an old gnarled tree, its thick trunk offering the stability needed to keep the structure aloft. The ladder leading up to the tree house was made of rough wood with knotted roped tied around the rungs for added strength.

Each time she came to his home, Lucy and Abe would spend entire afternoons drinking lemonade and sharing stories in their tiny hideout. Lucy told Abe all about The Elderwood and their friendship blossomed. If either of their fathers had found out, they probably would have been in trouble, but both of the children just yearned for something more. Something special that they could hold on to. It was that special relationship that she was eager for in this dire moment. She couldn't wait to see Abe.

The shoes on her feet were too bulky, and every step seemed like a stomp announcing her location in the forest. Instead of trying to carry everything on her back, she held her bow and quiver strap in one hand and kept her other hand tight around the amulet in her pocket, praying it wouldn't get lost in the dark of the woods. She slung her satchel across her back, and the rough fabric of the strap dug into her shoulder with a pinch.

The only light came from the moon and stars twinkling faintly through the canopy of trees overhead. Her hands shook and her heart raced as she heard the sounds of nocturnal creatures awakening. Lucy knew little about being in the woods alone, but she knew enough to fear the animals that prowled at night. Another snap in the brush made Lucy stop in her tracks, holding her breath as to not make a sound; hoping that whatever was coming her way would pass her by.

Lucy, however, was never that lucky.

A chorus of howls sounded from all around. *The wolven.* Lucy was so distracted by her own personal misfortunes that she didn't think to use her Fae hearing to her advantage, though now that she did, she realized she was surrounded.

Snarls in the distance spun her into action. She retrieved an arrow and nocked it, quickly discarding her quiver in effort to use both of her hands. She took aim at the rustling bushes ahead of her. *Great*, she thought to herself. *I've run from an anguishing life sentence of a forced marriage to Laurent Sloan, only to replace it with an agonizing death by the fangs of the wolven.*

On the range, Lucy had always been an exceptional archer, but the fear and adrenaline that pumped through her veins from the threat of the wolven was nothing she had ever prepared for.

She slowly dropped to one knee, inching her way to the ground, trying to remain silent. She knew she would only get a few good shots in before she had to run back for her quiver. *How could I have been so careless to drop it?* Without her arrows, Lucy would barely stand a chance against the enormous beasts. Her muscles tensed as she took shallow breaths. This was not a roadblock she had expected. Sweat beaded at her brow, but she refused to remove her hands from her bow in fear of the wolven taking her by surprise.

Another snap from the right signaled her to pivot quickly and release the arrow, just as a magnificent silver wolf-like creature came jumping through the brush.

With Fae speed and finesse at her advantage, Lucy rolled back toward her quiver, pulled another arrow, and nocked it into place. She released it straight into the dense leaves to hit another wolven. That quick release allowed her the seconds she needed to run. She snatched her quiver off the ground, pulled it onto her shoulder, and took off sprinting, her blood coursing through her tired limbs, her satchel hitting her back with each stride.

Fallen branches from the surrounding trees littered the ground as she sped off down the path. She assumed she was going in the direction of the mortal entrance, but she couldn't stop to check.

The sound of the wolven's panting breaths and snapping jaws filled the air. Their sharp claws scraped against the ground, kicking up dirt and debris as they ran close behind her. By Lucy's count, there were the two she shot, two on her tail, four on the perimeter, and another few still hidden within the trees. She was thankful for the small pack, though no matter how small, her chances of escape were still slim.

The yips and growls at her back gave her the motivation to move her legs even faster. *Don't look back*, she told herself. Her breath hitched, a sharp pain tearing into her side, reminding her she needed to spend more time strengthening her body. She couldn't spare a second if she wanted to flee from the wolven unharmed, but she needed to check the amulet, as it was her guide to the portal. Her hands were full with the weapons that were keeping her alive. She couldn't find a way to check the amulet without slowing; and slowing down would be the difference between life and death.

With a grunt of frustration, she placed one more arrow into the nock, angled her body to the wolven behind her, and loosed the arrow into the closest creature in sight. Desperate to use the amulet, she threw her entire bow at the line of wolven that were nipping at her back with another guttural roar, causing them to stumble and give her another foot of safety. Now, with her hand free, she could reach for her amulet to determine the distance to the portal.

Lucy dug her hand into her pocket just as a wolven jumped and landed on her back, digging its teeth into her bag, pulling her to the ground.

"No!" she screamed in terror. With the creature upon her, she was pinned as more wolven loomed closer, nipping as they tried to get their share of her.

The heavy beast shook the bag within its teeth as a fierce snarl escaped its massive muzzle. Lucy tried to wiggle her way out from under the wolven, but with no success. More weight pressed down upon her as a sharp pain from her ribcage caused her to scream out. The enormous creature was crushing her slowly. She heard a rib crack, and she forced back a sob.

She couldn't catch her breath and her heart was threatening to beat right out of her chest. In her panic, she fumbled for her quiver, grabbed an arrow, and jabbed it as hard as she could into the creature on her back. Lucy held fast to the arrow and continued stabbing, causing the wolven to whimper and stand down, the metallic scent of blood filling her senses.

Fear surged through her body as it pushed her to keep fighting. She screamed with rage as she stabbed another beast, and then another, until they gave her enough room to wriggle out from the quickly gathering pack, with only her satchel left to defend herself.

A glance at her amulet showed a shining white light beaming from the sigil inscribed upon it, indicating that she was near the portal. Hope filled Lucy as her eyes darted around the nearby trees until she found what she was looking for just to her right.

About seven feet up from the base of the tree, a carved symbol glowed, showing Lucy the way. Lucy ran in desperation as quickly as possible toward the tree with her ribs in agony. She held the amulet out in front of her, urging it to work and provide her passage. If she stayed in this spot longer, she would die.

She bid a silent farewell to her favorite bow, appreciating its power and protection, as she sprinted for the portal, desperate for a barrier between her and the hungry wolven at her heels. She kept the amulet tight in her grasp.

Running full speed into a solid tree felt like insanity for the millisecond that she thought of it, but once she made contact with the rippling sensation of the threshold, relief filled her. It felt as though she was splashing into a cool pool of water on a summer evening. Lucy's world went dark as she passed through the portal. She then became enveloped in a blinding bright light as the gateway pushed her onto the soft grass within the mortal realm. Joterra.

Lucy crawled away from the tree, twisting her body to brace for an attack she wasn't sure would come. As she gripped her ribcage, she saw the gateway through the tree close like a rolling wave, calming to stillness. The light from the symbol etched into the bark began to fade, blending in with the rest of the tree. There would be nothing else following her through.

Breathlessly, she struggled upright, scanning the woods for danger. She stood still, taking in the sounds of the birds chirping and the rustling of leaves as she tried to familiarize herself with her surroundings. While Lucy was free of the wolven, she was left exhausted and weaponless. The taste of adrenaline still lingered on her tongue.

It was much later in Joterra than she had expected. Lucy went from a darkening evening in Denora to another setting sun in this realm. She had to move quickly, so she wouldn't get lost in the unfamiliar, eerie darkness of the woods. Her magic had been depleted, and she was too weak to use it to heal herself. Lucy sprinted again, praying that she was going in the right direction.

THREE

The woods in Joterra were quiet on her journey toward Abe's old wooden house. Lucy was tired from running, but she couldn't slow down. Her green tunic clung to her torso from the blood drawn by the claws of the wolven. The sharp pain in her side reminded her of how close she was to failing with each step she took. *Keep going,* she told herself. She kept looking at her amulet in her muddied hand, knowing that once the sigil glistened with light, she would be nearing the portal.

Abe's property held the ancient tree which housed the gateway to The Elderwood, so the light would be a happy indication she was close to seeing her old friend. She knew the general direction of his house, but kept hoping for the light to arrive to announce that she was almost to her destination.

Time moved differently for each realm she entered. In Denora, two days would equal over a week in the mortal realm. It was one of the reasons why she and the citizens of Denora aged so slowly compared to those on Joterra — that, and Fae genetics were simply different from humans.

Her visits to Joterra were spaced farther and farther apart lately.

She hadn't seen Abe in a Denoran month; nearly five months in human time. Her father had previously allowed her to accompany her brother Wes on his work trips, but that was over now.

Corvus wasn't fond of her continuing with the family business, but that was why Lucy was here. She was going to prove to him he was wrong, and that this was the perfect position for her. Adding her to the Baum Bowyers could lessen the load her father and brothers were taking on creating the bows. Instead, they could focus their efforts on expanding the business through agreements within the realm, not relying on an arranged marriage to fix their potential issues.

Lucy didn't need a relationship, nor did she want one — at least not now. She would not simper and tend to another full grown Fae capable of taking care of himself. She wanted to lead her own life, even if that didn't follow a traditional role in Denora.

Laurent Sloan wouldn't give her the life she wanted. Lucy wanted more for herself, and her father wasn't giving her the opportunity to find it on her own. She believed what she sought was out there somewhere, and she wasn't willing to settle until she found it.

Stealing from her father and leaving without an escort wasn't the best plan she had ever made, but desperate times called for desperate measures. Each sharp inhale reminded her of the foolishness of her decisions, but it also reinforced what was at risk if she failed. *This will work*, she told herself. It would be a quick trip, there and back, before anyone noticed she had left. As soon as Lucy could enter The Elderwood, her amulet would automatically charge under one of the four full moons. Then she could get what she needed and take the trip back home.

The Elderwood was a special place with more magic than any other realm Lucy had ever visited. It had a time all of its own, but she could never fully figure it out. Sometimes when she went into the sacred woods from the mortal realm, she would spend a few short minutes there only to leave and discover hours had passed in Joterra. Other times, she would spend an entire day there, and only an hour or two had passed when she had returned. She and Abe had tried to time it on multiple occasions when her brothers and father were gathering materials in The Elderwood, but the timing was never consistent. Eventually, they gave up and decided that the special realm made its own rules.

Lucy made a vow to herself that she wouldn't spend more than five hours in The Elderwood. She was worried she could become trapped if she wasn't careful. It was such a beautiful but lonely place, and the thought of remaining there alone was unimaginable, so she did her best to follow the rules she made for herself.

Abe had played such a vital part in Lucy's life, especially when traveling between the realms. Abe never treated her differently because she was Fae. Instead, he embraced her differences and tried to learn about them, which allowed Lucy to learn about humans in turn. They spent so much time growing up together — and a decent amount of time getting into trouble together. One of their favorite past times was learning how to curse in each other's languages.

Once they were much older, Abe often talked of his family and always wanted to know more about Lucy's life in their time away from one another. It didn't bother Lucy much that Wes typically pawned her off on Abe. She thought of Abe as a true friend, more than anyone else in Denora.

She was a full-grown female, more than twice Abe's age, yet they treated her as though she needed to be looked after. Even Lucy's family didn't see her for who she really was. Seeing him was going to be the highlight of her trip, a close second being the opportunity to go into The Elderwood again; she could almost feel the soft breeze on her face just thinking about it.

Sweat dripped down her neck and pooled in front of her shirt, the walk was farther than she remembered, and the solitary journey caused an anxious buzz under her skin.

A glance at her amulet stopped Lucy in her tracks. The glowing symbol flickered, identifying that the entrance to The Elderwood was close by. Her heart beat erratically. She had never seen the light flicker like this before. *Was the power wearing thin? Would there be enough power to get through the portal? There has to be enough,* Lucy tried to convince herself.

She knew, as soon as she entered The Elderwood, the amulet would refuel its power. Then she could grab the wood she needed and spend a night catching up with Abe over a bowl of delicious food he called "chill". If all went to plan, she would heal herself, make her way back through the forest in the early morning, and return to Denora before breakfast. However, if the amulet ran out of power before she entered The Elderwood, she would be stuck until the next full moon on the mortal plane.

A full moon was the only thing that could charge the talisman. How long would that be? She quickened her pace, doing her best to ignore the darting pain with each step on the uneven terrain.

Lucy's fear was negated as the back of Abe's weathered house came into view. The two-story aged wood cabin unlocked the jovial memories of her childhood. The property looked more unkempt than usual; the grass overgrown and the garden choked with weeds. Regardless of the change, it still felt like a comforting embrace.

She veered to the east side of the house toward the portal, which lived among a line of trees. In the distance she saw Abe's tree house, long forgotten in his old age. Still, Lucy felt relief wash over her as she made it to his house before the night fell. A smile played at her mouth as she thought of the welcome reunion she'd be getting from her oldest and most treasured friend.

She took the small path between the trees as she walked out toward the front half of Abe's property. When she peeked at her amulet again, it surged with light showing that she was close to the portal, yet the flickering offered the same dire warning. *I need to hurry.*

She froze as she heard a group of male voices coming from the line of trees near the edge of the property where the tree to The Elderwood stood. Lucy hid behind a tree to listen closely to what they were saying while making every attempt to stay out of sight.

The quick movements sent bolts of pain through her body. It was getting harder for her to breathe with her injury.

"This is a great opportunity for you," one man said. He was wearing dark slacks and shiny shoes. He clearly wasn't prepared to be walking around in these woods. "Abe didn't see the potential here that you see," he continued.

"You won't find a better deal than this," the other smartly dressed man said. "You could take the money and never think twice about this old place."

"Listen fellas," a younger man in jeans and t-shirt responded. "I just got here this morning and have a lot of things to go through. When we spoke on the phone and I said I'd be here this week, I didn't realize you were going to be here so soon."

The young stranger ran his hand through his short, dark hair. He was tall and muscular, a bronze glow on his skin drew Lucy's attention. It was a stark contrast to her own pale skin.

Lucy couldn't figure out who he was, or why these people were on Abe's land. She was running out of time to get to the portal, and it was only feet from where the men stood.

"We just want you to get the most out of this deal," the first man replied. "Remember, the J. Pearson Land Developers only have your best interests in mind. Here are the numbers and we can come by with our lawyers to finish up the paperwork tomorrow."

"I'm busy tomorrow," the younger man said flatly, the scar on his chin visible as he turned to the man next to him.

"Well, the day after, then," the second man encouraged. "We cannot sit too long on this deal, or we'd have to draw up a new contract."

Lucy looked around, trying to find the tree she needed in order to enter the next portal. She inched closer to get a better view, finding the tree to The Elderwood. It's glowing sigil had a weak light pulsing from it. *Of course, it's the one tree they are standing directly in front of.* Lucy was thankful the trees between them hid her from view, but there would be no way she could get close enough to the tree without being spotted. Looking at the amulet flickering caused her heart to beat rapidly within her chest. She wasn't sure if she was going to make it before the amulet lost its power.

"Fine. The day after," the young man said as he took the papers in his broad hands and turned his back on the men. He shoved the papers in his back pocket next to a red bandana that hung out. Lucy smirked a bit as she took in his arrogant reply, insulting the men as he turned on them. The view as he walked away wasn't bad either. *Good,* she thought. *Get out of my way.*

"Okay. We will see you in two days' time then," the men called to him as they walked to their vehicle to leave.

As soon as the two men drove away and the young man was out of sight, Lucy sprinted over to the tree with her amulet tightly clenched in her fist. "Please, please," she whispered to herself as she got to the tree.

She put her hands down at her side, closed her eyes, and walked into the portal. But instead of feeling the cooling rush of the passage, she walked face first into hard tree bark. Her forehead stung from the rough edges, and she backed up with a hand to her head.

"No," she said to herself in disbelief. "No, no, no." Lucy reached out with her hand and touched the solid tree — her breathing hitched. Using both hands, she frantically patted every inch of the coarse tree trunk, scraping her skin, hoping she would find a way in.

When she looked back down to her amulet, her heart sank. Her biggest fear had actually happened. The sigil was dark, no glimmer of light to be found on neither the tree nor the amulet. She missed her window to enter the portal, and now she was stuck in the mortal realm until she could reactivate the amulet.

What have I done? How would this prove anything to her father? It would prove that she was nothing more than a useless female playing a male's game, unable to accomplish the simple tasks put in front of her. She kicked at the dirt at the base of the tree in frustration, launching the dry soil toward the greenery around her. Each mistake put her one step closer to being Lady Lucella Sloan, and it was the one thing she just couldn't bear.

Lucy threw down her satchel as she paced back and forth behind the trees. She continued kicking at the ground and muttering to herself about how she needed to take up Joterran astronomy when a voice caught her by surprise.

"What are you doing here?" the deep voice asked.

Lucy jumped, clearly surprised, and stared at the attractive stranger — the younger man from before. His strong jaw tensed in suspicion seeing another unwelcome visitor on the property. He was much more handsome up close. Warm caramel skin covered his narrow nose and high cheekbones, his dark eyebrows furrowed defensively.

"I'm here to see Abe," Lucy said pointedly. She grabbed her satchel and stalked toward the house, pushing right past the man. Her fingertips brushed the fabric of his shirt and she couldn't help but note the firm, taut muscles. The contact sent a tingle of electricity down her spine. She pushed that thought aside; she didn't have time to analyze what that meant. What she needed was to see her friend and make a plan out of this miserable trouble she had gotten herself into.

His eyebrows flew up. "Excuse me? Who are you?" he demanded of her, following Lucy as she walked toward the house.

"He knows me," Lucy replied firmly. Abe was the only person she could rely on. She needed him to plan out her time until the next full moon. Hopefully, it was in a day or so. She had never spent more than 24 mortal hours in Joterra, and the idea of it put her on edge. What a colossal mistake this was becoming.

"Yeah, well, he can't speak for you right now," he said, catching up to her, his deep voice carrying.

"Why not?" She spun on him with a look. "Where is he? Is he okay?" She started walking into his personal space, pointing her finger at him. "What happened?" She had never fought a human before, but she definitely wasn't above it.

"Slow down there, killer," he said with his hands up, retreating. He looked her over with interest, eyeing her tight leggings and torn blouse. His expression softened, and she realized he was not an immediate threat. If anything, he was the one who held the answers she needed. When she took a step back, he put his hands down. "Abe's gone."

"Where is he? When will he return?"

"He died last week," he told her, no emotion filling his reply. He straightened his posture and crossed his arms, withholding any additional words.

Her mouth popped open in surprise, realization filling her. The men were the same land developers who tried to get Abe to sell his property all those times before. She thought he had scared them off last year when they came knocking at his door; she remembered how he laughed as he told Lucy the story of how he brought out his unloaded shotgun and pretended to be crazy so that they wouldn't think twice about returning. No wonder they were back. They had fresh meat to try to convince.

Her poor friend. How could she have lost the one person who truly saw her for who she was? A thousand questions rattled in her mind as she struggled to come to terms with what was happening and what it meant for her. What would happen to his land now? To the portal? The grief tore through her heart like an arrow to the chest, but she couldn't risk breaking in front of this stranger. *Focus, Lucy,* she told herself, digging deep for some strength.

She analyzed his face more closely, looking for the similarities to Abe, wondering how they were connected. His tan complexion seemed so different from Abe's, yet his brown eyes hinted at the man she had called family for so many years. "You're related to him? Here to deal with the estate?"

Those brown eyes turned to steel. "Yeah, I'm here to deal with the estate." He looked her up and down, taking in her large bag over her shoulders and her disheveled appearance. "What did you want with Abe?"

Lucy realized why he was looking at her with such scrutiny and she tried to flatten her hair that had fell out of its long braid. The tussle with the wolven left her a little worse for wear. Dirt was smudged on her face and her hands were left scratched and bruised from the attack.

"I visit him every so often." She bent over and dusted off her pants with a groan of pain, forgetting her ribs were in such awful shape. She began looking around, trying to come up with an excuse for why she'd stay with him that wouldn't expose her actual mission. "And I helped him maintain his house," she lied. "I mean, he was getting old after all." Her words felt implausible as they left her lips.

"He was like 66," he replied, unconvinced. "Are you okay? No offense, but you look like shit. Did you *walk* here?" He looked around for a vehicle that she should have arrived in. "It's nearly 20 miles to the nearest town."

"Yeah, well, he liked the company. He's an old family friend," she stated, and that part wasn't a lie. "But yes, I walked. I was... camping." She wasn't entirely sure she was using the term "camping" correctly, but she wasn't sure what else she could say at that point. Clearly she could not immediately admit she was a Fae bowyer from another realm in a desperate attempt to flee an arranged marriage, could she?

"Then you'd know him better than me," he said as he turned around and started to walk into the house, his fitted shirt clinging to his muscular torso. "But, since he isn't around, feel free to leave." He sent a wave behind his back and closed the screen door behind him, letting it bang shut in her face.

Lucy scowled at his back, pulling the door open and walking into the house as he turned to look at her. "We had an agreement. I help him out and he lets me stay here." She held her hand to her ribs, the discomfort increasing.

"Not my problem," he stated, folding his arms across his chest once again, looking tough, but his eyes betrayed him. He looked her over, his eyes stopping on her arm wrapped around her injury. "Do you want me to call you a ride?"

"Look," Lucy said, moving past the broad-shouldered man into the kitchen. She winced in pain. "His calendar." She quickly placed her hand on today's date and willed the word 'Lucy' to appear as a scribbled note. It was only a quick illusion with her magic that wouldn't last more than a few minutes, but hopefully it would be enough. "My name on today — *Lucy*. He was expecting me and I have nowhere else to go. I won't even be in your way. I'll tidy up outside and then, when I've finished, I'll leave."

The man was clearly not used to people talking to him in such a brazen way, and he was close to fed up of the girl who barged into his life with no invitation. "Listen, *Lucy*," he said in annoyance, his full lips set in a grim line. "I don't need any help around here. I've got it covered. I'll even do you a favor," he said as he reached his hands into his jean pockets. He lifted the keys to his vehicle and jingled them in the air. "I'll give you a lift into town, and we can pretend this never happened."

The car, she thought to herself in a panic. She took an unsteady breath. "Please, let me help. Can we start over? I'm Lucy." She held out her hand in offering and spread a wide smile on her face, begging the stars to convince him to let her stay.

"I'm Micah," he said after a moment as he embraced her hand in a firm shake. Then he turned away from Lucy and walked out of the front door. "Car is this way."

Without a second of hesitation, Lucy closed her eyes and mustered all of the magic within her veins. She focused the spell within her mind, brought her fingertips together, and whispered the ancient Fae language to create a surge of power in the center of the vehicle. Her hazel eyes flicked open as she sent the bolt of energy, imploring the magic to find its way to the right spot.

Micah was already in the car using his keys when Lucy heard the engine start and then dramatically stop. Micah tried restarting the car a few times, to no avail.

Appreciation that Lucy had never felt toward her magic flooded her, and she swore to never take her Fae blood for granted again. *Mother was right,* she thought to herself incredulously. *The ancient magics taught to the young Fae were immeasurably helpful in times of need.*

Extreme fatigue began to build throughout Lucy, starting with a throbbing headache and the incessant urge to lie down. That small act of magic took more out of her than she was willing to admit, but she couldn't let this stranger see how vulnerable she truly was.

"Sorry, my car isn't working," Micah said with a frustrated sigh as he came back to the house. "I'll fix it up first thing in the morning and I can drive you to town."

"It's really no problem," Lucy replied with a feigned smile. "I am happy to help out here." She did her best to keep the desperation out of her voice, but wasn't sure if she was successful.

"I'm really not sure how you can help. I'm going to pack this place up and get out of here as soon as I can. I've got 'til the end of the week."

"You can't seriously be thinking of selling, are you?" Lucy demanded, forgetting that she was trying to be polite. "This house has been in this family for generations. You're just going to throw that away? Abe wouldn't want that." She stood with a scowl on her face, refusing to allow yet another thing to get in the way of her plan.

"Abe isn't here to decide, now is he?" Micah snapped back at her. "I don't care about this old, empty house." He looked around the room in contempt, seeing garbage and not the memories made by Abe.

"How do you even know Abe, anyway? Shouldn't someone who truly knows him be the one in charge of his estate?" Lucy challenged, not willing to back down from this argument. She stood firm with her arm crossed in front of her, holding her ribs, staring him down with an accusing glare.

If Micah sold this property, it was only time until they cut the trees down to make way for new development. If that one particular tree was ever cut down, the portal would be closed forever and there would be no other way to get into The Elderwood. *Shit*, Lucy realized. *This cannot be happening.*

"I do know him," Micah said, looking at her. "He was my grandfather."

A loud boom of thunder crashed in the distance, signaling a storm quickly making its way over the flat land. Micah looked through the kitchen window to the sky, observing the dark clouds that warned of rain. "Listen, the weather is going to hell, and it doesn't look like you have a car — though, I still have no idea how you made it out here. So I'll give you a room to sleep in and we can talk in the morning."

Lucy let out a huff of breath, then flinched at the pain it brought. She pursed her lips, but gave a curt nod of her head in agreement. She needed a place to stay, and maybe this house would have more answers for her — like how in all the realms she was going to save it from being sold.

"I usually stay in one of the rooms at the top of the stairs," Lucy said as she began walking up the steps. Before Micah could respond, she tripped on the stair and cried out as pain lanced through her side.

In an instant, Micah was there at her side, holding her elbow and hip gently, helping her up. "You're hurt?" he asked in surprise.

His rough exterior faded as he sprung into action to help Lucy. "I'm sure he's got a first aid kit here somewhere," he looked around, still holding her with his warm, rough hands. "Come on, sit down in here and we'll get you cleaned up." He brought her over to the main floor bathroom, sat her on the closed seat of the toilet, then went to find the supplies.

Lucy held her head in her hands, completely embarrassed by her present situation. The pain in her side was making her dizzy, but she didn't know this man. She couldn't show weakness in front of him; she wasn't in the right physical state to defend herself. The small bathroom was adorned in old floral wallpaper, yellowed with age. It seemed that it had not changed since the first time she visited the house so many years ago.

Micah returned to the bathroom with a brown bottle, a clean cloth, and a small red box. "Where are you hurt?" He asked her kindly, looking her over with warm sympathy.

The look in his eyes caused a flutter of anticipation to fill Lucy's stomach. He was much more handsome when he wasn't so guarded. His skin was nearly flawless, barring the large scar on his chin. She kept staring at him, taking in his chiseled jaw and perfect lips. Micah cleared his throat, bringing her back to reality.

"Oh," Lucy said, fighting the blush crawling up her neck. "My ribs." She admitted. "I'm okay, I can handle it." She first took off her thin belt and then went to grab the cloth and supplies from Micah, but he pulled away gently and shook his head.

"Please, let me help," he breathed. "This isn't my first rodeo fixing up some cuts and bruises." In her hesitation, he added, "I won't hurt you." His dark brown eyes seared into hers, compelling her to yield.

She kept her eyes focused on him, carefully lifting her shirt to reveal her injury to him. The blue and purple bruises stretched from the bottom of her ribs to the edge of her undergarment that covered her chest. There was a smattering of cuts and scratches along her side that bled slightly.

Micah deftly cleaned the wounds, his touch light as a feather. Lucy's body had never been touched by a man before, and she had never shown her bare body to anyone. Her skin pebbled and her heart jumped at the heat of his fingers on her cool skin. When he got up near the lace to her undergarment, he looked at her questioningly. "May I?"

All Lucy could do was nod her consent, too afraid that her voice would crack from the nerves raging war inside of her. He carefully lifted the lace near the curve of her breast and cleaned the wound there, glancing between her abrasions and her eyes, which were glued upon him. More pink rushed to her face as his hand brushed her curves.

Micah carefully put a bandage on her lacerations and pulled her shirt back into position. "There," he said with a small smile, revealing a dimple in his left cheek. "All done."

"Thank you," Lucy whispered, embarrassed but appreciative, still entranced by that dimple.

She had never had anyone touch her with such tenderness. Any injuries she had were brought to the healers, and they simply sent healing magic to whatever ailment she had at the time. There was no care and gentleness, no intimacy — everything with the healers was a business transaction. *Such as the way of Fae*, she thought to herself.

"How did that happen?" Micah asked her, worry furrowing his brow. "Are you in trouble? Is there someone you'd like to call?"

"Tripped," she lied, a half smile on her lips, no longer able to keep his gaze. The protective look from Micah made Lucy feel uncomfortable. She was not used to having others come to her aid.

He nodded again and disappointment painted his face. She was clearly not being honest. Though could he blame her? They were strangers. "Well, you can finish cleaning up in the upstairs bath-room. We can talk later, okay?"

Lucy gave a half-hearted smile and stood to walk back up the stairs. This time, she was careful to brace herself and use the railing for support. She paused on the staircase. "Thank you for helping me," she said to him without looking back. Then she continued to the room at the top of the stairs.

The kindness that Micah had given her at that moment was foreign to her. Whenever she had come home from a particularly rough day in the woods doing her own training, her father would have just sent her to the Fae medic to relieve her of her pain and injuries. It never mattered to the males in Lucy's life that she was hurt, only that someone else could fix the problem. But in the moment with Micah, he took care of her. Lucy's heart leapt at the thought, but that lightness didn't last for long.

Lucy's problems seemed to grow by the minute. She was now stranded in Joterra with no allies, no weapon, and now she needed to find a way to convince a mortal man to save a gateway he knew nothing about. Her day just kept getting worse.

WALKING through the house without Abe felt like tiptoeing through a sacred place. She didn't want to disturb anything within the house. It felt surreal that Abe was no longer around. She had never known someone so young who had died before.

After washing up all she wanted to do was lie down, but she had things that needed to be done. Lucy went to the main floor to sneak another peek at the calendar to find the lunar cycles and officially write her name now that the illusion was sure to be gone.

Abe always kept track of the lunar phases for gateway emergencies, so she knew she could calculate the time she needed to stay at this house until she could leave. Best case scenario? It would be tonight. Worse case scenario? It would be a month. She prayed it wasn't a month.

"Hello?" Lucy called as she walked through the main floor. She peeked in each room, looking for Micah while also scouting for anything that could help her last in Joterra until the full moon arrived. The rain splattered against the roof of the old wood house, creating a chorus of rhythmic tapping.

"In here," Micah's deep voice called out. He was kneeling on the ground, packing up old pictures into a cardboard box. The pictures had seen better days — the material not standing up to the tests of time. And to Lucy's guess, there wasn't much done to protect the pictures from the weather in this part of the mortal realm.

The summer days got very hot and the winter nights got very cold. It was amazing to see such diverse weather in such a short period of time. It was all so different from her realm. In Denora, the seasons stayed the same for many months at a time, and still the weather was never quite as extreme as Joterra with their highest of highs and lowest of lows.

"You said Abe was your grandfather, right?" Lucy asked as she walked over and sat on the battered leather couch next to where Micah kneeled on the floor.

"Yep."

"Was your mother or your father his child?" Lucy asked. She knew that Abe had a daughter, but she felt the need to test Micah to ensure he was telling the truth.

"My mom," he said. He reached into the box and held up a picture of her and Abe for Lucy to see. While Micah had dark hair with broad shoulders, his mother seemed more narrow, with long, light, wavy hair. She looked much more like Abe, who was tall with a thin frame, hair peppered with white on top of his head. "Vanessa."

"She's beautiful," Lucy replied with a smile. "You look more like your father then, I'd presume?"

"Yeah." He shoved the picture into the box. "Was raised by him, too."

"Were your parents not together?" Lucy asked, confused. Lucy's mother was not the nurturing type, but she was still always around. It was incredibly rare for only one parent to raise a child. *Unless...* she thought. *Unless his mother had died?*

"We will talk more about this arrangement in the morning," Micah said to her, changing the topic. "Don't get comfortable." His dismissal of her was obvious, a coldness creeping into his tone. His kindness from earlier was gone. Lucy noted the sudden change.

Lucy stood up and walked to the back of the house to the kitchen, not wanting to give Micah a reason to change his mind about her staying there for the night. She slunk over to the calendar hanging on the wall and jotted her name to match Abe's script.

How long had it been since she had seen her friend? Did anyone visit him in the meantime? Was he all alone when he died? The thoughts made her stomach coil. Anger filled the empty spaces within her heart. Her friend was gone, and she never even got to say goodbye.

That was the blessing and curse of a mortal life. A blessing because you live a full life, knowing you didn't have many days until your end. But a curse, as the days go by so quickly, sometimes you forget to live at all.

Lucy flipped the pages back to the last few months when Abe had been keeping track of the lunar cycles. Grief pierced her heart when she saw his written script on the paper, a fading reminder of the man who was once so full of life. Her fingers lingered on those letters written in pen for a moment more, tears threatening to make an appearance. She took a deep breath, steadying herself.

"Here," she whispered as she found the last full moon he had recorded, clearing the fog of grief that blanketed her mind. She slowly did the math, cursing herself for not being better prepared in case of emergencies like this, and tracked back to her current date. The next full moon was three more nights away. She needed to last three full days with this handsome, yet unexpected, mortal before she could find her way home.

CHAPTER

FOUR

Lucy's first night with Micah was quiet. She lay in the small bed, tangled in blankets from a restless night tossing and turning. The birds in the trees chirped loudly, the sound as bright as the sun gleaming through the window. *Get up*, she told herself, but she was more tired than she wanted to admit.

Rejuvenating her magic took a lot out of her, so she remained in bed, looking around the pale pink bedroom. Cardboard boxes were stacked against the wall, and a large wooden dresser stood empty, covered in a light layer of dust.

A loud click followed by the creak of the door jolted Lucy into a seated position in the bed. Micah walked directly into the bedroom she was sleeping in without so much as a knock.

"Do you mind?" Lucy yelled at him as she tried to cover her body with the crumpled blanket that laid around her. She did not have many extra clothes and just slept in her undergarments, not once assuming she would have this strange man barging in on her.

"Why are you in here?" Micah asked, his tone flat. His mouth turned down as he looked around the room, ignoring her complaint. He looked lost.

"I told you, this is the room I always use. Why are you barging in here when I'm sleeping? Get out," she snapped.

"You aren't supposed to be in here," he replied, still unsettled to have found her there. His face was emotionless and his eyes were unblinking as he surveyed room, taking deep steadying breaths .

"Well, I am, and I'm half naked." Lucy stood angrily, throwing the blankets to the floor. "Get. Out." She pointed toward the door, not caring that she barely had any clothes on. Backing down now would give Micah the idea that she was an easy target, and regardless of her current vulnerable state, she was anything but meek.

Micah's eyes finally snapped from his glance around the room to Lucy, taking in the fact that she really was half dressed. Her long, sculpted legs were bare, the thin lacy undergarments accentuated her curvy hips and full breasts. He quickly averted his eyes to the ground and headed to the door, closing it behind him.

What the hell was that about? Lucy thought to herself as she pulled a clean tunic and pair of leggings on and dragged her hair off of her back into a loose braid. She wasn't about to let some man try to boss her around. *I should have locked the damn door,* she thought as she angrily shoved her things into her satchel.

What am I even doing here? She sat on the bed with a flop and covered her face with her hands. *How many more mistakes am I going to make?* Lucy was so unsure of her place there without Abe to guide her. She needed a plan to get her through the next few days.

She finished getting dressed and stomped out of the room, only to run into Micah as he stood in the hallway, directly across from her door.

"Do you want to tell me what the hell that was about?" She challenged him with fire in her words. "I won't have you thinking you can push your way into any room that I'm in simply because Abe was your grandfather. He would have *never* done that to me and I shouldn't have just assumed you wouldn't have either. But do it again and I'll knock you on your ass."

Micah's gaze was on the floor as she spoke. "It was my mother's room," Micah said in a hushed tone, his face devoid of emotion. He looked past her into the room, not acknowledging the threat Lucy made.

Lucy wasn't sure how to respond. Didn't he know she was going to be in that room? Hadn't she said it? Abe always had her sleep in that room if her family was there overnight. Why would Abe put her in this room if it was so important to him?

"I'm sorry," Lucy replied, a shade calmer. "But that was still completely uncalled for."

"I didn't realize you were in there," Micah said, finally looking at her. He gave a small shake of his head, "honest." Sorrow and guilt filled his eyes, but Lucy wasn't sure who those emotions were for.

They held each other's gaze until Lucy believed him. She nodded, and he looked back into the room.

"I have to go through the boxes in her room. You can keep your things in it for now, but I'm going to be in there for a while today." His voice was quiet. Reverent.

"It's fine," Lucy said. "I'll grab my stuff and find somewhere else to go. Take your time."

She grabbed her satchel and cloak and walked outside to the front of the house. The sun was up and she needed to figure out how she was going to get through these next few days until the full moon.

Lucy laid out her cloak and sat in the grass, allowing the sun to warm her face as she looked up to the sky and took a deep breath, trying to center herself. *I can do this,* she told herself. *I just need to make a plan.* She opened her satchel to take stock of her remaining supplies — ignoring the dried on mud and blood from the previous night.

Half of the sweets she stole from her father's desk were gone. She ate them all for dinner in an attempt to avoid Micah and had the stomach ache to prove it. That ache reminded her of childhood days in her family home, stealing sweets from her father with her younger brothers. A twinge of sadness filled her. When would she see her brothers again? She pushed the feelings aside knowing she had bigger things to accomplish before she could see them again. She dug her hand into her bag to take out the remaining items: her last clean clothes were one pair of socks and an additional shirt.

Lucy piled her dirty clothes off to the side to clean later in some fresh water as she inspected her amulet. A weight was lifted from her chest when she saw that it didn't break in the scuffle with the wolven, but that relief was short-lived as she remembered the loss of her bow. Leaving herself so unprotected was not like her, and Micah barging into the room was just more ammunition for her father to reiterate that she had no place in the mortal world and needed a strong Fae husband to protect her.

'You are a female,' he loved to remind her. 'Your place is at home with your husband, Lucella, not traipsing through the woods like a child.' It didn't matter to her father that he was the one who taught her these woodworking skills — he was the one that taught her to love the craft.

It also didn't matter to him that she was the best bowyer in all of Denora, her father hated every moment of her leaving home. The only reason he ever allowed her to come to Joterra these past years was because he was busy establishing her older brothers, Hugh and Gregory, as the lead in the Southern Territory.

This worked out for Lucy because, while her father was busy in the south, her brother Wes didn't mind her accompanying him. Besides, the only other sibling who would have been allowed to come was her brother Tristan, and he was not interested in the slightest. He spent his time developing his combat magic with his friends, who were all soldiers in Denora.

Even back then, Lucy knew it wouldn't last forever. Her father, Corvus, told her it was just to keep her busy until she was old enough to be courted. She knew as soon as her younger brother Simon came of age, she would no longer accompany them on these trips. And just like that, she was stuck at home, longing for freedom.

She craved the independence she was given here in Joterra to be her own person with no one around to cast judgment. So often Lucy wondered how she could bring that same feeling back with her to Denora.

She set to work clearing the front of the house of garbage and debris, then began weeding the garden. It was slow labor with her injury, but her Fae blood was already speeding up the healing process. Since she was weakened, the healing magic wasn't coming to her as easily as it would in a Fae realm. If she could tidy up around here, maybe Micah wouldn't put up as much of a fuss about letting her stay until she could reopen the portal.

Once she was done with the garden, she again took notice of the thinning greenery in the forest. She wiped her brow on the back of her arm and started the trek into the woods to see what had changed since she had last been here.

Her pace was slow as to not agitate her bandages under her shirt. Walking through this side of the wooded acres of Abe's land was something she had not done in a very long time. When Abe was a boy, Lucy came with her father on every trip to Joterra. She and Abe were inseparable — they spent endless hours joyfully running through the woods together and telling stories in the tree house. Then, her father enacted his first embargo on her coming along. He believed Lucy's focus needed to remain on her studies and future courtship to produce an advantageous marriage agreement.

Lucy had not been able to be with her friend and consequently missed out on significant events in his life. She had missed seeing him become a man. She wasn't there for the death of his father. She missed seeing him fall in love and raise a family. Her absence shadowed all of the joys and sorrows that come along with living a full life. More than 30 mortal years had passed before Lucy was reunited with her friend when Wes finally allowed her to accompany him on his work trips, much to her father's dismay.

There was green forest for miles back then, but the woods felt different today. They sounded different. Where there should have been the buzzing sounds of life, it was quiet. As if the animals up and left, knowing it was no longer safe.

She walked toward the edge of the property that blended into the rest of the woods, the view absolutely astonished her. Where there was once flourishing landscape for miles around, was instead newly cleared land. The lush greens and browns of the forest were gone. Forgotten. All that remained was dirt and mulched stumps in the ground; plowed land prepared for planting season.

Why would they ruin their dense forests like this? Lucy thought to herself. *Where would the animals who relied upon the sanctuary of the forest go?* The wooded area on the other side of Abe's property stretched for miles. Abe had explained to her once that the human government protected the majority of the forest. But what would happen if those were to be developed as well?

Lucy walked back with a heavy heart, unsure of how to process the loss of land. She took her time to bask in the beautiful grove of trees that remained. It was even more vital that Micah protected the estate now. If he were to give up the property, it was certain to be flattened by the end of the year.

What would her family do if they could no longer enter The Elderwood to get the lumber they needed for their bows? Leaving without securing the future of The Elderwood would do more than end the Baum Bowyers — it would bring shame to her whole family name. Her father's anger would overrule any explanation of why Lucy left with the amulet and there would be no talking him out of the marriage.

As Lucy approached the house again, her body was filled with restless energy; uncertainty taking root and needing an outlet. She went straight for the weathered shed and took the axe to cut more wood for a fire.

In Denora, when she felt this way, she would normally take her bow and arrows and spend time in the forest in the company of its small, woodland creatures, practicing her aim. Unfortunately, her archery supplies were not available, so she had to release her pent-up frustrations in another way. She left the axe next to the chopping block and walked over to the leftover pile of tree stumps that Abe would sometimes chop in his younger days.

By the time Lucy heard footsteps approaching, a small pile of split logs surrounded the stump — evidence of her labor.

"I have something for you," Micah called to her as he walked over from the front door. She felt unsettled by his ever-changing moods and the deepness of his eyes that could distract her so easily. Lucy wasn't sure what tore at her nerves more, but she was thankful to have the axe nearby to steady herself with the potential to use if needed.

She heaved up the chunk of wood onto the chopping block and looked over at Micah as he held out a piece of paper.

"You know, I can do that for you if you need help," Micah said to her. His offer caused her lips to twitch up into a smirk.

She picked up the axe with two hands, swung it into the air above her head and let it come crashing down on the wood, completely cutting it in half with one fell swoop. She grinned from ear to ear when the wound on her body barely ached. Her appreciation of her Fae blood surprised her for the second time.

"Whoa," Micah said, staring at her. "I guess you don't need my help. How are your ribs?" Lucy was used to males telling her what to do, but this was not about control for Micah. He was looking out for her and putting her safety at the heart of the suggestion. The entire interaction confused her.

In response, she gave him a knowing look. With a mischievous glint in her eye, she repeated the action, successfully chopping another piece of wood.

His mouth hung agape as he tried to figure her out. He looked around the yard, his brows raised as he viewed the progress she had made. "You cleaned this place up pretty good. How long are you planning on sticking around?"

"Does that mean I get to stay?" Lucy asked, trying her best to hide the hope in her voice, resting the axe on her shoulder.

"You aren't really in my way and I'd be a fool to turn down free help," he said as he dragged his hand through his short hair. "You know, I'm sorry about earlier." He looked down at his feet, before finding the courage to look her in the eye. "I swear, I wasn't trying anything."

Lucy responded with a nod, cautiously accepting his apology.

He looked down at the piece of paper in his hands, and then back at her. Micah shook his head, almost to himself, as he lifted the paper to her again, an eyebrow raised in question. "Here," he repeated. "This, I think, belongs to you. I found it in Abe's old things."

Lucy placed the axe down and wiped her hands on her leggings as she reached for the paper. It wasn't just any old paper, though. It was a photograph of Abe and Lucy, from over 10 years ago.

"Oh," she was unsure of what to say. "Thanks." She couldn't admit to Micah that this was her, because otherwise how would she explain her body (which looked no older than 25) being in the same picture from more than a decade ago?

If she were human, she should have looked as if she were a teen — and his grandfather was clearly a younger man in this photograph.

"Is that you in the picture?" He asked, suspicion lacing his tone. He took a step toward her to look at the picture again. He side-stepped toward her awkwardly in his jeans that were covered in dust from his work within the house.

"Don't be silly," Lucy replied stiffly. "That picture is what, 10? 20 years old?" She feigned disinterest, but her heartbeat told another story as it pounded within her chest.

"Who is in the picture, then?" He asked, looking between the photograph and Lucy's face once more, scrutinizing the likeness between the two; disbelief transparent on his face.

Lucy pretended to peek back at the photograph as if she didn't get a clear enough view, but she knew very well when this photograph was taken. She remembered the day and made Abe promise not to share the photograph with others in an effort to keep her secret. Humans couldn't know about the Fae realms, or that she aged much slower than them. Lucy herself was mortal in her own way, but she would live to see a few thousand years if she was lucky, and that was pretty close to immortality for humans. It was too much for them to fathom.

"That's my sister," Lucy lied seamlessly. "I told you, family friends." She carefully took the picture and put it in her bag, her heart filling with love for her friend. She would cherish that picture for the rest of her life.

"You both look a lot alike," Micah stated, staring at Lucy with uncertainty.

"We get that all the time," she said with a strained grin. "Can you move this wood over to the side?" She pointed to the pile of logs and went to get another larger piece of wood to split, happy to not have Micah analyze her face a moment more. The heavy log bit into the palms of her hands as she heaved the piece onto the chopping block.

Again, she lifted the axe above her head with two hands and swung down hard on the log below her, splitting it in two.

Micah blew out an impressed whistle. "I can honestly say I've never seen a girl do that." He chuckled and looked at Lucy and her axe, appreciating the view in front of him.

Splitting wood was a necessary part to creating bows, so she didn't find the task difficult, nor a chore. There was actually not one part of creating bows for the archers that she found less than magnificent.

Her father had taught her and her brothers the trade from a very early age. Chopping the wood, finding the right size pieces for woodworking, shaping the bow with finesse, whittling the perfect arrows, promising perfection. Each part of the process took time and heart, and Lucy truly gave it her all. Her father loved being a bowyer as much as she did, and it was that love for the craft that connected them. It was the one thing that they could find common ground about, and it was what allowed Lucy to make the bows at all. The memory stung now that so much had changed.

"Me either, if I'm being honest," she shared with him. "My father taught me everything he knows about woodworking. Most females aren't interested in such... hobbies." She wasn't sure enough of Joterran careers for her to say she was a professional woodworker that specialized in weaponry, so she tried to keep that part to herself.

"So your dad is cool, then?" Micah joked.

"Oh, no, definitely not," she replied with a snort. She remembered Abe teaching her the word 'cool' when they were young, and *cool* was not a word to describe Corvus Baum. "This right here?" She lifted the chunk of wood. "This is the only way we relate to one another." She threw the piece onto the ground, then kicked it with her shoe. "For the most part, I don't exist other than to bother him, unless we are doing this together," she waved her hand at the wood around her. "But that happened less and less each year, and now it doesn't happen at all. So, there isn't much we talk about these days."

"Yeah," Micah replied. "I've got a dad like that," he began. "But for that conversation, we are going to need a drink. Want one? Now that I know you're a real person who Abe knew, you don't seem nearly as odd as before."

Lucy looked to the sky. The sun had moved further across the horizon, signaling that evening was soon to come. "Sure," she said, agreeing. "May as well. I'll go ahead and start the fire. You can fetch the drinks. And some food if you have any? I'm starving."

"You know," Micah said, looking at Lucy with a surprised smile etched across his face. "I don't think I've ever been on the 'drink fetching' side of a conversation when there was another side that comprised of 'starting a fire'. You may be bad for my manly pride."

"That's probably a good thing," Lucy said with a raised eyebrow and a twinkle in her eye. "Your pride is in desperate need of shrinking." She winked and then grabbed some wood and walked over to the fire pit, before fetching her flint and steel from her bag to start the fire.

Micah came back with a couple of sandwiches balanced on a stack of blankets and a few bottles of human alcohol. Abe had called it "beer" once before, which was basically the same thing as her ale back home — though, definitely more watered down. Lucy had the fire crackling and rolled over some more tree stumps for her and Micah to sit upon.

"Thank you," Lucy said to Micah as he sat down near her, handing her the food.

"Nothing like an ice cold beer after a long day of work," Micah replied, looking toward the fire. The sun had nearly set, casting long shadows across the grounds. Micah pulled a blanket from under his arm and offered it to her. The air was cooling as the sun disappeared for the night. Lucy was approaching the end of her first full day here, with just two more days to go.

"So, Micah," Lucy began. "Do you have, what is the word you used? *Cool* parents?" Lucy knew some of the Joterran slang, but always felt awkward trying to use it herself.

"My dad is alright," Micah began as he took a long swig of beer. "He holds really high expectations for me, which helped me be the man I am today, but sometimes it just gets old."

"What about your mother?"

"I can't wait to be done with this place," he said quickly, changing the subject.

Lucy looked him over with curiosity. His deflections and mood swings happened whenever he spoke of his mother or Abe. *What is the cause of these harsh feelings?*

"Why the need to get rid of this place so badly?" Lucy asked, frustrated with Micah evading the question.

"I don't want to remember this place," Micah admitted, opening up once again now that the topic of his mother was off the table.

"Why?" Lucy asked, with honest confusion. "This place is beautiful. And Abe is the nicest person I've ever had the pleasure of knowing."

At the mention of Abe, Micah's posture stiffened once again. "For one? Abe refused to leave this place, so I never really felt like I was a priority. I mean, have you ever seen him outside of this dump?" He shook his head and took a long swig from his bottle.

"A dump?" Lucy replied, unfamiliar with the term.

"This place is awful." Micah scoffed as he rolled the bottle in his hands, refusing to look her way.

"It is not!" Lucy pointed her beer bottle directly at Micah accusingly. "This place is a literal haven. It is silent, peaceful, the sky has your beautiful bright moon, and the trees are breathtaking." Lucy had seen much more beautiful places within her realm and others, but this part of Joterra really was stunning. She had seen pictures of busy cities that made her cringe — an enormous lack of appreciation for nature. Besides, her favorite place in all the realms lived just beyond one of Abe's trees, and that had to count for something, didn't it?

"It's too quiet," Micah objected hollowly. "Abe never left."

"Why do you keep saying that?" Lucy responded, exasperation filling her voice. "Where did you expect him to go that has you so irritable?"

Micah didn't answer, silence threatening to end their brief conversation early. He drank his bottle of beer and Lucy huffed out an annoyed sigh and looked up to the sky, praying that the full moon would magically make an early appearance so she could get to The Elderwood earlier.

"Did he ever tell you about her? My mom, Vanessa?" Micah finally asked quietly.

"Not much," Lucy admitted. "He spoke of her infrequently, though each time full of love and regret." Lucy glanced at Micah, sadness in his eyes matching her own. "I could tell it hurt him to remember."

"Good," Micah responded coldly. "I'm glad it hurt." He shifted uncomfortably on the tree stump.

"What did he do to hurt you so?" Lucy asked, realizing there was more to the anger he was feeling than hate. It was pain. She gripped the beer bottle tighter, unsure if she really wanted to hear what Abe did to hurt him so badly.

"She died when I was 9," he stated, staring at the fire. "He didn't leave this piece of shit land to come to her funeral." Micah turned and looked her right in the eye. "He never came to check on me. He didn't care." The steel in his gaze was his defense, a way to hold the pain in and expel anger in its place.

Sadness and guilt hit Lucy as a nauseating realization tore into her. Abe had lost his daughter before Lucy had reunited with him, but the agreement had been in place well before all of that.

Abe had signed a pact that he wouldn't leave his home for more than a few hours to ensure that the woods would remain protected. Her family couldn't risk anything, especially fire, coming to this part of the woods. Any destruction of the sacred tree would have closed the gateway to The Elderwood forever. Lucy's family couldn't risk losing the portal, and it caused Abe to lose his relationship to his only grandson.

Lucy struggled with finding the right thing to say. Even with their strained relationship, she couldn't imagine ever losing a parent. The loss would be devastating. A moment later, Micah stood up and left the fire pit without a word. How was she going to convince Micah to save a place he had so much animosity toward?

FIVE

The next morning, Lucy made sure to get up before Micah to avoid any more awkward morning interactions. Although, with her sleeping in Abe's old study, she was certain that Micah wouldn't have barged in anyway.

With the new understanding of Micah's anger toward Abe, it made sense why Micah put up such a strong barrier to avoid certain topics: Abe's belongings, memories, the property they were on. Each thing reminded Micah of his grandfather, and he worked hard to avoid it all. Trying to convince Micah that this place was special was going to be an even more difficult challenge, knowing that there were so many bad memories left behind.

Micah finished boxing up his mother's old room and had moved down to the main floor to pack up more pictures and to find the documents the lawyers needed. Lucy intended to stay out of his way as much as possible. She needed to come up with a plan to get him to understand how remarkable this land truly was.

In the privacy of her room, she removed the bandage to expose her milky white skin, free of any bruises or scars. Thankful for a full recovery, she hoped that moving her body today would get her mind to open up in order to see a way through all of this.

She was on her second day in Joterra, but Lucy had never been away from home for so long before. It was really beginning to take its toll on her, especially without a companion to rely on. Abe was the closest thing she had to a friend, and he was gone. Her heart shuddered at the thought, refusing to come to terms with reality.

Everyone in her life had an exponential lifespan, surviving for hundreds of years and living very full and vibrant lives. Here in Joterra, Abe lived such a short period of time.

In the last 15 years, Lucy saw Abe's body go from a mature and sturdy young man to an older gentleman. She would never say he was incapable, but the years of loss took a lot away from him, as the years seem to do, and seeing him age so rapidly scared Lucy.

When she asked her brother, Wes, about human mortality, all he had to say was that it was normal for mortals to age and die. His exact words were "don't grow too attached," as if Abe was something temporary and not worth remembering.

Abe was amazing. He lived in this house from the moment he was born until he died. He raised his daughter on this land, and lost his wife in this house. She became sick when Vanessa was in college and didn't make it past age 50. Vanessa moved away as soon as she entered college, excited for a new start away from the rural lifestyle. But Abe knew the significance of The Elderwood.

She wasn't supposed to talk about it, but it was Abe and Lucy's favorite thing to discuss. It was the most beautiful realm she had ever been, and she wanted Abe to understand the magnitude of such a dazzling place.

Even now, she yearned to see the lush forest waiting for her beyond the gateway. She yawned as she crept around the study, wishing she had a big cup of tea to wake her and warm her bones. The sun was shining, but the comforts of her home were deeply missed, causing an ache in her heart and a chill that cut straight through her.

The room was dark, with old navy blue curtains covering the windows. A dark, oak desk sat in front of the window, facing the door. A worn couch was off to the right in the room. On the left side was an entire wall of books that curved around to the adjacent wall. The built-in bookshelves were something out of a dream, and from ceiling to floor was a small library, cultivated by Abe and his family before him. She felt at home with the books surrounding her, reminiscing the stories she and Abe had shared in long days past.

As she walked out of the study, a bit of color on the bookshelves caught her eye. Lucy pulled the corner of a photograph from between two books, revealing the toothless smile of a seven-year-old boy. His dark curly hair poked out from under a baseball cap and his arms rested on his bruised, scrawny knees. A younger Abe sat on one side of the boy, and a beautiful long-haired woman on the other. The boy in the center had a fresh cut across the bottom of his chin. A cut that would surely leave a scar. *Micah.*

She gingerly touched the photograph, realizing that this hidden place between books wasn't so that Abe could hide Micah away. It was quite the opposite. The worn edges indicated that the photograph was handled frequently, softened and creased with time.

Lucy peeked back to the bookshelf where she found the picture. It was hidden between two books on the shelf closest to the door. One title was a worn book she had never read or heard of before. It was likely a Joterran author. Most of Abe's books in his study were nonfiction; information about the sciences and histories of the mortal realm. Well, either that or mysteries. He loved to talk about the mysteries he was reading when she came to visit. However, this worn title near the picture was not a mystery, it was a romance; a love story. It must have been his wife's. The other book that sandwiched the photograph was a children's storybook, probably Vanessa or Micah's.

The picture was between the only two items in the home that truly symbolized the love that existed in his life. *His family.*

She carefully slipped the photograph back between the books, sure to leave a larger corner out, hoping Micah would find it as he packed up. Micah made it clear it wasn't her place to get involved, and she was already in deep enough as it was.

THE DAY SLIPPED BY QUICKLY, the garden bed in the front of the house was tended, and the last of the yard behind the shed was cleaned up. Beyond that, all that was left outside was the great wooded area that stretched across the land.

The large trees offered shade and a whispering swish of the leaves above. Lucy removed the tie that kept her hair in her braid and combed her fingers through to release the tangles and ease the tension. She lifted her face toward the sky and let the sun's rays shine down on her, reviving her and brightening her mood.

The quiet reminded her of home, and her heart broke for the second time that day. Did her younger brother Henry notice she was gone yet? He always worried about her. She was a little more than a day away from being able to charge her amulet in hopes of returning home, but if she couldn't convince Micah to protect the property, she could never come back here again and it would be *her* failure.

Lucy walked to the tree that held the gateway to The Elderwood and sat down at the base. The tree held her family's sigil within its bark, the same design engraved on the amulet: a large tree with a bow replacing the tree roots. At the bottom was an arrow going through the bow and encircling the tree.

As her father liked to remind her, it represented the foundation of her family: The Elderwood trees and the honor of creating such important instruments for the realm. How would she live with the shame she would bring to her family if she failed?

She sat, thumping the back of her head against the trunk of the tree, hoping to shake some answers into her seemingly empty brain. She had to figure out a plan, and fast, but nothing was coming to her. If only she could talk with her father or her brothers. They were experts in this field and would know what to do. This is exactly what her father had been afraid of — allowing a female to be in charge of the business and it going up in flames.

She was going to have to figure this out with no one there to help her. If her mission fell flat, her family's generational business would be wiped out, and then what? What would her family do for money? Her marriage to Laurent would be set in stone. Her father would be desperate for Lucy to financially support the family as the Lady of the Northern Territory.

No. She shook her head and stood up.

If she wanted to avoid a life married to a stranger, she needed to persevere and stop sulking. Her father and brothers wouldn't be playing damsel in distress, sitting under a tree, waiting for an answer to come and hit them in the head. It was time to find a way through to the end of this, for better or worse.

"Hey, Micah?" Lucy called as she walked in through the backdoor of the house.

"In here," he called from the front, near the dining room.

The room was once beautiful, with ornate cabinetry and a table set for six, but now it was largely a place for unnecessary mail and old newspapers. Micah was going through and dumping the majority of the paper into a recycling bin, sighing heavily with every toss.

The more she thought of Micah's role here, the more her heart bled for him. He held such animosity for this place and for his grandfather, but his love and duty to his family kept him there, regardless. Micah put on such a strong act, pretending not to care, but his actions suggested differently.

In this room, Micah placed each meaningful piece of his grandfather's life in a box marked DONATION. He explained that he would be sending them to charities, which meant that he wasn't sending them to be destroyed, but to be shared. His pain shaded his true feelings, and Lucy wondered if he would begin to see them for himself soon.

The dim lighting made it hard to see much of anything, so Lucy pulled the curtains open and cracked the window to allow fresh air.

"Thanks," Micah said with a sigh as he put his hands on the back of his neck and looked up at the ceiling. "I'm never going to get this house in shape to sell."

"Maybe that's a good thing?" Lucy suggested, with a lilt of teasing in her tone. "This place has got some real potential," she said as she assessed the room with a mock serious expression. "Just imagine it now. Little Micah's running around in between the trees, their mother in the kitchen baking a birthday cake. Seems picture perfect."

"Not quite the salesman, are you?" He laughed at her, his broad smile stretching across his face. "This place is old and dusty and is probably going to fall to the ground in the next big storm." His eyes brightened at their light-hearted interaction. Lucy's heart fluttered in response.

"No, that won't be an issue," Lucy waved her hand at him as she leaned into the door frame, grinning in return. "Houses like this are sturdy. Reliable."

She knew enough that there was Denoran magic laced between the rafters of this house, keeping the roof from leaking and the winds from blowing the house over. Denoran magic could do a lot of things, but a perfect protection spell didn't exist. This just kept the house built to last. It would still be at the whims of nature — lightning, fires and the strongest winds.

"If only the people who lived in them were just as reliable," Micah replied as he threw another handful of old envelopes into the bin, sadness coating each word.

Each time Abe came up, Micah's suffering flowed over and caused him to see only hurt. How was Lucy going to overcome years of pain?

Anger can usually be subdued with reasonable explanations, but hurt? Hurt lingers. It doesn't work with common sense. Micah's pain over his mother and grandfather was something Lucy just couldn't fix. It would be the same if someone tried to explain to Lucy why her father didn't want her to be a bowyer. She understood his reasons, but the hurt she felt never faded with his rationale.

"Speaking of the people who lived here," Lucy segued. "Can I use some of Abe's tools out in his shed?"

"What do you need them for?" Micah asked with curiosity in his eyes. His hands dropped to his sides, the movement highlighting the rippling muscles under his shirt.

"I've completed the garden and general outdoors," Lucy explained. "I figured I could put some of the old timber to use?" Her eyes strayed from his face to his broad chest and muscular arms.

"Sure," Micah said, turning away from her, not seeing the interest in her gaze. "I'm pretty sure the keys are in the study. Probably one of his top desk drawers, if I had to guess."

"Why do old men think that's a good hiding spot?" she asked him with a smirk.

"I really have no idea," Micah replied with a huffed out laugh. "I don't know much about him at all, if I'm being honest. And it's just getting more and more clear as I go through his junk in this house." He ran his hands through his hair and over his face. Lucy could tell the stress was really beginning to weigh on him.

The two of them weren't in that different of a situation. Both Micah and Lucy remained in a negative relationship with a male figure in their lives. However, as Lucy was trying to gain recognition from her father, Micah was trying to make his grandfather disappear completely.

"I think you'll start to learn more about him as you dig a little deeper," Lucy offered gently. "His favorite places were his study, the kitchen and the front porch. He often read mysteries, never really explained why he loved them so much. Said he loved the detective series the most." She smiled as she recalled Abe in his rocking chair on the porch, always with a book in hand.

"He did?" Micah asked in disbelief.

"Why is that so unbelievable?" Lucy asked, evident confusion written across her face. "Don't all humans like mystery books?"

"That is a loaded question. First, why the hell did you say *all humans*? Are you an alien?" He laughed at his own joke, leaning against the wall.

"I'm just saying, in general. All people." Lucy tried to cover up her answer, hiding the blush spreading up her neck by pretending to fix her hair, loosely braiding it again.

Micah stared at her with a emotion Lucy couldn't identify. "Leave it," he suggested, an eager warmth in his tone. "Your hair is beautiful when it's down."

"Unlucky for you," Lucy said with flirtation in her voice. "I do what I want with my hair. Regardless of what a man thinks."

"Hey now, I was just offering a compliment," Micah joked.

"Thank you for the compliment," Lucy said. "But statement stands. I would be hard pressed to have it down in front of you again, simply out of spite." She lifted her chin in joking defiance.

"And I'm the one who needs to be brought down a peg or two, huh?" He began laughing in earnest now.

"If you like my long hair so much, maybe you should grow yours out?" she teased. Lucy pulled her hair out of the braid and walked over to him, holding up her hair and pretending to frame his face with it. "Oh yes, long curls look good on you." She smiled brightly.

Micah placed his hands on her hips as she stood close to him, his fingers pressing ever so slightly. "Not as good as they look on you."

Lucy jolted, surprised by his returning flirtation. Her eyes darted to his and her body stilled.

"I'm sorry, did I hurt you?" he asked with concern in his tone as he looked down at her side, inspecting her previous injury.

"No, I'm fine," she responded with a faint blush, still toying with her hair, bringing it away from his face. "Thank you, though," she said as she backed away from him and twirled her hair into another braid.

"Thank you for what exactly?" Micah asked. His hands lingered on her waist and slipped off as the distance between them grew.

"You took care of me when I was in a really vulnerable position, and you didn't take advantage like most men your age," she said. "It was unexpected and truly appreciated. You're a good man, Micah."

"It was nothing," Micah said, shaking his head with a grin. "I told you, it wasn't my first time helping to patch someone up." He rubbed his hand on the back of his neck, hesitant to continue. "See, it's so unbelievable that Abe read those detective stories, because he never read them before. He was always more interested in history and science." He looked to Lucy, an expression filled with hurt and love. "I didn't know him in his old age. And I didn't think he knew much about me... I'm a police officer for the city. A detective."

"See? Maybe there's more to him than what you remember." Lucy smiled and left Micah with that small bit of information.

Her heart was threatening to beat right out of her chest from the close touch Micah stole. Why did it feel so good to her? What did any of that even mean? She walked to the study and grabbed the keys from the top middle drawer. On her way out the door, she pulled the photograph free from the books and placed it on display to ensure Micah would find it. Maybe Micah just needed a little push.

THE SHED WAS COVERED in spiderwebs and dirt, but the tools inside were still in great shape. Lucy found the pieces she needed and headed to a clear spot in the yard to spread out her supplies and get to work.

First, she searched the tree line for a few branches that would be useful to her. Some with a nice thick bough, and others with straight, durable pieces.

Lucy worked relentlessly in the midday sun. While she was

working, she was supposed to be thinking about a way out of this situation, but instead her mind found peace and calm. Her thoughts were no longer racing, her body completely at ease in this place, far away from home.

Her skilled hands followed the same movements she learned when she was a young girl. Long pulls back and forth, shaping the wood, sanding it, creating the perfect bow. Sweat dotted her back, and as she wiped the moisture from her face with her arm, dirt and sawdust smudged it. She took her small pocket knife and engraved an intricate design along the arms of the bow. She even put a small etching of her family sigil at one end.

It was a short escape from her reality, and as the sun was going down, the grumble in her stomach was the only clue that time had passed.

Looking down at the finished bow made her heart leap. This was her happiness. Her sanctuary. Her solace. How could her father deny her of it?

"It's stunning," Micah said from behind her as he came closer. He stretched out his arm with an offer of a bottle of water.

"Thanks," Lucy smiled, genuinely happy to share this moment with someone. To be a bowyer was to be an artist, and so many people misunderstood that part of the practice. It wasn't just creating a weapon, it was composing a masterpiece. It was strength, poise, and power all wrapped into one.

"That smile isn't bad either," he added. "I'd tell you to do it more often, but I'm pretty sure you'd stop smiling around me completely just to prove a point, and we can't have that happening." He winked playfully.

"Well, sometimes the smiles are for me, and every now and then, one can be for you, too," Lucy said, pleased to share some of her happiness when Micah had been dealing with so much grief.

At the thought, her smile began to fade. She turned away from him, hiding her pain. It was difficult enough to see Abe's only family struggle so deeply. There was no point in letting Micah know how hard it was for Lucy to be here without a friend. She didn't know how to share that without divulging everything that tore at her heart.

"Thank you," Micah looked down, keeping his eyes on the bow so he didn't have to meet her gaze. "I'm sorry I've been less than friendly at times. Though in my defense, you aren't really always a ray of sunshine, either." He looked at her with a hint of a smirk.

"Thank you," Lucy fake curtsied.

Micah truly laughed that time. "Come on in." He waved his hand toward the house. "I'll make you some chili. I swear, the only thing this old man has in his freezers is frozen ground beef."

Lucy outwardly moaned, making Micah's eyebrows shoot up. "I'm sorry, but I am starving and Abe makes the best chill in the world."

"Chill? Do you mean chili?" Micah asked, humor glinting in his gaze.

"Yes, that," she pushed him toward the door with a blush. "Come on, let's see if you can make it as good as he used to. Maybe we can grab some drinks and make a toast to Abe. You want to learn more about him? I can tell you a few stories."

"THAT CANNOT BE TRUE!" Micah cried out in laughter. "I won't ever believe it."

"Oh, it's true alright," Lucy replied with a laugh. "He nearly burned the house down trying to make me that birthday cake. My brother, Gregory, was furious. He could have burned the entire forest down."

"Your brother? Did he come out here to visit Grandad often?" Micah leaned in closer to the fire to hear Lucy as she sat across from him. He handed her another bottle and their fingers lingered as they looked at each other with an alluring glance.

Lucy blushed and looked away. She was happy to share some of her most treasured stories about Abe. However, she made sure to leave out any telling information. For example, when he nearly burned down the forest, he was only 12, but Micah didn't need those minor details.

"I told you it was a family thing. My father and your grandad were in a business deal," Lucy explained, holding on to that little ember of hope in that small word. He wasn't *Abe* in that moment, but instead *Grandad.*

"What kind of business? What did you say you even did, anyway?" Micah asked with another swig of his drink near the fire pit.

"Woodworking, mostly," Lucy explained, the chili filling her and the beer loosening her lips. "It's been in the family for years, my grandparents and your grandparents and great-grandparents, and great-great-grandparents," she went on.

"What? I have never heard any of this before," Micah said, shaking his head in disbelief. He sat on the edge of his seat, scooting closer to her with every story told. Each inch closer made it evident to Lucy that Micah craved this connection to Abe that he had missed out on for so many years.

"I bet he would have told you," Lucy said with certainty. "He loved you. Vanessa, too." The sun had set for the day and the moon perched high in the sky, teasing Lucy. It was not full, but so very close.

"What kind of business did our families do together?" Micah asked.

"I'm not really sure how to explain," Lucy began to answer, and then quickly thought of half truths to share with him. The beer was fogging her mind, causing her to give parts of answers she didn't know how to explain. Why had she even mentioned the generations of business here?

"Wait," Micah began, watching her fumble over her words. "Are you really here to help Abe or are you here to try to get some money out of his estate?" Micah asked as he stood, closing himself off to her once again.

"What? No, of course not," Lucy stood as she tried to clarify. "It's the woods. The trees. We need them. They're important, special."

"These woods? There are less than 200 trees on the property," Micah replied. "How do these trees help your business?"

"Please, sit," Lucy grabbed his arm, pulling him back toward the log she was sitting on. He was hesitant, but when realizing he had nowhere else to go, he sat down with a huff and put a barrier of defensive tension between them.

"Are you going to tell me what you're really doing here?" he whispered to her, looking deeply into her hazel eyes, searching for truth.

"I'm not here for any malicious reason, I promise," Lucy breathed her response, her fingers trailing down his arm, pausing to feel the warm muscle beneath. "Abe was one of my dearest friends. I would never do anything to hurt him or anyone he loved."

"Fine, then tell me something real," Micah said in defeat, slowly pulling his arm away from her to turn and face her fully. "Tell me something about your family since you now know the entire messed up version of my own."

"Not much to tell, really." Lucy sat back, not wanting to admit how nice it had felt holding his arm in her hands.

Now *she* was becoming the defensive one, not wanting to share about her family. "My father owns the family business, and all of my brothers help him run it. I'm not allowed to help because I'm not a male, but he doesn't know how to handle me since I'm the only female in the family, beyond my mother, of course." Lucy continued to ramble. "It is frustrating because I'm the best bowyer in the family, you know? I'm better than all of my brothers, but that doesn't matter to my father."

"You're the only girl?" Micah asked.

"Yes," she went on. "It's infuriating. It was fine for me to be a skilled woodworker when I was a child, but now that I'm older I'm not allowed to have the same interests just because society deems it to be so?"

"Hmm," Micah said quietly as he stood up again. The fire was dying down, and the night was getting late. "It seems like there's a lot about your family that's a little confusing too, then. Huh?" He kept his eyes on hers.

"Yes. Want to know what else is confusing?" Lucy continued, the alcohol taking over her senses now. "Why do they call it chili when it makes you so warm? Or is it chili because you eat it when you're chilly?" She laughed at her own joke.

"I think it's time to sleep this beer off now," Micah said with a tight smile and a sigh. "Come on, I don't want you falling into the fire."

He walked her into the house and to the top of the stairs, keeping a gentle grasp around her waist to keep her from falling. Lucy basked in the feeling, allowing her weight to push into his side to be closer to him. He waited until she got into her room safely before he went into his own.

Lucy rested her head on the small couch in the study, smiling, knowing that she was closer to having Micah see the importance of this place. Slowly mending the rift between him and his grandfather. Step by step, Lucy would find a way into his heart.

SIX

A hangover was not something that Lucy was particularly accustomed to. She never really drank in Denora, and when she did she never drank to excess. The people she would indulge with would either be her brothers or the people at the taverns when she was seeking a cure to her loneliness. Waking up with her head feeling like it was being crushed within a vice was more than a little foreign to her.

What has gotten into me? Lucy asked herself as she got her bearings around the study. She held her hand up to the side of her head and quietly whispered the Fae words to cure the pain, giving herself a small amount of healing magic. Now that she was feeling more rested, the magic came a little easier to her.

Healing magic was helpful in minor situations; she was prone to slight cuts on her hands during her woodworking. Lucy had never gone so long without the magic coming to her fingertips with ease.

A tremendous burden was taken off of her knowing that her reserves were restored with rest and food. She knew her magic had its limitations, as she only knew a few dozen spells to use, but having the ability to use it in this faraway place was a sincere relief.

It was a quick lesson to not underestimate alcohol here. What an immature mistake. Maybe her family was right, maybe this wasn't the future for her. She couldn't get into The Elderwood, couldn't convince this man to keep up his family's end of a pact, and she couldn't even manage a few days in another realm without fawning over the whims of a random man. Who cared that he looked like a sculpted warrior under those cottony soft shirts?

A loud car engine perked up her fae hearing and announced a visitor approaching the property. Lucy quickly pulled her clothes on, braided her long brown hair and twisted it off of her neck. She held her boots in her hands and crept down the hallway to see if she could identify the visitor's purpose without intruding.

A knock reverberated through the house; the empty echoing reply felt ghostly in the moment. Even when Abe lived here alone, it was never this quiet. Never this empty. Abe was so full of life, it was as if the property hummed with positive energy. That entire spark of life felt dead now, gone forever. Her heart threatened to crack at the memory.

The pounding got louder until Micah pulled the door open with a lurch and gave a displeased acknowledgement to the men at the door.

"What do you want now?" Micah said to the strangers, no kindness lacing his tone, reminding Lucy of the first night she met him.

"Hello sir, it's great to see you again," an upbeat voice rang out, ignoring Micah's rude greeting. "We wanted to bring you the most up-to-date numbers for the property and to see if we could just get your signature and get out of your hair."

"I told you I wasn't ready to sign yet," Micah said, starting to close the door on the men. "I need more time to figure this out."

"We can give you another couple of days, but this offer will expire and then you will be left with this property on your own. I would hate to be the one to have to deal with the mess ol' Abe left here. The state and the bank won't be as helpful as J. Pearson Land Developers."

The man's voice rang familiar to Lucy. He was the same man who had tried to get Micah to sell the day she missed her chance at using the gateway. "Here is the paperwork from our company, check it out and get back to us before it's too late."

By the time Lucy got downstairs to give the men a piece of her mind Micah had closed the door on them, leaving Lucy and Micah in the same situation they had been in when they had first met: face-to-face in a silent standoff, battling for the future of Abe's land.

"You can't still be considering selling, can you?" Lucy asked, disgust dripping from her words. She looked at the papers in his hand, 'J. Pearson Land Developers' boldly printed across the top of the documents.

"Nothing's changed here," Micah said flatly. "This is an empty house that holds nothing for me."

"Nothing?" Lucy asked in disbelief, hurt at the idea that Micah still felt nothing for Abe. She had thought she was finally making leeway, sharing stories with Micah about Abe. Micah even called him 'Grandad.' What had suddenly changed?

"Nope," he punctuated as he walked toward the door. "Come on, I'll help you outside today."

Lucy couldn't get a read on his temperament. Was he upset with the land surveyors? Did she make less progress with him last night than she thought? How much had the alcohol tarnished her memory of just a night prior?

"I don't think I need any help," Lucy said as she walked after him, no harshness in her tone. "I'm nearly done, anyway," and that was the truth. Lucy had completely cleaned up the perimeter of the large yard and made it look more presentable than it had in years. The garden was weeded, the grass was cut, and she neatly piled the extra logs of wood for future use. There wasn't much else to do beyond putting away some tools from the previous night, which were spread out over a portion of the yard.

"I'll help you put the stuff back into the shed," he said as he eyed the tools. "Then I'll be needing those keys back." He gave her an even look, studying her every move.

Micah seemed much more untrusting of Lucy. He was barely looking her in the eye, and now he was demanding the keys when before he gave them to her so flippantly. It surprised her he had cared at all. Why was he following her around when there was definitely much more to be done inside?

She grabbed the keys from her pocket and held them in her hand. "Here," she called to him.

Just as he was turning, she tossed the keys to him, ultimately catching him off guard and earning her a look as the keys bounced off his chest and onto the ground. Lucy just smiled back sweetly and walked right past him to her bow and arrows she had made the day before.

The bow had no lacquer, so it was missing its protective coating, but it was still a piece of art. Lucy had no idea she would end up stranded in Joterra, but having the ability to create a working bow gave her a feeling of security that she was desperate for.

Her father always taught her to bring extra bowstring with her when she took her bow to the forest, and she was so thankful for that advice. As she was stringing her bow, she felt Micah's gaze cutting through her.

"Do you have a question lingering on your mind, or do you expect to pull an answer out of me with some mind-reading powers over there?" She teased, finally meeting his eyes.

"I just keep wondering how someone as young as you has such skill with woodworking," Micah said. "How old are you, anyway?"

"About your age, I expect, unless you are older than you look?" Lucy replied with a lilt.

"I was going to say the same thing about you," Micah said, holding her stare, no levity in his reply.

"If you are intending to insult me you are going about it in an odd way." She feigned indifference. "I am good at woodworking and must not be as old as I am, so maybe I am older and, therefore, look great for my age?" Lucy replied sarcastically.

"Does your sister also age so well?" Micah asked, his stare unblinking.

"Everyone in my family ages well," Lucy replied dismissively, moving away from Micah with her bow and a handful of arrows. "But not everyone is as good at archery as I am, so I guess I exceed in some things."

Why is he asking about my so-called sister? Lucy asked herself. Panic was creeping up, her heart pounding audibly in her ears.

"Let's see it then," Micah said. He stood so close behind her that she felt his breath on her exposed neck. He moved his hand over Lucy's shoulder to point at a bird in the distance. "Think you can get that one?" He whispered in her ear, causing the hair on her neck to stand up straight.

"I need a few practice shots to get a good feel of the bow first," Lucy replied stiffly, unsure of how to respond with Micah so close to her. She wanted to welcome his advance, thinking back to their comfortable companionship around the fire. But this was different. The energy he was exuding confused her — he did not seem his usual self.

What is going on with him? Trying to calm her body, Lucy rolled her shoulders back and took a deep breath. She knew her skill at archery was incomparable to most humans, so she didn't want to show off and let her true skill be shown.

She pulled the arrow, aimed it at a piece of wood and loosed it, missing her target. Micah snorted a laugh behind her as she drew another arrow, aimed at the wood and released the arrow, this time splintering the center of the wood.

A slow clap came from behind her. "Great! You murdered that log. I can see you'd be handy in an emergency." His jeering tone put Lucy completely on edge, and all semblance of holding back seemed to disappear in an instant.

Lucy stomped over to the chunk of wood and pulled the arrow

free. She then grabbed the stray arrow and came back to stand in front of Micah. Lucy scanned the tops of the trees to spy a small flock of gray birds resting on the upper branches just a few feet away from the bird Micah challenged her to hit.

Without a moment's hesitation, she pulled the first arrow, striking the bird he pointed out. Then, within the same breath, she nocked another arrow and loosed it, hitting another bird that had begun to fly away. She grabbed her last arrow and released it, bringing three birds to the ground in less than 10 seconds.

"*Yeah*," Lucy retorted sarcastically. "I'd be pretty handy." She looked him up and down with a mock analytical expression. "Not quite sure what you'd bring to the table, so *someone* would have to step up." She gave him another fake smile and walked away to fetch the birds.

As she went, her lumbering boots caused her to trip and fall nearly face first into the ground. *So much for that badass exit,* she thought to herself. Her hands were covered in dirt and she had a small rip in her leggings. She cursed under her breath and went to stand up. Micah was there, offering his hand to help her up, but Lucy pretended not to see it, refusing to accept help from him. She wasn't prepared for his demeanor to cause such confusion after what she thought was a meaningful connection just the previous night.

"You may have some skills with those arrows, but you aren't very stealthy. Anyone would hear you coming from a mile away." He smirked.

Lucy could not figure out if he was enjoying her obvious anger or if he had an ulterior motive, but regardless, she was inching closer and closer to losing her temper.

"It's the boots," she mumbled, not sure why she was even responding at this point.

"Sure," he faked sincerity.

"Is this a joke? Why are you behaving this way?" Lucy snapped. "Who cares how well I shoot or how nimble I can be? What the hell does that have to do with anything, anyway?" Her hair was falling from her braid and covering half of her face, making her fierce gaze much less intimidating. She pushed her hair out of her eyes and wiped the dirt onto her leggings.

"Just trying to see who you really are, Lucy." His usual annoyed tone seemed to be absent, but this was not his playful tone either. Micah was angry, and the hostility wasn't directed at his estranged grandfather. No; this anger was for Lucy, and Lucy alone.

"Get in line." She scoffed and walked away from him.

"No, I mean it," he said as he followed after her. "I don't get you. You worked with Abe, but won't explain how. You don't really talk about your family other than a few vague details, and you never, ever talk about yourself."

"And you do? All I know about you is that you hate Abe, you hate this place, and you like to behave like an insolent child when you aren't getting your way."

"A child, huh? Fine. Let's play a game, then." Micah walked closer to Lucy, determination set in his eyes. "For each point, the loser has to answer the question from the winner. No holding back."

Lucy's heart was racing. Why was this man having such a powerful effect on her? She should just walk away and find another path to saving the portal, but she hadn't walked away from a challenge in her entire life. "Fine." She saw how Micah's eyes glinted in the summer sun, making her heart jump again. "But I'm picking the game," Lucy said.

"Great." Micah replied. "What are we playing?"

"Seek-and-find," Lucy replied with a coy smile. "No going inside. No peeking. Count to 100, if the seeker can't find in three minutes or less, then they lose. "

"Hide-and-seek? Really?" Micah replied.

"Afraid to lose, Micah?" Lucy teased. She tried to keep an unaffected tone, but her hammering heart told a different story.

"Nope. You count first." Micah replied, giving her the red bandana he pulled from his back pocket.

Lucy pulled the bandana around her eyes and tied it in place, using gentle quiet movements so that she could track Micah's footsteps as he walked away from her and into the woods.

She didn't mention to Micah that tracking was all part of hunting in the woods, and she was quite good at that as well. It was Micah's fault for not putting two and two together when he saw her shoot down the birds from the tree. Though, in his defense, he didn't realize she hit them precisely in the eye where she had aimed.

"Ready or not," Lucy called, pulling the bandana off her eyes and pushing it into the waistband of her leggings. Abe had taught her this game when they were very young, and she had played often enough to know the sounds of this forest. Her Fae hearing was surely an advantage, but she didn't feel guilty when Micah was acting so childishly.

The woods were quiet, the birds all flew away since Lucy shot her bow. She walked between the green trees, the forest silent except for the soft rustle of leaves in the wind. She began walking toward Micah with full confidence, knowing he couldn't have gotten far.

He was a towering man with strong, broad shoulders, so he would need a place wide enough for him to hide. Behind a group of trees or a bush? Maybe he was lying down under one of the felled logs. She crouched down and felt the ground with her hand, staying perfectly still, waiting to hear Micah's movement muffled by the soft carpet of pine needles beneath his large frame.

It only took her a minute for her to come upon him, awkwardly crouched down behind a leafy bush, as if that would conceal his hiding spot.

"Found you," Lucy told him as she pulled the leaves out of the way to reveal his position, arrogance in her smile.

"Yeah, yeah," Micah said. "But you couldn't find me for a few minutes, so that was a pretty decent spot."

"I win. I get to ask," she announced, crossing her arms. "What do you like about being a detective?"

He rolled his eyes and looked up at the sky, avoiding the question.

"Excuse me, you were the one who wanted to play this ridiculous game of questions and answers. Now hold up your end of the deal."

Lucy was annoyed and was not about to let him back away when she wanted answers just as badly as he did. She figured she would start off with something easy that he would be more likely to answer. With her skill it was unlikely that she would lose a single round.

"I enjoy helping people," Micah said. "Now it's my turn."

"Absolutely not," Lucy protested. "That was not a genuine answer. You better give me more or all of my answers will sound just the same."

The threat was enough to get Micah talking. He let out a loud breath and looked at Lucy. "My mom enjoyed helping people. She was the kindest person I had ever met. She taught me everything I know about being a good person, and I'm trying to honor that."

The sadness in his tone diminished his anger, allowing Lucy to see through some of his harshness. "I'm trying to live up to the person she would have wanted me to be. Besides, my dad was strict growing up, so I was a rule follower. Being part of a police force makes me feel like I'm making a difference. Happy now?"

"Almost," Lucy replied, walking over to him with the bandana. "Your turn to count." She stepped behind him and her breasts pushed against his back as she reached around to put the blindfold on. She secured it with a simple knot. "Catch me — if you can," she whispered in his ear, and her Fae hearing caught the moment when his breathing hitched.

Just like that, she was gone. Lucy knew how to be quiet in the forest if she needed to be, and her powerful body gave her the edge she needed to get far enough away that it would be a challenge for Micah to find her in the allotted time. Lucy took a moment to watch him from afar, trying to figure him out. He was angry about the house, and then sweet and kind to her. He complimented her on her hair and smile and now was irritable and rude. *Is this what all human men were like?*

Lucy remained perfectly still as she took stock of the information she knew about Micah, trying to understand what was going on in his mind. He loved his mom more than he liked to talk about, and Lucy realized there was more to his pain than Abe. *His grief toward his mom is projected on Abe,* she thought. *It will take a miracle for Micah to forgive him.* Her heart ached for them both.

When his time to count was up, Micah took off the blindfold and looked around for any trace of where Lucy could have hidden. He nearly tripped over her boots — she took them off so she could move around more nimbly.

"Why are your shoes over here?" Micah called out. "That just means you couldn't have gotten very far!"

Lucy peeked from behind a tree to see him walking in the complete opposite direction of where she was hiding. She knew she would win, but she had no idea he'd be so bad at this game; it was kind of adorable.

All the same, it was more convenient for her. Lucy would get her answers and not have to be on the other side of the questioning. She enjoyed watching him, his muscular body tensing in frustration when he realized he was going to lose. The sun on his bronzed skin gave such a brightness to his deep brown eyes, so full of love and pain. *Why did he want to play this game?* she thought to herself. *What is he hoping to uncover?*

When the three minutes were up, she carefully crept up behind him and whispered "boo" to announce her arrival.

Micah turned with a frown, vexed that he again lost. His quick turn nearly knocked her over, but he held her by the waist to keep her from falling. "I should have known you were going to be good at this," he said with gentleness, letting her go. "Fine," he conceded. "What's your question this time?"

"How did you get your scar?" Lucy asked plainly. She touched under his lip gingerly, still standing close to him.

He took a small step back and touched his chin, feeling the discolored indentation from his childhood injury. At first, Lucy wasn't sure if he was going to answer, but when he finally did, she wasn't expecting what she heard.

"During a game of Entrance to The Elderwood," he said with the hint of a smile from the memory. "I know, it sounds silly," he ran his hand through his short hair and looked around the woods.

Lucy couldn't breathe. *The Elderwood?*

"Mom, Grandad and I used to play nearly every day. We'd hide under the dining room table and talk about how we used our talisman to get into the portal and then we'd run to the fort we made in the yard and pretend we just appeared there. We pretended the woods were a magical forest called The Elderwood and we would battle imaginary beasts and sneak cookies from the kitchen and have the best time... Once, I tripped on my way into the forest and face planted into a tree, it was awful." He chuckled at the memory.

Lucy stood still as a statue, eyes wide and searching for understanding. *Did he know about The Elderwood? Why would Abe play a game like that with him?*

"Why are you staring at me like that?" Micah asked her, his brows knit in confusion. "I was a kid. It's fine. It's not like it's some traumatic story." He walked toward her. "Here, your turn."

Micah carefully tied the blindfold onto her, but she barely felt a thing, so consumed with the idea that Micah knew more than he had realized. This was how Abe tried to teach him. *This was his plan.*

By the time she was ready to find Micah, she had been so distracted that she couldn't focus at all. Looking at the ground for footprints didn't help as she saw both hers and his scattered around the ground as if they were intertwined in an invisible dance.

She wandered aimlessly between the trees, digesting the enormity of the information he just presented to her while she also attempted to look for him. Her thoughts raced through her mind, causing enough chaos that her Fae hearing failed her completely.

Moments later, Micah came up behind her with a triumphant smile. Lucy could not believe she gave Micah such an easy win.

"My turn," he announced proudly. "I need to know more about

your family and Abe."

"Do you want to know about my family? Or about Abe? That's two questions," Lucy said, trying to redirect the question to buy herself time to settle her racing heart.

"No," Micah smiled knowingly, inching his face closer to hers. "I said your family *and* Abe. How are they connected?"

"I tried telling you before," Lucy said. "They worked together for years."

"Nope, that's not enough and you know it," Micah countered. "You made me give more, now you do the same."

"Fine," Lucy snapped, her patience wearing thin. "Abe had special wood we used for the bows and arrows we would make and sell. It's why I'm so good at archery; it's a family legacy. Abe's father and his father before him worked with my ancestors as well."

"Wood? Like his trees?" Micah asked in disbelief. "There's no way he would have ever let you cut down the trees on his property," he retorted, and Lucy knew he was right. "They were precious to him. Why are you lying?" Micah's anger was beginning to seep through the cracks yet again.

"I'm not lying," Lucy bit back. She threw the bandana at him. "You don't know anything about Abe! Stop acting like you know him so well now." She walked closer to him. "When was the last time you even talked to him, Micah? Hmm?"

Lucy had worked so hard while being here in Joterra alone, hoping to get through the journey without additional complications, but Micah was turning into the biggest and most unexpected complication yet. Her emotions were bubbling over, sending waves of anger and grief out into the realm, threatening to spill all of her secrets.

"Why would I bother responding to him? He abandoned me!" Micah began yelling. "Why would he think the letters would ever fix anything?"

"What letters?" Lucy asked earnestly, her eruption of emotion immediately ceasing.

"He sent me a letter every month for over a year. Then every few months, then once a year," Micah began explaining, his anger wavering. "I refused to open any of them. If he had something to say to me, he should have come to say it to my face! In the last year he sent one every two weeks — as if I'd somehow change my mind." He scoffed and threw the bandana to the ground.

"And you wouldn't open them?" Lucy demanded, needing more information about these letters. *They must hold more information for Micah about The Elderwood. He wouldn't have left it completely unguarded on purpose.*

"No," he raked two hands through his hair again, then covered his face. "No," he repeated, holding back emotions he wasn't sure he understood. "He must have known he was getting sick or something... He must have known and was trying to reach out." His eyes glistened in the sun. "Why wouldn't he just come talk to me? Why couldn't he try harder?" His whispered voice a plea. The desperation in his eyes made Lucy's heart ache with pain for Micah and Abe alike.

Abe had been trying so hard to reach out to Micah the only way he felt he could... *What was he trying to tell you?* Lucy kept thinking to herself. She paced back and forth.

"I think I have more answers to questions you haven't asked yet," Lucy began slowly. "But first, I need to know." She walked over and put her hands on his arms, calming him. "Do you still have the letters?"

"No," Micah replied, shaking his head in dismay. "I had the mailman return to sender."

"Return to who sent them? Then they're here," Lucy said with brightness in her eyes and a leap of hope within her chest. She took his hands in her own, holding them tightly, offering the hope she held within her.

"Yeah, I guess they would be," Micah agreed. "But what other answers do you have?"

"Let's find those letters, and I promise I'll tell you as much as I can."

CHAPTER

SEVEN

The house was still in shambles from Micah's attempt at boxing up important papers, and now it was in worse condition from the two of them searching for Abe's letters. The dining room table held loads of envelopes, but none of them were addressed to Micah.

The sun was setting, and the shadows were creeping into the house, casting a darkness that threatened to infiltrate Lucy's soul. She took a deep breath as she looked around at the chaos in front of her. She was so close.

If Abe had worked out a way to explain to Micah about The Elderwood, this was her greatest chance of getting Micah to protect the portal. She could return home and prove to her father that she was worthy of a seat at the table. She could put an end to the arrangement and save herself from a lifetime of unhappiness as Lady Lucella Sloan. If she could find these letters, maybe Abe's words would solve all of Lucy's problems.

Her breath caught at the thought of Micah's reaction to the truth. Would he accept the letters for what they were? Would he lay down the grief and anger he held?

"I've looked everywhere for any paperwork for the lawyers," Micah told Lucy, breathless from the endless search. "I don't know where else to look. This place is like a maze." He looked around in defeat at the boxes and papers strewn about the main floor of the house.

"His study," Lucy said with a question on her tongue. "You haven't been in there because I've been in there, have you?"

"True, but I'd already looked in there before you got here," Micah explained. "There weren't any important documents. Just books."

"But you weren't looking for mail before," she said with a glimmer in her eye. "In fact, I'd bet there's a lot you missed in the study," Lucy hinted, knowing there was at least one thing he had not seen.

Lucy led Micah up the stairs, hurrying as best as she could in her unlaced boots. She was in such a rush to get back to the house from their game in the woods that she didn't even bother tying them. As she stepped into the room, she slowed to get to the bookcase that held the photograph of Micah. She carefully took it and held the picture out to him.

"Here," she said gently, handing it to Micah. "See? He kept this. And from the worn appearance, I'd bet he looked at it often." Lucy pointed to the soft creases in the photograph.

"Where did you find this?" Micah asked in awe, taking the picture in both hands, holding it reverently.

"On the bookshelf. Here, between two books that clearly did not match the others. Look," Lucy encouraged as she took his arm and brought him closer to the shelf, pointing to the two books Abe valued above all others.

These small touches between her and Micah that once felt so taboo, now felt so warm and welcoming to Lucy. Micah's presence offered something that she could not quite put her finger on.

Micah delicately touched the spine of the first book. "My mother loved romance books. Even after her and Dad got divorced, she never gave up on love," he said with sadness. "They loved each other, but they just couldn't make the marriage work. Mom said they were better off as friends. I never understood why they separated."

"Your mom's view on love is something special. I think finding your other half is more important than people seem to believe." Lucy nodded in agreement. "I'm not sure I'll ever understand why people are willing to bind themselves with a vow of loyalty if they don't feel a strong bond of love."

"You don't see loyalty as part of love?" Micah asked her.

"It is not enough," Lucy said plainly. "Loyalty can come from a reliable pet, but love? Love ignites your soul. It leaves no room for question, because there is only that other person." She looked away, unsure why she was baring her soul to him. "When I find love, I want my partner to want me as much as I want them. I want love to fuel our growth, knowing I have someone who fully understands me. Sure, loyalty is involved, but that alone isn't enough for me."

Micah looked at her with a smile playing on his lips. Lucy wasn't sure she had ever been that candid about her views on marriage to anyone, let alone a man. "I think you'll find that," Micah said to her. "You wouldn't accept anything less."

"No," she replied, turning back to the books, a blush of pink appearing on her freckled cheeks. "I suppose I would not."

"So," Micah said, generously changing the topic as he noticed Lucy's demeanor change. "What else have you found in here?" His eyes scanned the shelves, eager to know more.

"There's another book," Lucy said as she pulled the children's book from the shelf. The pale blue hardcover book was faded with age, a small yellow bear printed on the front. As she went to hand the book to Micah, he kept his hands on the photograph. His eyes were wide with recognition and disbelief. For reasons Lucy could not fathom, he was reluctant to take the storybook. Lucy carefully took the photograph from his hand and replaced it with the book, keeping her hands in place as she worked to get his attention. "Micah?" she said delicately, hoping he wouldn't shut her out again.

"This was Grandad's... it got passed down to Mom and then to me," Micah shared with a faint voice. "He told me..." he cleared his throat. "He told me he'd hang on to it for my own kids, someday."

Lucy withdrew her hands as Micah clasped the book. As soon as he opened it, three or four sheets of paper slipped from the bottom of the book and onto the floor. Lucy and Micah looked at each other in shock, and Micah quickly bent down to grab the paper.

He unfolded it carefully, the letter on top, hand written in blue pen, was addressed to Micah.

Dearest Micah,

If you are reading this now, it means that I'm gone and that we never had the chance to make amends. I can't tell you how deeply I regret that, and I wish with all of my heart things could have been different. The land I had to protect is worth more than anything, even my own life. I've enclosed the title to the house, as well as my will. Please read the letters I've sent you. Read them carefully. There's more to this than I ever got the chance to explain. I've put the letters, and everything else you'll need, where we used to read together — where they will be safe until you find this.

I love you more than all the stars in the sky and every leaf upon every tree in The Elderwood.

Love, Grandad

MICAH STOOD, holding the letter and staring at the signature scrawled on the bottom of the page. "I have to find the letters," he whispered.

"We will," Lucy said with conviction. *We have to,* she thought. "They have to be in here somewhere," she said as she looked around the room. "He spoke of the place where you read together? They must be somewhere between all of these books." She looked at the walls of bookshelves filled from top to bottom, clearly unsure where to start. Lucy fervently pulled off the books nearest her and they crashed to the ground with haste. She flinched as the old titles hit the ground recklessly.

"No," Micah said, as he quickly lifted his head, a brightness in his eyes. "I know where they are."

Micah bounded out of the room and down the steps two at a time until he stopped in front of the dining room. Lucy followed quickly behind him, leaving the boots in the study so she would be more sure on her feet. The green bin he was using to get rid of the old paper was still on the floor, and the table had remained covered in mail.

"We already looked in here. Do you think we missed them some-how?" Lucy asked in confusion. Suddenly, Micah dropped to all fours and started crawling under the dining room table, muttering to himself. Lucy took a surprised step back as he squeezed his tall body beneath the old wooden table.

Lucy squatted down to see what he was doing and found Micah searching around the floor for any clue. "We used to read under here," he told her. "We would drape blankets or bed sheets over the sides and use a flashlight to read about magical places. Kingdoms with fierce knights. Immortal beings with magic." He stopped as he saw her watching him. "This probably sounds ridiculous," he said.

"It doesn't," Lucy said honestly, smoothing the surprise from her face and replacing it with attentiveness. She crawled under the table after him and sat cross-legged as he turned and laid flat on his back, his long legs stretching out far into the dining room. He was still searching the bottom side of the table for a clue. It was impossible to see much in the dimly lit room.

Lucy looked at the desperation written across Micah's face, understanding the feeling herself. Micah needed to find answers to explain the hurt he had felt for so long, and Lucy was desperate to find her place among her family. Fortunately for Lucy, the answers in the letters had the potential to contain solutions for both of them.

With that, she took a leap of faith. "Maybe you need a little light..." Lucy tentatively brought her hands up to her face, whispered in ancient Fae, and a small ball of light began to glow in her hands. Micah sat up in shock, slamming his head into the bottom of the table.

"Ow!" he yelped as he leaned back on his elbows, staring at Lucy with fear and wonder in his eyes. "What are you doing? How are you doing that?"

"I think you know more than you realize, but I'm willing to nudge you in the right direction just to be sure," she explained, trying to keep her tone calm and even. "The magical worlds your grandad told you about weren't fake. I think many of the stories you were told when you were a child were based on truth, just not *your* truth."

Lucy was explicitly taught never to use magic in front of humans, which is why she never had before, if you didn't count Abe, and she didn't. Her instructors taught Lucy that human brains could not comprehend magic, and more often than not, bigger problems arose. It was the reason she never mentioned the portal to Micah to begin with. But if Abe had tried telling him, maybe Micah needed to see more in order to really believe whatever Abe might have written in the letters.

"What does that even mean? Are you trying to tell me magic exists? Of course you're telling me magic exists. Look at you! So, are you telling me Grandad had magic? Or just you?" Micah couldn't stop rambling. He could hardly look away from her hands, afraid of what she would do.

A slight gasp from Lucy tore his attention back to her eyes. She was no longer looking at him, but instead at something just over his shoulder. Her eyes widened in shock.

"There," she pointed to the other side of the table. Tucked within the inside corner, where the table and the leg met, was a bound package, hidden from view. "Grab it," she told Micah.

He continued to stare at her, terrified.

"Stop being childish and grab it," Lucy told him, trying to be gentle and failing. "This is just the beginning," she said under her breath as he reached for the package. His eyes continued to nervously dart between her hands and the parcel.

He collected the brown, paper wrapped bundle and crawled out from under the table, eager to get further away from Lucy's glowing orb as she magically doused the light and let her arms fall to her sides.

"Open it," she urged him, eager to know what Abe had tried telling Micah.

"This feels insane," he muttered to himself, sweat gathering on his brow. "Magic worlds. Freaky flashlight hands. Hidden letters. What the hell have I gotten myself into?" He was hesitant to unwrap the bundle, as if he wasn't sure what he would find when the paper wrapping was gone.

"Micah," Lucy said, gently holding his arm to get his attention. His body tensed at the touch. His eyes stalled on where her hand met his body until he finally looked her in the eye.

"They aren't hot," he said.

"What?" Lucy looked at him with confusion.

"Your hands," he said as he touched hers. "I thought they'd be hot from the fire."

"Not fire," Lucy said with an easy smile. "Magic." She whispered another spell, then put her hands to her mouth and gently blew on her fingers as she lifted them. Tiny orbs of light floated ever so slowly into the air in front of them, gracefully twirling as they rose. Micah's eyes grew wider and Lucy feared he had stopped breathing all together.

"This is real," Lucy said as she elegantly twisted her hand, the lights following the movement. "And, you're right, it is a little bizarre; but I can promise you it is worth it." Her smile beamed under the glow of the lights as she slowly withdrew the orbs from the air and back into her hand, where she doused the light entirely.

"No. This can't be real. You're not real. I'm hallucinating." Micah rambled.

Lucy put her hands on either side of his face to try to calm him, hoping to get through to him, but he kept prattling about the impossibilities of it all. She pulled his face closer to hers and pressed her lips upon his, offering a kiss to quiet him and slow his thinking.

His tense body kept perfectly still beneath her lips. "I'm real," she whispered as she pulled away gently, feeling his body relax under her hands.

She gave him a little smile, offering some truth behind the uncertainty he was facing. Her hands lingered on his cheeks as Micah's eyes met hers. They stood there, locked in each other's gaze. Lucy gently smoothed her thumb over the bit of stubble that was growing on his chiseled jaw, then she slid her hands down to the front of his chest, wondering how she had even gotten to this moment.

The connection she was building with him was more than unexpected, yet it felt completely natural. She could tell him everything now, but where would she start? Perhaps, it was best to come from Abe. He had spent years finding the right words. This was a pivotal moment for the pair, and she didn't want to step in and ruin it — even if she was growing more impatient by the second.

He took a steadying breath and looked back at the package. He unwrapped it carefully, unsure of what he was about to discover. Once the paper was shed, a stack of envelopes tied in twine was all that was left. The top was the most recent and the least weathered; the one at the bottom had been worn with time.

Micah pulled the first letter from the top and put the rest of the stack on the dining room table. He turned the letter in his hands and opened it reverently, taking in the fact that whatever was in this letter was sure to be life changing. He looked between the envelope and Lucy, wondering what the connection was there, but she wasn't even looking at him, instead her eyes were glued to the letter.

"I'm going to need some time to read these," he whispered to her. Then he suddenly picked up the stack of envelopes and walked back up the stairs to the room he was staying in to read them in private.

Lucy stood alone in the dining room in surprise. *Do I go after him? Do I demand that I get to read them, too? No. They aren't my letters. Oh my stars, I showed him my magic. What was I thinking? What if this is too much and he just leaves?*

Her mind raced with thoughts that offered no assistance. Micah could come down and respond with emotions ranging anywhere between anger and fear or excitement and curiosity. Her mind ran the gambit of the possibilities, but nothing would be conclusive. She wouldn't know until he came down and talked to her.

Lucy didn't know what to do with her time, so she continued to pace in the dining room, hoping that he would read quickly and that Abe was clear about the reality of this beloved place.

An hour or two passed before Micah finally made his way back down the staircase to meet Lucy, right where he had left her in the dining room. She didn't think to leave the room, knowing that the fate of The Elderwood lay in Micah's answer to those letters.

"Hey," Micah said to her quietly, eyes red and puffy.

"Hi," Lucy rasped, having to clear her throat to continue. "Are you alright?"

"I'd be lying if I said yes." He forced a sad smile, "but, I think I will be."

"What did the letters say?" Lucy asked, trying not to sound impatient or pushy, but still desperately needing to know the answer.

"Let's go sit outside," he said. "It's a long story and I need some air." He walked through the house, out the back door, and sat upon one of the tree stumps near the empty fire pit.

He sighed loudly as he stared at the trees. Lucy quietly sat down beside him. He spun toward her, startled.

"I didn't even hear you behind me," he breathed.

"I took the boots off," Lucy shrugged.

Micah just laughed loudly as he went back to staring into the woods beyond them.

"What's so funny?" Lucy asked.

"You. This." He spread his arms to the surrounding property. "Everything? Nothing? I don't even know anymore." He dragged his hands down his face, a gesture Lucy realized he did whenever he felt stressed.

She stayed silent as he processed his feelings, ready to listen whenever he was ready. It wasn't easy, but she wasn't quite sure how to respond to that last comment, anyway.

"So," he began again slowly. "The Elderwood is real."

Lucy nodded.

"Magic is real."

She nodded again.

"And you are a witch?" he asked.

"Actually, that part is incorrect," Lucy replied, and Micah sighed with relief. "Witches are real," she began, and Micah looked back at her and tensed up again. "However, I am not one."

"You aren't human either. And you're really old. So what are you?"

"I'm really old? What the hell?" Lucy said with a surprised laugh.

"That picture is you. Not your sister," Micah began. "You don't even have a sister," he stated, looking at her, but no anger was in his stature. A look of surprise on Lucy's face prompted Micah to continue. "You talk a lot when you're drunk."

Lucy winced and covered her face. "That's why you were mean to me this morning? You knew?"

"I knew something was going on. I never could have predicted all of this." He leaned over on the stump and put his elbows on his knees. "Those trees are the important ones, huh?" He asked her.

"Not all of them," Lucy said, scooting over closer to Micah. "Just one. That one, right there." She pointed straight ahead of them to one of the older trees. "Most trees grow and age and die, but the portal was somehow ingrained within one of them, so my ancestors put a spell on that tree and a few of the surrounding ones to make it so they never age. They can still die if something happens to them, but it would have to be quite a force of power."

"Have you ever been there? To The Elderwood?" Micah asked, deference in his tone; quiet and contemplative.

"A few times with my brother," Lucy shared contentedly. "It was the most beautiful place I've ever been."

"Can I see it?"

Lucy sat up a little straighter, looking at Micah. She had never heard of any non-Fae going into The Elderwood before, but she had promised to bend the rules for Abe. She was unsure of the risks, but wouldn't it be a step in the right direction to mending the rift between Abe and Micah?

"Your grandad was my best friend," Lucy whispered, tears began to fill her eyes, threatening to escape and run down her cheeks. "I met him when I was young, he was only 10... I was the one who told him all the stories about The Elderwood," she continued, afraid to speak up, as if admitting this would somehow create more trouble for her. Her heart was heavy with everything she had kept inside of her since she had learned of Abe's passing. "I promised him that once I took over my family's business, I would bring him there, but... but my father wouldn't allow it." Tears raced down her face, and she wiped them away with the back of her hand, her lips trembling. "I was too late," she choked out. "I tried to come back, but I was too late," she sobbed.

She cried for the best friend she ever had, and the guilt she felt for missing her chance to tell him how much she appreciated and loved him. Lucy's grief hit her all at once, realizing she lost the one person in this life that fully understood her and accepted her as she was. Her chest felt as though it would combust, and she couldn't get a deep breath of air.

Micah lifted her in his hands, sat her on his lap and wrapped his arms around her to soothe her tears. He didn't say a word, allowing her the moment to grieve.

All she wanted was to see her friend again and make things right, but there was nothing she could do for him now. However, she could do it for Micah.

She took a second to contain her tears, and looked up to the sky, seeing the stars beginning to appear for the night. Lucy leaned into his warm embrace, pretending for just a few minutes that her future wasn't held in her father's palm.

"I wish I would have known more about all of this before," Micah said sadly, looking up at the stars with Lucy tucked closely to him. "I wasted so much time on hate when he was hurting and I did nothing to fix it."

"You didn't know," Lucy said to him as she put her hands on his cheeks, pulling his face to make him look at her.

"I didn't, but I do now…" Micah looked at her with grief-filled eyes. "You coming here was a weird slice of destiny. If we didn't meet, I would have never figured any of this out. I would still be filled with so much anger." He deftly guided a stray piece of hair out of Lucy's face and back behind her ear, caressing her cheek with a quick graze of his finger. "I'm glad you stayed."

"Me too," she whispered. "I'll fulfill my promise to him, with you… but we can't go yet."

"Why not?" Micah asked, pulling her closer to his body. She felt safe in his embrace.

"The amulet that will grant us access needs to be charged under the full moon," she lifted her head to the sky, with a hint of a smile. "But I think we are in luck, because that's tonight."

EIGHT

"This necklace is going to get us through a magical gateway and into another world?" Micah asked in disbelief as he held the amulet, turning it over in his hands.

"Small but mighty," Lucy teased. "Put it back on the windowsill so it can charge. I've never done this before, so I'm not sure how long it actually has to be in the moonlight."

"You've never done this before?" Micah asked incredulously. "I thought you come here a lot?"

"Well," Lucy dragged out. "Not exactly. I wasn't supposed to be here."

"You told me Grandad was expecting you!" Micah retorted.

"I know, and that isn't entirely true, but it's not really a lie either."

"That was the most vague thing you could have said," Micah groused. "I think we are past the point of holding back truths. Just be honest with me, okay? I'm still here, aren't I? I'm listening now."

Lucy took in a deep breath and released it with a note of defeat. "Alright. My father told me I wasn't allowed to come here to visit with Abe anymore because I am not allowed to be part of the family business. He was threatening... well, something that I wouldn't allow. I wanted to prove to him that I am capable and that he is wrong for trying to box me in and change who I really am."

"Who knows you're here, then?" Micah asked.

"No one?" Lucy cringed.

"Is that going to be a problem for you? Or is it fine because you're super old? How old are you, anyway?" Micah joked.

"You don't need to worry about how old I am. That's rude to ask a lady no matter what realm you're in."

Micah again laughed at Lucy. She bit her lip at the sound, trying to hide the want in her gaze. The two were sitting in the study under a couple of soft blankets near the window, watching the bright moon and waiting for the amulet to charge.

Both were too wound up to get any sleep, so they bunkered down near the amulet and kept talking late into the night. Micah brought up a plate of cheese, meat, and crackers to snack on, along with a bottle of red wine and two long-stemmed glasses. Lucy wasn't sure if only moonlight should be what touched the amulet, so they turned the lights off and lit a few candles to see. The flickering incandescence danced on the walls of the study, a slow, burning dance of want.

"Is your dad going to kill me if he knows you're here alone with me? Or is it not a big deal because you're like 60 years old?" Micah smiled and played with a curly strand of hair dangling freely from Lucy's braid.

"My father will not kill anyone besides me if this doesn't go according to plan," Lucy admitted. "That, or worse." She took a deep drink of the bold wine, licking her lips to catch every drop.

"What's worse than him killing you? That doesn't make sense," Micah replied. "Wait. He won't really kill you, will he? What is he threatening to do to you?" He sat up straighter and leaned toward Lucy in a defensive position. The mere thought of someone hurting her sprung Micah into action, as if he were ready to take on an invisible enemy.

"No, he won't really kill me," Lucy reassured him with a mournful smile. "But it may end up feeling the same. He's forcing me to wed a male that I have no interest in marrying."

"A forced marriage? Is that common where you're from?" Micah asked in disbelief as he sagged back down against the wall.

"Technically it is called an *arranged* marriage, and yes, it's fairly common. Most females my age are wed to other suitors that their parents arrange. It's usually a good enough match that it lasts and is worthwhile. Sometimes the pairing is awful and the couple just suffers through it, but not always. Many couples have found true love through this practice, but I... I'm just not interested in getting married to Laurent. Marriage is the last thing I want."

"Why not? What happened to all of that talk of love and loyalty?"

"That's the problem," Lucy said to Micah, looking deeply into his eyes. "I am hopeful to find love one day, but what they offer to me is not love. It's a business alliance. I don't want someone to marry me because it benefits their pocket book. I want someone to see me and decide they can't live without me."

Micah stayed quiet as he watched her, listening to her speak freely, moving closer to her as she spoke.

"I know it sounds ridiculous." She ducked her head and looked into her wineglass, wondering if she was drinking too much again and allowing her words to spill carelessly from her lips.

"Not ridiculous at all," Micah said, brushing back a stray curl behind her ear, a gesture she yearned for. She leaned into his touch ever so slightly.

"I know I am not a typical female in Denora." Lucy sat up, embracing this truth about herself. "I don't want to cook and clean and raise a brood of children without any help from my husband. I want someone who will be an equal to me, and I want to be an equal to them. My interests and pursuits are important to me, and just because I am female is not a good enough reason for me to change who I am."

"You sound just like my mom." Micah huffed a small laugh, his lips pressed together, holding a sorrowful grin. "That's why her and my dad never stayed together. They were friends, but she didn't feel like they were equals. My mom wanted to ride off into the sunset and change the world, but my dad was fine with the status quo. She left him and went searching for her knight in shining armor," he trailed off.

"Did she ever find him?" Lucy asked, inching closer to him.

"No," he whispered, then cleared his throat. "She got really sick before she could take anything else on. So, she didn't change the world, and she didn't find her soulmate. She never had true love."

"That's not true," Lucy said, brushing Micah's cheek. "She had you. There's no truer love there." He grabbed her hand in his and held it, not letting go. Lucy's center fluttered with anticipation. Each time they touched, it was easier and more natural.

"We were here a lot in her last few years," Micah said. "She got diagnosed when I was seven, so we came to visit every weekend. With my mom's treatments, I basically just lived with my dad, so my mom didn't have to worry about childcare between school and doctor's appointments."

"I'm so sorry that all happened," Lucy said, stroking her thumb along his hand.

"Me too," he replied. "I've been so mad at Grandad for abandoning me in those final moments. When I would visit my mom, we came here for the most part. She wanted me to spend time with her and Grandad. I think part of it was that she was so weak that she felt guilty that she couldn't play the way we used to, so I played with Grandad instead. The three of us were inseparable. I couldn't understand how he just stopped showing up. That he wouldn't leave here to come be with me when I was at my lowest point."

"He would have if he was able," Lucy said adamantly. "I swear it."

"I know," he said quietly, his fingers caressing hers in return. "I've spent over half my life being mad at him. It all feels so ridiculous now."

"It's not ridiculous — you were hurting. Your anger was a mask;

you weren't mad at him, you felt betrayed. Feelings of betrayal can only come from those you love, because you care about the decisions they make." Lucy bent her head down slightly, trying to get eye level to Micah who was looking away from her. "You loved him, and his choices hurt you. When your mother passed, you needed him and he wasn't there."

"Yeah, but he couldn't be there. It wasn't his choice." Micah tried to argue.

"I agree, and I'm glad you see it now. But it's fair that you didn't see it then. How could you have?"

"I should have tried harder. I should have responded to the letters. I just felt like I was drowning after Mom died. I couldn't sleep. I couldn't talk to Dad. I couldn't breathe."

Lucy reached over and hugged him as he silently remembered those somber days. "Grief can do that... No two people's paths through loss are the same. Abe was my best friend... when I —," Lucy began and then had to stop to clear her throat. "When you said he was gone, I blocked it out. I pushed through every hard moment since I've been here, just ignoring the way my heart felt; as though it had left me entirely. I just went on and acted as though I wasn't affected — that my life hadn't changed forever now that the person who I grew up with was gone... You lashed out in a mask of anger. My mask was my stubbornness. But both our love and hurt are genuine. They are both real."

"Does it ever go away?" Micah asked, biting his bottom lip to hold in the tears.

"I'm assuming it does, but I really wouldn't know. Abe was the first person I've ever been close with to pass over to the other side."

The conversation came to a quiet lull.

"I can honestly say I was not looking forward to coming here and dealing with Grandad's house." He looked deeply into her eyes. "But I wasn't expecting you."

"Is that a good thing or a bad thing?"

"Hopefully a good thing, but we are going to have to see how this whole amulet thing unfolds." He lifted her hand and placed a kiss upon her fingers and placed her hand back into her lap. "Also, you never told me what you even were. You're not a witch, so how are you magical and young?" Micah asked, still trying to seek understanding of his new reality.

"I'm Fae," Lucy explained, crossing her legs and pulling the blanket close to her, try to get comfortable and slow the erratic thump of her heart. "We live for a long time, but we aren't technically immortal. Our realm just ages slower than the mortal realm, I guess. And yes, I do some magic, but not much. All Fae go through education and we learn basics. Some who show promise can move on to the higher academies to learn more complex spell work. At the basic level, we just learn practical things."

"What have you learned in your 60 years of magic, then?" he asked.

"I never said I was 60 years old, Micah," she said as she looked at him carefully.

"How old are you, then? 70?"

Lucy bit her lip, unsure how to answer.

"80?" Micah asked in disbelief, leaning in closer to look at her face.

"122," she whispered.

Micah's mouth popped open in shock, his eyes wide.

"That's not even that old!" Lucy protested. "We live for a long time. We physically age, just much slower. Don't make it a thing." She crossed her arms over her body self-consciously. "That is part of what I meant when I said I didn't have anyone who has passed away before... Most Fae live for centuries, so when our venerable Fae leave us, it is a happy celebration of life. But this? Abe was too young for me to see it as a celebration." She shook her head, as she took a deep, steadying breath.

"Venerable Fae?" Micah asked.

"They are our eldest living Fae. They hold a deep seat of respect from the rest of the Fae for their wisdom and honor to Denora." Lucy tried her best to explain. "It usually happens once a Fae gets past the age of 2,000 or so."

"That is officially the craziest thing I've ever heard," Micah laughed, happy to accept the change of direction in the conversation. "So you'll live to be more than 2,000?"

"Possibly," Lucy said. "Most Fae do unless they are taken in battle or get one of the more rare sicknesses." At that last word, Lucy uneasily looked at Micah, remembering his mother passing from a deadly mortal disease.

"So Fae don't get cancer, then, I take it?" Micah said dryly.

"No, I'm sorry, we do not." Lucy wasn't sure why she was apologizing, but Micah losing his mother to something so common in the mortal world put Lucy on edge. She was thankful that Fae didn't have to deal with the same kind of mortality rates, and maybe that's why she felt guilty enough to apologize.

"That's a good thing for you — you don't have to say sorry," Micah said to Lucy, quelling her unease. "I guess you really do have a long marriage then, if it lasts over a thousand years?"

"Oh, please don't remind me," Lucy said with a groan. "That's a long time, even for me."

Micah looked over her body. "You look great for your age," he chuckled, but this time, a more seductive tone took over. Lucy felt her stomach flip at the tenor of his voice. "I hope I look that good when I'm 120."

Lucy barked a laugh. "Abe used to say the same thing to me."

"Were... were you and Grandad... *together*?" Micah asked, unsure.

"Oh, no," Lucy clarified quickly. "We truly were just friends. Abe only ever loved your grandmother."

"Good, because otherwise this would be a little strange," he said as he leaned toward her and kissed her. His lips were soft against hers, as if in question, waiting to see if this was what she wanted.

Lucy placed her wine glass off to the side and replied by opening her lips to him, accepting his kiss and offering passion in return. She dug her hands into Micah's short, dark hair and pulled him even closer. Their lips parted and a small moan left Lucy, causing Micah to grab her waist and pull her onto his lap.

Her leggings gave her only a thin barrier between her body and Micah's, her shirt loose on her waist without her belt to secure it. Micah slid his hands up her thighs as she felt a jolt of excitement run through her and their kissing became more sensuous. Lucy wrapped her arms around his neck as she rocked her body closer and closer to him.

His hands lingered around her waist before moving up her back, their kiss deepening as his fingers trailed down the skin under her shirt. Micah's broad hands grabbed her waist, squeezing gently. He couldn't seem to stop exploring her body and he moved them again to just under her breasts. He never took his hands off her. Through their kiss, his tongue greeted hers, tasting one another in ways she never imagined.

Lucy had never been intimate with a man before, and the most romance she had ever experienced was kissing Nicolas Strezo behind the barn on Tomlinson Farms. But that was child's play compared to the intensity pressing between Micah and Lucy. The aching need within her made her feel so unsure of herself. *Where would things go after this? Things couldn't continue once I return to Denora, could they?* She pulled away, breaking their kiss.

"I'm sorry," Micah said, tilting his head down in a blush. He removed his hands from under her shirt and placed them on top of her waist, while she remained on his lap.

"Don't be. You're not like most males I've met," she admitted to him breathlessly, still straddling his legs. She tilted herself back, looking at him with a smile full of longing, the pink blush still coloring her cheeks.

"I could say the same thing about you, but I don't want you to think I am saying it simply because you're an older woman," he winked.

Lucy shook her head and laughed. She swung one leg off of Micah and got back into a seated position, snuggling up close to him, wanting to be near him, but not knowing what else she wanted. "I mean it. Most males in Denora, where I'm from, are so focused on their careers and their status in the Kingdom."

"What about you? Are you a princess in your Kingdom?"

"No, not at all. My father owns a business the royals value, so we are just wealthy— which I realize is an amazing privilege."

"What about this Laurent guy?" The fierce look in his eyes hinted at something unsaid.

"He is a different story..." Lucy looked around the room trying to find the right words to say, but not wanting to poison this moment with thoughts of Laurent. "Denora is broken into three large sections. The Southern Territory is run by Lord Isaacs. The Central Territory is where I live and it is where the King resides. Then, in the Northern Territory, there is Lord Laurent Sloan."

"He's the ruler of the entire Northern Territory?" Micah's eyes were wild at the realization. "So if you marry him, that would make you...?"

"Lady Lucella Sloan, Lady of the Northern Territory." Lucy's entire demeanor changed, her face drawn and devoid of any lightness it usually carried.

She looked out the window, gazing at the moon in all of its mystery. The silver amulet glimmered under the moonlight, and Lucy wondered if she really wanted to return home at all.

"If you don't want to marry him, can't you just say no?"

"Unfortunately, that's not how any of it works. My father said yes, and that was enough. That is why I'm here, doing what I can to stop it." She gave him a weak smile and looked back to the window, hiding her feelings. *What happens once I stop it? What happens if I can't?*

"I think you should do whatever makes you happy. I assume that's archery?"

"Actually, I love to make the bows. That's partially why I left." She straightened again as she talked about her real purpose there. Micah looked at her and listened intently. "The Elderwood holds the wood we need to make the most coveted bows in all of Denora. My great-grandfather found it many years ago and forged an agreement with the humans here to protect it."

"That must be why Grandad's land is protected by the government," Micah mused.

"What do you mean?" Lucy asked.

"Land like this — the woods and the forests? It gets categorized by the government; labeled so they know what can and cannot be built or changed on the grounds. A lot of the land around here has been recategorized under residential or farmland, so it's easy to be sold. That's why so much of the forest shrunk. There's a tree-line far in the back of Grandad's property that's classified as protected forest, so it can't be sold. Grandad's acreage... His land backs up to the protected line, but it sticks out like a sore thumb. It should have also been classified as residential or farmland along with the rest of the land that surrounds it, but instead it's labeled as protected — even without being an actual forest. This land is unable to be changed or sold."

"Sounds like a tricky Fae had their hand involved in that," Lucy considered. "I'm sure my father's business would have been in jeopardy if the land was sold. I wouldn't be surprised if it was him or Jasper out here, making sure this property was saved."

"Maybe," Micah replied. "The paperwork I found with the will definitely didn't make much sense, but I guess paying off a higher up would do the job."

"Securing the gateway to The Elderwood is essential. My father would have done anything to ensure it's safety. Though, now that Abe is gone... someone needs to stay here to protect it." Lucy realized solemnly.

Micah stayed quiet for a long time after that, taking in the reality of his situation. He understood the words that weren't said. It wasn't that 'someone' needed to be here to protect it. It was him. Micah needed to stay.

"Well, then when do we get to go see it?" Micah asked, faking a casual tone, though his tense posture was enough to give away his true feelings on the subject.

"First thing tomorrow," Lucy said with a sincere smile. "We need the amulet to refuel all night just to be sure we can get in, and then I'll take you. It will change your life." Her smile was almost enough to make Micah believe her.

WHEN THEY WOKE up the next day, they found themselves in a tangle of blankets and arms. Their intimate whispers and touches carried on deep into the night, but Lucy made sure to keep some semblance of boundaries. However, waking up in the arms of Micah felt more like home than any place she had ever experienced. She wasn't sure what to make of it, especially as she would leave today after they came back from The Elderwood.

With that realization, Lucy sat up with a gasp. Today was the day she would finally finish what she had set out to do. Micah stirred with Lucy's sudden movements, yawning widely, still tired from the little sleep they had the night before.

He pulled her into her arms and kissed her deeply, his hands wrapping around her cotton tunic and her hands finding his bare, broad shoulders. A laugh tumbled out of Lucy's lips.

"I know I keep saying this, but I'm glad I found you here," Micah told her, holding her tightly in a hug. He nuzzled her hair. "I never thought I'd meet a person like you. You kind of drive me crazy, but in the best way possible."

"I feel the same about you," Lucy said, admitting her feelings for the first time. "I can't wait for you to see this forest. The Elderwood is the most beautiful place I've ever been. You're going to love it."

Lucy slowly twisted out of his arms, crawled to the windowsill, and grabbed the amulet. Micah sat up, more alert now that he had realized what Lucy was reaching for.

"Is it ready?" he asked, anticipation flooding his voice.

The sigil glowed in her hands. "Yes," she said as she looked at Micah with a smile to rival the sun itself. "It's ready. Let's go."

~

CLEARLY, this journey through Denora to the mortal realm had been nothing, if not unexpected. However, Lucy couldn't afford any more missteps. There was no way she would enter The Elderwood without being fully prepared. She wore her fitted outfit, tied her boots tightly and secured her bow and make-shift quiver of arrows to her back. Micah grabbed a hunting knife that Abe had in his shed.

The pair walked hand-in-hand to the tree that held the gateway and stood in front of it as they prepared to make the journey to the other realm.

"Are you ready?" Lucy asked Micah nervously.

"Ready as I'll ever be, I guess," he replied meekly.

"Okay, I will keep the amulet in my left hand, and you will hold it with your right. Your skin needs to be touching the amulet the entire time we pass through, understand?" Micah gave a nod. "Then I also want you to hold on to my arm with your other hand. Sometimes it can be rocky going through a portal, especially for your first time."

Again, Micah nodded and grabbed Lucy's hand. He curled his left arm around in front of him to hold on to Lucy's arm above her elbow, gripping tightly.

"Here we go," Lucy said gently. She held up her hand and led the two of them to walk through the gateway, but nothing happened.

Again and again, she took a step back and then forward, willing the portal to open to her, but all that remained was the tree bark. No source of passage to anywhere but where they stood.

She felt the power flowing through the talisman as it warmed in her hands. The light on the amulet glowed, but nothing else happened beyond that. The sigil on the tree remained dark.

"What is happening?" Lucy said to herself, letting go of Micah's hand as she forcefully pressed along the tree. "Maybe I can't bring someone who isn't Fae with me?" she suggested, distress coloring her words. She fervently tried again and again to gain access to The Elderwood, but it remained locked.

"I don't understand," Micah said. "Did it not get enough power last night?"

Lucy frantically analyzed the amulet. The light glowing brightly from the sigil was proof that they charged it enough to work, but why wouldn't it allow them entrance into The Elderwood?

"I don't know," Lucy said in despair. "It isn't letting us through." Her hands fell down to her sides, her face drawn and hopeless. *What did I do?* she asked herself, thinking about every single mistake she had made since she conceived of her plan.

Micah sighed and rubbed his hand down his face. "I need coffee."

"Are you making a joke? *Coffee?* That's what you're thinking about right now?" Lucy snapped at him, unable to bear the weight of the possibility that the amulet would not work. *It has to work, it has to. What did I do?*

"Well, the gateway isn't opening, and we barely slept last night, so yeah. Coffee." He turned and walked back toward the house.

"This is more important than a cup of coffee, Micah," she screamed at him, causing him to stop in his tracks. "This is my last chance!" Her breath hitched. "This can't be happening," she said to herself. Lucy began shaking with fear and anger. *Why does he not care? Why is he acting like this is not important?*

"For all I know, this is some extreme joke between you and Abe, and listen, you almost got me, okay?" Micah exhaled and dug his hands in his pockets and shrugged his shoulders. "Call it revenge from the grave, whatever. I'm getting coffee."

"No wonder you and Abe never talked!" Lucy shouted. "You don't listen, do you? When he was trying to apologize, you didn't listen. You never listened to him when he was trying to tell you about The Elderwood. You don't fucking listen!"

"And you do?" He replied indignantly, taking a step closer to her, pointing to her. "You're here because daddy doesn't pay enough attention to you? Because you can't just follow directions? You wouldn't even be here if you would just do what you were told."

"Fuck you!" Lucy screamed. With that, Micah threw his hands up into the air and walked into the house. He didn't turn back, leaving Lucy alone in front of the closed portal.

Lucy fell to her knees in the dirt, her breathing coming quicker as she panicked. *I can't return home empty-handed. I can't return home and tell them I left The Elderwood unprotected. I can't return home and marry Laurent.*

Thoughts were swarming through Lucy's mind as tears flooded and crashed down her cheeks. She sobbed at the base of the tree. How did things go so, so wrong?

NINE

The birds were the first sound to wake Lucy from her restless sleep at the base of the tree. She was sore from lying in the uneven dirt all night, but her body was again too weak to connect with her Denoran magic, making her feel less and less Fae.

Lucy had been gone from her realm for too long. The longest she had ever been away from home had been three days, and that was to another Fae realm. Today was day five in Joterra.

Surely her mother knew she was gone by now and told her father, but what could he have done about it? The talismans that allowed transport between realms were not given sparingly, and admitting to losing one was akin to treason of the Kingdom. It was simply not done. Besides, she could be anywhere, and if her father needed to travel the realms to come after her, he would have to find two things: Fae of significant power to ask to use their key and enough money to buy their silence. The shame she could bring her father kept growing tenfold.

The same self-doubts as before came pouring into Lucy's mind. Why did she think she could come here and prove herself to anyone? She couldn't complete a standard task that was necessary for the business. This was a worthless trip and when she returned home, shame would follow her right down the aisle as she married Laurent. Her future would be carved into stone forever.

A pang in her chest throbbed at the thought. But then, she thought of Micah... This entire time; she was so against marriage because she wasn't sure if she would ever find someone who really saw her for who she was.

Now, Lucy was with a man who saw her for who she truly was and accepted her. Was there any chance in all the realms that she could see where things go with Micah? Would she really have to throw away the potential of real love and wed Laurent?

She remembered screaming at Micah and cringed. *I'm pushing too much on him, too quickly.* Lucy shook her head. This situation affected his life too, and he needed to make the decision to protect The Elderwood on his own. The weight of his choices were wearing her down. She needed to figure this out if she wanted to give herself a chance to live her own life.

Lucy pulled herself off of the forest floor and slowly trudged to the back door of the house, hoping to get a large drink of water. She had stayed under the tree the entire previous day, trying to solve why the amulet wouldn't allow her passage. She dragged every possibility from her memory and recited spell after spell. Nothing she tried had worked.

The back door swung open with a creak as Lucy stepped into the kitchen. To her surprise, the entire room was a disaster. The table was turned upside down, chairs were strewn about the small room, and all the cabinets and drawers were opened and emptied. In the middle of the disorder sat Micah, shock plastered to his unmoving face. In his lap he held a very worn leather-bound book, gripping it so tightly his knuckles turned white.

"Micah!" Lucy ran to him, pushing an overturned kitchen chair from her path. She got to her knees in front of him, taking his face in her hands to get him to look at her. "What happened?" Lucy asked him gently, caressing his face with her fingers.

"It was where he kept the cookies," Micah whispered, staring blankly, his calm a distracting contrast to the chaos that filled the room.

"The letters," he said, looking at Lucy with red, tear-stained eyes. "You told me I never listen, and it's what my mom used to tell my dad... I was so angry at you. At Grandad..." He took steadying breaths. "I don't want to be that person. So I picked up the letters again and I read through them."

Lucy kept quiet, though the tension was killing her. *Why was he sitting on the floor like this? What happened? What had he found?*

"We didn't just read in the dining room. We played in the forest, in the living room, and on our journey through the house, we always made a stop in the kitchen. We always stole cookies on the way to the tree fort."

He held up the book as Lucy moved her hands to his broad shoulders, steadying his shaky breaths. "It was our secret, Grandad acted like Mom didn't know, but she knew. She snuck special treats in there for us, and me and Grandad hid our treasures there. Old coins we found. Fossilized rocks. I knew he had to have hidden more clues somewhere with the cookies, because it was our special place..." He looked around the room at the disorder that he caused in his search. "I couldn't remember which cabinet my mom kept the cookies, and I tore this place apart looking for them. I had to find them, Lucy," he said with desperation in his tone. "I had to figure out what Grandad wanted from me. I didn't want to turn my back on him, again. And this — it was in the drawer," he said as he held up the book. "Hidden in a false bottom."

The book was brown leather, wrapped in a thin strap. It looked older than anything else in the house, including the house itself, which was saying something. The front of the book was branded with the same sigil from the amulet, but with one main difference: the tree had no leaves. Instead, it was as if it were a tree in winter — bare branches creating a malevolent replica of the Baum family crest.

"This is different from my amulet," Lucy said in a near whisper, looking at the detail on the book.

"It's the first," Micah said to her, watching her response closely. "There's so much in here you didn't tell me."

"I told you everything," Lucy protested. "My great-grandfather found the portal. He paid the mortals here to keep it safe, and we use The Elderwood for the bows. That's it."

"Your great-grandfather didn't find the portal," he stated, clarity in his gaze once again. "It wasn't *your* family. It was *mine*."

"What? No. You're mortal, you couldn't have found the gateway. You don't have any magic."

"That's the thing. I'm not mortal... well, not full-blooded anyway." He shook his head and Lucy looked at him as if he was crazy. "Come on," he got up and pulled her out of the destroyed kitchen and into the living room, where they could sit next to one another. He grabbed two glasses of water from the tap and gave one to Lucy. "Sit."

"I don't understand why you think you're not mortal," Lucy said cautiously. "You're human, Micah. Are you okay? Did you drink too much last night? Did you hit your head?" She placed her water down and started checking him for injuries.

"Yes, I'm okay," Micah said as he carefully took her hand. "I want to show you this, but it seems to me like this is a big secret my family has been keeping for centuries. I don't think your family is supposed to know..."

"Just tell me already," Lucy urged impatiently.

Micah sighed and moved closer to Lucy so that their thighs were touching. He opened the book so it covered both of their laps. "Read this page."

As a young man, I traveled throughout the Kingdom and in between realms searching for more. I found myself in the mortal realm completely by chance, and continued to search the peaceful forests. The beasts were calm and kind, there were no beings around for miles. My amulet drew me toward an archaic tree, taller than all the others. When my talisman grew warm in my hands, I knew a gateway lay just beyond. Through that gateway, I found what I call The Elderwood.

Take heed. The Elderwood is no play place. Many ancient magics live beyond the shadows that we must never defy. The magic lives deeply rooted in the land, which allows the trees to be imbued with properties unknown to any other. When using the materials from the trees in The Elderwood, the wood will not splinter, break, nor fail. It feeds off of the magic used by the Fae that whittles it, creating the strongest of houses and most accurate of arrows.

I came to live in the mortal realm 500 years after the Great War to settle with my new wife once humans came near the forests. The Elderwood must be protected at all times, no one should enter or exit The Elderwood without extreme caution. And no one shall ever use the portal without a Lumen safeguarding the passage. I gave my one trusted companion an amulet to provide entrance to The Elderwood with his promise to keep it safe and out of the hands of any other Fae; and to keep my whereabouts unknown as I live out the end of my days with my family.

This book holds the history of the Lumen ancestral line as well as the accumulated knowledge of The Elderwood and what lies within. Use with caution, handle with care.

Alderic Lumen

"THIS CAN'T BE," Lucy stuttered.

"I know it sounds impossible," Micah reassured her. "But it's all true. There are pieces of information in this book that date back thousands of years. The archer," he took Lucy's cheek in one hand, desperately searching her eyes. "The archer created the amulet and gave it to your great-grandfather. You are the grandchild of the trusted companion."

"And you," Lucy looked into his eyes. "You are of the Lumen family line."

"Micah Lumen, pleased to meet you," he said with a smirk. "You couldn't get into the portal because the 'passing of the torch,' so to speak, didn't happen between me and Grandad. There was no one protecting it, so it wouldn't open to you."

"How do we fix it?" Lucy asked, looking back at the book, taking her hand from his and beginning to turn the pages. "How can we get it to grant us access?"

"I found it," he said gently, taking the book and turning to a page in the middle of the tome. "Most things we need are in the kitchen. There are a few things I don't understand, though. The stem of a lion's-tooth? Nettle root? Flay scuff?"

"Those are Fae terms," Lucy gasped, pulling the book toward her. "Lion's-tooth is a weed. Yellow in the spring and summer and it turns white and kind of fluffy when the seeds spread."

"A dandelion?" Micah asked in bewilderment.

"Nettle root is just the root of a nettle. They have stinging leaves, but healing properties if used correctly. I think I saw some on my way here," she said with bright eyes.

Lucy continued to read the text, learning how to complete the transference rite. Her eyes darted around the page, and then she began to look around the room.

"What is it?" Micah asked. "Is there something wrong with the spell?"

"Flay scuff... flay scuff..." she mumbled to herself. "It says flay scuff from the origin..." She got up and paced the small living room. "The tree. The tree is the origin! Flay scuff, it's what they used to call tree bark," Lucy said with fire in her eyes. "We have everything we need."

Micah closed the book and stood, holding the book under his arm. "Are you sure you're ready to do this?"

"Absolutely. You get the items from the kitchen and go find the yellow flower. I'll get the rest."

Micah nodded seriously and turned on his heel to the kitchen, stepping over the havoc he created, cleaning as he searched for the ingredients to the spell.

Lucy ran out into the woods near the house, searching for the nettle plant. Her head was spinning. *Was this really happening? Just yesterday Micah opposed this entire situation, and now he was ready to accept it all in effort to protect The Elderwood. Where did this change come from?*

After finding the nettle, and stinging herself while digging up the roots, she ran back toward the house and met Micah at the tree. He had the lion's-tooth stems and the other few common ingredients listed in the tome. The book was open to the inscription, the words to the rite seeming to glow a pale green light as they neared the entrance to The Elderwood.

Lucy stopped short, seeing the eagerness in Micah's stance. "What changed?" she asked him bluntly, emotions warring inside her.

"What do you mean?" Micah asked her, standing before the tree with his hands full.

"You told me yesterday this was bullshit, and that I was crazy and today you are ready to jump headfirst into another realm without a second of hesitation?" Lucy said to him breathlessly, tears on the verge of escape, the sting of his words still fresh. "This is not just visiting some place for a holiday, Micah. This rite will name you keeper of the gateway. You..." Tears were streaming down Lucy's face now. "You can't ever leave this property."

She knew the importance of The Elderwood to her family, but she also knew Micah's deep hurt. Abe's position as guardian to the gateway ruined their relationship. Micah held such anger and animosity toward his grandfather for decades because of the sadness he felt. Now he was ready to welcome the role with no questions asked? Something wasn't right here.

Micah stayed silent at first, unsure how to explain. "I..." he had a hard time forming the words. "I don't blame him for not coming. I had a lot of time to think yesterday and last night. And, you were right, Lucy."

Lucy raised her eyebrow. "Right about what?"

"I don't listen," he said with a sad smile. "But this book," he lifted the leather-bound tome in his hands. "This book has more than stories about The Elderwood. It had stories from every guardian of The Elderwood since its discovery. Grandad wrote in it... and so did my mom."

"Your mother?" Lucy was floored. "What did it say? Why was it written in there?"

Micah placed the materials on the ground and opened to the back of the book where a single piece of paper was folded; Micah's name written across in a beautiful scrawl.

My dearest son,

My diagnosis changes a lot about how I wanted this to go. Your grandfather and I have tried to prepare you for many years with games and stories to help you understand the true magic and wonderment of The Elderwood. Grandad was supposed to relinquish the position to me, and then I to you. I'm sorry we have to skip a generation and that the responsibility gets placed upon your shoulders sooner than it should have to. Please have faith in the truth that we are just one tiny part of this universe, and that beauty lies beyond our wildest dreams. I hope you get to see it one day. I hope you find beauty in our world as well, and live out your days with your family here on the property, just as I did so many years ago. I love you, sweet boy. Embrace the journey, accept the path that was destined, and make it yours.

Mom

"She knew?" Lucy asked breathlessly.

"She knew," Micah confirmed, a tear escaping and falling down his cheek. "Grandad was supposed to pass it on to Mom, and then Mom would pass it on to me when I was older and could establish a family... Grandad wasn't supposed to be the guardian for as long as he did, but he didn't want to give it to me until I lived. He didn't want to make me stop living my life before I was ready."

"He loved you so much," Lucy said, tears stinging her eyes.

"I know." Micah stated. "That's why I'm doing it." He took a deep breath and exhaled. "This is what was meant for me, and my family tried to protect me so that I could live a full life before I took over. But in that time, I didn't do enough with my life. My dad moved on and remarried. I was a detective to help people, but I never helped myself. I never kept a group of friends, I never found someone to love, I never made a family of my own."

"Why?" Lucy couldn't understand why he was sharing all of this with her.

"I think deep down, I knew it wasn't the path I was supposed to be on," Micah said, stepping closer to Lucy. "I think I was waiting for you."

He bent his head down to kiss her gently, their lips meeting through tears. Lucy felt the spark of something more between the two of them and beamed.

The weight that had been pulling him down and filling him with anger was gone, clarity shining through his deep brown eyes. This was the understanding Micah had been waiting for, and with it, his animosity toward his grandfather had left him completely.

Lucy was filled with an overwhelming appreciation for Micah, knowing how difficult this decision was for him. She was proud to see that Abe's words had made a difference — that her friend was able to share his love with his grandson even from the afterlife.

"I'm sorry for how I've been behaving." He looked down at his feet, ashamed of his actions. "I've been projecting all of my anger and sadness out to the world for far too long." He looked back up to Lucy, his eyes full of regret. "Thank you for seeing through all that; for seeing *me* through my struggle."

"I know you're a good man," she said as she pulled his face toward hers. "I'll let you keep working on proving it to me," she winked at him as she gave him a gentle kiss.

"Let's do this ritual and go see The Elderwood," Micah smiled.

Lucy nodded and put the ingredients for the rite into a large wooden bowl, then carefully used Micah's knife to chip a piece of the bark from the sacred tree holding the portal.

The transference spell was written in ancient Fae, and Lucy helped Micah to pronounce the words correctly. He then took a small sip of the brew they made and poured the rest of it onto the base of the entrance to The Elderwood.

Suddenly, the carving high on the tree trunk burst into green light, and the amulet in Lucy's hand emanated a warm green glow. Micah put the bowl down and held the leather tome close to his chest, not wanting to have it out of his sight for more than a moment. Together, Lucy and Micah clasped hands and leaned into the bark of the tree. The passage opened.

TEN

Most portals had a cool, refreshing sensation when you passed through, but entering this realm was something completely different. It was a warm breeze that surrounded Lucy and Micah. It was as if each burst of air had a mind of its own as it wrapped around Lucy's arm, her fingers, her neck. It sent a rush of electricity into her, the foreign sensation tingling from head to toe; joy bursting at the seams. Reds, blues and oranges, swirled in constant motion as she passed through the portal, reminding her of the sunset.

As she took another step, she felt soft grass under her feet. In a blink, otherworldly beauty welcomed her to The Elderwood. It took her breath away. She would never grow tired of the view.

She looked over at Micah as he stood wide-eyed and slack-jawed. She grinned and squeezed his hand to get his attention. He looked at her and then back to the view of the realm, unable to speak.

Lucy understood. She felt the same way the first time she came through the entrance. The tree that held the portal resided on a hill that perched high above the rest of The Elderwood, giving a perfect view of the forest for miles and miles.

Micah stood speechless, unsure of how to take it all in. Lucy gently pulled him a few steps ahead toward the overlook so he could get a better view. She pointed out the different parts of The Elderwood that she was familiar with and watched as he collected the information with awe.

The treetops were the first thing to capture your eye — nearly every color in any given direction. There were greens in every shade, yellows, reds, purples and oranges, even uncommon hues of blues and pinks. Deep below was a large lake that remained so calm and still even with the breeze; it reflected the trees in a perfect mirror image, creating a mirage of even more vast space.

Far off to the west from where the pair stood was a part of The Elderwood that her brother always told her to avoid. The grove was dark, as if cast in an eternal shadow, regardless of the position of the sun. The trunks were dark brown and black, the leaves a deep blood red. Naturally, Lucy was curious, but the negative energy the trees gave off made her sure to stay far away.

To the east were mountains that were covered in both snow and flowers. The chill of the snow didn't seem to impact the plant life at all. In general, the temperature within the realm was akin to a perfect spring day. Warm enough for the sun to kiss your face, but with moments of cool. Never enough to be truly cold.

The sky was its own masterpiece. A vast canvas of blue unlike any other, home to a sun and four full moons — each were said to have been connected with the four seasons. The satellites stretched across the horizon, offering an instantaneous, magical charge to her amulet. They would rotate throughout the sky, giving a bright beautiful glow at night, offering enough light for Lucy to accomplish her tasks without needing fire or Fae light to see.

At the moment, it was a beautiful, bright day. However, the night in The Elderwood was nearly as beautiful. Bioluminescent plant life sprinkled the landscape. It was a beauty to behold with unique flowers that would bloom only at night and more stars than Lucy had ever seen. She couldn't wait to bring Micah back here another time to see the sacred woods under the light of the moons.

"This is truly unbelievable," Micah said with a sigh of contentment.

"I know." Lucy looked out into the bright yellow and pink trees far into the forest. "It's why it needs to remain protected. If too many people knew of this place, it would be destroyed. Even the Fae are known to destroy beautiful things in the name of progress."

"I promise," Micah said quickly. "I'll protect it."

"Thank you." Lucy tucked herself into his arms in a hug and inhaled deeply, memorizing his scent. His sturdy arms held her closely, and she took a moment to commit that feeling to memory, too.

Now that they were in The Elderwood, her journey was nearing an end. How could she leave Micah after what they had discovered together? How would she leave him to figure out the Lumen family legacy alone?

Her thoughts threatened to ruin this moment with the worries of what was to come, but she forced herself to put them aside. She needed to take this minute, to appreciate the man who helped her get here.

There was something special about Micah, she realized. He accepted her for all she was, flaws included, and never asked her to change. Micah never balked at her directness and accepted her opinions without attempting to dissuade her. He liked her for who she was, not for what she could offer him. He offered her equal companionship.

"It's so quiet here," he whispered to her, his face nuzzled into her neck.

"No one has ever seen anyone else here," she told him. "No humans. No Fae. No animals, even. It's a very lonely place. In some ways it reminds me of home... the loneliness."

"You won't ever have to feel lonely again," he promised her.

Lucy smiled at him and took the book out of his hands and put it on the ground next to them. She placed her bow and quiver and the amulet down next to them as well, making sure they were safely secured before turning to Micah. Lucy reached around his neck and put her hands into his dark hair, pulling him in for an all consuming kiss.

In response, he pulled her close to him, meeting her kiss with a wild desire of his own. He found the hem of her shirt and pulled it over her head, exposing her smooth skin to the temperate air around them. An exhilarated thrill ran through Lucy as she pulled at Micah's shirt until he dragged it over his head and tossed it off to the side.

Micah's hands explored her bare skin, skimming her body from her neck down to the lace that covered her breasts. A soft moan left Lucy's throat, compelling Micah to kiss her neck and carefully remove the lace that covered her. Lucy tugged on his hair, pulling him closer to her naked torso as he kissed her, her center clenching at the sensual touch.

He picked her up and gently guided her down to the grassy floor beneath them, his strong arms lifting her with ease. Micah kissed her as he deftly removed the rest of their clothing until Lucy laid bare beneath him. She flushed with pink as a nervous excitement filled her, her arms covering her breasts; a smile the only thing she wore.

"Are you sure you want to do this?" Micah asked her, his heart racing with anticipation.

"Yes. I'm sure," she said as she pulled him down to her. He propped himself up on one bent arm, his body fitting closely to Lucy's as their desire led the way.

THERE WAS NEVER a time that Lucy felt more connected to another soul other than the time she spent with Micah under the great Elderwood trees. Her body hummed from the intimate tenderness, knowing Micah was more than just any male. She felt so close to him; an emotion teetering on the edge of "love" pressed into Lucy's heart.

But, there were too many things in her life creating pandemonium — she didn't want to drag someone she cared about into all of it. She couldn't add more to Micah's new life than she already had.

What they experienced together in this paradise was enough for Lucy to know that her future had really changed. However, the thought of that scared her more than she could have ever considered. How could she feel so deeply for a man that she could never have?

They drifted into a comfortable silence, with Lucy laying on Micah's chest, watching the warm breeze ruffle the leaves in the green trees above her. *How long have we been here?* she thought to herself. *We need to finish what we came here for and get back. We can't risk staying too long.*

"We really should get moving," Lucy said to Micah, nuzzling his neck. His stubbled chin lightly tickled her face. "I need a few boughs of wood from the trees nearby, and then we can make our way back."

"Lucy?" Micah asked in a solemn whisper. "What happens when we go back through that portal? Will you leave?"

She sat up and pulled her shirt on, looking at him with a war of emotions inside of her. "I have to," she replied. "This isn't my world."

"But it can be, can't it?"

"I'm not sure. I don't think it's ever been done."

"Alderic did it," Micah said, sitting up to get closer to her. "He left your realm and lived a long life. You can do it, too."

"I have to fix things at home. We can't get ahead of ourselves," Lucy replied, trying to be gentle, but she knew the words were like an arrow to his heart. She didn't want to leave him, but she really had no other choice. Had she? *Could staying with Micah even be a possibility?*

"Right." Micah turned away from her to get his clothes, trying to hide the hurt and defeat in his tone.

Lucy finished dressing herself and moved toward Micah, who was sitting quietly, staring into the colorful trees below. "Would you like to come with me?" She asked him, trying to bridge the gap she unintentionally created.

"I think I'm just going to soak this up for a bit," he gave her a forced smile. The hurt was apparent on his face.

"That's fine, I won't be long. My magic has replenished quite a bit from being back in a Fae realm, I should be able to move quicker." Lucy struggled with leaving him like this, but their time was coming to an end, and there was nothing to be done about that, no matter how much she wanted to change it. Lucy gave one last smile and made her way into the woods to complete the task that brought her here.

By the time she returned, Micah was staring oddly at the gateway. "Lucy," he called to her as she came into view. "Lucy!" Fear filled his voice. "Something's wrong."

The tree that held the portal to the mortal realm was glowing bright red, the light pulsating ominously.

"We need to leave," Lucy said urgently. She shoved a few pieces of wood into his arms and grabbed their belongings from the ground. "Hold on tight, don't let go," she told him seriously. He nodded, and they walked swiftly through the portal, holding the amulet tightly.

They entered into a world of smoke and flames.

"WHAT IS GOING ON?!" Micah coughed, the smoke and ash clouding his vision.

"Don't let go of me!" Lucy called back to him. She pulled him away from the smoldering heat, barely able to see through the thick black smoke filling the air. Under her feet, tree branches cracked and dirt softened their steps. They were still in the woods, but where was this fire coming from?

Flames in the near distance radiated extreme heat. Lucy continued to back away until the air cleared enough for her to see the source; the house was on fire.

"No!" Micah screamed. He dropped the wood and the leather tome and sprinted into the house.

"Stop!" Lucy called, in fear for his life. Running into a burning building was bad in all realms, wasn't it? What was he trying to get? *Why would he be so foolish?*

"Hurry up!" She heard a voice call out — a voice that did not belong to Micah.

She secured her quiver onto her back and positioned her bow with an arrow nocked in place. The man on the premises did not belong here, and she was sure that he was the one at fault for the fire. Lucy was going to find him, and she was going to make him pay.

Lucy quickly ran toward the commotion of voices, listening intently to decipher how many people she would be dealing with. She counted four different men's voices, along with the sound of a running vehicle. That was when she saw them; the perpetrators with a pick-up truck, the back filled with gasoline canisters. This was no accident.

"This way, Billy!" called one of the men. Lucy located him running near the house with another can of gas, ready to feed the fire. She pulled the arrow without a second thought, hitting the man in his thigh, causing him to crash to the ground as the canister tumbled away from him.

"Ah!" He yelled out to the others. "I'm hit! Someone else is here!"

Lucy tucked behind a tree, using her Fae hearing to identify where the men were gathering — knowing that the element of surprise could be used to her advantage.

They hadn't seen her yet, and they didn't know her true ability. She mustered all of her Fae magic within her veins and prepared to do whatever it took to safeguard The Elderwood. She listened as they shouted to one another, trying to find her location.

Lucy remained concealed and readied her bow. She swung out from behind the tree, loosed her arrow, then darted back to her hidden position with her Fae speed. The scream was the only indicator that she had hit her target.

She was doing her best not to kill any of the humans here, knowing that it was an unforgivable act and could be a call to inter-realm treason. However, getting them away from the forest, by any means necessary, is exactly what would happen if they didn't leave soon. There would be no bounds to her actions if it meant saving The Elderwood.

Where is Micah? Lucy thought to herself. *He needs to get out of that house before it falls down on him. Please, please, get out of there.*

As if he could hear her plea, Micah came tearing out of the house, coughing and holding a mass of items in his arms.

"There's one over there!" she heard one brute call. "Get him!"

At the idea of Micah getting hurt, something came over Lucy, causing her to move without fear of the repercussions. She walked out from her place beyond the trees and began wide, purposeful strides toward the intruders; her gaze fierce. Lucy's determination was palpable. She would not allow them to lay one finger on Micah.

This time, they saw her.

"There! The archer!" One of the men called. It was the first man she hit in the leg, and while he was unable to help the others with their destruction, he crawled his way back toward the truck.

"Take her out!" Another injured man called, a wound on his upper arm gushing blood. The other target she hit — but he wouldn't be the last.

The magic in Lucy's blood began to boil with the urgency of protecting what was hers. She kept eye contact with her prey, whispering to her arrow the ancient Fae her ancestors had taught her. The hair on her arms stood on end with the magic flowing through her body, ready to be unleashed on those who wished to do her harm. The arrow flew through the air, pinning the third man's hand to the car, rendering him immobile, screaming for help from his friends.

Lucy stood in the open yard between the burning home and the smoky forest behind her, no longer running from the miscreants trying to destroy Micah's land.

A flash burst to the right of Lucy, the trees going up in a blaze. She stuck her arm out to the fire, encouraging it to bend to her will. She stared into the flames and called to them in Fae, a spell she had never heard before, yet it came so easy to her lips. Her fingertips sparked with a pale green light just as that same light poured like smoke from the engraved sigil on the tree that held the passage to The Elderwood behind her.

It was as if The Elderwood was feeding the protection spells directly into her mind, giving her the words needed to take on this attack and secure the realm. The power and light surging toward Lucy poured around her, creating a wind storm.

She lifted her hand into the air, watching as the flames followed her movements. Keeping her arm held high, she watched the men remove the arrow from the man's hand, freeing him. Defiantly, he took another gas can and began running toward the house.

As she directed her gaze on him, her eyes shone a pale green. *You won't get away this time.* She smiled and threw the blaze in his direction, completely overwhelming him. Her victim screamed as the fire and light twisted and engulfed him completely. He fell to the ground with the gas can; the blast of fire multiplied from the exploding fuel. Lucy didn't blink as she slowly scanned the grounds, searching for her next target.

The magic within her was primal — other worldly and more powerful than anything she had ever felt before. There was no fear left within her. She knew she would bring down anything and anyone in her path.

One man was left, as the other two were still at the car. Lucy stood with her bow in one hand and the control of the flames in another, her hair whipping in the wind as the fire continued to spread. Her strange green eyes remained unblinking as she made contact with the last man, her lips turning up on one side as she prepared to end his life for the sake of everything she loved. Her anger grew within her, and her smile turned into a sneer. *How dare they try to take what's mine?* With that dark thought, she began to levitate off the ground, focusing on the demise of these treacherous mortals who tragically picked the wrong Fae to cross.

"Lucy!" she heard someone call, yet the voice seemed so far away.

She lifted her hand as the fire grew, preparing to aim the flames at the last of the men who were threatening to destroy everything.

"Lucy!" she heard again, bringing her back down to the ground. She blinked as the power she held over the flames dissipated, allowing her hazel eyes to return to their natural color. "Lucy, stop!" she heard the voice say again.

She looked over to Micah, finally realizing that he was yelling to her. Behind him, a wall of flames threatened to take over the entire forest. She gasped as fear flooded her body.

"Help me," he called to her desperately. He was pulling the garden hose from the shed, water spurting from the nozzle. "We need to stop the fire!"

The three remaining men took Lucy's hesitation as cue to leave, speeding off into the smokey forest in their truck, getting as far away as they could. Lucy cursed as the assailants got away. All but one.

She looked again between the house and the trees to The Elderwood. They couldn't save them both. "I'm sorry," she called to Micah as they reached one another. She grabbed the front of his shirt. "I'm so sorry. We can't save it all. We have to pick. The Elderwood trees or the house."

Micah looked at the house with sorrow, closing his eyes in a silent farewell. Then he began racing to the trees, knowing he could not wait a moment longer.

Lucy put her bow down and looked to The Elderwood entrance, praying for more assistance from the magic beyond the gateway. She outstretched both arms and held her hands high into the air, focusing on the fire and pushing it away from the portal. A swirling string of green light danced around her arms like a trail of shimmering mist, urging her power on.

She couldn't make the fire disappear, but she could displace it. A green haze clouded her sight as she guided it away from the portal. The inferno slowly crept from one tree to the other, leaving a wake of charred forest. Lucy continued to push the fire until it was condensed into one small section. She then compelled the fire to make a new path across the yard and to the house, grief fueling her power further.

This was more than a house, this was the home to her best friend. She was thankful Abe wasn't there to see the destruction, knowing that the house would soon be reduced to ashes. Somehow, she knew he would have understood; there was no other way to protect the forest.

Micah focused his attention on the trees. He sprayed water on the gateway and the surrounding trees, keeping the flames away as best as he could.

Lucy pushed her magic through the tips of her fingers, begging the flames to cease, but she knew she wasn't powerful enough. She had to keep pushing the fire toward the house. She sobbed from the toil; the exertion made her arms shake and threatened to crumble her body to the ground in surrender.

A sudden surge of power ran through Lucy's body, causing her to scream out in pain. The flash pushed even more magic out of Lucy as she wailed and writhed under the pure force of the power. A bright green light burst from Lucy's body, like rays from the sun, completely relinquishing the forest of the flames as they rushed down the path she created and into Abe's home. Micah was thrown to the ground by the sheer burst of energy.

The house continued to blaze behind Lucy as she fell to her knees in exhaustion, wholly drained of power. She grabbed her bow and quiver as she crawled to Micah, desperate to see that he was okay.

"Micah," she croaked, her voice fractured from the scream. The smoke made it hard to take a good breath, but she needed to get him to safety. "Please, be okay," she said to him as she rolled him over onto his back. He was disoriented, but otherwise uninjured.

He sat up and looked around in alarm, shaking his head as if to clear it. He grabbed onto Lucy, prepared to save her from any harm coming her way.

"It's okay," Lucy choked out. "They're gone. The portal is safe..." She looked over to the house, engulfed in flames. "I'm so sorry, Micah."

They held on to each other for support as they walked further back into the woods, away from the smoke, collecting their supplies they dropped on the way in: the book, the lumber from The Elderwood, and her bag. Micah also clutched a bundle of papers to his chest as they made their way out of the ash. They sat holding one another tightly, watching the house crumble before them.

ELEVEN

The following morning, smoke still lingered on the property. It hung in the air, thick and suffocating, causing Lucy's stomach to roil. Abe's house was rubble and cinders, nothing was spared from the intensity of the fire.

The fire department came and went, followed by the police. Detectives from the local department took pictures of the destruction and the evidence team looked for any trace of the arsonists. The gas cans were scattered throughout the front of the property, and tire tracks led away from the scene. Luckily for Lucy, there was no trace of the man she had killed — his body leaving behind nothing but ash.

"Did you recognize any of the men?" the officers asked the pair.

"No, but the only people who cared that this property existed are the ones who were trying to get me to sell. They are the same people who bought up the rest of this land out here," Micah explained.

"And what about the bow and arrow? Who's weapons?" they asked.

Lucy opened her mouth to give a reasonable lie, wanting to deflect the attention from her. Before she could speak, Micah answered.

"They're hers. She is an expert marksman," he said truthfully. "She scared them off. No one was too badly injured," he lied.

The officers went to finish their final evidence collection, giving Micah and Lucy a moment alone. "Why didn't you lie?" She asked him, upset with his carelessness.

"I will never lie about who I am, and you should never, ever hide who you are either." His trembling hands held her as he looked deeply into her hazel eyes. "And, I will never lie about who you are to me." He kissed her. It was becoming such a comforting gesture that she was unsure how she was going to be able to live without it when she returned to Denora.

"Micah, people can't know I am Fae." She searched his eyes, rubbing some of the ash away from his cheeks, knowing she likely looked the same.

"I know that," he replied. "But you are more than your magic." He held her in his arms as Lucy melted into his words. It was hard for her to believe he saw her for who she really was, but his actions reminded her of it regularly. It was so different from what was waiting for her at home.

Lucy realized she needed to tell her family what occurred, but she didn't know how she could ever explain everything that had happened. She needed to let them know she was alright and that The Elderwood was protected now. However, she feared the repercussions of her actions.

What if this wasn't enough to change her father's mind? What if her father never let her leave the house after this? What if her actions just moved up the arranged marriage?

No. She wouldn't allow it. She couldn't.

She fell into Micah's embrace and squeezed her arms tight around him, afraid to let go. "What's going on in that beautiful mind of yours, Lu?" Micah asked her.

"I'm even more scared to return to Denora now," she admitted to him. "I took a life today, Micah…" the words fell flat on her lips. "I'm not sure what that will mean — what the consequences will be. And what about you? What would happen if your police find out what I did here?" Her heart was racing.

"It's doubtful that the criminals who were here will show up pointing fingers. Let me take care of that end. Besides, you were protecting The Elderwood, there has to be some legal loophole there somewhere. Just like the land, it will be figured out."

Lucy took a moment to contemplate that, but realized there was an even more heavy burden on her heart. "I don't want to leave you... What if my father doesn't let me come back?" She looked at him, a tremble in her voice.

"When your dad comes back to continue business in The Elderwood, I'll deny him access and demand that you return to work this post."

Lucy coughed out a rough laugh. "That won't work."

"It will have to," he said seriously. "I'm the guardian of The Elderwood now. It isn't a Baum family legacy, it's a Lumen legacy." He let her go and bent down to retrieve a stack of papers he had shoved in a quilt. It was the bundle he rushed out of the burning house with last night.

"That's what you went back in the house for?" Lucy asked incredulously. She held the papers in her hands, seeing the will and legal documents protecting the property. In the middle of the stack was the picture from the bookshelf — a young Micah with his grandfather and mother. He went back to the study for them.

She looked at him thoughtfully. "So you're really going to do it? You're going to take over as guardian? You'll be here when I return?"

"I will."

WHILE MICAH WAS busy with the last of the police officers, Lucy snuck off for a quiet moment alone with her thoughts. She kneeled at the base of The Elderwood tree and looked out into the yard where Abe's house once stood. Her knees dug into the dirt below as she stretched her arms out gripping the rough tree trunk, as if desperate to hang on to reality.

It reminded her of the tree house she and Abe had used all those years ago. The tree house felt so sturdy at the time, but as the years passed, it became weaker, withering away to rags and rotten logs. Is that what a mortal life was like? Making it through the years to the best of one's ability, but still quickly coming to a devastating end all alone?

Alone. Abe was all alone when he died. The thought was enough to push Lucy over the edge into a grief-stained oblivion. Her tears came without warning and a sob escaped her chest; and for once, she didn't try to stop it.

She cried for her friend. For his house and his legacy. She cried for the future that Micah no longer had, now being tied to the portal for the rest of his existence. And she cried for herself, because *her* existence was going to be one without Micah.

She wasn't sure how she was going to go back to Denora and convince her father to let her return to Joterra. She wanted to live out her life with the mortal man who had nothing to offer except love and acceptance. It meant everything to Lucy, and nothing to her father.

I'm so sorry I didn't make it back to you, Abe. She said a silent farewell to her most beloved friend, looking up into the sky. *I promise I will do everything I can to make this right. I will do everything I can to protect Micah.*

She sat on the uneven ground, leaning into the gnarled tree of The Elderwood. Her shoulders shook with gut-wrenching sobs, feeling the uncertainty of her future with every gasp of air.

Lucy had every intention to keep that promise, but even in that moment, she wasn't entirely sure how she would ever be able to pull it off.

Stop this, Lucy. You can't give up now. Figure this out. She took deep breaths to calm her body, then stood up and wiped the tears away — she couldn't allow Micah to see her like this. He would try to convince her to stay. He would try to help her fix all of her problems —but this was something she needed to do for herself.

The view of the property broke her heart. The ruins replaced every weathered piece of wood, every dusty door frame. The fire left nothing in its wake; an attempt to erase every positive memory she had with Abe.

She refused to let his memory be wiped away so easily. Lucy placed a hand on the tree, closed her eyes, and vowed to keep her promise to Abe. She thought of all of her happiest moments with Abe and Micah in her time in Joterra.

Running through the woods as a young Fae with Abe.

Splashing in the stream on a hot summer day, laughing until her belly hurt.

Flashlights at night in the tree house, telling stories of other worlds.

Each memory was punctuated by a throb within her chest, threatening to break her to pieces. Her hand began to warm, the bark emanating heat. She opened her eyes and saw a bright green light seeping from the cracks of the bark. It was a comforting feeling, like the embrace of a long-lost friend. While she didn't understand what was happening, Lucy relished in the moment of peace the tree was offering her.

More thoughts of Micah swept through her, and she closed her eyes once again.

Drinking and laughing at the fire pit, sharing stories of Abe.

Tricking him during seek-and-find, helping him to break down the walls he had up for far too long.

Intimate moments under the moonlight as they waited for the amulet to charge.

Giving herself over completely to the man who accepted her for exactly who she was under the trees in The Elderwood.

Suddenly, her hand began to tingle and burn. She opened her eyes in surprise to see leaves and ashes swirling about in a chaotic whirlwind. Lucy pulled her hand away from the tree quickly, breaking the magic that had ignited, causing the leaves to drop to the ground suddenly. Where she had touched the tree, she saw a green glow on the bark in the shape of her hand.

In the silence, she took a deep breath, held her right hand close to her chest and examined the tree. It looked exactly the same as it always had. *Where did that magic come from?* She brought her hand back to the tree, though, as soon as she connected to the tree, her hand stung sharply, causing her to back away quickly.

She looked at her hand and gasped. Lucy saw what had caused the stinging sensation — in the center of her palm, red lines, like scars from a burn, created an image that she immediately recognized. The tree branded the symbol from the amulet into her skin, filling the entire palm of her right hand.

She tried to wipe it away, unsure of what it all meant. *Why did this happen? Why did The Elderwood do this? But that was impossible. Wasn't it?*

Her breathing increased and she was on the verge of losing her composure completely, when she remembered what she was focused on as The Elderwood burned this symbol onto her flesh: her promise to Abe to protect Micah.

She closed her eyes and calmed her breathing, knowing Micah would soon be done with his conversations and looking for Lucy. She looked at her palm again, tracing the lines with the index finger of her left hand. This display of magic was more powerful than she had ever experienced. How would she be able to explain to someone that a magical realm invoked a power all its own? Until she had the answers, she knew she had to keep this to herself.

She whispered the magical Fae words as she concealed the image within her hand, disguising it as her normal skin.

"All done," Micah said to her as he approached through the trees. The ground crackled under his steps, the dirt dry from the exposure to the fire.

Lucy turned and painted a smile upon her face, not wanting to worry him. "Great, everything go alright?"

"I think so. They are on the lookout for J. Pearson Land Developers, but can you believe that they said the company doesn't exist?"

"What?"

"I know," Micah replied, putting his hand on the back of his neck. "I don't understand it, but they said the rest of the land was bought by another company, and that this particular land was sanctioned as unsellable, which is why they had never attempted to buy it."

"So what does that all mean?" Lucy asked Micah, vaguely remembering their previous conversation about the land.

"It means that J. Pearson Land Developers aren't a real company, and they were trying to get this land — but I don't know why."

"I need to tell my father," Lucy said, concern lacing her brow. "Something is not right."

"I know," Micah said. "I will stay here and protect the land, but Lu," he looked at Lucy with an apologetic smile. "I don't know what I'm doing here."

Lucy reached up and held his cheek. "I know, I'm so sorry for having to leave you. I promise I will send whatever help I can as soon as I get home. I know you'll figure it out," she encouraged him. "Keep reading the book to see what other information you can gain from it, and I will talk to my father and see if something can be done. I promise I'll return as quickly as possible."

"I'll walk you," Micah told her as he lifted her bag.

"No," Lucy said in confusion. "You must stay here to protect the portal."

"I'm not going far, and I think we scared them off in the meantime," Micah said. "I can't bring you home, so the least I can do is walk you to the next portal." He began walking, ignoring her objections.

Even though the walk through the woods to the portal was more of a mental challenge to Lucy than a physical one, Micah still carried her bag and a bundle of wood from The Elderwood that initiated this entire journey.

Lucy kept her bow and arrows close to her, still feeling on edge from the attack on the property. Her body was exhausted from the massive amount of power she exuded in the battle to defend The Elderwood. She was quiet; unsure how to process the last week here in Joterra.

"What are you thinking about over there, my badass warrior?" Micah asked her. She laughed and shook her head.

"I'm no warrior," she said as she turned to look at him. He gave her an appraising look, rejecting the idea entirely.

"Look at yourself, Lu," he said to her; and she did. She was armed with a bow and quiver that she fashioned herself, and covered in blood and ashes. "You did it. You saved The Elderwood single-handedly while I ran and grabbed a water hose." He laughed at the thought and put his arm around her to pull her in close.

Lucy grinned at his smile, but not at the memory. She had really done that, hadn't she? What was that magic that had overtaken her? It was nothing like she had ever felt before — it wasn't her magic that she had used from deep within her, but instead it felt as though she was pulling from a well. A well of ancient magic, tied directly to The Elderwood itself.

She balled her right hand into a fist, hoping to keep what had happened to her hidden. She had never heard of any kind of magic like that before, and it both scared her and thrilled her. But what did it all mean?

She took a deep breath, trying to fill her lungs with fresh air. As she did, she inhaled his familiar scent, still lingering behind the smell of smoke. *How am I going to leave him?*

Getting to the portal took much less time than she had hoped, and by the time she reached the tree, she didn't know how to say goodbye. The few people within her life were always constant in Denora — her six brothers, her parents, her few acquaintances.

Her farewell to Abe was more than she could handle, and she wasn't sure if she was ready to say goodbye to Micah. Time moves so differently in Denora than it does in Joterra — when would she see him next? What if her father denies her the right to return again?

How long will pass before she sees those deep brown eyes once again?

Her mind was whirling with fear as she stopped in front of the gateway. She placed her bow and arrow at the base of the tree and Micah dropped her satchel and timber. She wrapped her arms around his muscular torso and firmly held him, not wanting to let go. He skimmed his hands along her back and through her hair, his embrace equally tight, his hands memorizing her curves.

He took his hands and tilted her face to gaze into her eyes. She dug her fingers into his shirt, holding onto this moment, taking in every small detail about him. His dark brown eyes that looked deep into her heart. His strong brow and jawline, and how she made him scowl at her at times, and laugh with joy at others. His lips— his perfectly soft lips and how they felt all over her body.

Saying goodbye was simply not an option.

She pushed him against a tree across from the gateway and kissed him passionately. Her hands wound around his neck then slid down his chest, stopping right over his heart. The deep thump she felt through his shirt jerked her to reality.

She carefully brought her hands down to his waist and invoked the magic in her veins to silently guide vines from the base of the tree to twine around his feet, ensuring he couldn't come after her. They wouldn't last for long, but they would hold while she left him. They would hold as her heart broke.

She looked at him with tears in her eyes as his eyes were wide and frantic, trying to understand what was happening.

She whispered one last thing to him. "This isn't goodbye."

Using her Fae speed, she swiftly gathered her bag and quiver and threw them over her shoulders. She held the pile of wood under her left arm and held her bow with the same hand. In her right hand, she clasped the amulet, and without looking back to say another word, she walked through the portal to travel home to Denora.

～

Passing through the portal felt different somehow. It was not the cool sensation she had felt in the past. It was not the warm embrace of The Elderwood. It was void of anything at all — no light, no temperature, no sound. It was as though a dark shadow encompassed her entirely as she passed through, weightless. As she exited, a small, familiar sound rustled in her ear, and just as quickly, it disappeared.

Dusk was falling as she entered Denora, signaling another end to another day. By her count, she had been gone for nearly two days in her realm.

She took a step toward the path, the moon lighting her way, and immediately came to a halt. Lucy ducked quickly behind a tree, holding her breath in fear of what she saw. The large, gray body of a wolven, prowled on the path ahead of her.

Of course, this is just my luck, she thought to herself. *Can't anything I do ever be easy?* Again, she was in the position of defending herself against a wolven. Her only hope of surviving was if the beast was alone.

She wasn't sure how she could make it out of the Nilban Woods in one piece if she had to face an entire horde of wolven again. Not when her energy and magic were so depleted.

She pressed her back into the firm tree trunk and peered around the corner to see where the wolven was located, noticing it was quiet. Was it hunting her already? As she looked, she saw the sigil engraved in the tree illuminated, glowing a bright green. *How unusual,* Lucy thought to herself. *Isn't it normally white?*

She slowly and silently placed her bag on the ground of the forest as she prepared her bow, strapping her quiver tightly to her back to not lose any arrows again. She placed an arrow in the nock and froze — her right hand was glowing.

She dropped the arrow and turned her right hand to get a better view. The symbol The Elderwood tree had branded into her hand was glowing a bright green light, the same as the sigil on the gateway. Panic filled her. *I don't have time for mystery magical scars while I'm being hunted.*

She returned the arrow back into position and pulled the bowstring as she leapt from behind the tree with a roar, ready to release the arrow into the large creature in her path. However, the creature did not move. The wolven was motionless as it laid on the dirt trail.

Lucy walked slowly over to the massive body, still prepared with her arrow to defend herself. She nudged the figure with her boot, turning it over to discover it was dead. From the center of its chest was an arrow. Her arrow. This was the same beast she had slain on her journey into Joterra.

Lucy marveled at the size of the creature. *I killed this massive beast?* she thought to herself. She reached down, pulled the arrow from the creature's chest and wiped the blood off on its fur. She walked back to her belongings, placed the arrow in her quiver, and continued on her journey home through the darkening woods.

Her red cloak now muddied and saturated with smoke. Her bag previously filled with candy and clothes, now holding the only photograph in existence of her and Abe. Her quiver soaked with the blood of her enemies.

Too many have doubted my strength for too long, she thought to herself. *Nothing is going to stop me from getting what I want. Not the wolven. Not those who try to destroy The Elderwood. Not Laurent Sloan.*

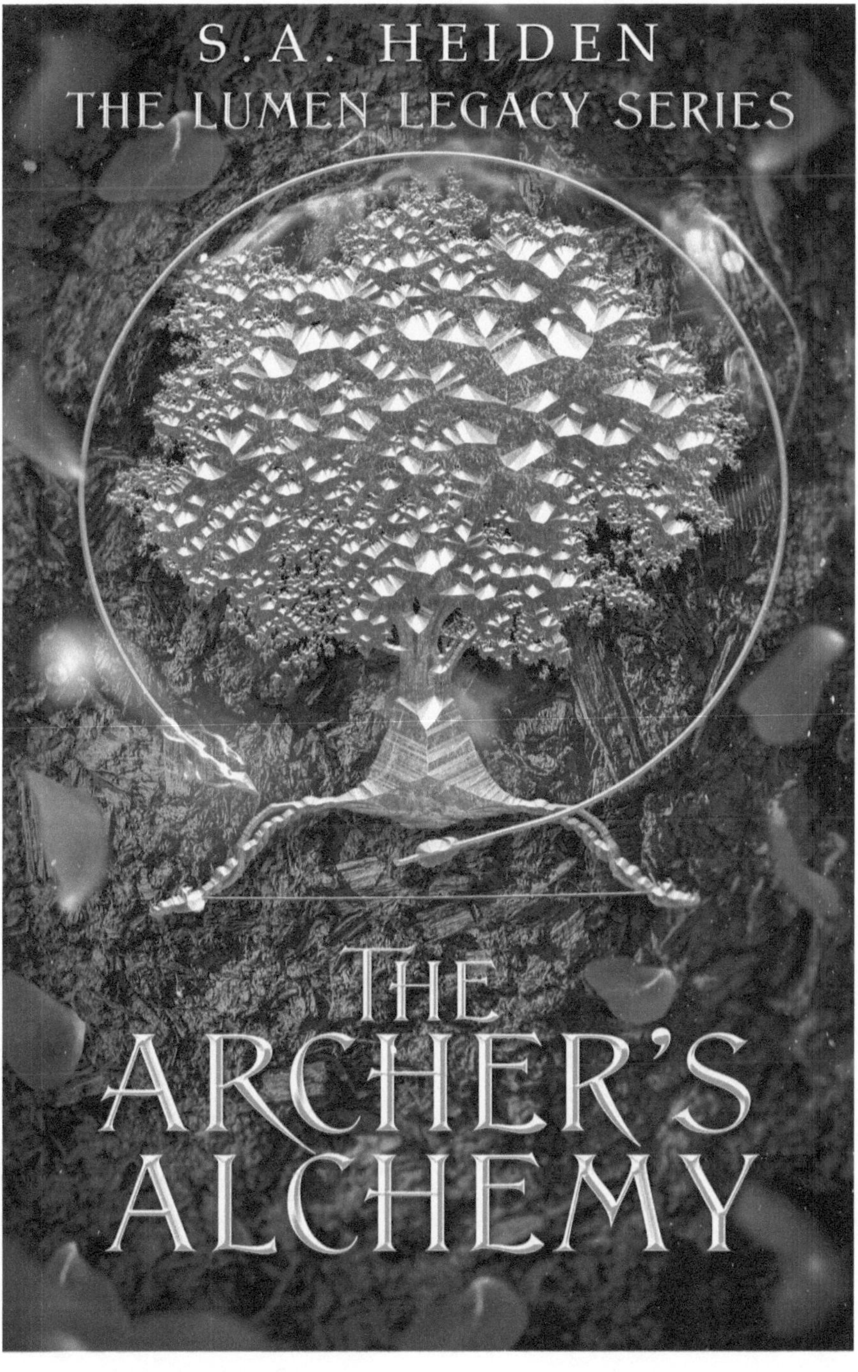

S. A. HEIDEN
THE LUMEN LEGACY SERIES
THE
ARCHER'S
ALCHEMY

For my Dad —
The strongest man I've ever known.

CHAPTER
ONE

LUCY

Ash and debris covered Lucy from head to toe. From her long, dark curly hair, across her light, freckled skin, and over her torn tunic—everything was smudged in a deep gray ash. Everything except for the arrow she clutched tight in her hand.

Her fingernails dug into the palm of her hand, but she refused to ease her grip. That bloodied arrow was the only thing grounding her. It stood as proof that she wasn't a feeble Fae female, but rather someone who could not be tamed. It was the only thing that reminded her that what she experienced was real.

As she made her way up the path to the Baum Estate, uneven breaths of panic pushed her further and further away from the calm and composed exterior she knew she would need for entering the halls.

The salvaged branches from The Elderwood were wrapped in canvas and held tightly in her other hand. Getting the bag into her bedchambers and out of sight would be difficult, but she nearly died trying to retrieve them.

The dark night covered her on her journey, and the rose bushes that lined the path back to her home rustled gently in the breeze. On any other

145

night, she'd appreciate their delicate scent, but not tonight. Nothing could soothe her—not with death and flame so heavy on her mind.

A hurried footstep shuffled from the nearby garden archway as Lucy entered the courtyard on the east wing of the estate. The sudden realization that other Fae were near caused an uneasy sensation to bloom in her stomach.

What if they see me looking so disheveled? Did they realize I was gone?

Too tired to think clearly, all Lucy could focus on was that she needed to quickly get back into her room. First, she needed the privacy to look at the strange mark The Elderwood placed on her. More than that, she needed to prepare for the inevitable discussion with her father that could change her life forever.

The loud snap of a tree branch came from off the path. Lucy stopped and turned toward the sound, a rush of adrenaline surging through her body. An odd magic began to flow through her veins, slithering through her, preparing to strike. Her Fae hearing picked up on a slight jangle of gold chains and relief filled her; though it was soon replaced by repulsion.

Jasper.

"I know you're there," she announced to the Fae male hidden in the shadows. The overwhelming feeling of her strange magic receded as she spoke. "You can tell my father I've returned."

She turned her head and continued inside, not needing to confirm that the lurking male had heard her. Lucy knew her father's second-in-command would make it to Corvus to inform him of her presence before she even stepped foot into her bedchambers.

"I'm done running," she said in a mumble, and though Jasper was sure to hear it with his Fae senses, she wondered if she said it aloud for his benefit or for hers?

Lucy may have been done running, but her plan was far from over. She needed to convince her father that the marriage he arranged for her must be called off immediately. If she could not do that, then her real battle would soon begin.

~

Lucy stared at the space she had called home for over one hundred twenty years. Her bedroom was exactly how she had left it, everything in its respective place.

Her ornate gowns were hung in her wardrobe hiding the pants and leggings she vastly preferred, the window overlooking Denora lay open with the soft breeze wafting through, and the wedding announcements that made her stomach churn were still in a pile on her bed. She sat on her bed, pushing the announcements to the side, looking at the space that seemed frozen in time. No matter how hard she tried, she couldn't comprehend how so much within her had changed.

Time moves differently throughout the realms, so her absence from her home in Denora allowed her nearly a week in the mortal realm of Joterra. Two days ago she was begging her father to allow her to take on the roles of the family business. When he said no, and instead discussed an arranged marriage, she ran away from home to try to prove herself. Now, she had returned as someone internally changed. Someone who had taken on the burden of saving her entire family's legacy and came out stronger in the end.

The breeze carried through her room to where she sat on her bed. Upon her return, she had hastily placed the branches from The Elderwood under her bed and out of sight, then freshened up for her meeting with her father. His second-in-command, Jasper DeValey, had already delivered the news of her arrival, which, knowing her father, would surely prompt an urgent gathering. Restlessly, she began pacing her room, waiting for her father's summons ever since, panic growing with every step.

Crossing the room to her window, Lucy leaned against the brick wall looking out to her family's courtyard and the landscape beyond. The Baum Estate was in the Central Territory, near the outskirts of the city. From her bedroom window, the expanse of the Nilban

Woods unfolded in the distance, reminding her of her journey that felt like a lifetime ago.

In those woods, she had her first experience with death as she fought for her life against a small pack of wolven. Her eyes darted to the wardrobe that concealed the bloodied arrow she hid, nervously ensuring it remained out of sight.

She could never have predicted that she'd encounter so much death and violence in such a short span of time. Lucy mindlessly rubbed the palm of her right hand as it throbbed—the feeling of The Elderwood's unparalleled magic writhing inside of her.

Why did you do this to me? she asked the strange magic, still so lost as to how this immense power lived within her. Her heart raced as each memory sliced into her like a knife, tumbling through her at a speed she could no longer control.

Her perfectly poised exterior threatened to crumble at the thought of everything she was trying to hold together.

Lucy smoothed the skirt to her red gown, took a deep breath, and turned away from the open window in an attempt to calm her nerves. A glance in the mirror was all it took for her memories to play in her mind on a loop.

Red.

The blood of the wolven she slaughtered on her way to Joterra.

The bandana Micah wrapped so delicately around her eyes as they played seek-and-find.

The wine they shared in the privacy of the study.

The flames of the fire as it overtook Abe's house.

The bloodied and burned mortal she struck down.

The brand that burned into her palm as she made a vow to The Elderwood.

Her lungs seized and she couldn't breathe.

She walked away from the mirror, trying to shake the memory, bracing the wall, begging for breath.

Her fists balled tightly as she forced her mind to refocus on the upcoming meeting with her father. She needed a clear mind if she were to sway him into understanding what she did. So much was riding on him finally accepting her for who she was. However, many things had happened in such a short period of time, and someone would have to be held responsible for the damages to the forest—and for the loss of life.

I am the one who saved the entire Elderwood, but I'm sure my father won't see it that way. Instead, I will be the one at fault for it all.

Lucy uncurled her fist to inspect the magicked scar from The Elderwood tree. It was either a curse or a gift, but she was unable to tell which. The deep red lines that formed the Baum Bowyer sigil filled the palm of her hand—though she still didn't understand why or how it happened.

With a feather-light touch, she brushed over the marking with her left hand, willing a concealment charm to keep it hidden.

Pacing the room, her body renewed its panic. With each passing thought, her heart pounded harder. *What will happen in these next days? Micah is so far... The only way back to him is to convince my father to just hear me. Really hear me.*

She stopped and sighed as she listened to the wind. The soft breeze on her face reminded her of working in the shade of The Elderwood trees. Closing her eyes, she took a deep breath in, and with it, the scent of Micah seemed to float to her on the wind—the warm earthy smell of the man she yearned for.

Lucy followed the aroma, her head tilted up, toes gently guiding her, but when she opened her eyes, she stood alone in her room, seeing nothing but the sprawling vista of northern Denora through the window.

Her eyes caught the glinting snow in the mountain scape far beyond the city in the Northern Territory. There, protected within the Leithe Mountains, was where Lord Laurent Sloan resided with his military forces. Lucy grimaced at the thought of him—the Fae to whom she was promised.

It was difficult enough that Lucy did not approve of the arrangement to Lord Sloan, but when the betrothal was made public, the servants of the Baum Estate had no qualms with whispering their gossip in the halls.

"Did you hear what Lord 'Slain' did this week?"

"Another attack on his own people."

"When will the King step in and do something?"

No one knew for sure if the rumors were true or not, but it was worth keeping in mind. On the other hand, these were the same Fae who gladly spread erroneous gossip that Lucy was overjoyed at the love-match. *Don't believe everything you hear,* she reminded herself.

A knock on her door drew Lucy back into reality. She took a step closer and nervously tugged at her gown. "You may come in."

Her brother, Wes, entered the room and she exhaled a soft sigh of relief.

"Lucella," he said in greeting, but the formality of her full name made Lucy's heart fall just a little.

He's upset with me.

He stood within the doorway, clad head to toe in his customary professional attire—long dark slacks and a crisp white tunic underneath a silver suit jacket with greenery embroidered on it. Always the perfect Baum son.

"Wesley," she replied in mock sincerity. She crossed her arms to conceal her hand and leaned against her bureau, waiting for her brother to give the scolding she was sure he had planned in his head hours ago.

Wes was the only brother in her family who had ever bothered to spend time with Lucy. Until her father recently put an end to it, Wes had allowed Lucy to accompany him on his trips to Joterra when she became restless at home and was avoiding her studies. It was during those travels that Lucy reunited with her friend, Abe, and felt as though she had found her calling within the Baum Bowyer family business. Now that she was older, Wes often needed reminding that she was no longer the little girl who needed an attendant.

Wes sighed and looked at Lucy with an irritable scowl. "How could you have been so careless?"

Lucy knew there would be repercussions for her taking the amulet to travel alone to the mortal realm, but she wasn't expecting Wes to be the one who would dole out the first chastising. It went without saying that her acquisition of the family heirloom would be a source of contention once others found out. Though in reality, if she had to do it again? She would. Burning a mortal to death, on the other hand? She wasn't so sure. The memory of his gruesome death made her squirm with unease. Lucy pushed the thought aside, not ready for others to know about it just yet.

"Yes, yes, I know. Get on with it." Lucy fanned her hands at Wes as she sat down at the edge of her bed, stilling herself. "Proceed. I'm comfortable and ready for the lecture."

"This is not a joke, Lucella," he said to her sharply, walking toward her. "You could have gotten killed out there! Then what would Mother have done? And with the amulet, no less! Father would have been beside himself!" His anger was palpable, but Lucy refused to hear it.

"Father would have cared about the missing amulet and the broken business deal. Nothing more," Lucy said dismissively as she turned away from him. Her fingernails bit into the skin of her flesh as she looked out the window on the other side of the room.

The words sounded cruel and vindictive, but she thought them true nonetheless, and the pain of that stung. Truthfully, everything inside of Lucy hurt, and her spiraling thoughts came crashing from her mouth.

"They care for nothing except the business. They don't care that there is a new guardian there, as long as one exists, correct? They do not care that Abe is gone. That he's- he's... dead." She gasped for breath, the hard truth of those words making her ill.

"He's dead?" Wes asked in a faintly He looked up and ran a hand through his dark brown hair. Slowly, he walked over to her and knelt on the wooden floor in front of her.

"Lucella."

She refused to look at him.

"Lucy," he said, his voice a whisper.

At that, she finally turned to him, traitorous tears in her eyes.

Don't cry, she told herself.

"I'm sorry about Abe," he said to her, solemnly. "I know he was your friend. I'm sorry we weren't made aware in order to support you through this." Wes gently took her hand in his and her heart threatened to crack right in half.

Lucy inhaled sharply, choking on the tears she held back with all of her might. She blinked furiously, her heart sinking with each passing second.

"But you have to know that our parents do care; deeply. Our parents loved Abe. And they love you, Lucy. We all love you."

Unable to hold it back any longer, tears poured from her eyes, each drop a memory of her dearest friend, Abe. With everything that had happened, she barely had any time dedicated to grieving her most treasured friend in all the realms. And beyond that, her thoughts of Micah left her strained. It had only been a few hours, but she already missed him more than words could describe.

"Everything has gone so wrong," she whispered, taking deep breaths to calm the tears. He raised his hand and a small burst of silvery light swirled out from his fingers. A delicate gust of air dried her tears, carrying them away on the shimmering wind until it dissipated.

"Then let us meet Father so you can tell him everything," he said. He stood up and carefully straightened out his clothes. "He is ready for us in his study." Wes's attentiveness toward her faded with each word.

Lucy looked up at him in question, apprehension clear upon her face. Wes, however, called on his rehearsed stoic expression, preparing for the audience with their father. Lucy recognized the facade he donned, knowing it was her turn to do the same. Her father did not appreciate overtly emotional displays from his adult children, and ensuring that she was up to his standard would allow the meeting to progress without additional complications.

Wes extended his hand and Lucy wrapped her fingers around his arm as he escorted her to the study where Lucy's actions would be judged.

Please, let him listen. She wasn't sure what she would do if her father didn't understand the risks she took and why. There was no other plan for her to attempt.

Please. She squeezed her fist tightly, begging for strength.

"FATHER, YOU DON'T UNDERSTAND," Lucy tried to explain for the third time. "I had no other choice!" Her patient exterior crumbled with each passing second.

"You talk of choices as if your future is not yet defined," Corvus Baum scoffed at his daughter. "You took a prized artifact that does not belong to you, traveled without an escort, and masqueraded as a true representative of the Baum Bowyer industry. Each step of the way you deliberately defied Denoran tradition. And your poor mother! She was worried sick!"

"I was gone for less than two days, Father," Lucy replied in frustration. "Surely *worried sick* is an exaggeration. By the time either of you realized I had gone, I was already back by nightfall."

Lucy paced around her father's study, trying to find the words to make him understand. She did everything she could to hold her tongue, but her father's Denoran views of females made each and every word from his mouth harder and harder to take.

If one of her brothers had made this choice, Corvus would have forgiven them immediately. However, because Lucy was a female, his expectations for her were skewed.

Lucy took a deep breath in, centering herself with the smell of bow varnish bottled on the shelves. She was astounded that they weren't listening to the crucial findings from her journey: Abe was gone, The Elderwood was unguarded and at risk, and there was now a new guardian who desperately needed support. She didn't dare mention that in her attempt to save The Elderwood, she had slain a mortal. It would have to come out eventually, but she wasn't ready for the emotional onslaught.

The meeting felt never-ending with the conversation going around in circles, Corvus never truly listening to what had happened while she was gone. He could not understand that her six days in Joterra had been filled with more than just her mistakes.

She sagged into the worn leather chair across from her father's enormous wooden desk as Jasper DeValey and Wes sat off to the side. Jasper's usual oily sneer was slick on his face as Lucy received her scolding, but she contently ignored him as she was apt to do.

Instead, she looked to Wes, desperate hope buzzing through her. His face hardened and he looked away, siding with their father. Lucy pursed her lips and forced her eyes straight ahead, realizing that, as usual, she was alone. *Here I am again, back at square one, trying to prove myself to every male in my life.*

Corvus sat at his desk—the same desk that Lucy had meddled in without his permission a few days prior. His colossal frame filled the space as true power exuded from his stature—it was one of the reasons the family business remained successful. Not only did the Baum Bowyers have exclusive access to The Elderwood, but Corvus Baum was a powerful Fae, and there were few who would dare to cross him.

"Please," she begged, "please, listen. I just borrowed the amulet. Then when I got there, The Elderwood was at risk, I—"

"The Elderwood is none of your concern," her father boomed, his fist pounding the desk. "If you had not gone to the mortal realm, we would not be in this dire situation."

"If I had not gone, the realm would have been destroyed," she challenged, her voice rising to meet his, a flare of fire thrumming in her veins that she did not expect. With shaking hands, Lucy stood as she held her ground, refusing to back down to her father. "Abe was not there to defend the property and if I wasn't there, all would have been lost!"

Corvus looked at her with wide eyes. Lucy had never known for someone to raise their voice to him before, and it was clear that he did not approve. His eyes narrowed and he quieted as she continued her tirade, her face flushed with anger.

"You should be *thanking* me, not punishing me, for doing my duty to protect our family's legacy." She stood stock-still, keeping the raging emotions at bay, unsure of the tingling sensation now writhing under her skin.

"This is *my* legacy, Lucella," her father replied with bone chilling calm. He gripped the edge of his desk and stood, a deep purple aura of magic radiating from his large stature, threatening to explode. "Your place is with your soon-to-be husband," he said as he stooped his tall frame to make himself eye level to Lucy. "It is not traipsing through the realms pretending to be something you're not."

Lucy took the reprimand like a slap to her face, physically taking a step back from him and his hurtful words. "And what is it you believe me to be, Father?" she asked, poison lacing her tone. Her blood simmered just below the surface. She pushed the rage back down, her fingernails digging into the palm of her hand as she desperately tried to regain her composure.

"Not a bowyer as you so often pretend," he said with a sneer. "The marriage to Lord Sloan will continue and you will not be leaving the grounds anytime soon," he declared. He sat and went back to the paperwork on his desk, the magic receding back into his body like smoke being filtered through a summoning charm. "You are not to return to Joterra, you will not travel with your brother, and all pretense of what you think your life should be ends now. Have I made myself clear?"

"You cannot mean that," Lucy said, breathless in her response. Her father had never spoken to her this way before. He had never made her feel as worthless as he did just then. "I have to go back! Please, Father."

Corvus did not look up to face her and Lucy's shoulders sagged beneath the realization of the truth in his words. His dismissal of her was absolute.

"Jasper," he commanded, still focused on the paperwork at his desk, oversized quill in hand. Wes and Jasper immediately stood at attention. "You and Wes are to go to Joterra to gain control of the situation. Inform the new guardian of his role and restore the power between realms. Prepare a formulated spell to repair the home. Report back as soon as you've returned."

Jasper nodded and looked at Lucy with a derisive grin. "Of course. I'd hate to see any more mistakes being made on behalf of the business. You should be ashamed to call yourself a Baum."

The lights flickered and the room darkened as Corvus slowly stood up, his shadow growing tenfold on the wall. His eyes narrowed as darkness seeped from the far corners, like spilled ink—Corvus's trademarked move. A promise of violence loomed in the air in dim candlelight.

Only the strongest Fae of Denora had an additional power or skill set. Corvus owned the ability to manipulate the shadows with his purple aura to make his presence seem more menacing.

And it worked.

"What did you just say to my daughter?" he asked Jasper with a deadly expression.

Jasper gulped down his next words, his eyes looking wildly around the room, nervously turning the gaudy rings on his fingers. "I just meant—"

Corvus's hand flew up in front of him as his gaze narrowed at Jasper. Ever so slowly, he pulled his fingers into a fist, squeezing so tightly they turned red.

A strangled cry left Jasper until he was wordlessly moving his lips. The ascot Jasper wore every day clamped around his neck, pulling tighter and tighter, making Jasper's already bulging eyes widen more.

"You will never speak to my daughter that way, ever again," Corvus said, emphasizing each word slowly. "She is a Baum and she is my blood. You will never disrespect a single person in this manor again. Is that understood?"

Jasper gasped for breath, pulling at the scarf around his neck, straining for air in a chaotic frenzy.

"Is that understood?" Corvus repeated, squeezing his fist tighter, his magic closing off Jasper's breathing completely.

Jasper nodded his head frantically as he turned purple beneath the pressure.

Corvus released him and placed his hand on the table. The shadows scurried off as the brightness returned to the room.

Lucy stood rooted in place, eyes wide and unblinking, taking in what had just happened with quiet, hyperventilating breaths.

He stood up for me.

Her shock must have been apparent, but she wasn't sure how to grasp what she had just seen. She had never seen her father display that sort of violence before, though she had heard the stories and knew he was capable.

Jasper quickly left the room, coughing and gasping for air. Wes looked between his sister and father with trepidation.

Corvus gave Wes a nod. "You're all dismissed."

Wes bowed and quickly followed Jasper out into the hall.

"Wait!" Lucy rushed after them, abandoning the idea of trying to convince her father. "Please Wes, please listen to me!"

Jasper rubbed his neck resentfully. A taunting curl of his lip made its presence known as he watched their interaction.

Wes faced Jasper, aware of his prying eyes. "I will meet you at the front gate when I have packed and changed for the journey."

"Don't be late," Jasper said hoarsely, rearranging the ornate golden necklace around his reddened throat. "We have a mess to clean up and I'd like to get it over with as quickly as possible."

Wes turned his back on him in dismissal, a rude gesture no matter what realm you were from. Lucy looked at Wes, hopelessness filling her heart. She needed her brother to be on her side. Without him, there would be no one else who could help her.

Wes hasted across the estate, not speaking a word to Lucy. She followed after him, afraid to break the silence.

He strode into Lucy's chambers, and as Lucy closed the door, he pulled her into the center of the room with urgency. He lifted his hands in the air and spoke the Denoran words to materialize a privacy charm, his hands swooping into a large half circle enclosing the entire room. A shimmering sheen filled the space around them, proving the charm to be in effect.

"Thank you, Wes," Lucy said, relief filling her voice. "I just need to get back and there is just so much to—"

"Lucy," he interrupted. "I have a feeling you are withholding important information and I am very curious to hear what it is you so conveniently forgot to tell Father." His serious expression bore into her soul, his knowing eyes alight with purpose. This was one argument she was sure to lose. "Why are you so desperate to return?"

Lucy looked up to the ceiling of the room, gave a heavy sigh and turned back to her brother, nervous to admit that he was right. Her thoughts were in turmoil, wary of what she was willing to tell him.

"Well," she began, hesitantly. "The new guardian is named Micah. He helped me to protect the property, and we..." Lucy paused, unsure of how to describe the enormity of what happened between them. "We, connected?"

Wes took a quick step closer to Lucy, looking at her in disbelief. "Surely, you did not do what I think it is you are about to admit." He paced the room, running his hands through his straight brown hair that always fell so perfectly it made even Lucy jealous. "In fact, maybe you shouldn't share with me."

This is so typical. If she were one of her brothers, the males would be sharing in cheers for the power of her magic and the bonds she had tied with Micah. However, since she was a female, they would hear nothing of it. She preferred not to dig herself into her own grave, so she went about this withheld knowledge from a different angle.

"He is my friend, Wes," she said gently as she placed a hand on his arm. In her mind, she was Wes's equal, and the constant belittling was pushing her closer to her breaking point.

"Friend," he said flatly.

"He is mortal and barely aware of any of the knowledge he is supposed to have of the realms and of magic. He needs assistance to learn what he is meant to do there."

Wes stared at her blankly, clearly unimpressed with her response.

Lucy withheld a frustrated groan and instead huffed out a sigh.

"I will talk to this new guardian for you," Wes said hesitantly.

Eyes bright, Lucy looked at Wes with the faint hope that she finally had someone on her side.

"I will tell him the basics of what he needs and set up a way of communication in case of emergencies. Is this acceptable?"

It was not a perfect plan, but it was something. The weight of the realms left Lucy's shoulders, and she pulled him into her arms for a hug. It was not an ordinary act to show this kind of familial affection, but Lucy was tired of doing things the Denoran way.

Wes's body first stiffened at the gesture, but after his initial surprise, he wrapped his arms around his sister, returning the hug. They held onto one another for just a moment, and Lucy reveled in the feeling of being just a little less alone.

"Thank you," Lucy whispered, tears threatening to pierce through the barrier she was tired of holding.

"I'm glad you're okay," Wes responded in a murmur. With one last gentle squeeze, Wes turned and walked from the room, dismantling the privacy ward as he left, and a flood of tears crashed down Lucy's cheeks.

CHAPTER

TWO

MICAH

Nearly three days had passed since Lucy left. Micah spent his time cleaning up the charred debris of what remained of Grandad's home during the day and he slept in the crowded confines of his car at night.

The trunk of his car was filled with his grandad's belongings Micah had sorted through before Lucy had come into his life—but that felt like a lifetime ago already. He was glad he was able to save the important documents for the lawyers, but signatures and legal jargon didn't seem to matter in the grand scheme of things.

Of everything he was able to save, it was the picture of his mom and grandad that he was grateful for. Micah had propped it up on the dash so that it watched over him as he slept each night, reminding him that he was on the right path.

He just had to be patient.

The vow he had made to protect The Elderwood meant he couldn't leave the property for long periods of time, and since someone had just come and torched half of the land, he was hesitant to leave it unoccupied for more than an hour or two. He took a few quick trips into town to get basic supplies, figuring it was safe enough, but he really didn't know. There wasn't much of a plan in place. All he knew was he was stuck here. Alone.

Under the heat of the sun, he sat in the yard near the fire pit, looking out into the ancient trees that got him into this situation to begin with. Most of the grove had evidence of char, and many trees were destroyed from the devastating fire from the arsonists. Only one patch of land was salvaged, and the green leaves of those magical trees swayed gently in the breeze.

The tree that held the portal was safe, and Micah would remain here to ensure it stayed that way. He just wished that Lucy would hurry up and come back to him, because he didn't know what to do next.

He took his time sorting and piling the destroyed wood, preparing it for the fire pit. He reached down and grabbed another branch and a strong zap coursed through his arm.

"Ouch!" He dropped it and shook his hand. *What the hell was that?*

The piece was a lighter color than the other branches.

He looked around at the trees nearby, all of them a deep brown. This small branch was pale; almost gray compared to the dirt it laid upon. He searched the littered ground around him. There were a few more pieces in a small stack off to the side, as if they were thrown there in a hurry.

It was then that he realized where it was from.

Lucy and Micah had traveled to The Elderwood to gather wood for Lucy to bring back to Denora. During the fight to save The Elderwood, some branches broke. Lucy took the pieces that were big enough to use, and the rest were left here in this pile. He stepped closer and pushed the stray branch back into the heap with his leather boot, careful not to touch it again with his skin.

He sighed in dismay as he looked at the broken branches. Lucy told him this wood was unique, with special, magical properties.

This is all I've got left of her, huh?

He assumed throwing it into the burn pile was probably in poor taste, so he left it to the side of the tree line, deciding to deal with it later.

He was exhausted and his body was sore from sleeping in his car, so he abandoned his task and sat by the fire pit. *I can't keep this up.* He put his elbows on his knees and ran his fingers through his hair, drowning at the thought of what to do next.

"Hello there," a voice said. Micah jumped to his feet, startled to see two men standing in front of him. He hadn't even heard them walk up. How could he have missed them?

The first one who spoke was tall and lean, with long brown hair. His light-gray eyes complimented his pale skin, and his dark blue uniform was emblazoned with silver and gold leaves. He stood with an air of confidence so different from what he had ever seen before that Micah considered he may not be mortal.

The older of the two looked closer to his father's age. His dingy long blond hair was swept into a low tie. He wore a white, high-collared shirt framed with tacky gold chains.

"Who are you?" Micah watched the strangers cautiously. "Where did you come from?"

"My name is Wesley Baum," the younger man responded. He spoke in a cadence that reminded him of Lucy. *Were they from Denora?* "I believe you've met my sister Lucella?"

"Lucy is your sister?" Micah asked in disbelief. He wasn't sure if he was relieved or worried. "How is she? Is she okay?" He took a quick step toward Wesley as he asked. He tried to keep the desperation out of his voice, but failed miserably.

"My name is Jasper DeValey," the other man interrupted before Wesley could respond. "Seems to me we have some business to attend to now that you are the new guardian of the portal." Jasper took an assessing scan of Micah and the land around—distaste evident upon his face.

The only proof a house ever stood on the property were the large beams of wood, charred and destroyed. Jasper eyed the tree to The

Elderwood, an emotion flashing over him that Micah couldn't identify, but it was gone as quickly as it came.

"I'm not sure how we are supposed to work in these conditions," he said with disgust.

Micah looked at the older Fae, wondering if he ever made a pleasant expression.

"Then let's get on with it," Wesley said with no intention of friendliness. He nodded toward the ruins, then glanced at Micah. "Please stay out of the way."

Micah took one step back and then another as the two Fae moved to stand ten paces apart, facing the wreckage that was once Micah's safe-haven. The duo lifted their hands high into the air and tilted their heads toward the sky, taking deep and steady breaths.

It started with a calm, velvety breeze racing through the trees, brushing against Micah's bare arms and sending a chill down his spine. Looking to the sky, he watched as the clouds slowly moved to block the sun. The two Fae were frozen in their peculiar stance, making the hair on the back of Micah's neck tingle.

Suddenly, the wind picked up around them, sending leaves and debris flying through the air. As the Fae men dropped their gaze to the ashes and destruction that was once Abe's house, they whispered in another language. Swirling light came from their hands and soared toward the empty space in front of them. The shimmering light twisted and turned around the broken remains of the cabin, covering each piece in a radiant luster.

The wind around Micah grew to a brutal current, crashing into the surrounding trees and making them bend and sway violently. He crouched down low, trying to avoid the magic bolting around him. The forest shook in the squall, the chaos threatening to uproot the trees.

What the fuck is happening? He watched in a panic as the shimmering magic picked up charred pieces of the old front door. They floated midair for a moment and then, caught in the gust of wind, zoomed past him again and again as the torrent circled around them.

The Fae men remained with their hands outstretched, having to shout the spell over the sheer volume of the wind.

Micah froze as the Fae men pushed more light from their hands, the radiance building with each erratic beat of his racing heart. He put a hand in front of his eyes to block the blinding light and swirling ashes, nearly falling to his knees from the powerful magic on display before him.

As if the wind ceased completely, the ashes and debris calmly came to a halt and floated in the empty land before them. The wind raged on around him, while he stood in the quiet eye of the storm, as though an invisible sphere protected them from the chaotic whirlwind just beyond.

This is unbelievable.

The ash and remains bathed in the magical light, bending to the will of Jasper and Wesley as they twisted their hands ever so slowly. As they pushed their magic into the space before them, the rubble and debris formed spiraling shapes that spun in the air above them, whirling around faster with each rotation.

"Close your eyes," Wesley ordered Micah loudly, keeping his attention focused on the house.

Micah wasn't sure why he needed to close his eyes—he had seen Lucy control magic before. Nevertheless, he obeyed, and did so just in the nick of time. A bright light abruptly flashed before him, making him cover his already closed eyes with his hands. Complete silence followed the radiant blast.

No more wind, no rustling leaves, not a sound to be heard.

Micah carefully opened his eyes and was astonished by what he saw. In front of him, where his grandad's house once stood, was a large wooden cabin, modernized and breath-taking. It fit in the outdoor space as if it had always been there.

"Now that's done, let's go inside to sit and go over the paperwork, shall we?" Wesley asked, dusting his hands with a clap as if the power he had displayed was a normal run-of-the-mill thing.

Jasper was a bit breathless as he followed Wesley into the house, ignoring Micah completely. He patted his sweaty forehead with a handkerchief as he walked.

"Uh, yeah," Micah replied, dumbfounded. *What the hell was that?*

Jasper and Wesley made their way into the newly built house as Micah trailed behind them, completely baffled by what had just happened. This was nowhere near the kind of magic Lucy had displayed in her time with him. Was that normal for Fae?

If Micah was speechless as they built the cabin, he was even more so now that he walked through the fully furnished house. The living room had a small wooden table, two brown leather chairs, and a couch. Across from the hall, where the dining room used to be, was an office. Micah's heart ached with the gentle reminder of Abe's old study. Empty bookshelves lined the walls, and the desk seemed to be stocked with parchment and quills—Micah didn't see a pen or pencil.

Peeking up the stairs, he noticed a hallway with additional bedrooms. He couldn't see inside of them, but he was sure they were likely supplied with the same modern furniture as the main level.

Walking to the back of the house into the kitchen he noticed the biggest changes. The old cabinets were replaced with walls of windows and the appliances were updated with the most modern technologies. A large, white marble island sat in the middle of the kitchen and a wooden table with chairs were off to the side along a wall that held an oversized window which looked out into the wooded grove that surrounded the property.

Micah ambled around the house with his mouth hanging open. It was so different, yet the wide windows that brought more of the forest into the cabin just seemed to fit.

You would have loved this, Grandad. His heart ached.

"Sit," Jasper commanded as he sat at the wooden table in the kitchen. With a flourish of his hand, he tried to push a chair from the table back a few inches, but all it seemed to do was wiggle a bit. On Jasper's third attempt, it was clear that he was directing Micah to sit, and Wesley used his own magic to pull the chair back with a roll of his eye. Jasper huffed in annoyance while Wesley maintained a smirk.

"H-how? How were you able to do all of this?" Micah sputtered, looking around in amazement.

"Magic," Wesley said with an air of impatience. His arrogance was hard to read. He didn't seem as mean as the older guy, but there was something about him, like there was something he was hiding.

Does he know something about me and Lucy? Does he know about the man Lucy killed?

"Yes, obviously," Micah snapped back. "But Lucy's magic looked different from that. It wasn't so..." he tried to find the word.

"Amazing?" Jasper supplied smugly.

"Extravagant," Micah replied, wiping the smile from Jasper's face.

"Lucella should not have used her magic here with you," Wesley said before Jasper could speak. "As for the magic you saw just now, it is predetermined magic. Prewritten, if you will. Lucella told us about the destruction of your home. We came prepared with the things you would need here in the mortal realm. A wooden home. Bedrooms, living areas, a kitchen with the common technologies." He waved his hand in the air. "The rest you can buy as needed." Wesley walked away from the table, inspecting his work with a self-satisfied grin.

"Like a pen?" Micah joked.

"A what?" Wesley replied, bewildered.

"Never mind," Micah muttered.

Jasper cleared his throat dramatically, shifting himself in the kitchen chair. "Now, as I was saying." He looked at Micah and pointed to the chair across from him with a jabbing finger. Micah sat slowly, still keeping his eyes on the two strangers. He didn't know them, and even though they said they knew Lucy, how could he trust them? He promised Lucy he wouldn't work with anyone but her.

Wesley was the brother Lucy spoke of regularly, but why did he keep calling her Lucella like she was a child being scolded?

This Jasper guy though... Micah couldn't put a finger on it, but there was something off about Jasper, something that made him stay on alert. Maybe it was the way his eyes bulged when offended; he looked like an insect being squished.

Normally, Micah had a good sense for reading people. Call it a trick of the trade or just practice being around people as a detective, but he could usually sense when people meant him harm and when they were not a threat; it was how he knew to trust Lucy, even when he first fought against that instinct.

Keep your cool, he reminded himself. *You don't know anything about these two or what they want from you.* He contemplated another moment longer. *Or what you want from them.*

"Abe held this position for many years before his passing. Our condolences," Jasper added in a flat tone. "I'm not sure why you are unaware of the transference process for the guardians at the gate, so I will try to be as succinct as possible."

Jasper spoke quickly and without remorse for Abe. Micah tried to listen as intently as he could, not wanting to miss any important information.

"You are not to leave the premises for more than a few hours at a time. You are compensated by the Baum family and we will send all funds to the same financial institution Abe used—your name is already on the account. I suggest the next time you go into your town, you stop in to provide any other contact information needed." He paused as he sniffed the air with disgust. "Ensure you stop by a merchant to buy some soap," he added, then abruptly stood in dismissal.

"That's it?" Micah looked at him, eyebrows raised. "I know nothing about this job and nothing about your realm. What is it that I'm supposed to be doing?"

"You have nothing to do except stay here and wait for someone to call on you." Jasper walked over to the living room, preparing to leave. "Other than that, follow the few simple rules left to you. We have nothing else we need of you."

"I won't work for anyone else but Lucy," Micah said stubbornly.

Jasper paused and turned, his eyes glinted with violence. "Miss Baum will not be here to help you. You will figure it out without her, as is ordered by her father."

"You want to talk about ordering someone around?" Micah asked angrily, standing from his chair and striding up to Jasper. When face to face with him, Micah stood nearly a head taller than the greasy, arrogant Fae. "I refuse to do shit for you, and you can tell that to your boss as well. If you expect me to work with you or your business, *Miss Baum* better be part of the equation."

Jasper's sneer grew with each word until his teeth were bared at Micah. He rubbed at the rings on his hands angrily.

Micah was happy to face down this snobby old Fae who clearly didn't realize what Micah went through that week. In the past seven days, his entire world was turned upside down thanks to these Fae and their bullshit rules. He wasn't about to let them control his life any longer.

"If you need any help, we will assist you," Wesley spoke for the pair. He looked between Jasper and Micah as they continued their stare down. Micah didn't move from his spot.

"Help? What kind of help do you need?" Jasper scoffed. "You are a mortal hired to oversee a *tree*. I think you'll be fine." He turned away from Micah and walked to the door once more.

"Lucy helped me. Her magic was more powerful than even yours," he told them. Wesley looked at Micah with interest, but Jasper had a completely different reaction.

"What did you say?" Jasper asked in a hiss, facing Micah once more. "Do you dare insult me?" Jasper met Micah's stare with his eyes bulging. "Are you insinuating that my magic is—"

"Lucy's magic is incredible," Micah interrupted. "When those thugs came and threatened The Elderwood, she was the only thing to stop them. Without her, the entire forest would have been in a blaze of fire," Micah said to them, proud of Lucy's determination.

"Pfft," Jasper scoffed. "Lucella Baum is nothing more than a disobedient child."

"Do not call her that." Micah squared off with Jasper again, his broad shoulders rippling under his thin cotton shirt. He refused to stand back as someone insulted Lucy. Not after everything she had risked, not after everything they went through together.

A vein popped out of Jasper's neck, his face ruddy and distorted with fury. Just as he opened his mouth to speak, Wesley stepped between the two and put his back to Jasper, looking directly at Micah.

"Agreed. She is not a child—far from it. However, she has made many mistakes we are here to correct," Wesley said to him evenly. He pivoted his body to Jasper, speaking to him sternly. "Remember your warning. Go outside and ensure the premises is secure while I go over the last few items with the guardian here."

Jasper gaped at them both, his mouth opening and closing like a suffocating fish, his hands stroking the scarf around his neck. Clearly, he had more to say, but decided to keep it to himself.

This Jasper guy is unbelievable. Micah kept his guard up, clenching his fists, prepared to take him on to defend Lucy's name.

Wesley, however, waited patiently as Jasper stormed out of the house. Once he was gone, Wesley turned back to Micah with a hint of a smile in his eyes.

"Jasper regularly forgets that he works for my father, and therefore works for me. Not the other way around."

He led Micah into the living room and stood before an undecorated wall. "I appreciate you standing up for Lucy like that," Wesley said—it was the first time he called her that in front of Micah, and it didn't go unnoticed.

"Of course," Micah said. "If she were here, she would have done it for herself."

"Would she, now?" Wesley tilted his head to eye Micah with curiosity.

"She's a spitfire, that one," Micah said with a grin, remembering her fierce temperament toward him in the woods. "Lucy doesn't deserve the hand she is being dealt. She's an amazing woman. She just wants to be heard."

"That she does," Wesley replied with a crooked smile. "She took care to ensure you would have what you needed here. She wanted to say goodbye in person, but it is not something that can be done."

"Goodbye?" Micah asked in alarm, his heart racing as dozens of questions flowed through his mind. "Why goodbye?"

"My father will not allow it," he said simply.

Micah's heart fell.

"In the face of an emergency, this mirror will allow you to contact one of us for support." Wesley ignored Micah's obvious disappointment and continued the conversation as if he didn't just turn Micah's world upside down once again. "This will help in times of need."

Wesley faced the empty wall, stretched out his right arm, and spun it in a circle three times. On the third rotation, an ornate mirror appeared on the wall.

Micah took a step back, but said nothing. Each new expression of magic put a bit more fear in him, but he knew better than to ask how the mirror came into existence. Instead, he asked a question that would hopefully help him. "How does it work?"

"You look into the mirror and say the name of the person you are looking for while sprinkling this powder in front of you," Wesley said as he handed Micah a small drawstring bag filled with a pale powder, almost like sand. "If there is an emergency, call out that The Elderwood is in distress and someone will come to your aid." With finality, Wesley turned on his heel and strode to the front door.

"So that's it, then?" Micah asked in disbelief. He shook his head and again was forced to follow Lucy's brother out the door.

Wes paused to face the house with admiration. "This is probably the best and most intricate spell I've ever written," he said, ignoring Micah's question.

Micah saw Jasper walking around the grove of trees that held the portal to The Elderwood, looking between them intently. He bent down and touched something, but Micah couldn't make out what it was.

"The property is protected from any unwanted visitors," Jasper shared as he approached Micah and Wesley. "The house has also been charmed to withstand the years, just as the previous dwelling was. Keep the fires to a minimum," Jasper said, as his lips curved up into an unbalanced smile. "A female with a bow and arrow can't keep all unwanted people away, but now that we are here with real magic, far more sophisticated deterrents were put in place to keep mortals like the J. Pearson Land Developers at bay."

He turned and walked into the forest with Wesley, the words leaving Micah feeling uncomfortable. *What does he know about that day?*

Wesley looked back with a stalwart smile and nod to Micah, as Jasper turned to look at the portal with a leering grin. Micah watched as they left down the same path Lucy took back to Denora.

Micah retreated into the cabin, marveling at the brand new home he was given. Sitting back on the new leather couch, he tilted his head to look up toward the ceiling. *Magic did all of this,* he thought to himself and chuckled with disbelief. *Magic.*

He bolted upright.

Magic.

He ran to his car.

In the front seat, under the other papers, hidden away from view, lay the great, leather-bound book, filled with the knowledge from his ancestors.

Alderic Lumen created the book and it was passed down for generations from guardian to guardian, sharing the secrets of the portal to The Elderwood and the magic that surrounded it. There had to be answers in there somewhere. Answers to help him understand his place in the world now; to give him purpose.

He walked back toward the house, tucking the book under his arm and holding it close. The trees that started all of this seemed to dance in the wind, taunting him as he passed.

Those trees hid the woman who pushed him to face the hard truths about his life. The one who called him out on all of his shit and opened his eyes to a completely new world. Those trees were the basis of his relationship with his Grandad, and his mom, growing up in their shade, the shadow of their power bearing down on his family. Yet, here those trees were, still thriving, thanks to Lucy's powerful magic that had pushed the fire away from them in order to spare the portal.

From the corner of Micah's eye, he saw the light change, almost like a shadow. He jerked his gaze toward the lurking darkness to investigate, but when he looked, there was nothing. Just trees.

He shook his head, swearing to get a better night's sleep in an actual bed, and headed back into the house with the book in hand. There, he pored over every word he could understand, desperately searching for more answers that could lead him back to Lucy.

THREE

LUCY

The morning was not going as planned and Lucy was in her room alone, yet again. She never realized how much she hated being alone until now.

After meeting Micah, she craved that closeness that she had felt in his presence. She lay back in her bed, closing her eyes and thinking of the mortal who held such a large piece of her heart. *How do I get back to you?* She pictured his broad smile beneath those deep brown eyes.

Lucy had so many things on her mind and wasn't sure which answer to search for first. She was desperate to know why The Elderwood seared her family sigil into her palm. It was nearly all she thought about since her return—that and Micah.

Even with the concealment charm, Lucy could feel the raised lines of her scar. From a quick glance, you couldn't see that anything was different, but Lucy knew what lay hidden.

She released the charm and stared at the lines glistening in the daylight. Her finger lightly traced the arrow circling the tree with a bow for its roots; the Baum Bowyer family crest, now feeling like a lie.

Surely, there must be a reason for this... gift.

However, for all her contemplation, she couldn't fathom an answer. All she knew was that on her return home, when she came close to the portal, the lines on her hand glowed a bright green. Was it to remind her of her promise to watch over Micah? Was The Elderwood angry at her for channeling its magic during the battle?

The magic slithered through Lucy's body, reminding her it was still there. It was a quiet, silken graze beneath her skin, though every once in a while it felt more active, dancing wildly.

She wasn't sure what it all meant, but she found comfort in the power coursing through her—reminding her of her strength in Joterra and how she faced any threat to The Elderwood head-on, no matter how dire the outcome.

The memory brought a jolt of anger. She remembered the men trying to destroy the portal and hurt Micah. Visions of the fire flashed in her memory, heating her blood. Her newfound magic churned within her in response and rose to the surface like a wave crashing through her and exiting her palms; a slow jade mist danced around her scar.

Lucy gasped—it had never done this before.

She watched curiously as the green swirling haze glided over her hand and up her arm, twirling around her playfully. It moved from one arm to the other, caressing Lucy in a feather soft embrace. A giggle sprung from her lips in fascination.

"Why are you still with me?" she wondered aloud.

It slowly drifted back toward her right palm and dissolved into her skin, becoming a part of her once more.

Lucy waited with bated breath, wondering if the spirited magic would return, but nothing happened. Her hand displayed its round scar, and the magic resumed purring under her skin.

A knock on her door startled her back into reality, and she quickly returned the concealment charm.

Madame Baum entered with a polite smile of contentment on her face, but Lucy knew better than to believe that. Her mother had been upset with her from the moment she was made aware of Lucy's disappearance. However, following proper Denoran etiquette, Lucy's mother would never admit her grievances. She would move about her day as though she was not bothered, silently withholding any negative feelings.

"Hello, Mother," Lucy offered kindly, sitting up on her bed to greet her.

"Good morning, Lucella," she replied tactfully. Her mother pulled out the small stool in front of the vanity with her beautiful gold swirling magic. "Come. Sit."

Her mother's usual light and cheerful smile seemed pasted on, her brightness dimmed somehow.

Lucy nodded in reverent compliance and sat before the vanity, allowing her mother to dote on her. Lucy felt the distance growing between her and her mother, and wanted to mend it if she could. Despite knowing her actions would hurt her family, Lucy had hoped they would understand upon her return.

"You must look your absolute best today, Lucella," her mother told her as she fussed at Lucy's lavender gown, flattening imaginary creases and wrinkles. Picking up a brush, she arranged Lucy's hair.

Lucy held back a groan as she straightened her shoulders, preparing for the day's events. The arrival of her magic distracted her from her impending meeting with Lord Sloan.

"Remind me again why you believe I must marry this male?" Lucy asked.

Anita stopped mid brush stroke for just a quick second, but it was enough for Lucy to notice. Her hands shook as she continued.

"This marriage will be a beautiful way to bring Denora together once again, Lucella, you know this," she explained. "You will be the Lady of the Northern Territory and have a prosperous marriage to Lord Sloan."

Lucy looked at her mother in the mirror's reflection—it was only at times like this that Lucy felt like she could truly look at her. Her face was tight with her lips pursed, trying to withhold something.

Does she really believe the words she says, Lucy asked herself. *Or is she trying to convince herself, too?*

"Mother." Lucy turned to face her, holding her mother's hands in her own. "This isn't what I want," Lucy spoke plainly, hopeful that her mother would listen this time.

There was no time to speak in riddles, no reading between the lines—at least one of her parents had to understand that she did not want to get married. In fact, it was the last thing she wanted. She had spent so many hours dropping hints at the fact with no success.

Lucy never wanted to come across as disrespectful to her family, but at some point she had hoped that someone would really know Lucy for who she was and see that this was not the future she wanted. Unfortunately, no one noticed, and since no one else was speaking up for her, she had to do it herself.

Anita's face was painted in confusion. "What do you mean, dear? This will be a wonderful opportunity for you."

"No, Mother, it won't," Lucy said sternly, standing up now to speak to her. "I want to be a bowyer. I want to be part of the family business." She walked across the room to the window, looking out to the Nilban Woods. "I want to create and explore—I want to find my own path." She turned to her mother. "Why is that so wrong?"

"Lucella, you understand Denoran tradition more than you pretend to," she began harshly. She used her magic to float the hairbrush back to the dresser and quickly returned the chair to the vanity. "Enough with the foolishness."

"Because I enjoy crafting bows, I am foolish?" Lucy challenged.

"Yes, Lucy," her mother said sharply. "You are foolish for the ridiculous choices you've made. I will *never* understand why you felt as though leaving to another realm on your own was a wise choice. It is completely outlandish behavior."

The words knocked the breath from Lucy, the pang of betrayal more than she was prepared for.

The pained look on Lucy's face was enough for her mother to

turn to leave. "I'm sorry you're so lost right now," she said over the shoulder of her gray gown, then she left the room.

Lucy took a deep breath, her blood rushing through her ears, unable to even hear as her mother closed the door.

How could she?

She tried to reason with herself as she looked in the mirror—trying to shake the feeling of devastation that swirled in her heart.

Why is there no one who will support me? Why is a business deal more important than my life?

Her long lavender gown was adorned with silver filigree along the bodice, with sheer, flowing sleeves reaching just past her elbows. It felt absolutely beautiful, and nothing like herself. She thought back to the woods on Abe's property... with Micah. When she could wear clothes that felt much more comfortable. Clothes that allowed her to run around in the forests and chop wood to create her elegant bows. She'd never be able to run in a gown like this.

And that's all she wanted to do—run away.

"It's time," Jasper's muffled voice came through Lucy's closed door. "Make haste."

"One more moment, please," she called, staring out her bedroom window, trying to find the courage to withstand the next few hours. Her stomach roiled with unease and every breath she took felt more and more shallow.

You can do this, she reminded herself. *Have the semblance of strength in front of Father and get through the day to make a plan back to Micah.*

She took a deep breath.

"You may enter," she called.

Jasper entered with an impatient huff, his permanent sneer on his face drilling holes through Lucy. "Why are you taking so long?" He asked icily.

"My apologies. Of course," Lucy replied with mock sincerity. "It would be so unfortunate for Lord Sloan to have to wait on a female. Goodness, we can't have that happening."

Her scathing reply left Jasper's eyes bulging, and Lucy kept her smile hidden. He spent so much of his time making Lucy feel like a worthless Fae, she thoroughly enjoyed pressing every one of his buttons.

"Your father and I have already cemented this union that will spread the Baum Bowyers throughout all of Denora. You should thank me for my business prowess, yet you are ungrateful."

Lucy eyed him suspiciously. It was rare for him to make more than a few commanding remarks to Lucy. She was thankful that he was usually not much of a conversationalist.

"What if I don't want to thank you? The business was fine without the Northern Territory—my future did not need to become a bargaining chip." There was fire in her response and in her soul.

"Your future means nothing to me," he replied as he waved her off impatiently. "The Baum Bowyers will take over the whole of Denora and beyond with this union. You'll see. Your father will see it, too." His arrogant grimace made Lucy uneasy.

What part did Jasper play in this betrothal? Why is he so concerned?

As usual, Jasper kept two steps ahead of Lucy on the walk through the estate to meet her parents and Lord Sloan's entourage. As they crossed the foyer, she released a sigh of relief. There were no carriages, no soldiers, and no hustle and bustle of the staff.

He isn't here yet.

Lucy considered the royals in Denora as nothing more than over-served, demanding Fae who held the citizens of the realm to an unrealistic standard. Being that Laurent Sloan was the Lord of the entire Northern Territory, she was sure he was just as bad at the rest.

His reputation for being a malevolent leader echoed through the homes of the Kingdom, but the Dukes, and the King himself, were all too afraid to do anything about it. Whispered voices talked of Lord *Slain*, and his wrath among his people.

The citizens of the other territories were thankful that he kept his people in the North, rarely needing to come into the Capital for any business. Although, that was to change with the marriage agreement.

Some of the fire in her dimmed with a sigh. Lucy couldn't understand why everyone thought her life was theirs to negotiate.

Her reality felt so small now that she had encountered so much beyond her realm. Here in Denora, she knew the expectations of a female Fae—and they were less than inspiring. She was to be a silent, beautiful figure who nodded subserviently to each request. Her mother, Anita, played the role wonderfully. Lucy preferred to live a life beyond service to her potential husband.

But in Joterra?

Her heart fluttered at the possibilities of a life in Joterra with Micah. In the mortal realm she could be exactly who she wanted to be, with no one there to try to change her. There she could shoot her bow and use her hands to create the most beautiful weapons for future archers. Dresses would be for special occasions only and she would never be looked down upon for wearing pants. Lucy could be exactly who she wanted to be without a Fae male, or anyone else for that matter, telling her she could not.

Jasper swung the doors to the garden open and stepped aside for Lucy to enter before him. His bow to her was negligible.

"There's my little flower," Corvus exclaimed as Lucy entered the room. She did her best not to blanch at the childish affection, curious of his change of tone from earlier that day.

The room was bright, with long oversized windows that stretched from the vaulted ceiling to the tiled floor. It was her mother's favorite room to host guests because of the beautiful view of the garden terrace, which was always expertly tended.

The sun refreshed Lucy, bringing her a sense of calm that she craved so very much. Her life had been turned upside down from the moment she left home, and she still had questions about this new magic that flowed within her. Her fingers dug into her palm as she remembered the soft green mist that made its swift, but short, appearance.

Lucy scanned the room, trying to prepare for the uncomfortable afternoon that was to unfold before her. Her father was seated comfortably before the fire, though the weather outside did not call for the additional warmth. Corvus liked to show off his power and influence by flaunting his wealth and his extravagant home. In his mind, a fifteen foot fireplace was a show of power, especially when he used a unique spell and a flourish of his hand to start the fire with golden sparks that crashed like thunder.

Jasper took a position behind her father and her mother stood near the plush armchairs and settees, awaiting her arrival.

One male stood at the far wall, but Lucy had never seen this Fae soldier before.

"Come, Lucella," Corvus called out to her. With a wave of his hand, a gray chair floated from one side of the room to the other, inviting her to sit. Lucy walked gracefully to the chair in her ornate gown with no hint of the clumsiness that she was so used to in the previous week due to the uncomfortable boots she wore in Joterra. She stood quietly and kept her lips pressed in a thin line, determined not to speak unless absolutely necessary.

Corvus, smiling like a pig in shit, turned to a man sitting across from him in a high-backed chair. She didn't even notice this stranger who sat with her father, still as a statue.

"This is my daughter, Lucella," Corvus proclaimed proudly.

The stranger stood to greet her with a sly grin and a boyish charm at odds with his regal stature. "Hello, Miss Lucella, it is a pleasure to formally meet you."

He was a handsome male, with long blond hair, nearly white as snow, and a straight, long nose over a thin mouth. He stood tall and elegant—beautiful in a way that Lucy had never seen in Denora; poised and quiet. Everything about him reminded her of the cold; even his posture was stiff. His commanding ice-blue eyes and the silver clothing hugging his muscular frame only added to the starkness of his pale skin.

Lucy wasn't entirely sure who this male was, so she curtsied obediently and sat, keeping a facade of pleasantry about her in order to appease her mother. She looked around the room distractedly and wondered when Lord Laurent Sloan would arrive with his entourage of soldiers and servants at his every beck and call.

"Lucy," Corvus began again. "This is Lord Sloan."

Her eyes swung toward her father at his declaration. Surprise painted across her face as she carefully observed the stranger across from her.

How is this man in front of me the terror known as Lord Slain?

Corvus smiled proudly as he turned to his daughter. "I thought it would be best for you two to get to know one another before we send the announcements out next week."

Her heart stopped, and she fixed her eyes upon her father.

Next week?

Lucy looked to her mother who was picturesque, propped on the plush settee, smiling placidly as the males spoke.

She knew… She knew, and she didn't even tell me.

As if reading her thoughts, Corvus continued. "We have moved up the wedding. We will hold it in four months."

"Why are you moving it up?" Lucy blurted, still staring at her father, the first words out of her mouth in front of Lord Sloan.

No, this can't be happening, she thought to herself, bile rising in her throat.

"Lord Sloan accepted my suggestion to have the wedding before the snow falls, as the long winter is on its way. We wouldn't want to delay such an extraordinary event in Denora, now would we?" His cautionary gaze was fixed on Lucy, demanding her words to be picked carefully in the presence of the Lord of the North.

"I see." She bowed her head and kept it down, refusing to look up at the males responsible for ruining her life, doing her best to compose herself.

"I look forward to courting you this month, Miss Baum," Lord Sloan said softly, the kindness in his tone clashing with what she knew of his reputation.

"Thank you, Lord Sloan," she replied sweetly. If there was anything Lucy knew, it was how to play the part when the time called.

Her father was sure to be shocked by her play of obedience, but she was no fool. Corvus got all of Lucy's harsh words and acts of protest, because she believed that deep down he once loved her with all of his being. Though it seemed a lifetime ago, she knew the feelings were still in there. Somewhere.

Lucy dared to look at Lord Sloan, trying to identify why this male sitting in front of her was one that others dreaded beyond all measure. He was tranquil and polite. Though, even with his soft white hair and gentle way of speaking, his features painted a picture of a predator to be feared. His long, thin nose and pointed chin gave him sharp features reminiscent of a bird hunting their prey.

Regardless, she would never give away her true thoughts of contempt to a stranger, let alone one she was set to marry. No, instead she would focus her efforts on trying to learn more about Lord Sloan. If there was any small detail she could collect in order to help her rid herself of him forever, she would find it. Then she would free herself from the manacles that Denora kept firmly shackled to every Fae female.

She was not the weak Fae her father once knew her to be, and she never would be again. She rubbed the palm of her hand in remembrance.

"This evening I would like to take you to dinner at the Capital," Lord Sloan said with a voice of velvet, his eyes sparkling. "I have some business to attend to in the city, and Tralont has extended his welcome to me."

Lord Sloan's familiarity with King Tralont surprised Lucy; she had never heard of anyone speaking so casually about a royal. Even the dukes spoke of the King with great reverence and respect.

"I will be busy and cannot return in time to escort you myself. My guard, Roger, will be there to greet you if I am delayed." He turned to speak to her father. "Corvus, will you handle the travel arrangements?"

"Of course, Lord Sloan." Corvus's smile faltered momentarily, not used to being told what to do. "Jasper," he snapped, directing him to begin the arrangements.

Jasper's face pulled into a grimace behind Corvus, but he quickly replaced it with a vacant look, prepared to serve.

Lucy eyed the silent guard, still standing at attention nearby. He wore Fae armor and the emblem of the North. *How did I miss that?*

"Wonderful," Lord Sloan replied with a curt nod. "I am also interested in protecting those *assets* we were discussing, so I will be arranging that today as well."

He stood and all the others in the room stood along with him, including Lucy. His height towered over everyone except Corvus. The ladies gave a small curtsey, Corvus and Jasper gave a deep bow, and Lord Laurent Sloan left with his guard in tow.

The door closed with a click, and Lucy whipped her head toward her father. "How could you do this to me?" Lucy's lips curled in anger.

"Lucella Baum, I will not hear another word from you," Corvus said, exasperated. "You are lucky Lord Sloan is willing to marry you and that the rumor of your escapades have not been dragged around the realm!"

"I have no other choice in the matter, do I? My life means so little to you." Lucy's eyes welled with tears as her anger filled her entirely. Once again, the tingling sensation of magic rippled through her, begging to be released.

To Lucy's astonishment, Anita stepped in before Corvus spoke again. "Your life means everything to us, Lucy."

Corvus stood, face flushed with frustration, preparing to lecture Lucy on her behavior once more. However, once he turned and looked at his wife, his anger faded from his features.

Anita stood tall, her hands folded tightly in front of her, with silent tears falling down her face. Her sad eyes fixed upon Lucy.

"This marriage does not mean we do not love you. Your father has only your best interests in mind, and we want nothing more than for you to be well taken care of. No female in Denora lives a happy and full life all alone."

"We will not continue to speak of this, and you will not bring it up again and upset your mother," Corvus demanded. "You will go to the Capital today to dine with Lord Sloan and you will be on your absolute best behavior."

Lucy looked at her mother with unbearable hurt.

How could she sit by and allow this to happen? The look Lucy gave her father was enough to kill, and the vibrating aura of her magic tempted to follow suit.

She swiftly turned on her feet to get as far from her parents as possible before her magic acted of its own accord once again. Though this time, she was both fearful and exalted by the new power seated deep within her, knowing the possibilities of this new magic were yet to be discovered.

She would never use the magic to hurt those she loved—but she didn't love Laurent Sloan.

CHAPTER
FOUR

LUCY

Storming back into her bedchambers, Lucy slammed the door shut, rattling the metal rails on her bed frame. Then she did something that she had not done in nearly 75 years. She spread her arms wide, lifted both hands into the air until they touched, and brought a powerful privacy charm over her room, strengthened by her otherworldly magic. Once she saw the pearlescent barrier in place, she let out a heart wrenching scream.

In agony, she released every painful moment she was ever ignored and demanded her voice to be uncaged. She screamed for the unfair wedding arrangement that she refused to accept. She screamed for the loss of her best friend, and the fact that no one understood her grief. And she sobbed, as she thought of the only person who understood her, and how he was so, so far away.

Lucy crumbled to the ground, exhausted by the burden of loneliness she carried with her.

I can't keep doing this. I need Micah.

Her hands braced the cold floor as she remained on all fours, trying to find her breath. Tears streaked down the tip of her nose and dripped ever so gently to the floor. She watched with ragged breaths as her teardrops puddled onto the wood beneath her.

Her ornate lavender gown was sure to tear with her huddled on the ground, but she could not find it in her to care.

What does it matter? she thought to herself despondently. *Nothing will change my fate. A torn gown will not change the mind of stubborn male Fae who care for nothing beyond themselves.*

She turned, sitting with her back against the wall, feeling the cold brick. Her racing heart hammered in her chest and she didn't know how to stop the raging despair inside of her.

That's when she felt it again: magic bubbling from deep within, starting in her broken heart and pouring through her like a wave. Her chest heaved as she felt the strange magic surge through her center like a blast of lightning until an emerald mist burst from her palms.

With her arms outstretched, a small sphere of green pooled in her hands. She stretched her fingers wide, numbly watching, curious to see if it would stay in her palm without her cupped hand there to contain it. Tipping her hand, she expected to see the mist pour over, but instead of falling, it floated. It changed form from a mist to a more solidified shape as it rose higher into the air.

No longer a sphere, the hazy magic turned into several small orbs, spreading through the room, circling Lucy as she watched in awe at the magic which seemed to have a mind of its own. Each orb began to stretch and divide, but right before it split entirely, the two rounded edges formed wings. The shapes then flapped in a graceful dance around Lucy's bedroom.

Butterflies.

Her eyes welled with tears again, as the beautiful, luminescent butterflies fluttered around her, bringing back a memory long forgotten.

Lucy and Abe, in the depths of the forest, adventuring while their fathers discussed business. They came upon a field of wildflowers during butterfly migration season. Running into the field, they startled the beau-

tiful winged creatures, creating a whirlwind of magnificence around the friends as the butterflies soared through the air. Abe grabbed her hand and pulled her onto the grass. There, lying on their backs, they looked up to the sky and watched the butterflies as they flew high into the clouds.

"I wish I were a butterfly," a young Lucy told Abe, wistfully.

"I don't want to be a bug," Abe laughed at her.

"I don't want to be a bug either," she laughed, then sighed. "I just want to be free."

Lucy's sobs filled the room again as her magic kept her company, gliding through the air, allowing her to feel just a little less alone.

BY THE TIME Lucy calmed herself, she was still without an appetite. In just a few hours, Lord Laurent Sloan would expect her at the finest restaurant in Denora and the very thought made her ill.

She paced back and forth in her lonely bedroom that had become a prison to her. The ornate furniture and soft comforts of her bed were a dazzling facade to the fact that Lucy was stuck in this cell of a room, not allowed to leave the estate.

She stopped at her open window, the breeze and fresh air clearing her mind for just a moment. A beautiful black raven perched on her windowsill. Lucy almost didn't notice it for how perfectly still it was.

"Hello, little one," she cooed to the bird. She slowly stretched out her hand, seeing if the bird would startle and fly away. Instead, it took a tiny hop forward.

Lucy pulled her hand back in surprise. Tilting her head, she analyzed the bird closer. It seemed to be watching her.

That's preposterous. Birds don't watch people.

Then the raven took another small hop toward Lucy. She smiled and reached out, carefully petting the bird with two gentle fingers. It was soft as silk, with the most lustrous black feathers.

"Thank you for visiting me," she whispered. "I wish I had some crumbs to offer you, but you don't want to be in this prison cell. Fly. Be free." Lucy bit the inside of her cheek; feeling so isolated was getting to her, but she wouldn't fall apart again. She turned from the window, a new determination filling her.

Her body buzzing, she pulled out the thin branches of wood she had hidden under her bed. Lucy touched the beautiful pale branch sadly. Her father would never accept this wood for the creation of a new bow while he was so upset with Lucy. He'd just as soon throw it in his fireplace out of spite.

His anger was unmistakable, and she knew he wouldn't approve any request from Lucy to construct a bow from the wood she collected from her journey. She'd rather ask for forgiveness later than for permission now.

Her hands skimmed the branches from The Elderwood with longing, and she felt the whisper of a shiver through her heart and down her arms. Her magic rose to the surface, as the bouncing green light slid from her palm, danced around her body and retreated into her skin once more.

Her eyebrows shot up in surprise, wondering why the wood triggered such a reaction.

You feel me, too... Don't you?

Unsure of what it all meant, she took the time to examine each branch as she took them out of their hiding place. She went through the steps slowly, analyzing each piece and determining which would be the best pieces to use for a bow.

It was the first time she was able to be herself without having to pretend that she was fine.

She was not fine.

Thinking about Micah filled most of her night; every inch of her hurt with longing. She needed to find a way back to him. As soon as she saw him, she would jump in his arms just to feel his strong embrace. However, the most frustrating part was that she had no idea when that could be. Her life was, yet again, under control of her father.

Control. That simple word put a fire in the pit of her stomach. *I won't let them control me again.*

The small strap of her tool bag poked out from under her bed. She took it by the handle and dragged the bag out. It had been so long since she had used these tools. Her father hadn't let her create any bows in nearly a year, and most of her focus had been on getting him to listen to her. The last bow she made with her father had been sold to one of the dukes for their son's 150th birthday. It felt like a lifetime ago.

Picking up her tools, one by one, she noted the familiarity of their heavy weight in her hands. These were sturdy and reliable instruments, and they had assisted Lucy in making more than one hundred bows.

What harm could there be in one more? she wondered mischievously.

Selecting the longest, sturdiest branch from The Elderwood, she sent a silent apology to Duke Renfro for taking the material meant for his sons, and decided she would have better skill with this bow than any of the Renfros anyway.

Then, she went to work.

For more than an hour, she shaped and shaved the wood, sanding it down to the perfect form. Lucy balanced it in her hands, watching it as it rocked back and forth, perfectly weighted. It was a lethal weapon of beauty and grace.

She picked up the engraver and paused, unsure what design to choose. Usually she engraved her family's sigil along with leaves, but something about that felt off. Her hand tingled in response.

Yes, I know you're still there. I don't think I need another reminder.

She held the bow in her hands and closed her eyes, thinking of how she had changed so much. She was no longer interested in flowers and leaves—that was behind her now.

In her mind, Lucy replayed her moments with Micah, the heat that rose between them, the flames dancing in the window. She thought of the fire she controlled to save The Elderwood.

That's it. Lucy took her time carving tiny flames up and down the limbs of the bow, connecting them with vines.

When she finished, she looked at the masterpiece that reflected who she was now. Lucy was not a timid leaf blowing in the wind. She was fire—ready to burn down anything in her path.

A smile played on her lips as she held the bow in her hands. She would play her role at dinner that evening, but she would not be the demure, silent female that a Denoran male expects. No. She would prove to Laurent Sloan how absolutely wrong she was for him. Then, she would find her way to Micah.

Her parents could try to carve her path for her future, but it was up to Lucy which direction she took. Would she follow the perfectly placed stepping stones to a future in the mountains as Lady Lucella Sloan? Or would she trample through the Denoran wilderness to get to the handsome mortal man in Joterra?

There was really only one option, and he had the most perfect dark brown eyes that she had ever gazed upon.

And he was waiting for her.

JUST LIKE BEFORE, Lucy refused to sit around and wait for someone else to save her. She would be happy to forge her own path and upset anyone who got in her way—no one else minded they were upsetting *her*, did they?

I may be on my own, but that doesn't mean I'm weak.

Closing her eyes, she focused all of her thoughts on the emerald energy that buzzed within her, asking it to assist her. The magic hummed with excitement as it answered her summons, pouring out of her palms in a rush. Lucy watched as the green mist swirled around her arms, waiting for her command. Lucy whispered the Denoran privacy charm, ensuring her footsteps would be silent as she traversed the estate, getting the things she needed for her trip.

Hmm, this feels familiar, she thought sarcastically.

She crept down the staircase that led to the kitchens, knowing if she were going to leave, she needed food to take with her. Last time she made the trip, she was less prepared than she would have liked. Lucy had already missed both breakfast and lunch and any risk of weakness would endanger her plan.

Once in the kitchen, she stalled, listening in wait to make sure she was alone. Unfortunately, she heard the voice of someone she definitely did not want to run into. Her mother.

"Bethilda, please prepare the fish for my husband's lunch, his meeting should be over shortly."

"Yes, Madame Baum," the kitchen master replied.

"And, has..." her voice trailed off. "Has Lucella eaten?"

"Not that I am aware of, Madame. She did not come down for breakfast and ignored the summons for lunch."

Lucy bit her tongue at the remark. *I didn't ignore the summons; I ignored Jasper. There's a difference.*

"Well, I would like you to prepare a meal for her. Some of her favorites, perhaps? I know she prefers the cheese and meat rolls from Durrant. Maybe some vegetable soup with warm bread and butter?"

"Yes, Madame. Right away."

"When it is ready, please find me. I would like to eat with her." A softness filled her voice that Lucy did not recognize.

Why does she wish to eat with me?

Lucy listened as her mother's footsteps walked away, then she waited rather impatiently as Bethilda prepared her father's lunch. Once the kitchen master left, Lucy had to act quickly.

Darting into the pantry, she gathered a large loaf of bread, dried berries and nuts that she often took with her into the woods, and a jug filled with water. It wasn't likely to be a long journey, but history proved again and again that her plans never quite worked the way she anticipated.

With her bag packed full of the food for her journey, a determined smile made its way upon her face. There was no doubt about it; Lucy was going to Joterra to be with Micah. Only one question remained—when would a window of opportunity present itself?

LUCY WOULD BE LYING if she said she was excited to eat with her mother, but if she was going to be leaving soon, it had to be done.

"Would you like some sugar for your tea?" Anita offered.

"No, thank you," Lucy replied.

The air was stifling, with an awkward silence hanging between them. What was left to be said? Lucy shared her issues and her mother dutifully ignored them—there was nothing else.

"I was just down by the Reiniers' last evening. Did you know Shoshana will marry Duke Renfro's eldest son?"

"Oh?" Lucy asked politely, though in reality, she did not care in the slightest. Shoshana was lovely, but Lucy hadn't spoken to her since she was quite young and was still required to take classes with the seamstresses.

"Yes, Maryanne is quite pleased. You know the Reiniers were very hopeful to marry to a strong bloodline."

Bloodlines.

An idea rose in Lucy's mind.

"How many weak bloodlines are there in Denora?" Lucy asked.

Her mother was smarter than she let on to the rest of the realm, but Lucy knew her mother was very knowledgeable regarding history and the families of Denora.

Perhaps she knows more about Alderic Lumen.

"Truthfully, more than is known. Most families of weaker magic do their best to compensate in other ways so that others don't see their true shortcomings."

"What do you mean?" This surprised Lucy. She was only aware of a few families who had weak magical capabilities due to their bloodlines.

"Most families who have... more *fragile* magic are well-known in the realm and they attempt to make allies in other ways. The Reiniers produce some of the most beautiful females in Southern Denora. Duke Renfro has an incredibly strong family line—he does not have to worry about the bloodline weakening with the Reinier line. Ethan Renfro can marry Shoshana and together they will bear beautifully strong Fae."

Of course. An arranged marriage for the sole purpose of strengthening Denoran tradition. The thought made her nauseous.

"However, there are also families who are weak who have nothing to offer. They do their best to hide it—they find other ways to be purposeful to the realm." Anita's voice dropped to a whisper as she leaned in close to Lucy. "Take the DeValeys for example."

The bulge of Lucy's eyes could rival Jasper's at the mention of his family line.

"*Jasper* DeValey?" Lucy asked in astonishment.

"Yes, dear. Are there any others?"

"I had no idea he was a weak Fae. How is that even possible? He has been working with Father for decades."

"Exactly," Anita said with a wry smile. "He is known for being in league with your father's business, so of course he must be a strong Fae." Anita winked.

"He isn't?"

"Absolutely not," Anita laughed as she shook her head.

Lucy stared wide eyed at her mother. How had she missed that?

"Think, darling. When was the last time you've seen Jasper use any magic?"

Her eyes blinked rapidly as she tried to recall a time. "Wait, what about Micah? Didn't Jasper and Wes have to travel to repair the house?"

Anita took a sip of her tea, a note of discomfort across her face at the mention of her mortal friend in Joterra. "Prewritten magic, yes. It's the only way Jasper has any success—that and Wes carried the majority of that spell."

"How can that be so different?"

Anita placed her teacup down and took a moment to choose her words carefully. "Do you know how prewritten magic works?"

Lucy squinted. "I probably should know this answer, but I am going to assume my tutors explained it during one of the lessons that I missed."

Her mother's pursed lips were light with the hint of a smile. "I see. Well, in short, prewritten magic is created by the caster. Wes created the spell for Abe's cabin to be restored, so his magic supported it," she said, pausing momentarily. "I am so sorry for your loss, Lucella."

A wave of silence overtook the room. Lucy wasn't ready to talk about Abe just yet. The hurt Lucy harbored over her mother's view of marriage was still fresh, and it was hard enough to speak cordially as it was.

Lucy cleared her throat and redirected the subject. "How many strong bloodlines are there in Denora?"

"Too many to count," Anita replied, taking another sip of tea. "Why do you ask?" Her perfectly shaded eyebrows furrowed in question.

Lucy just shrugged her shoulders. "Which are the stronger bloodlines in Denora? Any families we know?"

"I suppose it changes over time," Anita replied, setting down her teacup gently. "Bloodlines can weaken when mixed with others who are less powerful—that's exactly what happened to the Reiniers."

"Any others?" Whenever Lucy was upset with her mother, she always felt it was easier to ask questions than try to carry on a genuine conversation. It allowed her to seem polite without having to share her feelings on any given subject. However, in the past, her fury was juvenile. Today, her anger threatened to spill over—though she did her best to keep it contained.

"Hmm... The Brightons, Nostellas, Cridettes. Many of the families we celebrate with at the Winter Solstice."

"Which families would you suppose were the strongest?" Lucy wasn't sure how else to ask, hoping that her mother would give the Lumen name on her own without bringing any suspicion to Lucy.

"Well, ours, for one."

"Ours?" Lucy was completely caught off guard.

"Yes, dear," her mother replied with a soft smile on her lips.

"Just Father's side? Or yours as well?"

"Darling, do you think I am nothing but a pretty face for your father?" Anita asked in false distress.

"No, of course not," Lucy said quickly. However, the more she thought about it... *When was the last time I've seen Mother use her magic?*

"It is wise for females to use their magic strategically in Denora, Lucy," her mother told her seriously. Her voice dropped as she continued, as if worried about being overheard. "I know you think less of me because of my public subservience to your father, but not everything is what it seems behind closed doors."

Puzzled, Lucy looked at her mother at this strange admission. "What do you mean?" Lucy asked in an equally low voice.

Anita put her finger up to her lips to request quiet, and Lucy carefully nodded. With that, Anita stood up and walked a few paces away from the bed and stopped at the window. Her smile was wide and bright—something almost foreign to Lucy.

For so long, her mother had played the role of a silent figurehead for the family, never giving her opinion over important matters. She her practiced smile for the male Fae who came to do business with Corvus and the fancy estate dinners. She always smiled as she doted upon her husband.

But this. This smile was magnificent. It reached from one rosy, high cheekbone to the next.

It was real.

Lucy couldn't help but smile along with her as she watched, bewildered by the behavior.

What is she up to?

Anita turned to the window and took a deep breath in and out. She brought her hand up to her mouth and kissed her fingers, ever so softly, then blew over the top of her hand as though she was blowing someone a kiss. Her golden, shimmering magic drifted out the window to something down below.

Lucy stood and rushed over to the window as quickly and quietly as she could. Anita's eyes were bright and full of life as she put her hands on Lucy's shoulders and brought her closer to the window. From over her shoulder, Anita pointed at a rosebush in the distance, then whispered in her ear. "Watch closely."

The warm skin of her mother's arms pressed tenderly against her as she picked up on the scent of her delicate perfume. Being so close to her mother was a comfort she had not experienced since she was a very small child.

With a content sigh, Lucy bent further, trying to see what her mother wanted to show her in the plant. Suddenly, the entire bush grew dozens of bright red rose blossoms.

"Oh!" Lucy gasped as she clutched the window ledge, watching the green bush drown in large, red petals. She looked at her mother with wide eyes, as if seeing her for the first time. "How?"

This made little sense to Lucy. Her mother was known for using her magic for superficial beautification—pinning hair, smoothing make up, placing small details on gowns. But this? This was something she had never seen another Denoran female ever accomplish.

She has magic that works with nature?

"I've always been able to do these things, darling," her mother said, staring lovingly into her daughter's eyes.

"But you—" Lucy didn't know how to continue. She had never seen her mother do this kind of magic. Why did she hide such a beautiful gift?

"I know," Anita said with a sad smile. "I keep my magic private, because there is no room for a female who is stronger than her husband." She winked at Lucy, but the playful act took on a somber tone.

"Mother, I can't believe you have such wondrous magic! Female Fae shouldn't have to hide their magic when it is something to be proud of! And just because you are—" she stopped. "Wait."

Anita huffed out a small laugh as she saw her daughter register the last comment she made.

"You're stronger than Father? You can't be."

"I am."

"This is amazing!" Lucy trilled with delight. "Who cares what Father says? You should utilize your magic whenever and however you want!"

"I do, Lucy. Keeping my magic to myself is my choice. If your father had his way, I'd be flaunting my power all over Denora," she laughed.

"He is in support of your magic?" Lucy asked. Each time her mother spoke she learned something brand new.

How have I missed so much of this? How did I not know?

"He is. Why do you think he was so happy to show you the artistry of being a bowyer? Your blood runs thick with some of the most powerful magic in all of Denora," Anita said as she hugged her daughter. "What we do for you is out of love and respect for you and your magic. A strong pairing with another strong Fae is important— it allows for you to find equal footing within the marriage." Her voice trailed off at the change of topic.

Lucy stiffened under her mother's embrace, pulling back slowly.

"You deserve someone who will understand your strength and your need to always challenge yourself," her mother continued. "Lord Sloan is an exceptional Fae with powerful magic... Within a marriage, concessions are made."

"I will not be a concession," Lucy's tone fell. "I will not be with someone who gives me *permission* to be who I am," Lucy said with disgust.

"That isn't what I meant," Anita shook her head quickly,

reaching out to Lucy as she spun away from her. "Lucy, all I mean is that there is more to marriage than Denoran tradition."

"Then let me find it on my own!" Lucy nearly shouted.

The room fell still again. Lucy was breathing heavily as she turned to look at her mother. Anita's chest flushed pink, and the life that had once danced in her eyes was replaced with sadness.

"Mother, I realize you think you know what is best for me, but I am not you. And Lord Sloan is not Father." Her words that started out slow came quicker and quicker. "I am not promised a perfect love match and no matter how much I beg for you to let me make my own path in life, you silence me. Why? Why must I be silent?"

Her mother opened her mouth to speak, but then closed it again. They both knew there was no answer that could ever suffice. Instead, they remained face to face in a standoff. Two female Fae with unprecedented power: one willing to bend to the whims of Denoran tradition and one prepared the burn the entire institution to the ground.

"I will not divulge your secret, Mother," she said in hushed tones, forcing herself to breathe. "You are entitled to be as silent as you wish. I, however, refuse. I will not bend. I will not become something I am not simply because society deems it to be so." She took a step back and smoothed her gown, forcing herself to appear as calm as the magic writhed within her, mirroring her rage. "I will play Father's game, and I will smile serenely—but know behind each and every fake smile plastered to my face is a fire that is burning, ready to bring down anything that gets in my way."

Anita's footsteps fumbled. "Lucy, you misunderstand." She tried to find the words, but Lucy refused to hear anything more.

"Thank you for lunch," Lucy said with calm repose, devastated tears welling in her eyes. She stood next to her door, dismissing Anita from her room. "I will finish preparing for my evening alone now."

Her mother tipped her head down in defeat and took a deep breath, smoothing her skirts. Lifting her gaze, she walked to the door to leave. She paused only to wipe the tear falling from Lucy's eye with the back of her finger, staring at her daughter with sorrow.

Lucy held her pose, looking straight ahead, begging the tears to stop flowing, as she watched her mother walk through the door and down the hall.

CHAPTER

FIVE

MICAH

There and back, he kept telling himself. *Lunch with Dad, turn in my badge, pack up the apartment and back.*

He paced the newly renovated living room of the cabin in the woods, knowing that this trip could be risky, but also knowing he had no other choice. Taking these next steps toward his new role as guardian was important to him, and hopefully the closer he was to that, the closer he'd get to Lucy. Maybe with her, things would make more sense.

It's just me here in this middle-of-nowhere-house trying to figure out how to guard a magic portal with no magic. Got it. Easy.

Micah clearly had no idea what he was doing.

Leaving the property meant leaving The Elderwood unprotected, but since Wes and Jasper had visited a few days ago, nothing had happened. In fact, the house was so unbearably quiet he felt like he was going insane.

He glanced around at the unfamiliar space, not seeing any trace of who he was or where he came from. No mom. No Grandad. Everything was different now.

Micah wanted his own things to help him feel more like himself.

His record player. His workout clothes. Hell, his own pajamas. He had never expected to stay at the house for more than a few days, and now it had turned into his entire future.

This is my life now and the least I can do it make it feel more like home. The thought hung heavy in his mind.

Home.

My life.

Neither of those things felt real anymore. Micah's life, and everything in it, had been turned upside down. He squeezed his eyes shut as he pushed the thoughts away. There wasn't time to deal with it yet.

He grabbed the paper shopping bag perched on the arm of the couch and walked outside. Earlier in the day, he ran to the local hardware store to grab some equipment that would hopefully put him at ease as he left the premises. He didn't want to be gone for too long for a multitude of reasons—most obviously, he couldn't leave the portal unguarded. However, the bigger reason was the hope that Lucy would come back. It didn't matter to him how ridiculous it was —there was no one else he dreamed of late at night. No one else he craved the way he yearned for her. He could figure out the rest, as long as he had her.

All of this was unusual for Micah. Pining for a girl was something he had left behind so long ago, he didn't even think he had it in him anymore. He had worked hard building a life with no attachments. His carefully constructed boundaries kept him always an arms-length away from everyone. He built his system so rigorously to keep himself from ever getting hurt again.

Much good that did, he thought as he prepared to visit his old life and say goodbye.

The paper bag contained a set of wireless cameras he purchased to place around the cabin. He didn't expect to be gone long, but with the J. Pearson cronies starting the fire, he wasn't sure what lengths they would go to get the property. He needed to keep an eye on things until he understood more of how to legitimately protect the land.

He placed a camera by the front door, one to spotlight the back door, and another on The Elderwood portal itself. He connected the cameras to his phone and once he was sure it was working correctly, he got in his car to leave for his weekend journey to the city.

Something tugged at his heart as he drove away from the cabin.

Is this the right move?

The question hung heavily on his mind... but he wasn't sure what else there was for him. His life at the police department was important to him, and leaving felt like giving up on everything he worked hard for... But something deep inside of him warmed at the thought of his family and having the chance to walk in their footsteps. This was the task given to him by his grandad and mom. By choosing this life, he accepted the reality of magic and other realms... Hopefully Lucy saw that and accepted it for what it was: Micah choosing her, too.

There was no other choice for Micah to make. There was only this.

Glancing back in the rearview mirror, he could have sworn he saw a shadow hovering near the base of the trees, but when he looked again, it was gone.

"YOU'RE SURE ABOUT THIS, SON?" Micah's father, Richard, asked him for the third time.

Seeing his dad was important to Micah. He shared the same last name as his mom, but when he looked in the mirror, all he saw was his dad; his bronzed skin, dark brown eyes, broad shoulders.

Looking at his dad now showed more changes between the two than Micah had ever hoped to admit. His father's once dark hair was now peppered with silver, and the fine lines around his eyes were proof of time passing. Micah's heart hurt as he looked at the man that meant so much to him. When would he see his father next? Months? Years?

For the majority of his life, it had been just the two of them together. Once his mom got sick, he stayed with his dad most of the time. Richard always helped Micah forge his path in the world, never playing the overbearing parent role.

When his mom died, Micah was lost. He didn't speak up in class, he stopped going to sports, and didn't make time for his friends. All the kids from his baseball team called each other by their last names, and he couldn't hear "Lumen" without thinking of his mom. He loved the connection he had to her, by having her last name, but the reality of the situation was bigger than his young heart could handle.

It was only his dad and his new wife, Lori, who were able to coax him out of his shell and bring him back into the world. They tried doing some things Micah's mom, Vanessa, loved to do.

They started with volunteering at local homeless shelters and soup kitchens, just to help Micah feel like he was doing something good in his life. Lori made it a habit to bring him to the library weekly so he could pick out books to read, just like his mom used to do with him. They upheld Thursday family nights with movies and microwave popcorn. These small steps led Micah back to life again, and now it felt like a lie to have to leave that life behind after working so hard to get it back.

"I know it sounds crazy, Dad," Micah tried to explain as he took another bite of his lunch. "Mom left me some things at Grandad's that I didn't know about. Being there really helps me feel connected to them again."

"Things like what?" his father asked, hoping to get more out of his reserved son. Micah had always been closed off and private, but these were things he really couldn't imagine telling his dad.

Yeah, Dad, I've got magical blood and have to stand guard over a portal in a tree. That wouldn't go over well.

"You seem so different talking about them now." Richard shook his head in contemplation, a smile playing at his mouth. "I don't think I've ever heard you talk about your mom so much in one sitting since before she passed away..."

It was true. Speaking about his mom caused him heartache he refused to acknowledge. Somehow, forcing this path had made it easier for him to think about her without falling apart.

Maybe more good will come out of this than I realize.

The pair sat and finished their sandwiches on the outdoor patio of a local cafe, enjoying the sun. Micah looked around at the people bustling on the streets of the busy city, hurriedly going from one place to the next. This was sure to be the last big group of people he would be surrounded by for a long time.

He took a deep breath and took it all in. Soon, he would be alone again. The thought made his head hurt.

"I know. I feel different," Micah agreed with a quiet nod. "Grandad was smart with the property and did a lot of investing. His acreage is worth a small fortune, and he's set up an agreement with some farmers to use his land. I can live there and earn passive income while I get the land in good shape. I can really make it my own, you know?" Convincing his dad of this plan was important to Micah. He had to have his dad on his side.

"That house is so outdated. Does it even have internet access? If you are just looking to take a break, Lori and I wouldn't mind you coming to stay with us for a while."

"I've decided to take the money that Grandad left and make some major renovations," Micah lied. The property already changed, and it definitely wasn't done the way his dad would have guessed. "When it's all done and I'm settled, I'll have you and Lori come up."

Richard had spent the better part of their lunch hour trying to convince him to stay at his apartment and not to leave the police force, but Micah stayed calm and focused as he told his dad that this was really what he wanted in his life.

He was getting better and better at lying, and he hated every ounce of it. Hadn't he just told Lucy never to lie about who she was? And here he was doing the same.

He didn't want to lose his job at the department, and he didn't want to end his lease in the city—but what other choice did he have? The landscape to his future was clear; being the guardian of the gate was his life now. There was so much to say goodbye to, but there was also a bright new horizon for him. In time, he would get it all figured out. He and Lucy would figure it out together. Hope blossomed in his chest at the thought of a life with her.

Micah looked at his dad and took in the deep set lines across his forehead, the creases around his eyes every time he smiled. His father was aging with grace, and he was so happy that he had found love again after his mother. Lori was a nice woman, and she made Richard happy, too.

It made him think of Lucy. Her bright hazel eyes. Her soft smile that he had to earn. Her beautiful freckles that covered her nose and cheeks. The ache at the memory of her face spread from his heart to the rest of his body. He only hoped he could have the same kind of happiness with her one day.

"I'll keep in touch," Micah reassured his father, and he took in the moment, unsure of when he'd be able to leave his house to see his dad again. "Just a phone call away."

They both stood, embraced one another in a deep farewell, and went their separate ways.

Micah took the short walk back to his car, preparing to complete the last leg of his trip. He spent time with his dad, and now all he had left to do was resign from the police department and finish packing. His head was pounding—the stress of the last few days was really taking a toll on him.

Maybe a good night's sleep will make this headache go away, he hoped.

A SHARP PAIN knit in Micah's side as he gripped the steering wheel of his car so tight his knuckles turned white.

Almost there, I'm almost there, he coached himself, driving as quickly as he could back to the Lumen property.

Boxing up his life and moving it in one day proved to be harder than he initially imagined. His headache started at the lunch with his dad two days ago, and each hour it got worse. Speaking to the chief at the department was difficult, but he chalked up the nausea and dry mouth to nervousness, no illness.

Going through an entire upheaval of his life, he assumed the aches and pains were from the intense emotions running through him, but when he woke up in his empty apartment the next day, they didn't get any better. In fact, with each passing minute, things got progressively worse. He almost didn't finish packing—the headaches turned vicious, making him dizzy and unable to stand.

When he finally decided enough was enough, he left with pains lancing through his body, feeling as if his whole nervous system was hit with a bolt of lightning.

His only focus on his long drive back was to return to the cabin and pray whatever made him so sick would pass quickly. The lines on the road doubled before him, causing his car to swerve, narrowly missing the ditch to his right.

When he saw his cabin, he could have cried with relief, but instead he cried out in pain—his headache was so intense that bright flashes of light were clouding his vision. This migraine was worse than any he had ever experienced before.

Micah threw the car into park and lumbered toward the house, praying for the moment he could finally lie down and rest. His head pounded and his eyesight was hazy as he squinted through the bright sunshine, making his way from the car.

From the corner of his eye, he saw a large shape barrel out from somewhere behind the trees. He couldn't see clearly and didn't understand what was happening.

He whipped around, ready to take on an attacker, like the day of the arson, but nothing was there. Blinking, he tried to clear the spots forming in his vision. Everything felt like it was spinning. He turned again, frantically waiting for the onslaught, when the world seemed to tip on its axis. He took a step toward his cabin... then everything went black.

THE SOFT PADDING of footsteps across the floor was the first sound to register to Micah, but his eyes were closed and his head was still pounding.

Where am I?

There were soft cushions beneath him, and a savory smell of something buttery cooking in the air.

Maybe I'm at the apartment? Did I end up going to Dad's? No. I've got to get back to the cabin.

The memories of his last few hours were a blur, but then he remembered his drive. He remembered getting close to the house, but did he make it inside?

Another clink of glass brought him to reality. There was someone with him.

He opened his eyes and sat up quickly, the side of his head pounding, sending a surge of nausea down to his stomach. Groaning, Micah lifted his fingers to his temple and a burst of pain followed.

Squinting through the pain, he realized he was home, sitting on the couch in his living room. But he certainly didn't remember making it back to his cabin.

The noise in the kitchen stopped.

Lucy?

The forbidden hope of her coming to his aid made his heart practically leap from his chest.

Micah stood and tried to walk toward the kitchen, but his body felt weak and lightheaded. Stopping to refocus, he looked down at the beautiful hardwood flooring. Trying to center himself before he lost his balance, he leaned into the wall for support.

"Easy there, buddy," an unfamiliar female voice came from a few feet in front of him.

Micah's eyes trailed from the wooden floor to the woman's feet; bronzed skin with strappy sandals made of leather were wrapped up strong, muscular legs. She wore a fitted pair of shorts and a tank top, all in brown, making it look like a second layer of skin upon her athletic build, secured with leather straps. His eyes continued their trek up as he spotted her straight, short, black hair, chopped right above her shoulder which gave her sharp jaw line an even more aggressive look. Her full lips and high cheekbones made her breathtaking. With deep brown eyes, shaded with thick black makeup on the edges, her gaze seemed to pierce through Micah's soul.

"Who are you?" Micah asked her, trying to stand up straight, but the pounding in his head made every moment torture. His eyes strained as he fought to keep them open without wincing.

"Sit," she ordered, her voice smokey, with the hint of an accent he couldn't place. She pulled out a kitchen chair for him so he didn't have to walk much further.

"No," Micah refused, but he took a step closer and held the back of the chair for support anyway. "Who are you? Why are you in my house?" He tried to add strength to his voice, but each breath was a chore.

"You can call me Brax," she said with a roll of her eye and a sway of her hips as she walked away from him. She looked like a soldier wrapped in seduction.

I must have hit my head really hard, he told himself as he momentarily closed his eyes to try to figure out what the hell was going on.

"Okay, *Brax*, why are you in my house?" Micah asked again, looking around to see if there were other surprises waiting for him, but all he saw was his perfectly furnished and updated home Jasper and Wes left him.

Is Brax one of them?

"I was sent here by my employer," she stated. She walked up to the stove and stirred something in the pan, an aroma of rosemary and butter filling the air and making his stomach growl. "You should sit so I can look at that wound on your head," she said. "That must hurt." She gave him a pointed look somewhere between sympathy and disgust.

"Did you do this to me?" Micah said, taking a cautionary step back from her.

She turned the stove off and walked over to him, a mixture of arrogance and danger in her gaze. "No, I'm the one who found you on the ground and dragged you into the house and onto the couch. I'm the one who made you dinner. And I'm the one who's going to make your headaches go away."

Brax then took Micah by his shoulders and, with unexpected strength, she shoved him down into the seat and stepped in front of him. His legs were spread and she stepped suggestively between them, pressing her thighs against his. He looked up at her, ready to push her away when she put her hands on his head and whispered a language Micah had never heard. He knew it wasn't anything from Joterra, but he also wasn't sure if it was Denoran; it seemed different than when Lucy spoke in her Fae language.

Suddenly, his skin heated slightly, gave a burst of cold, and his pain disappeared. Micah groaned in appreciation and slunk his head back as he closed his eyes. It had been days with ongoing headaches, and being without it felt like the sweetest relief. "Thank you," he said sincerely, looking up at her.

Brax was still very close to him, and Micah looked around awkwardly. If he looked in front of him, he was face-to-face with her breasts, tightly wrapped a skin-tight cotton tank and leather straps and buckles. He tried looking around instead, and her smile grew.

"Am I making you uncomfortable, Lumen?" she asked as she cocked her head with a tease.

"How do you know who I am?" Micah asked, looking her in the eye. His stomach flipped and he became more uneasy as the interaction continued. "Who did you say your employer was?"

"I work for Lord Laurent Sloan," she said with fire in her voice, and Micah stilled. "He sent me here to help you protect his assets." She took a long step back, away from him, and turned toward the kitchen. "Seems you have had some issues with the portal, and I'm here until you figure out what you're doing." She winked at him over her shoulder. Her cropped hair swung with the action.

Micah couldn't breathe—Laurent Sloan was the man Lucy was expected to marry. Did that still stand?

Did she find a way to stop it?

"You're from Denora?" He tried to sound calm, but his emotions were at war. There was nothing in the entire world that would prepare him to hear that Lucy had to still marry that prick. If Brax were to say it now, he knew he wouldn't be able to keep his composure. Taking a deep breath in, he shoved those thoughts away. There wasn't time for them now.

"Look at you, a little mortal knowing about Denora," she said with a laugh. "No, I'm not from Denora, but I did take a quick stop there on the way to you. Interesting place." She stirred the food in the pan and served it onto two plates, licking her finger when a bit of the sauce spilled over. "Some of the most gorgeous males I've ever seen, though you aren't too bad to look at either." She gave him a long, seductive stare, biting her bottom lip, and Micah looked away.

It wasn't that he didn't appreciate her looks. She was alluring in ways he hadn't seen in a woman, but he had Lucy, and they had a connection that couldn't compare. He wouldn't consider risking that for all the ass in Denora.

There was only one woman for him.

"I could never live there, though," Brax continued as she brought the two plates of food to the table. "The males treat females like they are pieces of art. Statues formed out of the most beautiful marble. Breathtaking to look at, but they are expected to be nothing more than what the males carve them out to be." Her smiling facade was gone now, just simmering anger underneath her eyes so dark they looked black.

"When Lucy mentioned—," he stopped himself short. Was it smart of him to mention his tie to her employer's future wife?

Brax's eyes brightened in interest. "Lucella Baum? Oh, please continue," she purred. There was something unnerving about Brax. She was beautiful, but spoke as though she hid a deadly secret. She moved like a snake, ready to strike.

What is she supposed to do here? How does Laurent Sloan expect to use her?

He cleared his throat. "Yes, Lucy mentioned your employer, Sloan?"

"*Lord* Sloan," she corrected with a glint of violence in her eyes.

"Right," Micah said as he shifted in his chair uncomfortably. "Why did he send you here, exactly?"

"I told you already, I'm here to ease your headaches. I'm here to guard The Elderwood."

Micah didn't doubt it this time—there was danger in the air, and it all pointed to Brax.

SIX

MICAH

The wafting scent of bacon infiltrated Micah's room the next morning, waking him up. Micah's stomach growled in response—he was starving.

His new bedroom was all gray with dark green and white accents. It reminded him so much of the forest, which was beautiful, but he wasn't sure if his space reflected who *he* was just yet. The greens and grays were comfortable, but he had always been more drawn to the sky, with its bright reds at sunset and deep blacks at night. However, he was in no position to complain. Just a little over a week ago, he was homeless.

He had an awful time sleeping knowing that a stranger was in his house with him, but at some point in the night, he realized that if she wanted him dead, he would be by now. He still couldn't understand why Sloan sent her, but he also realized how powerless he was in changing anything about his current circumstances. No one seemed to care what a mortal man had to say in a group of powerful Fae.

Striding down the steps in his socks and sweatpants, he heard Brax singing a song in another language. Her voice carried through the main level, deep and sensual, the rawness in her voice exuding emotion. The words tugged at his heart, yet he had no idea what they meant.

"What are you singing?" Micah asked kindly as he walked into the room.

Brax turned with a smile, wearing black leggings and a cropped black tank top. Her feet were bare and her face had no makeup. Without the black shadows around her eyes, she looked younger and less abrasive. Her hair was in two messy buns on either side of her head, giving her an even more amiable appearance.

"It's a song my sisters and I love from back home." Her eyes were bright as she spoke of her family. She turned to the pans on the stove. "The song's title translates to *Warrior Beauty,* and it talks about this amazing warrior's sex-ploits and her independence."

"Sex-ploits?" Micah laughed as he walked to the coffee maker to brew a pot for the pair. He had to look around the cabinets a bit to figure out where the coffee was stored—it was all still so new to him.

"Yeah, you know, the sexual exploits people partake in? Don't tell me you're a prude," she pointed the spatula at him with a mock serious expression.

He put his hands up in fake surrender, appreciating the banter after so many days all alone. With his head feeling better, he was in a much better mood, though his thoughts on Brax's arrival still made him apprehensive. "Nope, took care of that during senior prom," he laughed as he dropped his hands and continued to make the coffee.

"I'm not sure what the hell *senior prom* is, but I'm glad you took care of that. Vytyrians are very sexual Fae and we have no shame on the subject." She grabbed two plates and piled a hefty serving of eggs, bacon, and toast on each.

"Are you going to cook like this every day?" Micah said as he looked at the mouthwatering plate of food. "Because I really don't mind if you do." He placed a mug of coffee down on the table for each of them and dug into his breakfast.

"I like to be useful," Brax said, as she bit a piece of crispy bacon. "This place is incredibly boring."

Micah snorted into his coffee.

"I'm serious. I was sent here to protect The Elderwood, but it's just an old gnarled tree that doesn't even *do* anything. And they told me to keep an eye on you." She looked him up and down. "No offense, you aren't much of a threat."

"I have no idea how to respond to any of that," Micah said honestly. He also had no idea why she was there or what protecting The Elderwood even entailed. He just knew he had to stay on the property. He needed more time to read about his duties in the book his grandad left him. And him not being much of a threat?

I'm a cop, damnit. I should be at least a little intimidating, right?

"I really don't mean offense," she repeated with a mouthful of eggs. "The Vytyr are trained warriors—I could take any human down in like, six seconds flat." She snapped her fingers, then waved her hand as she held her mug of coffee, taking a deep drink.

The way she spoke with such candor caused Micah to think she probably told the truth, so he made a mental note not to piss her off too badly.

Her presence still did not add up to Micah. If he was there guarding The Elderwood, what made Brax have to be there as well? Why did Micah have to be watched to do a job that was passed down through his family? And what was Sloan's stake in the matter? Wasn't it Baum property?

"Trained warriors? Like a soldier?"

"Don't insult me, Lumen." She pointed her fork at him, then speared another bite of food. "No. *Warrior*."

"Throw me a bone here. This is all new to me. A few weeks ago, I was a cop in a city and now I'm the guardian of a tree and magic is real. I'm not really sure what I'm supposed to be doing here."

Brax looked at him curiously, putting an arm over the back of her chair, letting her guard down. She wasn't nearly as scary as she had seemed, but he realized there was just a lot about her and the rest of the Fae that he knew nothing about.

"I believe you," Brax said quietly, taking a sip of coffee, continuing to stare at him. "Alright," she announced louder, bringing her arms in front of her on the table. "I'll teach you while I'm here. It'll give me something to do." Her abruptness was a bit of a shock to Micah.

"Really?" he asked, relieved by the opportunity to finally learn more about his place among the Fae. He hoped he could get some real answers about what he and Lucy were up against. Words couldn't describe how badly he missed her. He had no idea what the hell he was supposed to do and feeling uncertain made him feel useless and weak.

"Why not?" Brax said, a bored look on her full lips. "There aren't any other humans nor Fae around, and the tree is out there, *being a tree...* there's no threat to hinder us."

"Thank you."

"Lesson one."

Micah choked on a bite of toast. He definitely didn't expect her to start helping immediately.

"Warrior is more than a soldier. A soldier works for a realm, like the kingdom of Denora. They are tied to that realm and must obey the command of the officers above them. Warriors, on the other hand, are bred for combat. The Vytyr are instilled with *lyfar*—combat magic. We are the only Fae who hold such a powerful force of battle magic, but we do not hold the same Fae skill as others. I cannot say a spell and create practical magic like Denorans. However, we hold an advantage, because no mere mortal or Fae can ever take down a Vytyr. We are trained from a very young age. I learned to throw a spear before I knew how to write my name."

"If you don't work for the realm and are not a soldier, then who signs your checks?" Micah asked, confused.

"We decide who we support, and we get paid well for our services," she said plainly.

The way she described her position reminded Micah of a bounty hunter or mercenary. However, the memory of the things Lucy had told him about Denora kept nagging at his mind. Did they allow this in Fae realms? Was Brax being entirely truthful with him?

"Women are allowed to work where you're from?"

"Females, like anyone else, can do whatever they desire. No one is in charge of them but themselves—something Denora has not honored."

Micah's thoughts hung in his mind, remembering the pressures Lucy faced. She took major risks just to make her own choices in her life, and here was Brax, able to do anything she wanted.

Why was Denora so different?

"So, it was your choice to work for Lord Sloan?" He chose his words carefully, not wanting to provoke Brax.

"Absolutely. He is a kind and fair lord. The best among all Denorans. Any would be privileged to live in his territory or work alongside him."

She spoke with such veneration for the man who stood in the way of his and Lucy's happiness. It left a bitter taste in his mouth, but he would never admit this to Brax; not when her allegiance to Sloan was so apparent.

"Let me get this straight... You are Fae with magic that makes you a good warrior. And other Fae have magic that is used with spells?"

Brax nodded.

"And, where you're from—Vytyr? They appreciate women and Denora is a bunch of crusty old men making decisions?"

Brax's laughter filled the room, bringing a smile to Micah. "Yes. I like that description."

"Do the Fae realms of Denora and Vytyr have anything else in common? It seemed like you were speaking a different language than Denoran?"

"I'm surprised you caught on to that, Lumen. You're smarter than you look."

"I don't think that was a compliment," he said with a smirk.

"No, we speak different languages. However, the warriors in Vytyr are trained in many languages, ensuring that wherever we contract our work, we can speak with our employers, or taunt whomever we're fighting." She gave a roguish wink.

"Not everyone in Vytyr is a warrior?" Micah asked, perplexed.

"No, you loaf of bread. Have you not been listening? Vytyr allows people to make their own decisions. My mother was a warrior, and my sisters and I have followed in her footsteps. That is, everyone except for my youngest sister." Her eyes came alight with warmth again, as they always did when she spoke of her family. "Noelia is the budding artist among us."

"My mom liked art, too," he shared.

"Maybe you've got some redeeming qualities in there, Lumen," she said with a tease. Then she abruptly stood and grabbed her sandals. She put them on, lacing the leather up her muscular calves. "I am going to walk the property and secure the safety of the border. Do not go anywhere."

She walked to the door and opened it, leaving Micah and the dirty dishes at the table. Brax looked over her shoulder mischievously. "By the way, I don't clean." Then she left.

Micah let out a deep sigh, relaxing his muscles and rolling his shoulders.

What the hell have I gotten myself into? He looked up, thinking of his family. *I hope one of y'all up there is keeping an eye on me, because I'm lost.*

He got up and began cleaning the dishes from breakfast and the previous night. The new kitchen set-up was much more practical for daily life. The room was brighter now, with windows on three of the four walls—the last wall backing up to the living area and holding the stove and counter space. Over the kitchen sink was a window facing out to the west side of the property. On the opposite wall, where the kitchen table and chairs sat, were two large windows next to one another, offering natural light into the updated kitchen. The third wall held the door to the backyard and the fire pit where he and

Lucy spent so many nights. As he scrubbed the dishes, he looked out the window to see Brax in the distance, walking the perimeter.

He turned back toward the table and saw a dark shadow in the windows beyond. It was only there for a moment and then disappeared from view. From his position in the kitchen, he could almost make out the tree to The Elderwood on the east side of the house.

What was that? he asked himself. *It can't be Brax; she must be on the complete other side of the property by now.* His heartbeat quickened. *What if the arsonists came back?*

He looked around the room for a weapon, but kitchen utensils wouldn't likely help him in this situation.

He grabbed his phone to bring out the camera app he had installed before his trip. Micah pulled up the last five minutes of video from the recording directed at the tree, trying to see where the shadow came from, but nothing was there. The camera didn't pick up a single figure.

A loud cracking noise from outside made Micah's head jerk back toward the window. He waited silently, watching the woods, but nothing happened.

He sighed and shook his head.

It's just the forest.

He felt so on edge he wasn't sure what was an actual threat anymore.

Micah returned the phone to his pocket and finished cleaning the kitchen. When he went back to wipe the table, he saw the dark shadows again. He ran to the window to get a better look, and there, just beyond The Elderwood tree, stood a tremendous black creature with a feline body.

It had to be nearly four feet tall when on all fours, and its massive stature made it impossible to believe it was as quiet as it was. It slunk behind the tree that held The Elderwood portal and then disappeared.

Micah's heart was a jackhammer in his chest. He brought the

camera footage up again to get a closer look. However, just like last time, nothing appeared on the video.

Am I losing my fucking mind? I swear, something was there.

Micah rubbed his hands over his eyes, trying to clear the confusion building within him. He grunted in frustration, pushing his hands through his hair and onto his neck, letting them hang there for a moment as he thought of his next steps.

Outside, he decided. *I'll just go look around the tree and see what I can find.*

The surrounding forest was quiet. The wind was soft. The birds were silent. Not a footstep could be heard. Part of that calmed Micah, knowing that nothing lurked in the distance. However, another part unnerved him even more, wondering where all the animals went.

He took a straight path to the tree that held the portal and kept aware of his surroundings. Whatever was prowling around earlier was massive—he didn't need that sneaking up on him when he was alone.

As he stepped up to The Elderwood tree, what he saw stunned him. He didn't know what to make of it. The sigil engraved high on the tree trunk had changed. It wasn't just a basic carving. Now it had black, ashy smudges spread all around it—like it was burning from the inside.

This can't be good.

CHAPTER
SEVEN

LUCY

The Baum carriage was the epitome of extravagance. Crushed red velvet covered the seats and draped the windows, keeping the interior dark to the world outside.

Lucy pulled the curtains open to allow the light to enter the cabin. She watched as the children ran alongside the carriage, offering toothless smiles behind dirt smudged cheeks. She smiled and gave them a small wave. Lucy had not been to this area before. Usually when she had traveled to the Capital, they took a much longer, roundabout trip in order to visit extended relatives along the way.

"There is nothing to see out there except for penniless beggars and their run-down shacks," Jasper spat, snapping the curtains shut. He spent the majority of the ride fidgeting with his rings, clearly on edge. His temperament was worse than usual. She sighed and sat back; it wasn't worth the fight.

This dinner has to be worth it, she thought. *I need to focus on learning whatever I can about Sloan so I can use it to remove myself from this mess. Maybe leave Denora completely.*

The thought of leaving played in her mind more and more since her return, and her current companion did little to change her views. Jasper had come to hand deliver her to Lord Sloan. Corvus no longer trusted Lucy off the estate, so he put his most faithful employee to the task.

The Capital was busier than Lucy remembered. She hadn't visited in quite some time, and the residents were in a flurry with the arrival of Lord Sloan. It seemed as though the dukes were desperate to strengthen Sloan's connections to the Kingdom as it was his first visit outside of the Northern Territory in over 85 years. Lord Sloan preferred for most of his business to be done within his region.

Corvus visited the Lord of the Northern Territories nearly a year prior and convinced him to try a few of his custom bows in exchange for ore from the mountains to create sturdier arrow tips for the legion. Lord Sloan was very hesitant at first, but seemed to warm up after talk of alliances. Lucy never did figure out whose idea it was to arrange the marriage; however, given that everyone besides her agreed to the proposal, it would not change her thoughts on the matter. Regardless of who had organized it, she had no plans on following through.

The restaurant where Lucy was to meet Lord Sloan was the most lavish building she had ever seen. The outer wall was made of pure white stone, not a smudge of dirt anywhere in sight. Fae magic illuminated ornate sconces, sending a soft glowing light out to those walking nearby. Elite Fae in breathtaking gowns and tunics crowded the entrance.

Lucy was never one to care about those things, but then again, she had never had the pleasure of being around so many beautiful Fae before while wearing such a luxurious gown herself. Most of her life consisted of tagging along with her brothers and father—or ducking out of her etiquette lessons without her mother knowing.

But this? This was a completely new world to Lucy, more different than even Joterra or The Elderwood. This was the world of upper class Fae: royalty and wealth.

Standing under the dazzling lights, Lucy pulled at her lavender gown, checking to make sure the silver filigree was still in place and shining.

It was customary to dress with grandeur when dining with Fae of high status. However, she made it a point not to change her gown from her earlier meeting with Lord Sloan. She knew he, like most males, would take it as a slight that she did not modify her wardrobe for him.

Let him, she thought as she again fussed with the fine fabric.

It was unusual for her to feel insecure, but with so many females gliding across the floor in precious gems and metals, she worried she would stick out like a sore thumb.

Maybe that's all the better, she considered. *Let me stand out as someone who doesn't belong in this crowd, and Sloan will see that he's made the wrong choice.*

Jasper escorted Lucy through enormous metal doors, adorned in bright red tapestries; fine silver thread adding beautiful embellishments along the corners. Lucy placed her hand lightly on top of Jasper's arm as he walked through the crowd, clearly knowing his way.

Normally Lucy would not have been appreciative of Jasper, seeing as he was largely overbearing and full of rude opinions that made her eye twitch. Yet, here in this bustling crowd, she found herself thankful she didn't have to navigate it on her own.

Tucked away in the corner of the restaurant was a large table, fit for ten, but with place settings prepared for only two.

Extravagance. This must be the place, she thought sarcastically.

Lucy forced a smile instead of an eye roll and did her best to play the part her father forced upon her. She would have this dinner if it meant finding a way back to Micah.

Micah.

It had only been a few days for her, but it was much longer for him. She longed for the man who captured her heart and opened her eyes to real partnership. When would she see those deep brown eyes again?

Jasper guided her to her seat, and she immediately felt out of place at such a large table. To make matters worse, the empty place setting for Lord Sloan sat on the complete opposite end of the table.

I guess that means he didn't have much interest in hearing me speak. All the better, she thought as she unfolded her napkin dramatically.

I'll stuff myself and leave lethargic and full, and I'll sleep on my return trip home so I can avoid interactions with Jasper.

Her repulsive chaperone stood at her side, waiting with the air of utmost respect and chivalry—though Lucy knew better than to believe that farce.

As minutes passed, Lucy tried to avoid the eyes from the crowded room and began to fidget, pulling at her dress and touching her hair. She anxiously sipped from the oversized wine glass placed at the table. They wouldn't bring the food until the guest of honor arrived.

Clearly, that was not her.

It was almost as if a wave swept through the restaurant and hushed each patron, for all at once, the room quieted. Lucy looked up from her reverie to search for the cause—surely something must have happened for all of these very important Fae to stop their chatter and focus on something other than themselves.

Through a gap in the crowd, she saw him enter. Long, flowing white hair, flawless pale skin, and iridescent blue eyes meeting hers as he descended upon her, giving only her his full attention.

"Miss Lucella, it delights me to see you here tonight. Thank you for accepting my invitation." He bowed, took her hand in his, and kissed it ever so gently with warm lips. For some reason, she had expected them to be cold; as cold as the rumors. But here he was, flesh and bone, warm and apparently delighted to see her.

"Thank you for the invitation," she replied compliantly. "It has been quite some time since I've seen the castle and the Capital. I appreciate the opportunity to visit and see them once again."

Lord Sloan went to pull out a chair next to her until he saw his place setting across the long table. A server pulled out the chair on the other end and offered it to him, but he gave a curt shake of his head to decline it. "I will take my dinner here, from this seat next to Miss Lucella." Everyone within earshot took a collective breath in, attempting not to gasp at the shock.

"Yes, sir. I can switch your place with Miss Baum right away."

Lucy stood to change seats to allow Lord Sloan to be at the head of the table.

"No, no need," he reassured the wait staff. "Here is fine. Miss Lucella may keep her seat. She was already quite comfortable in it before I came. There's no reason to change."

"But, sir," Jasper interjected. "Surely you'll want the head of the table. Lucella would be more than happy to give that to you, wouldn't you?" He gave Lucy a stern look, expressing his disapproval.

"Absolutely," Lucy began again. She gave a tight smile as she gathered her skirt in her hands and attempted to stand and switch seats.

"Enough of this," Lord Sloan said loudly. Lucy froze. "It is perfectly acceptable for a female to sit at any seat she wants. In fact, I would prefer for her to sit there. She is my guest tonight, and I am honored to have her. Now, there will be no more talk of seating changes." He sat in the chair next to Lucy and, with a dazzling smile, asked the server to bring the food. "I am sure Miss Lucella is quite hungry after waiting for me."

A blush of embarrassment covered her cheeks as she returned to her seat. Every Fae in the vicinity eyed her curiously, wondering why the notorious Lord of the Northern Territory was so generous to this unimportant Fae.

"I am terribly sorry for being late, Miss Lucella," he leaned over and murmured to Lucy. His ice-blue eyes held Lucy's with sincerity.

"No apology needed. I understand you are a very busy Fae. And please, Lucy is fine."

"As you wish, Miss Lucy," he conceded.

"Just Lucy," she repeated with an easy smile. If she was going to have to spend the entirety of her evening with him, she couldn't keep being addressed in such a formal manner—it only added to her anxiety.

Lord Sloan smiled at her and then gave a nod to the servers as they brought out their food: a delicious-looking feast of soups, platters of meats and steamed vegetables, and a large basket of assorted breads.

Heaving a great sigh, Lord Sloan stood, straightened the hem of his jacket, and looked out to the crowd around them. Every Fae there was pretending not to be eavesdropping, but only a fool would dismiss Fae hearing for being anything other than a perfect tactic for acquiring new gossip. The icy Lord from the North peered into the bustling crowd and with a click of his tongue and a soft shake of his head, he lifted his hands in the air.

Lucy wasn't sure what she was seeing at first, until the crowd abandoned any pretense of disinterest to watch with wide eyes.

Lord Sloan's hands were above his head, and he murmured words Lucy could hardly make out. His hands spread apart, creating a half circle, and suddenly there was quiet; all that remained was a shimmering barrier like a bubble around the corner of the restaurant where they sat. The onlookers groaned with disappointment and turned back to their own sources of merriment.

"What magic is this?" Lucy asked, still staring at the shimmering sheen he had created.

Lord Sloan looked to Jasper and excused him from their presence with a wave of his hand. Jasper looked as though he might argue, but came to his senses and walked out into the foyer with a sharp look over his shoulder.

I'm sure that was for me.

Jasper wanted nothing to go wrong when he was ordered to escort her. Though what could go wrong in a room full of Fae? Besides, Lord Sloan's personal guard stood nearby at the ready.

"That, Miss Lucy," Lord Sloan began as he sat, "is a special privacy barrier."

The shimmering bubble reminded Lucy of the privacy ward Wes

had placed on her room when they had spoken before he went to visit Micah. But this seemed different. For one, it was much darker than any other privacy charm she had ever seen before. Another thing, most privacy spells did not stop noise from both sides. In her room with Wes, she could still hear the birds outside clear as day. But this? She was in a room full of people, but the noise was much softer, as though a thick wall separated them.

"I don't enjoy an entire room of Fae listening in on my conversations and staring at me as though I am an animal in a cage on display. This ward is specialized so that we can see out, but they cannot see in. It will also stop prying ears from listening, so gossip should hopefully be minimized. I was never impressed with the Capital's obsession with gossip."

Placing her napkin in her lap, Lucy then took another sip of the fruity wine, eyeing her company for the evening.

This is... unexpected.

She was relieved to be rid of Jasper, but thankful at least one of Sloan's guards remained; for propriety's sake.

The pair helped themselves to the delectable food placed in front of them, and Lucy audibly moaned as she bit into a slice of warm bread with butter and jam.

"Are you enjoying the food?" Lord Sloan teased as he ripped a piece of bread and popped it unceremoniously into his mouth. Lucy laughed at his candor and wiped her mouth clean with her napkin.

"I don't think I've ever had more delicious bread," she said as she smiled. "I'm sorry for the theatrics, I'll be sure to keep it down." She laughed as she prepared another piece.

"It's refreshing," he said as he stared into her hazel eyes. He watched her with such interest and regard, it was hard to peg him as the same man that others called *Lord Slain*.

"What is refreshing? Oh, the wine! Yes, it's quite flavorful." She took another sip as he continued to stare at her.

"The wine?" He laughed, his ice-blue eyes twinkled with delight.

"Yes, the wine is wonderful. But you..." His boyish smile returned as he spoke. "*You* are what is so refreshing. You're a wonder to behold."

At that, Lucy rolled her eyes. It was an involuntary reaction, and she internally cringed as she waited for the repercussions of such attitude in the presence of a great Lord of Denora.

Instead, he laughed! A big, hearty, full laugh that warmed Lucy down to her bones.

"You don't believe me, do you?" he asked her with a smile so wide, it made it hard for Lucy not to smile herself.

He scooted his chair closer to hers and leaned into her personal space to speak more intimately. "Look at the company we have." He directed his eyes to the rest of the patrons of the restaurant. "Each Fae here is a glutton for the delicacies this amazing chef has to offer. They indulge on the savory meats, exquisite wines, and mouth-watering desserts."

His voice was a low rumble, reverberating through Lucy. The warmth of his presence crept over her skin, her body reacting to their closeness.

"They take a bite and know it is delicious simply because this is the most prestigious restaurant in the realm. But that isn't what they are thinking about, now is it?"

Lord Sloan wrapped an arm around the back of Lucy's chair to share in her space. The deep tenor of his voice made her skin tingle.

"They don't care about the food at all. That female?" he continued as he nodded toward a beautiful Fae in a pale pink gown adorned with opalescent stones. "She keeps checking her jewels among her neck and ears. As she does so, she compares them to the rest of the females present, ensuring hers look the most elegant."

Lucy watched the female as she laughed and subtly placed her hand on her throat, brushing her necklace discreetly. The Fae covered her mouth in a fake laugh, and her hand next went to her earrings, dangling from her ears.

Lucy's eyes opened wide with astonishment. Lord Sloan was

completely correct. The female continued to scan the crowd, eyeing others' jewels draped carefully across unblemished skin.

"How did you know that?" Lucy twisted and asked him with a smile. She forgot how close he was, and when she turned, their noses nearly touched. She quickly looked back toward the crowd, giving herself a bit more space, her heart racing at the proximity.

"Look at that older gentleFae in the corner," he whispered, inching closer to her, his thigh touching hers.

Lucy didn't know what to make of it. Surely this closeness was not appropriate for any Fae, let alone the Lord of the North and his betrothed wife? Despite that, Lucy looked in the direction he suggested, shifting her body away from him slightly.

"He is here with his wife, and has absolutely no interest in her, nor his meal. Look at the way he shovels the food into his mouth, just to get the dinner over with."

Lucy saw the aged male Fae hastily swallowing the food, checking his watch between each bite. In the time they watched the couple, the female didn't stop talking for more than a few seconds in between eating and the male never made eye contact with her at all.

A laugh escaped Lucy as the male outright rolled his eyes at his wife and called for the check, even as she still had a full plate of food. Lord Sloan shifted back toward his part of the table and Lucy inhaled deeply, calming herself with slow, deep breaths.

"See, Miss Lucy? These people are here as a show of wealth and what they deem as *importance*. They don't bother with the taste of the food or any appreciation for the work that goes into a meal such as this. I enjoy that you find that appreciation in such a simple function as eating dinner. It is refreshing because I do not see it often enough in the rare occasion that I visit."

Lucy looked at Lord Laurent Sloan as if seeing him in a new light.

Is he what others say he is?

He seemed so different from any other Fae male she had met in Denora, especially those with a high status such as his.

"You are not what I expected, Lord Sloan," she said before she realized the words left her tongue.

"I will take that as a compliment," he said with a wink. "I aim to be different than my male counterparts."

"In what ways?"

"Well, to begin with, this meal?" He gestured to the food before them. "What a complete waste of resources. I hope you don't take offense, but you will not be taking the remaining food home once they box it up."

This caught Lucy off guard, unsure of his frank tone. "Of course not, Lord Sloan. I am here as your guest, it is yours."

"No, no, you misunderstand," he said as he leaned closer to her, reaching out for her hand. The tenderness of the action shocked her, making her heart leap. He held her left hand gently. "I also do not need this food. You and I, and everyone in this building, quite honestly, do not need food to this excess. However, on the trip here, I passed dozens of hungry families who could use this to feed their children."

Her mouth popped open in realization. She thought back to her ride to the Capital—the barefoot children, playing in the streets. "You're going to give it to them?"

"Yes, I was hoping we both could." His lips turned up into a smile. "Unless you would find that uncomfortable, then I understand completely."

"No, I would love to," Lucy said hurriedly, squeezing his hand in return. The warmth of his hands spread into hers, causing her core to flutter with excitement. "Honestly, I would find it more uncomfortable to ignore them as others do. They are worthy of our attention."

"Yes, they are, and I am so glad to hear you say that." Laurent's smile doubled, his white teeth gleaming from ear to ear. "I have always had many... issues, with the way that male Denorans conduct themselves. I find myself at odds with those around me."

"What do you mean?" Lucy asked, curiosity getting the best of her.

Every single thing out of his mouth from the moment she had met him had been the complete opposite of what she had been told to expect.

He was not the cold, heartless monster that others believed him to be. So far, he was the only male in all of Denora who thought of something other than status.

"We do things differently where I'm from," he said slowly, brushing her hand with his thumb, trying to find the words. "I take care of all the citizens of the North, no matter their station in life."

Lucy knew she was staring at Laurent with disbelief and that her unblinking gaze could easily appear as rude, but she just could not get her mind around what he was saying.

How could he be what I was fearing all this time? This must be too good to be true.

"I enjoy your fresh outlook, Lord Sloan. It's a pleasure to hear that someone is thinking of all of the citizens of their region, not just the ones who could fill their coffers."

"Thank you, Miss Lucy," Lord Sloan said with a smile and a nod as he released her hand. He took another sip of his wine and looked down at his empty dinner plate. "I apologize, but there is some small business I must attend to while we are here. Do you mind giving me a moment?"

"Absolutely," Lucy replied with a smile. "I understand." And she did. She didn't feel as though he was neglecting her, and she didn't feel that he would leave her unless he absolutely must.

Laurent stood and straightened his suit jacket. "I will have them send over dessert—you can start without me. Though," his voice trailed off as he leaned closer to Lucy, finishing his thought in a near whisper. "I would love to watch you enjoying the delectable sweets, so save a bite or two."

Lucy's heart leapt to her throat, a small gasp leaving her. Her cheeks flushed as she looked at Laurent, whose amusement lingered in the glint of his brilliant blue eyes. She watched as he left the domed privacy charm, walked into the main vestibule of the restaurant, and went out of view.

Lucy slumped back in her seat, reeling with the impossibility of how her night was unfolding. Laurent Sloan was nothing she imagined; in fact, he proved time and time again what a good and noble Fae he was.

How could the disparaging rumors be so mistaken?

A sharp sting in her palm caught Lucy by surprise. She dropped her hand into her lap, trying her best to be inconspicuous, even though no one could see her through the privacy charm. The imprint on her hand turned red, showing again through her concealment spell. She pushed more magic into the scar, watching it disappear from view, unsure why it decided to bother her.

The wine she drank coursed right through her, and she thought it was a perfect time to use the restroom. Unfortunately, with her elaborate gown, it could take a while. She asked Laurent's guard to show her the way through the unfamiliar restaurant.

"Of course, Miss Baum. And please, call me Roger," the guard said kindly.

She took his offered arm and he led her toward the foyer. More and more people were arriving—whispers and gossip met her ears every turn she made.

"Lord Sloan is here with a female Fae."

"No, she isn't royalty at all!"

"Haven't you heard? She's that Baum female!"

"What does he even see in her? There are so many others who are much more beautiful."

"She's so lucky."

The chatter amused Lucy. Earlier in the week, before Lord Sloan arrived, all the rumors were about his dark side and how vicious he was. Since he arrived, each Fae whispering to their neighbor wanted to gain the favor of the handsome Lord Sloan.

Funny how people's malicious words could change with the snap of a finger. I wonder what they will say about me next?

Their prattling about her didn't bother Lucy. She was not the most beautiful nor the most wealthy and she knew others would see her betrothal as a step down for Lord Sloan, but that didn't matter to her. Besides, Lucy wasn't planning on going forward with the marriage, anyway. There was still time to figure her way out of the entire arrangement.

Once Roger brought her to the middle of the foyer, he pointed toward the back where the restrooms were located.

Off to the right was a distinguished bar, stocked with the finest spirits available. The mirror behind the bar reflected dozens of fine cut crystal drink-ware in varying shapes and sizes. Some of the spirits were so rare, one tiny glass would cost a small fortune.

A flash of bright white hair caught her attention.

There, off to the side of the bar, was Lord Sloan, talking animatedly to another male Fae. She could only see the back of Laurent, his posture rigid with frustration. His shoulders leaned down, bringing his enormous height closer to the shorter Fae male in front of him. Lucy felt awkward watching the interaction. Realizing it was not for her eyes, she continued toward the bathroom taking one more glance at the pair.

She stopped dead in her tracks when she recognized the male. He looked right at her with rage in his bulging eyes.

Jasper.

Why is Laurent Sloan, Lord of Northern Territories, wasting his time with Jasper?

THE CARRIAGE ROCKED BACK and forth as the horses continued their return to the Baum Estate. Lord Sloan and his small entourage were en route ahead. The clip-clopping of the horses echoed down the narrow lanes in the Capital.

The ride home led through the outer cities, which were overcrowded and unsupported. With the summer months still underway, the sun was only beginning to fall, leaving enough light for the townspeople to roam about without difficulty. Lucy peered around the curtains, ignoring Jasper's scoffing, and took in everything she saw on the outskirts of a town she thought she knew well.

What she saw surprised her. The homes were stacked upon one another, leaving no space for children to play or for families to retain any semblance of privacy. The cobblestone streets were cracked, with weeds growing between the damaged rocks. Each street looked identical to the next: thin wooden houses with damaged windows, either broken and exposed to the elements or boarded up with warping wood, and doors that backed up to long, narrow alleyways that overflowed with rubbish and waste.

People sat outside of their homes, toiling over their work; whether it was scouring pots and pans, repairing old shoes, or washing clothes. One elderly female plucked the feathers from a dead bird laid flat in her lap.

Children in worn clothing were chasing the carriage in the streets; most had no shoes. They smiled, excited to see anyone of importance come through their small corner of town.

The distinct contrast between where Lucy sat and where the children ran outside made her heart sink. Lucy was clad in a beautiful, expensive gown with ornate jewelry, traveling in a velvet-lined carriage. The dress she wore was probably worth more than one of the homes on this street, and why? If she sold it, it would feed a family for a month.

Why does the King allow this? She shifted uncomfortably in her seat at the thought.

The carriage continued its trek away from the Capital, leaving the children and their weathered homes behind them. It hurt her to think about the poor children who were forgotten by the Kingdom. A nauseating sense of guilt grew within her chest.

How is this something we have allowed to happen?

It was just another nail in the coffin, finding Denora guilty of further injustices.

"Close the window. You're letting the stink in," Jasper barked, snapping the curtains shut, a look of disdain dripping down his face.

Lucy looked back to him with equal parts annoyance and curiosity. So many things about Jasper had never made sense to her.

Jasper's relationship with her father, Corvus, seemed most difficult for her to grasp. He had been riding her father's coattails for as long as Corvus had been in the bowyer industry. Even when they were young Fae, Jasper followed after him, always hoping to claim a position as his right hand.

It had worked, too. Jasper was so ingrained in the finances of the Baum Bowyers that, while many did not know his name, they at least knew his face, because he accompanied Corvus all throughout the realm.

Looking at him from across the carriage, Lucy recalled the day Duke Renfro came to the estate to arrange a business deal with her father. Normally, Corvus would travel to the dukes for their work, but on this occasion, since it was personal and not related to the Kingdom, Duke Renfro insisted on coming to him instead.

Lucy was speaking with her father, making yet another bid for her place with the bowyers, when Duke Renfro walked in with Jasper at his side.

Jasper led him to a chair and Renfro nearly shoo-ed him away with a look of annoyance, dismissing him. When Jasper cleared his throat to speak, the duke interrupted him.

"Stop blathering on. I won't be needing a beverage, this is a short visit. You are excused."

The look on Jasper's face was enough to curdle milk. His eyes flared with rage before they glossed over and he introduced himself to the duke.

"I am Jasper DeValey. I manage the finances for the Baum Bowyer industry and will be assisting Master Baum."

Lucy remembered him saying it with such greasy affect, wondering how hard it must have been for him to have swallowed so much anger. When she glanced at her father, she realized he hadn't even noticed. He was busy gathering the materials he needed for the duke's visit and didn't think twice about the conversation Jasper and the duke were having.

That day Jasper flashed her a look of pure loathing, forcing her to leave the study in a hurry, not wanting to be anywhere near those toxic males.

That bulging glare was seared into her memory, and she often wondered when the rest of the realm would see the real Jasper. Lucy knew he was hiding under a threadbare exterior, ready to erupt at any moment, and since her mother explained his lack of magic, it started to make more sense.

The carriage bumped over the cobblestones and came to an abrupt halt.

Jasper's eyes danced with fury reminiscent of Lucy's memory. His revulsion of the outer city pressed on Lucy's nerves.

His obsession with wealth and status is sickening.

The last thing Lucy wanted was to be stuck in a stopped carriage with Jasper, yet here they were.

"What is happening? Why have we stopped?!" he shouted to the driver.

Lucy peered out to see Laurent Sloan walking in muddied puddles, with boxes of food in his arms. His guard, Roger, came to the window to speak to Lucy.

"Sir, what are you doing out there?"

"Greetings, Miss Baum. Lord Sloan ordered additional meals to be passed out on our return to the estate."

"Meals?"

"Yes, Miss. Lord Sloan hoped that you could join him?"

Lucy's heart leapt from her chest. He was serious about giving the food to the families... "Yes, I would love to." She gathered her skirts and reached for the carriage door when Jasper held the door shut, stopping her.

"Absolutely not," he spat with disgust. "It is not safe for you in the dark of the streets, Lucella. Your father would never allow such a thing."

"She is entirely safe with us, sir."

"There will be no more talk of Lucella exiting the carriage. We are leaving."

Lucy could only glare at Jasper with frustration.

"Yes, sir," Roger said to Jasper. He turned to look at Lucy once more. "Have a safe trip home." Roger offered an apologetic smile and caught up with Lord Sloan.

He's hand delivering food to the families in need, and actually invited me to join him. Lucy looked on in shock.

Only a moment passed as the rest of the carriages continued on their way, leaving Laurent Sloan and his barrage of guards behind as they dirtied their uniforms, taking time out of their night to support the neediest families in Denora.

EIGHT

MICAH

Micah looked at the sigil on the tree; the black, charred edges remained. The last time the sigil changed, Micah was in The Elderwood with Lucy and he saw the symbol glow a bright red when his grandad's property was under attack and set on fire. This, however, was different. It didn't glow or surge; the carving in the tree did nothing at all. It almost looked dead—disconnected to The Elderwood completely.

That couldn't happen, Micah tried to convince himself.

He was thankful that Brax went on another one of her endless patrols. He appreciated having someone around so that he didn't have to talk to himself. However, she was a stranger, and he was still figuring out this new life that got dumped in his lap.

From his place near the trees, he saw in the distance something that made him pause, but this time, not with fear. A soft smile made an appearance on his usually stoic face as he walked to the old tree house that was left abandoned in the woods.

When the fire occurred, the tree house was far enough away that it didn't get destroyed—though time and weathering seemed to have dismantled it over the years.

Micah jogged over and slid his hand over the ridged wood of the gnarled tree, seeing the small fort he and his grandad used to escape to.

"What I wouldn't give for a good escape now," he said to the trees.

Being in the forest on his grandad's property had been a challenge all on its own, even before Lucy's magic. Each day he came outside, he saw flashes of memories; both good and bad.

More often than not, he chose to ignore the flashbacks. Pushing them away from his mind, focusing instead on what he needed to do right at that moment. Evading those hard memories was something he was an expert at, especially when he spent his life avoiding anything that could ever force him to remember. However, being here in the midst of everything, his mind couldn't escape them anymore, and each memory was slowly breaking him down.

He sat down at the base of the gnarled tree, not trusting the rickety ladder to enter the worn structure. He propped his arms on his knees and closed his eyes, heaving a sigh and feeling a sense of hopelessness that sank down to his very core.

He was alone again.

He had tried so hard, for so long, to not get back to this place, both figuratively and literally. He avoided Abe's property because he was just so damn mad at him for so long. He avoided the feelings, because he didn't know what to do with them—he never did.

Before his grandad died, Micah was willing to die with the anger he harbored toward Abe. He never planned on forgiving him or giving him a second thought. In his mind, it was a sealed fate.

But when Lucy came... Lucy changed everything.

God, I miss her. I'd do anything to have her with me now, he mused. But then again, maybe that was him trying to find other ways to escape.

He opened his eyes to the forest around him. His forest. This was all his now, whether he liked it or not. And really? He hadn't decided how he felt about it at all. It was easier to push it away and just deal with it a moment at a time than to think too much about it. He was here, this was his job, and he would do it.

Since Brax had arrived, he threw himself into figuring out his new role. Micah looked through the book his grandad left him and searched for answers, but ended up with more questions than when he started. He kept an eye open for the weird things that kept happening at the property and for talk of shadows or changes in the portal symbol. Unfortunately, he couldn't decipher the language, so he got nothing out of it.

Every bit of this new life reminded him of Lucy, and he missed his girl more than he thought possible.

He shook his head again, refusing to think too much about her. Micah couldn't fall apart when things were still fine between them.

Time moved differently there, and who knew what happened since she returned. Did her dad finally hear her out and let her join the family business? Was that why she was so busy? Or maybe she was in trouble? Maybe they found out about the man who died when she was defending The Elderwood? Was she okay?

The thoughts swarmed his mind, making his blood rage within him, thinking she could be facing something without any support. She was so far away and there was nothing he could do for her.

He couldn't help her.

He couldn't protect her.

Releasing a grunt of anger, he got up from the ground and began pacing.

Dwelling over this does nothing, he told himself again, reinforcing the concept of pushing away yet another issue from his mind.

With a final pat of the tree trunk, Micah turned back toward the house. He was thankful this new cabin looked so different from Abe's old one... He had a hard enough time keeping the memories at bay among a bunch of trees. Those rooms where he grew up would have been too much. It would have been too hard.

He sighed in relief, knowing he was going to walk into a kitchen where his grandad never sat, and sit in a living room where his mother never rested. But it was also a house where he never loved Lucy, and that part didn't necessarily feel fair.

He trudged past the small cluster of trees that surrounded the portal to The Elderwood. Looking at the carving, he expected it to look as it had for the past few days: charred with black. But this time, dark smoke slowly seeped from tiny cracks within the symbol.

He froze.

What the fuck is happening?

Shadows began to creep out of the engraved bark in bursts and puffs like it was being pushed through by an unknown force on the other side. Deep orange sparks jumped out as the smokey aura grew.

Micah's breath hitched. He took one step back, and then another as the ground trembled. Stumbling over the leaves and debris in the yard, he watched wide-eyed as a shroud of darkness encompassed the tree. Red sparks shot viciously in every direction.

"Brax!" he yelled. "BRAX!"

His head swiveled around, looking for a plan. Should he run? Defend himself? Wait for Brax?

Suddenly, the sigil on the tree began to glow an ominous blood red. The birds, who were once so quiet in the forest, began to caw and screech like mad, flying away as quickly as possible. Micah's eyes darted to the canopy of the tree above him, watching them flee.

A slow chittering began, and Micah whipped his head left and right, panicking as he tried to find the source of the sound. It wasn't coming from the air, and all around him was still.

Then a pulse rocked the ground beneath his feet. Micah bent his knees and spread his arms, trying to steady himself. *Boom.* Another pulse.

Boom. Another.

Boom. Boom. Boom boom boom. It turned into a rumble so violent his feet felt as though they were vibrating. He stepped backward, moving away from the trees, fearing that they would topple over and crush him.

Then, a resounding *crack* echoed through the air; the sound so loud he dropped to the ground on his knees and covered his ears. With his eyes shut tight, came silence.

The chittering had stopped. The rumbling ceased. He opened his eyes and squinted through the haze. The shadows began to recede. The sparks disappeared, and the tree was back to normal.

Except for one thing.

At the base of the tree, around the roots, the ground had split open leaving a puddle of smoke and ash swirling within it like lava deep underground.

Micah was entranced, staring at the dark, misty abyss before him. He took a step closer to get a better look. The shadows from the forest made it hard to see, and the depth of the split was too far away. Micah stood only another step away when another rumble came from below him. This time, more violent than before.

He could have sworn the earth growled at him; the sound splitting his resolve. The trees were shaking and swaying with the thunderous bellow.

A deafening *snap* and a tree branch came crashing down behind him. He jumped to get away from it.

The ground roared in response, sending a more powerful shudder coursing through the earth.

Micah looked up with wide eyes, his body trembling, realizing he was in prime position to be pummeled by fallen tree branches. Just like the previous branch, more were sure to follow if the rumbling continued. He spotted another limb cracking from the vigorous swaying of the tree above. Taking a step back to get out of the way, he tripped over the oversized limb that had already fallen.

From his position on his back, he looked straight up and saw the swaying bough crack once more. It was falling from the tree and headed directly for him.

He scrambled, trying to get himself back up, but couldn't seem to get his footing. The branch was only feet away, and Micah was paralyzed with fear.

Screaming, he threw his hands out in front of him. He closed his eyes and prepared for the monstrous bough to crush him.

But nothing happened.

He slowly opened his tightly shut eyes, knowing that any second the enormous piece of tree would come tumbling down on top of him, but when he saw what really happened, he couldn't breathe.

The 12 foot tree branch hovered in the air before him, wrapped in a red swirling mist. It was less than four feet away from crushing him, just floating in the air like it weighed nothing. Micah tried to figure out where the red magic came from. Was it Brax? Did someone know there was something wrong with The Elderwood and had come to help him?

No. There was no one else there.

His eyes widened, following the magic from the tree to where it originated.

The red swirling magic danced around Micah's splayed fingers. With each slight movement of his hands, the branch moved with him.

Gasping, he quickly shoved his hands to the side, throwing the limb away from him. The red magic let go of the branch and disappeared from Micah's hands.

He lurched to his feet, turned on his heel, and sprinted back into the house.

Once inside, he held the window frame with two hands. He leaned against the pane and scanned the trees for a threat. There was no evidence of any kind of disturbance. The forest was quiet and calm.

I'm going fucking crazy, aren't I? Should I call someone? He glanced at the mirror.

"Okay," he said out loud, talking only to himself. "Let's look at this logically. The Elderwood tree was smoking and sparking. The birds freaked out and left. A weird noise came from the ground, it rumbled like crazy and now there's a crack. And magic," his voice cracked on the last word. "I used fucking magic."

Micah released the window frame and paced back and forth. When he got to the end of the room, he looked out the window to The Elderwood and turned on his heel and walked back to the other wall. He continued this pattern of talking and walking until he calmed himself.

With each circuit, he peered out the window, though nothing seemed out of place. The tree still stood, the smoke was out of sight. His hands were magic free.

Did I imagine that?

"An earthquake," he said as he stopped mid-stride. "That's what this was. An earthquake. And there's some weird smokey shit because there's magic in the tree and the birds were afraid of the earthquake. And something must have hit my head."

He slumped down on the couch and closed his eyes.

Flowing brown hair, hazel eyes, and freckles invaded his mind. Lucy.

I need Lucy.

NINE

LUCY

I need Micah.

It was the only thing on Lucy's mind as she trundled through the fallen leaves crunching beneath her feet in the Nilban Woods.

It felt as though she was walking in a dream—the last time she was here, she had battled and defeated one of the largest wolven she had ever come across. Back then, she traveled with nervous steps; but today, no fear ran through her veins. Instead, pure power pulsed in her magic, and she was ready to wield it.

Learning about this magic was vitally important and that realization danced heavily in her mind. There were so many possibilities with this new magic she had yet to master, and with a the risky plans she had in mind, she could use all the help she could get.

The dinner with Laurent the previous night was more confusing than helpful. She had anticipated an evening with Lord Sloan would have provided her with ample information to guide her away from him. Instead, she had found hope in the most unexpected of places.

It was all too much to manage and now what she needed most, more than anything else in all the realms, was to be in the arms of the man who understood her most.

Luckily for her, Lucy's plan thus far was working flawlessly. She woke early, bathed, and finished packing her bag. She attended breakfast so her parents wouldn't even bother to look for her until at least lunch, and even then, Lucy would not truly be missed until her absence from dinner was noticed. Either way, it would all work out, as she expected to be home before nightfall.

She pulled her bag a little higher on her shoulder and continued her trek through the changing forest. Denora had not seen a winter in decades, and now that it was on the horizon, the hint of autumn made its appearance in little ways throughout the realm.

It seemed to happen so suddenly; almost overnight. One moment the apple trees in the orchard were blossoming as they always did, and the next, the leaves were as vibrantly red as the apples that had fallen.

She gripped her bow tightly in her left hand, keeping a keen ear available to hear any prowling animals. Her magic seemed to dance under her skin, getting more excitable with each passing moment. Lucy wasn't certain how she would enter the portal without the amulet, but she had a theory she expected would work, and each time she considered it, her magic responded with a gentle flutter from somewhere deep within.

When she last returned home from Joterra, the symbol that The Elderwood tree marked on her hand lit up with a green glowing light. It was the same symbol as the amulet and the tree carvings that activated the portals. If she guessed correctly, it would be enough to allow her to enter.

Lucy glanced down at the markings with a desperate plea for success. If this plan of hers didn't work, she would have to return home and plot out an entirely new strategy. And who knew how much time she had before she was sent off to see Lord Sloan again?

No. I will get to Micah.

There was no other option. There was no one else in all existence who could understand her the way he could, and she would do whatever it took to get back to him, if only for one moment wrapped in his warm embrace.

Beads of sweat peppered her brow as her anxiety grew.

This has to work.

Ahead on the path, she heard a scuttling of animals. She paused and focused her Fae hearing in the distance beyond. Gentle flapping wings. Small pattering feet. Then, a hushed caw.

Birds?

Lucy continued down the path cautiously, her bow in hand. She reached above her head and behind her to her quiver to count the arrows available to her.

Four.

She needed more branches from The Elderwood to create more, but four would have to do. Her heart beat erratically in her chest.

As she crested the small slope, she saw what caused the noise. A scant flock of birds hovered around the carcass of an animal. Ravens and vultures took turns pecking at the rotting meat, fighting over who got the biggest piece.

Lucy stayed off to one side, keeping out of the way of the birds and their meal. As she passed, she realized the carcass was the wolven she had struck down on her initial journey just a few days ago.

That means I must be close.

Her eyes darted down to her right hand; her palm was shining a bright green. Her heart jolted as she searched the trees for the same symbol glowing somewhere nearby. Looking left and right, she feverishly dashed around the woods, knowing the portal was just steps away from her

She stilled as the sight of the portal came into view.

A beautiful, large tree, leaves still green from the magic imbued within it, stood tall in front of her. Its brown bark displayed the glowing green sigil, signaling to Lucy like a lighthouse leading her in from the storm.

Her heart raced in anticipation; the only thing separating her from Micah was this.

Please, bring me to Micah.

Holding her breath, Lucy closed her eyes as she placed her right hand on the tree. The bark under her hand felt firm, and her heart sunk.

Please. Please, bring me to Micah.

Suddenly, the bark seemed to warm at her touch. She opened her eyes and was astonished to see the tree bark rippling under her fingers. Releasing her breath, she stepped through with complete confidence.

As she passed through from one realm to another, she was met again with the feeling of absence, unlike her previous trips to Joterra. No light, no color, no sound—everything was placid and empty. Except that tiny, familiar sound she had heard once before. Was it a voice?

Before she could analyze it any further, she stepped through the other end of the portal onto the lush grass of Joterra. Only, she wasn't where she had expected.

How did this happen?

As she exited the portal, she realized she was not on the outskirts of Micah's property, stepping out of the portal to Joterra, but was standing in the shadow of The Elderwood tree itself.

Lucy was directly in front of Micah's new cabin.

"How did I get here?" She asked herself quietly.

"That is a wonderful question," a female's voice spoke from behind her.

Lucy spun to see a tall, tan female, wrapped in tight leather as rich as her skin. Her short, chopped hair made her sharp features look threatening, and the kohl make up that lined her eyes helped to add to that image. She could tell that something fierce lay just beyond this stranger's sultry appearance, but Lucy was not going anywhere.

"Who are you?" Lucy demanded, pulling her bow and aiming it at the beguiling stranger.

Is this another attack on The Elderwood? Is Micah here? Is he okay?

Too many thoughts filled her mind, but she forced them away as she took stock of the enemy before her. She was clearly Fae, and definitely not from Denora. Whoever she was, Micah did not invite her here, which made her an intruder; and intruders were not welcome.

The fire in her veins ignited at the threat, and Lucy felt the magic of The Elderwood slithering through her body, preparing to attack.

Lucy brought her bow up closer to her line of sight, and the enemy gave a feral smile as she bent into a crouch, ready to charge.

"Brax?" Micah called from just out of view. The Fae barely flinched. "Brax? Is that you back there? Be careful with the portal, something is going on. It's not acting right."

Lucy's eyes darted over to where she heard his voice and then back to the female in front of her.

Brax? Micah knows her?

"Stay back, Lumen," the female Fae called. "There's a trespasser that needs dealing with."

"I'm not trespassing," Lucy spat in reply. "You are."

Brax's eyes lit up with ferocity as though she enjoyed the possibility of a fight.

"Lu?" Micah asked incredulously. Lucy could hear his footsteps as he ran toward the trees, finally coming into sight. "Lu!"

She was hesitant to take her eyes off of this strange Fae standing in between her and Micah, but Lucy couldn't help herself. She looked at Micah and her heart leapt with joy. He stepped directly between the females to greet Lucy and a smile broke over her face.

Lucy kept her bow in one hand and an arrow in the other as she flung herself into Micah's welcoming arms. His broad shoulders squeezed her tightly as Lucy clung to him. She could smell the familiar scent of him that lingered in the back of her brain since she had left him.

She pulled his face into her hands and she studied him. Micah seemed so different from when she saw him last. His hair had grown out and his five o'clock shadow was more of a short, scruffy beard, hiding the scar she had memorized. Her eyes landed on his full lips, then his chocolate brown eyes.

Those eyes. They pulled her in and kept her there, threatening to captivate her for all of time.

"I've missed you," she whispered, her eyes bright with adoration.

"Baby, words can't begin to describe how much I've missed you."

He grabbed her by her neck and pulled her into a deep kiss, making Lucy's heart explode. She couldn't get past the taste of him, the smell of him, the feel of him on her skin once more, but the sentiment was quickly doused as she heard someone clearing their throat.

Micah pulled back with a laugh and tucked his arm around Lucy's shoulders, facing the Fae.

"Lu, this is Brax," he said with a smile.

"What is she doing here?" Brax asked, stone faced.

"Who are you? What are *you* doing here?" Lucy retorted, taking a step toward Brax.

Brax ignored Lucy and looked at Micah instead. "If you were planning on having a female caller, all you had to do was tell me. You know I won't judge." She looked Lucy up and down. "Though I am surprised she's Fae. Who is she?"

"*She* is standing right in front of you," Lucy seethed.

"That is not her reason for being here," Micah replied, trying to ease the tension in the air.

"Why do you care who he's with?" Lucy said again, her magic bubbling up inside of her, ready to unleash on this horrid Fae.

"I don't," Brax replied, arching her eyebrow with distaste. "But I have a job to do while I am here, and taking out the trash comes with the territory."

Lucy's magic jumped from her hands and crashed into Brax, throwing her to the ground in surprise. Brax looked up at Lucy and saw her standing with two orbs of green light rotating in her hands.

"What the fuck is that?" Brax asked, staring at Lucy's magic and then to Micah, looking for an answer.

"It's me taking out the trash," Lucy said with fake kindness. Lucy pulled her arms back, prepared to unleash another blast upon the Fae, when Micah darted in front of her with his hands outstretched.

"Whoa, whoa, hey," he said, trying to calm her. "This is one big misunderstanding. Brax was sent here by Lord Sloan to help me with The Elderwood. That's all."

"Why are you telling her about The Elderwood, you kumquat?" Brax scolded.

"Because it's hers as much as it's mine." Micah reached a hand out to bring Brax back to her feet and then stood between the two beautiful, yet volatile, female Fae. "Brax, this is Lucy Baum."

"Baum? As in Lucella Baum?" Brax asked with amused curiosity.

"You work for Laurent?" Lucy asked her, eyeing her apprehensively. The swirling green mist whirled in her hands in a threat as she kept her body firmly in front of The Elderwood, blocking it from Brax.

Micah's head jerked back at the casual way she used Sloan's first name.

"Yes, I do," Brax said, smiling now. She cast a look at Micah in a taunt.

Does she know something I don't?

"I don't understand why you need to be here," Lucy continued. "The Elderwood is fine and Micah is completely capable."

"Sure he is," Brax laughed.

The forest floor crunched under Lucy's feet as she took another step toward Brax. Her magic flared in her hands as a hint of green light shimmered in her eyes.

Grabbing Lucy's arm, Micah gently tugged her closer to him. "Lu?"

When she turned to him, he saw the green more clearly, dancing in her irises as though the color was alive within her. Lucy blinked, and it was gone.

"I think I'll leave you two alone as I continue my rounds." Brax turned to Micah and pointed her finger at him in earnest. "I expect an explanation of whatever the fuck that was."

Micah nodded, his furrowed brow watching as Brax made her way across the trees and into the thicket of woods beyond them.

He slid his hand down Lucy's arm and stopped right before he got to her hands, then he cleared his throat.

"Oh," Lucy said sheepishly as she doused the orbs of green.

He grabbed her hand and led her to the cabin. He had no idea why she was here or what that standoff was about, but maybe putting some distance between her and the portal would help her clear her head... both mentally and physically.

Clasping their hands together, Micah felt a wave of contentment. *I can't believe she's actually here.*

Brushing his thumb over the back of her left hand, he soaked in the feeling. When he last saw her, she tied him up and dashed through the portal without so much as a goodbye. He wouldn't let her go so easily this time.

As they entered the house, he watched as Lucy's eyes took in the new interior her brother and that older creep had designed. With each passing day, it had felt more and more like home, and now that Lucy was here, it was as though everything was complete.

However, at the thought, his heart tightened; he knew she wouldn't stay.

Unless...

"What are you doing here, Lu?" His voice was soft, not because he was trying to be quiet, but because he couldn't let the shakiness of his words be heard. He guided her to the couch and sat next to her, still holding her hand tenderly.

"I needed you." She said it so matter-of-factly, just as she did everything.

He smiled broadly at the response. "My warrior." He pulled her in for a kiss, their mouths meeting in a heated moment of desire. Lucy's body melted into his, her lips growing more needy with each passing second.

With his powerful arms, he moved her from the couch into his lap to better hold her. Her body felt strong yet soft in just the right places, while his body felt starved without her affection. But in the moment, it was almost as though no time had passed between them.

Lucy raked her fingers through his hair and a growl of appreciation came from his throat, making Lucy huff a laugh between kisses.

"I think you liked that," Lucy whispered in a tease.

"I like everything about you." Micah pulled her closer, reclaiming her lips with his.

"If I didn't know any better, I'd think you've missed me," she said, pulling back to look at him.

Staring into her hazel eyes, his heart pounded in his chest.

She's perfect.

From the freckles on her nose to the curve of her lip, there was not one part of her that he didn't worship. She could command him to do just about anything and he would obey, just to see her smile. She was everything.

"Words can't sum up what I feel," he whispered, changing the teasing tone to something more serious. His eyes bored deeply into hers as her playful smile faded to an understanding lilt of her lips.

She nodded, reading his heart. "I know."

Micah stilled, unsure of what to say next. Should he lay it all on the line? Confess his never-ending love to her? Should he wait for her to share why she came back? To see if she was going to stay this time?

The seconds felt like hours, but Lucy didn't give any hint as to why she was there. He sighed and pulled her closer. She wrapped her arms around him, hugging him tightly, and nestled her head in the crook of his neck.

Micah held her as close to him as he possibly could. Rubbing his hands up her thighs, on her back, through her hair; it would never be enough.

"Why are you really here?" Micah continued to stroke her hair, losing himself to her scent... *roses and honey.*

She sat up, keeping her arms around him; her fingertips teased the hair at the base of his neck. Then she sat down on the couch next to him.

"Things aren't going as smoothly as I would have liked, and I just... missed you. I wanted to be with the one who knows my heart."

She shied away as she spoke, but Micah didn't mind. The soft smile on his face grew, and he dropped his hands to hers and squeezed. "I'm here. What's going on? How can I help?"

"I'm not sure you can," she admitted.

It hurt that she didn't think he could help. It's what he did—he helped people. Didn't she trust him? He turned to her to ask, but stopped. He wasn't sure he was prepared to hear the answer.

She turned away from him to the vast windows, looking out into the woods. "It's so beautiful here."

Micah agreed, but that wasn't what he wanted to talk about. He wanted to know what happened with her father. He wanted to ask what she was doing there, and if this time she would stay... Not to mention the portal, Brax, and the swirling red magic. Damn, there were so many problems.

"It is, but there have been some weird things going on that we should probably talk about. It's The Elderwood..."

"What happened to it? Was it that Fae female? Did she do something?" Lucy stood in a hurry, ready to defend land that wasn't being threatened.

"No, not that," Micah said. "The portal. There's something wrong with it."

"Wrong? What do you mean?"

"The sigil on the tree. It's changed. It has a dark, ashy smoke that seems to seep out of it." He rubbed at his chin, trying to find the right words. "It looks almost as if something inside of it exploded. And there's a crack in the ground. I don't know if it was an earthquake or what, but something is happening."

"Exploded? Fire?" Lucy's lips popped open in shock. Her fingers twitched at her sides.

"No, it's different. I don't know how to explain it. All I know is that it isn't a good sign. Something's gone haywire with it."

Lucy took a step toward the door, clearly prepared to go see for herself.

"That's not all," he murmured. The hairs on the back of his neck stood rigid as he remembered the creature in the shadows. A shiver shot down his spine. "There is something lurking around the tree, and I can't seem to get a read on it. It looks like an enormous cat, and every time I try to get close enough to see it, it's gone. I can't catch it on camera. I can't figure out where it's coming from."

"A feline? Is it small?" Lucy asked, focused on their conversation. She took a careful step closer to Micah.

"No. It's massive. It looks like a giant black panther, but its coat is so dark, like it's made of shadows. "

"A shadow beast?" She gasped in surprise. "But those are unheard of in Joterra..." Lucy went to the window, looking out into the forest. "In fact, they haven't been in Denora for thousands of years from what I've read."

"I haven't been able to find much about it in the book yet, but I figure Brax will help me find more answers."

She spun to look at Micah with a glare. "You're going to let that stranger look in your ancestral book?"

"I mean, I guess it depends, doesn't it? Are you going to stick around and help me or will you be leaving again?" His words had a sharper edge than he meant, but he couldn't stop them as they came out. The harshness lacing them hid the heartbreak. He was tired of people leaving him.

Lucy didn't respond. Instead, she stared at Micah, causing his thoughts to spin wildly.

I'm pushing her away. She never wanted to stay, did she...

"You know there was nothing I could have done about that," Lucy finally said. The hurt in her tone was quiet, but the defiance in her voice was strong.

Micah was already putting a wall between them before they even gave the relationship a chance.

"I know. I'm sorry." He shook his head, trying to relieve himself from the headache that kept growing.

Reaching out, he extended his hand to her, hoping she would take it.

If she takes it, there's still a chance... Take my hand baby, he silently pleaded.

She took his hand, and he pulled her back to sit on the couch next to him, her thigh grazing his.

A relieved sigh left him, but he wasn't out of the woods yet. There were too many obstacles between them. He had to figure out a way to make the two of them work—he wouldn't give up when they had barely had the chance to begin.

Lucy looked down, refusing to make eye contact. He saw her putting up mental walls, too.

"Do you remember the night in the study?" Micah whispered.

Lucy's eyes met his. She nodded almost imperceptibly, and a stray curl fell from behind her ear.

Micah's heart ached as he recalled the night. He needed to offer this piece of himself to her. He needed her to remember as much as he did.

"The flame from the candle lit up the wall in little shapes. We had red wine and cheese and you wore those soft, little leggings." He grazed a finger on the edge of her knee, not wanting to overstep, but wanting to touch her more than anything in the world. "You told me you wanted love—real love. You wanted someone who saw you and decided that they couldn't live without you."

Lucy's breath hitched as she lifted her head to Micah. They faced one another, their breathing erratic and shallow.

"That's me, Lu. I can't live without you." Micah's shaky words came out in a breathless tumble. "And it scares the fuck out of me."

Lucy's lips crashed into Micah's, swallowing his words whole. Her hands gripped his shoulders and she pulled him on top of her as they laid on the couch.

All at once, the pressure and stress that Micah had been carrying around in his tainted heart disappeared. Relief and love overwhelmed him, body, mind, and soul. The only thing he needed in this lifetime and the next was Lucy, there in his arms, as he made her happy every day for the rest of their lives.

The rest of mine, he realized.

Lucy was Fae and would outlive him.

He propped himself up on his arms, needing to look at Lucy. Her cheeks were flushed and her eyes were bright. There was no hesitation from her, so why did Micah feel so uneasy? He couldn't stand the thought of her running from him again. What if she left and found herself in the arms of Sloan instead?

She combed her fingers through his shaggy hair and looked at him curiously. "What's wrong?"

"I don't want you to close yourself off to me when things get hard," he whispered. "Don't run from me, baby."

Lucy's eyes welled with tears as she nodded. Then she pulled him in close and kissed him ever so gently, her hands exploring his body.

Micah tangled his fingers into her curly brown hair and kissed down the length of her neck, teasing with nips of his teeth and soothing strokes of his tongue. Lucy moaned as she encouraged him to continue, pulling off his shirt as he reached to pull down her leggings.

Micah needed more of her; he needed all of her. She was the sun lighting up his day and the moon and stars guiding him at night. She was the beauty of the wild-flowers in the grove and the foundation of the ground that nourishes his soul. Lucy was the answer to everything, and he made a silent promise to the stars at that moment that he would do everything within his power to always make her feel loved and seen.

Love.

The thought was nearly a shock to Micah.

This is love.

And for the first time in his life, he didn't run. Instead, he worshiped Lucy right there on the couch until the sun made its way down and all that was left were the shadows cast from the light in the hall.

"I'M sorry it took me so long to return to you," Lucy said in between soft kisses as they lay on the living room floor in a tangle of naked limbs.

"It's fine. Your brother, Wes, and some old dude named Jasper came and helped me take care of things here." He looked around at the new cabin they created for him. "Wes seems like he could maybe be nice if he wanted to be."

"If he wanted to be?" Lucy let out a reluctant huff of laughter. "Actually, that's a pretty accurate description of Wes." She sat up and began dressing, picking between the scattered clothes among them.

"Suffice to say, I don't think he likes me much. Did you tell him about us?"

Lucy paled. "No, of course not. I could never."

Micah's head jerked back in surprise at the admission. "*Never?* Why *never*? Am I not allowed to be something to you?" His voice was uncertain, with a pang of frustration that he tried to hide. He grabbed his jeans and began to clothe himself.

Lucy shook her head and offered a sad smile, scooting closer to him again. "No. It's not that. It's just... complicated right now. There's so much going on that I barely understand. I am doing my best to figure it out, but I haven't had many opportunities. I'm trying to find out more about your Lumen ancestry, but Jasper keeps following me around like a shadow—he won't leave me alone. Everywhere I go, there he is."

"Yeah, something about him rubs me the wrong way." Micah's face softened, happy with the change of topic. "When he came here, I'm pretty sure he just said things to intentionally piss me off. It surprised me you told them about the land developers." He stood as he grabbed his shirt and pulled it over his head.

"Pardon?" Lucy looked at him curiously, straightening her clothes.

"No. Pearson," he replied, helping her up. "J. Pearson? Jasper knew all about it and was talking to me like I was crazy when I said that I was worried they would come back."

"Micah—I didn't tell them who the land developers were." Her eyebrows furrowed. "I didn't even use that term because I assumed they wouldn't know what I was talking about."

"Then how did he know?"

"I have no idea, but maybe we're missing something. Once I return, I will see what Jasper is up to. I've never trusted him, and maybe my gut is telling me something more."

His stomach dropped.

"Once you return? You're leaving me again?" The sting of that reality was almost too much for Micah to bear. Didn't he just profess his love to her? Did she not feel the same?

"Micah, I have to. No one knows I'm here and I need to be back before the sun rises in Joterra." She glanced out the window to measure her time. "Besides, we need to figure out this Jasper issue. It is too odd for it to be coincidence."

We. It was the only thing Micah could hold on to. He'd never force Lucy into a decision she didn't want to make, and as long as she was still including him in her plans, that had to be enough.

"There have been some weird things going on here, too," Micah said to her as he dragged a hand down the front of his face. He took a deep breath, preparing to tell her about the red magic that saved his life.

"In Denora, as well," Lucy interrupted him. "My father is beyond angry with me, and he wouldn't let me come to say goodbye. I'm so sorry I couldn't come and see you sooner."

"Goodbye? What do you mean goodbye?" His response was faint, worry and confusion causing his voice to crack.

"Micah... I am doing everything to try to dissuade Lord Sloan from wanting to move forward with the arrangement, but my parents seem glued to the idea."

Micah's lips parted with disbelief, then quickly snapped shut. "Wait. Did you say you were trying to dissuade your parents, or Lord Sloan?"

"Lord Sloan," she whispered. "He arrived the day after I returned."

ELEVEN

LUCY

"I don't understand. What are you doing with him? Why so soon?"

"My father moved things up—the wedding is arranged for the Spring... Just a few more months away. He set up a dinner in the Capital so Laurent and I could get to know each other."

Lucy did her best to keep her tone neutral, to list the facts without any emotion behind them, because that's all that it was: facts.

Right?

"*Dinner*, Lucy? You're telling me you're going on dates?"

"Dates? What are you talking about?"

"You're spending time with him alone? Getting to know one another?" The anger had bubbled over in Micah once again, a line of frustration wrinkling in his forehead.

"It's not my choice, Micah!" Lucy retorted in frustration. "I am obligated to accept his invitations. It's what's expected of me! If I am to solve any of this, then I need to play my part."

"And what part is that exactly, Lucy?" Micah jumped from his seat on the couch and stalked across the room away from her. "Are you Lucy Baum, badass extraordinaire, who doesn't take no for an answer? Are you Lady Lucella, ready to take on a suitor?" He spun around to look at her, pain in his eyes. "Or are you my Lu? My warrior goddess, who I would move the stars for? Who are you today?" His voice rose and fell with an onslaught of emotion.

"What is that supposed to mean?" Lucy countered angrily.

Who does he think he is?

She stood up and walked to the windows, putting space between them. "What do you expect me to do, Micah? I already attempted one brash decision and it landed me stranded in another realm with a stranger and caused half of the star-damned woods to burn to the ground," she said in exasperation, shoving her hands at the window and the forest beyond.

"A stranger." His nostrils flared as he tried to get a deep breath of air. "A *stranger*, Lucy? That's what I am to you now?"

"No, that's not what I meant." Lucy shook her head and huffed an air of annoyance.

Why won't he listen to me?

The magical power in her veins thrummed with hostility. She had to tamper it down before it acted on its own accord once again. "Please. Let's talk this out."

Micah looked away indignantly, refusing any eye contact.

"Micah, I am here for you. I've traveled across the star-damned realms for you. Doesn't that mean anything?" She took a careful step toward him.

"I guess that depends on what it is you want from me." His voice was withdrawn and quiet. He took a few steps toward her, meeting her in front of the couch once again.

Lucy's heart fell at the comment.

"What I want from you? You are not a commodity I wish to use for my benefit... Micah, you're my friend. I just needed my friend. Is that too much to ask of you?"

Is friend the right word?

It felt like a lie, but she wasn't prepared to consider the other option. Not now.

Micah sighed. "No, of course it isn't. I'm sorry." He rubbed his eyes and groaned with his face in his hands, falling back onto the couch with a thud. "I'm so sick of these damn headaches."

"Headaches?" Her annoyance with Micah ceased immediately at the thought of him hurt. "When did they start?"

"I went home to turn in my badge and see my dad, and I don't know Lucy... something happened. I got so sick." He dropped his hands and laced them behind his neck, reminding her of the many times he did that in the forest with her. Especially when she was driving him crazy. The memory tore at her heart. She grabbed his hand and laced her fingers through his, sitting with him on the couch.

Just like the other times, her heart sang with their connection. Something about his touch just felt right, like there was nothing else that could complete her.

"My head was throbbing and before I got back on to the property, I thought I was going to lose it. I stepped out of the car and immediately passed out from the pain. I was lucky Brax was here to cure me —I thought I was going to have to go to the hospital. I didn't even know if that would be allowed?" Micah ran his hands through his hair, looking at Lucy with worry-filled eyes. "What happens if I get sick here and have to leave?"

"I- I don't know," she stammered out at last. Fae didn't have the same health problems mortals faced.

"Lumen, why didn't you tell me this?" Brax chimed in, leaning in the hall entryway that separated the kitchen and living area.

"What the fuck? Where did you come from? Have you been there listening this whole time?" Micah asked in surprise.

"Of course I was here. Now answer the question. Why didn't you tell me?"

Lucy glared at the strange female, ready to tear her limb from limb. How dare she be lurking in the back listening to their private conversation?

Was she there while they were naked and—oh my stars.

"What are you talking about? You knew. You were here," Micah said as he turned to talk to Brax.

Walking into the room slowly, Brax stopped in front of them and crossed her arms; her eyebrows furrowed above menacing eyes.

Feeling her magic pushing at the surface, Lucy took a deep breath, keeping it tampered down. She wouldn't have Micah injured in the crossfire if her magic went wild.

"You said it yourself—you were here to cure my headaches?" Micah finished tying his boots and stood, looking between Lucy and Brax with apprehension.

Yeah, you should be cautious. I'm going to maim this female, Lucy thought bitterly.

"I meant when you hit your head off the ground, Lumen. You bashed your head open and I had to heal you—but that's all I healed. Your body was perfectly fine before that."

"What?" Micah fully faced her now. "No, I passed out from the pain. I was definitely not *perfectly fine.*"

"My lyfar magic can sense sickness. We use it on the battlefield to find infection in wounds. But you? You were healthy beyond a head wound." Brax eyed him skeptically, her dark lined eyes narrowing in annoyance.

"That doesn't make any sense," Micah said as he took a step back. "I was dizzy, nauseous, and my head was splitting before you came around. Maybe your magic just didn't pick it up because I'm not Fae?"

"That's nonsense," Brax scoffed. "My magic does not discriminate like most Fae do. I am telling you, Lumen. There was nothing wrong with you."

"That doesn't make sense," Micah repeated louder.

"No, it does not," she agreed, turning to look at Lucy.

Lucy remained on the couch, watching the interaction and doing her best to keep control of her immense power. At the very sight of Brax, all Lucy wanted to do was blast magic into her chest and shove her out of the room.

"Maybe we can find some answers in my book?" Micah suggested, oblivious to the silent war being raged in Lucy and Brax's glares.

"What book would have answers for this, Lumen?" Brax asked him doubtfully, looking away from Lucy in boredom.

He walked over and uncovered the leather-bound book from behind the couch. "This book."

Lucy fumed. "I can't believe you told her."

"Who else is going to help me, Lucy? Do you think I look like a guy who can speak and read ancient Fae? Spoiler alert: I'm not. And you aren't always here, so someone is going to have to help me."

Lucy seethed with anger, but Micah wasn't wrong. She hated to admit it, but there was really no other choice in this situation, was there?

She had to continue to get close to Laurent to prove to him that there was a better fit for marriage than her. Micah had to stay at The Elderwood and figure out what was happening to the portal. They were both destined to carry out their tasks, far from one another, unsure of where the future may lead.

The reality of Lucy having to leave him hit her like a ton of stones. How could she leave the man who held her heart in the safety of his? How would she survive the night when she longed for his lips upon hers? How could she leave when she was finally exploring the possibility of real... love?

Her magic flickered in and out, anger fading with every thought.

Brax took the book in her hands and looked at it with great reverence.

"I will prepare this book in the study. You need to say goodbye to your visitor. I'm sure her daddy is wondering where she is," Brax said condescendingly.

Lucy took a step toward Brax, ready to unleash fury on her when she made a sharp turn around the corner and disappeared from Lucy's view. Instead, in front of her was Micah, with his hands up, ready to detain her from following Brax.

"So, you pick her to share all of your secrets with?"

Micah sighed, "I am just trying to do what I am supposed to: protect the portal. Sloan sent her to help me, so how awful can it be? I'm surprised you didn't know, with all of your time spent with him." His face was drawn, clearly unhappy with the turn of events in their discussion.

"Let me get this straight. You are judging me for being forced to spend time with Laurent and you are here cavorting with another female?"

"*Laurent*—first name basis now, huh?" He bit his bottom lip in anger, trying to withhold words.

Lucy stared at him as he did it—feeling furious yet also wishing she were that lip.

No, she told herself. *No. He is being ridiculous.*

"I'm going to pretend that you didn't make that last comment and instead leave you with this: I'm glad you're alright, and I am happy that there is someone here who can help you while I'm gone." The words pained her to say. "I can't necessarily say that I like her, but I don't want you to feel alone."

She looked out the window in a panic. The sun was rising, and if she wanted to get home without being caught, she needed to leave. Now.

"Work out what is going on with The Elderwood, and I will find a way out of all of this... Don't give up on me yet. Okay?"

Her eyes were fierce as she said it, but her shaky words betrayed her. Inside, she was falling apart, but she couldn't let Micah know. Not yet.

Micah's eyes remained fixed on hers as he nodded, his severe expression never leaving his face. Lucy couldn't be sure that he believed her, but there was nothing left to say.

She stood on the tips of her toes to reach up and kiss him softly;

his lips didn't move. Her heart sank as he didn't respond, and as she turned away, he grabbed onto her waist and pulled her back to him.

His returning kiss was forceful and heartbreaking and she couldn't decide if it was a kiss that said "I'll miss you", or a kiss that said "goodbye".

Either way, she couldn't stay to find out, for as soon as her Fae speed could allow it, she reached The Elderwood portal and was through the gateway without even pausing to see it.

What mattered most was that Micah did not get to see the tears streaming down her face—and that was all she could focus on.

TWELVE

MICAH

Micah's balled fists pounded into the wall next to the door frame. "Lucy!" he yelled again, trying to will her back to the cabin. There was no point—she was gone, and he couldn't force her to come back.

"Let her go, Lumen," Brax said from her place in the study. "We have work to do."

Micah turned reluctantly, glancing back once more, hoping that Lucy would appear.

What the hell just happened?

He squeezed his eyes tight as he dragged his hand down his face.

"What have you been doing this entire time? Where have you been?" Micah asked her.

Brax opened the leather-bound book at the desk, analyzing each page closely. "Around."

Her flippant tone made Micah's eye twitch. He wouldn't be getting any more answers from her; she was more stubborn than Lucy, and that was saying something.

As Brax turned the pages, her eyes grew wider with each inscription. She mumbled to herself as she read through them, quickly flipping through, searching for information.

Micah propped himself on the desk next to her, resigning himself to the fact that he had no real way to help. He had to rely on Brax, and he still wasn't sure where he stood with her. "We need to find out about that shadow cat, too."

"Nonsense," Brax replied. "There is no such thing as a shadow cat."

"Yes, there is. Lucy said they used to be in Denora."

"Miss Baum said that once upon a time there was, but we don't live in a fairy tale, Lumen. What she spoke of has not existed in a very long time." She continued to page through the book, scanning through the inscriptions. "Beyond that, they don't live here in Joterra. It would be preposterous of them to come to a mortal land. Their food source comes from the souls of the ancient Fae—not from mortals." She raked her eyes up and down his body. "They would starve."

Micah paled. "They feed on souls?" His eyebrows shot up. "What does that even mean?"

Brax turned on him with a look, leaning in with a wicked whisper. "I'm not going to spell it out for you, Lumen. Use your imagination."

Micah gulped and Brax smiled at his discomfort.

She turned back to the book. "Now, like I said. There's no reason to fear the creatures you think you saw. I am sure you mistook it for a forest cat. But there must be some more information on why you felt so ill and why my lyfar didn't pick up on it."

"How long were you standing there listening to our… conversation?"

Brax shooed the question away with her hand.

He sighed. "What about the crack in the ground?"

"I'll look into it. It is likely nothing."

"So black smoke, sparks and a fucking *earthquake* is nothing? Why didn't you hear it, by the way?"

Micah's frustration poured out of him with every word, but he knew there was no point. Each and every part of this had become more complicated than the next, and he wasn't sure what he was supposed to do.

"I heard you, and I came," she said matter-of-factly.

Micah looked at her in disbelief. Though, the more he thought about it, maybe he was overreacting. It probably felt like hours for him, but really, the rumbling was a matter of minutes. Not much time had passed by the time he got inside and Lucy came. At the thought of her, his insides twisted yet again.

He wasn't even sure if being mad was fair. Micah had spent so many years of his life being upset with people who didn't deserve it —the least he could do was try to rein it in as he lived on his grandad's property. Micah would never be able to apologize to his grandad for refusing his calls and avoiding all contact. He'd never be able to make things right... Being here on his land had to mean something more than just following in his footsteps. Micah knew deep down in his heart, things had to change. He had to try to honor his grandad in some way.

Micah slunk into the cushioned chair across from the desk and groaned. "This is a fucking disaster."

Brax took a quick look at Micah as he sat with his hands over his face, at a loss for his next steps. "What is going on with you and the Baum female?"

"What do you mean?" He mumbled.

"Well, you've just had a lovers' quarrel, and while it was extremely entertaining, I don't quite understand it. She is betrothed to Lord Sloan—is she not?"

He dropped his hands to look at her, but she focused on the book. Micah was at war with himself—he wanted to tell Brax everything. He wanted to finally talk to someone about everything that was going on without having to hold back any details.

Who better to talk to about Fae magic and forbidden love than someone who understood the bogus Denoran politics? But Micah wasn't sure how much he could trust Brax. More than that, he couldn't risk Brax going back to her employer, telling him everything that had happened between the pair.

Or maybe he did?

Maybe if Sloan knew Lucy was previously involved with another man, he'd back off. Maybe he'd see that she isn't into him and would let her go.

"It's complicated," was all he ended up sharing.

"It's less complicated than a mortal man having a Fae book. Indulge me."

Micah heaved another sigh and tried to figure his way through the story. "Well, when I first saw her, we didn't want anything to do with one another. I wanted to sell my grandad's old place, and she wanted me to keep it. God, she was such a nag about it all," he laughed. "She was so fierce. So beautiful... She's unlike anyone I've ever met."

His voice trailed off as he got lost in thought, sighing deeply.

"We went through a lot to get to where we are now," he told Brax seriously. "Hell, without her, I'd be a cop in the city, miserably unaware that life was passing me by."

"What do you mean by that? Miserably unaware? If you are unaware of what you are missing, how can that be miserable?"

"Because if I'm being honest, I was miserable anyway." As soon as he said it, he knew it was true. "I didn't realize it until now. Until Lucy."

Brax stopped what she was doing and looked over at Micah, enthralled by his words.

"Your life was miserable? What made it so bad?" she asked, truly curious.

"I was just kind of living life on auto pilot." Micah shrugged, not wanting to get too deep.

She gave him a quizzical look and he assumed it was the lingo.

"I was just doing the same routine every day? I did my job, worked out, came home and took care of my apartment, and repeated the same things every single day of my life. I didn't have many friends, so there wasn't much I did with anyone outside of work."

"What about lovers?" Brax asked as she pushed the book aside, leaning her elbows on the desk, cradling her head in one of her hands.

Being the center of Brax's attention made him squirm.

"I didn't have too many of those either." He shifted in his seat. "I had a girl for a while, but things didn't work out. I wasn't willing to change. I don't think I was a great listener."

Ugh. I'm seeing a fucking pattern here.

"So, what is this situation with you and Miss Baum? There is romance there?"

Micah wasn't sure he wanted to answer, but the look in Brax's eyes wasn't judgmental. There was a tender curiosity peeking from behind her tough exterior.

"Yeah," he said solemnly. "There is."

Brax nodded her head in understanding.

Micah had always been a good judge of character—it was one of the things that made him a good detective. He could read the intentions of a person by the inflection of their voice, the tilt of their head... He could always determine when someone was lying to him. He always knew who to trust; and he wanted to trust Brax.

The only person to ever make him question that was his grandad. He was the one person who didn't live up to who Micah thought he was... Though now, as he looked back, he realized he was able to count on Abe. That never faltered. Life just wasn't as it seemed, and Micah was too proud to just talk to him.

He shrugged off the thought, real emotion threatening to be acknowledged. "How about you? Got a guy? Or a girl?" Changing the topic was his best defense and he shoved the emotion away, refusing to bring it to light.

"Not at the moment. I have had many lovers who I've taken to bed, but none who have had the courage to stick around. It is a difficult thing to be paired with a Vytyrian." Brax straightened her shoulders and brushed imaginary lint off of her shirt.

"Why is that?" he asked, leaning back and turning toward her.

"Warriors move around a lot; we go from contract to contract and find work. I have gone to bed with Denorans from every territory, Vytyrians, the Karroz — the list goes on."

"Karroz?" It seemed like every time he thought he was getting the hang of things, new foreign words kept popping up.

How am I going to figure all of this stuff out?

"Yes, another realm. You'd probably find it fun, Lumen," Brax said with a sly smile.

"And why is that?"

She leaned forward and looked at Micah with devious eyes. "Dragons."

"Dragons?" Micah choked. "They're real?"

"Of course, Lumen." She rolled her eyes and turned her body back to the book. "By the stars, you're like a giant, hairy baby. There are so many things you need to learn."

"Tell me about it," Micah said with a huff.

It was just a customary Joterran phrase, but Brax took it literally.

"We will begin here," she pointed at a page near the middle of the book. "What do you know of this book and Denora?"

"Well," Micah began, taken aback by her abruptness once again. "I know there are Fae who live in Denora. They have magic. There is a Kingdom. And somehow I'm related to a distant Fae relative who decided to come here to live and then never left." He shook his head, listening to the words that came out of his mouth.

Magic. Fae. I'm not sure I'll ever get used to this.

Brax's eyes seemed to shimmer with mischief. "Alderic Lumen! I should have known you were related to him. He was a *beast* in the bedchambers." She leaned back with a smile on her face.

"What? How the hell would you know?"

"I'm older than I look. I've been around for thousands of years. Why do you think I am both so beautiful and knowledgeable?" She winked at him. "Only one who has seen the years that I have could be both."

Micah's eyes nearly bulged out of their sockets. "Thousands? More than one? "

"Yes. Four and a half, but the math changes with each realm you visit."

"You're four thousand years old?!"

"Yes." She rolled her eyes at his display of surprise. "Pay attention, you wet noodle. We have things to do."

She handed the book back over to him and he took it in his arms. Still dazed by their conversation, Micah remained silent.

"I will do another scan of the property to see what explains this crack you spoke of. You look through this book to figure out why your head ails you." Swinging the door open, she turned to speak to him. "Think about when it began, when you noticed it, and exactly how it felt. Then scan through the pages that you can understand. Look at the pictures, too. Maybe something will click."

"You can't go back out there. What about that shadow creature?" Micah was terrified of something happening to Brax and him being left all alone on the property. He didn't have anyone to rely on.

"Enough of that." She waved an annoyed hand in the air. "I will have my walk and be back soon. I'll put a call into my employer if it makes you feel better."

A look of hesitation crossed Micah's face before Brax spoke once more. "Don't worry, Lumen. I won't mention your fun with Miss Baum."

Then she left Micah alone in the house. He tried to look out the window to follow her, but her purposeful strides brought her to the trees quickly, and in moments she was far enough into the thicket that Micah couldn't see her.

What is she always doing back there? Am I right to trust her?

He squinted his eyes to see farther, but it was no use.

He lugged the book over to the kitchen table and plopped it down as he turned to grab a glass of water.

This is all so ridiculous. I can't believe that Lucy and I fought like that.

Closing his eyes, he tried to remember her beautiful face before it had turned to anger. Before he hurt her with his words. He had every right to be upset with her, didn't he?

Maybe this is why I was supposed to end up alone.

He shook his head again as he sat down at the kitchen table with the book, alone in the house that contained only wisps of memories, the dishwasher whirring the background.

For over an hour, he flipped through page by page, hoping something familiar would pop up. Carefully, he searched for anything that had the potential to answer his questions about his headaches or the mysterious creature prowling in the woods; something about the enormous crack in the ground. Better yet, he needed an explanation of what that red mist was—how magic came out of nowhere and saved his life.

Micah knew he wasn't making it up. It was there, plain as day. He didn't tell Lucy or Brax about the magic just yet, though. How would they believe that magic came to help him? That creature, though...

Why doesn't anyone believe me? If that shadow beast really exists, how did it get here from Denora?

More pages went by, and it was easier and easier for Micah to flip through. The majority of the entries were written in another language, and Micah had no idea how to read them. The pictures weren't very helpful. Every now and then there would be an image of a plant or herb, maybe some weapons? There were numerous entries with flasks and glass vials filled with liquids or powders. But for the most part, just ornate scrawl filled the pages, all written in dark ink on beige paper.

After what felt like an eternity, Micah flipped to a page and stopped. There in front of him was unmistakably familiar handwriting.

Grandad.

He brushed his fingertips over the words. When he read the inscription, Micah stilled.

The Curse of the Guardian

I am unsure who will see this after me, but I want it to go into record to ensure that no one makes the same mistake I did.

My wife is very ill, and I needed to leave with her in order to get her medical care. While I was away from home, I took a turn for the worse. It was a pain unlike anything I have ever experienced before. My head throbbed like it was in a vise; it felt like I was walking through a fog. I am mortal and have spent years experiencing many illnesses—but nothing like this. Once we got back to the property, all of my pain disappeared. It was as though I had imagined it all, which didn't make any sense.

A few weeks later, I had to bring my wife to visit family. The same sensations occurred. We had to shorten our trip due to my sudden symptoms, and again, as soon as I crossed over the property line to the house, all of my ailments vanished.

I spent time testing my theory, and discovered that extended time away from our home induces an enormous list of illnesses that I experienced, which were all relieved with my proximity to the grounds—though some took longer than others.

I was always told to stay to guard The Elderwood, and I was always encouraged not to leave, but I didn't realize there would be such a physical reaction. I never realized that is why my father, and his before him, never left the property. I didn't realize the ramifications of the curse placed upon us if we were to abandon our post—nor was I ever told.

So, to all future guardians—stay. The longer you are away, the more severe the symptoms become. I fear death would come to those who do not return to The Elderwood when beckoned.

Abe Lumen

Micah stared at the page, disbelief shaking him to his core.

Why would the Fae put a curse on someone just to guard a damn tree? An actual fucking curse?

He strode across the room with the book, dropping it on the small table in the living room. Heated anger rose to the surface. He balled his fists tightly and lifted them to his temples, his teeth clenching together in frustration.

I need to get out of here. If I don't get out of this fucking place, I'm gonna lose it.

Grabbing his running shoes and his phone, he stuck his earbuds in and ran out the front door, letting it swing shut behind him. He didn't care that he wasn't in his workout clothes.

He didn't think about the giant crack from the tree, the scarlet ropes of mist that sprang from his hands, nor the actual curse that threatened to hurt him if he left. Instead, he focused on the steady pound of his shoes on the earth. Each foot propelling him further away from that book, filled with a reality he refused to accept.

He ran from a cabin with no family, Brax and the Fae dipshit Sloan, Jasper, J. Pearson, everything. Even Lucy. He needed his mind empty of all the things crashing down around him.

Eventually, the music in his ears calmed him, and the quiet of the forest felt less foreboding.

His path around the property ended back at the cabin, and he walked in breathless. By busying his body, it quieted his mind. He was thirsty and sweaty, but clear-headed for the first time in days.

"Lumen."

Brax's voice startled him. She sat so quietly with the leather book in her lap. He didn't even see her there, sitting on the floor in front of the couch. Usually she was filled with movement, never still. But this... this was new. Her eyes held worry and sorrow.

The book laid in her lap, open to the page where he left off.

"I know," he replied, wiping the sweat from his brow. "The curse. That's why I was sick."

"No, that's not it," Brax replied seriously.

"Yes, I know I can die if I leave. I get it," Micah replied flatly, trying to forget.

"Listen to me, you overgrown turnip," Brax snapped at him. "The other side of this page is in Denoran and I assume you haven't miraculously acquired a lesson in Fae languages while I was in the forest, have you?" Her eyes were full of fire and impatience, hinting what truly lay beneath Brax's feminine exterior.

"Sorry," Micah replied with a defeated sigh. With a raised eyebrow he added, "do I want to know what it said in Denoran?"

"It says if there is no guardian to watch over the portal, it is open for all the dark and evil things to travel through."

"What does that mean?"

"It means the shadow beast is the least of our worries."

THIRTEEN

LUCY

"Throw it higher," Lucy called to Wes. She held her new bow high and aimed her arrow at the clay plate. Upon her release, the arrow whistled through the sky, striking her target dead center, shattering the clay into pieces.

Since her return, her head filled with a never ending whirlwind of uncertainty. Her secret trip to Joterra lasted only half of one Denoran day. She sulked in her room for the remainder of her night which made for unrestful sleep and a dreadful attitude.

Thankfully, her brother Tristan sought her out and invited her to an early morning archery practice. It was precisely the thing she needed to get her mind off of her troubles, if only for a little while. With each arrow, her mind calmed.

"This is always how high I send them for you," Wes said with an edge of annoyance. "How often have you been practicing?"

"Not often," Lucy said irritably. "Now send it."

Archery never failed to put Lucy's mind at ease. The predictable and repetitive movements slowed her body down and allowed her to breathe freely without the pressure of her reality weighing on her mind.

Lucy dropped her bow and looked at her brothers across the grassy field. Wes stood next to a tower of clay plates they used during target practice, preparing to throw another.

Tristan lazily sent magic toward the broken shards across the field, bringing them back into a pile to be recreated into a target once more. She chuckled at his less-than-enthusiastic position, lying back in the grass, his arm over his eyes to block the sun, one leg crossed over the other.

"Yes, Lucy, how often?" Tristan called. "You're pulverizing these plates and making the clean up harder than usual." He flicked his hand in the air as more pieces joined the pile. "I'm going to have to call Henry and Simon out here to take over. You're making me actually work."

"Not that often?" Lucy replied, wondering how much she had actually improved. "How much higher can you project them?" She asked with a hint of mischief.

"What are you thinking?" Wes replied, sensing Lucy's devious intent.

A flicker of mischief lit Lucy's eyes. "For each plate I hit, throw the next ten feet further. We shall continue until I miss."

"What happens if you miss?"

"I love a good wager," Tristan said, sitting up, finally interested.

"If I miss, you get a chance to hit the target. And if you strike true..." Lucy looked around, trying to think of an acceptable bargain.

"You'll give me your bow," Wes said with a triumphant grin.

"Absolutely not!" Lucy retorted, gripping her custom weapon close to her body.

"Oh no, Luce," Tristan replied with a laugh. "Are you scared of losing?"

"No," she replied firmly. "Fine. The farthest target I miss but you hit, you get my bow."

Wes's smile spread wide as he moved into position, his swagger implying he would have an easy win.

"However, if you miss, and I can hit farther than you, then you have to tell Father that I outshot you." Lucy's smugness was palpable.

Wes narrowed his eyes in thought, and then gave a sharp nod. Tristan's bellowing laugh filled the open air.

This should be interesting.

Lucy resumed her shooting position as her brothers did the same.

Tristan remained on the grassy knoll, but this time, he sat up to watch.

"Go ahead," Lucy said, and Wes's Fae hearing picked it up even from his distance away.

Lucy readied her arrow, sought out the plate in the sky, released, and hit her target with a resounding crack.

Without hesitation, she prepared her next arrow from her quiver, excited to take on her brother in this challenge. The following target was even farther out, but still easy for Lucy to take down.

Then the next.

And the next.

And the next.

Her brothers looked at each other in confusion. Tristan stood, having to keep an eye on the far target.

"Lucy, you aren't charming your arrows, are you?" Wes asked steadily.

"No," she said breathlessly, invigorated by the thrill of pushing herself to her limits. "Prepare the next."

Lucy's focus was absolute, and her body hummed with energy. She had never hit a target at such a distance before. Her blood thrummed within her veins, and her eyes were wide with delight. Lucy clenched her hands around the fiery details on her bow; it was the epitome of force and eloquence.

Wes gave a contemplative look to Tristan as he took another step back, nodded, and magicked the disc so far into the air it could hardly be seen.

Lucy's release was so quick, the arrow whistled in the air, hitting the target and turning it into dust.

Tristan's hand lifted, attempting to bring the pieces back to the rubble pile, but nothing came. He pushed his right hand out farther, spreading his fingers wide to call back the shattered clay—again, nothing returned.

"Maybe it was too far away?" Wes asked. Lucy smiled from ear to ear. The idea that her ability outshined her brothers' magic made the power within her body rattle with excitement.

"Throw another," he told Wes. "Lucy, don't hit this one." Wes careened the next plate even further, and Tristan held his hand out to retrieve the plate whole before it crashed into the ground. The disc came speeding back to Tristan intact.

"It wasn't too far." He looked at Lucy in question. "The disc you hit... there was nothing left of it," Tristan said, dumbstruck. "Luce— I'm not sure I understand."

Lucy's smile faltered.

How did I do that?

"I've always told you my bows outperformed yours," she said on a shaky breath.

"Let's call it a day, I think," Wes announced. "We will need more clay if you keep obliterating the plates." He shared a look with Tristan that Lucy did not miss.

They cleaned up and began the walk back to the estate. Lucy was unsure of what was happening and why.

My magic from The Elderwood must have something to do with this, she thought as she clenched her right fist. *I could really do with fewer surprises right now.*

Unfortunately for Lucy, more surprises were on the horizon.

RETURNING TO THE ESTATE, Lucy hoped to find her father alone in his study so they could talk in private. Each time she had seen him since she left Joterra, he was flocked by her brothers or his staff. All she needed was one moment of her father's time without Jasper breathing down their necks.

She was convinced that showing Corvus her bow would be the turning point she was looking for. He would see this immaculate contraption and know that it was the best he had ever seen. No other Fae, female nor male, could construct such a refined bow.

This is it, she told herself confidently. *This is what it will take to get him to see my worth. This will get me back to Micah.*

Nervous excitement filled her heart, and she tiptoed quietly down the corridor to his office door. Her plan was to peek inside and ensure that he was alone—if Jasper or another staff member was inside, she would return later.

I only get one chance. I can't let anyone ruin it.

For once, the door was open wide, signaling that Corvus must be somewhere nearby. He would never leave his study unlocked and unattended. She walked in, planning to sit and wait for his arrival, when a barrage of voices threw her off course. Corvus boomed down the hall, arguing with a more faint voice that she almost recognized...

Tristan? Why is he here? Is he going to tell father we were practicing?

She quickly ducked behind a large cabinet, and immediately the memory of stealing the amulet came rushing back to her.

I am so tired of sneaking around.

She closed her eyes with a frown and dropped her head against the cabinet frame.

"Why won't you let her try?" Tristan said as they walked into the study and closed the door behind them.

"Tristan, why are you bringing this up now? After everything we are trying to accomplish here, she does not need to hear that you agree with her. You need to stop giving her that hope."

"Unfortunately, Father, you're right about hope. I haven't expressed my opinions to Lucy about this, because I was fearful that you would do exactly what you are now."

"And what is that?" Corvus asked his son angrily.

"You're pushing any prospect of Lucy joining the business completely off the table. She is good, Father. She's better than all of us. Why won't you accept that this is right for her?"

Lucy's heart soared as she kept herself hidden in the corner of the room.

"You say this simply because you don't want to conform, either. You would rather join the Denoran army than involve yourself with the Baum Bowyer business."

"You're right. I would," Tristan argued.

Lucy held in a shocked gasp. She always knew that he wanted to become a soldier, but she never, in her wildest dreams, ever expected him to speak out against their father.

"That is the funny thing about this situation, Father. I am allowed to join the legion. I may leave and do whatever my heart tells me is right. You may not like it, but you cannot stop me. Lucy does not have that privilege."

The tension laid thick in the air. She had never heard her brothers speaking out against her father. She had never heard them actually admit that the Denoran policies regarding females were unfair. It was a much needed conversation at an inopportune time.

She panicked, looking around for an escape. Even if Tristan were to leave, she couldn't possibly speak to her father now; not after he was so riled.

How am I going to get out of here unseen?

"You do not know what you are speaking of," Corvus argued.

Tristan cut him off once again. "No, Father. I understand completely. It is you who chooses not to understand. Since it does not fit into your plans, you deem the entire concept unacceptable. You choose to not listen to Lucy, which means you choose to push her away."

"I am not pushing her away," her father boomed in response.

Lucy's heart stilled as the room went silent.

"When she is gone, she will not return. And it will be your fault." Tristan's scathing reply left Lucy breathless.

The door slammed shut and Lucy jolted in surprise. She calmed her breathing and focused her Fae hearing out as far she could. Realizing her father could hear her as well, she wordlessly pushed her concealment charm from the palm of her hand out to the rest of her body.

Sitting alone, she heard her father flipping through papers on his desk. He seemed agitated, but otherwise quiet. His movements stopped and he let out a deep sigh of defeat.

"I know you're there," he called into the room.

Lucy froze.

How did he figure it out?

"You may as well show yourself."

She hesitated, trying to determine what to say to her father but coming up short. How could he take her seriously when he knew she was eavesdropping?

Just then, the outer door to the study opened. "My apologies, sir," Jasper replied.

Jasper? Lucy could have died from relief. *Thank the stars.*

She furrowed her brow as she focused on their conversation.

"You know I dislike it when you hover at the door," Corvus reprimanded.

"I understand. I simply did not want to intrude." The outer door clicked shut and Jasper walked to her father's desk. "This is all for the best, Master Baum. You will see in good time."

"You better be right about this, Jasper," Corvus ground out. He released a sigh again.

"I believe it is the most suitable course of action. Our Bowyer industry will spread throughout all of Denora with this pairing and the business will grow to reach all the realms. You will be the most powerful Fae of all."

An involuntary shiver raced down Lucy's back at Jasper's repulsive obsession with power.

"I'm not sure it will be worth it. Lucella does not want this arrangement. If she declines…" His voice trailed off. "I will have to reconsider."

"Sir, without the North, your business is at a standstill," Jasper interjected. "Beyond that, if Lord Sloan uses his ore in weapons from another industry, the Baum Bowyers will one day fade to irrelevancy."

"And what of Lucy?" Corvus's tone weakened, as if in surrender.

"She will come around," Jasper replied. "I will make sure of it."

Lucy's magic fluttered within her and her thoughts slowed as she put the pieces together.

Jasper.

FOURTEEN

MICAH

"What else does it say?" Micah asked as he leaned over Brax's shoulder in the study. They had been poring over the book all morning, but the majority of their time was spent with Brax ignoring Micah or telling him to be quiet.

"I will tell you when I find something worthy," she said in a bored tone.

"You've been reading this thing for hours and all you've said so far is that without the portal being guarded, things can come through."

"Correct."

"But we figured that out days ago."

"Correct."

"So you're telling me there's nothing new in there?" Micah asked incredulously.

"Wrong. There are many new things, just none regarding our current predicament."

Micah slumped into the chair across from Brax, staring at the blank shelves in the study. Only one thing sat upon the middle shelf: the picture of his mom, grandad and him. The only picture had left.

He sat there solemnly, thinking back to how things used to be—before he became the guardian.

"You know, before Wes and Jasper remade this room, it used to be filled with books." Micah's lips quirked into a sad smile. "At first I didn't mind starting fresh, all the old dusty stuff gone, room for whatever I wanted to fill the space... I honestly thought that having my grandad's things gone from here would make it easier for me, but I think it's actually harder."

"What is harder?" Brax asked, finally looking up from the book for the first time in hours.

"Being here without them. At least before, when all of Grandad's junk was scattered throughout the house, I didn't feel so alone. It felt like part of him was still here with me." He dragged his hand down his face. "I'm sorry. I'm sure this is not important to you."

"I am listening." Her voice was quiet.

"The books... they reminded me of my mom. The old furniture reminded me of Grandad. He was always patching something up." He gave a soft chuckle. "I thought moving my stuff in here would take away the hurt I felt when I was here alone, but now all I see are my things. There's no trace of him or my mom. There's nothing here to connect me to them. It all feels... empty."

Brax listened carefully, then sat back in her chair. Looking up to the ceiling, she closed her eyes and smiled. "I will tell you a story, Lumen."

Micah looked at her inquisitively.

"When I first became a Vytyrian warrior, the pride inside of me swelled beyond belief. I had followed my dreams and made my family proud. However, after long years of traveling throughout the realms, I felt as though part of me was missing. I was not complete."

Micah's heart echoed with understanding, feeling like a shell of the person he once was.

"I came home for a visit and spent time with my family. I helped my mother cook our traditional foods. I assisted my sisters in their training. I felt happier, but I still could not fill that hole inside of me. My youngest sister, Noelia, has always been interested in art. Do you remember me telling you that?"

Micah nodded as he watched Brax's eyes brighten.

"I never fully understood it. She kept to herself and created her art, and I thought she was being foolish for chasing after such a silly hobby."

"I thought you said you loved her art?"

"Listen, you soggy cabbage."

Micah rolled his eyes and closed his mouth dramatically.

"I thought her art was foolish at first. Flowers and skyscapes? Waterfronts and plates of food? What was the purpose of such nonsense?" Brax looked at her hands, clearly wrapped up in a memory. "Then, Noelia brought me to the great willow tree, where she spent her days with her drawings."

Micah leaned in, giving Brax his rapt attention. It was rare for Brax to open up, and this conversation felt different from the others. It wasn't about business. It wasn't about The Elderwood or of any other Fae. It was about her.

"I didn't realize she quietly followed me around during my visit. I was always so busy, I didn't even notice... On a large sheet of white paper, my beautiful sister had replicated mine and my mother's hands, kneading bread, side by side. Each wrinkle of our knuckles, the shape of my mother's crooked pinky finger, my small beauty mark, right here." She showed him the small dark brown dot at the base of her thumb. Smiling, she rubbed it tenderly.

"That was only one of the many drawings she created for me. Another had my strong arms with my sisters, training in our Vytyrian uniforms. One with my feet kicking in the creek on a hot day. Each picture, one small body part, one small memory. Hands. Arms. Feet. The parts I love about me, like my strength, and the parts that betray me, like my eyes." She looked at Micah, with glossy eyes that refused to cry. "And it reminded me; I am not one thing. I am not just a warrior. I am not just a daughter or a sister. I am the sum of all of my parts, each one more intricate than the next."

"This is a beautiful story," Micah told her faintly. "But I am not sure why you're telling me this."

"Because, Lumen. You are not just the guardian. You are the sum of all your parts. A son. A grandson. A lover. A fierce protector, in this realm and all others." She leaned forward in her chair to look Micah in the eye. "You are Micah Lumen, and you cannot forget the parts of you that hurt. Take it all and let it shape you, let it fill you. Allow yourself to be both imperfect and whole."

Micah looked at her, speechless. An empty space inside of him swelled with gratitude for the Fae who sat before him and saw him for his imperfections and didn't judge. His smile warmed to the thought of their blooming friendship.

He was not alone.

She returned her gaze to the desk and flipped another page of the book. Her body went rigid.

"I—"

"Be quiet, Lumen," Brax interrupted in a demand.

"What?" Micah said in frustration.

Is she kidding me right now?

Micah tried again. "I wanted to say—"

"Whole."

"Yes, I heard you. I—"

"Lumen. Not whole; hole. The hole." Her eyes sprang to his. "I found it."

"You found what?" Micah asked, confused once more.

I cannot keep up with this chick.

"The hole, Lumen. Pay attention. Look." She pointed to the page. The words were in a language he could not comprehend, but the illustration was clear as day: a large shadow covering the base of a tree with sparking light, breaking away.

"What does it say?"

"Once the portal is broken, you must keep the realm contained. An open door that cannot be closed only leads to disorder. Find the basalt, smooth as glass, and build a wall. Combine purgheny, tormald, and golden crocidolite in a wooden bowl. Add water from a local source and leaves from the tree which holds the portal. Recite the incantation and protect the realm."

"An open door?" Micah asked.

"It says the portal is broken. How could your absence have broken an ancient door?" Brax stood and paced the room anxiously. "Something does not add up."

"What are all of those ingredients? I don't think I've ever heard of them before." He peeked at the book, trying to decipher the illustrations.

"Purgheny is a mineral used long ago for cleansing purposes. Tormald is a powder, inducing courage? Or strength? Then golden crocidolite is a gemstone of sorts—used to ward off evil. But I'm not sure why they are included."

"Why? Will we have trouble finding them? Are they odd Fae ingredients?"

"No. I have seen each of these ingredients all over your property. They aren't Fae at all. They are mortal."

"Why would a Denoran spell include those things if they couldn't be found in Denora?" Micah eyed Brax with doubt.

"It wouldn't." Brax's dark eyes met Micah's. "This is not a Denoran spell."

LARGE, smooth river rocks surrounded the base of The Elderwood tree and formed a large circle. Micah continued to find more and carry them over to the tree, creating a barrier three stones high. It wasn't much, but it rose to almost the middle of Micah's leg, and he hoped it was enough.

What else does this book say?

He flipped through the pages describing the protection spell written in a language he couldn't understand. It felt pointless.

Brax had read it for him and translated how Micah was to set up the stones. When she returned from securing the perimeter, they were to finish the spell and speak the words to keep the shadow creatures within the portal. He figured if he could get the rocks in place and the ingredients spread, then there would be only the one step left.

The sun was high in the sky and sweat poured down Micah's back. The rocks weren't overly large, but he needed two hands to lift each one. He spent the previous day finding the large, smooth rocks deep in the beds of the streams that ran through the property. Searching for them and bringing them to the tree took longer than he planned.

Brax left immediately after she gathered the ingredients and gave the instructions to Micah.

This better work.

Micah was hesitant to talk to Wes or Jasper. He knew calling for help in the mirror would bring someone, but he didn't have answers to any of the questions they would ask. He had no idea how any of this happened, and it was his duty to figure it out. The only person he would have been comfortable contacting was Lucy, and he sure as hell couldn't get a hold of her since their fight.

He kept trying to remind himself that even though it had been days for him; it was only one day for her. She was probably still stewing over their argument and sitting down to dinner; not even thinking about him because it hadn't been that long since they last spoke.

Not long for her.

His mind felt like it was being cleaved in two. On one hand, he understood Lucy had important things she needed to deal with at home. She left Denora and traveled to a different realm in order to get their attention, and now she had it—this was part of her plan.

Her plan never meant to include me.

Though, now that it did involve Micah, he struggled with the other side of it all—Laurent Sloan. How could she be spending so much of her time with him?

Was it that easy to forget me?

Micah heaved the rock into place and stepped back from the tree, watching the swirling black smoke as it writhed in the split in the ground.

This black, menacing fog seemed nothing like the green, swirling magic that came out of The Elderwood to help Lucy when the forest was under attack. He couldn't understand why The Elderwood's magic seemed so different this time.

It had been days since the crack in the ground appeared. When Brax examined it she couldn't identify the type of magic that caused it. All they were able to uncover about it from the book was that it was likely due to him leaving the property, allowing the creatures of The Elderwood to find their way out.

The only problem with that theory was that Lucy said that there were never any creatures in The Elderwood—so where did they come from?

A strange humming noise bubbled up from the smokey, black pit. Micah leaned in closer, trying to figure out where the sound came from. The humming cleared, sounding more like clicking fingernails on a tabletop. The noise grew until Micah recognized it as the same chittering from when the base of the tree split open just days before.

He knelt on the ground in front of the rocks, and bent his head toward the dark, swirling mist, trying to see what was happening.

Out burst hundreds of black, shiny insects. Crawling with their many legs and arms, their sharp fangs dripped a dark red ooze.

Micah threw himself away from the rock wall. He crawled backwards on his hands and pushed the sight away as he scrambled to put distance between him and the barrage of shadow-like bugs. As he shoved himself from the wall, a rock shifted and nearly fell. He watched as the terrifying insects climbed up the tree trunk.

No, no, this can't be happening! Where is Brax?! We need this spell—now!

Micah's panicked breaths were barely heard over the calamitous noise of the disgusting creatures covering the tree with their dark shelled bodies. His eyes stayed glued to the chaos before him.

All at once, the rocks around the tree began to glow, first a deep emerald green, and then it radiated a bright violet. A high-pitched humming reverberated through the forest as the rock wall began to vibrate ever so slightly.

The bugs crawled from the tree toward the rocks and—*zap!* The purple glow became a hard barrier that the insects could not pass. They tried to climb over the rocks, but instead climbed straight up. An invisible wall kept the strange small, dark creatures contained, as they slowly spread out and covered the trunk of the tree—the sigil hidden under the many legs.

How did that even work?

The spell was not finished and the ingredients still sat in a bowl next to the tree.

A low rumble gently ruffled the leaves around him.

Not again, Micah thought as he looked at the ground in fear, worried that the earth would split further. Would the shaking cause the rocks to fall? Could it split the wall apart?

But it wasn't a rumble similar to what he had heard before. No. It was more of a purring growl. Deep in his bones, Micah realized exactly what it was.

The shadow beast.

Micah took another step back, but then stopped.

My purpose is to protect, he reminded himself. *It's the same as protecting and serving those in need in my precinct. This should be no different. I can defend The Elderwood.*

He looked at the forest around him and the cabin nearby, a surge of deference flowing through him.

"I can defend my home."

He picked up a thick piece of wood from near the fire pit. He prepared to use it as a weapon, but hoped and prayed that the creature wouldn't breach the rock barrier he had created.

An enormous black paw made of smoke emerged from the black haze and slammed itself down on the ground with a distinct thump. Micah stilled, looking at the sharp claws shining menacingly.

It was only made of mist and fog. How could the creature's paw have made that much noise?

The crack in the ground was only a few feet wide, and as the creature emerged, its body took shape. Another paw, then its muzzle and head—all hidden by the dense haze filling the circle around the tree. Once the entire body broke through the crack, it started to solidify.

The paws and legs were first, the swirling mist receding and revealing the dark fur of a large feline creature. Then the body, muscular and strong, sleek fur shining in the light of day, its tail swinging ominously. Last, its face came into view—dark, swirling misty eyes, shadowed with black and swirls of yellow. Its teeth, dark and rotten, dripped a foul ooze, just as the bugs had.

The shadow beast focused on Micah and crouched down low before leaping at the barrier.

BOOM! It struck the wall and Micah's body shuddered in fear. He searched frantically for a break in the barrier. His lungs squeezed with dread, knowing that once the beast was out, he would have more trouble than he could handle.

I don't even know what I'm looking for. Where the hell is Brax?

The enclosure strained, but the shadow beast stayed contained.

This only made the feline more angry, snarling so loudly it shook the leaves on the trees. The bugs chittered away, nervously crawling over one another, trying to run from the sinister beast, dripping in shadow and rage.

Micah stood his ground, staring at the creature, swinging his make-shift bat in his hand, prepared to defend his new life.   .

The shadow creature took a leap at the barrier again, and still, it held.

Damn, this thing is big.

It lurked down low, hiding itself in the smoke that had seeped from the crack since its arrival. The beast pushed its muzzle at the rocks, pawing some of them with quick, purposeful strikes.

It's testing the rocks, looking for a weak spot.

Micah scanned the rocks quickly, praying that there was no point of weakness to be found. Then, he remembered the rock that moved when the bugs arrived.

No.

He sprinted toward the wall, hoping to push the rock back into position, but the shadow cat got there first. With all of its strength, the beast swatted the stones. The barrier held for a moment, but the force of the hit was enough to cause the rocks to shift. The cat's eyes met Micah's in a terrifyingly intelligent gaze as he reached out to stabilize the rocks. Micah froze, and his heart shuddered in fear.

It's going to get through.

The beast slammed its paws once more, and the barrier quaked, the glow of the rocks blinking in and out. Micah held his breath. It slammed again. The barrier sputtered, the light dissipating before illuminating once more.

No, no, no.

His wide eyes watched as the yellow-eyed beast reared up once more. *SLAM.* With one final hit, and the rock tumbled away and the purple glow of the light died completely.

Micah's heart threatened to give out on him. He stood rooted to the spot as the dark mist spread further from the tree. He tried to listen for the sound of the prowling beast over his erratic breathing, but it was no use.

One of the chittering bugs crawled on top of the rock wall. Micah watched it closely, his eyes darting between the bug on the stone and the shadow cat crouching in the smoke.

The insect slowly crawled from the side of the rock to the top, and then flew away. Out of the barrier.

Fuck.

The cat pounced out of the boundary in Micah's direction as he took three large steps back. The beast seemed to grow with each second; its colossal head coming up to the middle of Micah's torso.

Glancing at the branch in his hands, Micah prayed it was thick enough to do some damage to this beast without breaking and leaving him weaponless.

The cat prowled around him, like a lion playing with its food. With each step the beast took, the muscles in its body seemed to shift underneath.

The creature was pure force, but Micah wouldn't back down. He had too much to do here. He was the guardian. Besides, he still needed to work things out with Lucy—for her, he would move mountains.

Man, I could really use some of that Elderwood magic now.

The beast leapt toward him with a snarl, its teeth dripping a foul slime, prepared to tear the flesh from his bones. Micah swung the wood with all of his might, steering the creature off course, but not leaving much of an injury.

"Come on!" Micah yelled, adrenaline surging through his body, prepared to end this.

Again, the shadow beast crouched down low, staring directly at Micah, and jumped with claws unsheathed, ready to slash into him.

Micah whirled the branch again, just hitting the muzzle of the beast. The oozing liquid coming from its mouth covered the edge of the piece of wood, making it fizzle and disintegrate before him. The wood splintered and popped as it shriveled into nothing, and Micah had to throw what remained at the beast, hoping to push it astray as sharp talons swiped at him once more.

Micah, weaponless, sprinted in the opposite direction. His heart pounded in his chest, threatening to burst. His wide eyes scanned his surroundings, desperately searching for a weapon he could use against the monstrous creature—anything to hurtle at the beast trying to flay him alive.

A small pile of wood was stacked on the border of the forest—remnants and small sticks from The Elderwood that did not make their way back with Lucy. Micah shot a look behind him as he continued to run and saw the insects crawling through the forest. Their clicking legs brought them through the swirling mist as they abandoned their sanctuary of The Elderwood tree, becoming a scourge on the forest. The leaves in the trees shook violently under the tremendous weight of hundreds of insects as they aggressively claimed their fresh territory.

The shadow beast slunk back and forth, weaving its way closer to Micah; a slinking prowl, making the hair on Micah's arms stand on end. He put his back to the trees and found the sharp edge of a branch. Micah held out the short, thick stick as if he were brandishing a pocket knife. His hands trembled as panic washed over him.

"So, you're not afraid of me, huh?" Micah taunted the beast. "Well, I'm not afraid of you, either."

It was a lie, of course, but Micah wouldn't run from this. His chances of getting into the cabin were slim to none, and the beast would not leave him alive. There was only one option left—he would not let the creature devour him without a fight.

The shadow creature paused and crouched to the ground. Micah barely spotted it as it jetted out of the grass, darting toward him with full force. Micah held his ground and then ducked and rolled out of the way, making the creature miss him and clamber into the trees.

"Here kitty, kitty, kitty," Micah jeered.

He stood firm, his knees and elbows bent, ready to change course on a dime. He clutched the scrap of wood tightly, desperate to come out of this alive.

The feline gripped its claws into the ground to steady itself, keeping its swirling gold and black eyes on Micah, refusing to move quickly, eyeing its prey in a slow stalk.

When it reached a close enough distance, the beast stopped,

crouched, and pounced on him. Micah went down in a heap, the massive form of the beast crushing him beneath its weight. The snarl that escaped the creature made a trail of ooze slide from its teeth, falling to the grass just next to Micah's head, making the grass sizzle and burn.

The creature's head lifted with another deep growl. *THUMP.* Something shook the beast as it howled in pain. It took a step back, one paw moving from Micah's shoulder down to the ground.

With a freed arm, he sliced the face of the shadow creature with the stick he had grabbed, cutting across the beast's eye and causing it to shriek in agony.

It retreated from Micah quickly, getting away from the sharp piece of wood in Micah's hands.

"Lumen!" Brax called, running over with a spear in hand, her Fae speed astounding.

A silver spear stuck out from the back of the shadow beast, making it limp in pain.

"What the hell is happening?" Micah shouted as he and Brax kept their eyes on the creature. "Where the fuck have you been?"

The beast thrashed violently, shaking the spear loose. They stood, watching in utter shock, as the beast healed itself in an instant. The spear didn't affect it at all. There was no mark, no blood—nothing. However, the slice Micah left across the beast's face continued to gush a dark red blood, coating its black fur.

Micah backed up farther, thankful for Brax's timely entrance. There was no way he could have survived without her intervening.

The shadow beast looked at them with furious, yellow eyes. Brax stood at the ready, prepared to engage the creature, and Micah gripped the piece of wood as if his life depended on it—because it very much did.

The creature backed away slowly, slinking into the shadows surrounding The Elderwood tree, and Micah raced over to the rocks to rebuild the barrier, checking each stone carefully.

Brax followed him, checking his body insistently.

"Lumen," she called as he kept checking the barrier. "Lumen, are you hurt?" She continued to scan him for injuries, but could not get a good look at him as he hurriedly moved from rock to rock.

"Micah, stop!" she yelled, causing him to finally halt.

He took a deep breath, sat down on the ground a few feet away from the rock circle, and sighed in defeat.

Brax knelt in front of him to get his full attention. "Are you hurt?" Her eyes were wide with concern.

"No," he said simply.

She placed her hands on his shoulders and closed her eyes. He waited as her silvery magic spread from her fingers, magically checking him for bodily harm. She nodded, opened her eyes, and released a brief sigh of relief. Finally appeased, she sat next to him, watching their surroundings: the tree, Micah, and whatever might creep up behind him.

"What happened?"

Micah chewed on the inside of his lip, looked to the sky, and ran his hands through his hair and down his neck. "I was nearly done with the rock circle, and some scary ass bugs came out of the crack. The barrier, though... it worked. It was glowing purple, keeping all the creatures in. Then that big ass cat appeared and tried to eat me."

"It worked?" Brax said in astonishment.

"Yeah, you told me to move all the stones and get the stuff where it needed to be, so I did." He pointed at the rock wall he created and the wooden bowl of ingredients needed for the spell off to the side of the tree. "No help from you, I might add," he murmured.

"But it shouldn't have worked." She stood in a rush, checking the barrier and spinning back to look at Micah, her hair flipping with her quick movements.

He stood angrily. "Why would you tell me to do something knowing it wasn't going to work? What the hell, Brax? I thought you were on my side here?"

"Lumen, enough with the misaligned anger. It shouldn't have worked because you are not Fae." She stepped up to him, meeting his gaze. "I assumed you would prepare it and we would call in a Baum or Lord Sloan to finish the spell... Even I cannot create Fae magic the way the ancients have."

"What?" Micah's head pulled back, trying to comprehend what she had just said.

"Micah. You did magic."

FIFTEEN

LUCY

Her exchange with Micah had upset her more than she cared to admit, but there was nothing to be done about it now. She understood he was far away, dealing with his own issues, but Lucy wished she could be there to help him. She couldn't believe another female was alone with him.

How improper.

She clicked her tongue as she shifted in her seat in the garden. Though really, hadn't she just done the same with Micah? And hadn't she spent alone time with Laurent, as well?

Laurent. She groaned.

Everything was becoming more complicated. She looked out at the many flowers in the garden, appreciating their beauty in this quiet space. It was so rare for her to have a moment of peace. Her mother's bright red roses made her stomach coil with unease... She still had not forgiven her mother since their conversation, but she knew she'd have to speak with her soon enough.

The jangle of chains announced Jasper's arrival before she laid eyes on him. "Your father wants to speak with you," his oily tone declared as soon as he walked onto the garden terrace.

Lucy had barely sat down to warm herself in the sun before she was ushered off yet again. She wasn't sure when she would get her much needed time to think.

Nodding begrudgingly, she walked to her father's office, Jasper tight on her tail. After overhearing their conversation the day before, Lucy was careful with her words around him.

She knew this conversation with her father was imminent since her evening with Lord Sloan—but what Jasper had to do with it; she had little idea. His presence steadily increased since she had returned from Joterra, and any time she saw him was always too soon.

"What did you do this time?" Jasper whispered to her in the hall as they walked.

"Excuse me?" Lucy whirled to look at him, the image of the burned corpse at the front of her mind.

What does he know?

"What happened with Lord Sloan at dinner that has your father so determined to see you?" He took a brisk step toward her. "What did you tell him? What did you see?"

Lucy took a compulsive step back, creating a distance between herself and this odious male who kept provoking her.

"I don't know what you're talking about," Lucy lied.

Don't worry, I won't tell my father about your secret discussion with Laurent. Yet.

Rolling her eyes, she spun away from him. "Get out of my way so I can speak with my father." And with that, she upped her speed, and made it to her father's office without another comment from Jasper, much to his dismay.

"Hello, Father," Lucy said politely, entering the room.

"My little flower," Corvus boomed with a smile on his face. "Sit, darling."

Lucy's heart ached. It had been so long since she had talked to her father with such ease. He was happy and light, and seeing him this way almost made Lucy feel the same.

"Lord Sloan called in and said he had a wonderful evening with you." His full cheeks rose on either side of his face. "He was insistent on seeing you again today and asked if you would be interested in a carriage ride around the countryside. He is very keen to get to know you."

A flutter of anxiousness filled Lucy and her heart sank. This was not what she had in mind when she had planned to sway him away from her. Now he wanted more of her company? A sudden and unexpected thrill ran through her.

When he could have his pick of any female in all of Denora, why me?

Lucy bowed her head to hide her sudden unwelcome blush. "When will he arrive?"

"Soon," Corvus said, looking fondly on his daughter. "Lucella, I know that you have had a hard time accepting the roles of life here in Denora after I have spoiled you for so many years, but I appreciate you being more open to spend time with Lord Sloan."

"Father—" Lucy began, trying to explain.

"No. There's no need." He held a hand up to stop her. "I know this was not what you wanted, but I hope that you are also finding joy in Lord Sloan's company. I want you to be happy, darling. I want you taken care of." The softness in his eyes was new to Lucy and made her heart hurt. "I only want what is best."

There was not a word she could say to combat that. Of course, a father would only want what's best for his daughter. However, now that she knew her father could be compelled to listen to her, perhaps the only person she had left to convince was Laurent himself. She was certain she could dissuade him of this agreement.

Then, I'll be free...

Her heart wouldn't allow her to think on the topic any longer as her father stood to give orders to Jasper. "Prepare the carriages, and put Thomas on escort duty."

"Sir," Jasper's smarmy voice creaked out. "I would prefer to go with Miss Lucella, if you would accept. I do not want Lord Sloan and his guards having to deal with numerous Fae while here, sire." He gave a deep, ass-kissing bow, making Lucy roll her eyes.

Please, not another moment with him.

Corvus barely gave him a second look as Jasper's head was so close to the floor he could have licked it. "No business; just keep my daughter safe," he said in a quiet, threatening voice.

Jasper rose from the ground and the two men's eyes met; there was no mistaking the threat that loomed in the air. Jasper quickly dropped his gaze, bowing once again as Lucy left to prepare, wondering what the day's events held in store for her.

Laurent's carriage was subtly beautiful. It did not have the bright red velvet of the Baum's carriage, nor did it have the exquisite brass adornments. The metal rails of the carriage were an understated matte black and the material of the cushion was a soft leather, lined with fur on the edges for comfort.

"I don't think I've ever seen a carriage like this," Lucy said as she fluffed the soft fur in her hands.

"The Northern Territory gets quite frigid," Laurent explained from his seat across from Lucy. "Here in the Central Territory, the weather changes over time, but in the north, it is always cold."

"Don't you miss the warmth?" Lucy asked, genuinely curious.

"There are ways to find warmth in the dead of winter," Laurent suggested with a glint in his eye.

Lucy blushed under her pale yellow gown. She opted for something simple with soft gold leaves embroidered in the hemline. She was still so far from Micah, but she was doing everything within her power to find ways to feel close to him. She even wore her hair down, the way he liked.

"But yes," Laurent changed the topic, looking out the open window into the grassy plains before them. "I do miss the warmth of the sun on a beautiful spring day. Speaking of which, I hope you don't mind that today I have planned an outdoor adventure for us."

"Outdoor? Adventure?" she asked with sparked interest. His eyes met hers with intrigue.

"Yes," he laughed. "It seems to me you are not the typical female from Denora, and rumor has it you are involved in your father's business?"

Lucy looked away from Laurent and back to the landscape. They were approaching a tree line that reminded her even more of The Elderwood. She clenched her right fist.

"Unfortunately, my father does not believe females should be in the workforce and does not allow me to grow any further in the busi-ness." She looked at him, square in the eye, her face devoid of emotion. "He would rather I marry you."

Laurent's face dropped, but for a fraction of a second, his eyes flashed an emotion she could not read. It wasn't surprise, nor was it humor... was it... agitation?

"I'm sorry that you are put in this awkward situation, Miss Lucella."

"If you call me Lucella one more time, I am going to jump from the carriage and walk home."

Shock and surprise filled Laurent's face, causing Lucy to laugh.

"I'm sorry, it is habit." Laurent looked at her as if for the first time, smiling in astonishment at what sat before him. "You are remarkable. I really do mean what I said. I'm sorry that this is not what you want. If—"

"I would prefer not to talk about this topic at this moment, if you don't mind. It is a beautiful day and you've promised me an outdoor adventure and I'd much rather do that." Lucy couldn't believe she interrupted him, but she couldn't bear the topic a second longer. She was with Micah just the day before and now she was courting Laurent yet again?

Maybe Micah was right.

Laurent nodded and stopped talking. His lips still turned in amusement.

"However," Lucy stated as she looked around at the horses carrying Laurent's guards and the lone carriage ferrying Jasper. "I'm not sure my escort will be impressed with an outdoor adventure." She would do just about anything to remove herself from Jasper's presence.

"Ah, yes, about that." Laurent slipped from his seat and moved across to where Lucy sat alone. Lucy's breath hitched at the nearness. Laurent moved close enough to whisper in her ear. "What would you think about it just being me and you?"

She turned to look at him and he was mere inches away. When she went to speak, he delicately placed one warm finger over her lips to remind her to talk as quietly as possible—Fae hearing carried.

He removed his finger, and Lucy delicately bit her lip. The warmth of his finger lingered and her insides flipped with surprise.

Leaning in, she whispered in his ear in a challenge. "What did you have in mind?"

Without moving, she waited for his response as his mouth angled up her neck and toward her ear. His featherlight breath sent a chill down her spine, pebbling her skin and stirring an emotion she was not expecting. "Stay close to me, and pardon my hands. I have to hold you close for this to work."

Her head jerked back in surprise as she met his ice-blue eyes. With her mouth slightly open, she nodded subtly.

Laurent looked from her open, pouty lips, back to her wide, eager eyes. He put an arm behind her, placing his hand on her hip, and with one quick swoop, lifted her onto his lap, keeping a firm grasp on her back. He put his other hand across her lap and clasped his hands together to hold her against him.

She wrapped an arm around his shoulders and allowed her hand to lie on his chest. He gave a mischievous wink and a second later, he was standing, holding her in his arms in the middle of a small clearing deep in the woods.

Lucy gasped, tightening her grip on his shoulders as he held her with his strong hands.

He gently placed her on the ground as she turned and looked at the scene around her. Off to one side, a blanket with a full spread of food was placed on the soft grassy earth, supplied with wine and simple goblets. A large swing hung from a nearby tree, large enough to fit four people, piled with blankets and pillows for added comfort. Beautiful red flowers decorated their space. They twined in the swing ropes and lay scattered around the forest floor.

Lucy looked on, astonished. The amount of magic and time it would have taken to create such a beautiful atmosphere was jarring. Each rose brought stunning allure to the space. No one had ever made such a play for her heart this way.

Is all of this for me?

Then, in the center of the clearing, rested an archery target with a bow and arrows.

"How?" was the only word she could get out.

"It seemed from our recent night, fine dining is not quite your area of comfort, nor mine." Laurent smiled and held her hand as she took a deep breath in, the perfume of the flowers filling her with so much joy. "I much prefer to get to know someone for who they truly are, and you are just captivating."

She looked at the bow, spinning around to face him, her face bright and youthful. "How did you bring us here?"

"I am a very powerful Fae, *Lucy*," he said, emphasizing her name without any titles. "I am able to use magic similar to a conjuring spell if I work the incantation just right. It is far enough from the carriages that they won't hear us, but close enough so that I can return us when they have made their turn to complete the trip back to your estate."

"We get to shoot out here?" Her smile lit up her entire face.

He nodded, and she involuntarily used her Fae speed to swiftly reach the bow and hold it in her hands.

Lucy's blood hummed when her skin came into contact with the delicate wood from The Elderwood—it was one of her father's bows. The rush she felt was immense. She twirled the bow in her hands once before lifting an arrow. Her eyes were wild as she took aim. The speeding arrow pierced the center of the target, exiting the other side of the hay bale holding it in place.

"Excellent!" Laurent cheered from where he stood by the food, his attention solely on her. "Where did you learn to shoot like this?"

"It's in my blood," she said, hinting at her family's history within the bowyer business, but also offering a subtle nod to the ancient magic bestowed upon her from The Elderwood. Her hand tingled with the memory, not so much a pulsing, throbbing pain like it usually was. It was as if the magic was giving a faint approval.

She placed the bow down and sat on the blanket, her knees curled in front of her as she carefully smoothed out her gown. The small clearing in the forest was set up entirely for them. He supplied the picnic with savory snacks and delicious sweets, and the pillows and blankets were soft and luxurious.

Laurent did all of this for me.

She toyed with a soft flower petal between her fingers.

Me.

"Do you like it?" he asked her as she looked around, a smile softening her face.

"It's unbelievable," she shared in a daze. "This is..." She couldn't find the words. Never in all of her years had someone gone out of their way to make Lucy feel so treasured.

"I want you to know that I want you to be yourself around me. I don't want to change you. You are headstrong, but polite. Beautiful, but without vanity. I appreciate you allowing me your company, even when you do not wish to move forward with this arrangement your father has created for you."

Lucy looked away. He knew she didn't want to marry him, and yet he did all of this. Was he the one now trying to win over Lucy? His hand touched her knee delicately, making Lucy look up at Laurent.

"I do not fault you for these feelings," he said gently. "I merely want us to get to know one another."

"I would like that," she admitted. And it was true. Spending time with Laurent was a welcome surprise. Lucy reveled in the attention he gave her; his eyes that saw only her.

"As would I." His light blue tunic seemed to make his eyes brighten even more. "Please, tell me everything. I'd love to know more about you."

"Oh, there isn't much to tell," Lucy shared shyly, popping a cube of cheese into her mouth to avoid talking.

What is happening here? Wasn't I supposed to be dissuading him of our potential arrangement?

"I doubt that," he said as he helped himself to a piece of bread, removing his hand from her leg. "What I know of you so far is that you are the breath-taking daughter of Corvus Baum. You are an expert marksman, and you don't seem to be affected by wealth, status, or material things. Did I miss anything?"

"If you think a sentence could sum up my life, then carry on believing that," Lucy said with a devilish grin.

"I would never stoop so far as to assume you are anything less than enchanting," he said, looking into her eyes, trying to find an answer to a question he had not asked.

"I'm not sure why you keep saying I am this intriguing, enchanting Fae. I am not one to play humble, but let us please speak in realities. I offer no wealth, no great beauty, and no abundant knowledge. I am not sure what you gain from my presence."

The constant compliments were starting to overwhelm Lucy. He barely knew her and seemed completely taken with her—why?

He needs to see that we are not the match he believes us to be.

"I feel as though you are always truthful with me, and that is very odd for a male in my position," Laurent admitted. His arm hung over his bent knee as he spoke, his hair blowing freely in the breeze. "I have a knack for knowing when I am being lied to, though it doesn't seem to me that you have told me a single false statement since I've met you."

"Well, I did say it was a pleasure to meet you, didn't I?"

Laurent barked a laugh. "Well, my heart has been cleaved." He put two hands over his chest in mock heartbreak. "I guess that is true, though hopefully you feel differently now."

"I do," she said quietly.

"That was true?" he asked, full of surprise.

"I thought you said you had a knack for this?" Lucy teased.

"With you, there is just something I can't seem to put my finger on. I'm not sure I can tell with you," he said as he looked at her intently, trying to read her very mind. "I don't know why."

Lucy began to feel unnerved, being watched so intently. She hugged her knees close to her body and tried not to make eye contact, instead looking around at the beautiful afternoon before them.

Surely, he means no harm if he did all of this for me, could he?

"What do you want to know?" Lucy asked finally.

Perhaps I can twist my answers to get him to stand down. Maybe if he truly respects me, he will also respect my choice to say no.

He looked at her seriously, eyeing her attentively. "What's your favorite color?"

"What?" Lucy laughed. Her cheeks hurt from the smiles he uncovered.

"It is a very important question," Laurent said in false sincerity, a quirk in his lips admitting his humor.

"Well, then in that case I must answer honestly, now shouldn't I? Hmm. Some days I prefer yellow, because it reminds me of the sun. Others I prefer green, because it reminds me of the calmness of the forest. Red because it reminds me of the roses in my mother's gardens. Even brown," she said, immediately seeing Micah's deep brown eyes searing into her with intensity. She looked at the trees, trying to find the words she needed, but her heart was stuck on Micah.

She stood quickly, blood rushing through her body, making her lightheaded.

Micah. What am I doing here?

She walked over to the swing and sat, trying to create some distance. Her fingers ran over the soft fabric, taking deep breaths to calm herself. Sitting back, she closed her eyes. With Fae finesse, not a sound was heard as Laurent came and sat beside her.

"Did I upset you?" he asked her quietly.

"It's just complicated." Lucy opened her eyes and looked at her company—a male of status and prestige, whose focus was entirely on her.

They sat in silence for a long while, appreciating the world around them. Even with the awkward moment they had experienced, the quiet solitude of the forest gave Lucy the confidence that she needed to say the words she had feared.

"I enjoy my company with you, Lord Sloan. I never believed that it would happen, but you are not the Fae I thought you to be, and I am sorry for assuming otherwise. However, I am not sure I am ready to wed." She looked at Laurent with honesty and fear in her eyes.

"I meant it when I said I just wanted you to be yourself. I would never try to change you. Life can be like this—easy and full of wonder. I want a wife who will never lie to me and a partner who shares the same ideals as I do."

He took her chin in his hand, lightly directing her eyes to his. Lucy held her breath, wondering how a male could have such an affect on her. It was as though his eyes looked through her, directly into her soul.

"I see so much life and adventure in you, and I feel you mirror so much of what I stand for. You are exquisite and truly one of a kind. Any would be a fool to ever pass up a chance at a lifetime with you."

"That is what you ask of me? A lifetime?" Lucy's heart fell as another male tried to dictate the landscape of her future.

"Perhaps a chance?"

"A chance seems reasonable." A small smile grew upon her face, as she looked into the eyes of this potential friend.

Laurent didn't want her to change, he wanted her as she was. Maybe her feelings for Micah weren't enough for things to work between them... Laurent wanted to make the realm a better place... Maybe this was a better path for her.

A chance.

"I'm glad you agree."

Lucy peered up into the sky—the sun had moved across the horizon, signaling the passing time. "We should probably be getting on our way, should we not? The last thing we need is my father's assistant realizing we are gone."

At the change of subject, Laurent's demeanor shifted. "Ah, yes. Jasper," he said with an annoyed sigh. "I find it interesting that your father had picked him as partner."

"Why do you say that?"

"He is not as he seems. It is as though he can't decide his true desire in life." His face twisted into a grimace.

"How would you know so much about Jasper?"

Why does it feel like there is something important I'm missing here... His true desires? Does this have to do with their argument at dinner?

"As I said, I can read people quite well, and that male is an open book. Be careful around him, Lucy."

His ominous suggestion made Lucy's stomach tie in knots. Hadn't she always suspected something was amiss with Jasper? He was the one pushing for this arranged marriage. Didn't she see Jasper and Laurent discussing something that clearly upset Laurent?

What could it have been?

"You know, others have warned me about you as well," Lucy said carefully. She wasn't sure if Lord Sloan would take this poorly, but she needed to know. "Why do others fear you? There has been talk of attacks on the Northerners."

"Ah," Laurent sat back and nodded, pursing his lips in a concealed smirk. "Let me ask you this, Lucy," he said as he looked deeply into her eyes. "If I were to tell you that there was a safe place in Denora, where females could make their own decisions in their life, where less fortunate Fae were not ignored, where wealth and status did not equate to importance, and where all Fae could pave whatever path they wanted for their future—not just follow in their family's footsteps—what would you say?"

"I would say that it sounds like a dream," Lucy said honestly.

"Yes," Laurent replied, nodding seriously. "Many would feel the same. But the other territories of Denora would then lose much of their population to the north, would they not?"

Lucy nodded.

"It is much easier for the majority of Denora to spread lies and create fear than deal with the reality that maybe something is wrong with how things are traditionally done here; maybe Denora has work to do."

Whatever Lucy had expected him to say—it was surely not that. She stared at him in awe, hesitant to believe such a male existed in Denora. And here, with her, no less.

"Let's get one more round of target practice in, shall we?" He cheerily changed the subject. "We can't let all the trouble of me getting this bow for you go to waste. I need to see the Queen of the Archers in her element."

"Queen of Archers is a bit extravagant," Lucy laughed. "Though I will never turn down practice."

She took his hand and followed him to the target. Lifting the bow and arrow, she looked at Laurent, who again watched her closely.

"Would you like a lesson?" she asked with a teasing lilt to her voice.

Laurent's smile spread across his face, lighting him up like a young boy. "From you? I would be honored."

He used his Fae speed to advance directly behind Lucy, his presence sending flutters down her center. He put his face close to hers, whispering, "I'm ready when you are, my queen."

Lucy's breathing came in uneven breaths now.

My queen.

It sent shivers down her spine and an ache of wanting need. She pursed her lips, taking a slow breath and lifted her arms into position.

Laurent slid his hands down her arms. "Hold the bow like this?"

Lucy met his gaze and nodded, biting her lower lip. She looked to her target and pulled her arrow back.

His hands slid on top of hers, heat seeping from his body, making her legs quiver. She feared her heart would combust; the intimate touches sending her body reeling.

Laurent slid his hand along her arm, then down her side, just missing the curve of her breast as it stopped gently on her hip.

"Show me your magic, my queen."

*I*F HE CALLS *me his queen one more time, I believe I'm going to combust.*

Lucy's head spun with the thrill of showing off her archery ability to Laurent in their secret cove in the forest. Arrow after arrow, she hit her target, and with each hit, Laurent cheered her on. He wasn't afraid to get close to her, and each word felt as though he placed her above him.

My queen.

Two simple words had never affected her this way before.

Her right hand throbbed, the magic begging to come out to play.

"We should probably take a break," Lucy said, beaming.

"Unfortunately, it is nearly time for us to return." Laurent tucked a stray hair behind her ear, the action reminiscent of Micah.

It sobered her thoughts quickly.

"What about all of this?" She looked around at the beautiful setting he created for them.

"I will have it taken care of."

"This truly was an amazing day for me," Lucy said gratefully. It was so easy to be around Laurent and she could see herself forming a friendship with him. "I'm sorry we did not get to talk more and that the majority of our time was spent with me shooting."

"You are a force to behold," he said with an earnest smile. "I could probably watch you do that all day long." He walked with her to the picnic set up and grabbed a small bundle of flowers, tucking them behind her ear. He paused and stared at her with wonderment. "You are breathtaking."

Lucy felt the blush come to her cheeks. As she tried to hide it, he delicately took her chin and pulled her face back to his.

"Don't hide your beauty from me," he caressed her cheek with his thumb. His eyes were hungry and his lips were parted. "I will be thinking about this day for a very long time. And the pink of your lips and cheeks is something that is sure to keep me up at night."

Lucy's core melted in his gaze. She straightened her posture to counter his unyielding stare with a show of confidence. Their smiles mirrored one another.

He took her hand and walked her over to the swing, sitting. "If you don't mind, you can take your place back upon my lap and I will transport us to the carriage."

Normally, Lucy would feel out of place and uncomfortable with such a proposition—but there was nothing uncomfortable about Laurent any longer. She blushed as she sat on his lap; not from embarrassment, but because her thoughts had strayed to an unlady-like topic.

Lucy scooted her body so that her legs were high on his thighs. She wrapped an arm around his neck and didn't think twice about their intimate closeness. He put a hand around her back, his fingers gripping the top of her round bottom. His other hand slid up her thigh, keeping her in place.

He leaned in and whispered in her ear. "Don't make a noise." Then he inched closer to her until their lips were nearly touching. "Close your eyes," he whispered to her seductively.

She obeyed, a forbidden thrill of desire running through her.

His lips touched hers, lightly, and the surprise made her gasp.

Laurent covered her mouth with his own, and he kissed her more deeply, firmly pressing his lips on hers.

To her utter astonishment, she kissed him back.

It was rushed, yet slow—their lips kissing and tasting each other. Lucy slid her tongue across his, and he gripped her hips more firmly as she remained in his lap. She let out a breathy sigh, and he captured her lower lip, silencing her again as he gently sucked on it, making Lucy's insides blaze with need.

His hands slid over her thighs, up the back of her yellow dress, until he held her face delicately in his firm embrace. Their passionate kiss grew as Laurent pulled her closer and closer. The movement caused Lucy to clench her thighs together, yearning for more friction between her and Micah.

No.

Laurent.

Oh my stars!

Lucy opened her eyes and pulled away from the kiss in horror. "I'm sorry, I can't," Lucy told Laurent, putting her hands on his chest to stop his advances, looking down in shame.

"I'm sorry, Lucy." Laurent's cheeks had a hint of red in them, more color than she had ever seen on him. "I guess we got a little carried away." He gave her a half smile with an apologetic look on his face. "That was much too forward of me," he shook his head. "It will not happen again."

She nodded as she slid from his lap into the cushioned seat next to her. She looked around in shock. "We are back in the carriage?"

"Yes," he smiled again, looking at her intently. "Are you... alright?" Concern laced his tone.

Lucy took a deep breath, straightened the bodice of her dress, and sighed. She looked at Laurent. He sat next to her with his hair tousled, his clothing slightly askew, and the most vulnerable look on his face. His eyes searched hers as he sat completely still, waiting with bated breath to hear her response.

"Yes, Lord Sloan —"

"Laurent."

Lucy looked at him in bafflement.

He is the Lord of the Northern Territory. Surely, he cannot expect me to call him by his first name.

"Sir, it would not be proper."

"Lucy, you just sucked on my tongue. I think we can drop the formalities when it is just you and I."

Lucy let out a huff of laughter, shaking her head. She hid her blushing face in her hands. "I did that, didn't I?"

He reached over and took her hands away from her face, holding one to his cheek. "You don't see me complaining, do you?" He smiled again. "Please, Lucy. Are you okay?"

"I am." She smiled at him. Though that was a lie, and not her first. She was not alright. She practically mauled Laurent right after she berated Micah for even assuming she would ever do that.

"Please. You can be truthful with me. You do not look fine." He kept her hand in his, bringing it down to her lap.

"I think I am just overwhelmed by our connection." *Truth.*

"That's all?"

"I want to get to know you more before things move in that direction." *Truth.*

"And you wish to move forward with the arrangement?" His fingers gave a small squeeze to hers as he held her hand.

"Perhaps. I have not decided." *Truth?*

How in all the realms is that possible?

"I'm sorry to keep interrogating you. I just want to understand. Is… is there someone else?"

"No." *Lie.*

"I appreciate your honesty with me, Lucy," he said with a sigh, leaning back into his seat with relief.

"Then maybe you can unleash one of your truths on me, to even the score." Lucy said, scooting back, creating more space between her and the beautiful Fae male who made her insides curl with desire. She grinned to alleviate the tension she felt inside, but she wasn't sure if it was working in her favor.

Her cheeks flushed, and she fanned at her face, trying to rid herself of the redness she was certain covered her.

Laurent slid closer to her, returning her grin. "I have a secret, but I think I can trust you with it. If I share this with you, Lucy, do you promise not to share it with anyone else?"

"Yes, of course." *Lie.*

He smiled from ear to ear, then glanced out the window to see their location. "We are almost back, but I do not want others to overhear." He did a quick privacy charm, much smaller than his extravagant show in the restaurant. This bubble barely contained the two Fae, making it unknown to anyone outside of the carriage.

"I told you I have a knack for knowing when others are honest with me?"

Lucy nodded, remembering the conversation. Her heart raced with the urgency exuding from Laurent.

"Well, it is not just a knack. It is a magical ability."

Lucy stilled.

I've been lying to him.

"It is?"

"Yes. And you, my queen," he looked at her with adoration. "You are an open book. You are honest and kind and completely breathtaking. I trust you implicitly with this secret, as you are to be my wife." The color brightened in his cheeks once more.

Lucy stared at him in stunned silence, eyes wide. Her mouth popped open in surprise, unsure of what to say next.

No.

He spoke with a fervor she had not seen. "You are remarkable, and I cannot wait to marry you, Lucy. I've never met someone who didn't lie in my presence—even the smallest amount. You care for the poor the way I do. You do not think about wealth and status the way the other female Denorans do. You. My queen. My future wife. You are my equal."

He held her hands in his and kissed them tenderly.

Lucy had no words. She had failed miserably at getting Laurent to see her as unworthy. Why did she not try harder? How did she fall to his whims so easily?

The horses came to an abrupt stop and Laurent removed his privacy charm and slid to the other side of the carriage, creating the proper space.

Thank the stars, Lucy thought, relieved to not have to respond to that very surprising declaration. Her mind was racing. *How could he not tell when I lied?*

A sharp rap on the door made Lucy jump, but the interruption was greatly appreciated.

"Miss Lucella," Jasper's shrewd voice came from the other side of the carriage. He opened the door and stuck out his thick, sweaty palm for her to hold as she exited.

Lucy gave a quick apologetic glance to Laurent, opened the door to leave the carriage, then grabbed Jasper's hand for him to escort her out. As soon as her right hand touched his, her palm began to sting and burn.

"Ouch!" she gasped as she pulled away, taking a step away from him on the uneven path. She held her fist tight against her chest and peeked down, opening her hand so only she could see. The lines of her scar were bright red, the magic within her writhing in pain.

"Miss Lucy! Are you hurt?" Laurent sped out of the carriage to assist, but Lucy closed her hand tightly once more, hiding it under her other arm.

"I'm fine," she lied again. "It must just be sore from recent target practice."

Jasper's accusing glare landed on Lucy with disgust. "Your father has told you that you are done with the archery business." A wry smile came over his face. "Just wait until he hears about this."

Laurent forced Jasper out of the way as he grabbed Lucy's left hand and escorted her out of the carriage. Then he turned to Jasper with a look of utter rage.

Laurent's eyes were wide, his pale skin now devoid of any color —even his hair seemed more stark white than it had been. He quickly flicked his hand in the air, creating a privacy bubble around himself and Jasper, leaving Lucy and the guards to only guess what was being said.

Jasper seemed to crumble under Laurent's words, sinking low into a bow of apology and obedience. Laurent's shoulders shook with each word he spoke, and Jasper stayed glued to the ground.

A moment later, Laurent relaxed and straightened his shoulders, returning to full height. He removed the privacy barrier and turned to Lucy, leaving Jasper groveling in the dirt.

"I apologize for his rudeness to you, Miss Lucy. He will not speak to you in that manner again."

Jasper rose from the ground, giving a panicked look to Lucy and Laurent, unsure of what to say. He gave a slight nod to acknowledge Laurent and his eyes darted around nervously as he thumbed his oversized rings.

"Jasper. If you do not keep your word, I will find out." Laurent faced away from Jasper, but tilted his head to the side to ensure the sound carried to his weak Fae ears.

Jasper nodded again, looking at the ground.

I guess it pays to have the Lord of the Northern Territories as your betrothed.

CHAPTER

SIXTEEN

MICAH

"This isn't working," Micah groaned. He lifted his hands again to The Elderwood portal, pushing as much energy as he could into his mind, but all it did was give him a headache. "We've been out here for days, Brax. Nothing works."

The chittering of the beetles in the forest put Micah's nerves on edge. They hadn't moved since they swarmed into the trees, but they hadn't quieted down either. It was as though they were watching; waiting for something.

"There is a reason you were able to channel that magic, Lumen. Now stop being a dried up mushroom and keep trying."

"Why are you always insulting me with names of food?" Micah stared at her, perplexed.

"Try. Again." Brax glared at him intently. She held the book in her hands, flipping through the pages, looking for an answer about his magic.

They were able to identify that his aches and pains were caused by leaving the property, but nothing about the shadow cat or the red magic could be found.

Seeing Brax sitting on the tree stump by the fire pit put an ache in

322

his heart. He remembered his long nights with Lucy, sitting in the same place.

Damn, I miss her.

He paced back and forth, trying to find whatever strength he had inside of him that allowed the magic to come to the surface in the first place. It had happened more than once, he could make it happen again.

This is where I learned it all. This is where I will figure it out.

"Let's go through it again, Lumen. Think back to the first time you used your magic. What were you doing? Do not leave out any details."

"I was in the woods when the rumble started. The tree branch was falling down and somehow I was able to stop it before it crushed me."

Brax continued to flip through the leather tome, slowing as she reached pages with large pictures of glass vials and jars. "And the other day with the spell? What did you do?"

"I told you this a thousand times. I just did what you told me to do! I put the materials needed for the spell by the tree."

"But you didn't say the words."

"That's because I don't *know* the words," Micah ground out. They had gone over this so many times and always ended with the same result: they didn't understand how Micah was capable of the magic.

"Wait." Brax gasped as she read a page in the book.

"What is it?" Micah asked, coming near.

"Silence, you featherless chicken," Brax said.

Micah rolled his eyes, but kept walking closer. He tried to get a good look at the page she was reading, but he couldn't understand it.

"What language is that?"

"Ancient Fae..." Her voice was airy, as though she was afraid to speak the words aloud. "It has not been written for thousands of years."

"Well, what does it say?" Micah asked, exasperated.

She snapped her head up at him. Her gaze was wild, curiosity burning behind those dark-rimmed eyes. "Lumen. Did you ever go into The Elderwood?"

All at once, the entire forest went quiet. Micah looked up, the beetles in the trees still weighing down the boughs, but now eerily silent.

"Just once. Why?"

"What happened while you were there?"

Micah flushed, knowing well what he did there, but he wasn't ready to share that with Brax. "Uh, does it matter what I did?"

"Use your ears, Lumen. I asked what happened while you were there. I did not ask you what you did."

"I'm not sure if I understand the difference," he admitted with confusion.

She released an annoyed grunt and narrowed her eyes. "You got there. Did your body feel different? Did you see anything unusual while you were in the portal before you appeared in The Elderwood? Did you hear anything?"

Slowly, the insects began to chitter again. The rumble grew through the trees, passing through like a wave as though they were speaking to one another.

Micah replayed it all in his mind. Lucy held his hand as they walked into the portal, squeezing the amulet tight and preparing to be transported to another realm—as much as someone can prepare for that. He closed his eyes as he tried to remember.

"I remember seeing a bright swirling light—all different colors. My body felt weightless at first, but then it kind of felt like..."

"Like what?" Brax said, standing. She clutched the book to her chest. "Lumen. Tell me."

Micah looked at her, perplexed. "I was just going to say that at first it felt like I was weightless. Floating in a quiet void of nothing, then out of nowhere, my body felt suddenly heavy. Like the blood in my veins turned to lead. It was kind of awful." He looked at Brax as her smile grew. "It was just because I traveled through a portal into a new realm. It's normal, right?"

"No, Lumen. It's not." She opened her mouth and her eyes widened as a sigh escaped her. "I don't know where to begin."

"What was it supposed to feel like?"

She looked up to the sky, searching for the words. "Water flowing over you. Energy rushing through you. Air wrapping around you. Each portal is a bit different, but you... what you experienced was something else, Lumen. Something created specially for you."

"I don't know what that is supposed to mean," he said, a bit alarmed.

"Micah, what do you know about Alderic Lumen?"

"Other than he's my Fae ancestor who found The Elderwood? Nothing."

"Then I guess it is time for another lesson."

"ALCHEMY?" Micah said in confusion. "I don't even understand what that is."

"It's a source of magic that has been attempted by mortals for thousands of years," Brax explained.

She took a seat on the desk with her feet in one of the two chairs, Micah sat in the other, leaning over the book on the desktop, looking at the incredible pictures illustrated within it. Drawings of glass bottles and liquids, swirls and bubbles filled the page.

"You say *attempted*, so does that mean it didn't work?"

"Not for the mortals," Brax said, a smile slowly lifting on her face.

"You're losing me again," Micah said in annoyance. He pulled the beer he was drinking to his lips and took a long swig. It had been one hell of a week, and he really wasn't sure if he could take one more thing. The comfort of an ordinary beer helped stabilize him as he teetered toward the edge of insanity.

"The mortals tried using alchemy to create their own magic. They had heard of the gifts bestowed upon the Fae by the gods and wanted to even out the playing field. However, their focus was on transformation."

Brax pointed to the pictures in the book. "Minerals turning into gold. Metals into elixirs."

"Elixirs for what?"

"They wanted to create everlasting life." Brax said solemnly. "They wanted to live forever."

"Like the Fae?"

"We do not live forever, you absolute walnut." She let out an exasperated huff as Micah just rolled his eyes. "We live for a long time, yes, but not forever. Even Fae have an end, though expectancies differ."

"So what does Alderic Lumen have to do with this? And what does this have to do with whatever magic I have?" He chewed on his lip as he said it.

I have magic, he thought to himself, finally admitting it.

"You have to understand the alchemy first," Brax reiterated. "It will tie it all together."

"Then get on with it, you chicken nugget. We don't have all day."

Brax stared at him with confusion and disgust. "What did you just call me? What is a nugget of chicken? How can that even be an insult?"

Micah's face flopped with indifference. "You know what? It doesn't matter. Can you please explain this alchemy now?"

"Mortals," she sighed under her breath, shaking her head. "The alchemists of their time were able to create things akin to magic. Bright bursts of light that exploded in the sky in beautiful colors and pictures. Tonics to help heal life-taking wounds and illnesses. Some even believed in their potion making; creating love potions for those who they longed for. Do you follow?"

Micah nodded, following along, but still not understanding the connection.

"Alderic was always a very skilled Fae. His magic was strong and his natural passion for exploration is what guided him to The Elderwood. When I knew him, in our younger days, he had just found the portal to The Elderwood and used the wood to create the most amazing bow. He shot down more enemies than any other Fae to have ever crossed the battlefield. That is, until the wood from The Elderwood was shared with the rest of Denora, creating the strongest army in existence. Well—not stronger than the Vytyr. Soon after that, the amulet was passed down to the Baums, with the intention of allowing the Lumen line to fade from existence."

"In Alderic's letter, he said that he got married and settled on the land to protect the portal from the mortals who were moving in. What happened to him after that?"

"Now you are asking the right questions, Lumen." Brax had a twinkle in her eye, and Micah hoped it meant that they were finally getting to the point. "However, it is more than he just married. He married a mortal woman."

Micah's eyebrows furrowed in confusion. "Mortal?"

"Yes. That is why he became so interested in alchemy. His wife was the most breathtaking alchemist in all of Joterra. Her name was Sanni. She was incredibly gifted in alchemy, and together, Alderic and Sanni worked hard to find a way for their family to always be safe."

"Safe how?"

Brax ignored him and continued her explanation. "Alderic knew his Fae magic would stay within his bloodline, but not forever. Eventually, away from Fae lands, his ancestral line would have less and less of his Denoran heritage, until it was washed away completely. And, being that they were both incredibly intelligent, they created a fail-safe. And you, dear Micah, seemed to have found it."

Micah could have said that he was confused, but it wouldn't have made a difference. Everything about this made zero sense to him.

Brax showed Micah the entry on the page, pointing to the long paragraphs written by Alderic Lumen in a language he did not recognize, but Brax read it for him.

"In the book it reads:

The Lumen bloodline carries a strength in character that will last for generations. As Sanni and I live out our lives in Joterra, our lineage will be bound by the laws of mortality. The long-lasting love and devotion to knowledge and justice will strengthen our family as time passes.

While Fae magic brought me to the mortal realm, alchemy will bring us home.

With Sanni's knowledge, we will extract what remains of my magic and transform it. Together with alchemy and Fae magic, we will change the form of my magic, preserving it as it waits to be called on. We shall create a power so strong and unique that only the gifted shall be granted its magnitude.

As a worthy Lumen passes through The Elderwood, the magic will awaken. It will be restored in the Lumen bloodline and reside there for generations to come, as long as their legacy shares Fae blood once again."

"I have his magic?" Micah asked breathlessly.

"Part of it." Brax nodded. "The other part is unique to any other Fae magic: alchemy. They found a way to allow their magic to live forever."

SEVENTEEN

LUCY

"That's an interesting smile you have on your face, Lucella," Wes teased from across the dining table.

"Your face is quite interesting, too. You might want to see if you can have something done about that. May scare off the ladies," Lucy stage whispered.

Lucy couldn't hide her expression solely for the fact that she had no idea how she was feeling. Was it surprised? Worried? Quietly enthused?

The entire situation with Laurent had thrown her for a loop. This whole time she was so concerned with marrying someone without getting to know them. However, Lucy never considered that in getting to know Lord Sloan, she would find that he was a perfectly capable partner.

What am I doing? What about Micah?

She didn't have time to think about these intense feelings with her brothers there in front of her. Instead, she chose to ignore them until later, when she would be alone. While it had only been two days since she had her argument with Micah, she realized much more time had passed for him. It had probably been a week since their argument in Joterra.

She shook her head and refocused on her brothers.

Tristan laughed as he threw an apple into the air and made it hover with his magic. He juggled a few pieces of fruit as he made the apples twirl around Lucy's head in jest.

She swatted them away in annoyance. Tristan was never one to take things seriously. He enjoyed making his family laugh—even at others' expense.

Tristan pulled the fruit away from her head, back toward him. Lucy took the paring knife she was using to cut her apple and threw it at one of Tristan's. It hit dead center and lodged into the wall across the room, nearly six feet away.

The kitchen went silent.

Wes nearly choked. He walked over and stared at the apple wedged into the wall with the knife. The handle of the knife was halfway through the apple, pulp and juice dripping down the sides.

"What kind of strength training have you been taking part in?" Tristan asked in awe.

The pierced apple slid over the blade and dropped to the ground with a thud, making Lucy wince. The knife remained lodged in the wall.

"Luce—you sliced it in half from all the way across the room!" Tristan's eyebrows were halfway up his forehead.

"Lucky throw?" she suggested sheepishly.

"Nuh-uh, enough of this bullshit, Luce," argued Tristan. "Tell me what's going on. First, you demolish every clay plate Wes threw, and now you get a lucky throw with this apple? You hit it dead center, and this knife is so stuck in the wall it will take magic to force it out." He pulled and tugged at the knife without it so much as budging.

"Nothing is going on."

They can't find out.

"You forget I train with the best soldiers in all of Denora. Not a single male would have been able to nail that hit with a common kitchen knife, and definitely not in jest." He pulled over a chair, swung it around backward, and sat down next to her, pushing up the sleeves of his white shirt. His eyes narrowed and glued on Lucy. "Spill it. What happened in Joterra?"

Lucy got up to try to avoid the conversation when she met Wes's gaze. His brow furrowed, but he wasn't mad.

He's worried about me?

"Brothers... a lot happened in Joterra." She walked around the kitchen table away from them, desperate to find a way out of the situation. "I can't seem to find the words for most of it. Everything is changing now that I'm home. Especially with the impending betrothal to the Lord of the North." Her eyes darted around the room, never truly landing on her brothers. She couldn't lie to their face. She wouldn't. "Can't we just carry on?"

Wes picked up a plate and projected it at Lucy's head. Without thinking, Lucy threw her right hand up to block it, and a green force field radiated from her palm, protecting her entire body.

Wes stumbled backward and Tristan stood up in alarm.

Lucy gasped and closed her hand, holding it close to her body. She took a step back as the force field disappeared and the plate shattered on the ground. It was too late. Her brothers had seen everything.

"I knew something was different about you," Wes said quietly, taking careful steps toward her.

Lucy refused to hide from her magic, but also had no idea what to say. Their eyes met and Lucy could see the resolution in Wes's gaze. He was prepared to find out what exactly had happened.

"The orchards." He pointed to the back exit. "Out."

Lucy hesitated.

What did I do?

"Now," he barked. "No one says a word." He grabbed Tristan by the arm and led them both out of the kitchen, a backward glance ensuring that Lucy followed. He marched them past the gardens, past the grassy knoll where they had practiced, and straight into the apple orchards.

She realized why Wes picked this place—it would be empty and far away from prying ears at the estate.

Every few paces, one of her brothers would turn to look at her, their expressions filled with questions.

Fidgeting with her hand, she panicked, considering her options.

Do I tell them everything that happened? Do I pretend that what they saw is something one of my teachers taught me? No, they would see right through that.

Over and over, on the walk through the estate grounds, Lucy debated what she would share. By the time they arrived in the orchard, she still had no answer.

Wes and Tristan stopped ahead in the clearing and turned to stare at Lucy, waiting for an explanation. Tristan and Wes stood across from her as she prepared for an interrogation she didn't know how to navigate.

"You aren't being truthful. What happened?" Wes demanded patiently.

Tristan, however, was much less patient. "What in the realms was that?!" he yelped. "I've never seen anyone do that before."

Lucy paced back and forth quickly, looking from her brothers to the sky, praying for a magical portal to open up from the skies and take her away from this incredibly strange conversation she was about to have.

Here it goes.

"Wes. I told you The Elderwood was under attack, did I not?"

"Yes, you did, sister," he replied with waning patience. "And what does that have to do with glowing green magic that emanates from your hand?"

"You see," she began, twisting her hands and looking from brother to brother. "When the land was on fire, The Elderwood called out to me... It bestowed upon me a kind of *borrowed* magic. At least, I think it was borrowed?"

"What is borrowed magic? That doesn't exist."

"Well, it did for me. The Elderwood sent magic into my body so that I could control the flames of the fire and defend the land."

"You controlled fire?"

"I did. And..."

"There's more?!" Tristan's voice cracked.

"Yes, now shush," Lucy took a deep breath, trying to find the words to possibly tell her brothers that she levitated with all-powerful magic flowing through her veins. "When I was leaving, I placed my hand upon the tree that held the portal to The Elderwood, and it did this." She lifted her right hand, releasing the concealment charm to show them.

Square in the palm of her hand, red lines formed the Baum Bowyer sigil; the same symbol engraved on the amulet. The same symbol on the portals themselves.

Wes took her hand carefully to inspect it, turning it lightly, afraid to touch her. "What do you mean a tree did this to you?"

"Does it hurt?" Tristan asked, concern filling his voice.

"I'm okay, Tristan," she said with a weak smile, touching his cheek with her other hand. "It hurt when I received the mark. Since then, there are odd times when it may sting, but I don't know what it means. Sometimes it hurts for no reason at all. Sometimes I can feel the magic in my veins, writhing under the surface when I get angry, especially with Father... Then today it hurt when Jasper took my hand. But I don't know what that means."

"Did you say you *feel* the magic within you?" Tristan said, aghast.

"Truthfully, yes. I feel it all the time. It's... old magic. Ancient. It requires no spell work, no words. It responds to me, just knows what I need and when I need it. I feel it humming in my veins."

"Jasper?" Wes said with confusion. "He set it off?"

"I'm not sure. Sometimes it feels as though my body cannot control the magic when I experience heightened emotions," she said, remembering the anger she felt toward her father. It happened again when she experienced the thrill of using her bow. Her breath hitched as she remembered when she felt the magic begging to come out when she was propped upon Laurent's lap returning from their grove in the forest.

"Heightened emotions?" Wes said curiously.

"What else can you do?" Tristan asked. He grabbed her left hand and pulled her further into the orchard where there was a small clearing from a few chopped down trees. He brought Lucy to the center, then moved off to the side and stood by a tree stump—an expectant brightness in his eyes.

"Go ahead," he said with a flourish of his hands. "Show us what you've got."

"Tristan, this is absurd." Lucy crossed her arms in annoyance. "I'm not sure how this works! It just sort of happens."

He looked over at Wes. "See, Wes? This is all some big scheme. I'm sure she has no magic at all."

"Wha—" Wes began, but Tristan cut him off with a wave of his hand.

"No, no. It's fine. Luce here just clearly wants some attention from her big brothers since Father is so angry at her. And it makes sense! I'd probably do the same thing." He put his hands in his pockets and shrugged his shoulders. "I guess I just expected more from you, Luce."

"I am NOT making this up, Tristan. I—"

"Luce, Luce—it's okay! Really. We can pretend that you have some magic in you if it makes you feel better."

"Tristan, I don't want you—"

"Really, it's fine!" He sat on the stump and put his hands together in front of him on his lap. "You always were the least powerful of us all. It makes sense that you'd want that now." He gave her a sympathetic smile, as if he felt sorry for her.

"Tristan, stop interrupting me!" Lucy yelled, squeezing her eyes shut.

"I'm not, I'm just—" and suddenly he stopped.

Lucy looked up to find Tristan entirely wound in vines that

sprang from the ground. His feet were tethered to the tree trunk, his hands bound at the wrist. The vines were swirling up higher and higher, encompassing his face so that he could not speak.

"Oh!" Lucy yelped. She lifted her hand and the vines fell away, allowing Tristan to breathe freely. "I am so sorry!"

He took in heaving breaths as he looked at the lifeless vines at his feet. "That. Was. Amazing!" Tristan shouted. He ran to Lucy and picked her up, swinging her around in a circle. "Luce! You beast! I knew you'd be able to do it!"

"You knew?" The spinning made her queasy and confused. She hit his shoulders, forcing him to put her down. "Did you just provoke me so that I would lose my temper?" Lucy asked in shock.

"Of course," he winked at her. "You're too easy. You do recognize that your most revealing trait is your constant yearning for others to regard you on equal footing, don't you? I just had to pretend that you weren't."

Wes walked up quietly. "Well, now we won't have to pretend any longer. You aren't our equal, Lucella."

Lucy took a step back, hurt by his words.

Wes took a step forward. "You are much more powerful, little sister." His half smile gave him away.

Lucy's heart soared, feeling the loving words leave a mark on her forever. Her father would have to listen to Wes; he would have to agree to let her follow her own path knowing how strong she was.

"Though, I do worry where this power originated and what it means for you... What does the magic feel like?"

Tristan huddled closer, wanting to hear it all, a keen interest twinkling in his eyes.

Lucy stood and stretched her fingers, closing her eyes to channel the magic within her. "It feels like the forest. Like The Elderwood. It's enormous, and airy—it feels cavernous inside of me, like there is no bottom to this power. But then, the feeling changes." She wiggled her toes in her shoes, connecting to the earth. "It grounds me, roots me in place as something thrills through me. Like my body is humming. Like something is alive within me, with its own mind. It wants to be released. It wants to be seen."

"Open your eyes, Luce," Tristan whispered.

When she did, she saw him staring with wide, awestruck eyes.

A green halo of light encompassed her body, emerging from her hands. Light poured from them, a string of brilliance darting around her body, as if a playful sprite. She looked around, then at her brothers joyfully. They seemed so far from her. She suddenly realized she was in the air.

"Oh, my!" Lucy exclaimed. She flailed her arms, worried that she would lose her focus and plummet to the ground, but the magic held her. She looked at her arms, the emerald light bouncing around like a rubber ball. Lucy giggled with delight, and the magic slowly lowered her to solid ground.

"What else can you do?" Tristan asked excitedly. "Can you call for things to be brought to you? Try summoning one of those apples from that far off tree."

She lifted her hand and thought of the apple from the tree. Immediately, the apple came to her and landed softly in her palm.

"Now send it careening as far as you can!"

Lucy lifted her hand, and with a sharp push, the apple flew so far it left their line of sight.

"Woo!" Tristan gave an exhilarated shout.

"Lucy," Wes said seriously, bringing a hand up to his chin in thought. "You mentioned that you were able to control the fire? Were you able to create it?"

"No. The fire was already there, and I couldn't extinguish it. All I could do was redirect it... that's how the house was destroyed. The fire wouldn't stop, so we sacrificed the cabin to save the forest."

"Maybe. But maybe you just thought you couldn't control it, since you never tried?"

"How would that change my ability now?" Lucy asked, confusion coloring her face.

"Luce, people don't just randomly get powers that make them

exceedingly strong and precise. Nothing about this magic seems typical. Maybe you just need to train, learn how to hone it properly?" Tristan offered.

"I'm not sure I would know how," Lucy confessed, her heart beating erratically. This all seemed so impossible.

"Try this," Wes began. He pulled her away from Tristan and from the nearest tree. "Close your eyes," he whispered, calming Lucy. "Think about the spell we need to create a light orb. Don't speak it, just think about the effects of it."

Lucy held out the palm of her hand and did as he said, hoping something would work.

"Now, imagine that orb becoming a small flame. Small enough to control."

"What if it burns me?" Lucy worried.

"Don't let it," Wes ordered. "Control it. You tell it what to do."

Lucy focused her mind on a tiny orb of light, thinking about using that light to see her way in the dark. She remembered all the times she would sneak the light to read in her room when her mother told her to sleep. She thought of the nights in her father's office, working far into the evening, wanting to get her bow just right, needing an orb of light to see in the dark. She thought of Micah —when she created tiny glimmering lights that danced around the room like fireflies.

Then she thought of the small candles Micah used to illuminate the study while they waited for the full moon to charge the amulet. The way the small flame flickered back and forth, giving a dim light to the room.

"Lucy," Wes whispered.

She opened her eyes, and in her hand, was a small flame. She looked on in awe at the fire, wondering how this magic could allow her such wondrous powers.

"Now try to douse the flame," he said quietly, eyes still on the fire.

She hesitated for a moment.

I can't do this. What if it grows and I can't control it?

The fear crept over Lucy, invading every thought.

The fire grew, changing from the size of an acorn to a maple leaf, slowly spreading to the width of her hand.

"Lucy, you have to douse the flame!" Wes commanded.

"I can't! I don't know what I'm doing!" Lucy panicked and tears stung the backs of her eyes. The flame grew higher in her hands. "You need to run! I don't want to hurt you!" She couldn't see her brothers through the tears.

"We aren't going anywhere, Luce," Tristan said calmly next to her. "You can do this. Close your eyes."

"No! What if it spreads? You need to go!" Her eyes darted around wildly, looking at the trees that were sure to be consumed by the flames in her palm that she could not control.

"Lucy!" Wes yelled again.

Tristan stood directly in front of Lucy, blocking her view of Wes and all the trees behind him.

"Look at me, Luce." His voice was calm and his body was open to hers. "You won't hurt me. I know you won't. Close your eyes and get control."

"What if it spreads?" Her voice was breathless as fear threatened to take over.

"I will tell you. Right now I need you to talk to that magic inside of you—because I think it's trying to get your attention."

"What? What does that even mean?" The fire in her hand grew taller, blocking out Tristan's face from view.

"You said this magic is alive, and I know it doesn't want to hurt you, Luce," he said loudly through her panic. "And since you don't want to hurt me, I'm pretty sure it won't. You said it responds to you, right? You can feel this magic is different, but I think you're missing something. So close your star-damned eyes and figure out what's going on. Now."

Lucy felt the desperation in his voice, and her gasping breaths left her no other choice. She looked at her hand, the fire blazing out of control—but beneath that was something even more terrifying.

The lines on her hand were no longer red, nor did they glow green. The lines were now black, as if the magic within her had changed. Her fire changed from red to green, and the swirling black and green magic crawled up her arms. Her stomach began to churn, making her nauseous and dizzy.

This feels wrong. Something is not right.

"You can do this, Lucy," she heard Wes from far away.

Tristan gave her a stern nod of support through the growing flames, yet he never backed away.

She closed her eyes. The sound of her breathing made it difficult to focus, her panicked thoughts drowning her.

Stop it, she told herself. *You are Lucy Baum. Figure this out.*

She took three deep breaths, searching for the magic inside of her. Then everything went silent.

Lucy opened her eyes to an unusual dark mist. She was no longer in the orchard and no longer in the company of her brothers—all she could see was darkness and a soft green haze coming from somewhere far off.

She tried to follow the haze, since it was the only source of light for what seemed like endless darkness. Every time she took a step closer, it seemed to get further and further away. Her feet carried her farther, faster, desperately searching for the source.

"Where are you going?" she yelled into the abyss. "What are you?!"

She came to a halt, bending over to catch her breath. She looked around in dismay, each direction she turned was filled with shadows.

Am I even moving? she questioned.

She tried to take a step, watching her feet move, but knowing the misty green radiance was immobile in the distance.

I can't get to it.

Defeated, she put her arms on her head and screamed in frustration. "Why did you bring me here? What do you want?!"

The green glimmer bounced in response.

Her mouth popped open in surprise. The light bounced the same way it did when she first returned to Denora, when her magic played as she explored. She took another step, and again the emerald light stayed far off in the distance.

Maybe I can't chase the magic... I have to invite it to come to me.

She stood still and closed her eyes slowly. Lifting her hands into the air, she opened herself to the magic.

"Come," she whispered into nothingness.

The green mist soared to her and hit her like a wave crashing into a rocky shore. A tingling sensation rocked her from head to toe and just like that, she saw what the green haze was hiding.

A gasp left her lips, and her eyes popped open. She was back with Tristan and Wes, the orchard was safe from her fire, and she was no longer afraid.

The magic entered her and felt like something completely new. It zoomed through her bloodstream, joined with her nerves, and trilled through her mind. Then, her magic showed her something that had been hidden from view. It showed her an image that she did not quite understand.

A ring?

EIGHTEEN

MICAH

"Let's try it again," Brax called from the tree stump in the yard. "When the magic actually worked. What were you thinking?"

"Thinking?" Micah huffed out, clenching his fists at his side. "I was thinking I was going to fuck this all up. I was thinking that it was my fault that things were going wrong with portal and it was my job to fix it. That if I couldn't do this right, then people would get hurt. That Lucy would be hurt."

He looked back at the trees and let out a frustrated grunt, causing the insects closest to him to shift their weight on the branches. They still hadn't left. He kicked at the ground, looking at the barrier he constructed around the tree.

No one is going to get hurt on my watch. I won't let it happen.

"Now." Brax said suddenly. "Do it now."

Micah lifted his hands and tried again to summon the magic. He put all his effort into the task, focusing solely on the small stick from The Elderwood that was left in a discarded pile of wood.

Immediately, the branch radiated a red glow, then flew from the ground and bolted into his hands, causing him to stumble backward.

"That's it!" Brax announced with a wide smile, clapping as she walked toward him.

Micah stood speechless, an overwhelming relief washing through him nearly bringing him to his knees. He did magic.

It was real. All of it. There was something inside of him he could use to defend The Elderwood. There was something within him that connected him to all of this—he was no longer an outsider to it all.

Finally, a way I can help.

"Let's go again." Micah smiled with a fierce determination.

AFTER HOURS OF PRACTICE, Micah and Brax were at odds with his ability. Micah rested in the grass, exhausted from the endless attempts.

He did not have super strength at all times, he did not have the accuracy and precision of a skilled marksman, and he did not have the capability to do any special spells.

He had attempted to call a cup to him, but it stayed firmly on the ground.

He tried to create light, but all he did was stare at his sweaty hands.

Micah could not manage any spells that were common for Denorans, even with the correct spell work.

It was a fluke, he thought miserably.

"This is very interesting," Brax said at last, leaning against a tree stump in defeat. "You are as useful as a broom without bristles."

"What the hell is that supposed to mean?" Micah asked, disgruntled.

"It means you can't do anything worthwhile with it except use it to whack someone."

Micah's eyebrow raised in question, but then it came to him.

"You're right."

"I know I'm right," Brax said casually, swatting a fly away from her.

"No, listen," Micah interrupted as he sat up on the uneven ground. "I can't call the cup, because what would I do with it? Drink from it?"

"Are you new to cups?"

Micah gave her a look and ignored the jibe. "But I can call the stick. I can summon something I can use to defend myself and The Elderwood."

Brax paused, looking at Micah, considering his idea.

"I can't do spell work with Denoran magic because I am not Denoran. But I can ensure the magic of the barrier is firm, because I am working to contain the magic of The Elderwood."

Brax pivoted from her place on the ground next to him, put both hands on his shoulders, and looked him square in the eye with all the pride in the world.

"You are a guardian, Lumen. A protector. When you channel that part of you, the magic comes naturally. It isn't about making the magic work for *you*, it's about making the magic work for *them*. For those who you desire to protect."

"This is about protecting?"

Brax's eyes lit up, finally putting the puzzle pieces together. "And you can channel your power to save yourself when it is in direct relation to The Elderwood; when it needs you to help." She smiled widely as Micah nodded.

She kneeled on the ground next to him, giving him a friendly punch in the arm that felt more forceful than he was used to, and stood up.

"Lumen. You are a force to behold." She reached down and offered her hand, pulling him up to stand.

"I am the Guardian." Micah said proudly. His heart ached with remembrance. "I wonder if Grandad had the same abilities?"

"I would not know," she admitted. "I presume Corvus would have the answers to your questions." She looked around the property, dusting off her pants. "Where is your grandfather buried? I did not see his grave."

"Oh, I didn't have him buried here. He's with my grandma, in the city. It was just easier to transport him from the hospital there, and I figured he'd want to be with her again."

Brax's face twisted in confusion. "That doesn't make sense, Lumen."

"It does." Micah took a step away to put distance between him and the kohl-lined, sympathetic eyes bearing down on him. He didn't want her pity, and he wasn't about to discuss his feelings. "It wasn't a far drive from the hospital where he died. They called me when he was sick, but he went very suddenly. I didn't get there in time—it was a matter of an hour. I lived right down the block. I basically just had to deal with the funeral and cemetery arrangements." He tried to shrug off her look, shaking his head like it hadn't been a problem.

She walked up to him again, calmly. Slowly. "Micah."

He was caught off guard by her words. She rarely called him by his name.

"Why was your grandfather in the city?"

"I- I don't know." He took a step back, his mind rapidly going through each reason he could be there.

Was he already sick? Did he have an appointment and things got worse? Was he in the city for business?

"Why does it matter?"

She took his hand and walked him over to the stumps of trees, and sat him down. It was unlike Brax to be so quiet, so solemn— Micah didn't say a word. She placed the leather-bound book in his hands and opened to the page where his grandad had inscribed his note. The letter about the curse.

Micah looked it over once.

Twice.

Then, realization hit.

He looked up at Brax in panic, and then back down at the page.

"No." It was all he could choke out. "Why would he leave here if he knew he wouldn't have survived it? Maybe he got sick here and he called for an ambulance. Maybe someone brought him there?"

"I don't think any guardian would leave on their own, knowing the risk they would take. I'm not sure what happened, Micah. But it may be in your best interest to find out why he was so close to your home when he died."

His heart sank. His head swam with images of his grandad all alone, dying—desperately trying to get to Micah.

What did you do, Grandad?

But he had no time for his thoughts to spiral, because a second later, a low rumble began.

Both Brax and Micah swung their heads to the portal—they had been so busy talking and practicing these new powers, they didn't notice what had been building behind the barrier.

The sharp clawed bugs covered every inch of The Elderwood tree, but it was almost impossible to see because the entire wall of the magical barrier was covered with bugs and a thick, black mist. Its branches sagged down low with the weight of the insects—there had to be thousands.

Within the tunnel of mist, red sparks began to course through like lightning. Each strike set off a rumble within the ground. Every flash deeper and more powerful.

The bright sparks hit again, and behind the mist, Micah could make out illuminated yellow eyes staring at him through the deep cloud of smoke.

The shadow beast.

Its roar filled the forest, rattling the windows of the cabin.

Brax reached high into the air with two hands and called out in Vytyrian. From the palms of her hand, a silvery-gray mist formed, and within it, a spear appeared. It was as tall as she was, with a sharp metal point at the end. She gripped the spear in her hands and crouched into a ready stance.

Micah dug deep into the well of his powers, pushing his mind to focus on protecting The Elderwood, and called on two pieces of jagged wood.

Please work.

He stretched his hands out as a red rope sprung out to latch on to his weapons: one long branch, about as thick as a tennis racket handle, and the same small piece he used to stab the beast in the eye. He brandished his weapons with a fierce determination as confidence in his untapped magic rocketed through him.

Another roar and the insects vibrated so violently they fell off the tree branches. Micah's feet shook. The windows rattled again. The stones of the barrier quaked.

No.

Panic seized him as he stared wildly at the impending threat of the rocks falling and releasing the creature.

The shadow beast's dripping muzzle opened into a wide snarl that Micah could have sworn was a knowing smile. The beast roared again and Micah took off running toward the rocks, praying he would get there in time to keep them in place despite the shaking roar that threatened to topple the entire structure.

One last thunderous boom—a combination of beastly bellow and lightning—and two stones tumbled down and away from the structure.

The purple halo of light dropped from the boundary, and ever so slowly, the dark mist spread throughout the forest.

The shadow beast prowled out, with one resounding step after the other—its scarred eye searched for only Micah.

However, this time, it wasn't alone.

Behind it, three more monstrous beasts padded their way through the tumbling rocks no longer keeping them at bay.

"Well, now we know why it was such a loud growl," Brax began, but the scarred beast roared once again, making Micah's bones shake. "Or not."

"No, I think he's a bit upset with me for blemishing his perfectly black fur," Micah said quietly. "Don't worry, kitty. After I'm through with you, there will be nothing left for you to look at."

Brax stepped to Micah's right as she spoke under her breath. "You take Scar. I'll get the others."

Micah nodded, keeping his eyes on the beast.

As the leader snarled, the three fierce felines behind it came raging at Brax. She nimbly dodged the first, swinging her spear into the one in front of her, jumping over the creature as she tore the metallic point through its body. Its furious howl echoed through the trees as Brax made her way into a larger clearing, giving herself the space she needed to take on the three menacing brutes.

The wounded creature shook its body with a violent shudder, and in that moment, the gash was gone. Brax continued sparring with the beasts as they made their way closer and closer to her. Her Fae warrior speed kept her out of harm's way from their sharp claws, but it was anyone's guess as to who would tire out first.

"Lumen!" Brax cried. "My spear is doing nothing to keep them away!" She battled the felines as they snapped their oozing jaws at her.

Micah kept his eyes trained on the predator before him as they stood in a silent standoff.

Great, they fucking heal. How am I going to keep this beast away from me?

He looked down at the makeshift weapons in his hands.

I'm not sure how these sticks will help, but better than nothing.

He gripped the wood tighter, begging his magic to provide him with increased strength to have the slightest chance at besting the creature before him.

The leader of the shadow beasts crept toward him, his sharp, stained teeth more pronounced than before. The raging creature's eyes swirled with bloodthirsty violence.

It took a running leap toward Micah, and he stood with his feet firmly planted to the ground, refusing to leave the portal unguarded.

I am needed here. I'm not going anywhere.

He swung the larger branch toward the creature, cracking it on its side with all of his might.

The oversized cat went soaring away from him, a loud whimper proving his injury. Micah felt the magic coursing through his veins—the power of the guardians was there with him. He bobbed on his feet; the adrenaline mixing with his newfound strength.

"Here we go," Micah said to himself, a warning of brutality in his sneer.

The creature let out a fierce bellow, letting its venomous ooze drip out of its mouth onto the earth below. Another leaping pounce and Micah quickly ducked under it as it flew through the air, stabbing upward with his smaller branch. Micah slashed into the underside of the beast, creating a long gash that spilled blood everywhere.

The shadow cat fell to its side on landing, and scurried back to its feet, slinking away from Micah on a limp. Micah braced himself and held his breath as he waited for the beast to heal and attack once more.

"Come on!" he shouted, but as more seconds passed, he realized it wasn't coming after him.

I hurt him.

Micah looked down at the weapons in his hands, then back to Brax. She was absolutely remarkable—screaming at the top of her lungs as she jabbed and stabbed each of the creatures as they got closer to her, fending them off with expert skill and finesse. Yet, every time she injured them, their wounds would heal and she would be back to the same battle.

"Brax!" Micah yelled, and when he knew he got her attention, he threw the longer of the two sticks he had to her. He watched as the crimson rope of magic carried the stick directly to Brax without effort.

Damn. Magic.

Micah wondered if he'd ever get used to it.

She grabbed the wooden branch, using it to pelt the beasts in front of her. Their advances slowed. Brax's eyes alighted. She abandoned her spear and broke the stick in half over her knee. She used the sharp points of the broken ends to stab and prod them as they attacked her. The creatures whimpered in pain as they continued to fight.

But they didn't heal.

"It's working!" she called out to him.

The trio of felines looked for their leader, finding it huddled in the distance, rallying its strength. Brax pushed forward in her attack, no longer having to take the defensive route. She swung, stabbed, lashed, and jabbed as the shadow creatures tried to fight back. They were finally showing signs of weakness.

Micah's insides leapt with a fierce hope. His gaze connected with the leader of the beasts. "Come on, Scar. Let's end this."

The beast began a canter and then a sprint as it raced toward Micah. To his surprise, it stayed low, not taking another running leap. The creature's snarling mouth opened wide and kept laser focus on Micah's legs.

Shit.

Micah bent low, bracing himself for the onslaught, and stretched his arm out as far as he could without losing hold of the dagger-like piece of wood. The beast butted Micah's hand out of the way and knocked him down to the ground.

The shadow creature crouched low and slunk closer and closer to Micah. It snapped at his feet as Micah crawled backward, trying to regain his footing and give himself leverage—but the beast was too fast.

It bit into the side of his leg, grabbing his pant leg and large combat boot. It swung his head viciously, shaking Micah as it dragged him toward the misty void in the ground.

With as much strength as he could manage, Micah lurched up and stabbed the creature in its shoulder, forcing it to let go. The piece of wood got lodged in the beast's muscular body and Micah scrambled away, weaponless.

The creature's guttural growl was all it took for Micah to realize that this was the end. He held his hands out in front of him, hoping some magic would do something to save him. Anything.

The shadow cat's limping gallop did not slow it down, and it leapt high into the air—aiming straight at Micah.

His magic wasn't coming to him. Nothing was working. He was drained.

This is it.

A thunderous howl reverberated through the trees and Micah squeezed his eyes shut in defeat.

A high-pitched whistling raced past his ear just as he heard a yelp of agony.

Micah's eyes popped open just as the beast crumpled to the ground—an arrow straight through its scarred eye.

An arrow.

Micah's heart stopped as he looked back to where it came from.

Lucy.

She reached into her quiver and released another shot at one of the beasts coming close to Brax, successfully lodging the shaft into its back. Her eyes swirled with the same green magic from The Elderwood, with hints of darkness that weren't there before.

Wes ran out from behind Lucy, his hands swirling above his head, calling on his Denoran magic. He spoke loudly in a Fae language as he pushed the beasts away from Brax, grabbing them with some invisible force.

"Back to the crack in the ground!" Brax screamed over the chaos.

Lucy trained her eyes on the beast that nearly killed Micah. Her face was a picture of pure focus and intensity. Her hand glowed bright emerald as her fingers reached out to the beast and she lifted the massive creature with little effort.

Micah watched as the creature dripped oozing black blood from its injuries. It writhed in the air as Lucy flicked her wrist and sent it lurching toward The Elderwood, smacking its body on the enormous trunk of the tree.

Micah got to his feet and embraced the pandemonium around

him. Lucy's swirling green magic kept the shadow cat behind the rock barrier as Wes and Brax worked together to force the last three beasts back into the void in the ground near the portal.

Micah staggered over and stacked the rocks to prepare the wall for the magic needed to reinstate the protection spell. The beetles scurried about in a panic, some of them following the shadow beast, and others making their way to trees farther away.

As the last beast's tail cleared the rocks, Micah pushed the remnants of his magic into the barrier—urging it to work and hold. A bright purple glowing wall signaled his success, and he fell to the ground in exhaustion.

Brax ran over to him, grabbing his shoulder. "Lumen!"

Lucy's green haze in her eyes cleared as she saw Brax embracing Micah.

She rushed over and pushed Brax off of him in fury. "What did you do to him!?"

NINETEEN

LUCY

"Excuse me?" Brax grit out between clenched teeth. Her body hovered over Micah defensively, refusing to leave his side, even with Lucy's accusing remarks.

"What's wrong with him? What did you do to him?" Lucy shouted as Brax searched his body, her hands hovering above him with a silvery light.

Micah groaned in pain as Lucy neared his bloodied pant leg. His leg was pouring blood from the bite of the shadow beast.

Brax extended her arms toward his wound and Lucy's rage grew at the sight. The magic in her body vibrated menacingly, still heightened from its use against the creatures. Instantly, vines sprung from the ground and pulled Brax's hands away from Micah's body. This time, sharp thorns covered the vines, curling and tightening around Brax's arms.

"What the fuck, Baum!" Brax screamed.

Lucy's hazel eyes met her lethal gaze and the vines tightened again.

"Lu?" Micah's weak voice croaked as he opened his eyes, wincing in pain.

Lucy dropped her glower from Brax and searched Micah's face for a sign that he was okay. "I'm here, Micah. I'm here." Her hands landed on his chest, her fingertips pressing into his flesh, trying to convince herself that he was alright. She shook subtly with the terror of what a bite from that beast could mean.

"Lu, let her go." Micah held her hand weakly, looking over at Brax and then back to Lucy. "Let her go. She's my friend." He caressed her fingers, barely able to keep his eyes open.

If Brax's eyes could shoot daggers, Lucy would have been shredded. Lucy let the vines fall, but Brax's predatory gaze did not falter.

"Baum, I will allow you this one oversight, but make no mistake —the next time you attempt to harm me, you better succeed, or it will be the last thing you do."

"Is that a threat?" Lucy asked in a harsh whisper, her magic shooting through her like lightning, begging for permission to attack.

Instead, Micah interrupted. "Lucy, Brax is my friend. It's okay. She wouldn't hurt me, and I'd prefer if you didn't hurt her, either."

"Yes," Wes added, looking around nervously. "I think enough damage has been done today. Dare I say we work on fixing up Lumen here so we can talk about what in all the realms we just walked into?"

Micah groaned in agreement.

Brax went to put her hands on his leg again and Lucy eyes shimmered with green again, ready to stop her. Micah squeezed her hand tighter to get her attention. "She won't hurt me, Lu."

"If you don't mind, I'm trying to heal your lover. Now, if you would kindly leave me the fuck alone with your primitive magic, I can finish."

"Lover?" Wes asked.

"Primitive magic?" Lucy said in tandem.

Brax ignored them both as she placed two hands on Micah's leg and whispered a language Lucy had never heard before. It sounded like music and mystery—the magic inside of her hummed with recognition.

A soft, silvery glow emanated from Brax's hands as she passed back and forth, hovering over his wound. The silver light got brighter and brighter until Micah heaved a sigh of relief. Lucy had never seen healing magic like this.

Brax smiled at him and pulled him to stand. She nodded at Micah, the pair sharing in an unspoken conversation which made Lucy green with envy.

"How did you know the branches would work?" Brax asked Micah, shaking her head in disbelief.

"They were remnants from The Elderwood," he said to Brax and then looked at Lucy. "When you brought back a pile of wood from The Elderwood, you dropped the stack when we had to stop the fire. There were a few broken pieces that remained."

"So when you left that scar, it was from a piece from that pile?" Brax said as she nodded. "Of course."

"The Elderwood wanted to protect itself."

"No," Brax disagreed. "The Elderwood knew *you* would protect it. That's why it opened its magic to you."

"Can someone explain what those things were?" Wes asked, pointing toward the rock barrier Micah made. "And why there is a rock wall that glows?"

Lucy stood speechless, listening as the Micah and Brax spoke, sharing what had happened in her absence. She had been literally frolicking in the woods with another male and Micah had been here fighting for his life.

Her heart sank with every mention of the shadow beast and how it almost killed him.

What would I have done if he died and I wasn't here? She thought of Laurent. *Was I really ready to not come back to Micah?*

With the realization that she almost lost Micah, things seemed to click into place for Lucy. She didn't want Laurent and his pretty words and grandiose promises. If he were to die tomorrow, it would be unfortunate, but it wouldn't change Lucy's world. In fact, Lucy would daresay her life would be improved. But a reality in which Micah didn't exist was not a life she wanted to experience.

She couldn't.

With that sobering and distressing thought, the magic in her veins began to thrum, the dark lines along the sigil twisted beneath her skin. She held up her hand to look at the new black lines more closely, and the ongoing conversation abruptly stopped.

"What happened to your hand, Lu?" Micah said with concern, rushing to take her hand in his. He wasn't scared to touch her the way Wes had been. He held her palm in one hand and brushed her cheek with his other. It was his first time seeing the brand in her skin. "What is this? And how did you know to come here?"

At long last, she decided it was time to finally tell him about the connection she had to the tree when she left Joterra. Brax listened intently, not taking her eyes off the swirling black and green colors trailing Lucy's arm. Lucy did her best to explain, leaving nothing out even when Brax's unrelenting stare became too much.

"When the magic turned from emerald to black, it started acting differently—erratically. It made me queasy and everything felt off. I just knew I had to get to you," Lucy explained. "I knew something was wrong."

She kept her knowledge of the ring to herself. Lucy didn't know what it meant, but she was unwilling to trust Brax.

"Who did this to The Elderwood?" Wes asked, trying to regain control of the situation.

"That's the problem," Micah said at last. "I think it was me."

"What? No, Micah. It couldn't have been you." Lucy grabbed both of his hands with her own. "Besides, you have no magic. You couldn't have changed the portal."

"Last time you said that to me, I agreed with you. This time," he trailed off, running a hand through his dirtied hair. "Things have changed since you've been gone, Lu. I don't know how to explain it."

Wes pinched the bridge of his nose. "If you tell me you have some peculiar magic bestowed to you by some gnarled tree, I think I am going to need a drink." He kept his eyes closed as his face tilted toward the sky, shaking his head in dismay.

"No, I don't think that's what this is," Micah said. Wes let out a sigh of relief until Micah spoke again. "This is different magic—but I do think The Elderwood played a part."

"You have magic, Micah?" Lucy looked at him in disbelief.

"Yes, Baum. He does. Though it is very different from yours." Brax nodded toward her, surveying her with interest. "You have been gifted something very, very old—and powerful."

"You know what her magic is?" Wes asked urgently.

"Yes." Something shifted in Brax's demeanor and she stood before Lucy and extended one hand out in front of her. "May I?"

Confused, Lucy took her hands from Micah and cautiously placed one in Brax's.

Brax closed her eyes as the green magic rushed through her. She smiled and kneeled, putting one ear to Lucy's hand as if she was listening. A soft chuckle left her lips as she bowed deeper.

"What are you doing?" Micah asked her, looking between the females anxiously.

"You can communicate with it," Lucy realized in surprise.

"Yes. I can." She stood, still holding Lucy's hand. Her face was lighter, softer somehow. "I have not spoken to the primitive gods in many years. They have endowed you with something very special. Something I can't particularly understand."

"GODS?" Wes sputtered.

Lucy's face paled and her jaw went slack.

Gods?

"You speak to gods?" Micah asked her. His question seemed so run-of-the-mill. It was as if he were asking her if she knew how to fry an egg.

"The gods still exist?" Lucy in amazement. "No, surely this is something else."

"Do not underestimate me, Baum," Brax said sternly. "Yes. They exist. They are very wise and have been asleep for many years." She looked over at the tree. "I find it very odd that they had a connection within The Elderwood." She looked at Micah and poked him in his chest. "Why didn't you tell me?"

"Hey, I didn't know!" Micah said, rubbing his chest from her prodding. "So, are gods like, not around often or something?"

Lucy turned to Micah in surprise, and a nervous laugh passed between her lips. She forgot how little he knew about her realm. "Correct, Micah. In fact, they have been out of the public eye for centuries. I have never seen one, and neither have my parents. They left long ago. I've never met a Fae still alive who's seen them. Only our long forgotten ancestors would have been able to tell the tale."

"Then how could *you* speak with them?" Wes asked Brax, looking at her curiously. "You couldn't be much older than I am." He looked her up and down, a quirk of his eyebrow showing his interest.

"I am older than I look, Wesley Baum," she said with a tease. "Though, if you keep it up, I may invite you to do more than just look." She gave him a wink and Wes's cheek lifted into a half smile.

Lucy looked at her viciously. "I don't believe we have time for that rendezvous right now. What was your name again? Brax?"

"Let's not pretend that you don't know who I am. How infantile." She brushed her clothes off and looked over at Wes, speaking to him instead. "We have to figure out how to secure The Elderwood. We cannot figure out why it cracked open this way, though Micah's tome may have more answers."

"Each time we open it, we learn something new," Micah grunted in agreement.

As the three discussed The Elderwood, Lucy was distracted by a fluttering feeling that washed through her. She felt a pulling sensation deep in her chest, guiding her attention to the trees.

I need to see it.

"What?" Wes asked.

She didn't realize she had said it out loud.

"Can I see it?" Lucy asked at last. Her voice was small—

completely at odds with how she arrived. They looked at her in silence.

She cleared her throat. "The Elderwood. May I see the split in the ground? My magic feels... connected to it somehow. It is as if I am being pulled toward it as we speak. Maybe it will know how to fix it?"

"I'm not sure, Lucy," Wes began, but Brax cut him off.

"She's right. The magic inside of her is more powerful than my Vytyrian and Micah's guardian magic." She looked over to Wes. "Even your Denoran spells are nothing compared to hers."

"I know they aren't," Wes agreed. "But we don't know what any of this means. We can't just have her go near the gaping hole filled with shadow beasts and expect for her to not get hurt."

"She can handle herself," Micah stated. He took a step forward and put his hand on Lucy's shoulders, standing behind her. He looked down at her and kissed her on the top of her head. "She can do this."

The words of affirmation swam in her heart, and Micah's proximity woke up parts of her soul that she didn't even realize were dormant. Her heart fluttered with joy. It wasn't simply attraction or lust; it was true acknowledgement. He saw her and believed in her, something that so many others struggled to do for so many years.

"So this is what you meant when you said he was important to you," Wes said to Lucy, still staring at Micah.

Micah held his ground and stared back, keeping his hands on Lucy's shoulders, refusing to back down from his place with her.

"Please," Lucy said to Wes. "Trust me this once?"

Wes broke his stare and nodded at his sister. Brax led the way to the portal.

Micah held Lucy's hand as he walked with her to the tree. Her heart beat a mile a minute, eager to see what caused these ebony and jade ribbons to flow over her skin in anguish. Something was wrong with both her magic and the portal. She hoped she could connect with The Elderwood to understand what was happening.

When she approached the glowing violet barricade, her magic

flipped within her. A shimmering emerald stream of light leapt from her body, causing Lucy to gasp in alarm. It didn't hurt, but it felt like a part of her had detached from the rest of her body. Her magic crashed into Micah's barrier and melted into the other side, the violet force field doing nothing to stop it.

"What's happening? How did that get through?" Micah asked in worry.

"Like calls to like, Lumen," Brax said to him with calm reassurance. "The magic in Miss Baum knows it is coming home. Your magic did not feel the threat from hers, and it allowed entry. I would go so far as to assume they are old friends."

Lucy stood as still as she could as her magic wound through the tree branches, covering every surface. Though it was no longer part of her body, she still felt a vague connection to it. Recognition sparked through her as the magic swooped through the leaves, reuniting with The Elderwood's power again.

The deep black mist that swirled from the crack in the ground fled as the bright green magic invaded. She could feel her magic slithering through the leaves, searching... searching... but for what, Lucy wasn't sure.

The dark mist felt wrong to Lucy, as if something despicable hid deep within it. Her magic tried pushing it away, but it was unyielding. The darkness would run from the small specks of light, but there was so much of it compared to the minuscule amount of Lucy's light. There just wasn't enough magic within her to penetrate whatever darkness overwhelmed this barrier.

She remembered connecting with the magic in the orchard. All she had to do was allow the magic to enter her, and she was able to see things more clearly. She tried opening herself up the magic once more to see if there was something she had missed.

Suddenly, a flash of bright white light filled Lucy's mind, causing her to gasp and shut her eyes tight. When she opened them again, a white mist seemed to float in front of her. Just as the black smoke she saw in the orchard called her to The Elderwood, this light mist was showing her something else.

In the misty air, a vision came to her. It was Micah, walking around the newly updated cabin, his eyes wide; shocked to see the magic that created such a masterpiece. Wes was there, installing the mirror for communication. It must have been the day Wes and Jasper returned to help him. But Jasper... where was Jasper?

As if the mist heard her question, the world around her seemed to zoom away from the cabin and into the woods. After focusing again, she saw him: Jasper, standing next to the portal to The Elderwood, placing something inside the base of the tree. His magic glowed orange and then turned black as the tree shuddered. He was hurting the tree with whatever magic he placed inside of it.

Jasper turned and looked around, making sure he was unseen. With a last look at the tree, he returned to the cabin sporting a depraved grin.

It was Jasper.

Lucy took a step back, pulling her magic back to her. She blinked her eyes again with a gasp, returning to the world around her.

The black and emerald magic that wound over her arms began to fade. Then suddenly, the black receded completely, the green light ebbing, leaving only her original mark from the tree. Her fingers traced the lines.

This will never feel normal.

"It was Jasper," she said breathlessly. "It was him. He did something to The Elderwood."

"What happened to the black marks on your arm? Why have they disappeared" Brax asked her curiously.

"I'm not sure," Lucy admitted.

"What do you mean *Jasper*?" Wes asked.

"The Elderwood—it showed me. He was here with you, Wes, when you created the cabin for Micah. And he left you alone, did he not?"

"He did," Wes murmured. "He did something while I was here?"

"I don't know what it is, but he hurt the portal. He added magic; dark, wrong, magic."

"I wonder how he could get the magic to hurt the portal," Brax thought out loud.

"You speak of magic as though it has its own thoughts," Wes said incredulously.

"Are you suggesting that it does not?" Brax challenged.

"How could it? I conjure it, I bring it into creation, and I douse it when I am through. I control it, it does not control itself."

"You're wrong, Baum. It does control itself, it just has allowed you to learn the ways to use it. You speak its language, so it can agree to your terms."

Wes and Micah looked at her in confusion. Lucy remained shocked in place. It seemed impossible, but it was also only one of several impossible things to have happened to her that day.

Brax sighed and looked at Wes in question. "Have you ever attempted to use your magic, but the spell doesn't turn out right? Or perhaps you have to try two or three times in order for it to work correctly?"

"Yes, it happens to everyone," Wes said defensively.

"You're right. It does. But that is not because you are a weak male or unable to speak the correct Denoran words. It is because your magic and you are not on the same wavelength. You were not preparing your body to use it correctly, and therefore the magic decided to not come to you when called."

"That's impossible."

"It is not. You have worked your entire life to create beautiful magic; both strong and resilient. Where does the magic come from, Baum?"

"Well, every Fae has it," he said, scrambling for his words.

"Every Fae in Denora has your similar magic. Yes. And the Fae in Vytyr have Vytyrian magic. They are all unique, all separate. They all respond to different calls."

"That explains nothing," Wes retorted.

"The magic within us is gifted to us by the gods themselves. Do you not remember the creation story?"

"What story? I have never heard of such a thing."

"Come," Brax demanded, pulling Wes down to sit by the tree stumps.

Micah and Lucy walked after them to hear the story as well. Lucy's memory of this story had faded.

Could there be something to this?

"Before the realms became as we know them now, it was once one large territory. Creatures of all kinds roamed together, under the rule of the gods of lore. The gods had the power of unlimited magic. Some were skilled warriors. Some had healing powers. All magic was present in these gods—elemental, practical, some for beauty and good, others for evil."

Micah shifted nervously, pulling Lucy closer to him. His arm wound around her waist as she remained tucked under his shoulder. Lucy melted just a little in his presence, staying focused on the words Brax shared.

"When the gods tired of their day-to-day lives, they created life. They bestowed their magic on some of their creations—each group having unique abilities. The elementals could summon the four elements in order to bend air, fire, water, and earth to their will. Those with more practical magic conjured things from afar, created beauty and prestige, and brought light when there was none. A group was gifted the magic of healing others, and another group was blessed with warrior-like abilities."

"How does this explain my magic?" Micah asked.

Holding up a finger to silence him, Brax continued talking, ignoring his question.

"The gods did this expecting loyalty and adoration from their creations, and once they got bored, they sat by and watched them turn on one another. Those with elemental powers felt more important than those with more functional powers, like summoning.

Those with powers that created beauty feared those who would destroy."

Brax paced, looking down at her feet as she walked. It seemed strange to see this powerful Fae so lost in thought.

"Each unit of Fae felt threatened by the others," Brax continued. "The warriors came together and left first, not wanting to be forced into battle with any of the other Fae whom they so loved and cared for. Many of the healers went with them, fearing others would take advantage of them. So became the Vytyrians."

Brax flourished her hands as she spoke of the Vytyr.

Lucy rolled her eyes.

"The elemental magic stayed fused with the realm. Those Fae who could wield water, fire, air, and earth felt that they were most strong when united. However, the functional Fae were terrified about what that meant. They bonded together and created what is now known as Denora."

Lucy and Wes shared a tense look as Brax's eyes darted to theirs.

"Your functional magic allows you to bring light in dark places, move objects of your desire, and protect you with spells and charms. The elemental magic is different. No one knows what happened to it, because we have not seen it in centuries. Though it seems Miss Baum has found it. We can't be sure, of course, but there are ways to test the theory."

"I have never heard that story," Lucy said breathlessly.

"Then what's the deal with Jasper's magic?" Micah asked.

"I assume Jasper has magic that has been tarnished with time," Brax lamented.

"He has very weak magic," Wes interjected. "In my presence, he has not been able to do so much as a summoning charm. We performed the magic on the cabin together, but his help was minimal."

"Then why did he have that reaction when I said Lucy's magic was stronger than his?" Micah asked Wes.

Lucy beamed at Micah.

He said that?

"Because he is a self-serving male," Brax said. "Anyone can see that. Besides, it fits right in with the majority of Denoran men." She scoffed at the thought. "He'd never admit to having weak magic. Especially compared to a female."

"What about my magic?" Micah asked again.

"Your alchemy is different, Lumen," Brax said quietly. "I have never met your magic before. I daresay it is unique to you, and you alone. The original archer's alchemy."

CHAPTER

TWENTY

MICAH

"I think this calls for a beer," Micah said at last. Each time he thought he had heard the craziest thing, something new popped up. It was impossible to keep up with, and harder and harder to pretend that he was fine. He was so fucking far from the concept of fine that he wasn't sure if he'd ever be fine again.

"That's the first intelligent thing I think I've heard you say," Wes announced cheerily. Lucy glared at her brother, but Micah just rolled his eyes.

It wasn't worth the comment. For all he knew, Wes would call him a soup sandwich like Brax's ridiculous insults, and he didn't feel like going down that rabbit hole.

While Micah got the beers, Lucy started a fire. As all four magical beings sat around the campfire, it didn't take long for Micah to compare himself. Each person around the fire knew where they came from. Even Lucy understand her unique magic. But what about him? He knew he had magic, but he wasn't Fae—not really.

What am I?

The thought unnerved him. He was lost and confused and just a bit worried, which he didn't like at all.

365

"Brax is an interesting name," Wes said over the crackling embers. It wasn't quite dark out, but the night was not far off. Wes sat across from Micah, settling himself on the tree stump.

"I take it you haven't met many Vytyrian warriors?" Brax replied with a lift of her eyebrow.

"No, I have not," Wes admitted. "It is so odd for you to be here. In Joterra, of all places."

"I go where I am commanded," Brax replied casually, taking a swig from her bottle and placing it on the ground between her and Micah.

"That sounds awfully familiar," Lucy murmured.

"Please do not categorize me along with you and your plight, Baum." Brax's incensed tone drew an uncomfortable silence among the group.

Micah shifted uneasily. He knew the magnitude of power and viciousness that lay within Brax. Obviously, Lucy was a warrior in her own right, but there was no need for an all-out brawl right now.

Lucy's hazel eyes tinged with green as her expression hardened. "I would never want to side myself with a helpless soldier."

Brax's eyes darted to Lucy. "Say that again and see how helpless I really am," she challenged.

Micah grabbed Lucy's hand before she attempted to stand up and create a real fight. "We don't have time to bicker," he said softly.

Lucy looked at him in betrayal. "So you side with her?"

"I don't have to side with anyone. Neither of you are helpless—I think we can all agree on that. But both of your situations are very different. We don't need to jump to conclusions here."

"Why were you sent to Joterra?" Wes asked, trying to break the tension that filled the air, shifting uncomfortably on the tree stump.

"My employer entered a new business arrangement and had stakes on this property. I came to ensure nothing happened to it as he finalized the deal."

"Here?" Wes looked baffled. As if a lightbulb had turned on, his eyes alighted. "Your employer is Lord Sloan?"

"Lumen, why can't you be as intelligent as this male?" Brax replied in her deadpan way.

Micah laughed for the first time that day. It had taken a while, but he finally understood Brax enough to get her jokes. They were usually at his expense, but they didn't feel so bothersome anymore. Brax didn't have an affinity for compliments.

"Why are you so rude?" Lucy interrupted. "He is very intelligent. You know nothing about him."

"I know plenty," Brax said as she leaned forward, placing her elbows on her knees. "It is you who needs to learn, Baum."

"What do you mean you know plenty?" She looked between Brax and Micah accusingly. "How well do you really know one another?"

"Lu-" Micah began, but was cut off.

"Lucella Baum, age 122. Lives in Central Denora with her father, Corvus, mother, Anita, and four brothers, Wes, Tristan, Simon, and Henry." Brax spouted off facts about Lucy as if she were reading a report. "Brothers Gregory and Hugh live in the Southern Territory, directing the southern branch of the Baum Bowyers. You are betrothed to my employer, Lord Laurent Sloan, and apparently things have been going swimmingly, according to him. You spent a Joterran week here, with Micah, falling in love and bringing a mortal to The Elderwood, unescorted by your family."

Swimmingly, Micah repeated in his mind.

Piece by piece, his heart shattered, discovering more had been occurring than Lucy cared to let on. He wanted to be mad but he had no claim to her. Nothing had been discussed about where they stood —he couldn't even call it a relationship.

Of course, *he* had no interest in anyone else, but he would never expect to control Lucy's thoughts or feelings about it.

Lucy stood up in a rage, the bright green light dancing along her hand and curling up her arm.

"You are a female in Denora which means you have no say in the matter," Brax rattled on. "You are destined for a life of idiotic males telling you what to do and, from the looks of it, you are more powerful than all of them combined."

At that, Micah and Wes looked to Brax in confusion. Lucy stilled as she stood above her.

"So tell me, Baum." Brax stood up. "Are you going to let those males control your life?" She took a step closer to Lucy.

"Never," Lucy said adamantly.

Brax's eyes lit up wickedly, a small smile forming on her lips.

"Good. Maybe you are closer to learning than I thought."

"And what is it exactly that you feel I must learn?" Lucy demanded.

"That you are the only one in charge of your life. That you must never let a male determine your fate nor your future."

"Didn't you just say you were commanded here? How is that being in charge of your life?" Lucy spat.

Brax sat, unaffected by her anger. "Because I chose to come here. I chose the contract from Lord Sloan knowing that I could complete my job and be paid handsomely."

"You chose? What do you mean?" Lucy looked dumbfounded.

"Ah, yes. I know. It is such a foreign concept for a Denoran female," Brax continued. To others, it seemed as though Brax was being crass, but Micah knew she meant the words with sincerity. "Lord Sloan is an honorable Fae. He creates the contracts and sends them to Vytyr. Any of the warriors can apply for the position. I've had a longstanding partnership with him, and he agreed to my request for payment. I signed the contract and arrived here soon after."

"Your request?" Wes asked curiously.

"Yes," Brax murmured.

"What did you request?" Micah asked, equally curious.

Brax looked at Micah as though he was the only one there. "I requested a payment big enough so that I can go home." Her words were simple, but Micah heard the words she didn't say. Just like she mentioned before—her eyes betrayed her.

They softened as a barely noticeable shimmer foretold withheld tears. It wasn't for her to go home for a visit. It was for her to finish her days of being a warrior and be able to live out the rest of her time with her family.

"And Laurent agreed?" Lucy asked. Each time she spoke of him so casually, Micah felt as though he took an arrow through the chest.

"Yes," Brax said simply. "He differs from the Denoran males. Though I expect you've already figured that out." Brax's usual mocking tone was gone. She shifted her eyes to Micah, seeing his hurt. Brax looked down to the ground, grabbed her beer and took another drink.

Lucy was quiet. "Yes," she replied. "I suppose I have."

Micah refused to look up from his gaze on the fire.

Swallow me whole, he asked the flames.

"What makes this male so different?" Wes asked, oblivious to the fact that Lucy just admitted something life-changing for her and Micah.

Lucy looked at Micah in question, but when he didn't meet her eye, she turned to Wes instead. "He supports the poor in his territory. He is of high status, but does not flaunt it or abuse his power. He doesn't believe that females should have no voice in their life."

"As long as they aren't his future wife, right?" Micah spat.

"Micah," Lucy began, but Micah threw his hands in the air and stood.

"It's fine. I'm glad he's a good person. I wish you all the happiness in the world."

Then he grabbed another beer and stalked off into the trees, putting as much distance between him and Lucy as he could.

"Micah!" Lucy stood up and tried to follow him, but Brax took her arm.

"Give him a minute," Brax told her calmly.

"I need to talk to him," Micah heard Lucy say as he got further from the fire pit.

"Well, I need to talk to you," Wes said to Lucy in annoyance.

"Someone needs to explain more of this to me, because I clearly am missing some major details."

The voices carried through the trees as they argued, until they all faded away. The last thing he heard was Brax stopping Lucy.

"You can talk to Micah soon, but he needs a minute to calm down. After everything that has happened, it's the least you owe him."

IF MICAH WASN'T SO angry, the forest would have looked much more imposing. However, his mind was not on the broken portal, the shadow cat, or his alchemy. None of that mattered to him right now. All he could think about was Lucy in the arms of that asshole, and how he was stuck here pining after her while she went to Sloan.

She actually likes him. She defended him!

The wind in the trees was subtle, and the lightning bugs made their appearance alongside the stars. Night had fallen quickly, but this one felt different. For so long, Micah looked at every night as one step closer to Lucy, but it didn't seem as though Lucy had the same plans in mind.

His feet led him to the old tree house. He regularly found himself there when in need of refuge—half of the time he didn't even realize where he was going until he arrived. It was as if his mind knew it was the one place he could find solace. The one spot that remained that would connect him to Abe.

What I wouldn't give for a sliver of advice right now, old man.

He climbed up the weathered rungs of the tree house, skipping the third one that had rotted away to nothing. Balancing carefully, he shuffled over to the far corner that was most supported by the massive tree trunk. He slunk down and sat, staring up at the sky through the broken rooftop, watching as the clouds covered the moon and stars.

"Typical," he said to himself.

More things being hidden from view... Is that all my life is now? A series of events that are hidden from me until they come crashing down?

He closed his eyes and let the crickets lull him into calm. Micah wasn't happy with how things were going, but he also knew when there was nothing he could do.

He couldn't force Lucy to feel a certain way about him, and he'd never pressure her into something she didn't want. He couldn't master his magic without practice. He couldn't change his path in life; he was the guardian, and he accepted that for himself. He'd be lying to say he accepted without the thought of Lucy—he had hoped she'd be there with him every step of the way. He thought this visit to Denora would have been a hiccup in their future, not change its course completely.

Lucy is fierce and adventurous. She has big plans for her own realm, it's selfish to consider that she'd leave her old life behind and be forced to stay here with me.

"I am such a fool," he murmured into the dark.

"No, you aren't."

Lucy.

Micah sat up straighter and looked away from her as she climbed the ladder with ease. His body tensed as she sat down next to him. His emotions were in an uproar—he couldn't figure out if he was mad at Lucy or himself.

"Micah, please talk to me," she whispered.

He looked at her with despondence. "What is it you'd like me to say, Lu? That I'm fucking broken knowing that you want this other guy? That I can just accept that you're going to run off into the sunset with him? You know I can't do that."

"That isn't what this is," Lucy said. "I'm not running away from anyone."

"But you want him."

Lucy bit her lip as tears came to her eyes. "It's not like that."

"Then what's going on with you and him? You seem pretty fucking interested in all of his good deeds."

"I don't know how to explain." Her voice faltered.

Micah remained quiet. With his arms propped up on his knees, he held his beer bottle with both hands. Each thing he considered saying wouldn't change reality.

He wouldn't ask for specifics, because he didn't think he'd be able to handle it. He didn't want to know what her plan was, because if it didn't include him, he might scream. All he needed to know was how she felt about him. He needed to know it wasn't all just a ploy to get what she needed from The Elderwood—but he couldn't ask that. If the answer was what he feared, there would be no mending his heart.

Not now.

Not after everything.

"This place has so many good memories," Lucy eventually said, breaking the silence. "Abe and I were in this tree house all the time... I miss him."

"Me too," Micah replied. "I've been so busy I haven't even been able to read all of the letters he left me... He mentioned you in a few of them."

"You remind me of him sometimes, you know," Lucy said as she took his hand and held it in her lap.

Their touch ignited a fire in his heart, but he couldn't act on it.

"You have his eyes," she said quietly.

He finally looked up, meeting her hazel eyes, rimmed with red, tears shimmering.

"Please, don't cry," Micah whispered, touching her face.

Lucy leaned into his hand, crying more. "I'm sorry," she sobbed. "I wasn't sure what to do and I really thought I could help make a better Denora with Laurent. But when I got here and saw that shadow beast hurting you, it was as if my world was falling apart. I don't know what I would have done if anything happened to you. I'm so sorry."

Fuck it.

He pulled her into his lap and cradled her there as she cried. He stroked her hair, caressed her arms, and held her as if she was the only thing in this universe that could save him. And maybe she was.

CHAPTER
TWENTY-ONE

LUCY

Micah held Lucy's left hand firmly as they walked through the cabin upstairs to his bedroom; his broad hands fit in hers like a perfect puzzle piece. She felt the gritty mud and dirt that covered him from his encounter with the shadow beast. His steps were sure, no trace of the injury, but something lay heavy on his heart.

Releasing her hand, Micah walked further through the bedroom and pulled his shirt from his back. As he reached the bathroom, he turned the water on to the shower. He didn't look at Lucy, but she couldn't keep her eyes off of him. She followed him in and stood near the sinks, taking in the view. His tall frame slumped. His hair was a tangled mess as he peered through the room with vacant eyes.

I can't believe I hurt him like this. I don't deserve him.

His broad shoulders rippled as he made his way to her. His face was stoic and untelling—something that Lucy was surely not used to. She remembered his anger, his flirtation, and his adoration; but not this. Not an empty vessel.

Her brows furrowed, leaving a line of worry in the middle of her forehead. Sadness filled her, unsure what this all meant.

They didn't speak a word as they found each other in the dark room.

He reached for her and brushed her hair back from her face and off her shoulders.

"Micah," she began, but he silenced her with a kiss. Soft, immediate, and filled with all the words they could not say.

She melted into him, and he put his hands on her face, his thumb caressing her cheek. Lucy would do anything to hold on to this moment of contentment—they never seemed to last with him. Wrapping her arms around his shoulders, she pulled him toward her, needing him closer.

Micah slid his hands down her back and to the hem of her shirt, pulling it over her head. He threw it to the floor next to them, then he picked her up by her waist and abruptly sat her on the edge of the sink. The forceful movement caught her off guard, their gaze snapping together.

They stared into each other's eyes for a moment and thoughts of everything that had happened since she had left filled her mind.

Her time spent with Laurent, kissing him in the carriage.

Her dreams of both of them seemed at war in her heart.

Her constant state of indecision when it came to the marriage arrangement.

She thought of Brax and anything that could have happened with Micah.

It doesn't matter.

None of it mattered now that she was in his arms once again. Her fingers traced the tired look in his eyes that had appeared since her absence.

"Micah?" Lucy whispered to him in the solace of the dark bathroom.

Micah pulled back and kneeled in front of her. Each time he put more distance between them, her heart ached.

He untied her shoes, taking them off one by one and placing them on the tile floor with the other clothes. Lucy stared at him from her seated position, afraid to speak. He peeled off each of her socks, then stood in front of Lucy again, looking at her body, at her hands, everywhere but her eyes.

Micah moved in closer to her and her heart raced as he reached around to pick up one of her legs. He cradled one leg at a time, pulling her leggings off slowly, as though he was peeling each layer of distance away between them, leaving only them.

When she was left in only her undergarments, he grabbed two towels, put them near the shower door, and returned to her.

His eyes trailed her neck to her lips, and stopped on her eyes.

The hurt that lived there was like an arrow to her heart.

If Lucy didn't know any better, she'd think there was nothing there behind that darkened gaze. But Lucy did know Micah, and she knew this was about more than the shadow beast. It was about more than their time away from each other and the devastatingly confusing information he was gaining each day.

No. This was not Micah feeling nothing at all. He was feeling too much.

He was doing his best to keep it all in without breaking, but he was cracking. And Lucy wanted to put him back together.

Lucy stepped down from the edge of the sink and padded over to him, her bare feet cold on the white tile. She dragged her hands down the sides of his arms and stopped at his waistband, pulling his pants off. She stood and removed the rest of her undergarments, wordlessly telling him she needed him, too.

Her skin pebbled even as she opened the door to the shower and the warm steam filled the small space.

Lucy tugged on Micah's hand, and pulled him into the shower with her, the hot water spilling over their naked bodies, cleansing them from the filth of battle. His eyes remained unfocused as their bodies pressed together. He looked down, behind her, at his hands; but never at her.

The reality of the situation hurt, but the fault was hers. He waited here for her, while she allowed herself to be distracted by the possibility of a new Denora in the arms of another male. Of course he was hurting.

How could I have been so selfish?

Lucy grabbed the soap and lathered a sponge, then turned Micah so she could clean his back and his arms where he was covered in dirt and blood. With each movement, Micah relaxed a little more. She turned him to face her, so she could get his chest and shoulders, her breathing hitching at the proximity of him.

She scrubbed away the dirt. The quiet unnerved her. Feeling his eyes on her, she held her breath as she finally looked up, making eye contact with him. He stared at her, unblinking.

All she had to do was say it.

Tell him you love him, she swore at herself.

She felt it in every bone in her body, every ounce of her being yearned for him and him alone, but telling him now would be unfair. She couldn't manipulate him like that. Not after he had been through so much.

Micah took the sponge from her and turned Lucy. Slowly, he smoothed her hair over to one side and washed her back, then her arms, mirroring the movements from Lucy. Ever so slowly, he washed her as Lucy took shallow breaths, afraid to speak.

Look at me, she begged, terrified to say another word.

His eyes trailed to her lips. "Did you pick him?" he finally asked her.

Her heart sank like a falling stone in a bottomless sea.

"No," she whispered.

It's you, the words silent on her lips.

Micah squeezed the sponge on her chest, watching the bubbles cascade down her breasts to her navel. "Do you still want me?" Micah's eyes burned with hurt as they trailed her neck, her lips, and finally her tear filled gaze.

Lucy nodded, tears falling and blending with the stream of water from above.

Micah crashed into Lucy, pulling her into a deep kiss and grabbing her body with his large, firm hands.

Lucy gasped as she opened her mouth to his, tasting sweat, and soap, and Micah. He gripped her thighs and picked her up, pushing her up against the wall of the shower to keep her in place. Their soapy, wet bodies slid over one another as the cold tile warmed with the steaming water and their heated skin. With each possessive stroke of his tongue, Micah claimed Lucy as his own and with each moan, Lucy accepted.

She was his, and he was hers.

They didn't speak after that, the only sounds coming from the room being breathless cries, full of lust and love lost. Their joining bodies gave them the comfort they both needed as each processed what had happened.

They needed to know they were still rooting for one another. They needed to know the other was still there, still present—even if they were realms apart.

The water turned cold by the time they were done.

As Micah slept soundlessly next to Lucy, she stared at him and took in all of his features. His face seemed so relaxed as he slept, the stress and tension not present in his dreams.

Lucy realized in the dark of the night the importance of Micah... He would never be a great Lord of Denora, making the realm a better place for all those who needed a champion—but he was *her* champion. Micah was the one who would always be there for Lucy's battles, supporting her and giving her whatever she needed. And more than that, Lucy would give Micah the same love and affection in return. She didn't need lavish outings and fine dining. She needed a partner. Someone who would sit with her and stare up at the stars, discussing the beauty of the world around them.

Lucy looked through the window to the night sky just outside, and from the comfort of Micah's warm embrace, it was so very beautiful.

"WE NEED to test the magic to see what it can do," Brax announced as Micah and Lucy walked outside the next morning.

Lucy wore one of Micah's t-shirts with her leggings, and she hugged it tightly to her chest, taking in the smells of Micah.

Micah was still quiet, but there wasn't so much distance between the two of them now. His hands kept finding Lucy, touching her arm, her back, her hair. Lucy's body leaned into every touch, yearning for more of his attention.

"How do we test it?" Wes asked through a mouthful of eggs.

"We push it to its limits and see when it breaks," Brax replied.

"Can it hurt him?" Lucy asked, watching Wes move his plate to the side. She didn't have an appetite—her mind kept reeling with the same thought over and over.

I hurt Micah.

She barely slept, worrying over what would happen next; knowing she'd do whatever it took to regain his trust.

"No. We won't let him get hurt, I promise," Brax said, no jeering in her tone. "If anything happens to him, I can heal him."

Since their argument over the fire the previous night, they had seemed to come to a truce. Both females wanted to protect Micah and The Elderwood. They were both on the same team—for now.

Lucy nodded in assent.

"Glad to see you two have finally joined us," Wes said with a raised eyebrow in irritation.

Lucy's eyes widened at her brother's tone. What was she supposed to say to that? Obviously she and Micah needed time away to talk things over. Could he really be so unhappy with her over this relationship?

"Don't worry. I've already talked to Brax and she's explained everything, with no help from you." Wes took a dramatic bite of his breakfast and put his plate on the ground next to his place on the stump.

"I'm sorry." Lucy took a step toward her brother. "I didn't mean to disappear on you like that, I just had things I needed to take care of..."

"Yes, it seems as though there was much more going on here than I had realized." Wes gave Micah a cursory glance and refocused on his sister. "I don't think I'll ever approve of anyone you wish to be with, but what matters is that *you* want it. Right?"

Lucy's heart soared. She nodded.

"So, testing this magic," he said in a change of topic. "Can I start?" He wiped his hands clean and walked over to Micah.

"You seem a little too excited for that," Micah replied with a laugh. Lucy heard the sadness in his tone. It wasn't a genuine laugh, just another show.

I hurt him.

"It's good to release some magic when you're stressed. You'll see, it'll be fine."

Lucy stood off to the side as Micah and Wes faced one another in the yard. The Elderwood barricade glowed a faint purple in the background, reminding Lucy of the importance of Micah learning.

He needs to know how to protect himself when he is alone. He needs to learn as much as he can.

That reality struck Lucy with a heavy dose of fear.

If he doesn't learn, there may not be someone around if he... she couldn't even finish the thought. How could she leave him again?

Wes started by using his magic to lift a large branch from the forest floor, then hurled it at Micah. Lucy's breath got caught in her throat as she watched Micah's magic respond without delay.

Before Micah's arms flew out in front of him, an enormous red shimmer created a wall before him. The tree branch smacked against it and was projected back toward Wes. With exceptional Fae speed, Wes jumped out of the way to dodge the hit.

"Interesting," Wes mused, his hair windblown from his sprint. He walked back to his starting position with a smile on his face, nostrils flared and breathing hard. "Drop your shield and let's see if you can get past this next one."

"I don't always know what the magic is going to do," Micah replied. "I didn't mean to call on the shield... it just kind of happened."

"What were you thinking of, Lumen?" Brax asked from the sidelines.

"I thought the branch was massive and I wasn't sure if I could stop it," he admitted.

"You didn't trust your magic, so your magic did it for you. This time, *know* you can do it. Even if you miss, your magic will stop it on its own. Understood?"

Micah nodded and scrunched his face in concentration, forcing the shield to drop. He stood at the ready, his arms outstretched and prepared.

Lucy watched with bated breath as her brother lifted a variety of rocks into the air. Some were as small as an acorn, and others as big as Lucy's head.

Micah gestured to Wes with fierce determination in his eyes. Wes pushed his two hands toward Micah, and the wave of rocks came careening at him all at once. Micah's crimson magic latched onto each stone, stopping them midair. The rocks wavered as Micah stumbled over what to do next.

"Focus, Lumen!" Brax shouted in support.

"Find the thread that connects you to your magic," Lucy called to him, taking a few steps closer. "It will be deep inside of you and feel different from the rest. Your alchemy will be connected with the earth—find the connection and pull."

Micah's face contorted as he put all of his effort into the task. He squeezed his eyes shut tight. Lucy watched as the stones began splitting—one by one, each rock dividing into smaller and smaller pieces. Suddenly, the rocks disintegrated entirely; the dust suspended in the air. Micah opened his eyes, his eyebrows furrowed in concentration.

"Good, Micah!" Lucy cheered him on. "Now, what does your magic want to do?"

Micah's eyebrow rose in surprise, then he closed his eyes once more and his mouth set in a grim line. The speckles of rock remnants moved toward each other, creating one large sphere of dust.

With his hands stretched out and knees bent, Micah was clearly exhausted from using so much force at once. These were not minor spells and charms to move a chair or create an orb of light—this was critical life-or-death magic.

Micah set his sights on the sphere. He pulled his arms toward his chest, then together with a large step forward, he pushed out with vehemence, grunting through the exertion.

The cloud of dust was no longer a cloud, but instead an enormous boulder that cannoned toward Wes. Lucy knew he wouldn't get out of the way in time, and she pushed her magic in front of Wes, creating a green field that protected him and demolished the rock with a resounding crash.

Wes stared at the force field before him in shock. He looked between Lucy and Micah, panting heavily.

"You almost crushed me," Wes barely got out.

"Just returning the favor," Micah replied, equally breathless.

"Perfect. Now we know if you need to use your magic, you can," Brax said. "Interesting addition to the alchemy though," she looked at Lucy. "I'm very curious about what this all means."

"You and me both." Micah groaned and sat on the ground.

"No, no. Get up, Lumen. We saw how you responded to Denoran magic. Now, it's my turn." Brax gave him a crude smile and cracked her knuckles. "Let's play." She rolled her neck in a stretch.

"This is sure to be interesting," Wes whispered to Lucy as he stood next to her, still panting.

Brax gave Micah no time to rest, pouncing at him with a

warrior's call. Micah rolled onto his side to avoid her knee as it came thundering down into the ground, cracking the earth beneath her.

"What the hell?" Micah shouted as he leapt to his feet.

"No time to go easy on you, Lumen." Brax said as she stood. "Give me everything you've got."

Micah stood tall, curled his hands into fists, and rolled his shoulders back. "I'll do my best."

Brax came speeding after him. Lucy held her breath as she watched. Brax's fist flew out in front of her, but Micah dodged it in a flash.

He can move like the Fae?

He sped behind Brax and pushed her, causing her to turn. With a swoop of her leg, Brax kicked out and knocked him to the ground.

"Not bad, Lumen," Brax spat. "The Vytyrians can move quickly, with speed, finesse, and accuracy. See if you can hit me."

"But I don't want to hit you," Micah argued.

"Oh, but you wanted to pulverize me?" Wes called from the sidelines.

"If you don't hit me, I'm going to break apart your rock wall and let the shadow beasts take you down."

"You wouldn't," Micah said, standing up straight to speak with her.

She sped forward with a punch to his gut as she whispered, "yes, I would. We will do whatever it takes to pull the magic from you."

Micah spun and took the legs out from under her, causing her to crash to the ground. With Brax on her back, Micah brought his fist down to punch her. Just as his fist was inches from her face, she rolled away, causing Micah to put a divot in the dirt.

Lucy felt the ground rumble under his strength.

Brax did a flip, skirting away from him, a look of surprise and pride on her face. She zoomed to his left, ducked and popped up on his right, prepared to hit him.

Micah caught her fist midair with his hand. Brax pushed more of her force into her arm, trying to hit Micah. Instead, Micah held his ground, sweat pouring down his face as he kept her away from him.

She tried to punch with her other fist, but Micah caught that one, too.

It was an even stand off, neither stronger than the other.

"That's enough," Lucy shouted. "Let go of each other—there will be no winner."

Micah nodded and released Brax hesitantly. As he relaxed, Brax followed up with a quick head-butt. Micah fell to the ground in pain, and Brax acted as though nothing had happened.

"What was that for?" Micah groaned.

"We both know I couldn't let you win," she winked. She placed her hands on his head and healed him, giving him a firm clap on the back when she was through. "You were a worthy opponent."

"That was exhausting. Is this always what magic feels like?"

"Sometimes," Lucy said, bringing him a bottle of water. "Over time, you can build stamina so it doesn't feel so exhaustive. But all Fae need time to recharge. I'm curious what your magic will need to replenish."

"That is a good question," Brax said thoughtfully. "Denorans need to be in a Fae realm and limit time between usage to restore their magic. Vytyrians need to strengthen their body, keep themselves moving. We recharge during battle, which makes us hard to take down."

"You recharge during battle? Man, your adversaries are out of luck." Micah took a big drink of water. "Wait. You checked the perimeter like three times a day. Were you recharging then?" Micah asked.

"Sometimes, yes. Other times I was just bored." Brax waved off his comment. "Lucy, what about you? How do you replenish this magic?"

Lucy had never thought about it before. This particular magic that flowed inside of her felt different than her Denoran magic. It felt like it was always alive and ready to be used. She felt tired after the initial battle at The Elderwood when the land developers were trying to burn down the land, but that could have also been shock.

"I don't think I have to recharge it," she said, surprising even herself.

"That is impossible," Wes said, walking over to his sister. "All magic needs to recharge."

"Truly, I don't think I need to? Though, I haven't had to use much of my magic since I've received it."

"Show us," Brax said as she stepped back and leaned against a tree.

"You want me to go against Micah?"

"No, I think Lumen needs a break," Brax shared. "But your elemental magic would be a splendor to behold."

Lucy nodded solemnly. She kept forgetting that this magic wasn't just from The Elderwood, but it was likely the long lost elemental magic. Something completely different from anything she had ever known before.

"Remind me, elemental... that means I can control all four elements?"

"Yes, Baum. Fire, air, water and earth."

"I have an idea," Lucy said with a smile. "But Micah, I need your assistance."

"I'll try, but I'm not sure how much help I'll be."

"Sit here," she directed him to a place in the dirt. "And put your hands on the ground."

Micah looked at her inquisitively, but obeyed. Lucy's insides jumped with excitement. She could feel her magic moving inside of her, knowing it was going to come out to play. Her eyes glimmered with hints of green.

"I'm going to try something, and if you can feel it, I want you to pull it toward you. Alright?"

Micah nodded, and Lucy knelt in front of him. She called on her magic, and the green swirls of light bound from her hand and encircled her entire body. Lucy closed her eyes and placed her hands on the ground next to Micah's.

That was when she felt it. The ground trembled beneath her; the earth shifted subtly far below.

"Is that you?" Micah whispered to Lucy.

"You feel it, don't you?" Lucy asked, pleased with herself.

I knew this would work.

"I do, but I don't know what it is."

"Pull," she reminded him with a smile.

Then, with all of her might, she pressed down hard into the ground, her fingers clenching the dirt as her magic obeyed her thoughts.

Brax's gasp cut through the rumbling.

Wes swore.

Lucy opened her eyes and saw the emerald green magic swirling around Micah's ruby red, and under his hands, exactly what she had hoped for: liquid metal.

Micah opened his eyes and looked at ground in shock. Beneath his hands were small metallic pools of gold, settled among the dirt.

"What is this?" Micah asked in disbelief.

"I loosened the ground so you could find the precious metals."

"There was gold under Grandad's property?" He looked around in shock.

"Not exactly," Lucy said with a smile.

Brax came over and bent down to see the liquid hardening now that Micah lifted his hands. "You used your alchemy, Micah," she said in amazement. "How did you know how to do it?"

"I didn't," he told her. Then he looked at Lucy. "Did you plan for that?"

"Partially." Her smile grew as she looked at the astonishment on Micah's face. "I asked the ground to separate from the minerals and metals so that you could find them."

Brax turned to Lucy suddenly. "Did you just say you asked the ground? Or you asked your magic?"

"The ground, I guess." Lucy saw the concerned look on Brax's face. "Why?"

Brax stood up in a rush, still staring at Lucy. She walked away from Lucy, then turned back—words lost on her lips, her eyes wide. She paced back and forth, a panicked look across her face.

"What is it?" Micah asked her.

She ignored him until Micah walked over and held her arm gently. "Brax. What's wrong?"

"What's going on?" Wes asked in worry.

"Lucy, if you didn't tell your magic to do that, then..." Brax couldn't seem to say the words.

"Just say it," Lucy pleaded. Brax's reaction was scaring her. Lucy's heart thudded loudly in her chest as everyone waited silently for Brax to share why she was so thrown.

"Your magic has actualized."

"What does that mean?" Micah asked.

"It means Lucy's magic has joined with her body. They no longer need to communicate because they are joined as one," Brax explained.

"But that hasn't happened since the Originals," Wes argued.

"You're right." Brax bent respectfully into a low bow. "She is an Original."

TWENTY-TWO

MICAH

"You're wrong," Wes said furiously, pointing his finger at Brax. "Take it back."

Micah watched as the three Fae in front of him panicked as they spoke.

What does any of this mean? Why is Wes so mad? Why is Lucy so scared?

Brax stood up from her position in front of Lucy, looking at her with adoration. She turned to look at Wes with sympathy. "I'm sorry, I cannot. What I said is true."

"How can you be sure?" Lucy asked, a tremble in her voice.

"You can see for yourself," Brax said, nodding her head encouragingly. "Tell the rain to fall," she whispered joyously.

"What?" Lucy took a step back. "I can't do that. No one can do that."

Brax remained silent, staring at Lucy expectantly, a smile playing on her lips.

The only time Brax is quiet is when she knows she doesn't have to argue.

Micah's heart raced with anticipation. "Try it and see what

happens?"

He wanted to encourage Lucy, but their reactions were concerning. He needed Lucy to be safe, but wouldn't this protect her? To have powers beyond all other Fae?

He placed his hands on her waist, offering support and reminding her he was there.

Lucy looked up to the sky and closed her eyes. Seconds later, small droplets of rain fell from the blue, cloudless sky. She gasped and opened her eyes when she felt them on her face.

Micah stood in awe of the woman in front of him. She was perfect in every way, and now her magic was otherworldly. Her once hazel eyes swam with emerald.

Wes stared into the sky with wide eyes, his mouth hanging open in surprise. "This can't be," he murmured.

Brax gently touched Lucy's arm to get her attention. A soft smile reserved for very few appeared on her face as she spoke again. "Now, tell it to stop."

Her eyes were frozen on Brax. "Stop," Lucy whispered.

The rain ceased and Lucy fell to her knees. Micah caught her and held her in his arms.

"Lucy?" he asked in concern, but she covered her face, a gentle sob muffled from behind her hands.

He had never seen Lucy this weak before. Even in their time together, she was nothing but strength. If she was supposed to be all powerful now, why had she collapsed?

"Is she okay?" Micah asked Brax, fear coursing through him.

Brax bent down low, putting a hand on Micah. "She will be." He looked at Brax, seeking answers from her solemn look.

"But you aren't doing your magical thing," Micah argued. "Heal her." His voice was demanding. "Does she need to recharge her magic? Did she do too much?"

"She's not in need of healing, Micah. She is in shock."

"She's okay?" Micah asked breathlessly.

Brax nodded, then her eyes found Wes. He was still staring with unblinking eyes. Brax walked over to him and punched him in the stomach. He keeled over in two.

"What in the realms was that for?" Wes wheezed.

Brax put a hand on his shoulder and healed him from the pain. "Needed to help you take your mind off of it for a moment," she said with a wink.

Lucy shivered in Micah's arms, her panicked breaths increasing with each second. Micah had not seen her look this pale before. She uncovered her face and looked to Brax.

"How did this happen? Wouldn't I have realized?" Lucy asked her. "Why me?" Lucy's hands trembled with fear as she rattled off her questions, one by one, without pause.

Micah held her close and kissed her forehead gently. "We will figure this out," he reassured her. "Come on, let's go inside."

Lucy could barely move. Tremors racked her entire body. He lifted her into his arms and led the way back into the cabin as Brax pulled Wes inside after them.

Placing Lucy down in a chair at the table, Micah went to the sink to get a glass of water. "It's not uncommon to have a physical reaction to shocking information," Micah said calmly as he filled the glass. "When I had civilians who had experienced extreme trauma, this was a typical reaction. You need to drink some water, and I'll get some sugar in you." He looked through the cabinets for some candy as Lucy sat shivering, staring out the window past Wes, who sat across from her.

Micah's calm demeanor on the outside was just a show of strength for Lucy. Inside, his mind was reeling.

What does it mean that her magic has unified with her? Why is she having this reaction? Does the magic hurt her? Why is Brax so damn quiet now?

He shot her an annoyed glance as Brax stood near the kitchen island, watching the two men dote on Lucy.

"Luce," Wes said quietly. He took her hand in his and rubbed his thumb across her fingers.

"You haven't called me that since before you joined Father's business." Lucy's eyes were on Wes as Micah placed the glass of water down in front of her and sat to her left.

Wes gave a weak, tight-lipped smile. "Sometimes I try to be the Fae Father wants me to be, and sometimes I forget where my heart truly lies."

"And where is that?"

"With those that I love," Wes replied. "Tristan was right about you. You're more worthy than all of us combined."

Lucy looked away from Wes and continued to stare out the window.

"What does it mean, Brax?" Micah whispered, afraid to speak the words if the answer was not something he was prepared to hear. He looked at her, searching for answers; for hope.

Brax sat down next to him and took his hand. Micah couldn't recall a time that Brax touched him as a show of sentimentality. Her hands were softer than he expected. "Micah Lumen, you are a defender, so I know this is hard to accept—but Lucy doesn't need your protection."

"What happens when magic actualizes like this?"

"I have never seen it firsthand," she admitted. She looked down at her lap, deep in thought. "I have read little about it, and heard rumors for the rest. The Originals were the Fae who were given magic by the gods. They were more than Fae, because their power was absolute. You see, as years pass, the magic within us dilutes as it transfers from generation to generation. But Miss Lucy was gifted with magic that was looking for a home, straight from the gods of lore."

She withdrew her hand and moved her chair to face him. Wes leaned in further to listen.

"Once the gods ascended, some of their magic remained on the living planes of existence. Lucy's magic was living in The Elderwood for a very long time."

"So she isn't an elemental?"

Brax shook her head no in response. "No. This magic from the gods... It found its home with Lucy and has decided to form a symbiotic relationship with her."

"What does that mean?" Micah asked, confused and frustrated at never understanding any of these Fae terms.

"It means," Wes said slowly. "Lucy has changed."

The words should have rocked Micah right out of his seat, but in the same second, Lucy stood up quickly, scraping her chair across the tiled floor.

"Someone's here," she said as her magic crept out from her hand and twined around her arms and torso.

Brax stood as well, looking out the window. "Who is it? I see no one."

"The Elderwood is showing me," she said in a whisper. Her eyes were a bright emerald. "It's Jasper."

"What does he want?" Micah asked. One by one, each person stood up, looking through the glass, searching for Jasper's arrival.

"I'm not sure, but we need to call my father," Lucy directed. She seemed more confident than just seconds before, her eyes clear and her hands no longer shaking. "Wes, Brax, and I will go out to speak with him. Micah, you use the mirror and tell my father that his arrival is urgently needed. He will be able to stop this charade—we will take Jasper's power out from under him."

"What are you going to say to Jasper?" Micah asked.

"We are going to tell him The Elderwood is not his to take," Lucy said, taking a deep breath.

"We are going to tell him we will go down fighting," Brax said.

"We are going to tell him to fuck off," Wes added angrily.

Micah looked back to Lucy, his eyebrows furrowing in worry. "Are you sure you'll be okay?"

Lucy looked at Micah and gave him a soft smile. She leaned in, kissed him gently and whispered to him. "I am alright. I promise." Her voice was strong.

Micah nodded.

"Let's go take Jasper down," she added.

Micah couldn't help but smile as Lucy, Brax, and Wes left the kitchen to meet Jasper on the property. He watched as Lucy walked over with a determination that could not be destroyed.

There goes my badass warrior.

His heart thudded with pride.

He swiftly turned and reached the mirror, threw the calling sand and called out to the empty room. "Corvus Baum! The Elderwood is in danger!"

Only a second passed before the face of Lucy's father was clear in the mirror.

"What is the meaning of this?" Corvus asked, his wide body taking up the majority of the looking glass. He was regal in a deep navy suit jacket that only made his reddening cheeks look brighter.

"Hello sir, my name is Micah Lumen, I'm the new guardian of The Elderwood?" Micah was doing his best not to stutter, but he was not prepared for Lucy's father to be such an intimidating man.

"I know who you are." He eyed him judgingly. "What is the problem? Why are you saying The Elderwood is in danger?" The stern look on his face prompted Micah to jump right in.

"Mr. Baum," Micah spoke clearly. "There will be time to explain it all later, but The Elderwood is in trouble. We need you now."

"We?"

"Wes and Lucy are here, sir," Micah said, gulping.

"They are there? I told-"

"Please, sir," Micah interrupted. "I don't know how much time we have."

Tight-lipped, Corvus nodded. "I'll come at once." Corvus's face changed from anger to worry. "I need to find Jasper."

"He's here, sir."

"Why is he there? Did you call him first?"

A loud crash thundered. Micah ran to the window to see what had happened. Outside, Jasper stood alone in front of Brax, Wes, and Lucy. Wes was on the ground and Brax was helping him up. Lucy's green magic swirled, and from all the way where he was, he could sense the rage growing from Jasper.

"No, Mr. Baum," Micah said, racing back to the mirror. "He's the one threatening the portal. Lucy and Wes are out there right now trying to defend it from him. You need to hurry."

Corvus's face paled with fear.

"Do not underestimate him. There has been a change in him lately. We are on our way. Keep my children safe," he said solemnly. Then, just as quickly as he appeared, he vanished.

TWENTY-THREE

LUCY

Lucy's magic curled around her body in anticipation. Her heart thumped steadily in her chest as she stepped across the flattened grass to meet Jasper. They agreed to bring the fight to him in fear of Jasper getting too close to the portal. Ever since The Elderwood showed her Jasper's involvement, she knew there would be an uncomfortable accusation, but she did not expect it to be so soon.

"Are you sure he's out here, Baum?" Brax asked quietly from behind her.

Lucy had placed a privacy charm to ensure Jasper wouldn't hear them approach, but she wasn't sure what good it would do. He was still here, and there was still a serious problem they needed to rectify.

They needed Jasper gone.

She closed her eyes and asked The Elderwood to show her where he was, and clear in her mind, the vision came to her. Just like in the kitchen, her magic filled her mind with trees and leaves until suddenly, Jasper's face came into view. His menacing sneer made her stomach coil. He was just behind the line of trees.

"He's here." Lucy dismantled the privacy ward and watched as

Jasper came around the bend—the house in the distance behind them.

"To what do we owe the pleasure?" Wes asked as Jasper arrived.

Lucy expected to meet Jasper with his eyes bulging at the surprise of them halting his progress toward The Elderwood, but instead, Jasper smiled. Not his usual devious look, but happiness—elation, even.

"Oh, this is wonderful," Jasper called as he walked up to them. "All of you in one spot. This will allow things to move much more smoothly." He looked at Lucy. "It's such a joy to rely on you to never do as you're told."

"Nothing will go smoothly for you, Jasper," Lucy bit back. "You aren't getting anywhere near The Elderwood."

Jasper howled with laughter, bending over at the waist. His laughter unnerved Lucy—she had never so much as seen him smile before, and this overt display made a chill run down her spine.

"I don't care about The Elderwood, you naive female."

"What are you doing here, Jasper?" Wes demanded, taking a step closer.

"Just coming to get what I am owed." Jasper's eyes looked full of rage as they bulged from their sockets. He turned the rings on his fingers, his hands moving greedily.

"And what is it you think you are owed?" Lucy asked.

"Oh, there is no doubt. The magic here is mine, and I will not be leaving without it."

"You aren't coming anywhere near that portal," Wes ground out.

Jasper thrust his hands toward Wes, knocking him down in a crash, the ground rumbling from the force.

I thought Wes said he was weak?

"Are you not listening? I don't want the damn portal." Jasper snapped, his neck flushing red in anger. His view looked beyond Wes and Lucy, back toward the house. His eyes narrowed and he curled his lip in a depraved smile.

"You," Jasper's voice shook with rage.

Lucy turned to see Micah rushing toward them, using his newfound Fae speed to meet them. He gave a swift nod to Wes, letting them know he reached Corvus. An ounce of relief filled Lucy, but she worried it wouldn't be enough.

"I should have taken you out when I had the chance," Jasper snarled.

Brax stood defensively in front of Micah, as Lucy took a step toward Jasper. Rage bubbled in Lucy, sending her green magic writhing like hungry snakes around her torso.

"You will not touch him." Lucy's voice carried on the wind.

"There is only enough room for one Lumen," Jasper's oily voice replied.

What?

"You just had to make everything more difficult, didn't you?" Jasper took a ring from his finger and squeezed it in the palm of his hand. Immediately, bright orange sparks flared from his hold.

Lucy took a step away from Jasper, slowly getting closer to Wes, Brax, and Micah.

One Lumen?

"Don't worry—I can rectify that." Jasper pushed his hand out in front of him, and a orange orb of magic trapped all four of them. Immobile, their arms were down at their sides as if they were bound. Their mouths were closed and their faces' expressionless.

Jasper chuckled with delight as he neared the orb, pushing his hands up higher into the air, lifting them so that they hovered above the ground.

Lucy tried to speak, but she couldn't move her mouth. She couldn't move anything at all—she was frozen stiff in this orb of light.

"Yes, I imagine you're wondering how poor little Jasper, with his mediocre magic, could pull this off." He walked slowly, circling around the orb as he guided them through the trees to the house. "You see, my magic has been trapped, no thanks to the false Lumen ancestor."

False Lumen?

Lucy tried to scream, but nothing worked.

The only thing she could do was move her eyes to see that the others were captured just the same. Micah's eyes were wide with fear. Brax perfected her murderous gaze. If looks could kill, she would have taken out Jasper by now. Wes though, he looked as though he was trying to tell Lucy something, his eyes darting back and forth. But what?

"As soon as Alderic pulled his magic from his body, he took it from the entire Lumen line—hundreds of Fae lost their immense power because Alderic thought some fucking trees were more important than his family!" The words thundered among the forest. "My mother told me the stories for years—about how her horrible uncle ruined our lives. Stole our magic and stole our status among the Fae."

Uncle? Who is he talking about?

"This worthless mortal is not the last of the Lumen line," Jasper spat. "You see, I took my father's name—even after he abandoned my mother and her child. The Lumen name was tarnished by that point anyway; a legacy of weak Fae, our magic trapped."

Lucy's heart raced as Jasper spoke. Her eyes searched the trees for a sign of her father, but he was nowhere to be seen. She struggled, trying to move beneath the powerful spell. Nothing seemed to work.

"I've spent my entire life trying to find a way to unleash the magic. I think good ol' Abe was onto me after some time. Thank you for that, by the way," Jasper continued, looking at Micah. "If he ever successfully got to talk to you to tell you the truth, you might have been able to stop me. He knew once you refused the phone calls and letters for so long there was only one way to get to you—in person."

Micah's eyes opened wide in horror.

Lucy's heart shattered.

No, no, no. Please, do not let this be true.

"He got so far as a block away from you before his heart stopped completely." He paused to admire the jewels adorned on his hands.

"Some mortals found him on the sidewalk and sent him to your healers, but they couldn't save him. The only thing that could have saved him was returning here." Jasper's eyes were on the house as they walked, not even looking them in the eye as he told them this devastating news.

He was the one at fault for Abe's death. Lucy's mind raced.

Micah's eyes overflowed with tears that ran down his face, frozen by Jasper's magic.

"I tried to come to The Elderwood after that to figure out how to release the magic, but it wouldn't let me in." Jasper shouted as he lost his temper. He stopped to regain his composure as they got closer to the cabin.

Go ahead, Jasper. Show us the real you.

Lucy always knew there was something off with him, and now he was ready to show them all. She silently prayed for Corvus to hurry.

"Luckily for me, mortals are fools who are motivated by riches. The J. Pearson Land Developers tried to push the false Lumen into making the decision to sell. I needed him to quickly finish going through Abe's hoard of garbage to find the book." His eyes flared with wicked desire. "And like a bee to honey, you found it."

Jasper took a deep breath and stretched his neck, regaining his composure once more.

"I told those foolish mortals to keep a close eye on you, and they waited too long to return. I was notified after you had already entered The Elderwood, so I directed them to burn the property to the ground." Jasper's evil eyes looked back at Lucy. "Thank you for killing one for me. It made it much easier to dispose of the others."

He killed them all!

Lucy's heart shuddered. But then, a fiery rage grew.

He is going to pay for this.

"I should have killed you when we found you huddled in the rubble," Jasper sneered at Micah. "But you seemed so powerless at that point. It would have been easy enough to get the book from you when you didn't expect it, but then the portal betrayed me again."

Lucy's mind flashed to what The Elderwood showed her, when Jasper did something to it—ultimately opening the portal. She wanted to scream. Not being able to talk was pushing her to her limits.

Wait. Didn't Brax say if I wanted something, I just had to ask for it?

She focused her mind on the world all around her.

Let me speak.

Her mouth popped open as she took a deep breath in. "What do you want from Micah?"

Jasper stilled, his body going rigid. "I sensed there was something different about you when you returned... something wrong." He walked nearer to her, looking her up and down, trying to figure her out. "No matter now, you won't be around for long..."

"Tell me!" Lucy screamed.

"What do I want from him? I want what I am owed!" Jasper screamed back. "What is rightfully mine!" The veins on his forehead pulsed with rage.

"And what is that?" she asked.

"The magic!" he screeched. "Once I kill him, the magic will go to the only other Lumen. Me."

Lucy glared at him in disgust.

He will not touch Micah.

"Why would you admit your entire plan to us? You just love to hear yourself talk?"

"It doesn't matter anyway—you won't be around to do anything about it. Say goodbye now," Jasper taunted.

No, this isn't the end.

Lucy's panicked breaths came quicker. There was nothing anyone could do while they were confined.

There must be a better way.

That's when it hit her.

She closed her eyes.

Release me.

Suddenly, she was dropping like a rock in the sea, escaping Jasper's orb. Lucy thrust her hands out, her magic coming to her aid immediately.

An enormous gust of wind caught Jasper off guard and pushed him through the air, his necklace flying from his hands as he was tossed like a rag doll across the forest.

Lucy threw her hands to the orb, driving a blast of magic into it, releasing her friends from the spell. They dropped to the ground in a frenzy, Wes landing on his back, Micah and Brax landing on their feet, their magic preparing them for battle. Micah's hands misted with scarlet.

Brax sprinted toward Jasper, Micah tight on her heels. Lucy hesitated for just a moment to ensure Wes was fine.

"His rings," Wes gasped. "Stop him."

"His rings?"

"Go!"

Lucy took off running, catching up with Brax and Micah. What was she to do with Jasper's rings?

She realized Micah must be battling difficult emotions, but all he shared with the world was a mask of rage. His face was drawn and his eyes dead set on Jasper.

Jasper will pay for all of this.

Brax got to him first. With a tightly clenched fist, she thrust her arm at him to land a devastating blow, but she was thrown back with a bright orange gleam. Brax screamed as she flew through the air, unsure of when or where she would land.

"Save her!" Lucy called out in a screech. The green magic that twined itself around her shot through the air like a shooting star, catching Brax just before she collided with a tree trunk.

Micah lunged at Jasper, pushing him back down to the ground. Jasper's rings started to glow, then the swirling amber mist grew around them, creating a force field that shoved Micah away.

How is Jasper capable of this?

Lucy stared at the odd magic, trying to understand where he got it. She had never seen his rings glow before, and she definitely had never seen Jasper's magic this strong. He himself said that he was a weak Fae because Alderic locked up the Lumen magic.

So if it was true that he was a Lumen, why does he suddenly have more powerful magic?

Micah's red magic began swirling around his hands, preparing to attack Jasper. It was the strongest she had ever seen Micah. She took a step back as she watched the confrontation. Then, a small voice tugged in her mind. She couldn't place it, but she knew she heard it once before—when she had left Joterra for Denora.

Immediately, another vision came rushing to her. A group of Fae males dressed in dark clothes were making their way across the forest, leading straight to them.

"Tell me what you did to my grandfather," Micah roared. His crimson magic grew again, swirling around his entire torso. Lucy watched as Jasper snarled with contempt.

"I did nothing to him," Jasper spat. "His death was your fault, not mine. All you had to do was talk to him. You and that Baum bitch are a perfect match—so hard-headed that you don't care at all about the people around you."

Micah drew his hands in a circle and pushed his power out with all of his might, pushing Jasper to the ground again, making it impossible for him to get up.

"Don't you dare talk about her," Micah growled. "This is about me and you, you weak piece of shit."

"Oh, maybe you missed that last part," Jasper sneered. "Since you woke up the Lumen magic, I'm not so weak anymore." His hands thrust toward Micah, making his footing stumble just enough that his magic pulled back.

Jasper got to his feet, twirling the rings in his hands. "Yes, my Lumen magic has awoken, and I've been dabbling in something a bit different. Though you may be familiar."

His rings began to glow a bright orange.

"What is that?" Lucy asked.

A tidal wave of light grew from Jasper's hands, the orange magic from Jasper mixing with the red of Micah, creating a collision of magic that rung through the forest.

They stood in a raging battle, each trying to overpower the other —the magic seconds away from obliterating everything that came in its path.

Lucy's rage could no longer be tampered down. The anger within her grew, spreading throughout her body, reminding her of every single thing that Jasper was responsible for.

He was the one who forced this arranged marriage.

He was the one who scared off Abe, causing him to die.

He was the one at fault for burning down Abe's property and putting Micah's life at risk.

He was the one who damaged the portal, causing the shadow beasts to escape.

And now, he was the one who was trying to hurt Micah. And she would not have that.

The wind kicked up around her, and the emerald light danced along her limbs. Slowly, she was lifted into the sky, her hair blowing around her wildly.

She continued to rise into the air, searching for the intruders.

Jasper will not come out of this unscathed.

CHAPTER
TWENTY-FOUR

MICAH

The look on Jasper's face was pure hatred—it was so clear now that he was the one who was behind all of this. Micah should have seen it from the beginning when Jasper snooped around the property talking about the J. Pearson Land Developers.

Micah's power surged through him more than ever before. He wasn't sure if it was from his absolute rage at what Jasper admitted or something else, but his magic felt strong and ready to be used. Feeling powerful, he pushed more of his magic toward Jasper, throwing him to the ground.

Wes and Brax moved closer to join the fight just as a bright gust of power spread from Jasper's hands. Another tidal wave of orange magic forced the pair onto their knees.

Micah tried to push more of his power into Jasper, but he just wasn't sure how. He stood above Jasper, sweat pouring down his face, screaming at him to stop.

Jasper remained sprawled on the forest floor, pushing magic out to Micah with one hand and to Wes and Brax with another.

Straining to stand, Brax crawled behind Wes, stood and used his crouched body to project herself into the air, escaping the blast of magic. As she flipped, she called on two short swords, swinging them toward Jasper's outstretched arms.

The movement caught Jasper off guard as he was torn between who to fight off first: Micah or Brax. Jasper's magic faltered as the Vytyrian warrior came swooping down on top of him.

Wes stood, no longer being weighed down by Jasper's oppressive force. He looked into the air at his sister, seeing her levitating by the godly magic that flowed through her body. Meeting Micah's eye, he gave a quick nod that he was okay.

Brax's silvery magic was breathtaking—fluid like a dance. She swung the swords in front of her as they moved gracefully in her hands. Jasper sent small branches from the ground toward her like bullets as she closed the distance between them. Brax blocked each dart that came her way.

Even with his immense effort, Micah's magic was not enough to stop Jasper from his onslaught of attack.

"Enough of this, DeValey!" Brax shouted as she came close to Jasper and brought her boot down onto his face, forcing Jasper's concentration to end and his power to stop.

Thankful for the short reprieve, Micah quickly shook his hands out and rolled his shoulders back, returning to fighting stance when he saw Wes sprint away from the corner of his eye.

With his Fae speed, Wes ran to the vines that Lucy had previously used to hold Brax, his hair whipping behind him in the wind that Lucy created. Using a manipulation charm, he lifted them and hurried them over to Jasper, who was subdued by Brax.

"Lucy!" Wes yelled, trying to get her attention, but Lucy's eyes were on the distance beyond.

"More are coming," her calm voice boomed through the forest at a volume Micah couldn't comprehend. "Protect the portal."

Micah scanned the woods, looking for the incoming intruders, but saw none. However, when his eyes landed on the portal, he knew he would have his hands busy with his own problems.

The battling magic made the ground quake, and the swirling

black mist grew restless, twisting and twirling and growing with each passing moment. The beetles that never seemed to have left the tree branches were flying around nervously, refusing to land—the mass of them casting a shadow over the property.

Micah rushed over to the tree that held the portal, eyeing it carefully, trying to determine what needed to be done to properly protect it.

A low growl traveled through the smoke. The shadow beasts were prowling just on the other side—he could hear them, but could not see them. For now, they were not a problem. Though it would only be a matter of time until they returned to break through the barrier once again.

The rocks had shifted ever so slightly with the battling magic. Micah got down on his hands and knees to stabilize the wall.

There's got to be a better way than this, he thought to himself.

He continued to twist and turn the rocks, hoping this new formation would hold under pressure.

How many times have I fixed these rocks for them to topple over and let these beasts out? There's got to be a better way to close them in.

From his place on the ground, he could see past the rock wall to the base of the tree. There was a gold ring with a black opal in the center shoved between the tree roots, almost lost in the swirling black mist.

Where did this come from?

He reached in quickly, picked it up, and turned it in his fingers as he inspected it. It was definitely not his grandad's.

From behind him, a branch snapped. He spun around, seeing two large men in black tunics.

Before Micah even said a word, the taller of the two shot out his hand and a blast of energy came careening toward Micah. He didn't have time to jump out of the way, and shouted in fear as the magic neared him.

A ruby force field spread around Micah with a flash, protecting him from the Fae magic. The energy seemed to ricochet away from Micah and back to the caster, shoving the stranger deeper into the woods. The ring fell to the forest floor, away from the portal.

Micah kept his back to the tree as he watched the other Fae slowly stalking around him, looking for a weakness.

"That's an interesting trick you have there, Lumen," the Fae man said, eyeing the force field.

"How do you know who I am?"

"All of Jasper's recruits know you and the Baum female. We had to get to know our adversaries in order to break them down from the inside."

"What does that even mean?" Micah asked, confused. He kept his eyes on the Fae, worried to lose his focus. Using magic was new to Micah, and he didn't need it wearing thin.

"It means that everything you know will change," the Fae replied with a smile.

"If you think you are stepping one foot closer to this portal, then you're wrong. I'm here to protect it, and I will," Micah growled with fierce determination.

"Don't worry. Soon you will find yourself without a tree to protect and without a meddlesome bitch to get in our way." His sneer grew as he crouched, prepared to attack Micah.

Micah stood tall, looking at the piece-of-shit Fae in front of him. "What did you call her?" He felt the energy inside of him shift, preparing for the complete destruction of the man in front of him. His eyes narrowed as he pushed his shoulders back, ready to unleash the magic building within him.

The Fae's mouth popped open, his face contorting in fear. His eyes were wide with horror.

Micah lifted his arms, just as an enormous beast leapt over him and mauled the stranger right before his eyes. The Fae screamed in terror as the shadow beast ripped him limb from limb. Aghast, Micah looked on.

Taking several steps back, Micah walked directly into the rock barrier as it tumbled to the ground. The shadowy mist seeped further out into the forest, making it hard for him to see anything at all.

Shit!

He continued to crawl backwards until he pushed his back all the way against the tree trunk, watching the shadow beast tear the Fae apart. Directly next to him was the enormous crack in the ground.

His panting breaths were sure to give him away if he didn't calm down soon.

Why didn't it come after me?

He looked around, terrified, expecting to see more of the beasts. Everything around him was impossible to decipher with any clarity —the shadows spread too quickly and the rest of the battle was too far from where he hid.

The visceral snarl of the shadow beast echoed throughout the property, sending a shiver down Micah's back.

How am I supposed to use this alchemy when I don't understand any of it? Think, Micah, think, he told himself angrily.

He went back in his mind through everything he learned about the unique magic his ancestors bestowed upon him.

He thought back to the pages he read about the combination of power that was able to preserve Alderic's magic and send it into Micah. The magic had been altered through alchemy, granting him more abilities than the average Denoran. The force field he created seemed different from Denorans, but there must be more to it.

What were the abilities?

His mind ran through anything he could remember.

Alchemy. Metals into gold. Transformation. Curing diseases. Long life.

He thought of his mom and grandad. His entire life would have been different if only someone else was granted this magic... His grandad or his mom would have been better suited for this. His mom would have been cured from her cancer. His grandad wouldn't have died.

I wouldn't be here alone messing things up.

A scream got his attention. He searched through the dark mist, but could not see his friends. Wes and Brax were fighting together as a team, taking on a horde of thugs from the sound of it.

Where was Lucy?

He searched further, seeing only the flashes of bright orange and green light: Lucy and Jasper in a vicious fight for power. Lucy's magic was devastating, but Jasper had years on her. Could she best him?

He squinted through the dark shadows, searching for the ferocious animal that tore apart the Fae. He listened as Lucy and Brax took on attack after attack, refusing to back down and give up. His mom was like that, always refusing to back down from a fight.

And that's when it hit him.

Micah wasn't alone. Not really. Brax was his friend, and Lucy loved him. He knew she loved him just as much as he loved her. They would help him. They wouldn't let him down, and he couldn't let them down either.

He tried to calm his breathing, hoping to clear his mind and find a resolution to his problem. The rocks continued to shake slightly under the chaos of the forest, and the snarling beasts in the smoky shadows that surrounded him did not seem to be improving his situation.

I can do this. My magic is different. Alchemy.

He repeated the word in his mind, over and over.

What is Alchemy? Changing? Creation.

He looked at the rocks again.

Transformation.

Micah took a deep breath, climbed to the outside of the rock wall, and put his hands on the vibrating rocks, hoping that his idea would work. He pushed all of his focus into his hands, imagining the rocks changing—transforming into something more sturdy. His heart pounded, the repetitive *thump, thump, thump* slowed his breathing more.

"Protect," he mumbled.

Thump, thump, thump.

"Defend," he said louder.

Thump, thump, thump.

"I am the guardian!" Micah screamed.

Blazing hot energy surged through his hands, and a blinding purple light blasted through the trees. The force threw Micah away, knocking him down onto the ground in a daze.

He looked up to see the barrier, and he gasped for breath. There in front of him, where there used to be a falling rock tower sat a solid metal wall, half the height of Micah, completely encircling the tree. It glimmered and shined in the dark mist, the silver and purple-tinged metal dutifully encapsulating any of the beasts who tried to break through.

All except one.

The dark mist that surrounded him faded, giving Micah the ability to clearly see the forest around him.

Micah stood tall, searching for the shadow creature with the terrifying putrid yellow and black eyes. Though, it didn't take long to find it, because it was searching for Micah, too.

"Come on, Scar. Let's get this over with." Micah crouched down, panting. The amount of magic that he was using was wearing him down. He wasn't sure how much more he would be able to take, but he had to keep trying. There was no giving up.

The shadow beast looked at him for a long while, pitching its head with a curious tilt, and gave a slow blink.

Micah dug his feet into the ground, preparing for the onslaught.

The shadow beast stretched back from its front paws, then sat in the dirt.

What?

It looked at Micah lazily, as if waiting for something.

Micah took a step forward, ready to fight, but the creature just sat there, watching him.

What the fuck is happening? Is this the same creature?

He took a few steps closer to look at the beast more clearly. It blinked again as Micah came near, seemingly unfazed. Micah saw the scar left on the beast's eye, looking at him intently.

It must be the same... but why is it acting so differently?

Something was off about the beast... its eyes. They were more gold than black, as though the shadows had been lifted.

The beast stood again, and Micah quickly got into a defensive position. It took a few slow strides toward Micah, and then stopped. The gold swirling magic in the beast's eyes faded. The shadow cat leaned forward, grazing its jaw against Micah's head. Then, just as suddenly, the entire beast turned into a misty shadow.

Micah jumped back in surprise, watching as the mist returned to the void in the ground at the base of the tree.

Why did it leave?

He was breathing heavily, watching the black mist fade behind his new metallic barrier. Looking up into the trees, he watched as hundreds of black bugs flew around chaotically. They were nearly crashing into one another until they all flew at The Elderwood at once.

Micah ducked, throwing his hands over his head and... silence. Nothing happened as each bug returned to the portal, becoming dark mist once more. As the last beetle passed the barrier, the black mist dissipated completely. The forest looked normal once again— except for the giant metal wall, that is.

He crept closer, one step at a time, prepared for any other creatures to escape from the large crack in the ground.

Gently placing his hands on the metallic wall, he felt for the rumble of the creatures. He focused intently, but there was no sound.

Tilting his head up, he could see the sigil on the tree trunk. It no longer had the blackened outline—it looked back to normal.

At last.

A few feet from the barrier, a glint of gold flashed in the light. Looking at the ring more closely, realization hit. Only one person would wear these gaudy rings.

Jasper.

Micah's rage bubbled up again, taking the ring he squeezed it in his fist. Without warning, his red magic burst out from the palm of his hand, more recharged than ever. He looked down at the ring that had been reduced to ash.

That's how Jasper's magic grew, he realized. *Alchemy.*

TWENTY-FIVE

LUCY

Lucy threw her magic into Jasper again, pushing him farther and farther away from the cabin; and away from Micah. Jasper would never use magic on him again.

Jasper crashed into the ground, each time taking longer and longer to recover. Lucy was granted a moment to scan the property for her friends, The Elderwood's magic gifting her sight.

Wes and Brax were taking on a much smaller group of Fae now. The scattered bodies of the dead sprawled out among them.

Good, she thought bitterly. *The realms are full of enough evil already.*

She could see Micah in the distance near the portal, but shadows disturbed her view. Seeing him moving was enough for her to know he was okay. Enough to allow her to focus her thoughts back on the weak excuse for a Fae in front of her.

Pushing more magic into Jasper, Lucy kept him firmly planted to the ground, unable to move. From her place high in the air, she descended, keeping her eyes locked on the one who threatened to end the man she loved.

"You will never lay a finger on him," Lucy said to Jasper, using her

magic to send her thoughts into his mind. She glided closer, preparing to end his existence. A shadow of a smile appeared on her lips as she stepped back onto the ground.

With widened eyes, Jasper looked at her, terrified. "What magic is this?" He stumbled over his words, watching her as she approached. "What are you?"

"I am your worst fucking nightmare," she spoke into his mind. Her eyes shone green with magic and her hair began to stand on end, as if a field of electricity buzzed through the air. She rose her hands in front of her as emerald darts of light hovered all around her.

Jasper got to his feet and came stomping toward her, ready to fight back. He grabbed his rings, preparing to use his alchemy on her. Lucy knew better than to allow that. She lifted her hands higher into the air, garnering her power from within, ready to release it on Jasper to end him once and for all.

"Enough!" A booming voice carried through the trees, shaking the branches.

Jasper and Lucy both whipped their heads toward the sound.

Father.

Corvus Baum stood menacingly near a small clearing of trees. His purple shadowy aura exuded power and strength. With Fae speed, he stopped short in front of Jasper and Lucy. He snatched Jasper by the collar and lifted him from the ground, holding him by his scarf and chains around his neck. Lucy watched as Jasper's feet dangled in the air.

"How dare you attack my family," Corvus said in a lethal whisper. "It is the last thing you will ever do."

Lucy couldn't take her eyes off of her father as his enormous stature grew. He lifted his free hand, curling it into a fist as he drew upon his power, preparing for a fatal blow.

"Or not," Jasper whispered, his eyes glimmering with malicious intent.

Suddenly, Corvus shouted out in pain. His eyes squeezed tight as his magic wavered, dropping his fist and using two hands to try to detain the traitorous Fae. Corvus screamed once again as he dropped Jasper, cradling his hand to his chest.

Jasper fell to his knees with a strangled laugh, coughing as he tried to catch his breath.

"Father!" Lucy screamed, running to him. The hand he used to hold Jasper up by his neck was now covered in large, red welts—burn marks sizzling and melting his skin.

"Brax!" she yelled out. Lucy spun, anxiously searching for her and Wes.

She can heal him. Where is she?

"Brax!"

Corvus fell to his knees in pain, grunting in anguish. A sinister laugh echoed on the wind as Jasper clambered to his feet once again.

Corvus's glare, full of hatred and disdain, landed on Jasper.

"You traitor! After all I have done for you—you turn your back on me and do this?" He grimaced as he stood before his disloyal assistant.

Jasper met Corvus with a mirthless smile. "Turn my back on you? Me? No, Corvus. You have it all wrong." He inched closer, rage twisting his face. "You have turned your back on me so often that you have no idea what happens when you aren't looking."

Corvus glared at Jasper, squeezing his hand to his chest, using his free hand to try to pull Lucy behind him.

"There's nothing left to say, Corvus. I am no longer the weak Fae you can push about. I am stronger than you now." He took a step closer, a crazed smile breaking across his face. "I am more powerful." Another step.

Jasper's magic began to swirl in his hands.

No.

Summoning as much magic, power, and strength from around her, Lucy lifted her hands in the air.

I am more powerful than Jasper DeValey.

Lucy merely had to look at Jasper, and at once, he was trapped inside of a green orb of light.

Let's give him a taste of his own magic.

He was lifted off the ground, floating higher and higher. Lucy simply pushed off of the ground and levitated in the air before him.

As Jasper banged on the walls of the orb that confined him, Lucy tilted her head in amusement. The otherworldly magic seemed to take over her entire being, turning her into a feared predator on the hunt.

"Jasper," her primal magic spoke for her, taunting him. *"Your magic has no chance."*

She spread her arms wide once again, pulling more magic into her. The trees on the Lumen property rattled under the force of her power. The sky darkened and lightning streaked ominously through the horizon. Bolt after bolt of lightning crashed through the clouded airspace, terrifying Jasper.

"No!" Jasper shouted, falling to his knees.

Lucy nodded her head in reply. Turning her wrists ever so gently, she twirled her fingers through the air as little bursts of electricity jumped along her fingers. She focused her magic onto the green orb in front of her, and with a wicked gleam, she pushed all of the lightning into Jasper, striking him. With heaving breaths, she watched him writhe within the orb.

"You will never hurt anyone I love ever again," she screamed within Jasper's mind.

"This is bigger than you and me," Jasper tried to explain between bolts. He began to plead for his life. "Please! Please listen to me!"

"This is for Abe," Lucy finally spoke aloud, her voice hoarse as though she had been screaming for all to hear. Her heart ached, but this act would avenge the death of her best friend, and it would keep Micah safe forever. She raised a single finger, pointing it directly at Jasper's heart, the electricity surging down her arm.

"Lucy!" Corvus bellowed from the ground. Lucy's eyes darted to the sound as she watched as Brax and Wes rushed over to her father, healing him and pulling him to stand. From high above, she saw Micah run to the group, worry clouding his beautiful face.

They all turned, speaking to someone who had just arrived. Lucy tilted her head to look around Jasper's confining orb.

Laurent?

He and his most trusted guard, Roger, walked toward the group quickly, sending a burst of magic to take out a lone Fae straggler of Jasper's.

What is he doing here?

Laurent looked up and made eye contact with Lucy, a question in his eye, but amazement clear upon his face.

Beside him, Micah wore the same expression.

At the sight of them, something in her heart cracked in two, and her magic gave way. She felt the wind rush past her as she came plummeting to the ground.

"No!" Corvus shouted, his hand reaching out for Lucy.

"Jasper!" Brax warned them all.

Lucy turned her head just enough to see him falling along with her. The orb of light that had contained him failed when her magic sputtered, sending them both into a free fall.

Jasper's rings glowed bright orange as he sent a beam of magic directly at Lucy. She held her hands up before her in a panic, hoping her magic would come to her aid, but nothing happened. Her magic had gone dormant within her, she couldn't even feel it humming inside of her.

"No!" Micah screamed. His swirling red magic shot toward Jasper, grabbing at the rings on his hands. With an enormous tug of power, Jasper's rings came flying to Micah—taking Jasper's fingers along with them.

Jasper's piercing scream rang through the sky as he was left powerless, staring at his bloodied hand.

They did it. All that mattered was that they stopped Jasper.

Now that the threat of Jasper had passed, Lucy focused on the magic within her, but she couldn't seem to manage a single spell to slow her fall. Her mind raced as she thought of Micah and Laurent standing side by side, watching her magic with awe. But all that magic was gone now. There was nothing left to do; she was going to crash into the ground. Lucy squeezed her eyes tight, bracing herself.

Suddenly, a soft breeze ensnared Lucy. The magic curling around her felt warm and safe and vaguely familiar. Her falling slowed, and she knew she would make it to the ground in one piece.

She opened her eyes to find a shimmering ice-blue magic dancing around her. Her eyes found Laurent as he used his magic to bring her to safety.

Micah held the extracted rings in his hands; Jasper's amputated fingers scattered on the ground in front of them. His eyes were on her as well.

Brax detained Jasper in a magical lock with Wes, securing him and ensuring he wouldn't get away. Without his connection to his alchemy charged rings, he had lost his power. The vise on her heart seemed to lessen, knowing at least Jasper had been stopped.

Corvus ran to Lucy as she descended to the ground, his face full of fear and worry. Lucy had never seen her father so pale.

"My flower," he gasped. "My sweet Lucy, are you alright?" He scooped her up into his arms and embraced her tightly, hugging her so close she could barely breathe.

"Father," she sobbed. "I'm okay. I'm alright." She hugged him with a fierceness she had never felt before. Jasper attacked them and they had almost been killed. They almost lost everything.

Relief washed through her as the reality of the situation struck her. This entire time Jasper was the one who had put a wedge into their family. Now with him finally gone, they could make amends. They could rebuild the relationships shattered by Jasper and his need for power and control.

"I don't know what I would have done if I had lost you, Lucy," her father said into her hair as he held her tight. "I am so sorry for every-thing. I'm sorry I didn't see it all sooner."

From over Corvus's shoulder, Lucy watched the scuffle unfold almost as if in slow motion. Jasper stood, gripping something tightly around his neck, causing an explosion from the space between Wes and Brax. They both flew backward, releasing Jasper from his magical hold.

Corvus turned around just as Jasper ripped the chain from his neck and blasted a bolt of amber-tinted magic straight toward Lucy.

But the magic didn't hit her.

Corvus, with outstretched arms, stepped in the line of fire just in time, sending the magic directly into his chest.

He fell back with a thud.

Lucy moved to catch him and was assisted as Laurent sped to her aid, gently lowering him to the ground. Wes, Micah, and Brax sprang into action, trying to fight off Jasper in vain.

Lucy couldn't breathe.

Corvus lay in her lap on the ground—unmoving. Unblinking.

Jasper created a tidal wave of magic to push the Fae away, allowing him time to run.

Laurent squeezed her shoulder and tried speaking to her over and over.

But this was it.

Jasper killed Abe.

Jasper killed my father.

She gasped for air, searching for answers. Each glance around her felt as though the world was spinning. Then, all was dark.

TWENTY-SIX

LUCY

The bright light from the fire was too much for her eyes to endure as she came to. Lucy had no idea where she was or how long she had been asleep.

She propped herself up on one arm, her head swimming in pain. Glancing around, Lucy saw the familiar furniture of her father's study. The enormous fireplace roared from her place on his settee.

"Father," she croaked. It must have all been a bad dream. She shot up from her place on the couch, looking around the dark room.

Tell me it was all a bad dream.

Wes jolted awake at the sound of his sister's voice. "Lucy?" his groggy voice choked out, leaning toward her from his position on a nearby chair.

"Wes, where is everyone? Why are we home?" She searched the room for answers to the one question she couldn't bear to voice.

Where is my father?

Her heart broke at the reality. She knew the answer—but it couldn't be.

She stood, looking around.

"I'm sorry, Lucy," Wes's voice broke off in a sob.

"No," she begged. She crashed to the ground, grief weighing her heart down, shattering it to nothing. "No!" Her soul could not take another moment of pain—of hurt. She pulled her knees to her chest as she sobbed for the reality of this enormous loss.

Wes sat on the ground next to her and pulled his sister in close, holding her until there were no more tears left for her to spill.

Lucy stared at the fire, her existence feeling as though it was in flames itself, the only feeling left from the hollowness within her.

Long after her tears ceased, Wes spoke to her. "Brax and Micah are safe in Joterra," he cleared his throat. "I thought you'd want to know…"

Lucy nodded subtly.

"He wanted to come with you, but Brax was adamant that he stayed for his own safety."

Lucy tucked her chin closer to her body.

"Brax tried to heal you, but when you didn't wake up, we weren't sure what happened. We thought it'd be in your best interest to return to a Fae realm to recharge."

"How-" her voice croaked. She cleared her throat. "How long has it been?"

"You've been asleep for three days."

If she had any more tears left, she would have cried again. She had been away from Micah for almost two Joterran weeks.

Lucy sat up slowly, seeing her brother clearly for the first time since waking. He had bags under his eyes, and his hair was a mess. It looked as though he had not bathed since their return.

Lucy looked down at herself. She was in a clean gown—someone had been taking care of her while she was asleep.

"Mother came to care for you," Wes shared as he noticed her lightly touching the fine cloth.

"And Laurent?" Lucy asked in a whisper.

"He helped transport us home as quickly as possible. He has a magic unlike anything I've seen—he was able to travel through the realm with a blink of an eye. He took us from the Lumen property to the portal. Then from the other side of the portal right to our estate."

She knew of this power and was thankful for his presence, but why was he even there?

Her head spun with questions... but there was really only one that mattered.

"And Jasper?" she ground out at last.

"We..." He couldn't say the words. "We couldn't find him."

Taking his hand in hers, Lucy squeezed tight as she spoke to her brother. "We will get him. I promise you."

"You don't have to promise me that. It is a deal Jasper sealed in his own blood. This will go beyond vengeance—this will be a brutal punishment dealt straight from the Baums for every betrayal Jasper has ever committed."

Wes and Lucy sat in silence, holding each other's hands, staring at the flames that seemed to flicker and grow as they promised the death and destruction of their family's greatest enemy.

KNOWING that Jasper was alive somewhere, Lucy could not sit still. It was not acceptable. He had to pay for his crimes.

The magic within Lucy that usually soared and surged with her emotions barely ebbed. Now that she was well rested, she could feel it deep within her, but it was dimmed somehow, like the rest of Lucy's life.

She had hardly left her father's study since her return. There was something about being close to his things that made her feel close to him. His massive wingback chair that held his imposing stature, the large fireplace that warmed all on the coldest nights, the divot in the couch where he always sat... How could it be that this larger-than-life Fae just ceased to exist?

She would never hear his hearty laugh again, watching as the apples of his cheeks rose to crinkle the corners of his eyes.

She would never make another bow with him as he leaned over her shoulder to comment on ways to improve her technique.

She would never see the ire in his eyes when she upset him or the remorse they shared as they would make amends.

There would never be a new memory of the male who had shaped her into the steadfast, determined female she was today.

The pain seized her heart as she thought of him. She clung to the edge of the couch as the hurt became overwhelming.

How can this be real?

Moving from behind the couch to sit, she squeezed her eyes tight to rein in her tears. Taking deep calming breaths, she felt the weak flutter of her magic as it came to soothe her.

A gentle emerald mist presented her with a vision... Her father and mother, sitting on that same couch, cuddled next to one another, drinks in hand as they warmed their bodies from the heat of the fireplace. She couldn't hear a word they spoke, but their smiles were stretched across their bright faces, their cheeks red with laughter.

They were so happy.

She opened her eyes. Lucy wasn't sure why that vision surprised her—of course her parents loved one another, didn't they? They had been through so much together...

Lucy stood to go to her mother. Words couldn't describe what she must be feeling, to have lost a spouse... What could Lucy say to make anything better?

It is my fault that he died.

She dug her knuckles into her eyes to try to shake the thought. Deep down, she knew it was Jasper that had killed Corvus, but the same thought kept popping back up... If it wasn't for her, he would still be alive.

There was nothing else she could focus on. She needed to find Jasper and destroy him.

But how?

A knock on the door startled her from her spiraling thoughts.

She straightened and took a deep breath. "Come in," she called.

Lucy wasn't sure who she was expecting, but it certainly wasn't the Fae who walked through the door.

"Laurent?"

"Hello, Miss Lucella," he replied sheepishly, bowing his head and diverting his ice-blue eyes.

Lucy noted the formal greeting.

"I wanted to see how you were doing." He carried a bouquet of white roses, almost the same pale color as his flowing hair.

He looked completely put together and Lucy was sure she looked like she had been trampled by a stampede of horses, but she didn't care. She was no longer interested in concerning herself with love and the false lives she could picture for herself.

The only thing on her mind was vengeance, and she would have it.

Lucy crossed her arms over her waist, pondering her response. He knew she was not fine, she knew she was not fine, and he held the ability of knowing when someone lied to him.

She looked everywhere but at him. There was nothing to say, and she didn't care to play games anymore.

At her silence, he nodded in understanding.

"I've also come to offer my services," he said seriously.

That got her attention. Their eyes snapped together as her interest grew. He was a few steps closer to her now, his height looming over her frame.

"Services?" She asked. "How can you help me?"

"Miss Lucella," he said softly as he neared her. "I am in control of the entire Northern Territory as well as a vast army. Any battalion will walk out to battle at my very command."

Lucy still looked at him in confusion. Why would a group of soldiers put her at ease?

"Miss-"

"Enough with the *Miss Lucella* if you want to finish your next sentence," Lucy snapped, her patience thoroughly diminished.

A smile broke through Laurent's serious exterior. "Lucy. I wish to put my best Fae soldiers on the task of finding Jasper DeValey and bringing him to justice."

Lucy's eyes popped open in shock. A Denoran battalion exclusively formed to capture Jasper?

Of all the things that Lucy considered, there was only one word she could form.

"Why?"

It didn't make sense for the Lord of the Northern Territory to utilize his resources for something so trivial to the masses of Denora.

He got down on one knee and spoke to her in a near whisper. "If there is anything I can do to comfort my betrothed, I will move the moon and the stars themselves." He took her hand in his, smoothing his thumb over her fingers. "Come with me, my queen, and help me lead the soldiers in finding this cretin. Together, we can accomplish anything."

Her heart stilled.

Laurent did not realize what he offered her. It was not only vengeance on the table, but real partnership. Equality in the face of Denoran custom. Would he dare push back centuries of tradition?

"It is not the Denoran way," Lucy replied, carefully choosing her words.

"For you, I will take down every Fae who stands in our way and says it cannot be so." His words were a promise.

Her heart thought of Micah. She pictured his brown eyes that melted into her soul. There was no way that she could ever be with Micah unless Jasper was gone. She would do anything to keep him safe and keep The Elderwood out of the hands of those who wished to do evil.

The best way to keep Micah safe... was to say yes to Laurent.

And so she did.

TWENTY-SEVEN

LUCY

The carriage clattered over the uneven terrain as the Leithe Mountains appeared in the distance. Laurent sat in the seat next to her, which gave her the freedom to look out her small carriage window. Facing away from him, she managed to poorly mask the devastation upon her face.

Leaving her home was harder than she ever could have imagined. Her mother cried, but that was not a change from her waking moments mourning her husband in deep wailing weeps that penetrated her privacy charms when her magic failed from exhaustion.

"I'm sorry to be leaving so soon, Mother," Lucy had said to her in a near whisper. "I promise I will return for Father's funeral." Lucy's words shook as she held in her tears. Her mother had been through so much, Lucy needed to be strong for her.

"Sweetheart," her mother had replied with tear stained cheeks. "It is alright. Take care of yourself. Lord Sloan will keep you safe and return you to me soon."

The news slightly lifted her mother's spirits. All Anita wanted for her daughter was love and support and a future.

Saying goodbye to Wes went nothing like she imagined. Instead of sending her off with well wishes, he had tried to change her mind. The conversation replayed constantly in her head.

"Don't do this, Lucy," he had told her. "This isn't what you want."

The desperation in his voice rang in her ears even now. She knew he was right to some extent. She didn't want Laurent. However, she needed Jasper found and brought to justice—and for that, she would do whatever it took.

She told him to take care of Micah—to apologize for her. Lucy was too ashamed to go herself. There was nothing she could say to make this right. Nothing anyone could do. This was the only way.

Hugging her younger brothers goodbye was a challenge all on its own. Henry and Simon tried not to cry, telling Lucy they were mature now, and had to step up and serve the family business. Wes had swatted them over the head and sent them out to play. He would not steal their childhood from them in the face of such tragedy.

Oddly enough, Tristan was the only one who understood her position. As she said her goodbyes to him, he slipped her a silver dagger with a striking amethyst set into the pommel. The purple was nearly the same hue as their father's magical aura.

He ran his hand through his shaggy hair, still refusing to cry after all the time had passed. "Do whatever it is you need to do, and find a way home."

She wanted to tell him that there would be no reason to come home, but she had no more energy for words that would go unheard. Instead, she held her brother in a tight hug, slid the dagger into her boot, and left the Baum Estate to leave for the Northern Territory with her intended.

Laurent shifted in his seat next to her in the carriage, sliding his hand over to where hers sat on the leather cushion. The heat of his skin met her frigid fingers with a shock.

"My queen," he said in concern, sliding over to her. "Why didn't you tell me you were so cold?" He wrapped his hands around hers, offering her warmth.

Lucy offered a small smile in reply. "It's fine. I'm sure I will get used to the cold." Truth be told, she didn't even realize she was as cold as she was. She paid little attention to herself these days. Everything about her was numb.

"Once we get past the mountains you will see the castle," he told her, holding her close to warm her in the face of the brisk snowy mountains just outside of their carriage. He carefully pulled the curtain back a bit more to allow her to see.

The Leithe Mountains were monstrous, looming over them with malevolent prestige. The mountainscape went on as far as Lucy's eyes could see, crevices and plunging valleys hiding the boreal beasts that inhabited the land. The calynx prints in the snow were nearly as big as the carriage, and Lucy was grateful that they were largely nocturnal.

"How much longer?" Lucy asked. It had been almost an entire day of journeying. They left before sunrise, and the deepening shadows of the mountainside hinted at the night that swiftly approached.

"Just on the other side of this peak we will see the castle, and then enter the underground tunnels leading us to the carriage bay. I can bring us to the eastern wing once we are within the property lines."

"Why not do it from here?" Lucy didn't understand why they were taking this long journey when she knew Laurent had the capability to transport himself far distances with his magic.

"We have wards within the Northern Territory that prohibit magic. Even I cannot wield magic within the boundary lines. It helps us to fortify our borders and keep the people safe."

"You really would do anything for your people, wouldn't you?" Lucy asked, true understanding dawning on her for the first time.

It wasn't just that Laurent wanted his people to be protected, but he did everything he could just to make it happen; even if it meant making life more difficult for himself.

"I would," he said seriously, turning to look Lucy in the eye. "And you will, too. These will be your people as much as they are mine. Together we can create a realm where all are cared for—it's all that matters."

He turned away from Lucy at that last sentiment, staring into the distance, clearly deep in thought.

Lucy took the moment to study him. Strong angles lined his face, a seriousness that Lucy was sure came with a difficult life of safeguarding an entire nation. His posture was so at odds with how he was with her in the grove on their intimate date alone.

So much rests upon his shoulders, yet he finds time for the little things that make life meaningful.

His eyes lit, life coming back into them. "There," he said with barely hidden relief. Lucy followed his gaze.

Nestled high into the rugged, snow-covered mountains, the Fae castle sat as a testament to both nature's beauty and the elegance of Fae magic. The sight was breathtaking, with glistening ice crystals hanging from the windows like precious stones. The pale turrets nearly blended into the mountainside if it were not for the ice which sparkled like frosted glass.

An enormous bridge covered in ice suspended over a chasm, connecting the castle and grounds to the rest of the Northern Territory. Lucy watched as snowflakes flitted down slowly from the gray clouds blanketed above them.

If The Elderwood was the embodiment of springtime, this was winter incarnate.

"It's beautiful," Lucy said in awe. "Does it always look like this?"

"Yes," Laurent replied, suddenly looking concerned. "Is that acceptable? I know you are fond of your forests and warmth... I promise I will do what I can to ensure your comfort while you are here."

"It's wonderful," Lucy replied with a reassuring smile. "Thank you for bringing me here to see its magnificence."

"Of course I would bring you here, my queen. It is your home now."

Lucy didn't reply, but her frozen heart cracked at the reminder. She refused to think about it for long, but Laurent was right. Lucy had agreed to this; to a lifetime. And if it meant it would keep Micah safe, then so be it.

WITH EACH PASSING MOMENT, the carriage moved closer and closer to the castle, and Lucy knew there was no turning back. Her tensed muscles were the only outward sign of her panic, but she knew she could blame it on the cold. The air was biting, and she wasn't sure how anyone could get used to the frigid temperatures.

A sentinel guard stood at an outpost, bundled up with furs and leathers to fight off the cold. He stood tall, taller than any other Fae Lucy had ever come across. As they passed him, she stared into his deep blue eyes and was shocked to see tusks coming from his mouth.

"Your guards are not Fae?" Lucy asked in surprise.

"They are. I employ the Fae from a variety of realms, not all of them look the same as Denorans. My exterior guards are from Karroz. They can handle the extreme temperatures better than most other Fae."

Lucy just nodded. That seemed to make sense, especially since he employed Brax from Vytyr.

Brax.

Micah.

Her frozen heart ached. There was no time to think of them now, but she hoped Wes took good care of them as promised.

"The guard's outpost is the boundary line. We are free to enter the castle now. The carriage will next go to the underground tunnels, but there is not much to see for the remainder of the journey," Laurent told her. "Are you ready to relocate to the east wing?"

"Yes," Lucy said with a weak smile. She played the role of future-wife, hoping that Laurent would keep his promise to find Jasper. Every second of her time in the North should be focused on finding Jasper and getting back to her old life... or what was left of it.

Laurent slid one hand around the back of Lucy's neck and the other held her arm. In a blink, Lucy found herself standing in the foyer of an extravagant room decorated for royalty.

"Do you like it?" Laurent whispered to her, standing close over her shoulder. She felt his warm body press ever so gently to her back, reminding her of his comforting presence.

If I have to leave everything I know to be with a male I may never love, at least it is in a beautiful place with a partner who will care for me. At least I won't be alone, she tried to convince herself.

She smiled up at him, the closest thing to a real smile than she had had in days.

"It's wonderful."

Laurent beamed, his bright blue eyes bringing more warmth to Lucy than she had felt all day.

"Welcome home."

FINALLY GETTING AWAY from Laurent was a breath of fresh air. From the moment she agreed to go with him, from packing and through the carriage ride, he had seemed to always be nearby, waiting to dote on Lucy as though she were a breakable, fragile thing.

I've slayed men who have tried to hurt me, wielded other worldly magic, and have made the rain fall from the sky. I am not fragile.

She looked into the mirror with a huff and took a surprised step back at the image. Her hair was flat and dull, her skin pale and lifeless, and dark circles rimmed her eyes from lack of sleep. There was a heaviness about her that she had never seen before.

This is why those around me are walking around on eggshells, worried to upset me.

Her empty eyes devoid of emotion trailed her reflection.

I look breakable.

The admission, even if only to herself in the privacy of her quarters, hurt. She had been trying so hard to just keep moving. Trying to convince herself and others that she was perfectly fine. It was clear now that everyone could see right through it. And everyone had... everyone but her.

Her room was as extravagant as the rest of the castle. An enormous four-poster bed sat in the middle, delicate designs of flowers and leaves carved into the posts. The bedding was a soft silver, shimmering in the candlelight of the sconces. A wardrobe, bureau, and floor-length mirror were placed strategically around the room, and across from the door was a wall of velvet curtains.

Curious, Lucy walked over to pull back the velvet to see what was behind. A panorama of northern life was displayed in the wide windows. Far below lay a small city with a bustling town square, Fae walking to and fro, buying things at shops or walking with their families. It seemed almost too serene to be real; everyone calm and joyful. The only thing out of place were the sentinel guards roaming amid the citizens.

She watched those happy Fae as she sat alone in a castle room, trying to gain the courage to be the Fae she needed to pretend to be.

A KNOCK on the door startled Lucy, who sat in a silent panic. Her heart beat irregularly, but she did not know what else to do. She was dressed in a fresh gown and had cleaned up as best as she could, adding a little make-up to make her drawn face seem less sallow.

"Miss Lucella," Roger's voice sounded through the great wooden door. "I am here to escort you to dinner."

Of course, she realized.

Quickly, she walked to the door and opened it, greeting Roger and another servant.

Lucy smiled and nodded, following the pair of Fae through the castle as they navigated her through the corridors. She did not feel much like talking, but Roger was always overly friendly and did the talking for her this time.

"The castle is separated into three wings, Miss Lucella," Roger explained. "We are currently in the east wing, which holds the private living quarters of our more permanent residents."

"Who else lives here?" Lucy asked, genuinely curious.

"Lord Sloan, a troop of his most trusted guards, the lead house-keepers, and now you." He explained in a gentle voice, almost as though he was cautious of scaring her off.

They continued walking to the foyer where the corridor divided into three.

"That direction will take you to the center of the castle," he said, pointing to the middle passageway. "That is mostly for visitors and where the majority of the wait-staff live. There are small historical areas, a library for all who live within the castle, and a few other common areas. You must pass through the center to get to the west wing. This is the passage to the dining room and kitchens," he continued, pointing to the right. "It's toward the back of the wing."

"What's down the other corridor?" Lucy asked, curious why that was left out.

"That section is off limits, I'm afraid."

"What does it hold?" Lucy glanced to the hall on the left.

"Oh, nothing of concern. It's mostly old construction. Nothing particularly of consequence."

Lucy nodded in reply, seeing the tension in his stance.

"The west wing is where most of Northern Territory business takes place," he continued. "There are offices, conference rooms, battle rooms, a ballroom; pretty much anything you can imagine."

"Battle rooms and ballrooms, huh?" Lucy replied dryly. "Quite the juxtaposition."

"Lord Sloan must be prepared on all fronts—the politics of Denora are... precarious."

Lucy did not speak again as they approached a wide archway with oversized wooden doors with cast iron handles. Roger opened the door for Lucy, and she entered a room with an overly large dining table.

At the far end, Laurent sat with papers and scrolls surrounding him—his advisors whispering in hushed tones. Upon seeing Lucy, he excused the advisors, stood, and smiled.

"Lucy, you look splendid," he politely greeted her. "Please, sit. Dinner is just about to be served. I hope it isn't too late."

"No, no, it's fine," she reassured him. The day's journey was long, but she was ravenous after not eating much. It was, indeed, late, but she couldn't sleep now even if she wanted to. She was happy to have something to do.

However, once she looked at the table setting, her happiness faded quickly. Laurent sat at the head of the table, and eight chairs down, Roger seated her at the complete opposite end.

This was nothing like the dinner where he refused to sit far from her. This was nothing like the moment where he gifted her the head of the table as his honored guest. Similarly, this was nothing like the intimate lunch they had in the grove of trees, surrounded by flowers and sunshine.

No. This was typical Denoran business.

Lucy took a deep breath, holding back the disappointment, and sat with a fake smile pressed upon her lips.

"I'm sorry I wasn't able to help you settle into your new quarters. Are they acceptable?" Laurent asked her in between bites of dinner.

"Yes, thank you. Your castle is lovely." Lucy's insides churned at the fake niceties she was using.

Why am I acting this way?

She couldn't figure out why she went from being unabashedly herself to now hiding behind a simpering smile—something she would have refused to do before.

"I have been catching up on some business that has been on hold since I was gone," Laurent continued, not noticing that Lucy was behaving differently. "I anticipate that it will be like this for some time, but Roger, here, will help you get a lay of the land when I am unavailable to assist."

Another one of Laurent's advisors came into the room and began whispering in Laurent's ear, interrupting their conversation. Ordinarily, this would not have bothered Lucy, but she did not understand why his staff felt the need to barge in on their dinner and act as though she wasn't even in the room.

Once Laurent nodded and the male left their presence, Lucy asked the one question that had been consuming her every waking moment.

"How is the search for Jasper going?"

"Nothing so far, I'm afraid. But you need not worry. I have my very best troop on the frontlines, looking for any indicator of his whereabouts."

Lucy nodded and smiled, but inside her heart was breaking.

TWENTY-EIGHT

MICAH

"What do you mean she's gone?" Micah shouted at Wes. It had been weeks since Micah had heard from Lucy and there was no way that she had just disappeared.

"I'm trying to explain," Wes said, desperately. His hair was a mess and his face looked as though he had added years to his life in just a few short Denoran days. He dragged his hands down his face.

"Try harder," Micah said angrily, his body tense with barely subdued ferocity.

"She wanted to do the right thing... She wanted to keep you safe from him. Lucy hadn't slept a wink from the moment she woke up to the moment that she agreed to Lord Sloan's offer."

"What did he even offer her that I couldn't give her?" Micah roared in reply.

"Hey, slow down, Lumen," Brax said, pulling him back from Wes.

They were on the front lawn of the cabin—that's as far as Wes got before Micah saw him and charged outside, looking for answers.

"No! I won't slow down. This is bullshit!" Micah pulled away from Brax, shoving her hand off of his arm. "This isn't what she would have wanted. What is it? Huh? What did he offer?"

"He offered your safety, for fuck's sake," Wes said curtly. "Jasper is out on the run and he wants you dead, Micah. Do you understand that?"

"Yes, but we could work together to take him down!"

"Micah, he killed the strongest Fae Lucy and I have ever known!" Wes shouted back, his voice cracking. "Lucy did what she thought would keep you safe."

"She wouldn't pick him, she wouldn't!"

"Well, she did!" Wes screamed, stunning them all into silence as his exterior crumbled. "She's gone, trying to fix what Jasper ruined! And my mother is in fucking agony over losing her husband. And now I am the one who has to try to fix all of this mess, and I don't even know how! Is that what you want to hear? That we are all doing things we fucking hate trying to make things better?"

Micah's heart pounded in rage, but it couldn't have touched the agony Wes was going through. Micah remembered that pain... losing his mother. Then, hoping beyond hope that his grandfather could have been there for him to help make the grief bearable, but then he left Micah, too. That's exactly what was happening to Wes.

The realization subdued Micah's thoughts, draining his anger and replacing it with a sullen understanding.

Wes stood panting, trying to calm himself, looking down at the ground with clenched fists.

Micah took a slow step forward, and then another, until he was only a step away from Wes. He extended his arms and pulled Wes in for an embrace, wrapping his arm around Wes's shoulders.

At first, Wes stood as tense as a rooted tree, refusing to accept the offer of camaraderie.

"Death is confusing," Micah said gruffly. "You don't have to hold it all, man. That's what friends are for."

Friends.

The word felt foreign to Micah, but right nonetheless.

"Yes, Baum," Brax said gently, placing her hand on Wes's shoulder. "We're here for you."

Wes dropped his head on Micah's shoulder and finally let it all go. His silent sobs wracked his body as he released the pressures of leading his family business without a mentor, the sadness he felt for his mother and siblings, his sister's sudden exit from his life, and his devastating grief of losing the most influential male in his entire existence.

"You don't have to hold it all."

TWENTY-NINE

LUCY

Walking the halls of the castle was turning into Lucy's only pastime. It had been nearly a week of life in the Northern Territory, and each day was more depressing than the last. There was never any news about Jasper's plans. No one knew where he was, and each time she asked, Laurent changed the topic—and that was when Laurent was around.

Every day she saw less and less of him. At first, it was him being present for all three meals, then moved to just dinner and tea. Now it was a toss-up if she would see him at all.

Part of Lucy wanted to be offended by his lack of attention to her, but quite honestly, she was happy to not have to pretend in front of anyone anymore. The only constant in her life had been Roger these past few days, and she didn't care what he thought about her. He didn't force conversation and was happy to speak without her responses. He was easy to be around, because he needed nothing from her.

Each morning she planned her route at breakfast, ate alone for lunch, and then wandered the more interesting places she found before she broke away for dinner. Roger didn't seem to mind and narrated all the interesting, and more often than not the uninterest-ing, things about the castle. It gave her something to do, kept her body moving, and her mind off of her reality.

She had never been in a position where she felt there was no way to solve a problem. Even when she felt that her back was against a wall, she fled to another realm just to prove herself. When faced with violence, she exerted her power and strength and came out on top. When she missed her mortal lover, she snuck away and found the time to be with him.

Yet now, holding all the magic of the gods inside of her, she sits as a simpering female betrothed to a powerful Fae and therefore has no opinions? It didn't add up, and she couldn't figure out what in all the realms was wrong with her.

Today, she was pleased to be truly alone. Laurent needed Roger's presence and, surely, Roger was happy to no longer play the role of tour guide. Lucy promised to not wander off too far and mentioned perusing the library. However, what she didn't mention was that she was far more interested in the one area she was told not to explore. It was the only place in the entire castle that made her take pause, and each time she did, she felt the gentle tug of her dulled magic trying to breach the surface... She didn't know what it meant or why it happened, but she looked forward to finding out.

Taking the route to the center of the castle was easy enough, and when she came to the fork in the corridor that led to the portion of the castle that was off limits, she hurried down as quickly as she could.

If anyone asks, I got lost, she told herself.

The adrenaline rush from running in the hall was enough to almost make her smile. It was by far the most exercise her body had gotten since before her father died... At the realization, the smile that nearly made its appearance swiftly left.

The hallway changed from soft carpeting to bare wood and the walls became more barren as she progressed through. Roger had mentioned this area was under construction, but it seemed as if it had been forgotten all together.

What was wrong with this area of the castle? Surely, there must be a reason it looked abandoned.

Her footsteps echoed in the bare hallway, shadows shrouding her sight. A flutter of curiosity swam within her veins, her magic slowly waking for the first time since her arrival. The relief she felt was all-encompassing, feeling herself come back to life.

She brought her hands to her lips and whispered the Fae spell for light, and a small orb lit in her hands. Since the incident on Micah's property, she could not get her magic to work how it once did. Just weeks prior, the gesture was not needed any longer since she had actualized, but now she could not wield magic without the words. Lucy could not understand why, but she took comfort in the magic all the same.

The small light cast a dim glow all around her, but it was not enough to see in the dark space.

I should have listened more to my mother, she thought.

She froze in the middle of the corridor. She had been working so hard not to think about her family, pushing away the feelings of grief and depression that weighed heavily on her heart. But now, with that one little thought, emotion flooded her, making it hard to breathe.

My family.

She put both hands to her chest and closed her eyes, thinking of her family and what they must be going through as they plan out her Father's funeral without her.

I should be home with them.

Laurent's words from the day she arrived echoed in her mind, *"welcome home".*

This was not her home. Her home was with her family. Love sprouted from her heart at the thought of her six brothers and how fulfilling it would be to finally see them again.

All at once, her emerald magic came to her, caressing her arms in a gentle greeting. The sentiment rattled her insides, tearing her presentable facade apart at the sight of her magic returning to her.

Tears fell down her cheeks as she choked out a small laugh, smiling at the comforting presence she had missed so very much.

It glided over her face in a warm nuzzle, then darted down the hall, guiding her way.

"Wait!" She called in a whisper, hoping it would slow so she could follow at an easier pace, but the green light did not slow. She had to run to keep up, wondering where it took her.

Soon, Lucy found herself at another forked path, with a corridor going to the right, or stairs leading down. She peered in each direction, wondering which way her magic fled. Instinctively, she closed her eyes and asked within her mind, *where did you go?*

She opened her eyes and the stairwell down glowed an ominous green. Lucy used quiet footsteps as she descended, unsure of what she would find at the end.

She could have listed a thousand things in her mind, and not one of them would have led her to what she found in the middle of the long passageway at the bottom of that stairwell.

As her magic tenderly receded back into her, Lucy took one step closer to the scene in front of her. Huddled in the back of a cell, a male Fae with disheveled clothing and dried blood covering his body, shook and whimpered in fright.

"Please, please no more," he cried. "I have nothing else to say, and no more alchemy to give. Please, Sloan, you will drain me to my death."

Lucy gasped, and at the sound, the Fae male sat up attentively at the sight of his visitor. His eyes bulged in recognition and relief.

"Lucy! Please, Lucy! You need to get me out of here!"

Loud footsteps from the other end of the corridor made their way toward them, and Lucy looked up in terror.

Backing up a step at a time, Lucy nearly fell over as she ran from that basement cellar. Up the stairs, back down the dilapidated passageway, through to the forked hall and back to her bedroom quarters, where she threw the door closed behind her and tried to catch her breath. Disappointment threatened to drown her.

"Jasper has been here all along?"

HER MIND HAD BEEN RACING with disbelief and distress, not quite understanding how that pile of ragged bone and muck was really Jasper. It couldn't be... just that morning she asked how the hunt for Jasper was going and Laurent had told her that they were still on the search with no updates.

Her magic raced through her veins restlessly, causing discomfort and unease in her soul. Lucy didn't know how to slow any of this down—her thoughts, her emotions, or her magic. She was rapidly veering toward a mental breakdown if something didn't calm her soon.

She washed her face and fixed her hair once, twice, three times before a soft knock on her door made her nearly jump out of her gown.

"Yes?" She called with a shaky breath.

"Miss Lucy, Lord Sloan is requesting your presence for tea," Roger's voice sounded from the other side of the door.

Perhaps he is prepared to tell me of Jasper's arrival?

Lucy's heart soared with hope. She opened the door and offered a sheepish smile and nod in reply. She couldn't risk speaking when she was so wound up inside.

Her magic beneath her skin would not quiet, and it took all the concentration she had to keep it within her body. Lucy was not prepared for it to make an appearance in front of Laurent and have to explain any of it.

Following Roger down the hall, her eyes darted to the off-limits passageway, remembering the battered Fae found in the depths of what must have been their dungeon.

A fucking dungeon.

Her stomach threatened to bring up her earlier meal. Dungeons were not unheard of, but they were only found in the homes of the most ruthless Fae.

Once near the dining room, Lucy's heart felt as though it might explode at the impending conversation she would have with Laurent. Would this be the end of her fears? Now that he was captured, could she go home? The idea grew like a warm flame melting her frozen heart.

Seeing Laurent sitting so calmly piqued Lucy's curiosity and caused her to still.

He does not seem as though he has anything positive to tell me.

"Ah, my love, please come sit," he said cheerfully. "I am so sorry to have been neglecting you so much these past few days. I am happy to see you."

"Thank you, my lord," she said in a curtsey. "I'm happy to see you, as well. It is good to see you in such a jovial mood. Do you have good news to share?"

"Good news?" Laurent asked, bewildered. "Not particularly, I do not think."

"Any update on Jasper DeValey?"

Lucy's heart stopped, waiting to hear him say the words; that Jasper was captured and he would take care of the rest. That she no longer had to fear.

But that relief never came, for instead he replied with sadness.

"No, Lucy. I am so sorry. We think we have a lead in the Southern Territory," he said, taking another sip of tea, a new gold ring on his finger. "Don't worry. We will find him and have him pay. I will tell you as soon as I hear anything, I promise."

Lucy's magic flared in her body at the deliberate lie. She felt the heat of it flash in her eyes for only a moment, and Laurent looked at her with interest.

"Are you feeling alright, my queen?" Laurent asked her in concern.

The words made her stomach roil.

She would never be his queen.

"Yes, my lord," she said, her mask of meekness covering her contempt. While he could tell when others lied to him, he was never able to detect Lucy's deceit.

As for Lucy, she didn't need a magical skill to tell her that the Lord of the Northern Territories was lying to her face.

"Don't worry, Jasper may be a strong Fae, but I am stronger by far. You are safe here with me."

Lucy continued tea with Laurent as he filled the room with unimportant chatter, but all the while, she dove deep into her thoughts, her magic coursing through her, alive and ready to pounce.

I may have been so foolish to believe him once, but I will not be taken as a fool again and I will not be used as a pawn. Lord Laurent Sloan may be one of the most powerful Fae to have ever walked the realm, but I know something he does not.

Lucy smiled at the Lord of the North as he sat across from her, a green shimmer in her eyes.

I am no longer Fae.

To My Mom—
Thanks for being strong enough for both of us when everything gets too heavy.

ONE

LUCY

Lucy was many things, but patient wasn't one of them. She paced uneasily in her quiet bedchambers and flipped the amethyst dagger from her brother in her hands, anxiously replaying every moment of her evening tea with Laurent. Her feet took her from one side of her room to the other. She would approach the ornate wooden door that led to the rest of the castle, then turn and head to the window where she could see the village of the Northern Territories below.

Back and forth.

Back and forth.

It took every ounce of determination left within her to force herself to stay put in her room and not fly out to Laurent and demand he answer her questions.

It was rare for them to have any time at all together, and in the one moment she had with him, he hadn't been honest with her. The fact that he lied made her blood boil, but the more she thought about it, the more she considered that there had to be a reason that her husband-to-be kept the truth from her.

Laurent was not the icy, cruel Fae that others made him out to be. He was a kind and considerate male. He was worthy of his title of Lord and supported his people, didn't he? She trusted him to keep his word and protect her family and Micah from Jasper. That was why she was in the North. Lucy agreed to the marriage arrangement with Laurent solely for the fact that he promised to find Jasper DeValey. The rough handle on the dagger dug into her fingers as she clutched it tightly. He promised vengeance on the male who ruined her family.

She stopped herself in the middle of the chilly room and squeezed her eyes shut, trying to push away the harrowing memories she had avoided so diligently in the previous weeks.

Lucy's hands shook as she dug her nails into her palms, trying to take a deep breath. She felt her newly returned emerald green magic coursing through her body, trying to soothe her, but Lucy didn't want to be comforted.

Acknowledging her pain meant that it was real, and she couldn't allow herself to drown in it. Not now. Not when she had so much else to navigate.

Unfortunately for her, the sentient magic was insistent, winding around her forearms and blowing her long brown curly hair around her freckled cheeks. It swirled around her body and back to the sigil in her right palm, urging her to remember the real reason she was here.

She had made a promise under the shade of the great tree that held the portal to The Elderwood, and her magic refused to let her forget.

As she stood in the center of her room, Lucy felt her magic tugging, like it was trying to tell her something. Lucy wasn't interested in opening her mind or heart to anyone, however, her unusual, magical companion had never led her astray. Closing her eyes, she allowed the magic in, and exhaled slowly.

In a rush, her magic vibrated through her body as the memories from mere weeks ago broke through the mental wall she had put in place. Her magic showed Lucy images she couldn't bear. Of Lucy using her magic to stop Jasper as he tried to murder Micah. It flashed the evil gleam in Jasper's eye as he used his alchemy on those she loved. But the magic also reminded her of the vengeful force within herself and how she rallied her power to take Jasper down.

Lucy's eyes squeezed tighter as her stomach flipped at the next memory. The one of her floating in the air, ready to kill Jasper herself. Then her father...

No. I can't fall apart again, she told herself, driving a different line of thought.

She forced her eyes open, breathing deeply in the empty room that felt suffocating, focusing instead on what sparked her desire for retribution, not heartache.

Jasper DeValey.

Her mind still couldn't grasp that everything happened because Jasper was also a Lumen. It didn't matter though. Jasper may have been a Lumen by blood, but he was nothing compared to Micah... Micah deserved the magic he was gifted. Jasper deserved a shallow grave and a pack of starving wolven there to pick apart his remains.

Her heart twisted at the thought of the mortal man she left behind... Micah exemplified the best of humanity, though maybe he was more than just mortal with his newfound magic. He waited patiently for her to get her life together and come back to him. He offered his heart and his love to her, never wavering. And what did she do? She left him. Again.

I had no other choice, she reminded herself for the millionth time that week.

The entire idea that Jasper DeValey was alive and here in the castle made her stomach roil. Why hadn't Laurent told her? Did she not deserve to know that her father's murderer was in the same building as her?

A shudder of sadness threatened to bring her to her knees at the thought of her father. It happened every time he crossed her mind. Grief was alive within her, running rampant with its own agenda. Some moments she could withstand it, cast it aside to deal with later, alone in her room... Other times it would overpower her, and the tears would rush down her face in a torrent even before she knew it was happening. That was just how grief worked... one moment you were fine, and the next, you weren't sure how to breathe.

Maybe that was why Laurent hadn't told her about Jasper. Had her grief been subconsciously bleeding out into the rest of her life?

It *could* have been that he didn't want to upset Lucy that Jasper was there... Or maybe Jasper had just arrived and Laurent wasn't made aware. However, both of those seemed incredibly unlikely. Besides, Lucy asked for updates at every opportunity. Laurent knew how badly she'd want to be informed, no matter how much it hurt. So why did he keep it a secret?

Perhaps he thinks I'm weak.

Lucy sheathed her dagger in her boot, turned, and sat at the foot of her bed, taking a moment to truly consider that idea. She had been walking through this castle like a damned ghost, moving from room to room to give herself something to do, but never truly having a purpose. Even her magic was subdued, barely waking until recently; maybe her magic felt her weakness and wanted to run from her as well?

Mindlessly, her thumb glided over her palm, feeling the raised brand from The Elderwood. Her life had changed so much in such a short period of time... All she had ever wanted was to carve her own path for her future, and instead she was wearing down a path in the stone tile floor of her room as she did nothing to fix her situation but pace.

She shook her head and sighed.

Think logically, Lucy.

Worst-case scenario, Laurent was hiding Jasper's presence from her with malicious intent... but that couldn't be the case.

Could it?

Lucy ran her fingers through her unruly hair in frustration, but the simple act added another crack in her already broken heart. Such a common gesture, but it was one Micah did frequently. She thought of how she'd grab his hands and steady him, helping to calm Micah when he became overwhelmed. His dark brown eyes would melt her with just a look.

Stop that, she scolded herself. *You chose to be here, and now you are. You don't get to miss the man whose heart you broke.*

Flopping onto her mattress, she stared at the silken fabric that draped across her four poster bed. It stretched so serenely across the quiet room, a pale pink that offered calm, so at odds with her frenzied mind.

How do I keep ending up here? In these hopeless situations where I can't seem to make things right.

Regardless of the many options, there was really only one choice to make here. She could no longer think about Micah and the hollow space within her. She could not fall apart at the reminder that her father was gone.

No.

Lucy had to figure out what Laurent knew—and if he was hiding something, she had to know why.

Her thoughts dragged her back to the moment she saw Jasper in his cell.

"Please, no more," he had cried. *"I have nothing else to say, and no more alchemy to give. Please, Sloan, you will drain me to my death!"*

The memory of his withered body chilled her to the bone, but his words hung heavy in her mind. What did Jasper mean? Was Laurent hurting him? Is that why Laurent had avoided answering her question?

Sitting up, she pulled her soft white blanket around her shoulders. She couldn't tell if the shivering was from the cold, exhaustion, or fear; perhaps all three.

The ancient magic swirling inside of her pushed at her fingertips and Lucy invited it to the surface. She watched with amusement as the green mist danced from finger to finger trying to cheer her up. The sentient magic soared back and forth playfully, then stopped suddenly.

Lucy furrowed her brow, bringing her magic closer to her. A sound came from outside her door, like a shuffling of feet. She sat up, anticipating a following knock, but nothing else came. Her magic pulsed in the palm of her hand in warning. Another muffled sound made her stand in alarm.

Is someone outside my bedchambers?

Carefully keeping her magic in her right hand, she tiptoed to the door. Putting her ear to the large wooden door, Lucy heard hushed footsteps. As she opened the door slowly, she was surprised to see Roger, Laurent's trusted guard. He wasn't walking down the hall, and he wasn't summoning her for dinner—so why was he standing there?

"Can I help you?" Lucy asked through the crack of the door, keeping her magic out of sight.

Roger shifted, turning his bright smile to her. "No, Miss Lucy. Sorry if I have disturbed you." He turned from her door and continued facing the opposite wall, a longsword sheathed to his hip.

"Then why are you here?" Lucy asked bluntly. It wasn't like Roger to stand in the hall alone while she remained in her room. Roger regularly accompanied Lucy on her long walks around the castle, but he never stood by her doorway late at night.

Roger's eyes widened the smallest amount, Lucy almost missed it. "Just my rounds, Miss. Lord Sloan has asked his guards to do a few more patrols now that the soldiers are closing in on DeValey."

Lucy's eyebrow arched skeptically, knowing damn well that Jasper DeValey was locked away in the dungeons just floors beneath her feet.

"Hmm," Lucy replied, tight-lipped. "Well, thank you for your service. Good night." Then she shut the door before Roger could reply.

Appears Laurent is working hard to monitor things. Me, no doubt.

The idea made her fume. Lucy rebelled against every act of confinement her parents had placed on her; did Laurent truly think he could do the same?

What is it with males thinking females are so easily controlled?

At her thought, Lucy's magic jumped and swirled in her hand like a miniature storm. It was a power unlike anything she had ever seen. It never ceased to amaze her. Brax had told her that her magic had actualized; that Lucy was an Original.

It seemed both like a lifetime ago and within the same breath of a moment, but she was quick to avoid any reminders of that terrible day. It was her last time at the Lumen property. The last time she saw Micah. The last time she saw her father. It was when Lucy lost all sense of who she was as a Fae, as a daughter, as a lover... Everything changed.

It had to.

She took a deep breath, steadying herself. Her magic calmed and curled around her fingers in a graceful dance. Lucy had spent many nights awake, wondering where this miraculous gift had come from, why it chose her, and what it really meant to be an Original. It had never happened before—Lucy was the first.

When she learned that her magic had actualized, she was able to make the rain fall and the minerals in the ground bend to her will. The Elderwood's magic also showed her things... It allowed her to see far into the Lumen property to spot the intruders as they made their way across the land, ready to hurt The Elderwood and her family.

There hadn't been much time to learn more, especially as she came to the Northern Territory so quickly after Jasper treacherously turned on them. Once her father died and she left Micah, she shut down completely. Her life was in the capable hands of Laurent Sloan, and there was nothing left for her. She was alone, but as her magic zoomed up and down her arms playfully, she considered that maybe she was not as alone as she thought.

"What else can you do?" Lucy whispered to the bouncing green mist in her hand, a smile forming on her lips. She lifted her hand and cast a privacy charm on her room, not wanting Roger to hear her from the hall. No one in the North knew about her magic, and she had every intention of keeping it that way. For now, at least.

Since Laurent was in the business of keeping secrets from her, it seemed fair she had some of her own. It wasn't as though she planned to use this magic against anyone... It just felt good to make a decision for herself. To keep something good close to her before it could be taken away.

"You're always here helping me, aren't you?" She whispered to the bouncing mist. The simple question shook something awake inside of her.

Perhaps it wasn't The Elderwood showing her images in the distance. Maybe it was her magic? Could it be that it had been the one helping her all along? Could it help her here?

"Can you show me Jasper?" She spoke quietly, wondering if the magic could do as she asked—if it really was as sentient as she assumed. No one knew much of the magic she held within her, other than it was gifted from another time, another age—from the gods themselves.

Closing her eyes, with her arms outstretched, Lucy tried to clear her mind and allow a connection with her unusual power. With a burst of green light, a vision of her standing alone in her room appeared. She was in the same gown, the white blanket in a pile on her bed. A green mist cast a thin haze on the outskirts of the vision.

Lucy could see what her magic showed her.

Taking a deep breath to calm herself, she focused on the emerald mist. It crept under her door and slid down the hall undetected by Roger, or any other guards, meandering the castle late at night. The images passed rapidly, both blurry and clear, as she watched the realm through the lens of her magic. Doing her best to direct it to where Jasper had been, her green mist flowed quickly through the shadows, down the corridor to the left-most passage, to the off-limits section of the castle. Her heart beat quickly as she passed a servant bringing bushels of vegetables down to the cellar... No, Lucy didn't pass her. Her magic did.

With each turn, her breathing shook in trepidation. Sweat slicked down the side of her face and trickled down her back. The amount of energy this took was exhausting. Perhaps her magic *did* have limitations. Not on typical Fae spells, but on these otherworldly bits of magic she controlled—well, as much as one can control a sentient power.

She tucked that thought away for another day. Right now she had one focus: find Jasper. Her magic took her down the stairs to the dungeon and halted before a cell.

Lucy panted as though she herself had run through the castle to this spot. In truth, she remained safely tucked away in her bedchambers. She wiggled her toes to ground herself, reassuring her physical body it was not in danger. The rush caused her heart to pound with the thrill. It was working. Her magic allowed her to see whatever she wanted.

Squeezing her eyes closed tighter, she tried to focus on the image before her. All she could make out was Jasper sleeping on a filthy, thin mattress along the wall. No other Fae in sight.

He's still there.

Part of her felt relieved that her magic worked to show her what she had sought out, but another part of her twisted with disgust. She hated Jasper and wished him dead, but she still couldn't come to terms with the fact that Laurent wasn't truthful with her.

Lucy opened her eyes, amazed to see her bedchamber walls; her beautiful emerald magic still bouncing along her hands. A sudden thrill overcame her. She was able to use her power to do something completely unimaginable. Could she use it to see her family as well? Could she see Micah?

A pinch in her heart pushed that thought away, knowing the last time they spoke, Lucy had told Micah that she picked him—that she wanted to figure things out with their relationship. She never anticipated Jasper's attack and the death of her father. She never expected to go back on her word and pick Laurent instead. But it wasn't for love... her heart belonged with Micah, and that could never change.

Instead, Lucy focused on the Baum Estate. It had been weeks since Lucy saw her family and she'd do anything to hear their voices; to know they were okay.

The cold weight of the dagger in her boot made her think of Tristan and his wide smile before he tried to warn her not to come here. She thought of Gregory and Hugh in the South. Her little brothers. Her Mother.

But Wes... he was the one she wanted to see. He had taken over the family business for Central Denora all on his own. Was he okay? Was he mad at her for being forced to play messenger to Micah?

She squeezed her eyes shut once more, trying to see Wes. Lucy felt the magic reach toward him, pushing further and further from her... but it all went black. She tried again and again, but nothing showed.

Hmm... perhaps it is too far.

She sighed and fell back to her bed in exhaustion, disappointed that she couldn't reach her family. Her head throbbed and her muscles were weak. It was the first time she felt drained from using her new powers. Clearly, all magic had its limitations—even the Originals couldn't create miracles.

An ache settled deeply in her soul—a longing to no longer feel so alone. Sliding to the top of her bed, she wrapped herself in her lush blankets and rested her head. Curling into a ball, Lucy thought about her mother and brothers and the life she left behind, and prayed to all the gods who would listen that it would all be worth it in the end.

A soft knock woke her from her restless sleep. It was not a pleasant night, but most nights weren't. Nightmares of her father's murder passed through her mind each time she closed her eyes. Lucy had to relive the moment Jasper sent a killing blow meant for her, that instead found Corvus.

Sometimes her nightmares included Wes jumping in front of the murderous magic. Other times, it was Tristan. Each night she woke up in a cold sweat, gasping for air, spending the rest of the lonely night tossing and turning.

"Miss Lucy?" Roger's voice said from the other side of her wooden door. "Lord Sloan would like to dine with you for breakfast."

Lucy bolted upright in her bed, thrown by the invitation. Laurent had been so busy these recent weeks, she couldn't remember the last time they had breakfast together. Usually, her days involved arbitrary meandering throughout the castle wings and eating meals alone or with Roger. On occasion, Laurent would carve out a moment to eat dinner with her, but not always. However, since their tea last night when Laurent had lied to her face about Jasper, she assumed he would avoid her.

Either this breakfast is a way to try to distract me from the truth, or he is finally going to tell me. Her heart trilled with equal anticipation and fear.

"Thank you, Roger," Lucy called through the door, scrambling to her feet. "Please, just give me a moment to prepare, and I will be out shortly."

After rushing around her bedchambers, she pulled her hair into a mostly tame braid down one side, and wore a pale green gown with delicate cream lace at her sleeves. Slightly flushed from her hurried state, she made it to the door, opened it, and smiled at Roger.

"Good morning, Miss Lucy," Roger greeted her, his face drawn with fatigue.

"Good morning. Were you out here all night?" Lucy asked with a surprised smile on her face. The surprise was genuine, but the smile was not. The idea of a guard at her door at every moment made her incredibly uncomfortable.

"No, Miss. Lord Sloan has stationed guards throughout the castle as a precautionary measure."

Hmm, precautions for who they deny is in the dungeon?

"I see." Lucy tightened her fist, forcing the anger bubbling inside of her to subside. She tried to remind herself to think rationally. Laurent was on her side. There had to be a reasonable explanation.

She kept her head held high and her smile glued to her face as they entered the small dining area. Laurent sat dutifully in his seat at the end of the oversized table, and Lucy greeted him with a smile as she sat.

"Lucy, you look resplendent. I've missed our quiet mornings together," Laurent said. Then he did something that he had not done in weeks. He walked over to her, took her hand, and kissed her on the cheek. "Thank you for meeting me," he whispered in her ear.

Normally, this would be a gesture that would send shivers down her spine and heat pooling in her core, but the only heat she felt was in her face as her anger and impatience grew tenfold.

Keeping her practiced smile in place, she watched as he walked back to his seat, his long silver-white hair swaying gently over his navy blue jacket. He sat and resumed his regal stature, his piercing blue eyes connecting with Lucy's.

"Thank you," she replied. "I've missed our mornings as well. While our dinners have been lovely, I've been hoping to spend more time with you."

Her heart tugged at the deception in her words. She did want to spend more time with him, but was it to enjoy his company or to discover his truths? Or could it be both?

Laurent held her gaze behind steepled fingers, deep in thought. "I will do better about allocating more time specially for you, my queen. Daily breakfasts and dinners? Maybe an adventure just for the two of us, twice a week?"

My queen, blech.

She couldn't stand the phrase anymore. Lucy appreciated the gesture of him wanting to see her, but was also bothered by the fact that he had to schedule the time to do so. She took a small sip of her tea and picked at her warm bread.

He's the leader of the entire Northern Territory. You are not his only priority.

"Yes, I would enjoy that very much."

"We could talk about the plans for the wedding, if you'd like? I know your father set the date, but if you'd like to postpone to give you time to grieve, we can do that."

Her world stood still for just a second—even her heart seemed to pause between beating.

The wedding. How could I have forgotten? Of course he wishes to continue the wedding... that was the whole point, wasn't it?

A soft nod was all Lucy could manage.

Laurent's ice-blue eyes met hers from across the table and the kindness within them forced her into action.

There's no time like now.

"I'd like to talk about more than just the wedding," Lucy said, meeting his gaze.

"What about?" Laurent asked kindly.

"About Jasper DeValey and how I know he's in your dungeons."

TWO

MICAH

Slicing his axe through the air, Micah split the log into two pieces. The resounding crack tore through the trees in the otherwise silent yard. Leaning over, he grabbed one log, then the other, and tossed them over to Brax. Without even needing to look, the Vytyrian warrior caught them and piled them neatly onto the ever-growing tower of logs. Micah was already swinging to cleave another block when Brax called for a break.

"I think we have enough wood to last us at least three winters," Brax said in an annoyed huff.

"I thought you liked a good workout?" Micah asked, knowing full well that her Vytyrian magic recharged when she was exercising.

The muscles in his shoulders were screaming, but he wasn't ready to stop moving—he couldn't. He knew that if he stopped moving, he would have to face the new reality his life had become, but he was determined to ignore it for as long as possible. That was all Micah wanted to do: keep moving, one step at a time.

Physical pain was easier to manage and push away. Whatever was eating away at his soul? Well, that was harder to ignore.

He swung the axe hard into the tree stump, lodging it there for a moment to wipe the sweat from his brow with his forearm. Cutting firewood helped him to avoid his troubles, but it also reminded him of Lucy, and the fluid way she swung the axe when she was here. He should have known from that very moment that there was something special about her. Maybe things could be different. Maybe he wouldn't be in this mess.

Brax narrowed her eyes at him and leaned closer. "You and I both know I love the exercise. However, what we also both know—but for some reason won't acknowledge—is the reason we are endlessly chopping wood." She flung her arms out to her sides, gesturing at the multiple piles of logs settled around the property.

Micah took a swig of water from his worn down thermos and splashed some of it on the back of his neck. He didn't even want to look. Each pile was a reminder of the emotions he'd rather ignore.

A pile next to the house for his sadness; the never ending grief of missing his mom.

A pile near the tree line for his guilt; wishing he could have made things right with his grandad.

A pile near the fire pit for his loneliness; mourning the future he could never have now that he was stuck at this cabin.

A pile on the far side of the house for his heartbreak; a life without Lucy. It was by far the largest pile, and he couldn't stand to look at it.

"What are you trying to say?" He knew exactly what Brax meant, but he wasn't ready to have this conversation. Waiting for her response, his muscles tensed.

His dad told him that was called *flight or fight*. Micah had always had this reaction in him. When things got tough, he'd shove it all away and just wait for life to implode.

Brax looked at him with her usual fire in her eyes. However, instead of barking out a string of insults or going on a tangent about how she was right about something and how Micah was wrong, she just sighed.

"Nothing." She shook her head and looked away. "Come on, I'll make us lunch."

Micah watched her walk back into the house, and the tension in his chest slowly receded. He knew what she was going to say. Micah had been avoiding everything he was feeling and instead forced his body into staying as busy as possible in order to not think about it.

Not to think about *her*.

"You know," Micah called from behind Brax. "We make a pretty good team out here."

"Naturally. I make a superior partner in all things."

All Micah could do was laugh.

Of course, that's her answer.

Since Wes came and brought the soul shattering news that Lucy wouldn't be coming back—that she would marry Sloan after all—Brax had been a constant by his side. They completed daily chores, cooked and cleaned, talked and laughed. They had become a well-oiled machine in all things.

He was thankful for her presence... Without her, he'd be alone at the cabin because of the curse of the guardian—he couldn't leave the property for more than a few hours at a time before death came to find him. Since he wasn't particularly ready to die, he was glad he had someone to keep him company; even if she insulted him more often than not.

Swinging the backdoor open, Brax stepped into the kitchen and immediately went to work. She grabbed a loaf of bread, some meats and cheeses, and a few condiments.

"There is much to want for in this realm, but I will say one thing..." Brax looked at Micah with a mischievous smile. "Potato chips are probably the best invention your lot could have ever invented."

Micah chuckled as he washed up by the sink. Brax had been trying to cheer Micah up for months. Some days it worked. Others it didn't. More than anything, Micah remained in a perpetual state of uncertainty.

Why did Laurent Sloan want Brax to stay now that he had Lucy?
How long would that last? Could Sloan order her away?
Why didn't Lucy come back?

Realistically, Micah knew the answer to that. Lucy thought she was helping him, keeping him safe by staying away. If only she'd return and he could tell her he'd rather suffer at the hands of death itself than be away from her.

As if she could read his mind, Brax slid a plate before him at the kitchen counter and asked the question they usually dutifully ignored.

"Still no word from her?"

He shook his head in response. They didn't need to hash out the same words over and over again. Besides, it had been almost six months for Micah, but only a month or two for Lucy. Who knew how much grief she was experiencing? And maybe... just maybe... she *wanted* Laurent, and he just had to live with that.

That she picked Laurent, and not him.

"Let's say we practice more alchemy today, huh?" Brax changed the subject with fake optimism. "You got so close to getting those darts on target the other day. I bet we could get them closer this time—even if your aim is that of an infant."

"Yeah, maybe." He took a bite of his sandwich to avoid talking. Reaching for the bag of potato chips, Brax snatched them from off the table.

"No way, Lumen." She held the bag of chips to her chest as though they were a cherished gift. Giving him a look of pure disbelief, she pointed her finger at him and scowled. "Last time we shared the bag, you ate nearly the whole thing! And I hate shopping in your awful super markets. This bag has to last, so paws off."

"You're really not going to let me have any?" Micah asked with a huff of a laugh.

"Absolutely not." Brax gripped the bag even tighter.

"Wow, we're doing this, aren't we?" Micah said, shaking his head and smiling.

"I will fight you for them—let there be no confusion."

On any other day, Micah would have laughed at her threats and let her pig out on the salty snack on her own, but today was different. His body was full of tension, the frustration with his life always prepared to spill over into anger. Thanks to his guardian curse, even going to the store to buy his own chips was a danger to him, for fuck's sake.

Maybe a fight isn't such a bad idea.

With a wry smile, he carefully stuck his hand into the front pocket of his jeans to grab the alchemy ring he had taken from Jasper when Micah had sliced his fingers off. It had been months, but Micah kept it in his pocket in case of emergencies—with everything that had happened, you just never could be sure you were completely safe.

Squeezing the ring tight in his fist, he kept his eyes on the snack in Brax's hands, noting the foil lining of the bag—the alloyed materials could give his alchemy a bit of leverage.

Activating the ring with magical intent was the part he could usually get right when he practiced alone in his room. He only needed to let his intention be clear in his mind, then he'd send a surge of focus into the ring. Once the ring warmed, it was activated.

Step one, check.

"Lumen, what are you doing?" Brax asked in frustration. She couldn't see his hand in his pocket, but it was clear he was up to something. She held a hand out in front of her, commanding him to back down. Curling her other arm around the snacks, she shouted at Micah. "These are mine, you dry pork chop! Don't make me knock your ass out."

Next, Micah recalled the words for summoning that he and Brax had found in the Lumen tome left to him by his ancestors. In a flash, he pulled his hand from his pocket, aimed it at the bag of potato chips and called it to him.

"*Vennali!*"

The bag was pulled out of Brax's iron-grip, but she refused to back down. Right before it left her fingers, she clamped down with her Fae speed and strength to claim the salty snack as her own. With a pop, the bag split into two and potato chips went flying.

It was nearly in slow motion as Micah watched Brax witness her beloved snack fall to the ground in pieces. She threw her hands out to stop it, but the chips scattered so widely, she could only catch a few. Holding the salty chips in her hands, Brax looked at them as though she wanted to cry.

Her head snapped toward Micah in a glare, but the seriousness vanished when Micah caught sight of chips stuck in her hair.

He opened his mouth to say something, but instead a low rumble of laughter came out. It was really only a chuckle, but Brax was annoyed enough that she punched him in the side, causing him to bend down on one knee. He let out a groan that was half hurt, half amusement, then he ambled down to the floor and sat.

"You dunce." Brax slid down to the ground next to him, elbowing him to get him to stop. She picked a chip off the ground and popped it into her mouth. "Next time, I'll just buy two bags," she mumbled.

"You asked for it," Micah said, taking a chip out of her hair and throwing it at her.

She caught it in her mouth and chomped down in victory.

They both chuckled, the levity bringing them back to a moment of normalcy, but the quiet won out once again.

"Let's talk about that alchemy for a second." Brax turned her body to face him, gently bringing up his use of magic. "That was your fastest attempt at that magic so far. How'd you get it to work so quickly?"

"I wanted the chips." Micah shrugged like it was obvious, and then playfully swatted her away and got up to fetch the broom. He hated talking about his failures at magic.

The reality was that he had no idea how that worked so seamlessly. It usually took at least four big attempts to get the magic to activate, and then somehow he would fuck up the spell and it'd barely work. This time from start to finish, it was less than a minute, and it did exactly as he had planned.

What made this time so different?

Part of him wanted to chalk it up to practice. He'd been working hard and things were just coming together for him. However, deep down, he had a different idea. One that was probably more likely.

The rings made it possible when his magic alone wasn't strong enough. He was never meant to have Fae magic. It was all just a fluke—some off chance that he was here when Lucy needed a guardian. The rings gave him the power he didn't have on his own, and he wouldn't admit more weakness to the strongest warrior he'd ever known.

"Just a lucky try," he lied, but nothing about it felt lucky.

THREE

LUCY

Laurent and Lucy remained in a silent stare down as he processed her revelation of Jasper's whereabouts. Lucy held her breath, but kept her head up, her magic fluttering just beneath the surface, reminding her to show no fear.

A flash of shock and anger passed over his face. "This..." Laurent began, quickly masking his features to a more stoic expression of interest and caution. "This is quite surprising... How is it you know this exactly?" He shifted in his seat, keeping his focus on Lucy.

"I saw him with my own eyes, Laurent." A moment of worry washed over her, but she would not back down. Lucy needed him to hear her as an individual—not a simpering female. "I want you to understand that I am not afraid of shocking and unsettling news." She deserved to know that her father's murderer was apprehended. It was the sole reason she was in the North. "You should have told me of his arrival."

Laurent stood from the table and walked to her. He crouched down to meet her at eye level and took her hand in his, caressing the back of her hand with his thumb. "Do you know much about Denoran politics, Lucy?" He was hesitant to speak. His voice remained calm and even, with a hint of softness, as though making the next words easier for her to hear. "Especially when it comes to prisoners?"

Lucy blinked at the topic. "Admittedly, not much. But I am not sure why you are asking me that?"

"DeValey poses a threat to the kingdom of Denora. As my prisoner, there are things I must do to gain knowledge of his crimes—things that can make it hard for a Fae to sleep at night." He withdrew his hands and grabbed Lucy's glass of water and finished it.

Lucy's stomach flipped.

Is this why he hasn't wanted to tell me? Because he's torturing Jasper?

"Lucy, I am so sorry to have offended you." Laurent took a seat next to her at the table as he slid his hand into hers once again. "It is a recent development and I wasn't sure if you would feel safe here knowing he was also in the castle." His warm fingers smoothed over the top of her hand and his brilliantly bright eyes never left hers. "He is no threat to you, but I know you've been through so much. I didn't want you to have any more fear in your beautiful heart."

At his explanation, a flutter in her mind rebounded back and forth—her magic telling her to pay close attention. She weighed his words carefully, assessing if she could truly believe him.

It was no secret that she had been through a lot, but that didn't mean she was incapable of dealing with difficult situations. Perhaps he was only trying to protect her, in the only way he knew how.

She wanted to believe him. Though, unfortunately for Lucy, she did not own the same set of truth-detecting skills that Laurent held within his magic. Lucy could not determine for sure if he was honest with her or not, but she held enough hope in her heart, so she decided to believe him. For now.

"Laurent," she began, turning in her seat to better face him. "I do not need protecting. You've asked me once before to always be honest with you, and I am. I need that in return."

A smile stretched across Laurent's perfectly pale skin, reaching from high cheekbone to high cheekbone. "You are truly a marvel." He took her face in his hand and stared at her in wonderment.

"A marvel because I have confronted you about an unsettling topic?" Lucy asked in jest.

Laughing, Laurent shook his head. "Yes, there's always that. But you harbor no ill-will toward me for keeping this from you? And you don't hold fear from DeValey?"

His eyes bored into hers, searching for answers.

Lucy knew he was fishing for lies, waiting for her to share an untruth with him. Luckily for Lucy, that magic did not work on her. Perhaps it was because of the magic that made her an Original.

"I do not fear, Jasper," she said with conviction, not needing to lie. "I am angry at the crimes he has committed. As for you... I'm hurt that you felt you could not tell me."

Her eyes searched his as she thought about the one question that would always bother her: would he have ever told her Jasper was here?

Now it was Lucy's turn to watch his reactions, trying to find a tell that may give her a clue that Laurent was keeping things from her. "You once told me we would be in a partnership—equals. Do you still feel that way?"

"I do," he said adamantly. "There is much that happens in the political realm that you may not understand. Things that may make me seem like a monster. Things I must do."

Carefully, she placed her hand on his arm to get his attention. "You can tell me," she encouraged him. As awful as it could be, Lucy supported doing whatever it took to get the information from Jasper. He deserved to be brought to justice, and she needed to understand why Jasper did what he did—why he turned on their family.

Laurent's eyes sped wildly over Lucy's features—her eyes, her hair, her mouth. He smiled again and nodded. "I can. However, there are more important things in regards to making this realm better. Things I think I'd like to show you."

Pulling her to her feet, he clasped her hand with his and guided her out of the dining area. He walked with the vigor of a child on Winter Solstice, excited to open their presents. Two guards followed in their footsteps.

Where could he be taking me?

"What about Jasper?" Lucy asked him, trying to keep up.

"There will be time for everything, my love," he replied, barely slowing a step.

Taking in her surroundings, she realized he was not walking toward the dungeon, and Lucy's heart flipped with relief. As much as she wanted answers, she realized she was not prepared to see Jasper again so soon—especially with the thoughts of torture running through her mind.

Instead, Laurent was walking with her through the corridors, past the welcoming hall, and into his private wing of the castle.

A tinge of blush seeped into her cheeks at the thought.

He wouldn't be bringing me to his bedchambers, would he?

Fortunately, Laurent pulled her into his study instead, ordering the guards to wait in the hall and for any staff within the office to leave. She watched as two female Fae took their cleaning supplies and left the room in a hurry.

"Normally they clean during breakfast and are done by the time I arrive, but this couldn't wait," he explained. Pulling open the curtains, a wall of light entered the room, illuminating the ornate statues on his floor to ceiling bookshelves and highlighting the many maps he had placed strategically throughout the room.

"You couldn't wait to show me your *office*?" Lucy asked, a skeptical grin on her face. "What does this have to do with Jasper?"

"It doesn't," he replied, his eyes alight with a zest Lucy couldn't place. "It has everything to do with you. With us."

He stood in his office looking at her like a male starved, ready to devour her whole. His gaze felt predatory as he kept his eyes locked on hers, and Lucy wasn't sure if she loved the attention, or if it made her want to run in the opposite direction. Either way, it felt strangely good to be noticed.

With the grace only a Fae could have, Laurent rushed to her and grabbed her hips, pulling her flush against his front. A small gasp left Lucy's lips in surprise—he hadn't been this direct since their day in the woods, a day that felt a lifetime ago. His crisp scent filled the closeness, making her think of snow storms and linens. Squeezing her hips, keeping her in place, his nose trailed the inside of her neck, sending shivers wracking through her body. From his proximity, she could feel his length hardening against her thigh.

Her eyes widened at his boldness, but her center warmed with the reminder of what usually follows an act like this. She felt her cheeks blush at the thought, and looked away from the beautiful Fae in front of her. Laurent was handsome and fair and her future husband, and as much as he claimed to be hers, she wasn't his.

Laurent slid his hand up to her face and held her cheek once again, tilting her face back to his. His hungry eyes took in every inch of her and Lucy blushed more at the intimate act.

"You are breathtaking, my queen. That little smile of yours does me in every time. Did you know that?"

She shook her head, a hint of a smile still cemented in place.

If he thinks I'm going to drop the topic of Jasper just because of some pretty words, he has another thing coming.

"I want to show you everything," he whispered in her ear.

Her skin pebbled at his feather-light touch.

"But first, I cannot wait another moment to kiss you."

He captured Lucy's mouth with his own, and Lucy stilled. His tongue lingered over her lips, teasing his intent.

Lucy knew that accepting this kiss was accepting much more than a physical moment. It would be allowing part of herself to let go of Micah for good, and the mere idea felt like an arrow to her heart. But she had no other choice. She had to keep him safe. So with a deep breath in, she forced thoughts of Micah away from her, and opened her lips to him, tasting a hint of sweetness from his morning tea. He groaned into her mouth, devouring her with lips, teeth, and tongue, pulling her closer and closer to his body.

Lucy seized the chance to lose herself in him. She threw her arms around his neck and held on to him as if she were trying to hold herself together. She had been so devoid of any emotion for so long, with nothing but her grief to keep her company. Here, now, she didn't have to deal with her feelings at all. Instead, she could focus on the physical pleasure that drove her. She could just live, if only for a moment.

Walking her backwards, Laurent strode forward, never taking his lips off of hers, until Lucy's bottom hit the edge of a desk. With his Fae speed, he scooped her up and placed her on top, pulling her legs apart and standing between them. Lucy suppressed a moan at the enormous hardness that pressed at that special spot in between her legs.

Laurent raked his hands over Lucy's body. He dragged his lips to her neck down to the top of her breasts still covered by her gown. Lifting the bottom of her skirts, cool fingers slid up her legs, lingering on the tops of her soft thighs.

"My queen." Laurent growled in her ear.

The rumble of sweet nothings should have been Micah's voice. It should have been Micah's hands and lips that covered her. More than that, Lucy was sick of Laurent calling her his queen, especially when he refused to give her answers.

She didn't want to hear him speak anymore. She wanted to be consumed by this dalliance without the guilt and the shame that threatened to find her.

Capturing his mouth again, Lucy kissed him without restraint. It was desire and escape, lust and longing, truth and fiction; it was so many things, yet nothing at all. Nothing because this was the male she would live the rest of her days with, even if her heart belonged to someone else. There was no other choice, so she allowed herself a free fall into the heated desire—an attempt to feel something other than lost.

She pulled at his jacket, bringing him nearer to her as the heat rose through her veins and he gripped her thighs tightly. Rolling her hips off the edge of the desk, she tried to get closer, wanting the friction to ease her growing need.

Laurent's hands explored her curves, gripping her round bottom firmly. Wrapping his long fingers around her hips, he obliged her demand for more as he tugged her so closely to him that if he had just freed one button of his trousers, they would be in an entirely different situation. Trails of kisses peppered her breasts and up her neck, but Lucy tilted her face away, not wanting to kiss him again.

They rocked into each other again and again, his hardness meeting her pooling core with every thrust. Laurent pulled her bottom closer to the edge of the desk and kept his pace, moving one hand to her breast. She kept her eyes shut, refusing to acknowledge who she held on to, who she was using to allow her this release. Instead, she followed the pleasure, rolling her hips as he kissed and touched her. A gasp left her lips and she saw stars, moaning through her climax. Her hands clutched his jacket and his fingers dug into her curves as her body tightened then slowly relaxed.

Panting, she opened her eyes to take in exactly what had happened. She was propped up on the side of a desk with her skirt pulled up to her waist. Laurent stood with one hand under her skirt, one hand trailing from her breast to her hip, his eyes wild, and his cheeks flushed. It wasn't a blush of embarrassment, though.

No.

It was desire.

He pulled his hands away from her and helped her to her feet, carefully fixing Lucy's stray hairs that had gone rogue during their... activity.

What in the realms has gotten into me?

"I am so sorry," Lucy apologized, looking down and straightening her dress. Embarrassment may not have found Laurent, but it certainly flooded Lucy.

Laurent grabbed her by her chin and looked into her eyes with that same heated desire. "Please do not apologize. Especially not for that," he gestured with a raised eyebrow. "Before you ask, no—it is not customary that I engage in these excitements with another. More so, I have never allowed any guests into my office." He dipped his head and looked back to Lucy with a hint of insecurity. "And I should be the one apologizing. I did not intend to take things that far, but with you, I can't seem to help myself."

Her mind flashed to Micah and betrayal sliced through her like a sword. She took a deep breath and shook her head. She was not betraying him. When she left, Lucy made it clear that she chose Laurent. Things between her and Micah were over. She made the choice to leave, and she made the choice to do this with Laurent.

Grabbing her hand, he kissed it gently. "There is an actual reason I've brought you here," he said with a wink. "I want to show you something I've shared with very few people in my life." He walked over to a wall covered by a curtain and pulled it back.

Lucy had expected to see another window looking out into the courtyard, so she was astonished to see that behind the curtain was a large map of the Northern Territory filled with small papers tacked to different parts.

"What is all this?" Lucy asked in a hushed breath. This entire situation had thrown her. First Laurent ignores her, then he bombards her with physical affection, and now she is allowed to see his innermost private business matters? All of it had been confusing, but a hidden wall of notes was surely the most intriguing.

"These are my plans for the North" He brought Lucy a step closer to the wall to get a better look. "*Our* plans for the North," he whispered in her ear.

Letting go of his hand, Lucy walked closer to the map to read the words tacked carefully in different areas. The bottom of the map, where the village square was, had the most notes.

Food bank for those in need.

Clothing depository.

Winter Solstice gift donations.

Progressive tariffs.

"I'm not sure I understand?" Lucy admitted, turning to face Laurent. "What are all of these things?"

"The people of the North are no different from people of Central or Southern Denora. We have the same population struggles and the same groups of Fae who tackle the burdens of low income." He walked closer to the map, no longer looking at Lucy, but at his grand plans. "I wish to provide the North with an easier way of living. I've conducted the proper research and have scouted locations for a food and clothing bank, supported by our tariffs and given to those who need the support. I've even come up with a proposed tariff change to allow those who make more money to give more, and those who make less, to have to pay less."

"You're changing the tariffs?" Lucy asked in shock. "I didn't know that was even possible."

"I aim to make it possible, Lucy." He spun to face her, a lighted passion in his eyes. "We are—together."

"How?" It was the only question on Lucy's mind. Surely, this was all impossible under our current law from the King.

"Don't you remember seeing those poor families in the carriage after our first dinner together?"

Lucy's face fell. Of course she remembered it. The heart-breaking scene had been on her mind for weeks after. It was her first glimpse of the kind male Laurent was, as he hand delivered the food to those in need. She nodded, her brows furrowed.

"Wouldn't you like to actually help those people? Not look at them with sadness and wish that someone would do something— but to actually make a change and improve their lives?"

"Of course, but—"

"I know you do. It's why I have fallen for you so hard, my queen." He took her by the waist and spun her in a dance, smiling and laughing. "Together, we can do this. We will provide shelter to those in need when winter arrives. We will help Fae obtain good jobs to support their families." He held her in his arms and looked at her with a genuine smile. "*We* can make the difference."

"How will you convince the king of your ideas?" Lucy knew King Tralont was many things, but generous to the poor was not one of them.

"Tralont and I will have a meeting and I'll explain my plan. It will all be fine. In fact, that is why I've been so busy these past few weeks since we've returned. I've been preparing."

He placed her down gently and walked over to another large map of the entire realm of Denora. Standing there, he kept his eyes focused on the castle, deep in thought, with his fingers linked around the back of his neck.

Another reminder of Micah—it made her heart hurt once more. Shoving it away with more vigor this time, she reached out and placed her hand on Laurent's shoulder.

"This is truly amazing, Laurent. I'm sure your meeting will go well. You have only the best interests of our realm at the forefront of your plan."

"Yes. Tralont should have stepped in a long time ago before the population got to such an immense size. He can be a foolish braggart, but hopefully he will see the genius of this plan. He will have to."

There was a steel to Laurent's voice that Lucy noticed when he spoke of King Tralont.

Lucy continued to analyze the map. "What's this?" Where the North's soldiers were usually stationed, there was a large "M" on the note.

"My forces are split on a few different missions at the moment. One was gone on their search for DeValey, as you know. But others are on missions to support Fae in need. In fact, there is a large group on their way to the Southern Territories soon."

"Well, I think this is all quite wonderful." She took his hand and squeezed. "Thank you for showing me."

Without taking his eyes away from the map of Denora, he replied. "I would do anything for you."

FOUR

MICAH

"Come on then, you spongey lima bean." Brax pulled Micah out of the house and into the yard after lunch.

Hesitantly, he followed, but he knew it was pointless. Micah was able to use his magic faster than he ever had before, but it wasn't from some amazing feat of power—it was all because of that fucking ring. He should have just told her, but admitting he was nearly powerless was humiliating. Besides, she was just pissed because it cost her a snack.

Stopping when she got halfway into the yard, she turned and bent her knees, crouching into a fighting stance. "You were a tough guy when it came to my property. Now bring that magic back to the surface to put to good use."

"Your *property?*" Micah balked. "They were freaking potato chips!"

"And they weren't yours," Brax replied with a vengeful smile. "Let's get this magic to work. Come on."

Mental note: don't mess with a chick and her snacks.

"Let it go, Brax. We both know that was a fluke." He dug his hands into his pockets, trying to avoid her challenge. His fingertips touched the ring and a surge of regret swept over him.

He didn't want to use the alchemical magic from Jasper—he was the one who killed Lucy's dad. He even tried killing Micah! But there was something about it that just called to him. It made him powerful when he felt helpless. Wasn't that important in this new life he lived?

"I won't be able to do it twice," he called to her. "Calm down."

"Calm down?" Brax raged. "Absolutely not. You wanted your magic to work, and you made it happen." Brax held her fists up, prepared for combat. "Now—do it again."

Micah couldn't believe she wouldn't let this go. It was a fucking bag of chips. He wasn't even sure how he did it—it was a stroke of luck. Brax just wanted to drag him out here to make him pay for the emotional burden of losing her snack.

"We both know you are holding back," Brax taunted him, taking a step forward and shoving at his shoulders.

He took his hands out of his pockets to steady himself, then pressed his lips into a thin line. "I'm not doing this," he told her seriously. Turning to walk back to the cabin, he felt another shove at his back.

Micah spun around to look at Brax, his eyes narrowed. He had no interest in fighting anymore, but she seemed dead-set. Her cropped hair swung freely in front of her eyes as her crouched body shifted left and right.

"You can't run from this." Brax kept her dark gaze steady on his, refusing to back down. "It's been an hour. Your magic should have restored just fine. Now, come on."

Micah only stared at her, meeting her glare in a standoff. The anger simmering inside of him was not toward her; it never was. Time after time he took his anger out on someone who didn't deserve it, he learned that lesson the hard way long ago. He kept trying not to do that to Brax.

"So you're not going to talk this time, huh? Fine." She lifted her foot and kicked him directly in the chest, her leather boot sending him flying backward.

With a thud, he landed on the uneven ground, grunting in frustration.

"What the fuck was that for?" He got to his feet but kept his distance from her uncalled-for violence.

What did she have to be so angry about? Fucking chips? I don't think so.

"Why are you holding back, Lumen?" Brax asked again.

When Micah refused to answer her, she came soaring toward him with giant leaps, her warrior upbringing clear as day.

Before he found his magic, she would have clocked him easily, probably even knocking him out cold. This time, he had his Fae speed to his advantage—it was the one thing that came naturally these days. Brax lifted her fist in the air and Micah spun to the left, dodging her. She crashed to the ground, her fist caked in mud.

Baring her teeth, Brax turned on her heel and came sprinting toward him again. Her fierce gaze made Micah's insides tense—he had never been the target of her rage before. With another lunge at Micah, she closed her fist, prepared to strike. Micah wasn't quick enough. Before he could manage to block it, Brax collided with his cheek, forcing him into action.

Throwing his arm up, he swatted her windpipe, knocking her off course and easing the blow. He knew even the quickest Fae still needed to breathe.

Gasping for air, Brax staggered back a few steps, her hands at her throat.

"Just drop this, Brax. I don't want to fight you!" Micah roared.

He was teetering on the edge of sanity, with each day getting worse and worse. This conversation would lead to nothing but trouble.

He couldn't do it.

He couldn't handle it.

"That's the problem here, you rotten zucchini. You aren't ready to fight for anything." Brax dropped her hands from her neck and faced Micah again. For once, she was standing still, not attacking him with every insult.

"I *am* fighting!" He took a step closer to her, pointing his finger at her. "I've knocked your ass on the ground before, and I can do it again. Isn't this what you want from me?"

"You aren't fighting *for* anything, Lumen," Brax said with more significance in her voice, her chest heaving as she took in deep breaths of air.

Micah took a step back. Just like every other time, the urge to flee grew. He wasn't ready to talk about his feelings—it was too soon.

Why is she pushing this?

"We *need* to talk about it, Micah," she stated. She took a few slow steps closer to him and Micah tensed. "We need to talk about *her*."

There it was. The one thing he wasn't ready to talk about. There was nothing to say anymore.

He'd talk about his dead mother.

Or his grandad, who he thought had abandoned him as a child, but turned out to be the guardian of a fucking magical portal.

He'd talk about his loneliness he experienced when he was in the police force.

He'd even discuss his desperation for connection to his only remaining family, knowing he couldn't safely invite his dad here without eliminating every possible threat.

He'd talk about those things—but he couldn't talk about Lucy.

Not her.

"You can't push away every fucking problem in your life, pretending that you're fine. You're *not* fine." Brax's eyes betrayed her violent actions. She wasn't just angry, she was upset. At him.

"I'm fine," he said evenly as he turned away from her to head back into the house.

"Why are you doing this?" Brax's voice cracked with emotion, causing Micah to stop in his tracks. "Why won't you just face what happened and deal with it?"

Sighing, his shoulders slumped.

"You keep pushing me away, Micah. Talk to me."

He turned to look at her, meeting her brown eyes full of sorrow. "Why bother?"

Brax took a step back, eyebrows furrowed at his question. "Excuse me?"

"Why bother?" He repeated. "You'll leave next." He lifted his arms to motion to the empty property. "Just like everyone else."

"I... I'm not going anywhere," Brax stuttered, searching for the words. "Why are you suggesting such things?"

"As soon as Sloan says your job here is done, you get to go home. And I'm not mad at you for it, it's just the way things go." He sighed and looked up into the clouded sky. "You will go home and be happy with your family. And I will be here. Alone. There's no point in trying to fight it."

When Brax opened her mouth to speak again, Micah held up a hand, his face drawn. "Please," he murmured. "I don't want to keep arguing. I just don't have it in me right now."

Brax pursed her lips and straightened her shoulders, shaking off her vulnerable show of emotion. With an agitated nod, she agreed to a moment of peace. She put her hands up and walked to the tree stumps around the fire pit, signaling a truce; not forever, but just for now. Without another word, she pulled logs from an over-sized heap and started their nightly routine of a fire and beers before bed.

Most days, this was cathartic for Micah. They'd sit and drink and speak of nothing significant: maybe the weather, maybe the day's chores. Sometimes she'd try to pry more emotional responses from him, and most of the time he didn't mind. But if he was being honest, Micah had no interest in sitting outside and suffering through more unbearable questioning from Brax today. However, he also couldn't stand the idea of sitting alone in the quiet with his never ending thoughts.

There was no real win there.

As he watched Brax prep the fire, he realized there wasn't much of a win around for her, either. She was sent here to watch over a tree that either did absolutely fucking nothing, or acted up and tried to kill them all with shadow beasts. He was happy to have her for the killing part, but when the portal was dormant, there was nothing to do on the Lumen property.

Not only was Brax likely bored out of her mind, but she was probably counting down the days until she could go back to her family. Micah didn't blame her for that. If he had anyone to look forward to seeing again, he'd feel the same...

But that was the harsh truth about Micah's life—there was no one else to look forward to seeing anymore.

"I'll grab the drinks," he said to her, turning to walk back into the house. Stepping past the threshold of the doorway, his boot immediately crushed a crunchy chip they had somehow missed.

Micah smirked a bit at the thought of Brax's utter horror as her snack was flung through the air.

He dug his hand into his pocket to retrieve the ring once again. He had a few of them in a small box in his room—he collected them from Jasper's severed fingers for safe keeping. It ended up being a smart move on his part. Whenever he practiced his magic in private, his magic was always stronger with the use of the alchemy rings, but he couldn't figure out how or why. He wasn't intentionally keeping things from Brax, but this was something he just wanted to figure out for himself. He was tired of being the least intelligent one in every room.

There were four rings, one for each of Jasper's fat fingers. The amber colored one had never really worked for Micah—his only guess was that Jasper used all the magic from it. It was the same way when Wes and Brax took the necklace off of him after the tussle when he killed Corvus. The necklace was completely devoid of power after that.

Three of the rings were different, though—there were two ruby and one emerald. One of the ruby gems shone bright with a swirling magic within it. The other had a small bit of light, but barely sparked. The emerald ring was also bright with power—that was the one he had kept in his pocket. The green magic reminded him of Lucy.

It comforted him as much as it hurt.

On the few occasions when he used the rings to activate his magic, he noticed the magic inside of them did not wane the way they did for Jasper. He couldn't understand it, but with the rings, his magic felt immense. Without them, his powers felt almost muted, as if they were watered down.

It's why he hated practicing his magic with Brax so much. He could do it with a murderous asshole's weapons, but he couldn't do it with the little bit of magic already inside of him.

So far, Micah had been able to manipulate rocks and dirt, but that was the extent of his power. Jasper was able to do nearly anything with his magic. What made Micah so different?

If it were up to him, he'd never use the rings—they reminded him so much of Jasper, and each memory of him caused a disgusted shudder to snake through his body.

Maybe it'd be better to just ditch the rings completely. I could live a life without magic.

With beers in hand, and sidestepping a few stray chips, he made his way to the backdoor. But before he got there, what he saw in the window made him freeze in his tracks.

A long, curling black tail made its way around a tree trunk just outside his window. An oversized paw peaked from behind the leaves.

No. It can't be.

Bright yellow eyes locked with his from amidst the trees.

There was no mistaking it.

The shadow beast was back.

FIVE

LUCY

After her visit with Laurent, Lucy had spent time in her room mulling over what he had shared with her. If she were being honest with herself, it was hard to wrap her mind around it all.

Laurent had a plan for a better Denora—that in of itself felt remarkable. Could he really accomplish changing the course of Denoran tradition? Was it possible he could be the catalyst for so much more?

A faint whisper of a smile crept over her face as she remembered the way Laurent shared his positive intentions with her about their future; he always mentioned he thought of her as an equal. To consider a female as an equal in Denora was possibly the most ambitious aspect of it all. Even the situation with Jasper didn't seem to bother her as much as it originally did. Maybe he was still trying to do what was right.

Her mind buzzed with the possibilities, yet even with all of Laurent's amazing ideas, a nagging tug within her told her she was missing something beyond all of that. Something important.

So she decided to do the one thing she always did: search for answers.

Biting her lip, she contemplated where to start—this castle was still so new to her. She tried to trace her steps in her mind through the different wings of the castle and the various rooms she had explored. Lucy recalled the hall with three paths, one of them leading to the dungeons. Suddenly, her magic sent her a vision: a memory of when she first found Jasper in the dungeon. He was bloodied and disheveled, begging Laurent not to drain him of his alchemy. That he had no more to give.

Her magic rushed out of her mind, floating expectantly before her.

Alchemy to give? Why did he say give...

There was a reason she kept coming back to this moment, and Lucy needed to find Jasper and get him to explain what he meant. How did it play into everything?

Lucy considered sending her magic out through the castle on its own so that she wouldn't be spotted; however, she was nervous that exhausting herself of her magic so immensely may not be in her best interests at the moment. Luckily, the guards wouldn't think twice to see her walking in the halls during the day, since it was what she always did.

Steeling herself, she asked her magic to accompany her through the halls to the only person who could give her the knowledge she sought. Unfortunately, that person was someone she hated with all her being: Jasper.

What was even more unfortunate was that by the time she got to the dungeons, he was gone.

Out of breath from hurrying through the castle, she scanned the room in awe. There was no trace of him in the cell. It had been cleared and cleaned as though no one had been in it for years— though Lucy knew better.

Where did he take you?

Lucy looked around the dungeon corridors, trying to uncover any clues as to where Jasper went. Was he moved to another wing? A different location in Denora completely? Did Laurent kill him?

A shiver went down her spine at the thought. While she very much wanted to bring Jasper to justice, she still knew there was something missing in the grand scheme of things, and too many clues pointed to Jasper. She needed to find him and get the truth.

Perhaps that's why Jasper isn't here, she realized.

Each time she asked Laurent about Jasper, he changed the topic. And now that he knew Lucy was aware of his presence, he was moved? What was Laurent trying to hide?

As impatient magic led her through the castle on a wild goose chase, they searched for Jasper, carefully dodging the extra guards patrolling the castle. They had scoured the dungeon floor, the wait staff's quarters, and even tried to make their way into the guard's quarters, but didn't quite make it that far. Jasper was nowhere to be found.

Finding herself back in the main library with no additional leads, she called her magic back to her before anyone could question the strange green haze meandering the book stacks. It was daytime, and there were no shadows to hide in. Sighing, she took a seat in one of the oversized chairs by the windows that peered down into the market square.

Staring out into the sea of people below, Lucy thought about the change Laurent wanted to bring to his people. She could almost imagine the aiding-booths, a food stand full of meat and produce for hungry families, clothing stands for those who had worn down their jackets and trousers. Imagining the grateful Fae as they were supported by their realm made Lucy smile—really smile. Hope bloomed within her for the first time in a long time.

And Laurent wanted her to be part of it.

Her smile quickly dropped.

Well, he wanted her to be part of it, but also decided what information she could hear and when she was allowed to hear it. Just another way others tried to control her.

However, the difference they could make to the realm was more important than anything else she could have ever dreamed, and with each passing moment, she pictured herself doing those things. Finally making the changes she had always wished for in Denora. Even if Laurent had to be the one there by her side.

A fluttering sensation filled her from head to toe; actual excitement sending her to her feet. She would seek out Laurent and ask why Jasper had been moved—get him to answer the questions he kept avoiding. Then, maybe she could talk with him about more ideas for the future of Denora... Lucy knew he had always agreed with her views of female Fae, and perhaps they could work on laws for equality as well?

Walking down the halls to search for Laurent in his offices, Lucy passed a large glass display, showcasing pictures and scrolls of parchment safely tucked away behind the ornate glass.

The sight of ice-blue eyes caught her attention and made her pause.

Laurent.

The entire vitrine was dedicated to him and his accomplishments. There were medals of honor, plaques with his name engraved upon them, and flowers, magically preserved, on display. Her lips quirked into a small smile at the adoration the people of the North gave to Laurent. They truly loved and respected him.

There were three scrolls opened for others to read. One depicted his coronation when he became the ruler of the North. Another listed his heritage, going back generations from his father to his grandfather and more. But the last scroll was something that Lucy did not quite expect.

It read:

The Hero of the North

    On the precipice of war, newly appointed Lord Laurent Sloan made his way across the realm to honor Denora and pay tribute to his king. On his journey, he came across the knowledge of a secret rebellion group forming to overthrow the new young King Tralont. Once childhood friends, Lord Sloan knew the importance of the power balance within the realms, and did what any good and righteous Lord would do.

Returning to the Northern Territories, Lord Sloan subdued the rebellion group and ensured the halt of any future rebellion in its wake. It is said he had slain over 750 of his northerners in that battle, and because of his immense power and strength, Denora remains indomitable to this day.

Lucy stilled. There were rumors about "Lord Slain" for years, and all this time, it was his protection of the realm that had cost him that horrid nickname?

As if a weight had been lifted from her shoulders, so went a few of her reservations about Laurent. This entire time she had been holding back, waiting for the other shoe to drop with him, believing deep down in her soul that an arranged marriage was the last thing in all the realms she wanted. Yet, as she learned more and more about him, there was much to respect.

Sure, she didn't always agree with him on how he handled information she wanted to know, but he had been living alone for a very long time. Maybe they just needed to work on their communication?

Maybe love doesn't need to be immediate, she thought, picturing Micah's perfect face in her mind. *Maybe love can grow with mutual understanding; with equal parts respect and intention.*

Her parents' love had been formed from a prearranged relationship. Perhaps she could find the same? And even if it wasn't love, there was always hope for friendship.

Lucy realized that this was not the life she had dreamed of, but who ever achieved their perfect life? This new journey offered her the ability to change Denoran tradition. She could help other Fae find equality and support.

There was still hope with this new path she was on, and she wouldn't keep holding herself back.

Lucy met Roger standing outside of the door to Laurent's study, dutifully keeping guard.

"Hello Miss Lucy," Roger said, tipping his head toward her in greeting. "Is there anything I can do for you today?"

"I'd like to speak with Lord Sloan, if he is available?" Lucy asked politely. She hoped she wouldn't get turned away, but also considered that when he spent time with her earlier, it could have been an exception, not an expectation.

"Certainly," Roger replied with a smile. "He wanted to meet with you this evening, but I am sure he won't mind a minor interruption, seeing he is not currently occupied."

He turned and opened the door for her, walking in first to announce her arrival.

"Lord Sloan. Miss Lucy is here to see you."

Laurent sat behind the desk Lucy was propped upon earlier, and seeing him there made a rush of pink appear on her cheeks.

As if he could tell exactly what she was thinking, Laurent gave a knowing smile and stood. He came around to the front of the desk and sat exactly where she had, and waved for Roger to exit.

"My queen, to what do I owe the pleasure?" Laurent asked, his eyes raking over her body.

"I am sorry for bothering you," Lucy said, forcing her eyes to look away from his piercing gaze in order to get her question out. She was silly once and allowed a moment of physical pleasure to impede her questioning, but it wouldn't be happening again. "I wanted to ask you about the prisoner."

Laurent's demeanor changed rather suddenly, realizing it wasn't quite the social call he had hoped for. The flirtation from his eyes disappeared and instead a serious and concerned look colored his features. "What can I do for you?"

The question made Lucy stumble over her words for a moment. It wasn't *What do you want?* Or *What do you mean?* He was offering his services to her once again, putting her first, as he always had.

Her expression softened. "Jasper is no longer where he was when I... came across him. Is there a reason for that?"

What Lucy really wanted to do was ask Laurent why he was no longer in the dungeons, but perhaps that would have been a bit too brash.

Laurent smirked a bit, then nodded. "Unfortunately, he is a danger to those around him. It is for your safety, and for the safety of those who dwell within the North, that he has been relocated."

Her stomach did a strange flip.

Relocated.

"So he is alive?" A small part of her had believed Laurent had killed him, and she felt slight relief to know there was still time to find answers. Though, did she really still need them? Could she simply trust Laurent and his decisions?

"Yes, my love." Laurent walked up to her and took her hands. She hadn't noticed they had been trembling until he stilled them with his own. "You have nothing to fear. He is a crazed and dangerous male spouting strange accusations that could hurt those around us."

Strange accusations? What could be so dangerous about a male shackled in a dungeon?

"Do you not trust the guards who have him in their care?" Lucy challenged.

Where would be a safer place to keep a prisoner than a cell in a dungeon? Unless he just wanted to keep me from him.

He casually placed a stray hair back behind her ear and stroked her cheek softly. "He cannot be trusted, and I will not put my beloved in any sort of danger if I can help it."

Her eyes met Laurent's at the word.

Beloved.

He gave her a sweet kiss, then guided her to a chair. "Sit, you look quite shaken."

The truth was that she was absolutely shaken, but why? Because her father's murderer was still here? Because there were things that weren't quite adding up? Because her future husband had called her beloved? Or because the word had caused something to stir within her that she had not expected?

Shoving it all back down, she turned to Laurent and smiled. "Thank you." Trying to regain her words, she remembered what Roger had said. "Laurent? Roger mentioned you wanted to speak with me?"

"Ah, yes," he said, softly, a pinch of regret painting the air. "Your brother Wesley has contacted me."

Lucy's heart ached at the mention of her family.

"Your father's funeral is upon us. We leave for Central Denora in the morning."

SIX

LUCY

The carriage bumped over the rocky landscape of the Leithe Grove as Lucy and Laurent left the Northern Territory. The ride had been mostly quiet, except for the shuffling of papers from Laurent's side of the compartment. He was busy reading through documents, his brows furrowed, deep in thought.

"I'm sorry that I must bring all of this horrid paperwork along with us," Laurent apologized again. "I fear that if I get too far behind on my plans, then the king will not hear my concerns." A look of worry etched in the lines on his forehead, the only sign that hinted his true age.

Lucy smiled and brushed away the apology. "It's fine. I understand that your work is important." Truth be told, she was more relieved than upset. She didn't have the energy to make small talk. Her mind was elsewhere. "Perhaps while you visit, you will be able to speak with the king or one of the dukes about your plans," Lucy suggested. "There will be many officials at my father's... ceremony." Her voice cracked on the word.

She couldn't wrap her head around the fact that she was on her way to her father's Farewell Ceremony.

It was too much.

Pushing the thought to the side, she changed the topic. "When we get to the estate, I'm not sure how much time I'll have to spend with you. I told you it was fine for you to have remained in the North." She mindlessly toyed with the floral lace on her gown, staring out into the winding mountains surrounding their carriage.

"Nonsense," Laurent said. He slid closer to her and took her hand, calming her fidgeting. "Of course I will be with you, Lucy. You are my betrothed and I am here to support you in all things."

Normally, his doting upon her would have turned her cheeks pink and caused her stomach to flip, but everything felt too heavy.

She didn't even bother replying.

"Spend some time with your family, Lucy. I can keep myself busy. You do not need to worry about me while you have so many other important things to address."

Lucy's lips formed a tight smile. A small part of her wished he would stick around. She wasn't fully prepared to face her family, and having him there would have been the shield she needed. However, a bigger part of her appreciated that he trusted her enough that she did not need a chaperone. The stars only knew that if it were any other male in his place, they'd expect her to be followed around like a lost duck.

Well, every male but one other...

Her mind turned to Micah and the immovable trust he had in her.

The trust she destroyed when she left him in Joterra and hadn't returned... It had been months for Micah since he had seen her.

As if noticing the worry in her eyes, Laurent squeezed her hand, pulling her from her thoughts. "I will be with you any moment you need me, but I will give you the space to grieve with your family. Roger will always be nearby if I am not, and if you require anything, just let him know." His ice-blue eyes met hers with a fierce tenderness that she could hardly stand. "I will come to you. I will always come to you."

Lucy nodded again and Laurent let her hand go, turning back to his paperwork.

He may always come to me, but it isn't him that I need right now.

Her unfortunate reality was that she wasn't quite sure what she needed at all.

THE BAUM ESTATE was crowded with visitors from all over Denora and beyond. Local family and friends would arrive for the ceremony at a later time, however, there were still many guests from far away that had arrived early. A few guests would stay within the extra bedrooms of the manor, but most were settled in luxurious tents on the grounds of the estate.

There were canvas tents of all shapes and sizes, housing Fae from many different realms. Some were customers of the Baum Bowyer industry dating back to when Corvus first took over, like Matteo Lasso and Cristano Pedit, who took a few of the beige tents. Corvus's friend from childhood, Neddard Irvine, had an extravagant green tent, magicked with turrets and actual fire. He was in from Kerroz, where he maintained his mining business.

There were also more prestigious guests like Duke Renfro—the leader of the Denoran military—and his family. Even King Tralont himself would be in attendance.

Most guests were there to support Anita and her children, but there were still a handful of attendees who were there for the sole reason that Fae funerals were rare, and they didn't want to miss out on an opportunity to attend one. There would be music and food and lavish decorations.

The entire ordeal made Lucy nauseous, even if somewhere deep down she understood. Her father's death was so significant it would go down in history... The death of a strong Fae male by another Fae in his command? The scandal alone was enough. Add in the rarity of Fae death? You've got yourself the social event of the season.

But this was her family.

This was her *life*.

Choking down the lump in her throat, she continued past the grounds to the house. Everywhere she looked were faces of Fae she didn't even know. Where was her family?

Lucy wished it could just be those close to her for the final ceremony, not a mass of strangers coming to put their nose in someone else's business. Some Fae were so fucking flawed, they would never see the issue with it; they'd never see how badly it hurt to lose the ones you love.

The problem was that most Fae thought they understood. As soon as Lucy had arrived, she couldn't turn in any direction without being bombarded by condolences for her father. But it was only a moment until those condolences turned to interrogations about the upcoming wedding.

"Where will you hold the wedding ceremony? In Central Denora I hope?"

"Who will design your gown?"

"What cake will you be serving? Will Lisette be your baker?"

To be quite honest, she hadn't thought of any of those questions. The only question she had about her wedding was, "am I really going to do it?"

Truthfully, the last few days with Laurent had changed Lucy's viewpoint about her ideas of marriage. There was a connection that she felt when she was with Laurent—a camaraderie. She knew it was partially just a physical connection, but perhaps over time it would turn into more.

He had such amazing plans for the people of Denora, and being part of that gave her something to look forward to in a future with him in the North. It wasn't entirely romantic excitement, but perhaps, with time, those feelings would grow.

Regardless, this week was not the time for that. Laurent was busy planning his meeting with the king and Lucy just had to get through the funeral. For now, she was content to be here—in her true home.

Making her way across the garden terrace, Lucy saw her younger brothers Henry and Simon tear across the grass, laughing and playing with the other children who had come to visit.

Finally, something normal around here.

Seeing the estate booming with life made Lucy's heart warm. When she left the Baum estate for the North with Laurent months ago, it had felt so dark and dreary. Somber memories shadowed the once bright spots of her life. She wasn't sure if joy would ever return without her father's larger-than-life presence, and seeing the natural happiness of her young brothers gave her a ray of hope.

"Lucy," Henry called in a sing-song voice, darting past her. "I bet you can't catch us!"

"Wait!" Simon yelled after him. "You have to wait for us to hide!" He kept running after the children bounding through the yard.

"You forgot I am the reigning champion of seek-and-find!" Lucy called back to them. Her smile followed them as she watched the children run into the orchard and out of sight.

She rubbed her chest to ease the sharp pain of longing that struck. Seek-and-find was the same game she and Micah had played in the forest before they had fallen for one another. Or perhaps she had already fallen for him by then? There had always been something about Micah that just felt right to her... but there was no time to think about that now. She had to focus on what was in front of her.

Her family.

Grieving her father.

Then returning to the north to wed Laurent. She had to uphold her end of the deal.

There was no more time to live in the past.

With a defeated sigh, Lucy stepped through the terrace entryway and into the estate. Just on the other side of the door, Lucy saw Anita bustling around and directing Fae of all kinds. Some were delivering flowers or food, some were decorating, others were part of the cleaning staff. Anita rushed from one place to the next, making sure every detail was perfect for the most important part of this weekend. The Farewell ceremony.

Fae Farewell ceremonies were rare, as many Fae did not age and die like most mortals. The eldest Fae stayed to offer guidance and wisdom as Venerable Fae. After that, the Fae who lived to old age finished their lives with celebration as they passed from one plane of existence to the next. They didn't have Farewell Ceremonies. Instead, they simply had celebrations of life and those who passed on were usually prepared. They would carefully plan and finance the arrangements long before they were needed.

It had been centuries since the Addaxe Wars when Fae had last experienced a high death count due to violence. Since then, only those who had lived for over 500 years could speak to the unexpected passing of Fae, but Lucy was much younger than that. She, and many others, hadn't experienced a sudden Fae death in their lifetime.

Father, why did it have to be you?

She felt empty.

Corvus had been young and hearty and booming with life. It was simply unfathomable that he was... gone.

She couldn't bring herself to say the words, though the magic within her washed through her like a comforting hug. The gesture caused her eyes to sting.

Not now. I refuse to fall apart.

Thankful that her mother hadn't spotted her, Lucy took a deep breath and continued further down the hall. She knew Anita was likely having a difficult time with the funeral arrangements, and that order and precision were sure to be the only things holding her together.

Off to her right, the loud guffaw of her eldest brother, Hugh, pierced through her sadness and pulled a smile to her lips. It had been nearly a year since she heard that laugh.

Quickening her pace, she walked into the sitting room where her brothers gathered, drinking their father's favorite spirits and smoking strong cigars.

Leaning in the doorway, she took in the scene. Her three eldest brothers sat before a fireplace, lounging in deep, leather armchairs, with dragon-glass goblets in one hand and smelly cigars in the other. They all had easy smiles on their faces, their cheeks red, either from the warmth of the fire or the spirits.

"I should have known I'd find you three menaces up to no good," Lucy joked from the doorway.

"Ah, Lucella!" Gregory greeted her, walking toward her from his seat. "Wes here has told us you've been giving him a hard time." He winked with his customary sly smile all her brothers seemed to have inherited. "Keep it up."

Lucy laughed as she pulled Gregory in for a warm embrace. Hugh stood next, giving his sister a squeeze.

"Those things smell awful," Lucy said, gesturing to the large cigars in their hands. "Why are they so massive?"

"We broke into Father's secret stash," Hugh said with a laugh. "Cigars from Kerroz—only the best of the best." He took a deep puff in and blew out a circle of smoke. "Neddard said he's got another case in his tent. We hadn't seen him in ages, but he said it was the only way we could give a fair tribute to Father."

"I see you've been working tirelessly in the South," Lucy said with mock seriousness, ignoring the mention of funeral business. "Yes, such hard work sitting around blowing smoke rings all day. I'm sure Lisette just loves that."

"For your information, Lisette loves me, flaws and all." Hugh winked at her.

"And how many flaws there are," Lucy replied snarkily with a wide grin across her face.

"Wes, I think you were right," Gregory said, with a shocked smile on his face. "Lucy's become more brazen in her old age."

"Yes, I'm a crippling old Fae." She made Wes scoot over and sat next to him, taking a sip of the spirits in his cup. With a face twisted in disgust, she quickly handed it back to him. "This also tastes old. What in all the realms is this?"

"Amartium—dragon-flamed whiskey," a familiar voice said from the doorway. "Father's favorite."

She'd know that voice anywhere.

Tristan.

Grinning from ear to ear, she turned to greet her brother, but was met with an unexpected sight. It was, indeed, Tristan standing before her, but he had changed so much. His once long hair was now trimmed short to match his soldier friends. His eyes that had always twinkled in the light now seemed dull, like a bit of his brilliance was lost. But what stood out the most was his clothing. Truly, Lucy should have seen it coming, but still it shocked her. Instead of his usual casual tunic and trousers, he wore the uniform of a soldier.

He enlisted in the Denoran military.

Her smile failed only for a second, but Lucy was sure Tristan had seen it. Putting more enthusiasm into her greeting, she walked over to him and gave him a big hug. She may not have been thrilled that her brother had a new and dangerous occupation, but she was glad to see him. More than anything, she was happy he was following his heart. He had always wanted to join the military, and their father had been against it.

I guess there was no one to hold him back any longer.

The realization put a sting in the endless ache that was her heart.

"Welcome home, little sister," he murmured in her ear.

Pulling back, she looked into Tristan's eyes and replied, "I guess the same can be said for you." She looked over his uniform, her fingertips running down the crisp edges, the clothing noticeably brand new. "This is a recent occurrence?"

"Made it official about a week ago." As he spoke, he took a step back, straightening. He walked over to the couch and sat.

Lucy's hands dropped to her sides as she took in the change.

Tristan's entire demeanor felt different. He used to be the first to joke with his brothers, stealing their father's spirits and causing mischief. Now, he was turning down a drink from Hugh and sitting with a posture that would put Madame Paulina, their etiquette tutor, to shame.

Lucy and Wes exchanged a worried glance. While Hugh and Gregory were the eldest, Lucy, Wes, and Tristan were the closest. Tristan had always said he wanted to follow along with his friends and enlist, but this seemed different. He wasn't the happy and cheerful male, ready to follow his friends. This was something else.

"It's great to see everyone here," Wes said, changing the subject. The siblings sat in a semicircle around the fireplace—Tristan on one far end, and Gregory on the other. "I must admit, this..." His voice trailed off as he looked down at his glass. "This has been a harder transition than I ever thought possible."

Hugh and Gregory nodded, swirling the ice in their goblets. Tristan avoided eye contact and focused on the fireplace before them. The silence in the room was almost unbearable.

"We are here for you, brother," Hugh said, putting his broad hand on the edge of Wes's shoulder. "We know the business side of things will be a challenge. Don't give up. Gregory and I had each other while we figured out the business in the Southern Territory. You have..." His voice trailed off. It was clear Wes had no one. "Well, we will send a few of our finest workers to help you set up everything you need."

"Thank you," Wes said with a sad smile. "Mother keeps insisting on helping, but she needs the time to grieve and watch over Henry and Simon. I don't want to put more work on her."

"Perhaps Mother *wants* more work?" Lucy asked.

All of her brothers looked at her as though she was speaking in tongues.

"It is not insane to think that an intelligent female like our mother would like to put her mind to work instead of moping around for days on end," Lucy challenged.

Her brothers continued looking at her, then glanced at each

other. Clearly they disagreed, but Lucy didn't care what they thought.

"It couldn't hurt anyone to let her help is all I'm saying," Lucy said, putting her hands in the air, deciding it wasn't time for this fight.

No. There were enough difficult things on the horizon, and they all needed to stay unified to get through the day ahead.

Lucy checked the time on the clock sitting upon the mantle and her insides twisted with dread.

"Did you speak with Marielle yet?" Lucy asked quietly, changing the topic to what really mattered.

They all nodded.

Marielle was the Venerable Fae in charge of the Farewell Ceremony. She had explained to Lucy that in normal celebrations of life; the Fae honored the dead for days on end—sometimes even weeks. However, with Corvus's untimely death, it was more appropriate for a shorter commemoration of his life, giving them the time to mourn their beloved father.

Mourning was not typical for Fae, but Lucy became more and more familiar with the uncomfortable feeling—however unwanted it was.

Her eyes darted around the room, taking in her brothers as they steeled themselves for what was to come.

A brisk rap on the door frame announced their mother, Anita's, arrival. "Here you all are," Anita said with a weak smile. Lisette, Hugh's very pregnant wife, walked into the room beside her.

Lucy stood to give them both a gentle hug.

Anita forced another smile to grace her lips as she spoke again. "I'm glad you're all together. It's time."

CHAPTER
SEVEN

LUCY

Lucy wasn't sure what she had expected, even after speaking with Marielle, but this surely wasn't it. She stood with her family along the shoreline; the wind whipping her cloak back and forth in the brisk cold. There were spells for keeping warm, but Lucy refused to use them.

Not today.

She would feel every bit of this day. She couldn't risk forgetting a single moment... Not the words that were spoken. Not the chill of the wind. Not the empty emotions that threatened to drown her as she stood before the vast sea.

Side by side, she waited with what was left of her family, dreading the ceremony that she knew would truly be a final goodbye.

The steady beat of her heart quickened and boomed in her ears, drowning out the crash of the waves and the whispers of strangers. Taking a breath in, she felt she couldn't get enough air. Again and again, she gulped down the salty, damp air, but nothing was helping. In the midst of her panic, Lucy wasn't sure where to look.

Straight ahead was the open sea, ready to take her father's physical body and swallow him whole, forcing Lucy to say goodbye forever. To her right, her older brothers stood in a firm, straight line, barely moving, giving their deepest respect to their father. To her left, her younger brothers stood with her mother, all struggling to withhold their sobs.

Each direction offered no comfort.

She risked a quick glance at her mother and regretted it immediately. Anita stood tall, her beautiful brown hair curled the way Corvus had always liked, wearing a deep purple gown to honor the one she had loved more immensely than the open sky above them. Her hazel eyes were the only thing that depicted the true emotions warring inside of her, as tears silently fell in a torrent of sorrow.

Lucy squeezed her eyes shut, tears finding their way from her eyes as well. It was all too much.

She wasn't supposed to be saying goodbye this soon.

She couldn't.

As she braced her body to turn and run, a warm hand landed on her shoulder. With a gasp, she looked up, eyes wide with mourning. Wes must have known she was ready to flee. He gave her arm a gentle squeeze—the act grounding her. "It's time," he whispered to her.

There's no running from this...

Time and time again, Lucy ran from the things that hurt her. When her father told her she couldn't be a bowyer, she hid in the orchard and did target practice until her hands were numb and her heart was full. When her tutors refused to teach her anything worth knowing, she ditched her lessons and taught herself the things she wanted to know. When her parents arranged an entire new life for Lucy, husband included, she fled to the mortal realm in a desperate attempt to change her life.

But this. There was nowhere in all the realms that she could escape to that could change this outcome... Her father was gone, and there was nothing, *nothing*, she could do to change it.

And that hurt the most.

Nodding, she stepped forward with trembling legs as she and her family moved closer to the rocky shore.

Marielle gestured for the ferry master to initiate the ceremony, using her magic to send the elderly Fae the flowers from the hundreds of guests in attendance. Each guest had whispered into the flowers, offering words of love and encouragement to help the deceased brave the next chapter—whatever that may be. It was the very last gift a Fae could offer to their loved ones. Lucy focused on her breathing as the ferry master tucked the flowers safely into the stern of the ornate boat where Corvus lay.

The vessel was beautiful—a long, narrow body with emerald and violet accents bordering the hull. Her father laid in the bed of straw, every piece tightly woven into intricate patterns. Lucy watched as each of her siblings took their next position, walking closer to the shoreline—closer to saying goodbye.

I can't do this. I can't do this.

Her breathing hitched as her eyes darted behind her, searching. King Tralont, Duke Renfro, Laurent, Roger, family, friends, customers, faces of all people surrounding her—there was nowhere to run.

She took a step back and her foot bumped into her bow. Someone had placed it there in preparation for the next part of the ceremony. Lucy knew what was to come, but she wasn't sure what was going to be worse: taking her turn or when everything was over.

"We are gathered here to honor Master Corvus Baum as he makes his way past our realm and into the realms beyond." Marielle spoke to the crowd, amplifying her voice with a magical spell. "We ask all the gods in Porvanai to watch over his passage and send him to an eternal resting place, finding peace, just as the gods do."

Lucy's breath hitched.

"When our beloved Fae cross over from our plane to the next, we must always be there to guide them," Marielle continued, turning to the Baum family. "With our arrows, we will light the way as we show Master Baum our undying love and devotion. As his family floods his spirit with their magic, Corvus will send his magic to them in return. In the highest honor a father can bestow, Corvus will leave his legacy of power within his family, allowing the Baum bloodline to continue to thrive."

The boat drifted farther and farther away from the shore as Hugh and Gregory each took a bow and arrow into their hands and prepared to go first. With unwavering strength, they drew and released their arrows, then placed a hand over their heart in their last goodbye. The arrows arched through the sky, a trail of golden magic gleaming through the air. Landing directly onto Corvus's pyre, the spelled arrow burst into flames.

A lump grew in Lucy's throat.

I can't do this.

Wes took aim next. A graceful, silver stream twinkled in the sky and landed at the edge of the straw, growing the flame.

While Tristan took aim, Lucy began to shake.

How could she be next? She would have to shoot a flaming arrow at her father's pyre, marking this as the last time she would ever see him again. Was she ready for this? Couldn't they wait any longer?

Wes looked to Lucy, motioning for her to go when he saw the blatant fear overtaking her. Hugh and Gregory took notice as well and moved to help Henry and Simon send their arrows as Wes spoke with Lucy.

"It will be alright," he whispered to her, handing Lucy her bow.

"I can't do this," Lucy whispered, shaking her head, looking at the beautiful bow in her hands. Her eyes were wide and unblinking as they glossed over with tears. "I can't. I'm not ready to say goodbye."

An immense wave of anguish consumed Lucy, making her heart an empty vessel. Breathing quickly, her shaking turned into trembling. Her magic hummed beneath the surface, trying to soothe her, but nothing worked.

Wes rolled his lips into a thin line, his eyes searching hers, clearly trying to find the right words to say, but before he could speak, Anita came up behind her.

"It's okay, Wesley," she whispered, putting her hand on her son's cheek. She turned to Lucy. "Come, Lucella. You must go before me so I can initiate the spell."

"I—I can't," Lucy gasped, desperately trying to hold back the flood of tears. Her hand held the bow so tightly her knuckles turned stark white.

Anita just smiled at her. "My sweet girl, we both know you can. And you must. Your father deserves his final resting place with his ancestors above in the stars, and this is how he ascends. This is how Fae magic continues." She took Lucy's quaking hand and stilled it in hers, nodding at her in encouragement. "You are the strongest of us all... Your father would be so very proud of you."

Lucy squeezed her eyes tight and turned to the shoreline. Soon, the pyre would be too far away and the magic would not be returned to the bloodline. She had to make this shot so that her mother stood a chance to get her arrow to reach the far distance.

Taking a deep breath in, she closed her eyes. *I love you, Father.* She opened her eyes and took aim. *I am so sorry I couldn't stop him.*

As she released the arrow, she allowed herself to feel what she had been pushing away for so long: the fear of a life without her father, and the guilt that consumed her more and more each day.

Lucy watched as the shimmering green arrow arched high into the sky and landed gracefully on the pyre, the fire growing so large she could no longer see beneath the flames. She shuddered at the finality of the action. This was it.

This was goodbye.

Lucy turned to speak to Anita, but her mother was already in position, sending her arrow careening through the sky. Her graceful magic landed with a powerful thud.

Almost as soon as it connected, the fire on the boat grew to astonishing heights, roaring with the magic imbued within each arrow. Sparks of yellow, silver, purple, and green shot wildly from the burning straw. Then suddenly, the blaze calmed, as though the wildness of the flames left it completely. But the fire was still burning, however small it was, and it seemed to change as the water churned all around. The pyre continued to float farther and farther away from them, but from the far off distance, they could see a violet wave of power exude from the flames.

As if Corvus was sending his own arrows from the other side, a bright arch of violet light came speeding toward her family from the middle of the sea. First hitting Hugh, then Gregory, following each of her brothers in line in the same order they had sent their arrows. Wes. Tristan. Henry. Simon.

Lucy held her breath as she watched her brothers accept their father's magic, each inhaling deeply as the magic landed within their chest.

Henry and Simon cried as Anita held them tightly beside her, smiling softly at the magic finding its new home within Corvus's children.

Lucy watched, waiting for her turn, terrified of what would happen. Would it hurt? Would she get any at all? Was she deserving of his magic? It was her fault he was gone. All of this was because of her.

A shuddering sob wracked through her body, but she pushed it back, refusing to fall apart before the crowd. She took a breath, trying to calm herself.

Then she saw it.

A purple so deep it looked black came floating on the wind to Lucy. It was nothing like the soaring violet light given to her brothers. This was smoke and shadow, mixing and dancing in the wind.

Shadow.

Lucy's eyes went wide as she realized. She risked a glance at Wes, who was standing with his mouth open wide in astonishment, along with the rest of her brothers. Short gasps came from the onlookers in the surrounding crowd.

Anita only laughed. A joyous, relieved smile filled her as glistening tears reflected off her cheeks in the fading sun in the distance.

Her father had gifted Lucy his most treasured magic—the gift of his shadows.

Lucy took a step forward to meet the dark purple shadows, her toes soaking in the Lancast Sea.

I'm here, Father.

Spreading her arms wide, the magic swirled around her gently before entering through her heart, where each Fae held their magic.

As it flooded inside of her, she thought it would feel heavy, like the added magic wouldn't fit, but it was the complete opposite. She felt lighter than she had in years, feeling the joyous reunion of magic from her family line returning to Baum blood.

It was the most whole she had ever felt.

Anita kept her eyes on Lucy, pride still shining through her tear-stained cheeks.

Lucy's heart fluttered in fear and she tore her gaze away from her mother, back to her father's pyre. What would Anita receive from Corvus now? And was there enough time? She watched as the boat swayed back and forth, getting farther away. Would his magic reach her?

Lucy turned back to her mother, worried, but Anita was only smiling quietly to herself. There was no fear in her eyes.

An eerie hush came over the crowd. Squinting in the distance, Lucy thought she could see something making its way to them. Far off, a pale purple orb of light flapped in the air, bouncing up and down as though affected by the wind.

It was nothing like the magic given to her brothers and nothing like the smoky shadows given to Lucy. No, it was small and slow and graceful in a different sort of way.

Anita grinned from ear to ear, raising her hands to meet the beautiful light. "I'm here, darling!" Anita called out to the magic as though she had expected nothing else.

As it drew closer, Lucy could see exactly what it was. A small

EIGHT

WES

"Thank you for coming," Wes told King Tralont.

Wes had bid his farewells to his brothers and a few guests then promptly escaped to the study. He was hoping to find a moment to breathe, however, something always seemed to come up. Though, a knock on his door from the king was the very last thing he expected.

King Tralont came to offer words of sympathy and to check in on the status of the Baum Bowyer business. Wes appreciated it, but wasn't sure how to respond to the actual fucking king.

"Thank you for your kind words," he said, doing his best not to waver.

"I mean it, young Baum," King Tralont said for the second time. "Your father changed the face of our Denoran armies with his updated weaponry. Now, we are willing to give you time, but we want to ensure the quality of the bows remains constant."

Wes had already tried explaining that Hugh and Gregory had offered to send support from the South to support him in this new position, but it looked as though the king had a point he needed to get across. Wes didn't want to appear ungrateful for whatever the king offered, so he smiled and nodded enthusiastically in return.

"Duke Renfro is not far from the estate," Tralont continued. "He will come to assist you as needed. Consider him my liaison as you adjust to your new role here."

New role.

As if he had asked for it.

As if he had just gotten a cheerful promotion.

No. His father had died and now he was left to fill the shoes of a male who was greater than life itself.

Wes kept the shudder deep within him, refusing to appear weak in front of the Fae king. He nodded in a deep bow to show his gratitude and prayed he would stop talking.

He was tired—body and soul *tired*.

The Farewell Ceremony was more overwhelming than he expected, and it was draining keeping his emotions buried so deep inside of him.

He was now the face of the company business, and with Jasper betraying them all and Lucy's bowyer knowledge traveling back to the North in the morning, he was left with no one.

"I will send him within the next fortnight or so. Please, take the time to grieve and let Renfro know of anything you may need."

"Thank you, your majesty," Wes replied, his hand over his heart to show his allegiance.

When King Tralont finally left, Wes sunk into a leather chair and covered his face with his hands.

What the fuck am I going to do?

A knock on the door should have been enough to pull himself back together, but he stayed slouched in the chair, willing whoever it was to go away.

"Wes?" Lucy called from behind the closed door.

Unfortunately, younger sisters never care about things like patience or manners, so Lucy simply opened the door and strode right in.

"Are you alright?" Lucy asked, sliding into the chair across from him.

"Is there a line out there or something? I swear, one Fae exits, another enters." Wes said behind closed eyes.

"Have you seen Lisette?" she asked, changing the subject.

"Hugh and Lisette left with Gregory a little while ago."

"I can't believe we are going to have another baby in the family," Lucy smiled. "Did you see Lisette's adorable baby bump?"

"Yes, she mentioned she's traveling to the east to see her mother in the country before the baby comes. Hugh and Gregory are dropping her off there before they make their way back to the South." He released a deep sigh, already missing his brothers. "I can't imagine Hugh as a father." Wes smiled at the idea.

"Funny, they go south, and I go north..." Lucy's voice trailed off. "I'm leaving in the morning."

"I know." It was on his mind the entire day. He and Lucy had been through so much together, and when their father died, she just disappeared. Left to the North without so much as an "I'll miss you."

He understood why she did it, but it didn't make it any easier. He thought he had at least another twenty years of learning on the job before he'd be the one to take over. It was his own fault—he shouldn't have spent so much time fucking around. Now, there was no time to fix any of it.

"Is Tristan going to be okay?" Her voice was a whisper, almost like she was afraid to say it.

"He's finding himself," Wes sighed. "Not unlike yourself."

"I beg your pardon?" Lucy asked, hurt tinging the words.

"Is there a reason you are heading off to the North so soon? We could use you here at home." Someone could talk to their mother. She could help with the guests who hadn't yet left.

"This isn't my home anymore." Lucy stood up swiftly, walking over to a cabinet that held tools and polishes for bows.

The words hit like a sword to the chest.

Isn't it? Wouldn't this always be her home?

All he could do was nod. He had no more fight left in him, and from the way she lingered on the shoreline for hours after the sun had set, he wasn't sure she did either.

"Can I take a few supplies home to make a bow?" Lucy asked suddenly.

"Of course," Wes replied, smiling gently. "Everything here is yours as much as it is mine. Please, take whatever you'd like."

"I'll have Roger pick it up in the morning before we depart," Lucy said, then she walked over to her brother.

He pulled himself to stand before her, sensing her farewell. "Try out any of Father's magic yet?" Wes asked, trying to lighten the mood.

Lucy's lips quirked up into a sad smile, and Wes knew exactly how she felt. She nodded and threw her hands into the air, causing all the lights to flicker. With her hands still raised in the air, she curled them into fists, pulling the shadows from the corners of the rooms to where they stood in the center.

The effect was immediate and terrifying—the same as their father.

The shadows crept closer and closer, as though they had a nefarious mind of their own, their eerie wisps curling and clawing toward them.

Before the darkness touched them, she uncurled her fingers and pushed the shadows back to their rightful places, allowing the light to shine brightly once again.

"That will be a fun party trick," Wes teased, taking a deep breath.

Lucy took his hands in hers and squeezed them gently. "You will make Father proud and run this business better than anyone else in all the realms."

Wes's gaze pierced hers as he looked into her hazel eyes and replied, "And you will make Father proud as you find his murderer and make him pay."

The fire in her eyes was the only acknowledgment he needed.

He knew Lucy wasn't in the North just to play house—she was stronger than that.

He hoped.

~

THE NEXT MORNING, Wes thanked the stars for the spells to remove the lingering headache he acquired from the heavy pour of his father's amartium. He and Tristan shared the remainder of the bottle before his brother left to return to his unit. They granted him a soldier's leave to grieve, but dumped Tristan right back into the thick of his training as soon as the Farewell Ceremony was complete.

It tore at Wes, knowing Tristan was off serving Denora in the most dangerous way possible. Tristan kept telling him over and over that this was what he wanted, that this was the way to be part of the solution to Denora's problems, but Wes didn't understand any of it.

He was only thankful that their father's magic manifested in Tristan with improved strength and agility. Watching Tristan discover it as he nearly dropped a full bottle of spirits was quite amusing. It was as though Corvus knew from beyond this plane of life that Tristan would need the upper hand.

Denora had problems, sure; every place had them. But what were these problems that Tristan thought he could solve?

Wes would rather focus on the problems there in front of him. First and foremost, the silent warning given by the king himself. He was smart enough to know that the offer of Duke Renfro's services was more of a threat than a gift. It was clear: if Wes messed anything up, the king would replace him in a heartbeat.

I can't let my father down, Wes repeated to himself.

It was the only thing keeping him going. There was nothing else to say. Figuring it out was the only thing he could do to honor his father.

Walking into the study, Wes stared at the place that once seemed so familiar. Everything felt foreign now. It was one thing for the office to be his father's, but now it was his.

His desk.

His chair.

His business.

He took a deep breath to ease his flipping stomach. Sitting down at the desk, he looked around the room. He had never seen it from this angle.

"Well, here goes nothing," he said to himself. Opening the first ledger, he tried to read the contents but felt as though he was reading an unfamiliar language. It reminded him of Micah and Brax trying to read Micah's ancient tome.

He thought of them often, if he was being honest. Wes worried Lucy was making a terrible mistake in picking Sloan over Lumen, but there was nothing he could do about it. He had contemplated talking to Brax about it, but as much as the thought of her exhilarated him, she scared him a little, too.

Wes sighed and leaned back in his chair. Feeling defeated, he lifted his hands and called on his magic, forming a small ball of light.

"You give Lucella your shadows, Tristan your strength, and comfort Mother with the beauty of a butterfly, and what do you give me?" Wes said to himself sullenly. "Light." He made a fist and doused the light, frustration filling his entire being. "Sure would have been helpful, except I already learned how to summon light when I was a child."

He slammed the ledger shut and stalked across the room, only to get there, turn around, and return to the desk. There was nowhere for him to go and nobody to whom he could turn.

"If Lucy was here, she would at least insult me while telling me the most obvious thing to do, so why can't I figure it out on my own?"

An abrupt knock pulled him from his spiral. He ran his hands through his hair, ensuring he looked presentable, and then spoke, trying to capture the same commanding tone his father used to have. "You may enter."

The visitors the previous day had been full of surprises, so he didn't even bother to guess who it could be. Though, when his mother popped her head through the door, he was glad he could at least release the facade of power he was trying to emit.

"Hello, dear," Anita spoke, smiling gently. She had changed so much within the last day. Before the Farewell Ceremony, she was like a walking shell of herself. Now, there was more light in her eyes, more color in her cheeks. "I've come to see if I could help at all?"

Wonderful, Wes thought to himself. *I'm so blatantly pathetic that my mother has come to try to pick up the pieces I can't seem to manage.*

"No need, Mother," Wes said with a forced grin, walking over to her. He kissed her on the cheek as he said, "I have everything under control. I don't see how you could help much, anyway. It's all just the business side of things."

Anita kept her face stoic and blinked, as if carefully choosing the next words to say. "Wesley, I have helped your father with much of the business for many years. I'd be happy to help you now."

He almost scoffed. At no time would Corvus Baum ever let a female in a male's business industry. He made that perfectly clear when Lucy asked to be part of the Baum Bowyers. There was no way his mother knew anything more than he did. Besides, he was at his father's beck and call for years before this, and his mother was never included in any business conversations.

"I appreciate the offer, Mother," Wes said to appease her. "Right now I must get back to work. You don't need to worry."

The smile on Anita's face faltered for a moment, but she just nodded and looked down. "Well, I am here if you need anything at all." Her eyes barely met Wes's as she turned to exit.

When the door clicked shut behind her, Wes threw a privacy charm around the office. Screaming in frustration, he let go of his last bit of restraint. He kicked the high wingback chair to the ground and threw a large jar of wood stain across the room, watching as it crashed through the window behind the desk. He shoved the desk with all of his strength and wished that something, anything could take away this empty hole within him that seemed to only have space for anger.

He walked past the desk and his pant leg got snagged on a half-open drawer. Grunting, he ripped his pants away, leaving a hole in the cloth. Reaching for the drawer, prepared to shove it shut, he wavered.

There in the center of the drawer was a bejeweled amulet, forcibly reminding him what was at stake. The amulet was the key to the beautiful, fertile land of The Elderwood that remained the backbone of the family business.

He dropped to his knees before the desk and reverently pulled the drawer open a little wider. It felt as though he was breaking a rule, going through his father's things like this... but they weren't his father's things anymore. These all belonged to Wes now.

With a shaking hand, he picked up the necklace, inspecting it closely. He recalled the first time he saw this amulet.

"This is the key to our family's legacy, Wesley," Corvus had told him when Wes was young. "With this, we are given the special opportunity to bring the most remarkable weapons to Denora to keep our people safe." His eyes had twinkled as he said it. "We have an important job that we must never take for granted."

Wes squeezed the chain in his hands and carefully placed it back inside the drawer. He closed it, pulling the desk back into position, and then righted the chair. Taking a moment to breathe, he sat, removed the privacy charm, and got back to work. His father was right. Their job was important to all of Denora, and he would do it right.

A whistle of a bird called from the broken window, making his shoulders drop yet again.

"Day one, and what do you do? Have a temper tantrum and break a fucking window," he chided himself.

The bird's whistle called again. This time it was a familiar tune from his childhood. Curious, Wes looked up at the bird, which seemed to stare at him with knowing eyes. It was a beautiful, black raven, just sitting at the window, watching him.

He had no idea what to make of it, but couldn't linger on it for long. Wes opened the ledger once more and forced himself to keep going.

He had to keep going.

NINE

MICAH

"I pull the magic to me. I form my intent," Micah murmured to himself. "I feel the magic, and I take control."

It didn't matter. No matter how many times he whispered the steps to himself, the magic didn't make an appearance—not without Jasper's rings. Micah grunted in frustration, kicking the dirt on the ground, sending dust into the wind.

He was desperate to make this magic work. He kept replaying the events from when the shadow cat last appeared and how the beast nearly ripped his leg off. If it had returned, he needed a way to protect himself and The Elderwood from any more attacks.

The large metal wall that once surrounded the portal was gone. It did a remarkable job keeping the shadow creatures inside, both feline and insects. However, as time passed, the magic failed and the metal weakened, turning back into stone somehow. There hadn't been any disruptions since, so Micah assumed they were long gone. But what if they weren't? What if the beasts were ready for round two?

Brax used the river stones as a foot rest as she relaxed in the grass.

"Are you going to help me or just sit there?" Micah scowled. "If Scar returns and I can't use my magic to fight him, we're screwed."

"There's no way that shadow beast has returned," Brax said steadily from her spot where she lay in the sun. "Besides, it's been days and even you've said you haven't seen anything since."

Micah couldn't decide if Brax really believed what she said or if she just wanted Micah to believe it. Regardless, he knew what he saw, which was why he wouldn't back down.

"We need to keep working on my magic," he reminded Brax. "That's why we're out here. Not for you to sun yourself like some lizard." He stood near the edge of the shadowy tree line, keeping himself out of the midday sun as he continued his latest attempt to call for his magic.

"I'm going to pretend as though you have not spoken so that I do not have to insult you once more," she said as she waved her hand in dismissal. "Go ahead and practice. You and I both know that you aren't activating your true self, otherwise this magic would be working by now."

My true self?

Micah had had enough of her shitty attitude and the unfounded accusations that he wasn't trying hard enough. Every single day he was here on this property he was trying. He was trying to fit into this new life that was thrust upon him. It didn't even matter that he supposedly had magic. It was like giving a bear an axe and telling it to whittle a plane to fly—just because he had a tool didn't mean he knew how to wield it.

"It's such bullshit that you keep saying that," Micah said with barely confined anger.

Brax sat up with a jolt, looking him square in the eye, her kohl-lined gaze piercing straight through him. "Then tell me."

"Tell you what?" Micah snapped.

"Tell me you miss her."

Micah stilled, but the challenge in her eye was unmistakable. He knew her well enough to know she wouldn't back down, and maybe he owed it to her to be honest.

Brax had been Micah's loyal friend for the past six months. In the beginning, when Lucy had first left, there were days when he wouldn't speak at all. He couldn't. But Brax never forced anything from Micah. She let him grieve; just continued living for him, alongside him. She'd make sure he ate and dragged him outside to go for a run or to chop wood.

Every night she pulled him to the fire pit, making him sit there and listen to her, even when he had nothing to say. Some nights they sat and looked at the stars, some nights she'd tell stories of home or sing songs Micah didn't understand. But every night, a part of his heart healed, knowing that even though he felt alone, he wasn't—not really. Brax never left him. She didn't give up.

On one chilly night after a huge rainstorm, they sat around the fire and Brax told such a raunchy story about her having sex with a Kerroz ox-shifter that Micah had laughed so hard beer shot out of his nose. Since then, they were true friends, working together and getting through life, day by day.

The least he could do was be honest with the one person who didn't let him down.

"You know I do, Brax," he said with a sigh. "I miss her more than words can describe, but her being gone isn't why I'm not able to do my magic."

"You're entirely correct."

"What?" Micah was clearly lost now. "Weren't you just telling me the other day that my magic wouldn't work because I wasn't fighting for her? Wasn't there some nonsense about activating my true self?" Micah asked, exasperated with the increasingly annoying bullshit that spewed from Brax's lips.

"I recall saying you weren't fighting for anything, you pungent turnip. You are the one entirely hung up on your life connected to Lucy Baum's, and when you realize that one has nothing to do with the other, we may finally make some progress." Brax finally stood up and dusted the dirt from her black leggings.

"Oh, so now you want to help me practice?" Micah shook his head in disbelief. He rolled his eyes and walked over to her. "Fine. Let's go."

"Time to listen." She grabbed his hand and twisted so Micah flipped over onto his back. He grunted his annoyance as he tried to catch his breath. "Look at me, don't move, and listen carefully, because I've been very patient these last few months and I'd really rather speed up this process. Got it?"

Micah's lips were a sneer, but he nodded regardless. His shoulder was screaming in pain and he wanted this over as much as she did.

"Good. One: You aren't working to your true potential because you keep closing yourself and your emotions off to the world. You must accept all of who and what you are if you expect the magic to work. Two: I say you aren't fighting for anything because you aren't. You have this vague notion in your mind that you want the bad guy squashed, but there is nothing on the line for you. You don't care what happens at the end, because you aren't thinking about the end. You aren't thinking about what you're working toward now that you don't have Lucy to fight for. But you need to come up with something you care deeply about before it gets you killed."

A stinging pain rushed down his arm as she punctuated each sentence with added force to her grip.

"Three:—" Brax's angered voice suddenly calmed, pausing for a moment as her face softened as she took in Micah. "I am sincerely sorry about what happened between you and Lucy. Lost love is the most painful of all, but you can't let it break you. You cannot let a broken heart define you."

With a gentle nod, she eased off of Micah and helped him to stand.

They stared at each other for a moment before she said, "I'll give you a minute and I'll get us some water. Then we can begin again."

Micah could only watch her walk away as he took in everything she had said to him. He wanted to be mad; he wanted to scream that she was wrong and she had no idea how any of this felt, but that would be a lie all on its own.

The problem was, she was right—about all of it. He was absolutely closing himself off. It was what he did when things got too hard. And maybe he wasn't fighting for anything, because what the fuck was there to fight for? An empty cabin in a deserted forest?

He was no longer fighting for a future with Lucy. She left him... broke him. She built him up, healed his heart piece by piece, and then shattered it with a single stroke. She was gone, and he was an empty shell of who he once was—or maybe exactly who he had been before he met Lucy.

His eyes flickered to the tree that had started it all. The Elderwood portal was kept safely within an unsuspecting tree that looked similar to all the others; everything except for the engraving high on the trunk, about ten feet from the ground.

Careful not to step on the falling stones from the once solid metal wall, he took a step closer to look at the large engraving on the tree once more. The forest floor crunched under his boots.

They once thought it was the sigil for the Baum Bowyers, but his ancestral book had taught them it was so much more than that. The grand tree with a bow for roots and an arrow encompassing it was the symbol for the Lumen lineage. It started it all: the passageway to The Elderwood, the wood that made insurmountable weapons, a generational family business, and the source of all of his fucking problems.

It's because of this tree that I lost my family.

Grabbing the rings from his pocket, he put all four on and summoned as much power as he could, his rage guiding his intent. He wasn't sure what he was planning on doing, his emotions taking over all common sense.

He took a few steps back, feeling the magic inside of him grow. Squeezing his eyes shut tight, he felt the power surge through him. This was the power he wanted to manifest—this was the kind of magic that could make an actual difference. As he opened his eyes, two enormous spheres of red rested in his hands, his magic pooling in anticipation.

A large crack of wood sounded from the edge of the trees. Micah's eyes snapped to the sound, and there, at last, was the shadow beast, lurking in between the trees once again.

Scar.

Without a second thought, Micah hurled the magical spheres at the beast, but it dove out of the way and onto the open grass.

The back door of the cabin slammed just as his eyes met the beast's once again.

Prowling slowly on the grass, the shadow cat's two front legs reached out in front of him in a long stretch as its body transformed from solid to a shadowy mist. The last time it had done this, it seeped its way back into the portal of The Elderwood. This time though, it did something else entirely; something Micah could hardly comprehend.

Floating above the ground, the mist changed shape. First, there were two long forms...legs? The mist floated up, creating a torso, then long muscular arms. On top of that, a head. This was not the same shape as the shadow beast. The shadow dissipated completely and revealed the form of a man. Micah would have thought he was dreaming if he hadn't heard the clear thump of his foot meeting the ground.

A man with dark brown skin, golden eyes, and a scar across his face took a step closer to Micah. With a voice as deep as the ocean, the stranger spoke.

"I wish you'd stop doing that."

Micah felt his entire world spin. Was he seeing things correctly?

Brax came running over with her Vytyrian spear ready to attack, but mid-jump, the strange man waved his hand and Brax fell to the ground with a thud, her spear flinging in the other direction.

"Who are you?" Micah roared, taking a step back and trying to understand what the fuck had just happened. "What do you want?"

"Let's see," his deep voice rumbled like a purr. "You liked to call me Scar." He flourished his hand by the scar across his eye. "Clever," he retorted, though he did not seem amused.

"You were the cat?" Micah asked in disbelief.

"Cat." The man scoffed. "I am a feline shifter, yes. A *cat*? No. I am more akin to your... panthers, I believe you call them?"

Brax struggled on the ground, an unseen force still holding her down. She grunted as she yelled. "Run, Micah!"

"Why are you here? Let her go!" Micah would not hide from this stranger and leave Brax here, unable to defend herself. It wasn't in him to abandon someone.

"I'll let her go once you listen," he said, his golden eyes shifting to watch Brax with a predatory gaze. "I do not trust her to stay still long enough to hear me, so I apologize that I must restrain her." His eyes looked purely feline, but the rest of his body was the equivalent of a warrior. He was practically seven feet tall and the width of a tree trunk—solid muscle. He wore a dark brown cloth draped over one shoulder and around his torso, coming mid-thigh.

"Then get on with it, you fucking overgrown parsnip," Brax spat.

Micah flashed a look of warning to Brax to get her to chill out, but she didn't care. Apparently Brax was afraid of exactly zero things.

"My name is Quillan. I am a sentry of what you call The Elder-wood. I was summoned here by the dark magic that some evil Fae embedded inside the portal. It began to twist the insides of my realm, and I was sent here to fix the problem. I would like to first apologize for trying to kill you," he said, turning toward Micah. "Though by the sizable scar you've left upon me, I'd like to think we are now even." His beast-like eyes gazed upon Micah as though in contemplation.

Micah wasn't ready to speak, unsure what the cat-guy was getting at. He nodded, and the stranger continued.

"When you removed the tainted magic from the portal, our realm showed us that you were not the Fae at fault. Immediately it called to you as its guardian, and therefore, we standby to protect you in all battles." He gave a slight bow, keeping his eyes on Micah and Brax, clearly untrusting the duo. "There is much happening on the other side of the portal… Things you must hear for yourself."

"Why should we trust you?" Micah asked.

This all appeared too strange to be true, but then again, where did he even draw the line anymore?

"Because I could have let that Fae kill you that day, but I did not. I could have finished you myself, for that matter, and I chose not to." His golden eyes seared into Micah's. "You are The Guardian, and therefore, it is *imperative* you believe."

Micah wanted to argue, but the demanding look in Quillan's eyes told him it wasn't the best idea.

"Fine." Micah took a step forward, ready to make a deal with the strange shifter. If Quillan could bring him and Brax into The Elderwood to discuss these problems, maybe he'd get more answers. But before he could say another word, Quillan smiled, and turned into shadowy mist.

What the hell? That's it?

Micah took a step back as he watched the mist settle before him, wondering why Quillan had shifted back to leave so quickly.

Then, before Micah knew it, the magical mist dropped low and twined itself around his feet. With a swift jerk, it pulled tight as a rope, causing him to crash to the ground.

"Micah!" Brax screamed from far away.

"What's happening?!" Micah rolled to his side, trying to evade it, but the magic was far too powerful. Suddenly, he felt himself sliding along the grass. The beast was pulling him toward the portal. He dug his hands into the ground, trying to slow his trajectory. "Stop!"

The shadowy mist continued to drag him, never pausing for a moment. Micah continued to yell, thrashing his body in a desperate attempt to escape.

"Let me go!" Micah yelled, shoving his hands toward the shadows, calling upon his magic to blast it away. Nothing happened. Even the rings on his fingers had no reaction.

My magic is useless, he seethed.

As they got to the base of The Elderwood tree, the black mist lifted Micah into the air by his feet. Micah swung his body this way and that, but there was no use. He was up and over the last remnants of the stone wall and heading straight to the portal as the sigil began to glow.

"Micah!" Brax screamed, rushing toward him, the magic holding her down finally gone.

He reached his hand out to her, desperately hoping that she would get there in time. "Brax!" He screamed as he stretched his arm out as far as it could go, but it was too late. Micah was pulled into the portal, alone with the stranger who claimed to be friend, not foe.

Though Micah wasn't so sure anymore.

His mind reeled as he tried to get a handle on what was happening, but there was nothing he could fathom. Instead, his attention shifted to the portal he was passing through.

The last time he entered The Elderwood, he had felt a strange sensation of heaviness. This time, everything was different. Warmth penetrated his body, as though lightning was coursing through him. Bright colors of reds, blues, and yellows floated past him and an almost musical sound welcomed him as he stretched his arm through to the other side of the portal.

Somehow now upright, Micah stood on a bed of soft grass. Getting his bearings, he closed his eyes and shook his head. Forcing the dizziness away and tensing his body, Micah prepared to confront the man who basically kidnapped him. However, when he looked around at the beauty of the jaw-dropping Elderwood forest, he froze.

For a moment, he thought he was in a completely different place —it was not the quiet, uninhabited realm Lucy once brought him to. While Quillan stood beside him, they were not alone. Behind Quillan were at least a dozen other men and women wearing the same brown cloth draped over their bodies. They all had the same dark skin and golden eyes, eyes that stayed glued on Micah—each of them holding a large golden spear.

Micah carefully put his hands up as a gesture of nonviolence and took a deep breath of air, trying to calm his pounding heart.

"My people," Quillan announced. "I introduce you to The Guardian."

As though a wave crested over the crowd of people, each one crossed a fist over the chest, bowed their heads, and bent down on one knee.

Micah stood in shock. Looking at Quillan for an explanation, but all the stranger did was offer a wicked smile and said, "Guardian, welcome to your people."

CHAPTER

TEN

LUCY

Pull. Slide. Sand.
  Pull. Slide. Sand.

The repetitive motions lulled Lucy into a settled calm as she carefully created an exquisite bow. It didn't even matter to her that she wasn't at the Baum estate, but instead in the Northern Territories once again. The drawn out motions pushed away thoughts of her father, her family, Micah, Jasper, even Laurent. There was nothing but her and the wood in her hands, creating something one of a kind.

She took a deep breath and wiped the sweat from her brow with the back of her forearm. Even with the cooler temperatures of the North, the fire in the hearth and the labor of creating the bow warmed her.

Lucy's hands were covered in sawdust, and her bedchambers would need a thorough cleaning, but she was finally done. Another remarkable weapon, made by the amazing wood from The Elderwood, creating a bow that could out-shoot any others.

This will surely—

Her thoughts faded, and her smile faltered. For a single moment, she imagined showing this beautiful weapon to her father,

534

demanding for the eight-millionth time that she should be in charge of weapon design for the Baum Bowyers.

Then she remembered.

Her father had died.

It happened like that a lot the past few weeks. She knew for certain that her father was gone, passed on to another plane of existence, but it never stopped her from imagining, for just a moment, that he was still alive.

Holding the bow in her hands, the smooth wood grain flexed gently in her fingers. What to do with it now? She had her own bow —Laurent made sure of that when they first came to the North.

Is there anyone else in need of such a weapon?

Micah's beautiful face flashed in her mind. Her heart ached at the thought of him. She hoped he was doing well. Without the looming threat of Jasper, Micah was safe in Joterra. There would be no lurking Fae looking to steal his ancestral magic, and there would be no chance he could get involved in any other Fae incidents. There was no way for him to get hurt.

Even if she could change the course of her arrangement with Laurent, would Micah ever be safe with her? Lucy felt like a magnet to trouble, and she couldn't continue letting others get hurt on her account.

Instead, she would be right here in the North, keeping those she loved far away from her... Far away, safe and sound.

Her sacrifice of a life without Micah gave him a true chance to live. That's all that mattered anymore... She would find her own way to contentment. Lucy wasn't sure if happiness was still a possibility for her, but if the ones around her were taken care of, then that was all she could ask for.

Emerald green magic came crashing out of her hands and swirling all around her. A tug of the magic pulled at her, almost as if in question. *Who will take care of you?*

"I'm fine," she whispered to the empty room, wondering if her magic really could understand her. She stood and walked over to the window, noting the angle of the sun. The day had passed by without her noticing.

Standing and stretching, she looked around her room—a quiet space just for her. She may not have everything she had ever wanted in life, but what she had could be enough. Calling upon her magic, the green mist swirled around the room, removing any trace of sawdust or wood scraps.

It was funny to Lucy that she had once despised all acts of magic. When she was younger, she went out of her way to avoid it at all costs. Now it came to her as easily as breathing, as though it was an ingrained part of her—body, mind, and soul.

Soul.

The word strangled her heart. Was there such a thing? Did part of her father's soul come into her, gifting her new powers that allowed her to channel part of him?

She let her eyes drift close as she felt for that space within her. Shadow magic coursed over her to the dark corners of her room. Opening her eyes, she saw the room darken as the candlelight flickered out. Creeping tendrils of shadow curled toward her on the walls.

Why shadows for me, Father?

She released the magic and watched as the room lightened dramatically, returning to its otherwise normal state. A room that was given to her by someone who cared for her deeply.

Dressing for dinner, she realized exactly what she would do with her bow. She could no longer give it to her father, but there was someone near her who could appreciate its beauty. With a new determination, she picked up her tools and added a few final touches.

Looking down at the beautiful weapon in her hands, she was filled with a shade of gratitude. She wasn't sure if true happiness would ever find her again, but this hint of positivity felt close enough.

DINNER SEEMED a little more quiet than usual. Lucy wasn't sure if it was because of the time spent away during the Farewell Ceremony and that Laurent had work he needed to catch up on, or if it was something else entirely, but the silence pulled at the tension in the room.

"How are you feeling?" Laurent asked, a crease of worry on his brow.

"I am well, thank you," Lucy said politely.

"I sent someone to ask you for tea this afternoon, but I was told you did not answer... Are you upset with me?" His blue eyes met hers across the dinner table.

"Oh my," Lucy whispered in realization. She had a privacy charm on her room to block out sounds from the village below and the noise in the hall as she worked on her bow. "I apologize. I did not hear anyone at my door."

"I see..." Laurent looked down at his plate.

"Laurent, truly," Lucy said. She stood up and walked the length of the small dining room to sit next to him. "I was feeling a bit lost, and I put my mind to a task that would soothe me. I was..." Her voice trailed off seeing the hurt in Laurent's posture.

Now is as good a time as any.

She sat and placed her hand on his. "Let me show you." Lucy smiled at Laurent, then nodded to Roger standing behind them.

Roger walked to the table with a bundle wrapped in black velvet. He handed it to Lucy, who then presented it to Laurent.

"This is for you," she said with a shy smile.

Laurent's eyes perked up, perplexed by the gift.

He carefully unwrapped the bundle on the edge of the table, his hands slowing as he got to the beautiful creation inside. His eyes glanced to the bow and then to Lucy, the slightest bit of color coming to his cheeks.

"I wanted to offer a token of gratitude," she said sincerely. "You have been nothing but supportive of me for these past few weeks, and I am sorry I have been so unsure before. You have held your end of the deal and have found Jasper DeValey. I'm ready now."

Laurent's eyes darted to hers at the proclamation.

"Ready?" Laurent asked, uncertainty quivering in his voice.

Lucy only nodded.

"You'll have to excuse me, but I would love for you to clarify exactly what you are ready for, as my heart may not be able to contain the sorrow if I assume incorrectly." He breathed out a huff of breath, trying to hide his vulnerable state.

"I am prepared to move forward with the wedding," Lucy said, thinking of the words she had practiced in her head on her walk to dinner.

There was no other answer to her future. Keeping Micah safe meant staying away. Wes had the family business under control. She would see this through—an arrangement that would benefit her in more ways than one.

Lucy could find her place here.

With him.

Laurent smiled from ear to ear, then reached over and took her hand in his and brought it to his lips, kissing her fingers gently.

Lucy wanted her heart to soar at the gesture, but she found herself empty of the passion that would periodically run through her. It took every bit of energy within her to remain smiling, not to run screaming for Micah in the other direction. She knew it was unfair, saying she was all in with Laurent while still pining for someone else, but there was no other way forward. Leaving Micah behind was the best thing she could do for him, so she would do it.

"The bow has snowflakes," Lucy said, nervously changing the subject. "I thought it would be fitting for your position here in the North."

"*Our* position," Laurent corrected her, with a tilt of his head. "It is our position now."

"What? No. You are the Lord of the North and I will just be your wife."

"If you think you are *just* anything, then you are wrong."

Lucy could only look at him in bewilderment.

He isn't saying what I think he's saying... is he?

"Lucy, what have I told you over and over since we've met?" His eyes were wild with excitement, and he took both of her hands in his and gripped them tightly. "I am looking for a true partner. You will not be a figurehead for outdated Denoran tradition, Lucy. You will be my queen. Always."

Lucy's heart *did* leap this time. Whenever she considered they would pair in an adequate union, Laurent took it another step further to prove how clearly he saw Lucy. All she could do was stare at him incredulously.

He shook his head and gave a slight chortle. "It's time," he announced to Roger, leaning forward in his chair.

Lucy looked at the surprise on Roger's face and then back to Laurent. "Time for what?"

"It's time I show you everything."

Laurent guided Lucy, hand in hand, from the dining room to his study. Roger, keeping step on the other side of Laurent, muttered urgently in his ear.

"Are you sure about this, my lord?"

"Absolutely," Laurent replied confidently.

Lucy was still uncertain about what was happening. She didn't expect a gift of a bow and an agreement to move forward with their wedding to be the cause for such activity. With Laurent clutching her hand tightly, she did her best to keep up.

Roger moved ahead to open the doors for the pair, his face stoic and emotionless.

Laurent brought Lucy to the center of the room and let go of her hand. Facing her, he put his hands on her shoulders, and when he looked deeply into her eyes, she was surprised to see him utterly beaming. "I know we have talked much about my plans for our territory," he said to her. "There is so much more I want to share with you... But first, I must know."

"What?" Lucy asked, a nervous quiet to her voice.

"What does your perfect Denora look like?"

Lucy blinked. That was definitely not the question she had been expecting.

Laurent stood before her, watching her intently. The silence of the room put Lucy on edge.

"Well, I guess," Lucy began, feeling shaken by the vehemence in his words. "I guess I'd like to see more support for our families in need. I admire the things you are doing here for the Fae of the North, and I'd like that to happen in all areas of Denora."

A maniacal smile spread across Laurent's face. "Yes. What else?"

"Um," she continued, looking around uncomfortably. "I believe there should be a change among how male Fae look down upon females."

Laurent nodded excitedly, encouraging her to continue.

"I think there should be more freedoms for females. They deserve to make their own decisions for their future. What they would like to do with their lives." She cleared her throat. "Whom they would like to marry," she added sheepishly.

"Yes." Laurent wrapped his arms around Lucy's waist and spun her in the air. "Yes, my queen. I knew you were my perfect match ever since that day in the grove."

Lucy gasped as he swung her around once more, her hands tightening around his shoulders.

What has gotten into him?

"Laurent, I am pleased to see you are so excited about this, but I am not sure the reason."

Lucy knew something had to have happened. He was bouncing

around like a young boy, not at all acting like the leader of an entire territory.

"Because, my queen, I needed to make sure." He put her on the ground and grasped her by the waist, pulling her closer to him. Turning to the map, he whispered a Fae spell. With a wave of his hand, the map shimmered as a charm was lifted. Like a rippling wave, the images on the map changed and the words rearranged.

What she saw was not a typical map of Denora with boundary lines drawn between the Northern, Central, and Southern territories. As the images melted and changed, Laurent took a step back and Lucy took a step closer to see.

Pictures started moving across the parchment, horses and beasts traveling from the North to Central Denora. Naval warships traveled far into the seas on both the East and West coasts, making a wide arch as they headed toward Southern Denora. Then, the images rushed together in a clash of those moving hordes as they finally met in the center of the map.

King Tralont's castle.

This was a battle map.

All the blood drained from Lucy's face, but she refused to make a sound. Laurent couldn't see the true terror she was feeling, she had no idea how he'd react. What if he threw her into the dungeon for disagreeing with him?

She bit her lip and took in a shallow breath, forcing her face to look interested, not terrified.

"I have plans for the North, Lucy," Laurent said in her ear, and she nearly jumped at the proximity. "But my plans do not end there. Denora needs a change, and I am planning on being that catalyst. We will support the people in need; we will truly make a difference in Denora... but first, it needs a new ruler."

Lucy swallowed the lump in her throat, begging for strength to speak without a trace of alarm.

"You wish to be Denora's new king? What of King Tralont?"

"We will kill him," he said matter-of-factly, still looking at the map. "We shall kill anyone who stands in our way."

Lucy's blood turned to ice and her stomach roiled with unease.

"And you will be my queen." He laced his arms around her waist.

Lucy stood, petrified, as Laurent's words trailed through her mind like poison. She needed to get the fuck out of the room, and fast.

"Everything has already begun. The ships here," he said, pointing to the map from over her shoulder, "have already reached the southern shores."

A breathless gasp left her lips.

"Don't worry, my love," he said, his hands moving from her midsection to her shoulders, squeezing. "They are under strict orders to just gain control of the territory. Lord Isaacs is a coward and will release his power over the land with minimal force."

My love.

Each and every word from his lips made her more ill.

Curling a hand around her midsection, she hid her derision best she could.

"Are you alright, my queen?"

The words, once a flirtatious compliment, now cast acid down her throat.

Lucy would never be his fucking queen—she was an idiot for thinking otherwise. She should have trusted her initial instinct when she first confronted him about Jasper. How could she have been so clueless?

"I'm fine," Lucy lied, thankful he couldn't read her lies the way he could for others. "This is..." she couldn't find the words. It was disgusting. Vile. "So much information at once," she supplied.

"I know it seems harsh," Laurent said, turning to her, gazing deeply into her hazel eyes. He looked crazed with wide bloodshot eyes.

Lucy tried not to shun away from it, refusing to let him see the fear cast deep within her.

"But this is all for the best," he continued. "We will create a new Denora that is worthy of all of its citizens."

Her magic raced under her skin as though it was ready to blast out of her hands and kill the insane male before her, but she had to hold it back. If he said things were already in motion, she needed to understand all of it. Gathering the correct information here was key. She only had one focus now.

How do I stop this?

Lucy looked back at the map, studying it carefully. She would have to play into this—her stomach dropped at the thought.

Taking a step forward, she got closer to the map and out of the reach of Laurent. She couldn't stand his touch for a moment longer. "Your troops have already made it to the South to take control?"

"Yes," Laurent said seriously. She could sense his gaze watching her closely.

"Next, the North will march on the Central Territory?" It took every bit of effort for her voice to not crack. "To overtake the Kingdom?"

"Indeed." Laurent walked up to the map, pointing to the castle. "We shall take our stand and get the dukes under our thumb. Then there will be nothing else in our way." His eyes glinted with the promise of power.

"I have a question. I..."

Stop fucking talking, Lucy, she yelled at herself.

But she had never been one to stay quiet—no matter how much trouble it caused her.

"I don't understand why you want to take the throne," she admitted, pushing for him to explain. "You have so many ideas to support the people of the North. Couldn't you share those ideas with the other rulers of Denora and get them to see the benefits of your plan?"

"I've tried, Lucy," he replied with a surrendering sigh. "I've presented my ideas to them at every council meeting, but they do not agree with my views. They refuse to even consider them! The council believes that the people of Denora are happy with the current division of power, claiming that these class differences are needed for the stability of the realm."

Those words made Lucy's stomach turn. Of course, the wealthy officials would not care for those stationed below them. And it was doubtful that they would ever relinquish any of their power. But murder? There was never an excuse for murder.

"Therefore, you will take over Denora and give support to all the population?" Lucy asked, trying to understand.

"Well, not all the population." Laurent huffed a small laugh.

"Pardon?" Lucy stilled.

Here it comes.

"The population will look very different when I am done, as it should. There are too many Fae in Denora for us to have a sustainable realm where all are treated equally. By removing a portion of the population, we will have the greatest likelihood of success. We must decrease in size by a few thousand, at least." His voice trailed off, lost in thought as he gazed at the map.

He continued to ramble, but Lucy could no longer comprehend his words. He spoke of the murder of thousands as though he was discussing the weather. No remorse whatsoever.

"Sir," Roger called from the doorway. "Your meeting with the generals starts soon. Would you like me to bring Miss Lucy back to her chambers while you prepare?"

Lucy could have sobbed in relief to have the excuse to run from that room. Before Laurent could oppose, Lucy quickly turned and faced him.

"Let me allow you to get back to work," Lucy said with a painted on smile. "It is already getting late and I do not wish for you to get behind on your important work here."

Laurent looked at her, as if debating if he would allow her to leave. Something within him softened as he smiled at her. "My meeting will run very late... Can we discuss more of this in the morning, my love?"

It felt like a test.

"I look forward to it," she replied sweetly.

She had to ensure he believed in her support. He couldn't be given any hint of what she was truly feeling or what she was about to do next—it was a risk she wasn't willing to take. So, instead of running in the opposite direction, she stepped close to Laurent, pressed her lips against his cheek, and told him something he wouldn't understand until it was far too late. "Your plans are awe-inspiring, and I look forward to the outcome."

The outcome being someone killing you, you psychotic megalomaniac.

Laurent's ice-blue eyes burned with passion as she gave a slight curtsey and left the room, the smile on her face physically hurting.

It took everything in her not to run.

ELEVEN

LUCY

Lucy paced back and forth in her room, willing her mind to focus.

This can't be happening.

She replayed the conversation in her mind over and over. Had Laurent Sloan really admitted to her that he was planning treason against the king? Did he really expect her to be part of it?

The thought cast a cold sweat over her otherwise flushed body.

She was going to be sick.

Lucy believed Denora had its flaws, but to murder people in order to take over? She couldn't fathom it.

Her magic sprung to the surface, as if feeling her growing panic. It bound away from her skin and scattered around the room like a caged animal looking for an escape.

Escape. That's it.

She had to leave this place and warn others of Sloan's plans. He had mentioned the first invasions in the South... Her heart stopped.

My brothers.

Were Hugh and Gregory in danger?

She needed to see Wes. They'd go to the King and inform him of

Sloan's intentions. But what did she know, really? Were there others involved in his plan? Surely he couldn't have a large backing behind him—not with his plot to murder the king.

Could he?

The emerald magic continued to zip around the room until suddenly it stopped by the door and shimmered, as though it was beckoning her.The last time she followed her magic, it led her along the darkened corridors only to find Jasper's decrepit body, withering away in the depths of the dungeons.

Should I follow you once more?

Jasper had warned her that Sloan was not what he seemed... He said Sloan was draining him. Was Sloan siphoning Jasper's magic to empower his forces with alchemy?

It was possible—that particular magic was powerful, but rare. Unfortunately, there was no time for guessing games.

Lucy had to find out.

With careful movements, she opened the door from her bedchambers to the empty hallway beyond. Thankfully, no guard stood by her door.

Not yet.

Following the green light, Lucy tiptoed down the corridor, praying to all the gods in all the realms that she could track down the one person she never thought she'd seek out for help...

Jasper.

Lucy held her breath as she traversed the long corridors in the thick blanket of night. She had spent weeks getting used to the layout of the castle, and it had almost begun feeling familiar to her. But now, each shadowy corner made her stomach lurch, as though Lord Sloan would see her deceptive words and come barreling out to throw her in his dungeons at any moment.

If only she could hide.

She came to a halt.

Of course, she realized.

Looking around her to ensure she was still alone, she quickly closed her eyes and summoned her father's magnificent power over the shadows. This magic was still new to Lucy, and she wasn't entirely sure how to command it just yet, but pure force of will would have to do. She lifted her hands in the air and called the darkness to her, then squeezed her fingers into a fist and curled her arms around her.

Taking off down the passage, she wore the shadows like a blanket, making her nothing but a darkened blur out of the corner of someone's eye. It was late, and it was likely that the rest of the castle was asleep at this hour, but Lucy couldn't risk anyone seeing her. Not now.

The emerald bouncing light led her straight past the dungeons. Lucy wasn't surprised—the last time she looked for Jasper there, he had been relocated. Even Sloan himself had admitted to moving him to a more secure location.

Where was the light taking her? What would Sloan consider the safest area of his castle?

That's when it dawned on her. Her magic was leading her through the east wing; straight to Laurent Sloan's personal chambers.

The thought of being caught sneaking around his private rooms sent a healthy dose of fear straight through her. Sloan was decidedly insane. He was a manipulative liar and had planned to kill the most influential male Fae in all of Denora. Would he hesitate to kill her if he thought she was up to something that could derail his plans?

Getting caught was not an option.

Stopping in the hallway to refocus her thoughts, she hid in a small alcove under an oversized tapestry hanging near the windows. Her hands were shaking, the nerves threatening to lock all of her muscles into place until she couldn't take another step.

Her magic returned to her side, swirling gracefully around her arm, waiting for her signal to keep going, but Lucy wasn't sure how to continue forward. She was on a path to Sloan's private rooms to kidnap his prisoner and leave, preferably without him knowing. Was there any possibility she could pull it off?

Doubt swept through her mind and a veil of paranoia began to smoother her. Jerking her head left and right, she waited for the moment that Sloan would jump out and drag her away, until suddenly a golden glimmer caught her eye. Lucy stilled. The dim candlelight caught the metallic edges of the decorative vitrine a few paces away. It was the same display that showcased Sloan's many medals and accomplishments. Her mouth turned into a sneer.

Just days ago, she had been admiring Sloan for his action to save King Tralont's reign. She was foolish. He stopped one rebellion just to start one himself.

He was exactly as the rumors had described. *Lord Slain*—only interested in his own selfish initiatives. And now she was under his thumb, too.

She squeezed her eyes shut.

Stop this, she told herself. *You are Lucella Baum, and you don't let a single fucking person in this realm or the next control you. You are powerful. You are unstoppable. You are a damn Original. Now. Get. Up.*

Opening her eyes, she shivered as pulse of her magic cascaded through her. Lucy was more powerful than any other Fae she had ever come into contact with, and she would not be bested.

This would not be the end of her.

She only had to glance at the shadows lurking in the corners of the dimly lit hallway for them to come swooping toward her, her intent clear in her mind. Lucy would take hold of her father's gift and become little more than shadow and mist as she walked through the halls.

Looking down at her hands, she saw the magic forming. Her hand was nearly transparent as a dark fog covered her, cloaking her from view. A wicked smile crept onto her face as she was reminded of the many times she had snuck into her father's office. Only this time, as if by ironic design, it was her father who gave her the power to slip through the corridors unnoticed. She felt comforted by the presence of his magic within her, shielding her from danger, as if this was Corvus's intention for her all along.

The emerald mist sprung forward, ready to lead Lucy to Jasper, but she wasn't sure if she needed it. It was as though an innate force was leading her right to him, and for once, she trusted her magic over logic.

The corridor was empty when she reached Sloan's private suite, which meant he was still in his meeting and Roger was sure to be by his side. Taking a deep breath, she dropped her shadows. Tiring herself out before she even got to Jasper was not a risk she was willing to take, and whoever watched over him would see her one way or another. Her magic would better serve her if she was focused.

Now to get in, she considered as she took in the enormous metal entryway.

Putting her hand on the door, she felt the safety charm she assumed was in place. It reminded her of the same security her father had on his office. A darkness in her rose at the thought, especially as his killer was nearly in her grasp.

"Open," she commanded the door. As soon as the words left her lips, the lock disarmed and allowed her into the space. The familiar hum of power beneath her skin was a quiet cheer of success.

Lucy took in the rooms before her. Off to the left was a bathing chamber, where she stood was a welcoming chamber with a sitting area and fireplace, and to the right were his bedchambers. That's where the prisoner would be. Her magic tugged her toward the right, confirming her suspicions.

She knew there wasn't time for a clever plan, so after a few careful steps, Lucy charged into the room, her magic vibrating under her skin.

"What are you doing?" A large guard with enormous tusks asked in surprise. He was one of three hulking ox shifters surrounding a large steel box. His brows furrowed and his face reddened with anger. "You shouldn't be in here."

He and the other guards slipped in front of the steel contraption, which stood taller than them all.

Lucy offered him a saccharine smile and continued walking toward them. Her heart was pounding, but she forced herself to proceed with a look of carefree ignorance.

"Ah, give it a rest," the other tattooed guard said with a laugh, stroking one of his tusks as one would a beard or mustache. "Clearly she's in here for a little late night comfort from Lord Sloan."

The guards laughed with him, dismissing Lucy's presence.

Typical male bullshit. I guess Sloan doesn't hire these Kerroz guards for their intelligence. Her eyes twinkled. *This should be easy.*

"Hmm..." Lucy came nearer, her eyes focused on the closest guard. "It certainly *is* late. You must be so tired."

The guard tilted his head in confusion. With her eyes on him, she heard the other guards stir, watching her.

Taking gentle, graceful steps, she placed her hands on the enormous chest of the tusked guard and smiled sweetly. Standing on her tiptoes, she rose to eye level with the guard. His head jerked back with surprise, clearly unsure of what to do. Leaning closer to him, she whispered into the guard's ear.

"Sleep."

Without looking back, she twirled away from him and faced the other guards. She lingered as their gaze swung from Lucy to over her shoulder at their friend and back to her.

A quiet thump of the guard collapsing behind her only put a greater smile on her face. Their expressions twisted from confusion and into fear as she took another step toward them.

"You, too," she said quietly to the tattooed male. "Sleep."

"What are you?" The tattooed guard ran for the exit, pushing his companion out of the way. Lucy only winked at the other guard in the room as he stood frozen in fear before her.

Another thud from the next room brought a hint of green to Lucy's eyes, which she saw in the reflection of the steel structure.

"Two down," Lucy said, watching the last guard trying to fight off the effects of his impending slumber. She casually padded over to face him, then blew a small gust of air from her lips. At last, he toppled over, crashing to the floor. "Three."

A wave of satisfaction broke over her, knowing her magic wouldn't let her down. She subdued three Kerroz guards with a simple word.

But her smile faded when she turned to the enormous steel box off to the side of the room. What she needed was inside of the towering structure. As she neared the it, it was clear what it was… Not a box, but a cage with three sides of solid metal and one side with iron bars.

Stepping around to the front, she looked through the bars and saw Jasper crouched in a corner, terror contorting his face.

"L-L-Lucy?" He stammered, his stringy hair covering his face smeared with dirt. The fear in his voice turned into amazement, perhaps relief, as his bulging eyes took her in. "You've come here to save me?"

"Absolutely not," Lucy spat.

Whatever relief she thought she would feel upon finding Jasper was gone. She didn't want to save him. Lucy hated Jasper with a passion that lit a fire deep in her soul. He killed her father.

"I'm here to ensure you get the sentencing you deserve."

For a single moment, she thought about killing him right then and there. The hatred that sparked inside of her knew it would take all of one single thought. Just one thought, and her magic would carry out the task. She could crush his windpipe. Stop his heart. Slit his throat right there in his cell.

Each idea seemed more tempting than the last, but she would never stoop so low as to become a murderer like him. She wouldn't sully her father's memory with that kind of violence.

"You're coming with me."

"You are saving me," he blubbered, scrambling to his feet. "I always knew you were the best of your family."

"Don't you dare talk about my fucking family!" Lucy roared as she stepped closer to the steel bars. "You will not speak unless I ask you a direct question. Do you understand?"

"I cannot believe it, just wait until—" Jasper continued to spout more nonsense, but Lucy held up her hand and snapped her fingers once. Immediately, the sound ceased. There was no more noise coming from Jasper's lips after that. He opened and closed his mouth like a fish gulping air, but he made no sound.

Lucy gave him another smile, but he would have been foolish to take it for anything other than ruthlessness. "You will be coming with me, but I am not here to save you. I'd just rather be the one to dole out your punishment."

She needed to ask him more about Sloan and his plans, but getting out of here in one piece was top priority, and they were running out of time.

Lucy waved her hand and the door to the cell swung open, allowing her to step through. Jasper gasped and jumped back, falling over himself and crawling backward to get away from her.

With a simple point of her finger, vines sprung from out of nowhere and twined themselves around Jasper's hands, keeping them in place.

"Come. We're leaving." Lucy started to walk, then paused realizing she hadn't quite finished her plans after this point.

Getting out of the castle without running into Sloan or Roger was imperative, but how? Taking a moment, she called upon her Original magic, hoping to get a glimpse of where they were so they could find a safe passage out. Her emerald magic filled her mind's eye, but Lucy wasn't able to find Sloan anywhere. Perhaps she was drained after sending the guards into a deep slumber.

Jasper was glaring at her, his eyes bulging with the need to speak.

"What is it?" Lucy snapped, impatience waning on her.

"The boundary line." Jasper's eyes widened in amazement when he heard the sound of his voice, then he quickly went on. "There's a large boundary line that does not allow any magic to pass, not even Lord Sloan can conjure. It lasts for the length of the bridge—it acts as a defensive protection from those beyond the castle. We need to get past the boundary line and then you can use your magic to free us."

Lucy thought back to her travels when she first reached the Northern Territories... Sloan had brought them in the carriage until he crossed the bridge to the guard's outpost, only then was he able to bring them into the castle using his magic to travel instantly.

"Time to go," Lucy announced. Jasper tried to open his mouth to argue, but no sound came out.

Lucy smiled to herself.

She was finally able to shut him up.

Gripping his collar, she shoved him in front of her. "Lead the way."

Lucy kept her shadows close, cloaking her and Jasper as they traveled through the castle. Each noise made her startle. At any moment, Sloan would return to his rooms to find slumbering guards and a missing prisoner. They had to get to the bridge as fast as they could before he caught wind of what had happened. It was only a matter of time.

Shuddering to a stop, Jasper turned and looked at her, sweat covering his pale skin.

"What is it?" Lucy asked him, knowing he couldn't speak until she allowed it.

"This is the door to the exit, but the guard, Mairlor, is on the other side."

Lucy remembered the tusked sentinel guard in his icy outpost—another Kerroz shifter.

"My magic will work from here. I'll make him sleep, then we make a run for it across the bridge."

Jasper opened and closed his mouth again, trying to speak but failing.

"Speak," Lucy commanded, rolling her eyes in frustration.

"Your magic will fail on the bridge. Your powers won't work again until we pass completely."

Lucy nodded in understanding. "You will keep up. If you fall behind and get us caught, he will do much worse to you than I ever could, and you and I both know it. Do you understand?" Lucy wanted to bring Jasper to justice, but she wouldn't get caught on his behalf.

Jasper was asked a direct question, so he could have replied, but instead he nodded his head quickly. They both knew the reality of the situation, and while Lucy was no fan of his, Jasper was better off with her than Sloan.

Turning back to the door, Lucy closed her eyes and focused her magic on the guard at the outpost. Forcing the command for the guard to sleep, Lucy hoped it would last long enough to get them across the bridge.

Nudging the door open slowly, Lucy winced as it creaked, the sound echoing across the large castle foyer. Peeking her head out, she saw the guard asleep at his post.

"Now," she told Jasper, shoving him out the doors. "Run."

Together, they sprinted across the icy bridge, careful not to fall into the deep chasm below. Over and over, Lucy thought to herself that she would fix this, fix all of it, as long as she could get away.

She would go to her mother and be the daughter she needed her to be.

She would help Wes with the Baum Bowyer business.

She would return to Micah and make things right.

They were halfway across the bridge when Lucy begged the stars for extra time to get away before they were found.

But as history would have it, Lucy's timing was never quite that lucky.

"Stop!" Lord Sloan's yells echoed from the doorway of the castle.

Her stomach dropped.

"Keep running!" She ordered Jasper. "He has no magic on this part of the bridge. We need to outrun him!"

Lucy's Fae speed made her quick, but Jasper was old and weak, especially after being imprisoned. He couldn't keep up with her, and as she pulled him along, Sloan was gaining on them.

Just a little further, she thought to herself, seeing the end of the bridge. They were almost there.

"Come on!" She screamed, pulling at his arm to urge him on; but it was no use.

Lord Sloan crashed into them, knocking Jasper to the ground. Lucy lost her grip on Jasper as Sloan grabbed her shoulder and spun her to face him. His hands clutched her, his fingernails digging into her shoulders. She tried to pull away, but his undoubtable strength kept her from breaking free.

"What is the meaning of this?" Sloan growled.

"What do you think?"

"Lucy, come back inside." Sloan's voice was cold and detached, as though he was holding on to his last bit of restraint.

"I'm not going with you. You're a monster!" Lucy bellowed. Her voice echoed through the icy mountains and reverberated from the cavern below. "I can't let you do this."

"So you side with the weak Fae who murdered your father?" He seethed, his ice-blue eyes momentarily shooting to Jasper. "You and I are united!" He shook her body, pulling her closer. "You belong with me!"

"I belong to no one," Lucy said through clenched teeth as she stood tall.

"I forbid you from leaving here," Sloan said, his teeth grinding as he spat the words, leaning close to her face.

"You do not control me," Lucy said. Looking her nose down at him, she added, "no one controls me."

"All of Denora controls you, Lucy! That's the problem!" His fingers dug into the sides of her arms, bruising her. "Together we can be more."

Lucy shoved his chest with both hands and snarled, "Get off!"

With a derisive laugh, he just held on to her tighter, yanking her to his chest.

"Oh, Lucy," he crooned, his nose in her hair and his words like acid to her ears. "It didn't have to be like this. But you will learn, I am the more powerful Fae here."

And with those words, Lucy remembered what Brax had said about her powers.

She was an Original—the rules of Fae magic did not apply to her.

Gasping for air beneath his unrelenting grip, Lucy screamed, shoving him away with all her might. With a shimmering blast of emerald light, Sloan flew backwards, landing on his back in the middle of the bridge. The bridge that didn't allow magic.

Lucy's chest heaved with panting breaths, and her eyes darted back to Jasper, making sure he was still nearby. She couldn't let Sloan have him.

Sloan's gaze darted to Lucy as she stood before him in the bitter wind. He scrambled to his feet. "How?" Sloan demanded in disbelieving rage.

"You will not use Jasper for his alchemy any longer. He will be punished for his crimes, and then we are coming for you." Lucy felt her magic coursing through her body. Her hair twisted wildly in a gust of warm air that seemed to surround only her. The green mist swirled around her, prepared to protect her. "You no longer have access to his alchemy."

She reached out to get Jasper back on his feet when Lord Sloan began laughing—a slow, sinister taunt.

"I don't know how you were able to hide this from me, but I will figure it out. I will figure *you* out." His eyes landed on her grip on

Jasper, and his deranged glare flew to her once more. "You think this will stop me?" His maniacal laughter continued as he stood up. Walking toward her, his sneer turned rabid. "There are others with alchemy I can use to get what I need. You can't save everyone."

Other alchemists?

Lucy's blood turned to lava as she registered the threat.

He meant Micah.

"You're going to want to take that back," Lucy snarled.

"Where do you think you'll be able to run where I can't catch you?" Lord Sloan asked arrogantly. "Once we get past that boundary line, my magic will reappear and I will return you to where you belong."

"You're delusional," Lucy snapped.

"I am your future king, and soon you will see you are my fucking queen! Mine!"

Enough of this.

She wouldn't waste another second on this madness.

Grabbing the back of Jasper's collar, she changed course and pulled him toward Lord Sloan.

Sloan's eyes brightened with delight as Jasper's bulged in fear.

"Yes. Let us return him to his cell and get back to where we were." He held out his hand for Jasper. "I am very interested to hear more about your... magic."

Lucy stopped short, just far enough to stay out of his grasp.

"I just wanted to make sure you hear me clearly," Lucy said with a venom she never knew she held. "I will *never* be yours."

Lord Sloan lunged at Lucy to seize her. With a blink of an eye, Lucy and Jasper were gone and Sloan swung his arms in the empty space in front of him.

Sloan hollered, swinging his head back and forth wildly, looking for them.

Lucy reappeared behind him, then whispered into his ear. "You're going to lose."

Before Sloan could turn around once more, Lucy and Jasper were gone again.

The only thing Lucy heard as her magic took her and Jasper away from the North was Lord Sloan's screams as they echoed through his icy domain.

TWELVE

MICAH

This was more than anything Micah had ever expected. The last, and only, time he and Lucy were here, The Elderwood was vacant. Trees and plants in every direction, but no life—not even an insect in sight. Now this? Not only animals roaming the land and birds soaring through the skies, but people—real people!

And they were still on their knees, bowing to him.

"Uh," Micah started, hesitantly. "Please, there's no need." He waved his hands for them to stand, awkwardly sidestepping and looking to Quillan for an explanation. As expected, he ignored Micah.

However, Quillan didn't ignore the people before him as they looked to him for answers. Nodding his head, Quillan motioned for them to rise.

Micah remained silent, hoping for someone to talk—to explain what was happening here. But instead, they all looked at him expectantly.

Well, fuck.

"Hello," he said, clearing his throat. "I'm Micah."

Each of the people lifted their spears into the air and drove them to the ground in unison, creating a loud thud. Their faces remained stoic, eyes never leaving his.

Micah just blinked.

"Thank you all for welcoming The Guardian with such passion," Quillan said to the group.

That was passion, huh?

"I must bring our honored guest to the grand counsel. Remember, we are here to listen to all concerns. Please find your advisor and share whatever burdens your heart. We will be working toward a better future for the lives of all."

Concerns? Burdens? What has been happening here?

"Come with me, Guardian," Quillan said to him quietly. "We have much to discuss."

WALKING through The Elderwood was an experience like no other. The trees were magnificent, each one a different color. Seeing the typical green and red trees was fine, but a bright blue tree? It seemed impossible.

He wondered if it was anything like Lucy's realm of Denora. However, from the way the leaves glittered in the breeze, he wasn't sure if there was another place like this anywhere in creation.

As they traversed down the long stone path that led them down the side of the hill, Micah took in all he could about this place. The waterfalls off in the distance were still breathtaking, with the most clear blue water he had ever seen. The strange moons in the sky still took up much of the expansive horizon before them. Everything looked perfect.

What could possibly be going wrong here?

Suddenly, he paused, an eerie sensation creeping through his blood. From what he remembered, the forest was not all sunshine and rainbows, though. The last time he was here, there was one place that sent a shiver down his spine. Remembering the darkness that dwelled at the edge of the forest, he turned to the west to see it.

His blood ran cold.

There it was. The forest that seemed cast in eternal shadow—so at odds with the rest of the realm. Blood red leaves blooming from black branches fluttered ominously in the wind.

His stomach dropped.

Why am I really here?

Could Quillan have lied to him about peace? Was this some terrible ruse to get him here and hurt him?

"What is the matter?" Quillan asked, seeing Micah tense and worried on the path beside him.

Micah stopped in his tracks. "I'm not going with you to some evil forest for you to kill me. I won't let you." He took a step back, preparing his body for a fight, and calling on the magic deep within him.

The smile on Quillan's face faltered. "If I wanted to kill you, I would have done so already," he replied, completely unamused. "You *do* realize you have done much worse to me than I've done to you. Correct?" A blazing fire lived behind those amber eyes.

"Then why are you taking me into a cursed forest?" Micah demanded.

"We aren't going there," he said, looking over to the dark red leaves. "We are meeting somewhere else. Everything will be explained in the counsel. Now, please, move your feet so we can get there and I no longer have to listen to your incessant mumbling." Quillan turned and continued to walk toward the forest.

Everything inside of Micah's brain told him to run. It was idiotic of him to be following a stranger who once had gouged a hole in his leg with his teeth.

Didn't he know anything about following random strangers?

Yet, something within him urged him to keep walking, to find out what Quillan urgently needed him to know.

There must have been a reason he was still alive.

So Micah continued, somehow knowing this visit would change his life forever; whether it'd be for better or worse, he wasn't sure.

~

BY THE TIME they came upon the building, Micah's heart was beating out of his chest. It wasn't for lack of exercise—something about this place just felt different, almost as if the air itself was thinner.

The monumental structure before him would have taken his breath away if he wasn't already having such a difficult time breathing. It stood at least two stories high, with a large golden dome for its roof, its surface reflected the bright afternoon sun that peeked between the canopy of leaves. There were large windows, from the floor all the way to its vaulted ceiling, which only added to the brightness of the room. The walls were a pale pearl color that shimmered in the sun, even with the structure nestled into the shadow of the looming trees.

"This is our counsel building, The Dome. The advisors come here to meet as needed when trouble arises... Unfortunately, that has been frequent as of late. Hopefully, with your arrival, that will change."

Micah could only nod, still taking in this new place. Still wondering if he was welcome there or not.

Quillan opened the wide, ornate doors and led Micah inside.

The interior was as beautiful as its exterior. Large windows scaling the length of the walls opened at the top to let the greenery of the forest trail inside. A filtered light gave a pearlescent glow to the walls, accenting the clinging dark green ivy. Small ornate fountains were placed throughout the building, giving off gentle and relaxing sounds of the forest. It was as though the inside was as wild as the rest of The Elderwood—as though nature came first, and the people came last.

A clearing throat brought Micah back to his reality. Standing in the middle of the otherworldly room, he took in what he assumed was the grand counsel. Around a large oval table, made entirely of wood, three men sat watching him intently.

"Sit, Guardian," Quillan told him gently. "You're going to want to sit."

Micah nodded and took a seat at the far end of the table made for eight, seating only four.

He felt completely out of place.

The three strangers smiled at him gently, all wearing the same style of clothing worn by Quillan and the others. Brown fabric draped around their muscular bodies; and while the fabric was simple, they sat with the poise and importance of royalty. Each man looked to be in their late thirties or early forties, but knowing the Fae, they were likely much older than that.

That is... if they were Fae.

"We know you have many questions," the first spoke. "My name is Fergh. I am the lead advisor for the biosphere here. I ensure the safety of our plants and wildlife—as we have many." He outstretched his hands to the plant life all around them. The soft lines around his eyes crinkled as he attempted a show of kindness, though barely a smile appeared on his freckled face.

"I am Rowan," the man across from him said next. He had long braids pulled back with a strip of leather. "I speak for the safety of our people."

Safety, he scoffed in his mind. He was tired of always being the last to know what was going on, and he wasn't going to sit around and make idle chatter.

Before the third man could speak, Micah cut him off. "What am I doing here? First, I'm attacked by this dude as a cat, and then I get dragged here and no one will tell me why."

Rowan looked to the third man who had not been introduced, but all he did was nod, his steepled fingers hiding a small smile on his face.

"We apologize for Quillan's... abrasive manner upon your first meeting," Rowan said, looking at Quillan with judgment.

Quillan remained standing beside the table, smiling.

Jackass.

"As he was *supposed* to tell you," Rowan continued, "there was a dark magic that affected our realm. Our understanding is that a Fae male put something tainted within the base of the tree that holds the portal here. It caused the magic within our realm to suffer."

"Trees were withering," Fergh said with distress. "The animals were in hiding and even the morning birds did not sing the songs of a new day." Fergh took a deep breath, steadying his shaking hands. "The magic that lives within our people is tied to our land. With the magic in the plants suffering, it started a chain reaction of devastation. That is... until you removed the tainted magic."

"We are truly grateful for your interference with the immoral Fae. We hope he has been brought to justice." Rowan's face was the picture of sincerity.

Micah's stomach curdled at the thought. He hadn't heard from anyone, and he wasn't sure what came of Jasper.

"So you've brought me here to thank me?" Micah asked, still not seeing what they wanted from him.

The three men looked at one another seriously, then back at Micah. "Indeed, we wanted to thank you. However, there is more. We are in need of your assistance." Fergh shifted in his seat, almost uncomfortable to admit they needed help.

"Since the magic in the land was affected, our seers have been ill. We did not have the ability to see into our future for the weeks that our magic was harmed," Rowan said, glancing back at the third man uneasily.

"Seers?" Micah asked, sitting forward in his seat.

"Yes," Rowan replied solemnly. "Now that the dark magic has been lifted, we have been able to see what is to come." His eyes widened in fear as his voice dropped to a near whisper. "Another Fae is on their way here to disrupt the prosperity of our land."

"What do you mean?" Micah asked, not understanding the

threat. "You were all here in secret for who knows how long. Can't you go back to acting like you were never here?"

"Perhaps," Fergh replied. "Unfortunately, the Fae who threatens our future doesn't want anything to do with us. They want the magic of our land—the magic we cannot give-up. It doesn't matter if we hide or not."

Micah nodded, thoughtfully. "How did you do that, anyway? Make it seem as though there was no life here?"

This time, the third man spoke. "We have a special magic that allows us to change things as needed. When visitors come through the portal, namely the Baums, a magic spell allows them to see only what they have come for—the wood of our trees." He smiled and crossed his hands on the table, his fingers adorned in rings of all colors. "We have allowed the Baum and Lumen families to enter our realm to gather the wood they require because they take only what they need and never take in excess. It is what holds the balance."

"So can't you do this to whoever this bad guy is?" Micah asked, still not seeing the issue.

"No," the third man said with severity. "The seers have all agreed. He will come to take the wood—all the wood. He will level our realm until it is nothing but piles of dirt, siphoning every ounce of magic within."

Micah felt the gravity of that. Another entitled jerk coming and expecting to take whatever he wants, no matter the repercussions.

"Well, how can I help?" Micah asked. "I don't have the same kind of magic you guys do." It had been less than a year since he learned magic existed, and he had only recently discovered he had magic of his own. What use was he?

"You're a Lumen," the third man said with pride. "We have every faith in you that you will continue to protect the portal." He turned and nodded at Quillan, then looked back to Micah with his deep brown eyes. "We shall help you."

Micah turned to see what was happening. As Quillan stepped closer, he held in his hands a large bundle wrapped in a thin cloth.

"This is for you, Guardian," Quillan said with reverence. "We have heard of your alchemy and have provided you with the tools you need to be successful."

He pulled the cloth off to reveal a large axe with a wooden handle. The axe blade gleamed in the light of the room. Embedded in the knob at the top was a beautiful red jewel.

"The metal is a mix of iron and steel. The wood is crafted from one of our most cherished trees in our realm—it is harvested for only the most revered weapons we must create." Quillan turned the axe handle toward Micah, offering the weapon to him. "The red sunstone can be imbued with your power to utilize your magic and alchemy as one."

Micah looked around the room in amazement. It was a gorgeous weapon, but how did they know about the alchemy? His stomach turned with unease. Grasping the axe, he noted the way the sunstone glittered in the light. The handle was smooth and the blade was heavy, yet it was perfectly balanced.

The third man rose from his seat at the table and walked over to Micah slowly. "May I?" He extended his hand to the weapon.

Micah could only nod, still at a loss for words.

Turning the axe over, the stranger displayed the other side of the handle. At the shoulder, where the wood and metal met, was a deep engraving.

Micah stilled.

It was the same sigil Lucy had on her amulet that allowed her entry into The Elderwood.

"If you ever need to come here, you now have the ability to do so." The man smiled at Micah, as if he knew something Micah did not.

And that didn't surprise Micah at all.

THIRTEEN

LUCY

"Come on. You've given me enough trouble as it is. Stop slowing me down," Lucy bristled as she dragged Jasper the final steps to the Baum manor.

It was an exhausting journey with multiple stops along the way. Her Original magic was beyond powerful, but even that had its limits. She could jump miles at a time, but each use of her power drained her. When they finally arrived in Central Denora, she couldn't so much as cast light to guide their way, let alone jump through space and time once more. Instead, Lucy had to grip Jasper by his damned collar and drag him through the Nilban Woods, a small part of her hoping some wolven would come looking for a snack.

The entire time they trudged to the estate, Lucy had one thing circling her mind: how was she going to tell her mother that her brothers were in danger?

Could Anita handle another horrific incident at the hands of someone they were supposed to trust?

And what if, somehow, she misunderstood, and they weren't in danger? What if Lucy put fear and worry into her mother's heart for no reason? Was it worth the risk?

Over and over, she battled with herself internally as she battered Jasper, tugging him along as his feet reluctantly took one step in front of the other.

At the sound of their struggle, a few of the estate staff came peering through doors and windows. Normally, Lucy would have preferred not to be seen. For this occasion, however, time was of the essence.

A gardener came around the curve of the walkway, hands full of tools. Upon seeing Lucy and her captive, he froze, unsure what to do.

Frustrated from hauling Jasper halfway across the damned realm, she huffed out a request. "Please, go get my brother."

The gardener's eyes widened as they took in Jasper's disheveled appearance and vines tethering his hands. The male dropped all of his tools and took off running for Wesley.

He'll know what to do. He has to, she hoped.

"Lucy?" Anita's voice spoke quietly from behind them.

Lucy turned to see her mother holding a bushel of roses from her garden. They fell to the ground in a flourish as Anita rushed to Lucy and embraced her in a hug.

"What are you doing here?" Anita asked Lucy, scanning her body and taking in her messy hair and the dirt peppering her clothes. "What happened to—" she began, but stopped as soon as she saw the Fae male standing behind Lucy.

With narrowed eyes, Anita made a beeline for Jasper. "You."

That's all Lucy heard as her mother tightened her hand into a fist, pulled her arm back, and punched Jasper so hard, he collapsed right at the terrace entrance.

Anita stood over his unconscious body, panting as she kept her focus on the monster who terrorized her family and murdered her husband.

Lucy's eyes burned at the pain her mother had to endure by his presence, but she forced a smile instead. "I wish I would have thought to do that."

Before either could say another word, Wes was at the door, standing with a look of pure astonishment.

To be fair, it was quite a sight to stumble upon.

Lucy covered in dirt, Jasper knocked out cold, and his mother with reddened knuckles.

LUCY WAITED as Wes stared at her in wide-eyed silence, apparently taking in everything she had just told him. She couldn't blame him, though. If someone would have told her that Laurent Sloan was in cahoots with Jasper, using him for his alchemy, and had plans to overthrow the entire Denoran kingdom, she'd probably be in shock, too.

"So, what do we do now?" Wes asked. His voice sounded small. Scared. It was so at odds with how Lucy had always viewed him and a wave of hopelessness crashed over her...

She had raced Jasper here, hoping Wes would have some answers —at the very least a plan. She was so tired of running from one place to the next, and she couldn't keep doing it by herself.

Wes sat slumped behind his father's desk in a chair that seemed much too big for him. It was as though he was a child playing as an adult. It had been only a couple of days since she had seen him last, and already he looked more tired.

Jasper lay unconscious on the floor in front of them, his legs sprawled at odd angles after they'd dropped him there. With his head pinned against the front of the desk, they could at least see when he woke up.

Anita, however, stood in rapt attention, taking it all in. She did not shudder with fear, nor did she balk at the bastard at their feet. She kept a keen awareness, her mind contemplating... calculating. That surprised Lucy the most, if she were being honest.

Since when did Mother become so determined?

"It is obvious what we do, son," Anita said to him, pulling Lucy from her musing. She turned to face Lucy, her eyes blazing with resolve. "We must stop him, at any cost."

Lucy nodded in agreement, knowing in her heart it was the only course of action.

"But first," Anita began, scowling as she spun toward the unconscious lump on the floor. "It's time to wake *him* up and hear it from him."

She pointed her magic at Jasper and soft curls of gold mist formed chains, which wrapped themselves around him, lifting him and plopping him unceremoniously into a chair. Then, with a snap of her fingers, the magic walloped Jasper in the face, waking him up.

Lucy snorted at the brash behavior of her mother.

She approved entirely.

Jasper gasped and his eyes bulged as he woke. He opened his mouth to speak, but didn't make a sound. His mouth bobbed open and shut like a fish out of water.

"Oh," Lucy said, remembering. "You can speak freely now."

Jasper stretched his mouth wide and screamed in their faces. It was a long, drawn out yell that was completely unintelligible. His face turned a ruddy red and his eyes bugged out wider than ever as he kept at it, his voice cracking at the end. When he was done, he heaved in a deep breath and eyed the Baums with oily hatred.

With a sneering face that could sour milk, he glared at Lucy. "Do you know how horrific it is to be stuck with you, yet unable to speak?"

"Do you know how horrific it is to hear you speak?" Lucy spat back.

"Enough of this," Anita announced, taking a step closer to Jasper. "I need to hear it from you." Her shoulders were pulled back as she looked down her nose at him, the venom in her gaze something that seemed to chill the room.

Wes stood and walked to the front of the desk, watching Jasper with menacing intent.

Lucy angled herself to be closer to her mother, prepared to protect her from the horrid Fae at any cost.

All three Baums were ready to strike at the very hint of magic. Lucy wasn't sure who wanted his death more.

"What do you want me to do? *Apologize?*" Jasper scoffed. "I clearly never meant for things to go this far, but I'm not sorry for what happened. I'm only sorry that I ended up here, on the *losing* side."

"Silence," Lucy said, unwilling to hear him spout any more wretched words.

Jasper scowled. He tried to speak, but nothing came out.

Lucy smirked at him before turning away, facing her mother and brother once more. Seeing their expressions brought a whole new level of pain to the next words out of her mouth, but they deserved to know the truth. "I think Hugh and Gregory may be in danger."

"Why?" Wes asked, his brow furrowing with concern.

Anita gasped softly, covering her mouth with her delicate fingers.

Secrets won't bring back the dead, nor will they save the living... no matter how badly they hurt.

Taking a deep breath, Lucy continued.

"Sloan mentioned his soldiers were on different missions in the South, and when I got a good look at his map, it appeared that this was step one of his plan. He's sending his ships south, but directing them to stay far away from the coast to stay unseen. When they arrive in the Southern Territory, it will be a surprise as they dock. They will try to take over the land, then it's only time until they work their way toward Central Denora." Lucy looked at her mother, and then Wes. "If Sloan is prepared to kill, then his soldiers are, too. We need to find a way to warn them—we need to give the South a chance to fight back."

Wes swayed on his feet. Anita quickly pushed her magic to the chair behind him, bringing it closer, as he fell into the seat.

"What is it, Wes?" Anita asked him in alarm.

Wes looked at his mother, his face pale and a shallow devastation clear in his eyes. "I have been trying to call my brothers since they left... There has been no answer." His voice trailed off into a whisper.

Any shred of hope that Lucy had been holding on to was clipped —it felt as though her heart plummeted straight through her body and to the bottom of the rocky Lancast Sea.

"Then they have already arrived," Anita said matter-of-factly. She straightened and walked to the window, her hands clasped in concentration.

"We must get to them." Wes lowered his face into his hands and shook his head. His voice was barely a mumble. "We need to save them."

Lucy never expected things would end up moving so quickly. They went from planning to inform her brothers about potential trouble to saving them from the terror that is Laurent Sloan?

She thought they had time... Months... weeks at least. But this? They were down to days! There was no time left to plan. They had to move *now*. "I need to get to Micah, too," Lucy whispered.

At that, all three Fae in the room looked at her, including Jasper, who had stopped struggling long enough to hear her next words.

"Why would you involve him in this?" Wes asked, lifting his head to look at her.

"Sloan told me he needed an alchemist... Not Jasper in particular," she said, her eyes darting to Jasper just as he sighed in relief. "Just someone who can form the magic he needs." Her eyes moved to Wes's, who was looking at her in harrowing understanding. "He's the last alchemist that we know of... We need to warn him."

I need to keep my promise to keep him safe.

The sigil burned into her hand tingled with recognition of the promise she made at the base of The Elderwood portal.

In a flurry, Wes stood. He had always been a male of action, prepared to do what was necessary. "I will come with you." He rushed to the desk to grab his coat and looked down at the papers and ledgers sprawled on the desk. His face flared in realization. "I-" He bit his lip, trying to form the words. Desolately, he dropped his coat back into the chair. "I have to stay here." He placed his two hands on the side of the desk and dropped his head in defeat.

"What? Why?" Lucy asked. Why wouldn't he support her in this? Didn't he care about what happened to Micah?

"King Tralont graced me with a visit and warned me that if I didn't keep the business moving as Father had, he would replace me with someone else."

"He can't do that!" Lucy demanded. "This is *our* family business!"

"There is a simple way to solve this," Anita said, waving her hands at her children, shooing them away as she walked to the desk. "I will stay here and run the business. Wes, you will go with your sister to warn Micah. We will throw Jasper into the cellar and lock the doors. Our staff will be under strict orders to not let him out." Standing before the desk, she whipped her head to Jasper with a ferocious glare. "Though not one soul here would ever consider freeing a leech like you."

"Mother, you can't be serious," Wes said with a half-smile on his face.

"Denoran tradition has always said that the eldest male will lead the family, but I am telling you now it is *me*." There was a fire in Anita's eyes that Lucy had never seen before, but it cast warmth within her heart to see it now. "I was helping your father run this business while you were in diapers, and well before. I will do what is needed while you do the same."

Wes stood in shock at Anita's resolute declaration.

"You need to help your sister set this right before there is no family business to attend to. Go with Lucy. Fix this." Anita's determined countenance left no room for argument.

Wes nodded, then looked at his sister. "Let me prepare and we can leave."

Lucy watched as he approached their mother, a curiosity in his eyes mixed with love and concern. He kissed Anita on the cheek and headed to the door.

Lucy couldn't help the grin that spread across her face. Her mother was finally coming into the powerful magic she had within her. She was no longer being stifled... but what had changed?

With quick steps, Anita crossed the study to the hallway doors and opened them wide to call for Thomas, the head of the estate staff.

"Put this lout down in the root cellar with the rest of the vermin." Anita cast the golden chains across to Thomas as the male stood tall, eyeing Jasper with equal amounts of hatred and loathing. "No windows. No sunlight. No escape. Do you understand?"

"Yes, Madame. I will ensure no one is privy to his whereabouts and no one will stumble across him," Thomas replied.

"It will be as though he doesn't exist," Anita said dismissively, then turned away as Thomas led Jasper from the room to his next prison.

The room was quiet for a moment, like the calm before a storm. "You can say it, you know," Anita said to her, seeing Lucy's inquisitive gaze. "Nothing's ever stopped you from speaking freely before." There was a hint of mischief in Anita's eyes, but despondency, too.

"Why now?" Lucy asked plainly, a tinge of sadness coloring her words. "You've always held your magic back, always played the role of doting housewife... What changed?"

"Nothing. Everything. You name it," her mother sighed.

"This is about the magic, isn't it?" Lucy asked. "The butterfly?"

"Your father's magic? Yes, partially. But, this is more." Anita turned away, walking back to the windows, as though she couldn't face Lucy.

"More?"

"What you've said has stuck with me, Lucella." Anita looked down at her hands, then closed her eyes. "I know my magic is wonderful and powerful, and I know that I've kept it closed off for many years." She lifted her head, turned, and gazed into Lucy's eyes. "Your father and I had a wonderful partnership. There was kindness and respect, but most of all, there was love." Her hazel eyes lightened at the memory and a smile played on Anita's lips. "I owe it to Corvus to be my own person now. I cannot hide behind another male just to ensure that the Denoran ways are upheld, and I should have seen that before. I should have listened to you, Lucy."

"Mother, I didn't mean it like that."

"You did, but you were right." Anita said, her expression soft. Walking up to her daughter, Anita held Lucy's cheeks in her hands. "You are brave and kind and true... just like your father. It has been an honor watching you grow up to turn into this remarkable female."

It was hard to keep eye contact with her mother as tears threatened to fall.

"I will not shy away from my power," Anita promised her. "I will not let this family crumble under Denoran tradition while we fight tirelessly to save it. You and Wes go and save your Micah." She dropped her hands and walked over to the wing-backed chair behind the desk. With shoulders back and a fierce determination in her gaze, she sat, and Lucy could have sworn the chair was made for her and her alone.

She was the epitome of elegance and power, and if anyone tried to challenge her, they would surely fail.

"You and I will talk more when you return," Anita said to her. "But Lucy?"

Lucy stood, waiting for her mother to speak.

"Make him regret it."

FOURTEEN

MICAH

With axe in hand, Micah stepped through the portal to return home. It felt strange being alone there, knowing he had a way to travel back and forth through the realms without anyone else needing to guide him.

Without Lucy.

It should have made him feel strong—independent. Instead, it made him feel lonely.

Returning played out exactly as he assumed it would. Brax was left pacing in front of the tree and proceeded to curse at him when he stepped onto the Lumen property.

"What the fuck was that?" Brax cried. Then she fell into a battle position, ready to fight Quillan, assuming he'd be stepping through next. Her eyes were wild as she surveyed the portal, seeing it close as the rippling bark turned to solid form once more. "Where is he?"

Micah stilled at a loss for words, staring over Brax's shoulder as she berated him about utilizing his magic and not getting captured by cats, but he could barely focus on her. While he expected Brax's volatile reaction, there was something he certainly did not expect.

In the middle of the yard, from seemingly out of nowhere, stood the one thing that could both shatter his heart and mend it completely.

Lucy.

Everything inside of him screamed for Lucy—her embrace, her touch, her scent. Why was she here? Was she hurt? His eyes darted over her perfectly curved body.

Is this a dream? Did I hit my head?

She wore a midnight blue tunic synched with a thin leather strap, black leggings, and a pair of boots. Her long brown hair fell in waves over her shoulders. She looked exactly as he remembered— utterly breathtaking.

He took a step toward her, and a hint of regret shone from her eyes.

Micah paused, remembering his new place in her life. Lucy was marrying Sloan.

She left me.

He couldn't figure out why she was there. It was likely she was just there to enter The Elderwood to get supplies to make another bow. Maybe she was taking over that part of the family business. Maybe there was something else with the business that she needed to discuss. Maybe she had a message from Sloan.

His mind was reeling. But at the root of it, it didn't matter why she was there... All that mattered was that she was.

It was really her.

Unblinking, he walked around the screeching Vytyrian warrior toward Lucy. Steeling himself for what was sure to be more heartbreak, he smiled at her.

"Lumen, what is your problem?" Brax began, but stopped as she turned.

"Hi," Lucy said sheepishly. "We need to talk to you."

"We?" Brax asked.

That's when Micah heard it: retching in the bushes.

Wes stood up and walked over, his skin pale and clammy. "Let's just say Lucy's fancy magic is not as fancy in practice." He wiped his mouth unceremoniously.

The little bit of hope he was holding on to left Micah completely. If Wes was here, then he doubted she was there to speak about where their relationship stood... but then again, Micah didn't know the answer to that, either.

What did he expect from Lucy, anyway? For her to run into his arms and apologize for leaving him high and dry with no explanation? To say sorry about telling Micah she chose him, and then changing her mind as soon as things got hard? Perhaps she was there to invite him to her fucking wedding.

Damn. Nothing she could say could fix this... Could it?

Brax just sighed in annoyance. "Well, let's go inside then, shall we? Instead of standing out here staring at one another like a bunch of moldy potatoes?"

"Potatoes?" Micah asked, looking at Brax, the random insult pulling him back to reality.

"Yes, you nitwit. They have eyes?" Brax just stared at him dully.

Wes snorted and threw his arm around Brax. "You know, I think I've missed you."

Brax recoiled, pushing his arm off of her. "Please continue to do so." Then she walked ahead of him into the house, swaying her hips a bit more prominently as she went.

Micah's gaze turned back to Lucy, and he offered her a weak smile, tipping his head toward the house to invite her in. She was there because she needed him, and that had to be enough for now.

They walked in, side by side, without saying a word to one another.

"LET ME GET THIS STRAIGHT," Wes said to Micah as they all sat in the kitchen. "The shadow beast was a male shifter. There are actual real living beings within The Elderwood, and they gave you some magical fucking axe to wield as their guardian and savior?"

"Actually, that about sums it up," Micah replied.

Brax just crunched on her salty potato chips sullenly, listening to what she had missed. "It's not fair," she mumbled. "I should have been dragged over, too."

Micah laughed at her. "You wanted to be dragged into a portal by a beast?"

"I mean, when you say it that way, Lumen, it sounds even better." She winked coyly in his direction.

Micah snorted and stole one of her chips, earning him a glare from Brax once again.

"It's good to see you two getting on so well," Wes replied, eyeing them both curiously.

Lucy hadn't spoke since she first arrived. It made Micah uneasy.

"Well, when you're stuck with someone for nearly six months, they grow on you," Brax said with a saccharine smile.

Micah didn't know what to say. It was true. They had no other choice but to figure things out together. Thankfully, Brax was the perfect person to have stayed with him.

The more Micah thought about it, he realized fate had thrown them together, and somehow, they just worked. She was his best friend. He didn't know the last time he'd had a best friend, but the thought warmed the frozen parts inside him. He looked over at Brax and let out a breathy laugh as she chomped down on more chips. He doubted he could ever tell her what she meant to him, but he meant it all the same.

No longer willing to keep the tension at bay, he finally asked the question they were tiptoeing around. "What are you doing here?" His eyes landed on Lucy this time. He needed *her* to be the one to say it— to say anything.

"There have been some... developments. All of them bad." Lucy looked at Brax in apology. "There are a few things I have to say, and I don't think you are going to like them."

"There are many things you've done that we didn't like, Baum," Brax replied with ire in her tone. "May as well spit it out and add it to the list."

Micah gave her a warning glance, imploring her to calm down.

Brax returned the look as if to say, *you can't make me.*

With a sigh, Lucy began her tale. It definitely wasn't anything Micah had expected, and with the way Brax put her beloved snack to the side, he didn't think she expected it either.

At the end of her explanation, the room was dead silent. Wes looked as though he had seen a ghost, the pallor of his skin dull in the light.

Brax, however, was seething. With her eyes narrowed on Lucy and her teeth clenched, her jaw twitched. She shifted in her chair to lean toward Lucy, her motions stiff, as though she was restraining herself from doing something brash. "You're wrong," Brax stated, pointing an accusatory finger at Lucy and refusing to believe what she shared. "Lord Sloan is not the Fae whom you describe."

"I have been wrong about a lot of things," Lucy said bleakly, sending a quick glance toward Micah. "But I am not wrong about this." She shook her head and stood her ground.

As much as Micah was thrown by it all, he believed Lucy. He wasn't sure if it was his loyalty to her, his hatred for Sloan, or for the circumstances of the situation, but he believed her. .

"I'm going for a walk," Brax declared, storming out of the room. The slam of the door on her way out seemed to echo in the silence.

Wes let out a long huff of breath. "Well, that was awkward."

Lucy and Micah just looked at him in disbelief.

"Yeah, all of this is a bit awkward," Micah replied with a touch of irritability.

Wes put his hands up in surrender and walked out of the kitchen toward the sitting room, plopping down on the couch with his hands over his face.

"Can we go for a walk?" Lucy asked Micah gently. "I've missed this place, and I.... I was hoping we could talk?"

Micah knew this was coming. May as well go outside in case his magic wanted to lash out like it did every other time he was upset. At least he wouldn't break any furniture. "Sure."

His footsteps always happened to lead him to the tree house near the back of the cabin, but today he wanted to avoid it. It had been his safe haven whenever he needed to think things through, and if Lucy had something else bad to share with him, he wasn't sure if he'd ever be able to sit there among the trees in peace again.

Their path took them the long way around the property, but Micah knew it well by now. It was the same path he took on his daily runs; it was flat and serene. However, he had a feeling this conversation would be anything but calm.

"So," Micah said awkwardly. "Seems like trouble in paradise."

Lucy looked at him with furrowed brows. "There was never any romance there, Micah. You know that."

"Do I?" He challenged. "Because it seems to me that *we* were ready to move things forward with what we were, and instead you took the coward's way out."

"The *coward's* way?" Lucy stopped dead in her tracks, her voice rising in disbelief. "I agreed to an *arrangement* because it would benefit the cause of finding my father's murderer. I agreed to a *deal* because I knew it would keep you out of harm's way."

"Harm's way? You think I'm doing fine right now, Lucy?" His voice rose with every word.

"You're in one piece, aren't you?"

"No!" His jaw dropped at the realization that she had no idea what she had done to him. "No, I'm not in one piece, Lu. I'm fucking broken."

Micah took a step away from her, and then a step toward her, reaching out to touch her face and then thinking better of it, dropping his hand. He didn't know how to deal with this—how to talk to her and be there with her when she wasn't his.

"All I wanted was you. Us," he said in a near whisper. "But you chose him."

"I didn't choose him for love, I chose him for revenge."

"How'd that turn out for you?" Micah scoffed. He turned away from her, not wanting to talk anymore.

There was nothing that could fix this.

"I never stopped thinking about you," she admitted softly. "It was only you, but I couldn't be selfish. Finding Jasper would keep you safe. Sloan promised me he'd find him. I had to go. I had to keep you safe."

"Seems like promises aren't really your thing then, huh?" Micah replied, venom dripping from every word. He stormed away from her, no longer able to keep his resentment in.

"Please!" Lucy cried, stopping Micah in his tracks. "I want us to be better again. Can we please just..." but the words died on her lips.

Turning, Micah finished them for her. "Just forget this happened? Just pick up where we left off?" He took steps toward her, his temper fading in the shadow of her sorrow. "I wish we could, but we both know we can't."

Lucy's tears streamed down her face, her hazel eyes glinting in the afternoon sun. "I'm so sorry."

"I know, sweetheart," he said, wiping the tears from her cheeks. He wanted to hate her.

He wanted to find the reason for all of his outrage and leave it there, allowing it to grow and rot into something else entirely... but he knew he couldn't. Micah was mad, but he wasn't an idiot. He couldn't turn away from all of this.

"Unfortunately, it seems like we have bigger things to deal with right now," Micah told her. "We should probably work on that first."

Lucy nodded, turning her gaze downcast.

The gesture shattered the tiny pieces left of his broken heart. It didn't matter how angry he was, he never wanted to be the one to hurt Lucy. She could run him over with a fucking truck and he'd still be there, ready to love her.

He was a fool.

However, one way or another, their lives were twined together, entangled with The Elderwood and his alchemy. Alchemy that apparently Sloan was on the search for. Micah needed to figure out how to survive being around Lucy without letting his ruptured heart get in the way.

Micah lifted her chin with a finger, forcing her to look at him. "I'd like us to be friends again, if that's okay with you." His eyes seared into hers, looking deeply for the love that was once there, and now lost. "I don't think I can keep up with the whiplash that's been forced between us. But we were always a great team," he said, with a crooked little smile. "So let's be *that* as we bring down Sloan and make him fucking pay. What do you think?"

Smiling back at him, Lucy nodded again. "I think that's a good plan."

Rubbing his thumb over her cheek, Micah let go of her chin and they continued on their silent walk around the property. He knew it wasn't the best plan, and it was only temporary, but there was no other choice.

One thing was for sure, though—together they would crush Sloan, and that would probably make him feel a little bit better.

FIFTEEN

LUCY

The walk through the wooded area of the Lumen property brought so many memories back to Lucy. Each creek held a memory of her and Abe splashing in the water and each leaf shimmering in the trees reminded her of the games they would play on the early summer mornings when she would come to visit with her father. Her heart stung at the memory of two important figures, both stolen from her by the same male.

Jasper may not have killed Abe by his hand, but he played a significant role in it nonetheless.

He's going to pay for this, Lucy seethed.

Her anger bubbled up inside of her once again, clashing with her sorrow, and threatening to drown her in self pity.

Lucy's emotions were a wreck. She was walking in a beautiful forest with the man she loved who refused to love her back, planning to kill the male she was betrothed to. She was even hiding her father's murderer in her family root cellar! All the while, she was surrounded with memories of those who had died, leaving her alone in this wasteland of a reality. The juxtaposition was laughable.

What a fucking mess.

She scoffed at the thought, causing Micah to look over at her.

"You alright?"

"I just keep thinking about how awful all of this is," she admitted. "I miss my father. I miss Abe. I keep making awful choices thinking they're good ones, and now I feel stuck."

"I get it," he said, shoving his hands in his pockets as they made the turn toward the cabin.

She still couldn't get used to how different it was with its modernized look. It wouldn't have suited Abe, but it seemed to be the right fit for Micah.

Lucy glanced over at the portal to The Elderwood, longing in her eyes.

"What I wouldn't give to go back in time," she joked. "I'd go into The Elderwood to experience the pure beauty of creation, not a care in all the realms." It used to be her safe space, a place of beauty and calm.

"I don't think it'd be as quiet as you remember" Micah said, a small laugh in his voice. "Would you like to see it again?"

Her eyes brightened instantly. "The Elderwood?"

He smiled in return. "Yeah. You've got your fancy hand thing to get us there. I'll take you to see The Elderwood at its finest."

"Do we have time?" Lucy asked, looking back at the cabin for any sign of Wes or Brax.

"We won't be long. Besides, if Sloan is on his way through the realms destroying everything, maybe you want to see a bit more of what you're fighting for."

Tentatively, he held out his hand to her, and her heart soared with relief. She smiled at him, and with his hand warming hers, they walked through the portal to The Elderwood.

LUCY SHOULD HAVE REALIZED that when she came through to the other side, it would be different—Micah had warned her of such things. However, she evidently did not understand how different, because when she saw a fawn bending down to munch on a patch of grass, she squealed in delight.

Gasping, she scared the small deer away, but she kept her eyes trained on it as it bound down the hill. As the deer crashed into the forest below, it startled a flock of birds from the trees. The birds soared through the sky above her, wings of all different sizes and colors. Her gaze followed them as they landed one by one near the small lake at the base of the mountains.

She nearly fell to her knees as she watched the wild rabbits scamper off at their arrival. Animals of all sized drank from the clear water of the lake; wild horses cantered in the sandy shore, turtles lazed on warm rocks, and large fish jumped in and out of the water.

"I can't believe this is the same place," she murmured to Micah, who stood close by her. In all the times she had visited, she had never seen this side of The Elderwood—what had caused this change?

"I know." The warmth of Micah at her back comforted her. "Let's go for a walk. There are a few people I'd like you to meet."

"People..." She could barely form the word, so astounded by the change.

Smiling, he guided her down the path to a group working around a garden.

Lucy's heart thumped nervously as they neared, a million thoughts running through her head.

Have they always seen me here? Do they even want me here?

The group stopped what they were doing as Micah approached, and in unison, they bowed their heads in deep reverence, placing a fist over their chest.

Lucy could only blink, stunned by the act.

"It's wonderful to see everyone again," Micah said, bending, trying to get them to look him in the eye. "This is my... friend," Micah stated awkwardly, "Lucy Baum."

They all stood upright, and Lucy gave a quick wave as she laughed nervously.

"Some of you may know her from her visits here in the past."

They looked at her and nodded, showing no sign of emotion, their amber eyes trained on her.

"She is here to help keep you safe," Micah said seriously, earning their attention. "Lucy Baum is a fierce warrior and fights for the good of your people. She has always admired your home, and I wanted her to see the people who took such great care of the realm; those who allowed her to enter."

"I am eternally grateful," Lucy said, nodding her appreciation.

As one, they lifted their staffs and pounded them on the ground.

Lucy jumped back a little in surprise, but Micah just chuckled.

"I think it's a good sign," he joked under his breath. "Come on, let's keep walking."

They waved their goodbyes to the group and walked toward a grove of bright orange and magenta trees.

"Friend?" Lucy asked him, her eyes dragging over his muscular form. "Is that what we are?"

"I'd like us to be," he replied, his eyes meeting hers. "Friendship is important in any kind of relationship. Right?" He slid his hand through his hair.

Lucy smiled at the familiarity of the move, his stress getting the best of him. "Yes. I haven't had a real friend since Abe." She sighed. "He would have loved this place so much, I just know it."

Micah's lips quirked up in a smile. "I agree."

Lucy paused under the shade of a bright pink tree and sat beneath it on a bed of grass, her eyes burning at the idea of Abe here —happy and healthy. She pushed the thought away and tried to relax, laying back on the soft earth. Tucking her hands under her head, she looked into the canopy above her, watching as the sunlight trickled in between the leaves. Small birds and bugs fluttered this way and that. To think, she once thought she was alone here when the entire realm was booming with life.

She patted the ground next to her. "Come on down," she joked.

Micah laid down beside her, assuming the same position. Their elbows touched slightly, and a burst of electricity shot through her. She missed his touch. She missed his lips; his broad shoulders as they embraced her.

Sighing, she let go of those desires. There was nothing to be done about that now. Not here. Not after all this time.

The birds chirped above them in the trees. She watched as they bounced from branch to branch.

"It feels nice here," Micah whispered, breaking their silence.

"It does. I wish I could just lie here and allow things to slow down." She propped herself up on one elbow, looking over to Micah. "But we can't slow down. Not yet. We need to stop Sloan."

Micah sat up and put his elbows on his knees. "I know." He glanced over at her, as though he was about to say something, but then closed his mouth and turned the other way.

"What is it?" Lucy asked.

"It's just... I think that's our problem," he began to explain, still having a hard time looking at her. "We rush into everything, don't we?" He offered her a half smile, filled with more sadness than joy. "We rushed into a fake friendship built on lies. We rushed into me becoming the guardian. We rushed into thinking we could build a life together while we were realms apart. And now this. We keep rushing all over without ever slowing down. Without allowing ourselves to feel."

His words seemed to pierce straight into her.

Did she force him into these roles he didn't want?

Lucy sat up straight, tucking her feet underneath herself, as anxiety pooled in the pit of her stomach. "Do you regret becoming the guardian?"

"No," he said quickly, reaching out his hands to her and stopping short.

Each time he did that, Lucy's heart stung.

"I'm glad I became the guardian. I know how important it is, and I'm happy to have taken the role. It's just... everything has been so quick. I just wish we could get to a normal pace and do things the right way."

"What do you mean?" Lucy asked, confused by what he meant.

"Never mind. Come on," he said, changing the topic and brushing the dirt off his legs as he stood. "We have a lot to take care of if we want to stop that asshole."

She didn't want to leave, not after being here for such a short period of time, but she knew he was right. Nodding, Lucy followed him back to the portal so they could pick up where they left off. They needed to make a plan to accomplish the one thing that mattered above all others: take down Sloan.

"THESE ARE the rings that Jasper left behind," Micah said, holding out four rings shimmering with jewels encased in gold. He placed them down on the living room table as they sat on the leather couch. "At first I just kept them in a drawer, afraid to look at them, but the more I thought about it, I realized I could probably use them."

"Why did you want to use them?" Lucy asked, taken aback. These were the same rings Jasper used to hurt The Elderwood... to kill her father.

"Because my magic isn't coming to me the way that it comes to you," he said, a bit of bite in his words. "I was able to use the book to figure out how to imbue some of my magic into them. It's not much, but every bit helps. Then I learned I could also garner some of my strength from the gems themselves. Come on." He grabbed a ring and led her out the front door to the forest's edge.

It was hard for Lucy to watch the man she cared for wear the rings. It made her nauseous if she was being honest. But she knew Micah must have been on to something, because when he slipped the ring on, it glowed a bright red, his magic responding immediately.

He levitated a branch over his head, his outstretched arm guiding it back and forth through the air. "With the ring the magic comes quicker, and I don't tire myself as easily."

Lucy watched as the red mist that gripped the branch flickered in and out, almost like lightning. The branch trembled in the air and Micah's magic failed him.

He jumped out of the way as the branch came crashing down. "Unfortunately, I'm still not great at making the magic work for me. Some days are better than others, but..."

"Most days are shit?" Wes offered.

Lucy nearly jumped.

Where did he come from?

"Yeah," Micah admitted, running his hand over his face. "Brax has been trying to help me, and I think we are getting there. It's just taking time." He looked around in confusion. "Speaking of Brax, you still haven't seen her?"

"You mean when you two just left me at the cabin and went frolicking in The Elderwood without me?" He threw his hands up in the air. "What is it with people just forgetting I'm around?"

Lucy scrunched up her face in guilt. "Sorry."

"Well, the answer is no, I haven't seen her." He paused, then cocked his head toward the trees, his brow furrowed.

Lucy heard it, too.

Something was rushing toward them from the forest.

Wes and Lucy shifted in front of Micah, readying themselves for a fight. Lucy pulled her magic to the surface, the green orbs curling around her arms. Wes's silvery magic was like a whip in his hand as he whispered the words to summon the magical weapon.

From the trees, out crashed Brax, looking windblown and grief stricken.

With a deep breath, Lucy stood up from her defensive position, but she didn't let her guard down. While Brax was not an unwelcome guest, something was still not right. Lucy's green magic slithered around her, ready to strike.

"What's wrong?" Micah called, running to her.

"I'm sorry," Brax said weakly. She placed her hands on her knees to catch her breath.

"What happened?" Wes demanded.

Brax stood and shook her head in hesitation. "I didn't believe you," she said, looking at Lucy. "I couldn't believe you. Lord Sloan has been nothing but good to me—to *all* who work for him…" her voice trailed off.

"What happened?" Lucy asked again, fear filling her.

"I contacted him."

Lucy's heart dropped.

"I used a bespelled mirror to reach him, to see if what you said was true. I asked him what else he wanted me to do here, or if there were other places I could be of use. Maybe he could use me in other missions, maybe in the South."

"No," Lucy's mouth popped open. "You may as well have just come out and shouted that we were here."

Fuck.

"I know. I'm sorry," Brax said, her eyes set with a quiet determination. "He asked me about you—about you both," she said, looking at Lucy and Micah. "I tried to tell him something to steer him astray, but I think he knew I was lying. He knew. He knew!" She roared. "I don't know how."

"What else did he say?" Lucy demanded, grabbing Brax by her shoulders.

The next words out of her mouth would navigate their course of action, and she had to know what he knew.

Brax's eyes were full of fire as she spoke. "He's on his way to Central Denora… He's making his way to the Baum estate."

My family.

Lucy's eyes widened in alarm, and she looked at Micah.

He gave her a swift nod, knowing she had to leave.

She grabbed Wes's hand and squeezed, holding him tight.

"Ah, not again," Wes moaned.

Within the span of a blink, they disappeared from Joterra and landed in her room back in Denora.

CHAPTER

SIXTEEN

LUCY

Lucy quickly threw a privacy charm over Wes as he landed, sputtering and keeled over in her bedchambers. She didn't have time to wait for him to master himself before finding their mother. With Sloan's power to travel with just a thought, he may as well already be here.

Lucy thought back to when he transported her from the woods into his carriage, how she sat in his lap and imagined a life with him. The very memory that once gave her butterflies now appalled her.

Manipulating her magic to split the privacy charm, she left a bubble around Wes to allow him to regain his composure, and tightened one around her body as she ran to the door.

"Stay here until you're steady," she told Wes over her shoulder as she made it to the hall. "Then come find us immediately. I don't know how long it'll take Sloan to get here."

All Wes could do was throw a hand in the air as his head bobbed between his knees, trying to ease the contents of his stomach.

Lucy ran down the stairs, hoping to discover her mother alone so she could prepare her for Sloan's arrival. Magic swirled beneath her skin, her panic rising with every breath as she raced around the

594

estate. Where could she be? The gardens? Her study? Lucy sent a silent prayer up to the stars to ask for guidance and protection. It was one thing to go against Sloan on her own; it was something else entirely to have her family at risk.

Green light sprung from her hands and flew ahead of her erratically, leaving a trail of light in its wake as Lucy followed quickly behind it. She had no idea what she would walk into, but with her magic so frazzled, she could only assume it wouldn't be good. Perhaps her magic knew something Lucy did not?

Stretching her Fae senses throughout the estate as she searched for her mother, she reinforced the shields around her, hoping it would be enough.

"Oh, yes!" Anita said, her voice coming from the parlor. "They should be back soon."

Is he here already?

"I don't mind waiting for my betrothed," Sloan's voice replied, a touch of coldness seeping over the words.

Lucy ran faster, keeping her privacy charm tight to her body so he wouldn't hear her approach.

"Yes, we are all so excited about the wedding! How are your people in the North taking to the news?" Anita continued making small talk.

Lucy's stomach churned. Sloan had a special magic and could always tell when someone was lying to him. What would he do to Anita when he realized she was spouting off nothing but falsities?

She couldn't let herself find out.

Racing to the doorway, she paused, fixing her hair and blouse from her quick travel, and dropped the magical shield.

"Mother," Lucy said, cheeks flushed from her rush. "I'm glad to see you. Wes wanted to discuss some business with you upstairs."

Anita's eyes flared in relief at the sight of Lucy. "No problem, dear. Lord Sloan and I were just talking about the wedding and how you had some wedding day jitters." Anita smiled at Lord Sloan and feigned an airy laugh.

Laurent Sloan just stood there and smiled at Lucy, a smile so cold and dark she wondered how he could force the gesture at all. He nodded in agreement with Anita, his sneer made proof he believed none of what she said.

"I told him you just needed some motherly bonding to prepare you for the big day." Anita said it with such ease, Lucy was shocked at the seamlessness of her lie.

"Mother, get upstairs, please." There was no more time to pretend, and the command came out more forcefully than she intended. Lucy kept eye contact with Sloan, refusing to let her mother get involved in whatever was about to unfold. She couldn't risk her getting hurt.

Losing one parent at the hands of this monster was enough.

Sloan put a hand on Anita's arm to stop her, his fingers curling around her wrist.

At Anita's gasp, Lucy's eyes tinged with green. "Don't touch my mother," Lucy barked as she felt the wave of magic spring to her fingers. All pretenses of civility were far gone.

Lord Sloan just smiled, placing his very best mask of kindness on his face, slowly tightening his grip on Anita. "No need to worry, my beloved. We—"

But Lucy cut him off. "I know why you're here. And you and I both know everything my mother said was a lie. Now let her go before you fucking regret it."

Sloan must have read the steel in her eyes, because for the briefest second, he released Anita, allowing Lucy to rush forward with her Fae speed and pull her out of his reach.

"There's really no reason for this, Lucella," Sloan said each word carefully. Though something just under the surface of those ice-blue eyes was filled with allure. "It's time to come home now. We can discuss your... unusual departure in private."

"This is my home, and I have nothing to say to you." She took a step back, trying to get Anita to the hallway exit.

"On the contrary," Sloan replied, his lip curling. "I think we'd have much to discuss for our future."

"You want to hurt people," Lucy said, the sheer disgust in her voice evident. "I can't let you do this."

"Now, now. Let us not get ahead of ourselves," he said dismissively. "Return to me, and all will be forgiven." He held out his hand to her, expecting her to take it.

"You're fucking delusional if you think I would ever stand by you," Lucy hissed through clenched teeth.

"You will!" Lord Sloan snarled, his face twisting with violence as his temper flared.

Lucy took another step back, holding her mother behind her and away from his outburst.

I need to get her out of here. Where's Wes? Panic bubbled in her chest.

He straightened his shoulders, trying to regain his composure. "You and I will do this, and you will be by my side every step of the way. You and that *magic* of yours." He took an angered step forward as though he would grab her, but then thought better of it.

His words turned Lucy's wrath molten. The magic in her body swarmed through her hands and curled around her and Anita in a protective stance, prepared to oppose Laurent Sloan. "Never."

The one word was enough to tip Sloan into a fury. "You will be mine," he roared as he cast a blue rope of ice toward her.

Anita stepped in with a graceful swish of her hand, shifting Lucy to the side and sending Sloan's magical ice ropes into the wall with a deafening crash.

Anita spun her arms in front of her in a circular motion, creating a vortex of ribbons in a shimmering gold. Then, she pushed forward with two open palms, blasting a powerful force of magic directly into Sloan. He barreled across the room and hit the wall with a clatter.

"Don't you ever attempt to hurt my daughter again," she said with a deadly edge to her voice.

Lord Sloan pushed himself up from the ground and narrowed his eyes in hatred at the two Baum females. His usually perfect hair was in disarray, tangled strands of white covering his revenge-filled eyes. With a grunt, he threw his hand out, sending shards of ice careening toward them. Lucy's arms dashed up to protect her mother and herself, but Anita got there first, turning his icy magic into nothing but gentle flakes of snow.

Laurent Sloan screamed as he sent burst after burst of magic toward them. Each time, Anita's unyielding power met his, dismantling his spells, blow for blow. Sloan released a deranged bellow as he pressed on.

Lucy watched in stunned silence as Anita's powerful magic bested the great Lord of the North, not one hair out of place. Lucy cast a shield to keep her and her mother safe from any more icy attacks. Wonder and pride raced through her at her mother's remarkable skill.

"You are going to regret this," he hissed at Lucy, capturing her attention. "You are supposed to be by my side as we make Denora better. We are meant to be together! But instead you want to do… what, exactly? Thwart my plans so you can play house with some weak little mortal?" He scoffed, then spat at the floor. "I will get my hands on his alchemy and your magic. You are *mine*!"

Anita's arms shot in the air, and glass from the windows crashed to the floor around them. Vines came pouring in from the outside garden, slithering in front of Anita and Lucy like snakes. Anita's fierce gaze remained on Sloan as she controlled her magic, her fingers curling into tight fists. Swooping toward Sloan, the vines tried to bind him, but he cast blades of ice, cutting them down.

Lucy dug her heels into the ground, strengthening her shields, her body humming with power.

"I can't hold him," Anita said, her voice trembling as she attempted to continue the attack. "But we can block him, don't let down your shield!" Steadily, the vines retreated from Sloan and instead began to weave together in front of them.

"You can hide now," he shouted over the din, "but you *will* come crawling back to me! What we have is real! You belong with me!"

Sloan threw darts of ice at the wall, but Anita's magic wove the vines into an impenetrable blockade. Channeling more power into the shield, Lucy focused all of her anger on keeping Sloan away from her mother. A gust of wind lifted her into the air, a green haze tinting the shield she formed. With her hair flying wildly, her magic raised her higher and higher until she could see above the wall of vines, Sloan still screaming through the chaos.

Anita's magic grew tenfold, matching his rage. "If you'd like to die today, I invite you to stay where you are." Her words promised violence and Lucy couldn't have loved her mother more in that moment. Anita continued to build her magic until the vines were a towering wall of protection. Then she slammed her hand on the vines, causing a dark, gray wall of swirling magic to build.

The magic vibrated loudly, unlike anything she'd ever experienced before. With gusts of smoke, the magic billowed around the vines. As each second passed, the wall of misty magic seemed more solid than smoke, slowly blocking Sloan into a corner and cutting him from Anita's view. But from her height, Lucy could see the wall rippling, turning into something else entirely. The vines melted together, forming a solid gray wall.

"This is just the beginning," Sloan said with darkening promise, and before Lucy could even blink, he disappeared. She waited, looking for his reappearance, but it never came. Taking a deep breath, Lucy floated back down to the floor.

Anita stood at the ready, breathing heavily, her hands pressing against that shadowy magic that stood tall and strong in the face of their enemy. Her eyes were scrunched together and her brow was furrowed in concentration as she worked tirelessly to keep this blockade before them, keeping her daughter safe.

Lucy gently placed a hand on her mother's shoulder, and Anita startled—the only proof she was nervous at all.

"It's okay, Mother. He's gone... for now," Lucy whispered, calming her.

Sighing, her shoulders slumped, and she released the giant wall of magic she had built to protect her daughter. In an instant, it turned back into smoke and began to dissipate.

"What was that?" Lucy asked, marveling at the enormity of the magical wall her mother had produced. The solid form changed back into vines and they fell to a heap on the floor.

"When I felt as though there was a chance that Sloan could break through my wall of vines, I called on your father's magic. I wasn't expecting it to, but... it appeared as stone, transforming my vines into something unyielding."

Lucy's dark shadows swirled with recognition.

"An immovable force field," Lucy said, warmth coursing through her.

"Leave it to Corvus to be stubborn as a rock in both life and death," Anita said dryly.

Lucy looked at her mother incredulously and burst into a fit of laughter.

"If he was one thing, he was consistent." She chuckled along with her. Then Anita looked over at her daughter, a serious expression appearing on her face. "Seems like we have a lot to talk about... Follow me."

CHAPTER
SEVENTEEN
ANITA

The halls were quiet as they walked side by side from the foyer to the gardens. Anita always felt most like herself when she was outside, and today was just the same. She needed the comfort of her garden if she were to have this conversation with Lucy.

"What happened while you were away?" Anita asked Lucy softly, worried her questioning would scare her daughter away like it usually did.

"We saw Micah and Brax," Lucy began. "We warned them about what was to come." Her voice trailed off, as if she was unsure of what to say next. "I know you don't approve, but I just needed to make sure he was safe."

Anita stopped on the stone walkway to the back gardens, reaching out for Lucy's arm to face her. "What do you mean you know I don't approve?" She furrowed her brow, but Lucy just stared at her, unfazed.

"I'm well aware you don't want me paired with a mortal," Lucy said, pulling away from her mother and continuing her walk down the path.

Anita kept her pace with Lucy, contemplating how to share what she knew. "From my understanding, he is no longer mortal. Is he not?"

Lucy whipped her head to look at her mother. "What do you know?"

Anita rolled her eyes but offered a soft smile. "Do you really think I don't know what goes on around here?"

Lucy said nothing, which was typical for their conversations.

With a deep sigh, Anita continued through the gardens, making their way to the east side of the large maze of foliage. She kept her hands clasped in front of her as she always did, and the sway of her large skirt shifted in the breeze. Long moments passed until she finally arrived at the section with the butterfly bushes—her favorite. The memory made her smile.

"Do you know why I love this place so much?" Anita asked Lucy, changing the subject. "The butterflies come here to lay their eggs and start the next cycle of their lives." She ran her hands through the leaves of the soft green bushes. "They eat the leaves of the plants to give nutrition to their bodies, lay their eggs in the safety of this little garden, then the caterpillars come out in beautiful shades of greens and blues and pinks, only for them to once again wrap themselves in their silk, hiding away from the rest of creation."

Lucy said nothing, watching Anita with questions clear upon her face. She also looked as though she was ready to walk away, like she usually did when it came to the two of them. But Anita couldn't let her do that today. There was too much that needed to be said.

"They stay that way in their little silk wrapping for days, did you know that?" Anita continued, walking through the garden and smelling the beautiful violet flowers that were planted in orna-mental pots. "Inside, they turn to goo. No more caterpillar. Not yet a butterfly. They become something else completely—something in between. And when they emerge?" A smile lit her face as she focused on the memory.

"Why are you giving me a lesson on insects?" Lucy asked from the other side of the square in her usual sassy tone Anita had come to love. It often reminded her how powerful Lucy was—something she could never forget.

"Your father and I used to sit right there on that bench for hours, watching the butterflies." Anita pointed to the wood and stone seating just behind Lucy.

"You're telling me Father sat around and watched bugs with you?" Lucy said in disbelief, her cocked eyebrow slightly hidden by her voluminous, unruly curls. "He must have hated it."

"It was *his* idea," Anita countered with a fiery challenge in her eye. "There was something about the in-between that always made him take pause. It took a lot to slow that male down, but for some reason, the butterflies did..." Anita drifted off, deep into remembrance. "Once, we were picnicking right here, drinking wine and snacking on cheese and bread until late in the day." She grinned, happy to share this memory with someone for the very first time. "We let time get away from us, and found ourselves sitting in the dark under the stars." A giggle escaped her lips, and she put a hand up to her mouth to soften the sound.

Lucy looked on with curiosity in her gaze, a faint, begrudging smile playing on her lips at her mother's story.

"We didn't think butterflies came out of their silk wrappings so late at night; but there was one. Just once. I don't think I've ever seen anything like it, and your father said the same. The butterfly was bright purple; so bright it nearly glowed in the dark. Have you ever seen such a thing?"

Lucy shook her head slightly, but Anita continued on, wrapped in the memory.

"Your father took his magic," she said, lifting her hand to act out what Corvus did. "And he blew on the tips of his fingers ever so gently, allowing the smallest bits of light to pepper the sky above us, like a shimmering mist that floated through the air." She threw her hand in the air, the way she remembered Corvus had, wishing she could repeat the same beautiful magic he once created.

It was quiet for a moment. Anita tried to reel in the wave of sadness that was threatening to crash over her. She needed to speak to Lucy about him. She needed to stop shying away from the memories that stung because they healed her as much as they hurt.

"Like this?" Lucy whispered, then she lifted her hand high in the air. With a wave of her fingers, tiny orbs of light floated all around them.

Anita's broken heart soared. "Very much like that." She smiled through watery eyes, looking at the daughter she was beyond proud of. "You know what happened next?"

Lucy shook her head again.

"The butterfly floated around us for the next few hours, just shimmering its violet light around the beautiful glittering sky your father created for us. He..." She took a deep breath, calming her shaky words. "He told me the gods must have sent him that violet butterfly, and I believed him." Anita walked closer to Lucy and held her hand. "That same month, we found out we were pregnant with you. And when you were born, we knew you'd be the most amazing thing to ever happen to us."

Lucy's smile faltered as she bowed her head, no longer able to look at her mother.

"You have other children." Lucy's words were a mumble. "You cannot truly think I believe that a butterfly made you change your entire way of thinking simply because I was born."

"You're right—we have many children, and all of them change us in different ways. Hugh and Gregory taught us to be patient and loving parents. Wes and Tristan taught us how to be strong, how to guide each of you and mold you. Henry and Simon taught us to bring a little fun back into our lives. And you, Lucella..."

How do I tell her that she changed my world?

"Do you know what your name means? They are two Fae words for *light* and *warrior*."

Tilting her head, Lucy looked back up to her mother with tears filling her eyes.

"I did not give birth to you for you to fall to the whims of society.

I gave you life so you can fight for the things you want. To build the life you want for yourself. Lucy, you were that in-between... We knew you'd be more than a female Fae in the Denoran courts. We knew you'd be more than just our daughter. You'd become *more*."

"You can't honestly say that," Lucy said, tears full of hurt and pain slipping down her cheeks. "You were so quick to throw me into my endless schooling with my tutors, never listening that I did not want to go. Father would never let me join the family business, saying I was simply a female who would never be able to be worthy of such a position. And then, when I upset everyone, I was married off to the first Lord who had enough money and space to handle my temper. Don't tell me you paved the way for me to be who I am today —you've stifled me!" Her words came clipped and full of emotion.

Anita knew this conversation was coming. She had been dreading it for the last hundred years, if she was being honest with herself.

"Lucy, whose idea was it to teach you how to make a bow?" Anita asked quietly, never taking her eyes off Lucy. "Who encouraged Wes to take you with him to Joterra?"

Lucy stared at her, surprised by the turn of questions. "Well, I... When I..." But she never finished her sentence.

"I told your father you were ready to learn the trade because you were a natural, it was evident from the first time you picked up a bow. I saw you getting restless and I told Wes to take you, to show you the ropes. I knew you needed the adventure. You needed more than what Denora has to offer."

Anita watched as Lucy's eyes widened at the admission.

Keep going, Anita, she told herself. *Help her see the beauty and strength that lives within her.*

"And darling, of course everyone hates their classes. Do you think I was overjoyed to sit around and learn how to do needlework when I could very simply create beauty with a flourish of my hand?"

Anita turned and paced before Lucy, the nerves within her body getting the best of her. She had always hoped Lucy would put it together herself one day. Anita never wanted to take ownership of anything that helped mold Lucy—she was her mother, she always did the best she could. Even if Lucy didn't see it.

She turned once again to look at Lucy, who was standing there, dumbstruck.

"This marriage to Laurent Sloan was supported by me because I knew you would be your own person, no matter what. No male can change you, Lucella Baum. You are a force to be reckoned with, and I'm sorry I didn't see how badly you wanted out of the arrangement to begin with. You've always been... opinionated, but this time I should have listened. I thought with time you'd see we weren't against you at all."

Slumping into the bench behind her, Lucy's face went slack. "I don't understand... I've been so upset with you... with Father... and this whole time—what? This whole time I've been screaming from the tops of my lungs that this wasn't what I wanted and now, now when everything is too fucking late, I find out that it was all for nothing?"

"What was all for nothing?"

"Being so mad at Father!" Lucy yelled. "I've run from him, put so much distance between us that it was never able to be mended. I ruined everything and now he's... he's dead. He's dead because of me!" The words crashed through the garden like a rushing torrent.

Anita hurried to Lucy, holding her by her shoulders and forcing her to look her in the eye. "It was *never* your fault for your father's end. That responsibility lies solely with the cretin holed up in the cellar waiting for his judgment." Her eyes burned with pain.

Looking up at her mother, Lucy's face crumbled. "If I had just listened, this never would have happened."

"We raised you to follow your heart, Lucy. We—"

"I didn't do that either!" Lucy sobbed, cutting her mother off. "I'm heartbroken. I chose Laurent over Micah all because of a fucking vendetta and now I'm left with nothing! Nothing but anger and pain." The sobs wracked through her body and Anita held her through it all.

"You are strong, Lucella Baum," Anita told her, fiercely determined to get her daughter to listen. "There is so much riding on the next few days as we navigate this new reality Lord Sloan wishes to force upon us, but it is our destiny to stop him. I feel it in my bones." She felt the presence of her husband deep within her, encouraging her on. Tugging Lucy's chin up to look at her, their hazel eyes mirrored one another. "You will overcome this. Your life has not ended, and if my instincts are correct, you and Micah Lumen will have time to work this all out."

Lucy nodded through the tears, wiping them away with the back of her hand. "I don't know how we are going to get through this."

"Together," Wes said, coming out from behind one of the larger bushes. "We will get through this together."

Anita startled. She didn't hear him approach—perhaps she was too distracted by their conversation.

"Dry your eyes, my love," Anita told Lucy. "There is time to figure this all out. We will put one foot in front of the other and we won't give up. Do you understand me?"

Lucy took a deep breath and looked at Anita, her eyes shining a pale green.

"Lucy, are you okay?" Wes asked her. "Your eyes are glowing again. That only happens when you get lost in your magic."

Anita smiled, pulling Lucy's chin up to look her in those beautiful eyes more closely. "You will glow. You will get lost in your magic. And you will take down anyone who has ever doubted you. You are Lucella Baum, and you were born to become something more."

Lucy nodded at her, with an unshakable resolve settling in her gaze.

"I will go to the King," Wes stated. "I'll try to convince him to stop Sloan before it's too late. Perhaps we can intervene before he's even begun."

Anita nodded her agreement, proud to see Wes finding his

footing in his new position. She knew he had more inside of him than he had ever dreamed, but it would take time for him to find it... and she would do whatever it took to make sure he had the time to do so.

"I need to go to the South," Lucy said, turning to Wes. "I must see our brothers and make sure they are safe. I'll figure out what's happening there and report back. Then, hopefully the king will do something to step in and stop this madness."

Wes gave her a determined nod, and Anita just watched in adoration at the beautiful souls she had raised. They were good, noble, and honorable Fae.

Corvus would be so proud of them all.

EIGHTEEN

MICAH

With another swing of his axe, the blade came rushing down toward the tree trunk, expertly heaving it into two pieces. The same maneuver as always, but now with his gift from The Elderwood. The sunstone in the hilt of the handle glowed with otherworldly radiance, and in the light, Micah thought it looked exactly like his own magic.

"How do you feel?" Brax asked him for the tenth time.

"I'm fine," he replied. "Stop asking after every damn swing."

Micah was still frustrated with Brax for contacting Sloan, and as much as he was trying to get past it, the action felt like a betrayal. The second she contacted him, it put Lucy in danger. In that moment, Brax was careless, but she was his best friend. She'd never do something to hurt him—not intentionally.

Stretching his shoulders, he cracked his neck to calm himself down and recenter. It had been two days since Lucy had to run home, and the tension of not knowing if she was alright coiled around him like a snake. He wouldn't be able to take a deep breath again until he knew she was okay. He prayed she got there in time before anything bad happened. There was nothing else he could do except hope it went well and wait, impatiently, to hear from her.

That was his life lately. Rushing from one bad thing to the next—a time bomb just ticking away like a big fucking joke.

"I ask after every swing, you caved in cantaloupe, because I need to know when your magic wanes." Brax jumped down from where she was standing on the tree stumps and walked over to him. "So far you've swung thirty-seven times, and the magic has sliced through the wood like it was carving warm butter. That is not your strength alone—that is your magic."

Micah turned to look at her, his face clouded with doubt.

It couldn't have been thirty-seven times. I'm not tired at all.

"Hmm, strange, isn't it?" Brax said with a grin curving up her lips. "You're powerful and are using your magic without weakening in the slightest."

"It must be the gemstone," Micah said, looking at the red tinted jewel. He wondered how something so small could have such a powerful effect.

"That is my thinking as well," Brax replied.

"Then why did my magic drain when I used the rings from Jasper?" Micah asked. "It's all alchemy, isn't it?"

"Pfft," Brax sounded. "Just as there are varying powers of magic, there are varying elements to strengthen your alchemy or weaken it."

"And now you're the expert on alchemy magic?" Micah said blandly.

"No," she replied sweetly. "I'm simply smarter than you. Which isn't saying much."

Micah rolled his eyes and swung the axe again. He cleaved another piece of wood, this time focusing on his magic. Tuning in on each swing, he tried to sense it. The problem was, he didn't know what he was looking for.

He never quite found the well of power inside of him, but he also didn't feel tired at all. Instead, he felt refreshed. Re-energized.

"I think Jasper never mastered alchemy," she said as she watched him line up for another strike. "There must be some gemstones that are more apt to taking and holding power for your alchemy than others. His rings would wear thin after as much as two uses."

"So either he sucked at alchemy, or he picked the wrong stones?" Micah asked, swinging again.

That makes forty.

"Perhaps both," Brax said matter-of-factly. "He's an imbecile."

"This magic *does* feel different," he admitted at last. He wanted to stay mad at Brax, but that wasn't fair. He had more than his fair share of shitty situations, and Brax always helped him through it. She had proven over and over that she was a loyal friend. Sometimes friends just fuck up. Casting the remaining annoyance away, he looked at her. "I just wish I understood it better."

"Your alchemy powers the gem, which activates the magic within the axe. It is a weapon specially made for you to wield without tiring." Her eyes shimmered with interest. "It is a wonder to behold." Her head snapped to Micah again, and her voice turned stern. "You better learn to use it correctly."

"Yeah, yeah," he waved her off. "I'm working on it."

"Try using the axe for something *other* than chopping wood," Brax suggested. "This is a ridiculous amount of logs to store for no reason."

Looking around at the piles and piles of wood around them, Micah replied, "Good point."

"Go over there, where we won't be crushed by an avalanche of logs, and try to harness your magic to do things you've done before. Call over an item. Or perhaps try to raise the stones as weapons as you once did in front of Wes?"

Micah walked over to the open area and recalled the day she had mentioned. Lucy had been there with him, and together they had pulled the metals from the ground, turning them to gold. It was the day he learned she was more than Fae.

Or maybe not Fae at all.

That part he still didn't understand.

With his axe in both hands, he squeezed the handle tight and looked at the stones on the ground at his feet. He aimed all of his intent at them, ordering them to raise up and form a large boulder.

But nothing happened.

He looked at Brax and shrugged his shoulders.

"Try again, you wrinkled prune."

"That insult doesn't make sense. Prunes are already wrinkly."

Brax just stared pointedly at him, directing him back to his task.

With a roll of his eyes, he focused back on the rocks. He saw them just sitting there and had no idea how he'd get them to move.

Closing his eyes, he tried to picture it all in his head. The stones lifting one by one, the pieces grouping together to form a large ball, just like the one that he aimed at Wes. He remembered how tired he was that day, and he prayed that this time when he made the magic work, he would have any energy left over to continue practicing.

To his shock, when he opened his eyes to perform the magic, the massive boulder was already there in front of him, hovering in the air.

"Trying to throw another boulder at me, Lumen? I thought we were past that," Wes said from the edge of the forest.

Instantly, Micah dropped the rock pile and it landed with a loud thud.

"Where did you come from? I didn't even hear you come up." Micah looked around, hoping he had brought someone with him.

"Yes, explain Baum." Brax's eyes were wild with caution. "How did I not sense you before your arrival? Have you learned to travel the way your sister does?"

"Thankfully, no," he blanched. "I hate that form of travel. Give me my own two feet any day."

"Then how?" Brax grated, her eyes narrowing with suspicion.

"It isn't nefarious, calm down. My father blessed me with the gift of light," Wes said with a mischievous smile, producing a ball of gleaming light in the palm of his hand. "But my father was full of secrets, and this light does more than brighten spaces."

He tossed the ball into the air before him, and the small light crashed into his chest, encompassing Wes and making him glow. For all of one second, he was illuminated by the strange magic before it faded away, leaving Wes looking exactly the same as before.

"What does it do?" Brax asked curiously.

Wes jumped up and down, clapped his hands, and stomped his feet. Not one sound was heard. It was as though he wasn't there at all.

Waving his hand over his body, he dismissed the spell so he could explain. "It allows for lightness on my feet as well. It has proven to be useful to sneak up on people unsuspectingly."

"Why are you trying to sneak up on us?" Brax asked accusingly.

"Relax. That was just practice," he said with a sigh. His usual charm seemed muted, like he couldn't find the energy to be himself.

A cool shiver went through Micah's body at the thought of Wes needing to use that magic to sneak around.

"Practice for what?" Micah asked.

With a weary glance, Wes explained. "Lord Sloan's visit was less than pleasant."

"Is Lucy okay?" Micah asked, panic rising in his chest.

"Yes, she's fine," he clipped.

"Why are you here, then?" Brax asked, trying to get to the point.

"From the sound of it, Sloan's plans are already unfolding in the South, and I've come to ask you to ally with us against him if he rises in Central Denora." The somber expression in his eyes filled Micah with dread.

They are already expecting the worst.

"You know we are on your side, but what can we do?" Micah asked. "I'm stuck here, remember?"

"Yes, but Brax has many allies who just so happen to be undefeated warriors." Wes lifted a brow at Brax, imploring her to consider.

"You want my people to fight against Lord Sloan?" Brax asked, incredulous.

"Most definitely," Wes said, thrown by the question. "We must stop him by any means."

"There has to be a misunderstanding here. He would never hurt others for power." Brax took a step away from them, clearly choosing sides.

Micah shook his head, crestfallen. "I know he's done a lot for you, but you really don't think there's any truth to what they've been telling us?"

"No. I don't." Brax crossed her arms, staring daggers at them.

"Listen, you called Sloan and gave away Lucy's position," Micah countered. "And you felt awful about that, didn't you?"

Micah couldn't understand why she would feel so bad about betraying them just days ago, yet she still believed that he wasn't exactly how Lucy had described.

"I am sorry for betraying your trust before by calling Lord Sloan. However, he has a right to be upset that his bride-to-be was here with her ex-lover." Each word out of her mouth had more bite than the last.

"That isn't fair and you know it," Micah said softly.

"Well, I—" Brax began, but Wes cut her off.

"He came to my house and tried to take Lucy," Wes snapped. "He cast battle magic upon my mother in our own home. You cannot tell me that unhinged Fae is anything beyond a power hungry psychopath."

"He did what?" Micah snarled.

"Sloan put his hands on my mother and attempted to bind Lucy with his ice ropes and whisk her away back to the North." The anger in the air was palpable and Wes's eyes were anything but calm.

"Is she okay?" Micah asked, barely able to restrain himself.

If Sloan hurt one piece of hair from her perfect head, I'll take my axe and scalp the mother fucker.

"Thankfully, yes," Wes said, looking at Micah now. "She and my mother didn't let him get away with a stunt like that." His gaze narrowed and flicked to Brax. "But clearly Brax would have been willing to."

"Of course I don't want anyone to get hurt!" Brax shouted. "Maybe it was an accident? Maybe he just lost his temper because Lucella Baum is an infuriating Fae."

Her eyes darted to the left, then the right, but never landed on Micah. He knew Brax was avoiding looking into the eyes of her friend and admitting she was worried about something beyond her control.

"What ties you to him so deeply that you cannot see him for who he is?" Wes asked her.

But Micah knew.

Micah knew that Laurent Sloan was her ticket back to her family. Brax relied on him to earn the money she needed to retire and spend the rest of her days with her family—her sisters. Any threat to that plan was not acceptable.

But could she really just ignore the flashing signs before her? Could she not see him for the monster he was? Or did she see it and choose to ignore it, because that was what would benefit her?

"He's marching on the South, Brax," Micah said with measured strength in his voice. "He plans to take over and become Denora's next king."

"Maybe Denora needs a new king," she spat back.

An exasperated sigh left Wes, and as he opened his mouth to counter her argument, but Micah simply held up his hand, stopping him.

"I want to show you something, Brax," he said, the calm tenor in his voice still present.

I hope this fucking works, he said to himself.

Taking a few steps back, Micah held onto his axe with two hands. Gripping it by the handle, he lifted it high into the air and squeezed his eyes shut tight. Slowly, he swung it in a wide circle in front of him, skimming the ground and soaring above his head. Feeling the magic coming to his fingertips, he began to swing faster and faster.

Then, as the axe got to the top once more, he paused, and opened his eyes. Just as he had hoped, the magic was there before him, a large wall of glowing red magic.

"What is this?" Brax asked him, anger still there, but fading.

"My magic," he said softly, the words gentle as though he was afraid he'd scare her away. "Can you see it?" His words were shaky as he tried to hold the magic in place.

"See what?" Brax asked, looking at him, her weight shifting from foot to foot.

"Come closer," Micah told her. "Stand next to me." Sweat trickled down his neck, pooling on his back.

Taking slow strides to him, she glanced between Micah and Wes, unsure of what Micah wanted. Then, as she stood there with Micah, his magic did exactly what he had hoped.

"It's our reflection," she stated, looking at the glimmering magic. The red wall shimmered in and out with silver, creating a mirror.

"Yes," Micah said, as though it explained everything. "It's us. It's you and me in my magic." He looked at her reflection, speaking to her—his best friend. "You were the one who taught me how to use my magic. You showed me how to rein it, how to nurture it, and how to understand it. Without you, this would not have been possible." He said the next words slowly and with the utmost sincerity. "Without you, there would be no me."

"That's nonsense," she scoffed, trying to walk away.

Micah reached out to stop her, still holding the axe in the air with one hand. "Wait. I mean it, look—look closely."

He couldn't have her walk away just yet. He was lucky his magic worked for him the first time, there were no promises he'd find a way to make it work again.

She paused, giving a warning glare to Micah, but when her gaze found the wall of magic, her eyes widened, and she gasped in surprise.

There in the reflection, it was not just Micah and Brax as they stood. Instead, there was a set of moving images... Memories of them together.

Sparring in the shade of the trees.

Fighting over the bag of potato chips.

Laughing side by side as they chopped wood.

Smiling shoulder to shoulder under the stars.

"It's us." Brax's voice caught and she tried to clear it. "How?" Her glossy eyes looked to Micah's as he dropped the axe and the reflective magic disappeared.

Taking deep, heaving breaths, he rested his hands on his knees; the magic taking more out of him than he thought it would. "I channeled all of my power into reminding myself, reminding *you*." Standing up straight, he looked her in the eye, refusing to let her walk away and choose the wrong side without him knowing how important she was to him. "You're my best friend, Brax, and I can't do this without you."

"It... It doesn't make him what Lucy says he is," she whispered, yet something in her tone told Micah that her conviction was failing. Doubt crept through her words.

"Believe it or don't," Wes said crossly. "It will not change the course of our future. And for your sake, and mine, I hope you figure that out."

CHAPTER

NINETEEN

BRAX

Brax's bedroom in the Lumen cabin was simple: a soft bed with rich earthy colors, a large brown leather chair near the window, and a simple wooden dresser near the door. The room was otherwise empty of her belongings since she didn't take many personal items with her on assignment. She always kept with her a few changes of clothes, her weapons, a picture of her family, a looking glass for communications, and a gift from Laurent Sloan.

"Where is it?" She cursed under her breath as she tore through the drawers of her dresser.

I know I left it here at home. Did I put it in the...

The simple phrase stopped her, catching her off guard, unable to finish her thought.

Home.

She called the Lumen cabin her home.

But that was what it had become... hadn't it? A place she yearned for at the end of each long day; a place to rest her head at night and feel safe.

Somewhere she belonged.

She dropped into the leather chair in front of the window and

618

gazed out, chewing on her lip. It had been years since she truly felt as though she belonged somewhere. There were the years at home as she grew up in Vytyr, but since she had gone out on missions, Vytyr felt more and more like a memory of days long past. Not her future.

Brax couldn't stop thinking about what Micah had shown her—their friendship on display before them within his unique magic. He showed her everything they had been through: the laughter, the anger, the moments of peace. Their connection was something that people wished for all their lives—a true friendship.

It was worth fighting for, wasn't it?

She gulped down air, the weight of her decision before her making it hard to breathe.

Even Wes had been right, though she'd never admit it in a million years. She could be 20,000 years old and still refuse to ever concede to that shriveled up fig. Whatever she felt about the situation was irrelevant; all that mattered was the truth. She needed to figure out what was really happening one way or another—so she would, with the help of Lord Sloan himself.

Shooting to her feet, she grabbed the leather satchel off the edge of her bed. Reaching her hand down to the very bottom, she found what she was looking for with a sigh of relief.

Lord Sloan had given her two complete doses of traveling powder, for emergency use only. When he first gave it to her, so many years ago, he told her it could be used to get her anywhere she needed to travel. The enchantment was written on a tiny piece of parchment and the bespelled powder was in two separate vials in a small drawstring bag. One dose to get her to her destination, and another to bring her back.

She never thought she'd use it—that was, until today. She desperately needed to find answers to the questions that plagued her mind. Micah was busy with learning how to wield his axe, and she knew she could leave without his marshmallow brain noticing. He'd probably understand if she had explained, but for whatever reason, each time she tried to voice her emotions, the words wouldn't come.

Brax couldn't come to terms with the betrayal of the male she revered more than any other.

What *was* Lord Sloan truly planning? It couldn't be what the Baums assumed, nor what Micah interpreted it to be. What was the real truth?

She couldn't ask him outright. The last conversation they had through the looking glass did not turn out the way she had expected, and she didn't want anyone else to get hurt. Besides, going behind Micah's back to speak to Lord Sloan had unexpected repercussions, and she couldn't imagine dishonoring their friendship again.

Her heart raced at her plan, but her mind was set, because more than anything, she had to choose a side. She needed to know if the accusations around Lord Sloan hurting others were true.

They simply couldn't be.

Laurent Sloan was a mighty and fair lord, with enough power that he need not hunger for any others. Baum had to be wrong about him. There had to be a misunderstanding that she could set straight.

There was no other option.

She tucked one vial of traveling powder deep in her pocket and palmed the other. She'd make it to the South and uncover the truth, once and for all.

THE THREE TERRITORIES of Denora were recognized for different things. The North was known for its steadfast cold as the icy mountain range kept the borders protected. The North contributed to the realm by mining all the ore for weapons and tools, but otherwise the Northerners kept to themselves.

Central Denora was where the wealthy officials lived with their families, serving King Tralont and his kingdom. Most businesses were run through the center of Denora. Lavish dinners, elegant clothing, and snobby Fae seemed to be the highlight of the capital, and Brax did her best to avoid it.

The South, however, was very different, indeed. The streets were always filled with working-class Fae peddling their wares or walking down the main road to and from their jobs. The docks kept many of the Fae employed with fishing and ship maintenance, but more than anything, it was a welcoming place for the masses to gather and celebrate life.

That's what Brax loved the most about it—each day people were truly living in Southern Denora, working by day, and revelling by night.

Merchant Lane was her very favorite, for once the sun set, each of the street vendors would close up their shops and they would all meet at the local ale houses. There, they'd sing the songs of great wars past or drunkenly brawl over the last turkey leg like complete oafs.

She loved it.

However, arriving in Southern Denora with the traveling powder Lord Sloan gave her was very different this time around... and the incredible change took the breath right from her lungs.

Brax took a step forward on the cobblestone road, the sun nearly set as shadows crept from the corners of the buildings. There should have been workers and customers and people on the streets, but Merchant Lane was abandoned. The shops were left unattended— their wares still in the stalls, as though they had left suddenly, unable to properly care for the root of their livelihoods. Brax glanced around the lane to the large buildings that surrounded it... not even a flicker of a candle in the window of a home gave so much as a hint to where the Fae were.

The eerie silence pressed down upon her as she slowly tread down the vacant lane, looking into each window and door, holding her breath in hopes of finding someone, anyone, who could explain what was going on.

These Fae relied on their shops to provide for their families... they would not just leave things behind that they valued so deeply.

Where are they?

She stretched her Fae hearing as far as she could, and all she met was muffled silence. Not a stray cat searching for food in garbage. Not a child giving their mother a hard time about going to bed. Not a laugh, or a cough, or a clang of dishes from the alehouses. There was no sign of life anywhere, not even the faint whisper of voices carrying on the breeze.

Merchant Lane was empty. Not a single sound.

Quickening her pace, she rushed down the street toward Town Square. There must be answers somewhere, and the officials in town would know something.

Her heart pounded in her chest, a mix of anxiety and fear, because she knew deep down that whatever caused the lane to be abandoned could not be good. Turning the corner in a sprint, she slid to a stop and fell to the ground, her arms and legs scrambling to back up as she stared in horror at the tapestry of devastation that lay before her.

Everywhere she looked was utter chaos. Flames flicked in and out of the windows of burning homes. Fae were huddled and crying, mouths open mid-wail. Soldiers were stalking down the square, forcing magical bindings on the helpless Fae they dragged behind them.

But not one single sound or smell met her.

A ward.

A powerful, menacing ward, blocking out all sounds and smells from those beyond it.

Scurrying to the shadows of a building, she watched the scene surrounding her. Panicking Fae tried to fight against the soldiers, but were beaten down to submission. The chilling sight of their faces contorted in anguish, yet still in utter silence, made Brax's skin crawl.

She took one slow step forward, and then another, until she felt the magical barrier at her fingertips, a weak vibration that caused her hand to snap back to her chest. Looking closely, she saw the shimmer in the air, pulsing ever so gently. Placing her hand up to it, it went through seamlessly.

It allows movement between sides...

There were many different kinds of wards that could spellbind an entire area as this. Some focused solely on sounds, and apparently others on smell. There were few which could act as a physical barrier, stopping anything from traversing between sides. Brax was thankful that this one allowed her passage—she only prayed it wouldn't sound an alarm that could give away her position.

As she stepped through, desolation ravaged her ears.

"Please, someone help us!" Fae mothers cried for their children.

"Get back in line," a soldier screamed, pushing a Fae male to the ground next to a group of others.

The fire in the buildings roared behind them all, the cracks and booms of the blazing embers sounding in the distance. The smell of smoke made her cough and gag as it crashed into her.

Rushing to an overturned wagon, she hid as she worked to control her breathing. The desperate cries for help from the Fae tore at her heart.

Becoming a Vytyrian warrior was an honor given to only those of purest spirit and intention. They did not hurt the weak and defenseless, and they only represented the divisions of their choice. Brax had fought in dozens of battles in her many years of life, killing numerous Fae in the process, but each moment of bloodshed had been for the betterment of the realm. She chose the sides she fought on to ensure the safety of those who would otherwise be left unprotected.

But this? What was the reason for such violence?

Keeping low, she crept to the edge of the overturned wagon to better analyze her battle grounds. She spied a group of Fae locked in a magical barrier. A shimmering rope penned them together like livestock.

Her eyes scanned the crowd on the border of Town Square; there were at least a dozen groups detained by these magical enclosures. The clusters of Fae were separated; some had only males and the others had females and children. The smoke and ash made them all look filthy in their worn clothes—clearly the working-class Fae that made these businesses successful. As the light from the fire flickered nearby, she saw it was not only ash that covered their skin, but blood as well.

Her heart sank. Did these Fae commit any crimes? Surely a child cannot be held accountable for the actions of the mature Fae here. Why were they being included in this horrific round up? Staying close to the shadows, she continued on, looking for clarity.

Brax dodged several soldiers as she slipped from one hiding spot to another, carefully staying out of sight. Finding a row of hedges at the edge of a property, she hid, staying low to get her eyes on the center of the disorder.

In the middle of Town Square, the Fae in the holding pens looked different. They were clearly more wealthy, wearing fine fabrics adorned with jewels. That didn't seem to give them any upper hand though, as they were equally bruised and bloodied as the rest of the detained Fae.

Watching closely, she waited until the soldier watching the nearest pen turned and walked away to another group of prisoners.

Prisoners. Her stomach wound tight at the thought. *Could Laurent have done this?*

She raced to the enclosure and questioned them in a hushed whisper. "Why are you all trapped here? What are your crimes?"

An elderly Fae with long gray hair looked around nervously, ensuring the soldiers were nowhere in sight before he spoke. "We have no crimes," he said with fervor. "The soldiers came here and rounded us up during our dinners. Some of us were putting our children to bed, for goodness' sake. Now we are here in the middle of this filthy fucking street, being pushed around like cattle."

"Who is in charge? What do they want?" Brax asked, urging them to answer before anyone came back.

A younger Fae male leaned over to whisper to her. "The Lord of the North," he said.

Brax's veins turned to lead.

"They informed us that we have no choice but to follow him and his rule, otherwise they will imprison us," the young Fae male spat. "He's giving us no option at all. If we don't follow him, he will kill us."

"Those who have already defected have been collected about four blocks from here," the older Fae said. "They are to be tried first. I think he wants them to change their mind and support his side."

"His side for what?" Brax snapped.

The two male Fae glanced at one another, and then back to Brax. "War."

As if the ground rushed up to meet her, Brax's head spun. She forced herself to kneel, putting a hand on the ashen dirt to steady herself.

Lucy was right.

They were all right.

Lord Sloan is doing this.

"Get out of here," snapped the elder Fae. "They're coming!"

With a quick breath in, she ran for cover as two soldiers took count of their prisoners before them. Brax reeled as she listened from a shadowy alcove.

"What are we supposed to do with all of them?" The soldier asked his companion.

"I have no clue," the other replied, looking down at the Fae. "But we aren't bringing them all back to the North, so I assume nothing good."

The first soldier sneered, then spat on the prisoners. "About time you elitist pricks get what's coming to you. Not so strong and powerful now without all those riches, huh?"

The second soldier just laughed. "King Sloan will rectify all of this."

King Sloan.

Her blood, which was once frozen with dread, turned to molten rage.

A sneer worthy of the most vicious Vytyrian warrior graced her face as she took in the enemy around her. There were too many soldiers for her to kill and still get away, but luckily, like most flaccid zucchini, these males all underestimated females. And that was precisely where she would focus her energy—on the females and children who were forgotten and left off to the side, unwatched.

She ran to them without a second thought. There was no way in this life or the next that she would stand by as innocents were hurt due to a male on a power trip.

As she got to the group, the females bristled, unsure of what she was doing there. Silently, Brax analyzed the magic containing them. From the way it was flickering, it looked as though it was weak spell work, but she wasn't able to perform Denoran magic. She'd have to find a way around it.

"I am going to help you get out of here," Brax whispered to a group of females nearest her. "It may take me a moment because I do not know the spell, but I *will* get you out." The determination in her eyes mirrored that of the young females before her. Brax touched the magical bindings keeping the Fae within the pen. A crushing wave of despair overtook her—she had no idea how to dismantle the charm.

"There's nowhere for us to go!" hissed an older Fae female with long white hair, her face colored with fear. "Get away before you make things worse!"

"It is a tether charm," one of the younger prisoners told her, shuffling closer to the edge. She had violet, wavy hair and brown eyes so dark they reflected the flames from the buildings all around them. "I can break it, but half of these old hags are too afraid to get caught. Every time I get close, they push me away." She shot an angry look at the Fae huddled behind her. "I only stopped because I don't want to draw any more attention to us."

Brax nodded in understanding, looking at the beautiful Fae before her. Beneath the soot and grime from the chaos all around them was the strength of a warrior. Behind her, she held tight to two young Fae children. Brax understood why she stopped; keeping the children from being noticed was imperative.

"I told them we needed to get the fuck out of here before it's too late, and all they said was to wait for them to let us go home." The young female stepped closer to Brax, drawing her attention back to her. "Be frank. What are their plans for us?"

"You won't be going home today," Brax said. "I'm sorry." Her eyes glanced around the group: females of all ages, each with a bit of fire in their eyes. "But you do not need to die here at the hands of males who care nothing for you. Save yourselves and your children from these monsters."

"What do we do next, then? Huh? Do you have an answer for that?" The older Fae scowled.

"You live," Brax said in anger. "You get up, you leave here, and you live to see another day. You fight for a future for your children. Now stop your ridiculous complaining so I can find a way to release you."

"I can do it," the younger Fae told her. She rushed over and called to her magic and a beautiful pink mist gracefully swooped around the spell.

"You are very powerful," Brax said to her knowingly. "What is your name?"

"I am Ruthani," she replied as she worked to pick apart the spell like a knotted string. Thread by thread, she worked until the spell collapsed completely.

The females shared in a silent cheer and clasped hands as they rushed to leave their holding place. Brax stepped to the side to give them room to escape, pointing toward an empty lane for them to run.

"Please," Brax implored, stopping Ruthani as she followed the others. "Tell me how you did that so I can release the others."

"You mean to free us all?" Ruthani asked, suspicion in her eyes as she held the young children close to her. "Why?"

"Because I will not sit idly by and watch innocent Fae suffer because they happened to be in the wrong place at the wrong time," Brax retorted. The ice in her voice meant for Sloan crept out with each word. She couldn't believe he did this.

Ruthani nodded, casting a furtive glance behind her at the young children hiding behind her skirts, then meeting Brax's eyes once more. "If you can be quick and help me keep my siblings safe, I will help you unlock the spells on as many pens as I am able."

Brax opened her mouth to refuse, to insist she flee to safety instead, but a blood-curdling scream cut her off. Gripping Ruthani and her siblings, they ran to the row of hedges to hide. In the center of Town Square, a female was held by the back of her long braid of hair to watch as a group of four male Fae fell to their knees in pain.

"King Sloan will accept nothing other than greatness," the soldier's voice boomed across the cobblestone square. "Let this be a lesson for all."

Then, with a flick of his hand, the female screamed again as the heads of each male fell to the ground.

The Fae all around Town Square took in a collective gasp at the blatant violence, but Ruthani made not a single sound, only moving to cover the eyes of her two young siblings.

"You will not deny my help," she whispered to Brax. "We will get these innocent Fae out."

Brax looked over at Ruthani, and took in the grim line of her mouth and the mettle in her eyes that refused to back down. She had no other choice than to agree, knowing she needed the help to get this done quickly.

"Then when we are done, Sloan is next," Ruthani said, staring into Brax's eyes with the spirit of a Vytyrian.

Brax could only nod, the promise of his demise more than enough to fuel them on.

CHAPTER

TWENTY

LUCY

Running through the blazing streets of Southern Denora was not what Lucy expected when she arrived, but she had little choice in the matter. She traveled directly to the Baum Bowyer office to speak to her brothers, but instead of finding Hugh and Gregory, she was met with an abandoned building in the midst of a nightmare.

Smoke towered high in the sky and the screams of Fae carried in the distance. Buildings were on fire and the streets were empty, save for a few Fae soldiers clad in navy blue uniforms which blended with the quickly darkening sky. Upon each shoulder was a silver mountain.

The uniforms of the North.

Lucy froze.

Sloan is here.

A scream pierced through the air and Lucy's emerald magic coursed through her body, ready to be used. There was no time to hesitate. Lucy shook off her nerves and focused on that scream, letting it propel her into action.

If there are Fae in trouble, I must help.

629

Staying tucked into the shadowy corners with the help of her father's gift, she followed the sounds of screaming toward Town Square. Along the way, she crossed paths with more soldiers. Lucy was able to keep out of their sight, but each terrified step toward the cacophony made her heart race in her chest.

She couldn't force herself to accept that this horrific landscape was the Southern Territory. What was once a joyous and bustling town had been razed to the ground; everywhere she looked were upturned wagons, homes on fire, and businesses left abandoned. The notion that her brothers were here somewhere in this chaotic madness of fire, ash, and ruin was unbearable.

Sprinting from one street to the other, she followed the commotion, only to be shocked once again when she ran headfirst into none other than Brax.

Pulling her shadows away from her, Lucy revealed herself and was met with an equally surprised expression from the Vytyrian warrior.

With her quick reflexes, Brax held an arm out to stop the Fae next to her—a beautiful female with purple hair, holding the hands of two children.

"What are you doing here?" Lucy asked her breathlessly.

Is she secretly supporting Sloan? Did she bring Micah here?

"I... I didn't know," Brax said, shaking her head slightly. Her mouth hung open, still in shock, Lucy assumed. "I came here to be sure. I needed to know the truth. I would have never..."

But Brax didn't need to say anything. Lucy understood completely. She, too, had been completely brainwashed by Sloan's *good intentions.* He was a manipulative liar, and apparently quite good at it.

"I'm sorry I didn't believe you," Brax said, her lips pursing with anger as her eyes welled with an emotion seeped in devastation. However, not one tear fell from the warrior's eyes; her hardened exterior locked in place.

Lucy just nodded. There was nothing else to say, was there? Not about the past.

Now it was time to make things right.

"We are freeing the females and children," Brax said, gesturing to the female beside her, catching on to Lucy's line of thinking in the presence of her silence.

Lucy glanced at the small children at their side. "Take them to my mother," Lucy said pointedly. "She will have the means to care for them and keep them safe."

Brax nodded.

"We need to save as many as possible. This is going to get ugly. Do you have a way to get them away safely?" Lucy looked around, a pit forming in her stomach at the destruction of such precious life.

"I do," Brax replied. "What are you doing here?"

"I need to find my brothers. They weren't at the offices or their homes. We need to understand what happened, and I..." The words turned to ash in her mouth.

I can't lose anyone else.

She wanted to say the words, but she couldn't.

Perhaps Brax understood, because she didn't push the matter.

"They are likely in Merchant Square along with the other nobles," the violet-haired Fae said.

"Lucy," Brax began. "Do not hesitate. Do whatever you need to do."

"When you are done, go straight to Micah," Lucy ordered. "Keep him safe. And... here." Lucy handed her the amethyst dagger she had tucked in her boot for safe keeping. "Stay out of sight and free as many as you can."

A sharp nod from Brax, and she was off with her companions to the next group of females. However, Lucy went on in a different direction.

Toward the fire.

Toward the screaming.

Right into the heart of chaos.

~

EMERALD MAGIC SPUN around Lucy's arms, preparing to defend her. Without knowing what to expect here, she was thankful for the extra protection.

In the large open area the town normally used for their bustling Merchant Square, were now six enormous wooden platforms erected in a large circle. In the center was another smaller stage, big enough for only three others. A Fae commander stood in the middle of the stage, peering over the edge to the ground below, giving orders to the soldiers standing on the street.

Lucy's eyes scanned the crowds. Each large platform held Fae of nobility or money—all of them male.

Brax was right to think the males would underestimate the females here, not worrying about them until later. She needed to buy Brax more time to get the innocent Fae out, but what of these males grouped together in these clusters? How would she get them free?

Reaching down deep into her magic, she asked it to shield her from prying eyes. She needed more than her father's shadows. If she were to be seen here with Sloan around, there was no telling how he would react.

Feeling a cool sensation rush over her, her shadows and an ancient magic covered her from head to toe, masking her from the surrounding Fae. Looking down at her hand, all she saw was shadow and mist. Knowing she was well hidden, she rushed closer to the crowd to scan for her brothers.

Where are you? Where are you? She thought to herself, using her Fae eyesight to see as far as she could, hoping to find them.

For once the stars listened, because as she inspected the second wooden platform she found her two brothers, kneeling but not shackled.

They were alive.

Relief washed through her so fiercely tears threatened to burst from her at the very sight. She hadn't realized how much she dreaded not finding them. If anything had happened to them, she wasn't sure if she'd ever come back from it.

In a blink, she appeared on the ground next to their stand. Still shrouded from view in her father's shadows, she stepped close enough to see them from below. With a whisper on the wind, she called over to her brothers.

Shoulder to shoulder, they heard her at the same moment. First, their eyes were set on the platform before them, and then their heads whipped up in unison, searching for her.

Letting her magic fade from her face, Lucy waited for them to find her.

Locking their gaze with Lucy, their eyes bulged in terror. With soot covered faces, they shook their heads in silent warning, pleading for her to go.

Lucy steeled herself for it, knowing they were only trying to keep her safe, but she'd never leave them. Ever.

She shook her head in anger, refusing to let them push her away. She was here and she could help. Surely they couldn't be so stubborn as to refuse her assistance in the midst of all of this?

Hugh tilted his head up to get her attention, then gave a pointed glance behind her to another stall of Fae. It was difficult to see with soldiers everywhere.

She looked back to Hugh, making a show of not understanding what he wanted her to see.

His eyes filled with sorrow as his shoulders slumped. He whispered the words, willing them to her ears. "Tristan."

Her mouth popped open in shock.

Tristan is here? Was he captured?

She swung her head back, searching for the bright eyes that had always been so full of humor and joy.

When she finally spotted him, she couldn't contain the gasp that left her lips. The shock rocked her entire body.

Tristan was there. The light in his eyes was dimmed by the

devastating reality around them, but it was him nonetheless... But not as a Fae prisoner. Tristan was wearing a navy blue uniform.

He was a soldier in Lord Sloan's army.

No. No, it can't be.

Her head jerked back toward Hugh and Gregory, the misery searing through them. All Gregory could do was nod.

"Save him," Hugh whispered to her once again, his magic meeting hers with a heaviness that nearly brought her to her knees.

Her eyes gleamed with tears, but she refused to cry. There was nothing she could do but continue to fight, even if it meant dragging Tristan home kicking and screaming.

She would make him see.

Nodding, she turned toward Tristan and in a blink was hidden in the shadows near him. The soldiers continued to mill about, talking quietly among one another. Some of them were clearly drunk as they took swig after swig from a dark brown jug.

Tristan's eyes, though... They weren't rejoicing. They were terrified.

Lucy's insides twisted, not knowing how to get to him safely. Her magic must have felt her worry though, because it snaked its way along the dirt and debris, crawling over to Tristan, creeping up his leg like a vine.

Lucy sent a tendril of shadow in its wake, keeping it hidden from view.

When he felt it, he jumped with a start, but at the recognition of the emerald green mist just barely visible around his ankle, his gaze popped up. He scanned the crowd, looking for the source as Lucy dropped her shadows. When his eyes finally found hers, they swam with regret.

He opened his mouth to speak, but shut it quickly. Glancing around him, he walked to her, his eyes wide with fear. His face was completely panic-stricken.

"Where?" He whispered in a daze. "Where did you come from?

Why are you here?" His eyes searched her, darting around her face and her body, likely ensuring she wasn't hurt.

"I heard about the invasion. I had to make sure our brothers were safe," Lucy said, putting her hand on her brother's arm, calming him. "Why are you here? Are you... are you with Sloan?"

The words hurt as they came out. She couldn't see any other reason for him being here, but she prayed she was wrong all the same.

His head hung down in shame. "It wasn't supposed to be like this," he said dejectedly. He tried to raise his head to look at her, but couldn't bring himself to do it. "I *am* here as his soldier,"

"What was it supposed to be like?" Lucy bit back, sounding harsher than she intended.

He took a deep breath and looked her in the eyes, shaking his head solemnly. "He told us he would create a new Denora. He spoke of equality among the classes; equality for females. He told us he wanted to make a home Denorans would be proud of, and we all agreed." He inhaled deeply, as though the words were too hard to voice. "But when we got here, it was clear there were some soldiers who knew more—knew the plans they didn't share with everyone."

He looked around at the Fae soldiers among them, and Lucy took stock as well.

"The soldiers with the large mountain and star patch on their uniforms? They are his generals," Tristan explained. "When we got here, they divided us all and sent us to gather people in Town Square. They made it sound like we'd scare them a little, make them realize the error in their views. But then, they started shackling those who rebelled with this magic I've never seen before."

"What kind of magic?" Lucy asked, trying to scan the Fae prisoners to see what he meant.

Tristan pointed to a group of Fae nobility down the street. "Their wrists are shackled with what looks like normal metal, but alongside it there are gemstones that glow." He ran a hand through his hair. "I've never seen anything like it," he admitted. "When they... when they started hurting people, I tried to help some of them. I tried to free them." His eyes looked to Lucy's in panic. "The shackles don't respond to my magic at all. Like it's something else entirely."

Alchemy, Lucy realized. *He's found a way to use it in his rebellion.*

"We must get out of here, Tristan," Lucy said firmly. "Come with me."

Tristan nodded and followed her, the relief visible on his face.

"We will tell our brothers. I will take you home and come back for them."

"Perhaps not," an icy voice drawled behind her.

A shiver swept over her skin as she took in the voice of the male she'd been wary to avoid. Spinning, she eyed him with disgust.

There stood Lord Laurent Sloan. His fine navy uniform bejeweled with blue and white gems reflecting the orange and red fire beyond. His stark white hair that so often wafted in the breeze was secured in place by a large, ornate crown he had fitted on his head. That, too, covered in glowing gemstones.

More alchemy, Lucy realized with a scowl.

"As lovely as it is to see you, my beloved Lucella," Lord Sloan said with oily affect, "you were not invited here. But I'd be happy to escort you to a more appropriate location." The threat that loomed behind those words was clear.

"I will not be going with you anywhere," Lucy snarled.

"Oh, I think I have something that will change your mind," he laughed.

Lucy grabbed onto Tristan's arm at the same time that Sloan grabbed hers. She tried to transport them out of there, to blink and return to home, but her magic did not respond.

"Don't fucking touch me," she spat, pushing his arm off of her. She took a step back, shaken by her magic failing.

Sloan laughed again and put his hand out toward her and Tristan. Tristan stepped in front of Lucy, trying to protect her from whatever it was Sloan was about to do.

A bright blue glow lit from one of Sloan's fingers, and he covered Tristan in the sapphire haze.

Realizing too late what he was doing, Lucy tried to tug Tristan out of the way, but there was no use. It was as though his body was covered in a thick shield that her magic could not touch.

She gripped his arm tightly, but the shield around him zapped her in response.

"What did you do to him? Let him go!" Lucy yelled at Sloan, but all he did was stand there with a satisfied smile on his face, grinning from ear to ear.

"Is it hard to accept I know something you do not?" Lord Sloan chided. His eyes bored into Lucy's—the glare sending spears of ice down into her gut.

"Which is what, exactly?" She took a step closer to Tristan, preparing to force her magic into whatever shield Sloan tried to wield against him so she could transport them far, far away from here.

"That my alchemy is stronger than your... *unique* magic," he whispered to her. "By the way," he said, bending closer to her, speaking directly into her ear. "I can't wait to peel you apart, layer by layer, and learn how that magic of yours works."

Lucy blanched, tilting her head away from him and grabbed Tristan by the back of the neck, ignoring the shocks of pain radiating through her from Sloan's alchemical shield.

Release him, she commanded her magic.

But nothing happened.

She stood there, blinking. Her magic had only ever failed her once before, when her heart was torn and she didn't know what to do. But this? She knew exactly what she was doing. There was not a sliver of doubt in her mind, yet her magic could not break the spell.

"Release him," she said aloud, compelling her magic to work, shouting her command into the universe.

Alas, the blue, shimmering shield remained on Tristan.

"He will be coming with me," Sloan said. He waved his hand and

Tristan walked toward him, his eyes bearing the only emotional response.

Fear.

"You can't do this!" Lucy roared, her magic forming at her fingertips, preparing to unleash on Sloan and his entire fucking army.

"I can and I will, Lucella. However," Sloan drawled, watching Lucy closely. "I'd be willing to form a trade." His disdainful laugh drained the warmth from her body.

"A trade?"

"Yes," he said simply. "But before then, here's something to remember me by."

He lifted his hand to a nearby soldier and gave a firm nod. The soldier saluted in return and turned to the group of Fae he was patrolling. Reaching into the penned area, he grabbed a male by his hair and lifted him into the air.

Lucy's breath stilled.

The soldier unsheathed his longsword and swiftly beheaded the Fae right there on the platform, his blood covering the others surrounding him.

Shrieks of terror unleashed around Town Square.

Then the soldier lifted the next Fae male and beheaded him all the same. Then another.

And another.

Lucy couldn't pull her gaze away from the horrific act. Sloan's soldiers murdered the helpless Fae in cold blood.

How? How could anyone be so cruel?

Her eyes narrowed to slits as she swiveled her head to Sloan, her magic roaring through her veins. He was watching her with a smile on his face. Summoning her magic to build, she prepared to blast Sloan away into dust.

"If you leave now, I will allow your brothers to live." Sloan's words cut through her like a knife.

Her breath faltered and her magic paused.

My brothers.

"I'll see you in a week, my beloved," he crooned.

With a hand on Tristan's shoulder, Lord Sloan and Tristan vanished from sight.

Lucy released the air trapped inside of her lungs and fell to her knees. The sound of soldiers yelling and Fae prisoners crying rose and fell from behind her.

The rumors were true... They were murdering Fae.

And Lord Laurent Sloan captured three of her brothers.

TWENTY-ONE

WES

When Wes took his position as head of the Baum Bowyers, he never imagined most of his time would consist of sitting around and worrying.

Since his father's death, patrons of the business were giving the family time to grieve. As much as that would have bothered Corvus, Wes didn't mind a bit. The family had more than enough money to carry them the next few months, perhaps the next few years, if he played his cards right. He was in no hurry to feign a hectic work schedule while there was so much else to concern himself with. However, while the rest of his family was working tirelessly, he wasn't doing much of anything.

Anita was forever bustling around the house, watching over his younger brothers and ensuring the safety charms were active. Lucy was off visiting the South to find Hugh and Gregory and bring them home safely.

And what am I doing? He mused. *I sit and stare at a fucking desk.*

There was nothing for him to do until Lucy returned with news, but the inaction was getting the best of him.

As soon as Lucy returned, they could go to the king and request his support. Wes just hoped they would get to King Tralont before he sent any of his delegates to take over the Bowyer business.

I have time. It's been days, not weeks. The king wouldn't even know production had slowed.

A sharp knock on the door pulled Wes from his spiraling thoughts, and he straightened his desk to suggest he was working.

"You may enter," he called, assuming it was his mother or their house steward, Bernard, who took excellent care of the manor.

Wide wooden doors swung open and Bernard stepped through.

"You can place the food at the coffee table, Bernard. I am not quite hungry yet." Wes's mother was sending Bernard with food roughly five times a day, in hopes he would keep his energy up. It was kind, but he wished she would let it go.

"Today is a bit different, sir," Bernard said, the aged smile lines on his face creasing. "A female is here demanding to speak with you. She has... well. Perhaps it's best you come see for yourself." He took a step back and raised his eyebrows, inviting him to follow.

With a tilt of his head, Wes stood carefully and followed Bernard to the front of the estate.

"At least we can say your mother's wards are working," Bernard chuckled lightheartedly. The quiet padding of his leather shoes echoed in the empty manor. "This stranger kept trying to take a step into the courtyard, but Madame Baum's magic held." A glimmer of pride crept from his eyes. "And for some reason, this Fae kept insulting me with names of arbitrary vegetables."

Wes took a surprised breath in and rushed to the door, seeing the Fae at the end of the cobblestone path.

"You better let me in, you rancid rutabaga!" Brax yelled from the other side of the courtyard. "We have to talk."

"What was so surprising about her arrival?" Wes asked Bernard as he quickly dissolved the wards to allow Brax to enter.

"It wasn't her so much as it was the rest of them, sir," Bernard replied.

"The rest?" Wes asked, looking over at Bernard.

Bernard only pointed to the trees beyond the path, redirecting Wes's gaze.

There, slowly leaving the tree line, was a group of at least fifty Fae, all females and children, covered in soot and ash.

Dropping his hands to his sides to stare in disbelief, Brax took it as a cue that she was safe to enter. "About time," she snarled, stepping up to the pathway. She got about a third of the way down before she turned and beckoned for the others to follow her. "Come," she said, her voice gentle. "You'll be safe here."

The softness in her words sent an unfamiliar jolt of warmth through Wes.

A female with violet hair stepped forward first, a look of determination clear upon her face. Behind her, a small group of children followed. Then more Fae joined the queue until they were all walking to the manor.

Wes walked out to meet Brax, confusion marking every inch of his face. "Who are these people, Brax? Why are you here?" His eyes danced over her skin, noting the ash and dirt covering her, but no injuries. A breath of relief left him at her safety.

She looked so different from the last time they were together. Her cropped hair was windblown and in disarray, the kohl that lined her eyes smudged and blended with the soot covering her face. But more than that, her eyes were wide… not in fear, so much as in concern.

"I went to the South," she said solemnly, her chest rising and falling with the deep breath she took as she spoke.

Wes opened his mouth to ask about his family's safety.

About Lucy. Hugh. Gregory. But no words could form. If she looked this poorly, then clearly things were not alright in the South, just as they had feared.

"I saw Lucy as I was freeing the females and children," she said to him, glancing over his shoulder as Anita walked through the doors. "She said they would be safe here with you, Madame Baum."

Wes's mother put a hand up to her face in shock at the sight before her, but quickly turned to Bernard and started giving him orders to prepare the rooms for guests.

"Absolutely," she said with a wide smile, then went to take the hands of some of the terrified Fae to welcome them into their home. "I think some warm tea and fresh bread and jam are in order, don't you?" Anita smiled at a young girl who immediately took her hand and gave her a toothy grin.

One by one, they followed Anita into the manor as Brax and Wes remained outside, ensuring no stragglers were left behind.

The female with the violet hair lingered at Brax's side as well, looking over Wes with distrust.

"Wes, this is Ruthani," Brax said, smiling gently at the stranger. "She helped me to free all the Fae here. She is a hero."

Ruthani looked to Brax with skepticism and shock. "No. I am no hero. I only helped."

"You did what I could not, and it is because of your willingness to stay that we saved those people."

Seeing these two females, covered in ash and despair, brought Wes back to the moment Lucy returned from Joterra after fighting off Jasper's goons when they set the fire.

These were Fae running from a monster and finding their way to safety. But more than that, they were warriors, rebelling against evil, and refusing to let the innocent suffer in their wake.

"Let's go inside," Brax said to Wes. "We have much to discuss."

By the time Brax finished her tale, the room was deathly silent. Anita was sitting with her hand permanently over her mouth in shock and Wes was slumped on the couch next to Brax in utter disbelief.

"*King Sloan?*" Wes repeated. "How can he get away with this?"

"He won't," Brax replied sharply. "Not if we have anything to do with it."

"What are we supposed to do?" The panic in Wes's voice crept in, and he took a swig of amartium to try to hide it.

"We gather anyone willing to fight against him," Brax said matter-of-factly.

"What about Lucy?" Anita asked quietly. "Was she able to get anyone out?"

"I'm not sure," Brax said, looking at her hands. "Ruthani and I were busy freeing those you see here, but the female clusters were much farther away from the males. They wanted to keep the males front and center. I'm not sure how much luck Lucy would have had in rescuing anyone."

"The Fae I spoke with were very guarded," Anita replied, confirming the terrifying conditions of the South. "Many are worried about their husbands and sons."

"And rightfully so," Brax replied. "It was... horrific." She shook her head in disgust.

"If we are going to go against Sloan, we will need to know more about his plans," Anita said decidedly. "Wes, bring Brax to the vermin in the cellar. See what you can get out of him."

"Vermin?" Brax asked, looking from Anita to Wes for an explanation.

"Ah, yes. We have Sloan's loyal follower in the root cellar," Wes said. "Jasper DeValey."

"You have that withered fungus *here* and you didn't tell me? What are we waiting for?" Brax jumped to her feet with a fiendish smile and strode to the door.

The right side of his lips quirked up into a smile as Wes walked behind her.

This is sure to be entertaining.

"What's so funny, Baum?" Brax asked, stopping in the hallway to let him lead the way.

"Honestly?" He paused next to her. Crossing his arms in front of his chest, he smiled and shrugged. "I can't wait to see you call him strange names and beat him up a little."

"Hmm, that's interesting, coming from you," Brax replied, smiling back and beginning to turn back down the corridor.

Reaching out, he gently took hold of her arm, slowing her to a stop.

Brax turned to look at him, questions lighting her eyes.

"You're sure you're alright?" Wes asked her quietly, carefully wiping the soot from her cheek with his thumb.

She bit her lip and leaned into his touch ever so gently, Wes almost missed it. "I will be." Her eyes burned with the intensity of that truth and the words behind it that she did not say.

Wes nodded in understanding. No one was alright, not anymore. No one would be until Sloan was stopped and the people were safe.

And they would stop Sloan by any means necessary.

Dropping his hand, he tilted his head to the right, leading her down the hallway to the cellar stairwell. Milton stood at the top of the stairs, acting as guard for Jasper's makeshift cell.

Milton gave a quick nod and let Wes and Brax down the stairs.

The heaviness of the entire situation weighed heavily on Wes, and Jasper played a major role in all of it. His mind was reeling with what could have happened to Brax in the South; with Lucy and her wellbeing. However, his smile returned when he listened as Brax called to Jasper, knowing what came next was sure to cheer him up.

"Jasperrrr," she sang. "You have visitors."

Wes's chuckle just grew stronger at the sound of Jasper's whimper, and he wondered if it was a bad thing to laugh at Jasper's demise or a good thing that he was smiling this much at all.

"What do you want from me?!" Jasper shouted between gasps of air.

Brax kicked him again, a wicked grin on her face. "Nothing yet." She spun to look at Wes. "This is making me feel a lot better."

Wes thought watching someone beat the living daylights out of someone would bother him, but it was putting him in a pretty decent mood himself.

"Good," he replied. "Though we should ask him what we came down here for. My mother is probably wondering where we are."

"Oh, fine," she sighed and rolled her eyes. After another swift kick to the gut, she placed her foot on his side and rolled him over. Crouching down, she touched his arm to spread her magic through his body. "Here. I'm not healing you completely, but I need you to stay alive long enough to be of use to us."

Jasper mumbled more insults, but they were promptly ignored.

"Listen, you curdled fish," Brax spat.

Wes tilted his head in confusion from the nonsensical insult.

"How do we stop Sloan's alchemy?" Brax balanced her arms on her knees, staying low to hear Jasper's response.

"You don't," Jasper responded with a maniacal laugh, spitting blood on the cellar floor. "First step, the South, and then he will move to the king."

"Obviously, there must be a way to combat the alchemy. Don't play dull with us," Wes scolded.

"And you think I'll tell you?" Jasper's laughter grew. "The more stones he has, the more powerful he will become. He will kill you all! He—"

Before he could finish his sentence, Brax knocked him out with a hit to the side of his head.

"We barely got anything out of him," Wes said, looking at Brax with annoyance.

"We know he's an idiot, we know Sloan has more stones, and we know Jasper doesn't have the answers." Brax gave him a pointed look.

"And how do we know this?" Wes asked her. "You didn't give him much of a chance to talk."

"First of all, he told us things we already know, as if he was so special to know about them at all," she replied. "Additionally, he says there is no way to stop the alchemy, and Jasper is a fool who thinks his own alchemy is unstoppable."

"Right," Wes said, still confused. "But that doesn't help us."

"Sure it does," Brax said, smiling brightly. "Jasper is currently in this root cellar surviving on what looks to be raw potatoes, and he has no alchemy powering him."

"That's because we didn't let him have his gems," Wes replied, still not seeing what Brax was getting at.

"Exactly," she said, bopping Wes on the nose with her finger and turning for the exit. "Without the gems, he is nothing."

"That should have been obvious," Wes murmured.

"Yes, you're right, but bloodying him sure made me feel better."

Wes couldn't help but smile as he followed her sashaying hips up the stairs.

Whatever Brax is, she sure is something.

AFTER BRAX SAID her goodbyes to Ruthani and the other Fae, and gave her thanks to Anita, Wes offered to accompany her through the Nilban Woods to the portal that would return her to Joterra.

"I am completely capable of making the walk alone, Baum," Brax replied with a distinct tinge of vexation.

"Believe me, I have more worries for myself on the return trip than you going anywhere alone," he laughed.

"Then why the suggestion of a chaperone?"

Brax and Wes walked slowly, her speed clearly proving she was not upset about his company at all. If she had wanted to, she could have sped off through the trees to the portal before Wes could ever have the chance of catching up.

"You are the first thing that has made me smile in quite some time, and maybe I'm just not ready to let that go just yet," he said quietly.

The ground was littered with damp earth and fallen branches, so each footstep they took was muted. The wind rustled through the trees; the leaves shaking ever so slightly in its dance.

Brax turned to look at him and smiled brightly. "Well, I *am* breathtaking, so your cheerful attitude is to be expected when I grace your presence." Her hair fell from behind her ear and brushed across her high cheekbone.

Wes laughed again. "You are definitely that."

Wes questioned over and over if he should push her hair back behind her ear or if she would break his hand if he attempted it. Either way, his heart raced at the thought.

"There is much for you to still smile about, Baum," she said seriously.

"There is," he agreed, "but there is also..." He paused, changing his mind. There was no point in talking about this with Brax—with anyone.

"What is it?" Brax asked, stopping them in the middle of the forest path. She placed her hand on his shoulder and forced him to face her. "You can tell me. You don't have to hide."

"I'm not hiding," he said defensively.

"You are," she countered. "There is nothing wrong with being sad—you've gone through so much in such a short period of time. It would be more strange if you were not."

"That doesn't mean I'm hiding."

"You hide because you are pretending to be something you are not. You can be broken and still be strong. You can live in the darkness and still search for the light."

The determination in her eyes forced his attention.

How could he admit he felt broken in front of this remarkable warrior?

"I'm not hiding, I'm just..." but the words never came. Because what was he?

"You're lost," she answered for him.

Wes froze at her response, his stomach sinking at the truth in them.

I am lost.

Taking a step closer to him, she placed both hands on his face and leaned closer until there was only a breath between them.

"I want to tell you something that I don't want you to forget, okay?"

All Wes could do was offer a subtle nod, the smell of her intoxicating—like a bright winter day mixed with a dark summer night.

"No one wants you to be your father."

The words struck him like a bolt of lightning. He had definitely not expected that. And more than that, she was wrong. "That isn't true. People are relying on me to do the things he was capable of doing."

"The realm needs you to be Wesley Baum and no one else." Brax inched closer, her lips nearly grazing his. "You are different from so many others, and that is why you will do wonderfully in this new position. Allow yourself to be seen for you—stop trying to be someone else. Do the things you want to do, not what others expect of you."

He closed the space between their bodies, wrapping his hands around her taut waist, feeling the strong muscles beneath his fingers. "What if I want to kiss you?"

Before he could make a move, Brax kissed him with a fervor he would have never expected.

Her lips were soft, and her tongue teased the edge of his lips. As he opened for her, desperate to kiss her with the same enthusiasm, she pulled back.

"*I* kissed you," she said with a mischievous grin. "If you wish to kiss me, then you must figure out who you are in all of this and claim it. And when that time comes, come and claim me."

Then, she shoved him away and took off running for the portal, laughing in her exit.

Wes could have chased after her. He could have used all of his Fae speed to try to catch up to her and make her stay, even if it was just to kiss her again. But he knew she was right.

He needed to figure out what in the realms he was doing and stop waiting around for something to happen.

Instead, he needed to *make* it happen, and he would.

~

WES WASTED no time at all when he returned from his walk with Brax. He went straight to Bernard and requested his assistance. The very next day, as he paced in the study, his waiting was over.

"Master Baum," Bernard said, entering the study. "Your guest has arrived."

An older Fae with a formal green military uniform followed behind him.

"Hello, Young Baum," Duke Renfro said with a polite, if not forced, smile. "You called for my presence?"

TWENTY-TWO

LUCY

Lucy crashed into the center of the study at the Baum estate, despair drowning her every thought.

"No…" Her voice was faint.

This can't be real. I have to go back.

"Lucy!" Anita's voice cried as she and Wes raced over to her, surprised by her unexpected entrance.

"He took him, he…" the words were a jumble as Lucy said them, over and over again.

Wes pulled her to her feet and set her in the chair in front of the fireplace. The sound of the fire crackling sent a shiver down her spine at the memory of the fires surrounding Southern Denora.

The South.

Where her brothers were held prisoner.

Where she lost Tristan.

Her teeth began chattering, the shock settling deep into her bones. It was almost a relief as it muffled the burning logs.

"He… he…" Lucy rambled again, trying to understand what had just happened. Coming to terms with what she allowed to happen.

"You're freezing," he said, rubbing his hands up and down her arms in an attempt to warm her. "What happened? Did you see our brothers?" The desperation in his voice tore at her heart.

With her head still bent down, she lifted her face only enough to make eye contact with Wes. Her heartache apparent as she very faintly nodded in answer.

"It was terrible," Lucy said, looking away again. "Sloan was there with his entire army... They..." She couldn't say the words. The nausea threatened to turn her stomach inside out.

"Darling, I understand that what you saw must have been terrible," Anita told her, holding her hand tightly. "Brax came with the others. She told us some, but she left to return to Micah... Please, Lucy. Your brothers. Are they alright?"

Lucy took a deep breath, then closed her eyes, finding the strength to share the danger her brothers were in.

Could her mother handle it?

"They rounded up every Fae from their homes and brought them to the Town Square. The females and children were placed into large tied off areas, and all the males were brought to the center of the square. They were separated on these enormous raised platforms."

Wes quietly pulled over a chair for their mother, then sat on the ground with Lucy. No one dared to ask a question, allowing Lucy to tell her story at her own pace.

"Brax was there. She was helping the females and children to escape. I sent them here knowing we could help." Lucy pulled a hand to her chest, rubbing at the pain buried deep within her. Her skin was still caked in soot and blood from the Fae she couldn't save.

Wes nodded, confirming they had arrived.

"The males—they were to pledge their fealty to *King* Sloan," she spat. The words were bitter on her tongue.

Anita scoffed at the name.

"If they don't agree, they..." she couldn't finish the thought.

Lord Sloan was an evil-hearted Fae who would stop at nothing to get what he wanted.

"Sloan's killing them?" Wes asked, quietly.

"Yes," she whispered.

A small gasp left Anita's lips. "So Hugh and Gregory... they were there? You saw them?" Anita asked quietly.

Lucy nodded. "I saw them. They were there... They know the danger they are in. I only hope they are willing to play Sloan's game before they get the chance to escape. Sloan told me to leave before he killed them, too."

Her hands shook at the thought.

She couldn't leave right away though, she didn't trust Sloan. Instead, she hid and watched as more and more soldiers rounded up Fae and imprisoned them. Lucy tried to create distractions for Brax to have the time she needed to get the innocent females and children out, so she toppled over tents and created small explosions on the other side of the square. Her anger drove her, and the destruction she made came easy. She wasn't sure if it would be enough, but she had to at least try.

Then she spent the rest of her time hiding in shadows, watching Hugh and Gregory shackled on the podium. Lucy spied on them for hours, trying to convince herself to leave them and come back with a plan, but it was nearly impossible. It wasn't until another soldier spotted her that she finally left, worried her magic would wane and she'd be stranded there.

Wes stood and began pacing the room. "They are smart, they will find a way out of it. Thank the stars Lisette left to the east instead of returning home with them."

Anita only watched Lucy, observing every movement she made, every glance, every facial expression. "What is it, Lucy?"

Lucy couldn't bring herself to say it.

"There's... something else. Isn't there?" Anita asked, her question heavy with emotion.

Lucy nodded, finally looking her mother in the eye. Tears rolled down her cheeks at her guilt. Her frowning lips quivered as she formed the words. "I found Tristan."

Wes stopped his pacing.

Anita held her breath.

"He was there with Sloan's troops, but he didn't know," Lucy said quickly, looking to her brother, her bottom lip quaking. "He had no idea. He didn't support any of it." She sniffed, trying to get a breath down. "We—We tried to leave. Hugh told me to take him and go, and I—I tried."

Anita covered her mouth.

Lucy choked down a sob, squeezing her hands into fists. Her fingernails broke skin as she buried them deeply into her palms. She needed to tell them.

"Sloan took him. His alchemy… I couldn't penetrate it. I couldn't stop him. He took Tristan, then he killed those Fae as a warning to me. I tried waiting. I tried finding a way to get them out, but there was nothing I could do. Nothing." Lucy wrapped her arms round herself, curling into a small ball, rocking back and forth as sobs overtook her.

Everything about this kept bringing her back to the moment she lost her father. Having to tell her mother that he was dead. That Lucy couldn't save him in time. Feeling so detached from reality as she replayed every moment in her head, trying to find the path where she could have saved him. Could have stopped Sloan.

Her breathing got faster and faster as her magic felt further and further away from her. Gasping, she couldn't get a breath down. She couldn't do this. Couldn't do this again. She couldn't lose another person she loved. She couldn't handle it.

"Lucy," Anita whispered. "It's okay." Putting her hands on her daughter's shoulders, she sat on the ground next to her, trying to pull her back to reality.

"How is it okay? He's gone. I let Sloan take him. Now all three of them are there with that monster. I've failed." Her voice was raw as she choked out the words between sobs.

"No, you didn't, honey," Anita said, taking her hands, sending small swirls of magic down her skin. Her smile was soft and sad.

But why wasn't her mother angry at her? She should be angry, she should be furious that Lucy kept putting her family in danger. That she was the one responsible for this fucking mess.

She couldn't do anything right.

"Lord Sloan is a disgrace to the Fae, and no matter what you could have done, he would have tried to hurt us," Anita said assuredly. She lifted her hands to Lucy's arms, sending a spread of calm through her golden swirling magic. As she touched Lucy's hair gently, her sense of dread receded.

"What are you doing?" Lucy said in a panic.

"You were like this after Father died, too," Wes said quietly over her shoulder. "Mother needed to calm you before you hurt yourself."

Lucy could barely remember it. She remembered waking up next to Wes, but she also remembered faint moments of her mother's sad eyes watching over her carefully, combing through her hair.

"No," Lucy said, distantly. "Please, don't put me to sleep. Please."

There wasn't time for her to fall into a spiral of darkness. She needed to prepare. She needed to fight back.

"You aren't going to sleep," Anita said, pulling her hands to Lucy's shoulders again, sitting her up straight, looking her directly in the eye. "You are stronger now than you were before. You are going to take a deep breath, we are going to get up, and we are going to make a plan to take down this son of a bitch for everything he's done."

Lucy stared wide eyed at the female in front of her, as though seeing her for the first time. She nodded vigorously.

"Good," Anita said. "Come. It's time to show our true hand."

STANDING around her father's study, Lucy tried to find an inkling of hope, but came up empty. Anita sat at the desk, pulling out a paper and quill.

"We are going to write our plan down?" Wes asked her, a heavy skepticism in his words.

"We are going to be *thorough*," Anita countered. "Sloan wants a trade, you said?"

"Yes, but what?" Lucy replied. She paced in front of the desk, biting her lip as she wondered about the safety of her brothers.

"I think he is after something valuable to him." Anita's eyes were bright as she pulled out a piece of parchment and a map from the desk drawer.

"I didn't even know that was there," Wes mumbled.

"Valuable like what?" Lucy asked.

"His alchemy is nearing the end of its power, I'm sure," Anita said, pointing to the North on the map. "You said when Jasper used the magic before, it would wear out after a few uses, correct?"

Lucy nodded, feeling foolish for not thinking of it before. "He wants to power his alchemy. He wants Jasper back."

"Possibly," Wes said, catching on. "But we can't give him up. We can't give him the source of his power against us."

"There will be no stopping him," Lucy said, a shiver coursing through her again. "We can't let him come here with Henry and Simon around."

"Yes, I've already sent word to Lord Klimek," Anita replied, writing a few notes down on the parchment, then tearing off a small piece. "They leave in the morning and will be safe in a quiet village in the east."

"What?" Wes said in shock.

"They will consider it an adventure and will be much safer away from us. Klimek has been instructed not to let us know exactly where he is, that way we do not need to lie about it. He will send a messenger bird to us as needed."

Lucy stood stunned at her mother's efficiency. It was the perfect plan to keep her youngest brothers safe.

"What about the rest of the staff?" Lucy asked.

"We will send them away," Wes responded. "They will have no idea why we are sending them away, and only a few know of Jasper in the cellar. Their honesty will keep them safe from harm."

Lucy nodded in agreement as Anita wrote another note and tore it from the parchment.

"Bernard and Milton will refuse to leave your side," Wes said thoughtfully.

"Perhaps. I will not force anyone away, but we will highly encourage it." Anita gave a short two-note whistle and a black raven came flying through the window, perching at the desk in front of her. Anita tied the piece of parchment to the bird's claw and told it to return to Klimek. Then she whistled again, and another black bird landed on the desk. She tied the second piece of paper to its claw. "Bring it to the staff quarters. Don't miss anyone."

"Mother, why are you speaking to birds as though they understand you?" Lucy asked with uncertainty.

"Because they can," Anita said, smiling. "I think it's time I tell you the rest of my secrets. They will be handy in the days to come."

Standing abruptly, Anita waved a hand in front of her, sending glittering gold magic over her body. The golden specks first touched her hair, turning it a dark color, so black it seemed to swallow the light around them. Next, the glitter landed upon her face as her nose began to elongate. With a gasp of surprise, Lucy watched as her mother shrank before them, slowly transforming.

Lucy looked over to Wes in alarm, but by the time she looked back at her mother... she was gone. Instead, in her place, was a black raven, looking at them carefully.

Backing up a step, Lucy reached out for her brother's arm. But Wes only walked forward, smiling.

"You clever Fae," he chuckled. "I should have known it was you all these years."

Lucy looked at Wes in disbelief. "What in the realms are you talking about? What happened to Mother!"

Wes didn't seem worried at all. He whistled off a familiar tune, and the bird chirped it back.

Recognition soared through her. The raven at the window after her trip to Joterra. A black bird following her in the trees, watching over her as a child as she traversed the forest. The dark wings that soared over the orchard where she and her brothers would practice their archery.

With a small pop, a puff of smoke filled the air, and Anita returned to her normal Fae body. She stood before her children, her hair color fading from its dark black back to its beautiful brown to match Lucy.

"It's been you all along?" Wes asked in awestruck disbelief. "Why didn't you just tell us?"

"Your father and I felt it was best to keep that one a secret," Anita winked.

"So you're a bird?" Lucy sputtered.

Anita only laughed. "No, dear. Do you remember when I showed you my magic's likeness for nature?"

Lucy nodded, remembering the night she came into her bedchambers and showed Lucy her powerful magic, making the bushes sprout amazing flowers in a heartbeat.

"I can also communicate with some of the smaller creatures of the wild. I seem to have a natural affinity for birds, and they agree to do my bidding."

"You have bird minions?" Lucy said blandly.

"No," Anita said, grinning through her words. "They are my friends. They help me when I need to send messages but can't be seen sending the message myself."

"So Father knew about this, too?" Wes asked.

"Yes." Anita smiled. "He liked for me to sit in his meetings, but since Denora is full of males who have an aversion to females, we agreed my appearance in my bird form was more useful. I'd sit in the sun of the window ledge and be an extra set of ears for your father. We were a great team for many years."

No wonder Mother kept offering her support to Wes; she knew more than him all this time.

The distant memory seemed to fade with a touch of sadness.

"Alright. Henry and Simon are going off into the woods, Hugh and Gregory are smart enough to play Sloan's game for now, Lisette is safe in the east, Tristan is a prisoner, there are a bunch of Fae females and children in our guest rooms, and our mother is a bird." Lucy's dejected summary made for a bad joke.

Anita's laugh was full and bright that time. "That about covers it," she said.

The three of them sat in silence for a moment, taking in the dire reality before them. There was so much to do.

"Wes, you ensure Milton and Bernard know of the plan and give them the option to stay or leave. They are part of this family, and I want to keep them safe, but we could still use a bit of help if they are willing." Anita gave the orders like she had been doing it for years; as though she wasn't just a silent figurehead.

She wasn't, Lucy realized. *She just played the role so damn well.*

Lucy stared in awe at her mother. So much pride ran through her at her mother's strength and power.

"I'll make sure Jasper's still alive down there. Then I will prepare the rest of the guards here at the estate and ensure our people are safe." Anita turned to Lucy, a smile of understanding filling her.

"I have to make sure Micah is safe," she said on a whisper.

"Yes, you do. Do what you must to keep him and The Elderwood safe."

And with her mother's blessing, she left, urging her soul to find the other part of her heart.

CHAPTER

TWENTY-THREE

MICAH

"War?" Micah asked Brax for the third time.

He couldn't wrap his mind around it... A war of powerful beings who would fight one another using magic—actual fucking *magic*. Fae lives would be obliterated...

"There hasn't been this kind of division since the Addaxe Wars—and that was centuries ago. But this..." Brax shook her head in dismay and continued pacing in front of the living room windows. "This will be a complete annihilation if someone doesn't stop him soon. He now has the North *and* the South, we cannot let him take Central Denora."

The hairs on the back of Micah's neck went taut at the reality of their situation.

So much death.

Didn't Lucy say that unexpected Fae death was more or less unheard of?

"How can they stand by and let this happen?"

"Lord Sloan's powers..." Brax shuddered, unable to continue. Placing a hand on the windowpane, she stopped her anxious walking, staring out into the world beyond the sanctuary of the cabin.

660

Micah watched as his friend retreated into herself, quiet and unsure for the first time since he'd known her. It left him unsettled.

Since Brax's return, the light in her had dimmed. Her bronze skin always shimmered with power, but now she seemed ashen and dull. It was as if everything in her was buried somehow.

Brax had seen so much in her extended lifetime, watching as nearly four thousand years of Fae history came and went. She had survived in numerous wars and had come out on top.

But this is what she feared?

This was what threatened to break her?

"If that's the case, then we are going to need reinforcements." Micah leaned back into the couch cushions, bringing his head to his hands, rubbing his brow for the oncoming headache he was certain to acquire. Where would they find people to help them?

"Yes, Lumen." Brax slowly sunk down into the chair across from him. "We need to call upon our allies."

He dropped his hand and sat up, looking at his friend who had been by his side since the beginning. She looked so torn, her elbows rested on her knees as she sat, lost deep in thought.

"It is time to call on the warriors of The Elderwood," she said confidently. "They would not appreciate their Guardian turning into mush—then who would watch over the portal?"

"The Elderwood?" Micah asked, dumbfounded. "Why would they fight in this battle?"

"Because you are their only line of defense from here," she pointed to the floor, "before the evil takes over there," pointing to the portal.

Micah followed her pointed finger out the window and to the forest beyond. As much as he wanted to argue, she was right. If anything happened to him here, who would protect them?

She stood up abruptly and walked toward the door. "Come on, you snack thief," she said, the hint of humor in her otherwise defeated eyes. "Grab your axe and let's go pay your friends a visit. I want to see this place for myself."

"And you're sure they are going to help?"

"No, I'm not," she admitted, the brightness in her eyes gone once again. "But that's why I'm coming with you. I will make them listen."

In no time at all, Micah found himself sitting at the same large oval table in the domed room with Brax on his right and Quillan on his left. Only Fergh and Rowan came to speak with him this time, the other unnamed advisor nowhere to be found.

"We apologize for the short notice, but it was imperative that we met. There are new developments with the safety of your realm, and this couldn't wait." Micah tried to explain to the two male Fae sitting before him.

"What's the problem?" Fergh asked.

"You were right," Micah said solemnly. "Your seers were correct... There is a Fae in Denora who wishes to take over all of the realm."

"Our seers are never wrong," Rowan said seriously. "We have warned you that this would happen."

"If this Fae takes over Denora, his next stop will be to me, then to you," Micah told them, trying to tame the rattle in his voice. "And, I hate to break it to you, but if he's able to level Denora, then I don't stand a chance."

"What do you mean?" Fergh asked, his otherworldly eyes troubled.

"If he plans to come here, I won't be enough to stop him."

"But you are the Guardian," Rowan said, his voice cracking with surprise.

"I am a mortal man who acquired magic less than a year ago with zero understanding of how or why it works," Micah contested. "I wish I could say I could take this guy down, but I know I can't. Not alone."

"Guardian," Quillan's deep voice rumbled. "What is it you're asking of us?"

Micah took a deep breath. By the look on Quillan's face, it was clear he knew.

"I need you to come to Denora to fight. I need help."

"We do not fight for Denora," Rowan said, almost insulted.

Fuck, this is exactly what I worried would happen.

"Please, hear me out before you make any decisions," Micah pleaded.

Both males looked to one another and then back at Micah, and nodded. Quillan kept his stoic eyes on Micah.

Sighing, Micah told them the entire situation. He explained his magical alchemy, about how Jasper tried to kill him for the power to come here. He told them all about the Baums and how Corvus had been murdered, and how Lord Sloan now wanted to take over all of Denora, not caring how many lives he must take in the process. He explained that they were already in the Southern Territories, taking over and hurting innocents.

The shift of Rowan's chair was the only hint that they were uncomfortable at all. They stayed quiet and attentive, listening to Micah's tale.

He left out the part of Lucy promising herself to Lord Sloan.

He left out the part where his heart was torn to shreds by her choice.

"What I'm saying is that without your help, Sloan will come after my alchemy next." He cringed at the admission of weakness, but he had no other choice. "If I'm not around, it won't take much for him to turn his attention here."

"How does he know about our realm?" Fergh asked in concern.

"Because Corvus Baum made a deal with him before we realized his involvement in all of this... It's why Brax is involved." Micah turned to face Brax, her body still rigid with unease. She always had her defenses so high for strangers.

Micah realized how lonely it must be to have to be on guard all the time. To have no one around to rely on. Being the one who has to look out for others and never the other way around. He put his hand on her arm, calming her. Reminding her he had her back.

"Why are we to believe she is no longer in collusion with the Fae lord?" Rowan asked, eyeing Brax suspiciously.

"I'm here, aren't I?" She said, narrowing her eyes at the two Fae males before her. "You can either stand by his side and fight, or risk a male of evil intentions knocking at your doorstep."

"There is no reason to threaten us," Fergh said with a wave of his hand and a defeated sigh. "We will provide our resources to you. Though we will need to come together in our counsel to determine who and how many will assist."

"Really?" Micah asked in relief at the same moment Brax asked, "Why?"

"Yes," Fergh said, eyes softening as he looked at Micah. "For one, our realm holds more than its Fae and its wood... Much more that is precious to all... But also because our leader taught us to never hide from the fight that matters."

"Who is your leader?" Brax asked. "Why are they not here to have this conversation?"

The third advisor came from the doorway. Micah hadn't realized that he had been standing there. "I think this is their leader," Micah said to Brax.

Her face tensed with a shimmer of knowing. As if fighting a smile, she kept her eyes on the male.

"This is my friend Brax," he told the Fae. "Brax, this is..." He looked back at the man in realization. "Actually, I don't think I ever got your name."

"It's great to see you again," Brax said with a wry smile. She shook her head gently and gave a light laugh as she stood up and embraced the stranger in a hug.

"Wait, you know him?" Micah stood, trying to understand how that could even be possible.

"Micah, you empty walnut," Brax turned, her arm slung around the male. "Meet Alderic Lumen."

"Wait a minute," Micah murmured. He couldn't seem to stop his mind from spinning. "You're Alderic? Like. *The* Alderic Lumen?"

The Fae just continued to smile at the group. He nodded as if it was not the most reality altering thing in Micah's existence.

Micah turned from the table and walked away from the group, not trusting what would come out of his mouth next.

"Where are you going?" Brax called after him.

"I need a minute!" Micah stormed out of the room and ventured through the trees to an empty courtyard behind the domed building.

The stone court had beds of flowers nestled in the shade of the forest. There were benches made of wood scattered throughout and a large fire pit in the center. It was clearly a place for large gatherings or celebrations, but Micah was glad to find it empty now. He needed a moment to deal with another bomb of information being dropped in his lap.

Why the fuck wouldn't he have told me who he was when I first met him?

He paced, running his hand through his hair. In his other hand, he kept the axe held tight in his grip. It steadied him somehow to have this weight grounding him as his thoughts spiraled.

Alderic Lumen's been here this whole time. He could have helped me with this alchemy. He could have been around to help us fight off Jasper during all his bullshit.

Micah kicked at a rock and listened as it scattered off into the trees beyond.

"I'm not the last Lumen," he said to himself in disbelief. He had felt so alone for so long, believing he was the last of his line... and now this?

"No, you're not," a deep voice replied.

Micah spun around to see Alderic standing before him, a gentleness to his face.

"Why didn't you say something before?" Micah asked, not understanding the endless secrets of the Fae.

"When it was my turn to introduce myself, you cut me off." Alderic shrugged. "I guess it didn't seem important at the time."

"Not important?" Micah scowled. "I was mortal before your magic changed me. You're my ancient fucking ancestor and I have no idea what I'm supposed to do."

"And we've been guiding you," Alderic said casually. He picked up another rock from the ground and tossed it in his hand as though he was mulling over a grocery list.

"You sent a fucking cat to bite my leg off and left me a book in a language I can't fucking read." Micah's lips pressed into a thin line, trying to hold back his temper and failing miserably.

"In our defense, we didn't know you weren't the one hurting our realm," Alderic said with ease. "But yes, I wasn't expecting our languages to change so much over the past centuries. The mortal land is very different than our Fae realm."

Micah just looked up to the cotton-candy colored sky and shook his head. "This is too much."

A snap of branches behind him made him turn, expecting the worst yet again, but it was Brax walking up to join them. "Come on, Micah," she said softly. "It can't be that bad. Besides, now we have the opportunity to ask more questions. Right?"

Since her return from the South, she had mostly stopped insulting him. He didn't know what to make of her kindness, and if he was being honest with himself, it kind of put him on edge.

Alderic's face lit up and he extended his hand to the benches, inviting them to sit. "I've always preferred to be outdoors anyway," he said with a wink. "I'd be happy to tell you anything you'd like."

"Fine," Micah replied with a punch of attitude. He turned to Alderic Lumen; his great-great-he-didn't-know-how-many-greats-great grandfather. "How does the alchemy work?"

Brax slapped him on his arm, chiding him for his attitude. "Sit up, stop acting like a child."

As much as he wanted to fight her about it, he knew she was

right. There was something innate within him that tended to push away his family. He didn't have time to act this way. What they needed more than anything else were answers and allies. Micah nodded, sat up, and looked to Alderic to continue.

"The alchemy was Sanni's most incredible discovery," Alderic said with a smile. "She was brilliant. The other mortals in her realm didn't take her intelligence seriously. They always said she had her head in the stars and needed to come back to reality." He smiled, lost deep in thought. "That's how I found her. It was late at night and she was laying in a field, completely silent. I had not figured out the time difference between Denora and Joterra yet, and as I walked through the lush landscape of the forests of Joterra back then, she was just lying there. I almost fell upon her!" He chuckled. "I remember she was so mad at me for crushing one of her gemstones with my clumsy footing. But when I convinced her I wasn't a rogue bandit and asked if she'd let me repair it with my magic, her eyes lit with fierce wonder. A bit of residual magic was trapped inside of the gem I fixed for her. It seemed to glow, even in the darkness of the night."

"You put your magic into the gemstone? That's how we get the alchemy to work?" Micah asked, trying to understand.

"Yes and no," Alderic smiled. "Sanni had no magic, so the alchemy acted within the bounds of science. Elixirs to improve health were more akin to modern medicine. Changes to rocks and minerals were chemistry. However, when magic and her alchemy united, it wove a new tapestry for magic the universe has never known."

Brax scooted forward in her seat, prepared to learn as much as possible.

Micah's head tilted as he took it all in, a question in his mind he wasn't yet ready to ask.

"Her alchemy and my magic together allowed for new magic to arise. For Sanni, my magic within the stones allowed her to cast her own spells, utilizing the alchemy in a new way. For me, using her stones amplified my powers, almost giving it a jolt of extra energy. That's why your magic is so unique." A proud smile graced his barely aged face.

"But I can't do the magic without the stones," Micah said bleakly.

"What?" Alderic had clearly not expected that reply, his smile faltering.

"When I try, my magic is next to nothing unless I have the gemstones to amplify it." Micah explained.

"No, your Lumen magic should come first, the gemstones just support you." Alderic stood and paced the small stone platform. He ran a hand through his hair and Micah noted the similarities between them.

"It's true," Brax supplied. "He was able to do some of his magic, but it has waned tremendously. Now he gets the most power from the stones."

"It's probably the fucking curse," Micah huffed under his breath to Brax. "We could have done without that one, so thanks." The bitterness in his voice was enough to make Alderic stop.

"The what?" Alderic looked at Micah, completely perplexed.

Micah stood up to come face to face with Alderic, his anger just simmering beneath the surface. "The curse," he spat. "The one you put on every Lumen descendent so that we could never leave our post."

"I don't know what you mean. What curse? Where did it come from?" His eyes were wide.

"You're the one who gave it to me," Micah snarled. "Your entire fucking family line."

"That's impossible," Alderic breathed, taking a step back. "Sanni and I put the utmost love and care into that spell. You should have received a blessing of magic, not a curse."

Brax stood slowly and put a hand on Micah to calm him. There was a look of realization in her eyes and Micah knew she had put something together that they had missed.

"When Micah went through the portal," Brax explained gently, "he was given your magic." She looked between the two Lumen males before her and a sadness painted her face. "However, before that, when he agreed to remain as guardian of The Elderwood, he and Lucy Baum completed the transference rite. Somewhere in that initial guardianship rite, there must be a mistake."

That's when it hit Micah. It wasn't the magic that caused the curse, because Abe had the same curse with no magic. It was the rite. Brax figured it out.

"The rite allows for the guardian to stay on the land and protect the portal," Brax said. "But it also ensures that the guardian can never abandon their post. If they were to ever leave, they would get very ill. With enough time away from the portal, the guardian would... die."

Alderic's face paled.

He had no idea.

"There was never meant to be a curse," Alderic said softly. His gaze jerked to Micah, his eyes wild with grief. "Surely, you must believe me. I would never wish ill upon my family—my own blood."

Micah's brows were still furrowed with anger, but he dipped his head in agreement all the same. As much as he hated the curse for killing his grandad, he believed that Alderic never intended that outcome.

Taking a quick step toward Micah, Alderic put his hand on Micah's shoulder and another across his own heart. Looking deeply into his eyes, Alderic told him, "I will do everything in my power to find a way to break this curse. I am so sorry for... for... all of it."

Micah nodded.

"How do we imbue the stones with his magic so that we can use them on the battlefield?" Brax asked.

Micah was grateful for the change of subject.

"I will tell you what I told my son," Alderic smiled. "Your magic is strengthened by alchemy, but there isn't anything special needed to imbue those stones."

"What do you mean?" Micah asked. "Jasper—another long lost Lumen—made it seem it was impossible to do without the right spell?"

"It's within you already," Alderic said. His eyes were bright in wonder. "*Everything* you need is inside of you."

"If we remove the curse, will my magic improve?" Micah asked, hopeful for an answer.

Brax smiled gently and shook her head. "I don't think so. I think the curse is tethered to the physical body and where it lies in relation to the portal. I don't think it calls to your magic at all."

"I, too, don't think it is related. But I will do everything in my power to break the curse quickly," Alderic said, his face grave. "I give you my word."

Another barrage of footsteps approaching made all three of them turn at the sound.

"Sir," Quillan said as he came around the side of the domed building. "You three are going to want to come out here. We have another visitor."

Alderic's face turned serious as he followed Quillan.

Brax and Micah could only exchange quick glances of concern as they trailed behind.

Micah's head was spinning. First, he finds out his magical ancestor is still alive. Then, he discovers his magic is supposed to be more powerful than it actually is.

What's wrong with me?

It was the one question that had been plaguing his mind this whole time. What was different about him that the magic didn't work the right way?

He could have sulked and moped over the question for hours, but what he saw before him changed his entire course of thinking.

There, in between at least four different guards, was a Fae female, full of freckles and ash and blood.

"She came through the portal and refused to tell us who she was until we told her where the Guardian was," one guard explained. "Some villagers said she was familiar, but she refused to confirm who she was or why she was here until we brought her to him."

The next words on Micah's lips were an answer to his pleas.

"Lucy Baum."

TWENTY-FOUR

LUCY

"Micah," she breathed, the tightness in her chest subsiding for the first time in hours. When she had first arrived in Joterra, there was no sign of him nor Brax anywhere, and immediately she panicked, thinking of her visit to the South and finding her brother's home empty.

Lucy had only hoped that she'd find Micah in The Elderwood. However, upon arriving, she realized she had no idea where to look, so she approached the first guard she found and demanded that he bring her to Micah; to their trusted Guardian.

"Why wouldn't you just tell them why you were here?" Brax asked, clicking her tongue in disapproval.

"Because I no longer trust blindly," Lucy said, an undercurrent of vexation lacing her tone.

Lucy was still angry at Brax for not believing her, for going behind their backs to try to prove their theory wrong. Inevitably, Brax came around to their side, but so much could have been avoided with her trust that they all thought they had from her.

Brax's eyes dropped ever so slightly at the dig, but she again raised her head to the Fae before her. "Lucy, this is Alderic Lumen."

Lucy's mouth popped open in shock.

"She is here for the same cause. Lucy Baum is a trustworthy and noble Fae." Brax nodded her approval in apology.

Alderic sighed, then turned to Micah. "I will assemble our advisors and we will discuss our next steps. Convincing our people to leave our realm may take some time." His brow furrowed with concern, but something in his posture spoke of a male with conviction.

Micah's Fae ancestor is still alive here...

"I thought Rowan and Fergh said all of you would fight?" Micah said, worry cracking through his usual solid exterior.

"Many of us will, yes." Alderic looked past them all to the realm beyond them. "But for all of us to come together to fight this evil, we will need time to prepare. Brax, I'd like you to join us for the conversations, if you don't mind."

Brax nodded and gave Micah's arm a squeeze.

"Micah, take some time with your friend. We'll summon you when our decision has been made." But before Alderic left, he leaned over and whispered something in Micah's ear. Words so quiet even Lucy's Fae hearing couldn't pick up.

For a long moment, Micah just looked at him with raised brows, clearly bemused.

Alderic clapped him on the shoulder and walked away with the slightest smile, winking at Lucy as he passed.

As the guards turned to exit, Brax followed, leaving Micah and Lucy alone in the courtyard.

Lucy had imagined she would find Micah and run into his arms. She had thought she'd wrap her hands around his neck and feel his warm embrace around her middle as it filled with butterflies at his touch.

But that was not what happened.

They stared at one another, silently taking each other in.

Micah with his axe in hand, devastation and concern in his eyes.

Lucy across from him, full of dirt and grime from her time in the

South. She didn't even give herself time to clean up before she had to come to Micah.

To the one who held her heart.

But perhaps he no longer felt the same, as he stood far on the other side of the stone path, feeling like another realm away.

He took a steady step toward her, and Lucy held her breath.

"Come on, Lu," he said softly.

The nickname was like music to her ears and lead in her gut.

"Let's get you cleaned up." He took her hand and led her away from the building, past the endless trees, never looking back or speaking to her once.

She followed, sending a prayer to all the stars in the sky that she could fix what she broke.

MICAH BROUGHT her to the water's edge of a small, familiar lake. The view was stunning. At the base of the mountain, the water trickled down from the snowy tops, creating the perfect place for animals to drink. She saw the trails of deer and other smaller creatures in the brush. Some tall grasses lay just beyond them, where animals could hide. Colorful, little rocks peppered the shore line—pinks, oranges, and yellows to blend in with the sands. Though every once in a while, there were blues and purples shimmering with beauty.

The only animals she saw now were small aquatic creatures like turtles and fish as they swam freely in the clear blue water. A small waterfall cascaded into the lake towards the side of the mountain, nearly out of view from their position in the front.

It was beautiful, and Lucy was not.

Finally looking down at herself, she saw what made all the villagers pause when she arrived. She was covered in soot and blood.

Whose blood is this? She asked herself, but she didn't know—didn't want to know.

She couldn't remember. There were so many people she had

helped in the South, and still so many lives taken. Shuddering, she forced the bile down, not willing to tarnish the breathtaking coast more than she already was.

Micah took the red bandana out of his back pocket and dipped it into the water.

The same bandana they had used for seek-and-find.

He kept it all this time?

She held her breath as he cleaned her, first wiping the dirt away from her hands and arms as he rinsed them at the water's edge.

Each movement reminded her of the first time they met... Her sitting on the edge of the closed toilet seat in Abe's old bathroom as Micah cleaned her wounds from her scuffle with the wolven.

So much had changed since then.

He immersed the red cloth into the water and brought it up to her face, gently wiping away the ash lined with trails of tears.

Everything is so wrong.

The back of her throat burned and her eyes began to water, but she couldn't cry. Not now. Not when Micah was dealing with enough of his own shit—Alderic Lumen was real and he was here. Clearly, that had to be so much for him. Lucy had to hold it together for Micah.

As if following her thoughts, Micah smiled at her. A soft smile, full of sadness. He dropped the bandana and scooted closer to her, rubbing his thumb across her cheek.

"You can let it go," Micah whispered tenderly.

Lucy refused to blink, for if she did, the tears would flow and would not stop.

"When it gets too heavy, you don't have to hold on to it all," Micah said again. "Let it go."

Even if she wanted to, she could no longer hold back the tears. They cascaded down her cheeks, mirroring the waterfall just beyond them.

A choked sob escaped her chest and her hands flew up to her face to cover her mouth as she wept, her body curling into itself.

She felt broken inside, like the tears were crashing through her and ripping her to shreds. Tearing her into pieces that could never be put back together again.

Micah embraced her as she cried, pulling her closer and holding her tightly, like it was the only thing keeping her whole. And maybe it was.

"It's okay," he murmured in her ear. "I'm here. You're okay. It's okay."

"It's not okay," she sobbed. "Nothing is okay, everything is wrong. It's wrong!"

"Shh, slow down, slow down," he whispered, trying to calm her. "What happened?"

His eyes were like windows into her soul, seeing her own sorrows reflected in his perfect brown eyes.

"My brothers," she said, taking a deep breath to calm her racing pulse. "Sloan has them. Hugh and Gregory are captured in the South, and Tristan..." Her voice broke on her last brother's name. "He took Tristan and we need to get him back." Another choked sob escaped from her lips. "He said he'd return him to us for a trade."

"You don't believe him, do you?" Micah asked, tension lining his entire body. "He'll cross you the first chance he gets."

"That's the problem," Lucy said, her voice barely above a whisper. "I know I shouldn't give in. He wants Jasper. He wants his source of alchemy back... If we give him Jasper, then he has access to more magic that could kill thousands. But without Jasper, then his target is *you*." Lucy could barely get a breath down at the thought. "That was the whole point of all of this." Her voice cracked through her tears. "I went with Sloan to keep you safe..."

She couldn't bear to face Micah. She squeezed her eyes shut tight and curled into herself again, feeling the warmth of Micah's body. Reminding her she was here with him, and that he was safe. That through all of this, she needed him to be safe.

But Tristan...

With her head on Micah's strong chest, she listened to the steady thump, thump, thump of his heart. His kind, loving, full heart.

The heart she broke.

"I don't know what to do," she whispered. "If we give him Jasper, then more people get hurt. If we don't, then we don't get Tristan back, and you become his next target."

"I can take care of myself," Micah reassured her, forcing her to open her eyes and look at him again. "But you're right. There's no easy answer here, but I know you'll figure it out." He squeezed her tight.

She sat curled in his lap and his fingers delicately stroked her arm. He leaned down to nuzzle her hair and kissed her brow so gently Lucy thought she would crumble.

They sat there in silence for a while, taking in a gifted moment of calm in a reality that appeared to never slow down.

"You're here for reinforcements?" Lucy asked, putting together what she heard from Alderic earlier.

"Trying," he responded.

"And... Alderic?" Lucy asked. "He's here?"

"Mmmhmm," he replied, clearly not interested in talking about it.

She let it drop, not wanting to pry. Micah had always had a hard time sharing those emotions, and she was not in the position to demand anything from him.

Not now.

Not anymore.

She had ruined that part of their relationship when she chose Sloan.

The realization made her nauseous. Lucy used to think of the Lord of the North and see his regal stature and his handsome features. Now when she thought of him, the image of his maniacal face as he killed those innocent Fae burned in her mind.

She shook the thought away, refusing to let such evil and hatred fill her mind in such a beautiful place.

"When I was younger, and I'd come here with Wes, I used to camp out at this waterfall," she told Micah, forcing her mind to think of something else.

Anything else.

"I never saw traces of animals. It was always just me—alone. I'd find little colored rocks on this shoreline, and I'd toss them in and make a wish."

"What did you wish for?" Micah asked, his voice deep and warm.

"I wished for a life full of adventure," she told him. "And love. Real love." She bit her lip, reining in the tears, happy to be facing away from him. "Now I have too much adventure, and I lost the only love I've ever had."

TWENTY-FIVE

MICAH

With each declaration from Lucy's mouth, Micah's heart ached more and more. She had told him the last time they were together that she had picked Sloan in order to save him. It had infuriated him—the idea that she thought she was doing him a fucking favor by leaving him behind.

But with her curled in his lap, baring her soul to him about her love, all he wanted to do was kiss her. He wanted to hold her freckled cheeks in his hands and pull her pouty lips to his and make her forget all the pain that she felt.

It would take one kiss. Just one perfect kiss for him to fall right into the same patterns from before; make him fall deep and hard for her, and never let her go.

But he couldn't.

He couldn't risk falling apart again. Not right before they dove head first into battle against Sloan. A battle that needed them all thinking clearly if they wanted to succeed.

Micah was tired of people coming into his life just to leave again. He was tired of hurting.

But then he remembered what Alderic had whispered in his ear, and he sighed.

"Come with me. I want to show you something," Micah said to her, helping her to stand.

Lucy sniffed, her eyes puffy from crying, but otherwise mostly clean. She dipped her head and followed, slipping her hand into his.

His heart jolted with the feel of her. The rightness of her.

He pulled her along up the side of the mountain, bringing her toward the first ledge of the waterfall.

Just as he had expected, the view was magnificent. They weren't so high that it was dangerous, but high enough that they could see the water below them and groves of trees in the distance. The landscape of The Elderwood never ceased to amaze him, and from the look on Lucy's face, he knew she felt the same way.

He pulled out of her hand, feeling her reluctance to let go. He didn't want to, but he needed both hands for this. Placing his axe down, he bent over and untied his boots, throwing them to the side, away from the ledge.

Lucy's face twisted in confusion.

He pulled off his socks, then shifted out of his heavy pants, standing before her in just his shirt and boxers.

Before, the movements would have made his arousal apparent, but he had no intention of seducing Lucy right now.

"Take off your boots," he told her, smiling slightly.

She raised her eyebrow to him, but nodded and did so, throwing them with Micah's.

He reached out for her, and she stepped close to him. Once Lucy grabbed his hand, the electricity between them heightened again.

"Alderic told me something today, and I think I understand what it means." He gripped her hand tightly and took a step toward the edge of the mountain. "He said, when you're at the edge of your hope, and you aren't sure what else to do.... We don't back up and hide from it all. We jump, feet first, and have faith that what molds us today stays with us forever."

With a twinkle in his eye and a tug on her hand, he jumped with her into the water.

Lucy screamed on the way down, but not in fear. No. It was joyful laughter that he hadn't heard from her in far too long.

Splashing into the refreshing body of water was completely different than he had expected. It wasn't cold at all, but a perfect temperature. It seemed to have a natural buoyancy that pulled them to the top on its own. As they swam around the surface, Lucy's gaze met his. Her eyes were so bright, full of love and wonder.

"Just jump, huh?" She asked him with a smile. They were still near the waterfall, and the spray of the crashing water landed on her face like glitter. Lucy was completely clean now thanks to their swim. A trail of dark brown curls floated behind her.

The curve of her lips as she smiled at him was his complete undoing.

Fuck it.

He wrapped his long arm around her waist and pulled her to him, capturing her mouth with his and tasting her once again.

A breathy gasp left her as their lips and tongues collided, reacquainting themselves once again. She tasted like roses and honey and he could not get enough of her.

They kicked their feet under the water as their arms wrapped around one another in a desperate rush to get closer. Almost as if a wave pushed them, they floated under the waterfall. The crashing water above them broke their kiss as they looked around at where they landed—a small alcove behind the waterfall, just out of sight.

Micah kept his hand wrapped around Lucy's waist as he pulled her further into their hidden space, his length hardening with every lingering thought of Lucy in his hands.

Far back in the little alcove, small ledges jutted out at different intervals. His feet felt the tip of one and he was able to stand on it and stay above water. He lifted Lucy onto another one a few feet in front of him, plopping her down in a seated position before him, their faces level.

"I love you," she told him, her fingers trailing his face. The touch sent bolts of need through him.

Micah stared into her gorgeous hazel eyes, knowing in his heart how he felt but being too scared to admit it.

What if she hurt him again?

What if she finds someone else to spend the rest of her days with?

He took a deep breath.

Just jump.

"I never stopped loving you," he told her. Gently pushing his fingers into her hair, he caressed her face with his thumbs. "I'll always love you."

This time, their lips met slowly, savoring each word they announced. Lucy ran her tongue over Micah's lower lip, and he opened his mouth to her. Lucy's moan had him pulling her closer, her chest pressing against him.

"I want to feel you, all of you," she breathed in between her kisses.

A small echo over the watery alcove repeated her words in his ears.

She tugged at the bottom of his shirt and he complied, pulling it over his head and throwing it to the back of the alcove and out of the water.

Lucy's tunic floated around her midsection, lifting just enough for his hands to find her bare stomach. His fingers trailed her skin, exploring the silky smoothness of her body, wishing he could see all of her.

Reading the desire in his eyes, she smiled as she removed her top. Micah held his breath as he looked at her, sitting before him in just her lacy undergarment and a pair of thin leggings.

Taking it as an invitation, he wasted no time burying his face in her neck. As she panted with arousal, he never stopped kissing her, worshiping her. His hands traveled to her breasts, squeezing them as she moaned breathlessly. As his kisses traveled lower, he pulled her lace down and captured her breast in his mouth, flicking her pink bud with his tongue.

"Micah," she cried out, pulling him closer. Begging for more.

He scrambled for her leggings, trying to pull them down and failing in the buoyancy of the water.

Lucy put two hands behind her back and removed her lacy garment, uncovering the most perfect breasts Micah had ever seen, but before he could bury his face between those perfect curves, she jumped down to the ledge he was standing on.

Swinging her arms around his neck, she pressed her bare chest to his and kissed him. Again, it was slow, and he moved with her as she turned them so he had his back to the ledge. She pulled his boxers down just to his thighs and palmed what was hidden there, sending a shudder of pleasure straight through Micah.

"Sit," she told him between kisses, and Micah obeyed, feeling the hardness of her nipples as he rocked himself back onto the ledge.

Lucy took a step back and shimmied out of her leggings, making herself completely bare to Micah. Then, with her Fae grace, she climbed up onto Micah's lap and wrapped her arms around him.

He was trembling. Shaking uncontrollably.

"Are you okay?" She whispered to him, their bodies pressed close to one another.

"I'm scared," he told her. His eyes gazing deeply into hers—the only person he had ever fallen in love with.

"We don't have to do this if you don't want to," she said, pulling back with surprise and barely concealed hurt.

"No," Micah said, holding her in place. "I'm not scared of this—of us. Not anymore." He closed his eyes and pressed his forehead to hers.

"Then what?" Lucy wrapped her hands around his neck, her fingers playing with the hair at the base of his neck.

"I'm afraid of losing you, Lu," he told her, the rushing water outside their alcove hiding the quake in his voice. "I'm afraid of what tomorrow brings. But even if we were to die tomorrow, I'd never regret loving you. Choosing you."

Micah knew the risks of love when he couldn't even leave his post as guardian, but the rest of his family knew the risks too, and they took it. They never missed out on a chance for love. For family.

"I choose you, too." Lucy pulled his face to hers and kissed him with a passion that told him she was just as scared of tomorrow as he was. Her chest pushed against him and his hands found the firm roundness of her bottom. Caressing her from hips to breasts, he felt Lucy move, lowering herself down onto him.

They stayed in the cave for what felt like an eternity, hoping the sounds of the crashing waters would hide their cries as they came together, again and again, leaving no room for regret.

TWENTY-SIX

LUCY

Lucy wasn't sure if it was the buoyant magic within the lake or finally letting go of the worry and strain after missing Micah so badly, but she felt as though there was a lightness to her.

Hand in hand, they left their watery alcove, hearts united as one. Lucy took the time to squeeze out some of the water from her hair and tame it into a braid while Micah retrieved his axe, the rest of his clothes, and her boots.

As she watched him in the distance, a realization came to her. She would do anything in her power to keep him safe, would do anything at all to protect him. Anything except leave him again.

Her heart was his.

"Got them," Micah said, walking over, holding her boots up. The smile on his face was lighter now, too.

"Thanks," she replied as she put them on.

Micah took a deep breath in and looked back at their hidden spot behind the waterfall. "So what do you think the chances are they already made up their mind but decided not to interrupt us?" His face pinched in embarrassment.

Lucy laughed. Her first real, honest laugh since her father had died. "I'd have to say it's pretty likely. They're Fae—good hearing, remember?"

"Oh, yeah," he said, the tiniest bit of blush covering his cheeks.

Smiling, Lucy pulled him into another kiss. "It's fine. Let's go find Alderic and hear their decision."

LOCATING Alderic was the simple part. He was in the same domed building that Micah suggested he would be. Getting his attention away from Brax was what proved to be difficult.

"Wow," Lucy said to Micah. "Some friendships don't fade with time, do they?"

Lucy and Micah watched as Brax and Alderic sat side by side, laughing and talking animatedly. It was nice to see Brax so happy, but the idea of Alderic being there still confused Lucy.

Why had there been no record of him after all this? Why did he hide from them?

Micah cleared his throat, getting Alderic and Brax's attention.

"Ah, Lumen," Brax announced. Then she looked at Alderic. "Lumen."

The duo broke into a fit of giggles again.

"Sorry, sorry," Brax said, seeing the annoyance on Micah's face.

"I take it conversations went well?" Micah asked, the hope apparent in his voice.

"Yes," Alderic said with a smile, but then his face turned serious. "We understand what is at stake, and we are prepared to fight alongside you."

Relief flooded Lucy.

"The South…. It was…" Lucy tried to tell them, but the words died on her lips.

"It was the worst thing I have ever seen in all my life," Brax said for her, a hushed solemnity in her words.

Lucy could only nod. "Our Denoran armies are split. Some

soldiers are supporting Sloan, and I'm not sure if King Tralont has enough soldiers to triumph in battle."

"Our people will unite and fight together," Alderic replied with ferocity.

"I know some warriors who have a soft spot for the freedom of females and children," Brax said with a wink.

"And with your power, Miss Baum," Alderic said to her, "we know you will lead us to victory."

"My power?" Lucy repeated. Then a new question came to her mind. "Alderic, you have been here in The Elderwood for a very long time... what do you know about the magic inside of me?"

It hadn't occurred to her to ask before that moment.

"It was dormant for as long as I can remember," he said with a slight smile. "It woke up the very first time you crossed through the portal."

Lucy's heart jumped.

"You should have seen how it would sulk around when you were gone," he chuckled. "It waited around for you all the time. Then when the time was right, it left with you." There was a glint in his eye, as though he knew something she did not.

"Where did it come from?" Lucy asked, desperate for answers. "Please, tell me. Help me understand."

"How about I show you instead?"

The magic inside Lucy sprang from her hands and twirled around her in a dance.

Alderic barked a laugh. "Oh, so now you come to say hello."

"What is happening?" Micah whispered to Brax.

"You're about to find out," Alderic replied. "Follow your magic, Lucy. It seems to want to show you for itself."

THE EMERALD green mist zoomed in and out of tree branches, joyously floating along a trail to another part of The Elderwood.

Where are you going?

The other times they were in The Elderwood, her magic didn't appear. Lucy had assumed it was simply because she didn't need it here when she was safe, but perhaps it was something else.

Keeping up with the trail, the footsteps of Micah, Brax, and Alderic lumbered behind her. What did Alderic know that he hadn't told her yet?

Taking a sharp turn, the magic stopped at the entrance to the dark forest. Lucy took a giant step back, cautiously watching as her magic bounced up and down.

"I figured it'd take you here," Alderic said.

"Isn't it unsafe?" Micah asked, catching up to Lucy and putting a hand on her shoulder, as if to stop her from following the magic into the dark woods.

Lucy had no intention of entering such a terrifying space, but realistically speaking, if her magic went in, then so would she.

"No," Alderic scoffed. "It's not unsafe at all. Why would you say that?" He looked at the three of them as though they were insane.

"Hmm, maybe because it's a forest of black trees with blood-red leaves?" Micah said.

"Maybe it's the shadows that crawl over the forest that don't seem to touch anywhere else?" Brax supplied with sarcasm.

Lucy's heart warmed seeing the two friends so seamlessly banter.

"Oh, right," Alderic said, wide eyed. "It'd probably help to take the glamor off." He waved his hands in the air and said an ancient Fae spell.

As if the world around them was melting, the forest scenery began to change. The dark shadowy sky swirled with color, the black and deep brown tree trunks turned hazy, and the red leaves rippled in and out like a stream of water. Ever so slowly, their view before them changed.

The shadows disappeared, revealing a brilliant forest, surrounded by trees of gold and silver, the bright yellow sun shining down on them. White flowers of all kinds covered the grassy plains in between the towering trees.

"What is this place?" Lucy asked in awe, watching as the soft breeze caught in the branches of the illuminated trees. "Why was it hidden?"

"This is the reason this realm exists," he said earnestly. "The most sacred place among all Fae."

Brax's wide eyes stared unblinking as she walked through the entrance and into the grandeur of the forest. "Is this... it cannot be." She looked back at Alderic in wonderment. "The gold and silver trees. The endless fields of white flowers. Is this...?"

Alderic smiled as if reading her mind. "It is."

"It's *what* exactly?" Micah asked, frustrated that he was clearly missing something.

"The true name of our realm is Porvanai," Alderic said solemnly. "The resting place of the gods."

Lucy's head spun at the declaration.

Porvanai was layered deeply within Fae religion... so deeply some considered it myth.

"Is anyone going to explain this to me?" Micah asked, breaking the silence.

Brax walked deeper into the shimmering forest and Lucy's eyes followed her magic as it sprung along with joy, twirling itself around the glittering trees.

"All Fae come from the gods," Alderic explained. "Gods are the only truly immortal beings on this plane of existence; even Fae lives will expire." He lifted his hand to the miraculous trees before them. "This is where the gods come when they are ready to rest. They do not die, but they can retire in peace, here forever."

"Are they asleep?" Micah asked.

"Some, not all," Alderic replied. "Most keep to themselves and remain here in their forest—we call it Thrinuin. Others roam around when they get curious."

"Like my magic?" Lucy asked, her voice nearly a whisper.

"Yes, like yours," Alderic laughed. "In all my time in Porvanai, I have never seen a god reach out to another the way this one did to you. I truly believe it belongs with you somehow."

"A god cannot belong to another," Lucy said.

"No, it cannot," Brax agreed.

"Maybe it was just looking for a little adventure," Micah suggested. "It can't die, right?"

"Correct," Alderic said.

"Then when all is said and done, it will return here," Micah said, as though it was obvious.

Alderic, Brax, and Lucy slowly turned to look at him.

"You know, Micah," Brax said slowly. "I think that's the most intelligent thing you've ever said."

"Do you know who it is? Whose power this came from?" Lucy asked.

"No," he shook his head. "No one knows, and I don't think we will ever have a way of finding out. But that doesn't matter anymore, because it's you now. It's your power—and so far you've done everyone proud." He winked.

But Lucy couldn't agree. She thought of Abe. Of her father. Tristan and her brothers.

"Even them," Alderic whispered to her, as though reading her mind.

Her emerald magic came bounding back toward her, shimmering with knowledge that Lucy was finally starting to understand.

"Now you see why it is so important we keep the realm safe," Alderic stated fervently. "You are not just a guardian of an ancient forest. You are the Guardian to the Gods."

Micah inhaled deeply and stood up straight, as though he was taking in the enormity of his task.

"I will go to Vytyr," Brax told Micah. "Alderic gave me Sanni's old potions to travel there. It won't take me long."

"Thank you... You'll know where to find me," Micah said in reply.

Lucy's hope fell.

She had already promised herself she would never leave him again, but she had to. There was no way for him to leave the property safely until Alderic broke that curse. But she had to go back, she couldn't leave her mother unprotected at the estate. And she wouldn't be leaving him forever.

Not in that sense.

The panicked look in her eyes softened as Micah met her gaze, nodding gently. Letting her know he understood.

"I will continue to train," Micah said to the group. "Do you think Quillan would be interested in giving me some lessons on this thing?" He lifted the axe in his hand.

"I am sure of it," Alderic said proudly. "I will have all the advisors prepare our soldiers."

"What will you be doing?" Brax asked.

"I will be in my study, finding a way to break this horrid curse I've caused." Alderic's face crumbled in dismay.

"I must return to my family," Lucy said softly. "My brother is trying to get the king to listen, but I need to make sure my mother is safe at the estate. She will probably need help with the extra Fae there."

Alderic, Brax, Micah, and Lucy stood shoulder to shoulder in determination, looking into Thrinuin, knowing they wouldn't hide from this fight. Then, they looked at one another closely, realizing that this may be the last time they'd all be in the same place together.

"Then it is settled," Brax said, clapping a hand to the back of Alderic's shoulder. "We prepare for battle."

TWENTY-SEVEN

MICAH

"Are you sure this is going to work?" Micah asked Quillan as he stood next to Brax in the open space of the lawn outside of the cabin.

"I am certain," Quillan replied, stoic focus and determination set in his brow at all times. "Move the axe as I've shown you and enter that space where your magic resides."

"What do you mean *enter the space*? The magic is just... in there somewhere." Micah imagined his magic just swimming through his veins, only occasionally willing to show up.

The faint sigh from Quillan put a sparkle of amusement in Brax's eye, but thankfully, for once, she kept quiet.

"It isn't fair for you two to keep telling me to *use my intent* and *find the space where my magic reside*s when I've had magic for such an infinitesimal amount of time compared to you. I haven't had it for centuries. I haven't had it all my life, learning to grow with it. I've had it for months. That's it."

He didn't mean to snap, but he was drained.

He was losing his patience.

He was just so fucking tired.

A softness came over Quillan then, and he walked up to Micah slowly, his large palms out in a peace offering.

"You're right," Quillan replied. "You haven't had the time nor the training. You don't know our histories and you don't know the nuances to your magic yet."

Micah sighed. It was rare that someone saw and acknowledged the difficulties he was facing.

"But none of that matters." Quillan's harsh words came out like a whip and ended Micah's moment of relief. "Today, or tomorrow, or the next day, an unrelenting, powerful Fae will come here prepared to take your magic."

Quillan took a step closer to Micah, and Micah took a small step back, not used to seeing Quillan so hostile.

"He will come here and kill anyone in his way to get *your* alchemy." Another step toward Micah. "Your Lucy. Her family. Brax. Me. My entire village." A powerful glint in his golden eyes brought forth the predatory power Micah recalled from Quillan's form as the shadow beast. "You would leave the gods without a resting place? You are willing to risk all of that simply because this is *hard*?"

"Of course not," Micah bit back, trying his best to stand his ground. "I'm just saying I don't know how."

"Then find it within you to figure out how," he said fiercely. "Lives rely on your dedication to this cause."

That was it. That was the problem... Everyone relied on Micah to do this the right way, but he was given nothing in return. No training. No support. No fucking option to even take the job. He was just there in a destiny he did not want, or at least one he had not intended.

He wanted to fight back. He wanted to yell at the Fae in front of him that he would do anything to protect those people, all of them, but he didn't know how his magic worked. He didn't know if he could do it.

"I know," Micah said, running a hand through his hair. "I just..."

The words got stuck in his throat. Was this the future that he wanted? "Can you help me?" He asked faintly.

"Lumen," Brax groaned. "We've been trying to help you utilize your magic, you buffoon," she spat at him, throwing her hands up in frustration.

"No—" he tried to explain, but Quillan cut him off.

"Guardian," Quillan said quietly to him, his deep voice a near rumble. "You are a protector, are you not?" He closed his eyes and sniffed the air, his head bobbing slightly as if he was savoring the scent.

Micah didn't miss the feline way his neck curved into the movement.

"Yes," was all Micah could say.

"A protector in this life, as well as your life before," he said, opening his golden eyes just inches from Micah.

Micah nodded, remembering his position in the police department. Remembering the lives he tried to improve. It felt like a lifetime ago.

"Close your eyes," Quillan instructed.

Micah looked at him doubtfully. He felt like a fool closing his eyes in front of these people, but then again since he found out magic existed, he fell in love with a beautiful Fae woman, he found magic of his own, and now was speaking to a man who could turn into a fucking cat, he decided the rest of his life was sure to be equally strange.

Quillan just gave him a look as if to say *"really?"*

He sighed and closed his eyes.

A moment later, Micah felt Quillan lean closer to him, standing a breath away. Micah tried to steady his breathing as Quillan's strong hands weighed down on his shoulders.

"There is a power inside of you that has nothing to do with your magic," Quillan said to him quietly. "It is a place that speaks to who you are as a person. Your generosity. Your patience. Your intuition. It is everything that makes you who you are."

Micah took a deep breath, searching for that place within him.

"Your magic does not come from your mind," Quillan said, softly tapping a finger to Micah's temple. "It's deeper than that. It is a well that lies within all Fae; and you, Micah, even though you don't feel as though you were Fae before this... you were. No mortal could have taken on the magic from Alderic. No mortal could have pulled magic from thin air to save his friends."

Micah thought about that. It had been something that had bothered him this whole time... How he went from a mortal man to a magical Fae in the stretch of one moment. But perhaps something Quillan was saying was true. It did make sense. How could anyone just be empty of magic one moment and filled with it the next?

"Your Fae heritage is more than the blood within your veins," Quillan's voice rumbled. "It is in the loyalty your family had for our people. It is in the sacrifice your family made to keep a life changing secret."

Micah's heart sank at the thought: the reality of that sacrifice. His throat tightened.

His grandad.

His mom.

Now him.

Was their family cursed to live this life alone? The responsibility of an entire realm in his unprepared hands?

"There's more that burdens you," Quillan said as if in realization, squeezing his shoulders. "Speak, Guardian."

But Micah wasn't sure he could say it. Could he voice that he hated that his entire family had this obligation to shoulder?

Part of him wanted to say he never wanted the job, but was that true? The tightness in his throat seemed to make a blockade the size of his fist.

The very thought of leaving here...leaving his position as guardian... It made him uneasy.

It was no longer about what he left behind in his life before this.

Giving up this role would mean giving up every bit of the magic, the good and the bad.

It'd mean no more cabin.

No more Brax.

No more Lucy.

Even if things weren't perfect between them, there was still so much they had yet to figure out. Once all of this was behind them, maybe they'd have a real shot...

But more than that, he wanted to learn more about the magic and his family. He was tired of the secrets and lies and wanted the truth—the whole truth. Maybe spending time with Alderic would answer more of his questions. Maybe this role didn't have to be as isolating as it was for his family before him.

Micah cleared his throat. "When I first was... *appointed* to this job, I was still deep in my grief. I don't think I was ready for it. For any of this."

Micah opened his eyes, nervous to see Quillan upset at his admission, but instead, he remained stoic. No judgment upon his face.

Micah glanced at Brax standing over his shoulder. She nodded at him, giving him the strength to continue.

"I was mad when I found out about the curse; about all of the ways my family had to sacrifice their wants for this cause. But the more I am involved, the more I understand." Micah took a deep breath in. "I want to be here. I think, somehow, I was always made for this. Not because of my grandad or my mom, not because of the cabin I've always visited, but because I am a protector. I've always wanted to ease the pain of others and bring justice to those who deserve it. I want to do the job the right way."

Quillan squeezed his shoulder and took a step back, dropping his hands. "You are the Guardian." He lifted a fist to his chest, held it over his heart, then bowed his head. When he looked at Micah again, there was a smile on his face. "I think you've found where your magic lies."

"What do you mean?" Micah asked, confused as always. "I only said that I'd keep trying."

"Yes."

Micah waited for him to continue, but Quillan just stood there silently. All knowing.

It's awfully fucking annoying always being the only person in the room not knowing what the fuck is going on.

Brax smiled and walked up to Micah, reading his annoyance.

"I know you've heard me talk about magic and intent, but I don't think you've ever allowed yourself to accept your magic," she said. "You've just kind of went along with it."

"I've accepted it," Micah responded in defense. "I've been here this whole time, haven't I?"

"You've been here because you weren't given any other choice," she said with a wistful smile on her face. "But listen to what you just said. You said you wanted to be here. That you were made for this. Do you truly believe that?" Her eyes remained on Micah's face, searching for answers he perhaps could not say aloud.

Micah's breathing hitched, just in the slightest. He had said that, hadn't he... And did he mean it? Did he mean all of it?

He squeezed his eyes shut and looked deep within himself.

Even without Brax. Without Lucy. Without his grandad and mom. Would he choose this? Would he choose to stand guard over a mystical realm and take over the magic that was hidden deep within his veins all this time? Would he stand against injustice and fight for what was right?

The answer was yes. To all of it, always. That is who he was.

The Guardian.

"Yes," Micah said, and as he spoke, a flare of red magic came crashing out of his chest and swirled around his body.

It felt like a crackling fire and a raging wind, then suddenly a warmth grew deep inside of him.

His magic, buried deep, nestled near his heart.

It was there all along.

"You found it," Quillan said, a statement, not a question.

Micah nodded, amazement filling him. He looked at his hands as they held his red swirling magic, the axe nowhere near him.

It was him doing this.

Him.

Not the axe. Not The Elderwood.

The magic was his.

"Then let your training commence."

"Stop doing that," Micah grunted as Brax hit him in the side for the fifth time.

"Then stop leaving it open," Brax snarled. She spun and kicked at his side again, and Micah blocked her foot with the handle of the axe.

This had been going on for damn near an hour and Micah was spent. First the training with Quillan, then combat practice with Brax.

He stood up straight to prepare for another onslaught of Brax's Vytyrian fighting tactics, but instead, she kicked him in the side again.

"Damn it, Brax, will you knock that off?" Micah yelled, clasping his side in his hands.

"No," she said as she swung at him, managing a blow to his shoulder.

Hit after hit, she never stopped coming for him. He could barely block half of them, let alone manage to get a hit back at her.

Micah fell to the ground in a heap and threw his axe down next to him. Lifting two empty hands up to the air, he shouted, "That's it! I need a break!"

"You don't get a break. Pick up your weapon," Brax demanded. She stood over him, panting from exertion. There was an intensity in her eyes that Micah didn't understand.

"No," he said calmly. "I'm taking a break." He leaned forward to stand, placing his axe on the ground to steady him.

"There are no breaks in war," she said as she kicked him backwards, his body hitting the grass with a thud. "Pick up your axe and continue."

"No." Micah looked at her through a veil of simmering frustration.

Brax lifted her foot again to kick him, but Micah's magic responded first, grabbing onto Brax by her ankle and flipping her feet over head, and onto the ground.

"Yes, finally," she said with violence dancing in her eyes. "Again."

"No, Brax," he said louder. "I'm done. What's gotten into you?"

"We aren't done until you can beat me," she said, preparing to advance on him again.

"Then I guess you can beat my fucking ass all afternoon because I'm done fighting," he said through gritted teeth.

"You aren't done!" Brax cried, nearly shrieking with frustration. Her eyes were wild and her nostrils flared as her breaths heaved. She bobbed on her toes and yelled at him again. "Get up!"

He said nothing.

"Get up!" Brax screamed, taking a step closer to him. "Get up!"

But Micah heard it... the crack in her voice at the command.

"Why?" Micah asked her quietly.

Brax opened her mouth to reply, but no words came out. She looked away quickly and took a step back.

Micah got up and walked over to her.

She picked up her fists and got into another fighting stance, her breathing uneven and her feet heavy on the ground.

"What's going on Brax?" His voice was a near whisper in effort to keep her calm, approaching her slowly as he would a wild animal.

Her stance didn't falter, but a lone tear escaped her eye and fell down her cheek. "Because you need to be ready."

"We're doing that, Brax. We're getting ready." He brushed a tear off her cheek with his finger. "What's this about?"

"No. Not *we*. You." She shoved him back, then wiped the back of her arm across her face, erasing any sign of tears. "Now fight!"

He grabbed her fists lightly in his hands and brought them together to his chest, holding her there. Her hands were shaking and she was panting for breath, her gaze darting everywhere but to him.

"Tell me what this is about and I'll do anything you say," Micah told her earnestly. "This isn't about you wanting to whoop my ass, so what is it?"

Her hands quaked under his. He had never seen her look so shaken. Slowly, her eyes rose to meet his. More tears welled there, not yet cascading down her beautiful bronze cheeks.

"We need to do everything we can to prepare you," she said quietly. "I've seen…" She bit her lip, trying to find the words. "I've seen what Sloan has done to people… to good people." Her eyes darted across his face, taking in his features as though she was memorizing them in case she never saw them again. "But I've never fought alongside someone I've loved. You are my best friend, and I can't let anything happen to you."

"You're my best friend, too," he told her.

That was the most important thing at that moment. Not that they would fight together. Not that they would train and prepare for battle. What mattered was that they were friends who loved one another—because that was the only thing worth fighting for.

Love.

"You're the only real friend I've ever had," she whispered.

"You know, that makes sense," Micah said lightly, releasing her hands and holding her arms. "You aren't very nice."

Brax snorted in laughter, and Micah smiled back at her, pulling her in for a hug. He held her there as she sniffled, her body slowly relaxing into his.

"I know this is scary," Micah told her, resting his chin on the top of her head. "It's never easy risking things so close to us… but we know this is the right thing to do. We will fight, and we will win, because there is no other option here." He gave her a gentle squeeze and let her go, pulling her away from him to look at her. "We can do this."

Brax nodded, her eyes still full of worry.

"This calls for a fire," Micah announced.

"And a beer," Brax finished for him.

He smiled, recalling the times over the last few months that Brax would pull him out of his dreary moods with a fire and a beer. While she ran inside to grab the drinks, he picked up his axe and went to light the fire.

Without Brax around, he wanted to try something else with his magic. He lifted his hand and commanded his magic to arrange the firewood in just the right way. Then he held onto his axe in one hand and the matches in another.

"Light," he told the match, and instantly it burst into flame. He had no idea how this power actually worked, but he felt it there within him now. Ready to be used.

As Brax returned, they sat on the tree stumps and looked out into the fading sky above them; the sunset turning the world into hues of orange and pink.

Brax still looked completely broken, and it lit a fire of resilience in Micah's soul. He would do anything for his friends, even if it meant training until he was more sweat than man. He hated seeing Brax like this.

"Come here," he said, lifting his arm for her to come closer.

She scooted toward him and leaned her head against his shoulder silently. "You're a good person, Micah. And I'm better for knowing you."

"I feel the same about you. Thanks for always being here to help me."

"You're welcome. Now make sure you don't die, you overgrown radish."

TWENTY-EIGHT

Lucy's magic had been quiet since the return from The Elderwood. She wasn't sure if it felt at peace from visiting its previous home or uneasy at the battle to come—probably both.

That was one thing she was learning each day, you could feel many conflicting emotions at once, and they don't always make sense together. Lucy felt happiness and terror; love and fear; hope and despair.

Sitting in the garden, she closed her eyes as the sun warmed her face and the scent of the flowers filled her with calm. Another set of opposites, peace and trepidation.

She kept going over what would happen next in her mind. Soon Sloan would arrive looking for Jasper. They would give him Jasper as a trade for Tristan, and ensure the safety of her brothers... but it would just allow him to become stronger.

Unfortunately, there really wasn't any other way. She needed her family safe and *together* in order to take down Sloan.

A group of children ran through the garden, surprising Lucy and pulling a smile to her lips.

"Stop running, you hooligans!" The violet haired Fae called, chasing after them. When she turned and saw Lucy sitting alone, she stopped to apologize. "I'm so sorry. I'll go get them and tell them to stop."

"Please, don't." Lucy reached her arm out to get her attention. "Really, it's fine." She smiled as she watched the kids running after one another, playing a game of sorts. "It has been a long time since we've seen happiness in this garden, and I welcome it entirely. Let kids be kids while they can."

She nodded, her violet hair falling from her fraying hair tie. "I'm Ruthani," she said with a wave. "I'm sorry my hair is such a mess right now." She tried to flatten it closer to her scalp.

"Stop apologizing," Lucy told her, a sharpness in her tone she didn't intend. "You were imprisoned with your family and are fleeing for safety. Do you really think I care about how your hair looks? Your hair is beautiful."

"Thank you. My mother used to hate that I would color it such bright colors, but my father always loved it. She ran her hands through it again. "Sure wish I could tame it now, though."

"Come here," Lucy said, pointing to the bench beside her. "I'll help you get it out of your face, so it's easier to chase those rascals." She tried to add more lightness to her tone, but it was hard. Why did this young female think Lucy cared about how she looked in the midst of civil unrest?

She sat hesitantly, and Lucy turned her head to braid her hair into an elegant crown.

"You aren't quite what I expected," Ruthani told her, her gaze still on her siblings playing in the mud.

"And what is it you expected?" Lucy asked, her fingers moving at lightning speed as she braided.

"You were betrothed to Lord Sloan, were you not?"

Lucy straightened her spine and took a deep breath, considering her response. "I was."

"And it was your choice?" Ruthani continued.

Lucy clenched her teeth. "It was." She put the last section of hair into a stronger tie, then dropped her hands.

Ruthani turned to look at Lucy, eyes full of scrutiny. "Then what happened?"

Lucy considered telling her a half-truth—considered making the answer easier to hear, more palatable for a stranger.

But Lucy never was one to water herself down for someone else.

"I agreed to a business deal so that Sloan could help me catch the Fae who murdered my father," Lucy told her with fire in her eyes.

Ruthani didn't balk for a moment.

"And when I found out that he was the Fae responsible for so much death and destruction, I turned my plans on him instead. So yes. He was my betrothed, and now he's the target of my wrath."

"Good." Ruthani smiled as she looked back to her siblings, her entire demeanor changing. She was no longer sitting as though she was nervous and on edge.

"That was not the response I expected from you," Lucy admitted to Ruthani, regarding her carefully.

Turning her head back to Lucy, Ruthani's eyes were fixed, full of bold determination. "I needed to be sure you were someone we could follow."

"Follow?"

"Brax told us you could be trusted, but I needed to be sure. We will not walk in the footsteps of some love-sick female, but perhaps we can follow a female who straightens the crowns of others." She smiled as she lifted her eyes to her braided crown of hair.

"Who is this *we* you speak of?" Lucy asked, noting the significance of her words.

"The Fae here are scared," Ruthani told her, "but we are not weak." Then she stood and turned to Lucy. "Thank you for the weapon, it came in use," she said, offering the amethyst dagger back to her. Brax must have given it to her for protection during their time in the South.

"Keep it," Lucy murmured, still thrown by the conversation. "Use it to keep you and your siblings safe."

Ruthani nodded, sheathing it. "And thanks for the hairstyle," she said with a wink as she walked away.

Lucy stood and watched in awe as Ruthani gathered her siblings. The interaction left her heavy with emotions she couldn't describe.

Seeing Ruthani with her family opened up feelings within Lucy that she had been trying to avoid. The people who mattered most to her were on the front lines of this conflict, and worse, they were all spread out; no unified front.

Hugh and Gregory were in the South, no doubt captured alongside Tristan, Wes was desperately trying to get the royals of Central Denora to believe his claims, her mother was trying to run the business and keep Jasper in line, and her father was... dead.

Each time she thought it, it was as though an arrow shot through her heart again and again.

When will the grief ease? She wondered. *Will I always fall to my knees in despair at the memory of his death?*

There had to be a way to defeat Sloan, but how?

There was nothing left to do but keep going, and if they all died tomorrow, at least she could say she went down fighting. Looking up to the bright blue sky, Lucy squeezed her eyes shut and pleaded that they all made it out alive.

"I believe you've just been played, sister," Wes said. Her eyes shot open to see her brother sitting on a nearby bench.

"How long have you been there?" Lucy asked, incredulous. She was certain he was not there a moment ago.

"The entire time," he said with a wink. "It's not my fault you aren't very observant." He stood and walked toward her.

"Wesley Baum, I daresay you are keeping secrets. When I see father in the afterlife, I am going to give him a piece of my mind for giving you, of all people, the ability to sneak up on others," Lucy said with a scowl. "As if you weren't already nosey enough."

"Stop complaining," Wes said, chuckling. "You're just annoyed that Ruthani played you like a fiddle." He pretended to play a violin and did a little jig in the middle of the garden.

"Why would she do that?" Lucy asked him, still reeling from the strange interaction.

"Ruthani is strong. She reminds me of you and Brax; determined to do the right thing. I think she was sizing you up."

"Well, I—"

But before she could finish her sentence, an alarm blared all throughout the estate. The deep reverberations of the siren vibrated Lucy's bones.

Someone's coming.

"Get the females and children back inside to safety," Wes told her, seriously. "I will identify who comes."

Lucy took off in a flash, ensuring the protection of those who needed it most. Then she went to collect Jasper.

If Lord Sloan was here for an exchange, then he would get one.

And she would get Tristan back.

"Move your feet before I remove them for you," Lucy threatened, dragging Jasper through the manor to the front foyer entryway.

Anita had helped settle the Fae guests and put Milton in charge of keeping them safe and quiet during the trade. No one wanted Sloan to find out that they had secretly taken his prisoners right from under his nose.

Wes positioned himself at the door, and Anita stood at the ready, her magic steadily gathering. They looked perfectly poised and calm, the complete opposite of how Lucy felt.

Lucy's heart hammered in her chest. She was so thankful her younger brothers were away and somewhere safe. There could be no more mistakes, no more risks to their family. This final trade would bring them all back together.

Pulling Jasper to a wrought-iron chair in the grand entryway, Lucy tied him securely, ensuring his captivity.

"You don't understand," Jasper gasped, looking at the door in sheer panic. "If he takes me, he will kill me!"

"That wasn't the tune you were singing to Brax the other day," Wes said.

"It's true! You can't hand me over!" Jasper pleaded. "I will do anything. Anything!"

"Will you change your ways and help us thwart Sloan?" Lucy asked pointedly.

Jasper recoiled in disdain. "No, absolutely not. I'm desperate, not an idiot."

Lucy rolled her eyes.

"But anything but that!"

"Silence," Lucy commanded, sending a silencing spell over him once again.

"You'd think subservience to us would have been preferred," Anita said to no one in particular.

Lucy looked at the grand front entrance as her fingers trembled with nerves.

What if Sloan takes Jasper but doesn't return Tristan?

What if Jasper's magic allows Sloan to become too powerful?

What if there's no stopping him after this?

She had to shake the thoughts out of her mind. Dwelling over the what if's would do nothing to help her here. The only option was to keep going, even if every thought pained her. She couldn't go back and change time even if she wanted to... and she did. Desperately.

The soft folding and unfolding of Anita's arms shifted her attention to her family beside her. Wes stood directly next to Lucy, prepared to receive their brother and bring him to safety. Anita was a bit further down the hall, guarding Jasper for their barter.

She replayed the plan in her head over and over again. They would each prove their side of the bargaining chip, they would send Jasper over to Sloan, Wes would get Tristan and hurry him off to safety, and then they'd close the doors to Sloan and his soldiers as they figure out their next steps.

All that mattered right now was Tristan and her brothers and getting them home safely.

Her entire body was on edge as they waited in silence.

"Are we sure we are ready for this?" Lucy asked her family. Patience was never a virtue that took kindly to Lucy.

They looked at one another, worry heavy in their stance.

"There's no other choice." Wes turned to the door. "He's here."

With his shoulders back and a steadfast expression on his face, Wes opened the doors to Lord Sloan and a small squad of soldiers as they approached the entrance.

"Ah, what a warm welcome," Sloan called out with false sincerity. "I see we are ready for the big event." He rubbed his hands together selfishly.

"Show us Tristan," Wes demanded, staying clear of Sloan and his soldiers.

"Do you doubt my word?" Sloan asked facetiously. "Tsk, tsk. I am the only Fae of honor here."

"Honor?" Lucy spat in disgust. "Your plans to murder the king and hurt anyone who gets in your way is the opposite of such titles."

Sloan just smiled at her as though he was seeing her for the first time. "My dear. How I've missed you."

"Tristan." Wes demanded.

"Yes, yes," Sloan replied, waving to his soldiers. "Bring the boy forward."

The group of a dozen males in navy uniforms parted as a soldier escorted Tristan to the front of the crowd. His eyes were wide with fear, but he was otherwise intact.

Anita drew in a quiet gasp as Lucy held her breath.

He was there. He was there and he was unhurt.

Thank you, she said to the stars.

Wes walked back and grabbed Jasper by the collar. "Here. Give us our brother, take your prize and leave." He shoved Jasper at Sloan's feet.

Sloan looked at Jasper, flummoxed.

Jasper fell to his side and pushed himself away from Sloan by his feet, his hands still tied.

"I believe there has been a misunderstanding," Sloan said seriously, the forced civility now gone. His ice-blue eyes met Lucy's with anger and disdain.

"And what is that?" Lucy asked. "You want a trade. Take him, then give me back my brother."

Sloan broke into a low laugh, the sound like gravel in his throat. "I do not want that sniveling coward. Keep him. Kill him. I don't care."

"What? You don't mean that," Lucy said, taking a step forward.

As though he was talking to a petulant child, he rolled his eyes and sent a bolt of magic straight to Jasper's chest—killing him instantly.

"I do," Sloan replied, a sinister smile creeping over his face. Taking another step toward Lucy, he continued. "I do want a trade... but I want something worthwhile. I want a magic that compares to no others."

Lucy couldn't breathe.

How did she not see this before?

"I want *you,* my beloved."

"What? No." Wes nearly shouted the words. "Absolutely not. That was not the deal."

"It most certainly *was* the deal," Sloan replied, keeping his cruel eyes locked on Lucy.

"She's not coming with you," Wes snarled.

"Oh, she will," he hissed. "That magic will be mine, and then we will go have a little chat with that mortal you're so fond of, hmm? Or perhaps I can do that *after* I kill your brothers."

Micah.

"I will give you the time to think it over," Lord Sloan replied, casually looking at Anita. "I've got three of your sons," he called to her. "Three sons for the price of one daughter? Well. That must be worth it, don't you think? I'll even let everyone in the manor live."

With a sneer, he turned on his boot and walked back through the entrance.

"Wait," Lucy called weakly.

Sloan paused without turning.

"No," Anita commanded. Throwing a silencing bubble over Lucy, so she could not continue. "You cannot have her."

"I'll be back," Sloan replied, continuing his walk.

Lucy watched as the soldiers carried Tristan away, his face scrunched in concern.

She wanted to yell at them to wait. To come back.

She wanted to scream that Laurent Sloan could have her if he freed her brothers. If he left her loved ones alone.

But the words didn't come as each of the soldiers left through the door and Anita rebuilt the wards around their home.

Tristan was gone again, and Hugh's and Gregory's lives were added to the barter.

The entire Baum family line rested in her fate.

And she would give herself over to her enemy if it meant saving the ones she loved.

TWENTY-NINE

WES

"You are out of your mind," Wes snarled at Lucy as she stood before him in his office.

"I am of perfectly sound mind," she replied, but the passion was gone from her words.

"You will not give yourself, and your magic, to some monster who wants to take over Denora!" Wes shouted at her.

He paced before the fireplace, trying to calm his mind.

This can't be happening.

"I will not live to see my family die because of my inaction," she scowled back at him.

"Lucella. You must hear what you are saying." Wes stood before her and put his hands on her shoulders, bending down to enter her line of vision. "If his alchemy is as strong as it was before, then you will not be able to overpower him. He will bend you to his will and command your magic. He will be unstoppable. Do you understand that?" The desperation in his voice was clear, but it had no effect on Lucy.

As he looked into her eyes, he saw her surrender and it terrified him.

It didn't matter what anyone told her, she would trade her life for the life of her brothers. It didn't matter that it would make things worse. It didn't matter that it would allow Sloan to become more powerful.

"Before you make any drastic decisions, please go check on the others. I need to make sure Mother is okay," Wes requested as he pinched the bridge of his nose and spun away from her.

Sighing, Lucy walked to the door, then paused. "If the roles were reversed, you would sacrifice yourself for us."

"And you'd try to stop me, too," he replied dejectedly. He turned to look at her, their sorrowful eyes meeting the hard truth.

No matter the decision, everyone in their family would be hurt by the outcome.

I will find a way to fix this, he swore.

As Lucy left the room, Wes closed his eyes and called upon his father's magic. A brilliance went through him, a levity cleansing him of his worry.

He had only used this magic a few times, each time utilizing it to travel without being heard. However, when he used that magic, his family always seemed to be shocked at his arrival. Knowing his father, there had to be more to it. Letting the ethereal light pass through his body, he let go of any reservations holding him back. There was no time to learn this magic slowly. There was no time for hesitation.

"If you're listening, Father," Wes said to the room around him, "I'm ready to harness the rest of your magic. Help me help our family."

Wes stood in the center of the room with his eyes closed and arms open wide, feeling the radiant light covering him from head to toe until a weightlessness encompassed him. Opening his eyes, he looked down at his body, astounded at what he saw.

"You sure love a play on words, don't you, old man?" Wes said with a breathless laugh. Taking a deep breath, he welcomed more of the light in, watching as his skin glimmered like stars around the room. The effect was nearly blinding.

Lucy had his shadows, and Wes always thought that was the more remarkable magic. However, Wes had the opposite, and he had never truly understood what it meant until now. Sure, he could create light and have a lightness to his feet, but as he looked down at where his hand should be, he realized what else this magic allowed. Wes could bend the light, making him disappear from view.

"I believe it's time to put this magic to the test," he said to himself, excitedly. He left his study and turned down the hall to find his mother.

At the first intersecting corridor, he walked past Bernard and Milton.

"Are you going to leave?" Milton asked Bernard, scanning the hallway for prying eyes. He looked directly at Wes, but didn't even acknowledge him.

Poor lads, Wes thought. *They don't see me coming.*

Wes never enjoyed listening in on other people's conversations, but he'd be lying to say it hadn't come in handy more than once.

"I would never leave Madame Baum and these children," Bernard replied, horrified at the thought.

"Nor I," Milton replied. "Then we will remain and carry on until our last dying breath."

Their words were hushed, and the enormity of their loyalty almost made Wes take pause and thank them. However, Wes was on a mission, and there was so little time left.

Passing through the hallway, Wes found Anita in the library, poring over books with different stones illustrated in them.

"If you're going to stand around, you may as well help me search for an answer," Anita said suddenly.

Wes dropped his magic and looked at his mother in surprise. "How did you know I was here?"

"It's your father's magic," she replied with a sad smile. "When we were in the garden, I thought I felt the presence of your father because of the story I was telling. I didn't put it together until later that I just felt his magic within you."

"Nothing gets past you, does it, Mother?" Wes asked in admiration.

"Sloan's declaration certainly did," she whispered, turning her gaze back to the open books before her. "There must be a way to stop him with alchemy. He is not invincible."

She huffed as she flipped page after page, searching desperately for an answer.

"Mother," Wes said, in realization. "I think you're right... and I think I have a way to get help." He grabbed Anita's hand and stilled her progress. "I need you to keep Lucy busy. Don't let her leave. Give her things to do to keep her feeling important and useful. The moment she thinks all is lost, she will arrive on Sloan's doorstep without our knowledge."

Anita vehemently nodded, knowing Lucy's stubborn streak better than anyone.

"Lucy is not to be trusted," Wes replied. "I will be back as soon as I can."

"Where are you going?" Anita asked, concern etching in the fine lines of her face.

"To gather our allies."

ARRIVING at the Lumen property took more time than Wes initially wanted, but he knew Lucy would come here to say goodbye before she turned herself over to Sloan.

Micah needed to hear the truth before Lucy tried to spin it in her favor.

"Lumen!" Wes yelled, beckoning him as soon as the cabin was in his eyesight.

Micah ran outside in a spurt of speed that surprised Wes.

Hmm, seems he's found his magic.

"What's wrong? Where's Lucy? Is she okay?" Micah asked in a hurry, searching over Wes's shoulder for Lucy.

Wes clasped Micah's shoulder, reassuring him. "Lucy is fine."

Micah's shoulders dropped in relief as Wes watched him. The way his tension fell knowing Lucy was safe.

"Micah, you love her, don't you?" Wes asked, seeing it clearly for the first time.

"More than anything," Micah replied as though it were obvious.

"And you would do whatever it takes to keep her safe from harm?"

Micah tensed again. "What happened?"

"Where is Brax? She may as well hear this at the same time." Wes said, looking through the trees in search of the warrior who made his blood heat, and not always in a bad way.

"I'm right behind you, you putrid turnip."

A flare of fire surged through his body at seeing Brax, but more than anything he was simply happy he didn't have to say this more than once.

"Say it," Micah urged.

Wes nodded, seeing the determination set in Micah's stare. "There is no way to sugarcoat this. Sloan came for the trade, but he didn't want Jasper. He wants Lucy."

"Well, he can't have her," Micah growled.

"Correct, but Sloan made an offer she couldn't refuse. The safety of our entire family for her and her magic."

The color dropped from Micah's face. He knew as much as Wes did that Lucy would put the life of those she loved before her own.

"No..."

"Yes," Wes replied. "She's more powerful than all of us, so we have to work together without her knowing. We must figure out how to stop her from making the biggest mistake of her life."

"We'll just tell her to wait. That there's gotta be another way. She has to see that Sloan having all that magic is only a recipe for trouble." Micah paced on the uneven grass lawn before him, running his hand through his hair.

"She won't listen," Wes countered, then asked the question he was praying would change the course of their upcoming battle. "Have you learned more of your alchemy? Can you take him down?"

"He has been practicing," Brax answered for him.

"No," Micah replied, cutting Brax off. "I'm not strong enough. I won't make enough of a difference."

Wes feared that answer, but it wouldn't change their next steps. "Will you fight with us? I have a plan, but it will only work if everyone is on board. And Lucy can never know."

"I would do anything for her," Micah promised.

"Then listen carefully," he said, looking from Micah to Brax. "There are many moving parts here, and yours can't falter."

BY THE TIME Wes returned to the Baum estate, it was almost dark.

I think I've had enough of single days turning my entire life upside down, he thought to himself.

Just that morning he was prepared to get his brother back and fight the good fight against Sloan with Lucy by his side, and now he was at risk of either losing Lucy or losing his three brothers.

Neither option was acceptable.

However, this time he wouldn't sit back and watch as life passed him by, the way he did when his father died. The moment Wes took charge of the family business, his life turned upside down then, too. It seemed so trivial now that he thought about it. He was so upset about having to take over and make the decisions for his family just days ago, and now he was traveling through realms and making secret plans to take down a maniacal tyrant.

Hurrying to the library, he found his mother poring over piles of books on a variety of subjects. She had "Stones and Rock Formations" open on one side and "The Myth of Porvanai" on the other.

"Any luck?" Wes asked.

Anita just slumped back in her seat despondently. Her hair was a mess, as though she was pulling at the edges as she searched. With a wave of her hand, her smudged make-up was perfected and her hair back in place.

"Where's Lucy?" He asked, tension rolling through his muscles.

"Don't worry, she's still here," Anita replied. "I guilted her into doing some housework. I told her I needed things done before I was left alone without any children to care for me."

"Mother!" Wes scolded with a shocked smile. "You did not."

"Of course I did," she said, waving her hand at her son. "I needed to keep her busy while we figure out an answer to this. I will not be losing *any* of my children."

The words were a challenge that Wes was happy to take on.

"I agree. I have a plan, and you probably won't like it, but I need your help."

THIRTY

MICAH

Micah swung his axe through the air, slicing at such speed and strength, he could easily take down multiple Fae attackers at once. Now that he had found where his magic resided within him, it was almost difficult to keep the power at bay. His magic was dormant for so long it seemed to flare with strength and purpose—a purpose he had been seeking for a very long time.

He could feel it coursing through his veins, zooming through his lungs, lacing every muscle—he was pure Fae magic and strength, and he was happy to wield it.

If only it was enough to stop Sloan.

He swung the axe again, roaring through the movement, pulling his magic along with him as he created a devastating blow with each swipe.

Micah would do nearly anything to keep his mind from his reality at the moment. As soon as Wes left, Brax got her supplies and hurried off to do as Wes requested. Micah went the other direction and traveled into The Elderwood to tell Quillan and Alderic of the new plan. Unfortunately, the entire timeline had moved up dramatically, and they asked for time to discuss before they gave their answer.

That didn't matter to Micah, though. He barely heard their request as he rushed back to the portal to return home. He would travel to Denora to protect Lucy using his newfound strength. She would be protected by her family and those who loved her. He was halfway across the property to the other portal when the truth hit him.

I can't leave.

Stopping in his tracks in the middle of the forest, Micah fell to his knees in anguish. The love of his life needed him to fight for her, and instead he was stuck on the sidelines, unable to make a difference at all.

He screamed, allowing all the pent up anger and frustration to spill out of him. It didn't matter how many times he chopped wood or ran through the forest, the resentment still thrived inside of him.

Fucking curse.

He walked back to the cabin and began to head inside when the portal to The Elderwood rippled with light. Changing course, Micah went to greet Quillan, and was shocked to see who was with him. Alderic stepped out and smiled, looking around the new realm. According to what Quillan had told him, Alderic had never left his realm before.

"Hello, Micah," Alderic greeted him as more warriors came through behind him.

"Have they agreed to band with Denora?" Micah asked, hope coating every word.

"Yes," he replied grimly. "Quillan is checking their vitals here in this new realm, ensuring they will be at their peak performance." His footing slipped, and he grabbed Micah's arm.

"Are you okay?" Micah held his arm and guided him to the tree stumps around the fireplace.

"I'll be fine," Alderic reassured him. "It has been a long time since

I've visited a mortal realm. The air is different, and as you know, time moves differently here."

"Why are you here? You could have sent Quillan, or requested my presence back in Porvanai?" Micah couldn't understand why Alderic had come, especially if it wasn't necessarily safe for him.

"Because there is much we need to discuss."

"I'm not sure how much time the Baums have until Sloan comes to collect his bounty," Micah told him. "Lucy will do it. She will give herself over to that asshole if she thinks she's protecting her family. We can't let her."

The rage he felt tensed through his body, but Alderic just sat there smiling at him.

"What?" Micah asked.

"You're in love," Alderic stated, but it wasn't a question.

Micah nodded, then he recalled the words Alderic told him when Lucy came to The Elderwood. "How did you know before? You hadn't met her for more than a few minutes, and you knew exactly what to say to me... how did you do that? Is that part of your magic?"

"No," Alderic chuckled. "I had five sons. I've seen the signs of love in young males before." He sat, lost deep in thought.

"What happened to your family?" Micah asked him.

"Our family," Alderic corrected him with a smile. "They did what most do. They grew old, created families of their own, and died."

"Weren't they Fae?" Micah remembered Lucy saying the lifespan of the Fae was much longer than mortals.

"Yes and no," Alderic said vaguely. "Unfortunately, there isn't time to talk about that just yet. Shall we save that story for another day? I'd like to share more about our family with you."

There was no arguing that—they were running out of time. He nodded and sighed, looking at the warriors as Quillan prepared them.

"Good, good," Alderic said, wringing his hands. He looked around the group cautiously, his eyes darting from Fae to Fae, hesitant to speak what was on his mind.

He stood and Micah watched as he approached Quillan and the other warriors.

"Quillan, I know you are aware of the risks we take in joining this cause, and I just want to say thank you for your devotion to our people and to the fight against evil." Alderic placed his hand over his chest and bowed.

Quillan bowed in response.

Micah watched carefully, reading Alderic's body language. Nervous smiles. Fidgety hands. Shaky breath.

Something bad is coming, he realized.

His heart fell.

He followed Alderic. "You said they are here to fight. All of them? The soldiers from The Elderwood—from Porvanai—will be there to guide us?"

Quillan gave a resolute nod, and brought his spear down beside him with a great, agreeable thump.

"Actually," Alderic began, his voice trailing off.

No.

Micah knew what that meant. He knew this was the face of someone preparing to declare devastating news. He'd seen it before in his dad's eyes when he was told his mom had died.

"To break the curse, we must cut off all connection to the portal," Alderic said finally, as though he had to rush to say it before he lost his nerve.

"Cut it off, how?" Quillan asked, his usual emotionless face full of worry.

"Cut it *down*, to be frank," he said with a sad chuckle.

Quillan took a step back, but Micah only inched closer. He needed to hear it, he needed to hear the words.

"You're telling me," Micah said on a hushed breath, "that the only way to end the curse is to close off the portal? Forever?"

He couldn't even fathom it. This beautiful realm that he had just been introduced to? The family he found there? The *answers* he found there?

"Yes," Alderic said softly.

"If we close the portal, what would that mean for each of its inhabitants?" Quillan asked, trying to understand.

"The gods would be safe within Thrinuin, but I am not sure how Lucy's magic would return when her life comes full circle... As for the rest of the villagers," Alderic said, looking at Quillan. "They would be safe within the realm as they've always been. We will continue to live and to thrive."

"But we would never see you again," Micah said flatly.

"No, you would not." Alderic said sadly.

Lucy would never be able to use the wood again, either. Would their family business still thrive? Would everything Corvus built be gone forever? Everything Lucy fought for, all for nothing?

It can't be all for nothing...

"Wait," Micah said, sensing more about the issue at hand. "How would the warriors return after they've helped us?"

"That is the bigger problem." Alderic's eyes glanced to Quillan with devastation, and then to Micah with apology. "If you break this curse, you will be able to go to Denora and fight against this immoral Fae... but then we cannot accompany you. Anyone who leaves could never return home."

The words came like a punch to the gut; the wind knocked out of Micah at the realization.

"So either I fight... or you fight?" Micah asked sullenly.

"That is how it seems," Quillan replied. His mouth opened as he said more, but Micah heard nothing.

The blood rushing through his ears drowned out everything else around him.

Either I'm trapped here or they're trapped there.

"I need... I need time to think," Micah replied, leaving the Fae in the center of the yard as he walked deeper into the tree line.

His feet pounded into the uneven terrain, following a dull path into the woods.

He couldn't believe that this was what it all came down to. If he accepted the end of the curse, Denora wouldn't have the allies it needed to take down Sloan. Lucy would be hurt over losing access to The Elderwood, but she'd understand... But would Micah's presence be enough for her? Would she even be able to look him in the eye if they lost the battle? Would there *be* an after if they lost at all?

But if he kept the curse, then he wouldn't be there with Lucy. He wouldn't be able to wield his alchemy against Sloan to help Denora gain victory. What if something happened to her and he never saw her again? Could he even live with himself for remaining at the property while the battle raged on?

Before he knew it, he was standing in front of the tree house yet again. As always, his feet brought him to a place of comfort... but nothing could comfort him now.

Why couldn't he have it all?

Why couldn't he break the curse, keep his allies, and help Lucy fight this fucking prick? Why was his life a never ending list of sacrifice?

Squeezing his hands, he realized he had never put his axe down.

This place was full of magic and secrets that he had never asked for. Grabbing the broken rungs of the tree house ladder, he climbed the gnarled tree until he was standing in the teetering tree house.

If I had to pick, I'd pick ending this curse. I could come and go as I please. I could fight alongside Lucy. I could make my own path in life...

But he knew he would never leave her defenseless.

He squeezed the axe until his knuckles turned white and heaved it up above his head and let it come crashing down on the tree house. Again and again, he swung the axe as it sliced the wood into chunks, letting the pieces rain down below him.

Boom.

Into the wall, collapsing a corner.

Boom.

Into the base, creating a man-sized hole.

Boom.

Another swing into the wall across from him.

If he couldn't chop down the fucking Elderwood tree, he'd chop this down.

He heaved his axe above his head once more, but then the entire structure began to sway. This way and that, the tree house rocked back and forth, causing Micah to lose his footing and grab for the walls to steady him. Realizing he didn't quite think this through, he jumped down from the hole he cracked open in the side of the tree house and landed on the ground.

Taking a few steps back, he watched as it shuddered once, twice, and then crashed to the ground in a heap.

Decades of memories reduced to a pile of warped scrap wood.

He leaned against the trunk of a nearby tree and knocked his head into the bark over and over.

Get a grip, Lumen.

He wanted to say that he had grown more than this over the past year—that he had learned and matured, but really, he was still the same lost little boy who missed his family.

So he did the only thing he could think of... he walked back to the house to speak to the only other Lumen left.

THE KITCHEN WAS quiet as he walked in, Alderic and Quillan waiting for him with bated breath.

He wasn't sure who would be disappointed or thrilled by his decision, but he knew not everyone would be happy.

As he opened his mouth to speak, Alderic stood up first and stopped him. "Micah, can we talk before you share your decision? I want you to hear a little more before you feel as though you are rushed into anything."

Micah took a seat. Part of him was relieved to not have to make the choice yet. However, another part of him anxiously awaited the moment when his decision was final—just so he could move on.

"Do you know anything about my magic?" Alderic asked Micah.

Micah shook his head no.

A weak smile spread over Alderic's lips, revealing the young Fae he once was. He brought his hands up before them and twirled his fingers, revealing a shimmering mist that formed a small hole. Sticking his hand through it, it disappeared.

A look of confusion crested over Micah's face as he tried to understand what happened. A tap on his shoulder made Micah turn around in shock. Alderic's hand was floating midair, poking out from another hole in the air.

"Portal magic," Alderic explained proudly. "Each Fae has their general powers, but some Fae hold extra magic... special to them. This was always mine." He removed his hand from the hole and closed the small portal he created. "When I was young, I didn't understand my magic. I didn't realize that with my eager want for adventure, I was creating portals to other realms that didn't want to be found."

"You created the portal?" Micah asked in awe.

"Yes, that one among many, I'm afraid," he said apologetically. "By the time I realized what I was capable of, I'd opened dozens of portals from our realm to others. Some portals I was able to close, as they were too dangerous for our realm. However, others I loved too much to let go."

"Like The Elderwood," Micah offered.

"Yes," Alderic said. "Sanni and I went there often, enjoying the beautiful trees and the magnificent bioluminescence at night. It was more than anyone could have ever dreamed, and I'd dream of it often." He looked down at his hands, taking a deep breath to find the words. "After I'd crafted my first bow, I was wonder-struck by its unique capabilities. When I thought of the ways we could use this new material, it was all too easy to return. How could I pass up the opportunity to strengthen Denora's defenses? How could I pass up the honor to give Denora such power?"

"What about the people there?" Micah asked.

Quillan answered this time. "We didn't let him know we could see him. He came and sat under the cover of our trees and never took more than he needed. It was why we felt the urge to trust him."

"It was Sanni's doing, really," Alderic laughed at the memory. "She was there singing and dancing as I collected the wood I needed, and she caught the eye of some of the children there. She sat in the shade, with her eyes closed, softly humming, when a small boy named Quill came up to her and asked her to sing the song again."

Quillan smiled. "We all loved Sanni." He put a hand over his heart and bowed in remembrance.

"She loved you all, too," Alderic said with a satisfied smile. "After that, Quillan's parents came to us and removed the glamor on the realm, allowing us to see the villagers. After a time, they showed us Thrinuin and made us promise to keep the realm safe from harm." His brows set in a determined line as he recalled each moment. "Sanni and I worked together to take my portal magic and place it in an amulet with her alchemy, so only those with the key could enter the portal."

"Lucy's amulet," Micah said in a whisper.

"Sanni and I kept it safe, using it sparingly, until we decided our time had come to finish our lives with our friends." He pulled a chain from around his neck where a simple gold ring hung. "When our children were well established at the small cabin, we left them, making them promise to keep the secret. Making them promise to keep the land safe." His hand clutched over his chest, his eyes furrowing with distress.

"Are you okay?" Micah asked, standing to approach him.

"I'm fine," Alderic said, waving him off. "It is just... with the realization of the curse I'd planted on my family... it breaks my heart to know I've caused anyone pain, especially the ones I love so dearly."

Micah sat back down slowly when a question came to him. "If only those with the amulet could enter, how was Lucy able to come and go freely without it?"

A twinkle came to Alderic's eye as he answered. "The gods

granted her special magic. They found her worthy of the knowledge of Porvanai and granted her something unique."

"If we close the portal, everything changes," Micah said sadly.

"Yes, you're right. It does."Alderic leaned forward in the kitchen chair, making Micah really look at him. "Just remember, with the portal closed, there is no more need for a guardian."

"Yes, but with the portal closed, then that god inside of Lucy never gets to go home. Lucy's family business will be gone forever. And I..." He almost couldn't say the words. "I finally found a family who understands me... I'm not ready to let it go."

"Are you sure, son?" Alderic asked him carefully.

"I'm sure. The warriors can still go and fight against Sloan to stop him. Lucy will be protected, and I will be here when it is all over."

Quillan's eyes softened at his answer, sadness filling them.

"If that is your choice," Alderic said, pain lacing his words.

"I'd do anything to be there for Lucy, but it's not me who she needs. Besides, sometimes doing the right thing means doing the hard thing."

Alderic nodded, and the three Fae walked back outside to meet with the warriors. "Micah, can you go grab your axe for me? I want to explain the alchemy to our warriors."

With a nod, Micah jogged off to the broken down tree house, regretting his outburst now that he was left with nothing to comfort him.

At his return, a few of the warriors had walked back through the portal, leaving their numbers from closer to thirty warriors down to near a dozen.

"Are they getting the rest of the fighters?" Micah asked, handing Alderic his axe.

"Not quite," Alderic said with a resolute smile. Then, as Micah, Quillan, and the other soldiers stood in the grass, Alderic swung the axe and chopped the tree cleanly in half.

THIRTY-ONE

LUCY

Leaving was the only option.

Lucy had gone through the different possibilities for hours, but each of them ended with unacceptable results.

You made a promise, she scolded herself. *You told Micah you'd stop running.*

Squeezing her eyes shut on her bed, she tried again to see a different path out of this mess. She didn't want to run. Every time she had done so in the past, it left her with an unfavorable outcome.

But this was different... This was life or death, and as she analyzed every avenue, it always came down to her or her family. In Lucy's mind, there was no acceptable reality in which she survived and her family did not, which made her decision easier.

Her life was not more important than theirs, and she would do whatever it took to keep them safe. Alive.

The truth was, she wasn't sure if she could survive another death in her family. Her father's murder rocked her to her very core, and the idea that she would have to experience more Farewell Ceremonies due to her inaction was unimaginable.

This is the only way.

She sat in the center of her bedchambers, staring at the brick walls and trying to gather the right words to make Wes and her mother understand her choice. With the estate staff gone, Anita had been giving her chores to do throughout the house, clearly to just keep her busy. Lucy could have ignored them, but instead, she worked through them as she solidified her plan. Besides, knowing she was going to be putting her mother in even more pain once she left made her uneasy. It was best to keep her mind off of it.

Life with Sloan would be difficult, to say the least. The idea of having to join him for dinners and live under the same roof as him made her ill, but being near him would allow her to keep fighting against his tyrannical power. It would keep her family safe as she smuggled out messages to her family about his awful plans. She could bring him down from the inside and make her way back to her family.

Unless...

Unless he found a way to overpower her completely. Then he would force her to bend to his every whim.

She sighed, knowing the likelihood of a happy ending for her was slim—but there was still a chance. There was a chance she could get to Sloan, outsmart him, keep her family safe, and find her happily ever after with Micah once and for all.

Even if she failed, she had to try. Her sacrifice would give her family more time to gather allies and prepare the king for Sloan's attack. And maybe, in the grand scheme of things, that's all that her family really needed: time.

If only they would see it the same way. It didn't matter how many times Lucy went through it—there was no way her family would let her surrender to Sloan. Instead, she would have to leave in the dead of night, when no one would expect it.

Old habits die hard, huh?

Closing her eyes, she took a deep breath in and out. She didn't want to do this, but she had no other choice. Opening her eyes and holding on to the little bit of courage she had left, she left her bedchambers and headed to the study.

Anita sat at the couch and Wes was in the wing-back chair at the desk.

"Ah, Lucy," Wes called to her. "I'm glad you're here. It's time for us to talk." The tenor of his tone told Lucy he was likely awake half the night, his voice raw and tired.

"I know what you're going to say," Lucy began, but Anita stood and held her hand up.

"We know you plan on leaving us when we least expect it," Anita told her.

Lucy froze.

"Probably in the middle of the night, and then we won't even get the chance to say goodbye," Wes replied with a sigh.

"How... What?" Lucy asked, astonished.

"Lucy. This is what you do. You aren't nearly as unpredictable as you'd like to think," Wes replied, stone faced.

"Darling," Anita said, trying to soften the mood. "We know we cannot control you, so we would like to help make this as smooth of a transition as possible." Her eyes gleamed with tears as she spoke, apparently hating the words and hating that Lucy would be sent away with that monster. "So, please, let us take you there. We can say goodbye to you and greet your brothers in tandem, hmm?"

Lucy couldn't believe it... they were letting her leave. Part of her rejoiced, knowing she could have the closure she so desperately craved... but another part of her was suspicious of their acceptance. Maybe they believed in her ability to thwart Sloan on her own? Maybe they agreed that the betterment of the family was more important. Either way, she was getting what she wanted.

"Thank you," Lucy said vehemently. "This is what I want. Thank you for finally listening to me and accepting that I am old enough to make my own decisions."

Wes bowed his head, his steepled fingers touching his lips deep in thought. "I'm thinking we should go to him on our terms... not his.

Let us have the day together, and then we will collect our brothers at dusk."

Lucy's heart raced with anticipation... Soon she would save her family.

~

THE DAY WENT by in a blur as Lucy kept her impending departure on the forefront of her mind. She walked in the gardens with her mother and took in the vibrant colors and scents that she would no longer have in the cold of the North. She drank amartium with Wes, dug through their father's favorite weapons, and shot them into the sky in fits of laughter.

She thought about going to visit Micah one last time, but she couldn't do it. There was no assurance she would actually follow through with what she needed to do if she fell into his arms once more. Again, she was breaking her promise to herself to never leave him. Unfortunately, keeping him safe would always be priority, whether he understood it or not.

Instead, she wrote letters to explain herself to all of those who mattered to her most in all the realms: her mother, all six of her brothers, and Micah.

She saved his for last because she had no idea how to put into words the enormity of her feelings for him. How do you tell someone they changed your destiny? How could she ever find the words to say that the stars are brighter because of his existence? That the moon has new meaning and the rustle of the leaves in the trees will always call his name? That her heart will belong to him and him alone for the rest of time?

The letter she wrote didn't carry the immensity that was her love, but it told him enough all the same.

She piled the letters neatly on her bed. They weren't goodbye letters, and she told them so. She would find a way back to her family, one way or another. Even if they were no longer in this home, even if it wasn't for centuries—she would make it back and reunite with them when the time was right.

When Sloan was no more.

~

"It's time," Wes told her as he buttoned a fine suit jacket.

Anita walked into the room behind him, holding a bundle of small vials.

"What is that for?" Lucy asked.

"Wes made arrangements for us to have the traveling powder for our use in case of emergencies," she explained, her beautiful dress a shimmering gray. "In case we are in need of a swift exit."

Lucy's eyebrows furrowed, but she nodded in agreement. Lord Sloan may be pleased to have Lucy in his grip once again, but it didn't mean he would make it easy for her family to leave.

Taking the vials from her mother, she placed them on the coffee table before her. With a wave of her hand, the bottles multiplied. Instead of just five, there were ten, then one hundred, then more, as the vials fell off the table.

"Lucy! What in the realms are you doing?" Anita yelped, backing away from the enormous pile of traveling powder.

Ensuring your safety, she thought to herself.

With those vials, they would always have a means of escape. Lucy wouldn't be there to whisk them away in the midst of trouble, but with the potion, they would have the power to do it themselves so she could see them again.

And that was where true freedom was found—in the power to make your own decisions about your future.

That wasn't exactly what was happening with Lucy, for it was not her choice to be imprisoned with Sloan. However, it was still her choice to save her family, and it made each moment of impending suffering worth every bit.

"This way, if you need more while I'm gone, you have it," Lucy smiled at her mother gently. Anita returned the gesture, but it barely met her eyes. Instead, a line of worry etched between her brows.

Wes checked the time and hurriedly took Lucy and Anita's hands. "Let's go. Bring us to Hugh's house, first. There's something I need to get."

With a gentle squeeze of her fingers around the family members who would stand by her side as she ensured the safety of all Baums, she took a deep breath and brought them to the South.

In a blink of an eye, they were standing in the middle of her brother Hugh's kitchen, the room dark and musty since his absence.

Wes and Anita dropped Lucy's hands and instantly began scouring the room. For what, Lucy was unsure.

Wes took off down the hall. Anita opened the kitchen cabinets, rummaging for something and cursing each time she closed a door and opened a new one.

But what was most curious of all was their clothing.

Wes was not in the fancy suit jacket he left in and her mother was undoubtedly not in a gorgeous glittering gown.

Why in the realms are they in fighting leathers?

Lucy watched as Anita wore a fitted long sleeve tunic under a leather vest with worn leather pants. Her hair was woven into an ornate bun at the top of her head and secured with pins—a far cry from her usual elegant updos with flowers and barrettes.

"Mother?" Lucy asked, forcing calm into her voice.

"Yes, dear," she replied, still searching through the cabinets.

"Why are you dressed this way?"

"It was a glamor, darling," she replied calmly, as though they were speaking of the weather. "I am looking for Hugh's fentyr-salt. Do you know where he keeps it?"

"Why are you looking for salt?" Lucy asked, her face contorted in confusion. "What is Wes doing? Why are we here and not with Sloan getting my brothers back?" The last words out of her mouth were more of a shout than a question, but she had had enough. "This is not the time for silly games!"

"You're right," Wes said breathlessly as he approached the room from the hall behind her. He stood before her in deep brown leather, clad from neck to toe. "We are not in the business of fooling around when our family is in need, and we don't intend on starting today. That is why you will not be going over to Sloan just yet, Luce."

"What?" Panic rose within her and her stomach roiled with unease. "What do you mean? I have to go there! We have to save them!"

Anita put her hands on Lucy's shoulders, calming her. "And we will." She handed her a pair of leather pants and helped her take her dress off. "But if you really think we were going to let you go so easily, then you, too, are foolish, my warrior of light."

"We have a plan," Wes announced, opening the oversized canvas bag he dragged through the house. Thrusting his hands inside, he pulled out weapon after weapon, expertly made by the Baum Bowyers themselves.

Lucy watched as she quickly dressed herself, too confused to defy.

"Sloan expects us to fight for you, and if we tried alone, we would likely fail. But what he doesn't expect is the rest of the Fae who will fight for Denora. And that, dear sister, is a fight we will surely win."

He handed Lucy a bow with a quiver full of arrows, each engraved with what she thought was their family crest. In fact, it was the Lumen family crest all along.

Micah.

Her heart ached for the one she loved.

Was there a chance that they could win this? That there was a way to both save her brothers and be free of Sloan forever?

She looked at Wes with the most pride she had ever felt. He planned all of this? How had she missed it?

"There is a benefit to being light on your feet," he winked at her. "But now we must hurry. It is about to start."

"What is about to start?" Lucy asked, but no sooner did the words leave her mouth as she heard it.

An explosion rocked the ground beneath her feet.

Wes smiled grimly.

"War."

~

Running through the streets of the South reminded her of her last visit. However, instead of the females and children penned in magical cages, they were freed. Instead of the uncertainty and confusion of what she saw clouding her judgement, her mind was clear. And instead of the fires blazing from the homes of the innocent, Lord Sloan's fleet of wagons was burning to a crisp.

Wes had explained as they made their way across town they had allies placed around the South, ready to fight against Sloan. A few were insurgents in Sloan's military forces, and others were from Denora's military, sent by Duke Renfro himself.

Lucy couldn't believe that he convinced the most arrogant Fae in all of Denora to side with him, but then again, Sloan was threatening to take that spot, and clearly Renfro couldn't let that happen. What would his poor ego do?

Her mind reeled at her new situation. She wasn't about to surrender herself to Sloan. She would not let her brothers die at his hands.

They were going to fight, and for the first time in days, she felt like they really had a chance.

THIRTY-TWO

WES

Adrenaline vibrated through Wes's body as he watched the battle unfold. Nearly everything was going according to plan.

To his right, Denoran soldiers provided by Renfro were actively fighting Sloan's. A loud clang of metal rang through his ears as swords met and great blasting lights of magical defenses lit the dusky landscape. The roar of battle cries sounded through the South, and he watched on from afar as he sent his petition for success to the stars peeking their way through the clouds above.

To his left, his mother stood at the forest line, digging deep into her remarkable power over nature. She looked like a completely different person in her leather pants and vest. In fact, Wes wasn't sure he had ever seen his mother in pants before. Within the length of a breath, she changed into her raven form and flew into the forest, leaving Wes and Lucy with the rest of the battle.

"Where did she go?" Lucy asked, shouting over the ever present sound of clashing. She tightened her quiver closer to her body as she gripped her bow in her other hand, strumming her fingers down the bow—a nervous habit Wes had watched Lucy do for years.

"She has her own plans," Wes said, not sure where his mother went. He knew it was important, and he trusted her implicitly—there was no time to question it.

However, Lucy was one he did *not* trust.

Turning, he held her tight in his arms and bent down to look her directly in the eye. "I need you to make a vow to me, Lucella."

The color in her face drained.

Vows were made between two Fae only in the most desperate of situations. They were looked down upon by the elders for their violent consequences. Once a vow was made, it could not be undone. Ever. If a vow was broken, the Fae would not just die, but terrible torment would spread over both Fae and their families.

"You must not give yourself willingly to Sloan. This is bigger than you and me; bigger than our family. We are all here to fight for the livelihood of Denora—for the future of all our realm. Do you understand that?"

He looked into her eyes, urging her to see the truth; begging for her to comply and promise she would not make any dumb moves while the battle unfolded.

She opened her mouth to speak, but Wes cut her off again.

"If I believe that you are out there trying to sacrifice yourself for our brothers, I will not be focused on the battle before me. Mother will always be looking over her shoulder for you. I will be scanning the crowds, praying you are still with us. We cannot afford to lose our footing in the fear that you aren't keeping your word."

The words were harsh, but Wes did not have the time to tiptoe around it. He knew this conversation was pertinent, and he also knew that if he had tried to have it earlier, Lucy would have just left. She would have transported herself right to Sloan's feet, knowing her family was safe at home.

But they weren't safe now, and they needed her to fight.

Battle magic raged behind them as the fight crept closer and closer to their position. Renfro's soldiers were formidable, and with their support, they would surely take Sloan down.

Lucy glared at her brother, her eyes turning a bright green. He recognized it as the steadfast sign that her magic was ready to pounce.

Wes smiled, knowing he had her then. Shoving his hand in front of him, he spoke the solemn words he had never dared to speak before.

"With this vow, I am tied to you. Under the guidance of the stars and the blood of the gods, I will keep this promise, or face the wrath of the unknown."

Lucy shoved her hand in his and repeated the words. Then she added, "I will not sacrifice myself for my family."

A pang of worry shot right through Wes, but before he could amend a single word, she ripped her hand from his and they were met with a flash of white light, sealing the vow between them.

"You better not sacrifice yourself at all, Lucella," Wes growled at her, pointing his finger in her direction.

Lucy just smirked as the green glow of her eyes grew. With a soft jump, she was floating midair, her hair raging in a wind that circled only her. "Don't worry brother," her ethereal voice sounded. "I have no intention of letting Sloan win today."

He watched as she joined in the fray, shooting arrow after arrow into Sloan's soldiers. They never saw her coming and each of her victims dropped to the ground with a thud. With each kill, she summoned her arrows back to her, allowing for a never-ending supply.

Wes would have laughed at her brilliance, but he had other tasks that required his attention. Even after the soldiers began their attack on her from high in the sky, he knew Lucy was more than capable of taking care of herself.

Summoning his lightness, Wes sprinted to Town Square. With his invisibility magic pressed tightly around him, he remained unde-tected as he took stock of their progress.

The soldiers were deep in the thrall of battle. Very few green uniformed bodies of Denora covered the ground. However, it seemed as though more and more navy blue soldiers of the North were finding their way to the battlefield. But how?

Renfro had said his spies gave him the numbers, and he built this team accordingly. He even brought extra soldiers to make the slaughter more prominent—how were they so outnumbered?

Where are you? Wes thought to himself, scanning the crowd for Sloan.

There was no way he was actively fighting, not with this many of his soldiers doing the work for him... but he had to be close by to give his commands.

Wes bypassed the small tents used by the soldiers. Sloan was calling himself *King*—there was no way he would encamp with anyone below him. No. His ego had inflated an impressive amount, which meant that wherever he was, it must be fit for a king.

And indeed it was.

At the very back of Town Square, Wes saw it at once. The old meeting place for government affairs was transformed into a castle of ice, the frozen crystals glistening in the light.

Renfro didn't mention this, he cursed. *Sloan must have warded this with his alchemy so enemy spy masters didn't pick it up from above.*

A delicate flicker of candlelight in a window was enough proof that someone remained inside the building, and Wes would bet any amount of riches that it was Sloan, biding his time until he struck.

Just then, a raven came and landed beside him. With a rustle of its feathers, it transformed back into Anita, her eyes wide with the chaos of violence surrounding them.

In that moment, Wes was thankful that Anita was the only one who could see him when he was using his father's gifted magic.

"I'm sorry I've been gone so long. I tried to send the word out to as many as I could." Her voice was raspy and her eyes were wild as she took in the clash of swords and the screams of injury as Fae battled Fae.

"Who did you tell?" Wes asked her quietly, trying to think of any who he had missed. He lifted some of the magic, allowing himself to be seen.

"You'll see if they accept the call," she said with a fierce look of determination in her eyes.

That would have to do for Wes, because they could use all the help they could get.

"I will go to the forest line and begin my line of offense," she said.

"Don't block every path in," Wes reminded her. "We are still counting on the warriors from The Elderwood..." His voice trailed off, concern filling him. They should have already been there.

Anita nodded and took off in her bird form as Wes turned back to face the castle of ice.

He still had a few tricks left, so he rushed to get in place before more of his surprises arrived.

CHAPTER
THIRTY-THREE

MICAH

"What did you do?" Micah asked Alderic, breathless. His mind spun with the repercussions of Alderic's action... The Elderwood portal—it was gone.

It happened in what felt like slow motion, but Micah couldn't stop him. Alderic took the axe and the light for the portal lit up as though he was going to step through it—but Alderic didn't enter the portal. Instead, he swung the axe with all of his might and chopped the tree down, using his magic to ease it down as it fell.

"I did what I should have done centuries ago, Micah." Alderic's eyes were wide, looking at Micah with such love and sorrow. "No one should be held prisoner to the past."

"But I wasn't a prisoner," Micah begged, dropping to his knees on the hard, uneven ground next to the tree. "I chose this. I chose to stay." His voice wobbled on every word. The guilt threatened to consume him. "You..." His eyes darted to the warriors standing by, Quillan in the lead. "You're stranded here. You can never make it home again."

Quillan's gaze remained stoic as he replied. "We are here to serve the Guardian."

"How am I a guardian if I have nothing to guard?" Micah spat the words. "This isn't right." He shook his head, looking over to Alderic, panic and dread filling his every thought. "Fix it, fix it now."

With a forced smile, he shook his head. "I cannot. But what I can do is offer you a chance to live your life once again. A chance to *really* live."

Alderic lifted the axe to hand it back to Micah, and as he did it, he stumbled. Micah reached out to steady him.

"What's wrong?" The alarm in Micah's mind was blaring. The portal was closed. There was no way for Alderic, Quillan, or the other warriors to make it home again. There was no wood for Lucy to use in her family business. There was no way her magic would ever rest in Thrinuin again. He felt his world spinning.

"I am very old," Alderic said with a weak laugh. "Porvanai gave me a way to live without aging, and that will have stopped now that I have left."

Horror struck Micah. "So, you're going to die?"

"Eventually, yes," Alderic said with a soft smile. "But not until you return victorious. Not until we have the time you need to find peace with your life as a Lumen."

The words were a gentle embrace on his heart, knowing he could have both of the things he wanted above all else... A connection to his family, with both Alderic and his father, now that he was able to leave.

And Lucy.

He could have Lucy. He could leave this place and be there for her.

"I don't know what to say," Micah said to him, realizing the sacrifice Alderic made on his behalf. Then he looked at the warriors, knowing they would have no way to return to their loved ones. "I don't know what to say to any of you." His words turned to a whisper.

"There is nothing to say, Guardian." Quillan stepped forward as he spoke. "You are still our Guardian, fighting for the life of those who matter. Fighting for the innocent in the face of evil. Our allegiance to you knows no bounds; no realm can stop us from following you."

Micah's heart lifted in hope and Alderic smiled at him, all knowing.

"It started with your amulet," Micah said in hushed tones.

"Then with your alchemy," Alderic said proudly.

Micah looked at the Fae before him, and for once, he counted himself as one of them. He was a Fae with powers that could make a difference in the fight against evil.

A red ball of magic grew in his hands and determination set in his brow. Feeling the immense power coursing through him, he gripped his axe tight in his fist.

"Now, let's follow our allegiance to all Fae and take this mother-fucker down."

THIRTY-FOUR

LUCY

The surge of magic running through Lucy was overwhelming. Her ability to strike her opponent directly in their heart from high in the sky only added to the adrenaline guiding her.

From her view, she could see the devastating battle raging on below her. Fires spread from the soldiers' tent village, the smoke creating a billowing haze that amplified the blinding light of battle magic. The slaughter of Fae life made her ill, knowing Sloan was at fault for all of this death. She tried to push more of her magic into taking down her enemy, but there were too many, and they were too widespread.

Lucy called to her Original magic and sent commands of all kinds.

"Stop," she called, but only a few of the soldiers closest to her were affected.

"Freeze," she demanded, but those who submitted to her power thawed quickly in the pressure of battle.

"Cease," she stated, hoping some would drop dead of their own accord.

Alas, nothing worked.

Nevertheless, Lucy pressed on, knowing moving forward was the only way to end this. And yet, the worst part of it all was not the exhausting fighting, nor was it the dread that seized her each time she thought about losing any more of her family. The worst part was that Lucy realized it was still the calm before the storm.

She hated to say it, but Sloan was brilliant. The decision to take over and become king had not been made in the midst of a cup of ale on some arbitrary night. No, he had been playing this long game for centuries. It made sense to her now that she saw his tactics up close.

He first made others fear him, murdering hundreds in the name of loyalty to Denora. For that, he earned the title '*Lord Slain*'.

Next, he added mystery to his repertoire. He lived alone in the castle with limited waitstaff and allowed himself to become nothing more than fable and myth, letting the people of Denora twist their own tales about him.

Then he worked carefully, slowly biding his time. He watched people... He took hold of what the Fae really wanted and needed in Denora, and he made them promises. Promises of more wealth and better opportunities for jobs. He promised them better quality food and support for the poor. He promised them a better Denora, and by doing so, he created loyal supporters who would follow him to the ends of time.

Until, finally, he tied it all with a beautiful bow, and showed them his true colors. He was not in the South to make the realm better. He was there for total domination, and his followers, so blinded by his lies, would never turn their backs on him.

That was why they were down there, right then, fighting for his charming words and insincere promises.

Lucy watched as the battle grew more violent. More Fae, from both sides, were left broken and bloodied on the ash covered ground. As each moment passed, more and more of Sloan's soldiers made their way through the crowd, meeting the Denoran soldiers in a clash of brute force.

Where are they coming from? Lucy asked, searching the ground from the sky for an answer.

She scanned high and low, looking for something that felt amiss. Further into town, Lucy saw the Fae male prisoners, still in their magical cages, unable to escape and fight with the rest of Denora. Biting her lip, she continued to survey the land, pondering how she would free those innocent Fae.

At the edge of the square, the soldiers erected a small tent village for their lodgings. Lucy would not have thought anything more of it, but something caught her eye. It wasn't more than a small shimmer at the corner of a tent, but with the dreariness of the battleground, it was unmistakably out of place. Taking a closer look, she knew she was right.

A ward.

Sloan's alchemy powered his magic to unprecedented levels, even holding the ability to subdue Lucy. However, she was still housing the incredible powers of an Original. Using that form of her magic drained her if she used too much, but there was no better time to use it than while fighting for the lives of the innocent.

Holding her hand out toward the shimmering space, she sent her magic to release the spell. "Reveal yourself," she announced. Emerald magic soared like a shooting star through the sky and landed directly on the canvas. With a crackle, the air around it vibrated, breaking apart the charm. Piece by piece, like a distorted puzzle, the ward dissolved before her.

Lucy's lips curved into a well-deserved smile, knowing that not all of Sloan's tricks would be impregnable. But as she watched it disappear, she could barely breathe.

Once the facade had worn away, she saw that there weren't tents at the edge of Town Square as she first thought.

It was all an illusion.

Instead stood four multi-level structures, large enough to hold hundreds of Fae.

Her heart plummeted through her body as she watched the Fae

soldiers in Sloan's command pour from the building. An officer stood at each of the enormous structure entrances, dispatching waves of soldiers to fight.

Quickly sending her magic to investigate, she found only one structure had been emptied, and another had just begun to join in the battle. But that meant Sloan still had two more buildings full of rested soldiers in reserve to dispense at any given moment.

He outnumbers us ten to one, Lucy realized, devastation filling her entire being.

She forced herself to breathe, squeezing the bow in her hands and tightening her quiver closer to her body.

Even with the immensity of her realization, she had no time to dwell over it, for just then, the trees in the forest began to shake, creating a creaking rumble that spread through the clamor of battle. First, it was just a minor quake, but then the colossal trees in the forest were swaying as though they were nothing but grass in the wind.

Lucy searched through the chaos for her mother, praying she would find her in time to protect her.

Flashes of her father's last moments came to her. Corvus falling to the ground, his body still and his eyes lifeless.

She refused to let her mother incur that same fate.

Close to the edge of the forest, Lucy found Anita forming vines that lashed out to enemy soldiers. The vines twirled and snapped in the air like tentacles with a mind of their own. Anita stood strong, her feet planted firmly on the ground as her arms twisted and directed them, grasping the leg of one Fae Northerner and flinging him into the dirt at top speed. Fae after Fae, Anita battled as fiercely as the military trained soldiers, defending her realm and her family.

Lucy would have watched on in admiration if it weren't for the wavering trees that traveled closer and closer to Anita's position.

In a single breath, Lucy appeared at her mother's side, yelling for her attention. "Something is coming!"

Throwing her hands high into the air, Lucy summoned a protection ward around them just as whatever was making its way through the forest appeared through the tree line.

First, hundreds of birds came soaring through—eagles, hawks, ravens, even little sparrows. Then, deer and elk rammed their antlers through the brush and right into the gut of an oncoming Northern soldier. Lucy and Anita stood close to one another as the birds dove away from her barrier at the last minute.

"I know," Anita replied over the rumble of stampeding animals, a smile blooming over her face. She looked at Lucy with a wicked gleam in her eye. "I invited them."

"You *what?*" Lucy said, her head jerking back to look at her mother in bewilderment.

"I told the woodland creatures that we needed help before Sloan destroyed all the good Fae left in the realm." Anita stayed focused on the animals pouring out from the trees, a curl to her lips showing her delight. "They said they'd discuss it and get back to me. Looks like they've come to their senses." She nodded to herself in approval, her hair still perfect in its sleek bun.

"And how are a bunch of sparrows going to help us?" Lucy asked in disbelief. She considered asking her how she could communicate with them, but decided against it. They had much bigger things to overcome and that could wait until after.

Because there *would* be an after.

"Don't underestimate the little ones," Anita told her disapprovingly, tightening the leather vest around her waist and then moving to tighten Lucy's around her shoulders. "When cast together, they create a mighty force to be reckoned with. Look!" Anita pointed to a small flock of birds just as they all attacked a singular Fae soldier, pecking at his eyes and shredding his skin.

"I never expected such violence from a tweeting song bird," Lucy said with a shudder.

Anita turned and looked back into the forest line as though she was anticipating something—or someone.

"What are you looking for?"

She sighed. "I asked more to come, but I guess some of them had no intention of helping us."

"What other creatures did you speak with?" Lucy asked, taking stock of the animals before her and coming up blank.

Then, a low growl sounded from behind her, making the hair on the back of her neck stand on end.

She spun in a flurry and raised her bow and arrow to the enormous wolven before her, pushing her mother behind her. One by one, an entire pack slowly made their way out of the dark forest, their glowing eyes locked on Lucy and her bow.

This was not Lucy's first interaction with the wolven, though it was the first time she had strong enough magic that she no longer feared for her life. They probably smelled the blood of the battle and made their way over to feast on whatever was left.

Lucy drew her arrow back, targeting the alpha that stood front and center. They would not hurt her or her mother today. Lucy took a deep breath to release the arrow, but Anita put her hand on her arm to stop her.

"No, Lucy! They are here to help!" Anita's smile reached from ear to ear.

"Excuse me?" Lucy said to her mother, thinking she must have heard her wrong.

"Thank you for coming," Anita said, speaking to the wolven instead, slipping out from behind Lucy with her hands clasped in gentle greeting. She took a few steps forward and the wolven stayed where they were, their hackles raised in warning. "The Fae in blue, with a mountain or snowflake on their shoulder," she continued, pointing to her shoulder as she spoke. She cleared her throat. "Ahem... eat *them*."

The alpha barked a response, then led the pack of thirty wolven onto the battlefield. It was almost laughable seeing the mature wolven, which stood as tall as a grown Fae, grip the soldiers in their maws and shake them like rag dolls. One by one, they took out Fae enemy soldiers, and our Denoran army backed away slowly to allow them room.

"It's working," Lucy proclaimed in hushed amazement. Her eyes were wide in shock, seeing the Denoran soldiers steal the advantage once again.

That was until a fresh wave of soldiers came charging through the battlefield straight for the wolven. But this time, it wasn't just any soldiers...

The tusked Kerroz guards from the North.

Lucy remembered seeing them guard Sloan's castle, but she never thought they'd choose to fight in a battle that had nothing to do with their realm... Unless Sloan promised them more?

They came running at top speed, shifting into their forms in their stride. Their bodies grew to double (and some triple) their size. Short, dark fur covered their bodies as they ran on four legs, like an enormous bull. Their two jagged tusks jutted out from their mouths as they grew two incredibly sharp horns atop their heads. They were designed for destruction, and that was what they brought.

Colliding with the wolven, they thrust their horns and tusks into the wolven's soft flesh, wounding them. Over and over, the creatures fought, racing toward the other's death.

"It's as though each time we get a handle on this, Sloan has something else up his damned sleeve!" Lucy fumed, her nails biting into her palms. "I need to get back into the air to help," she told her mother, looking into her beautiful eyes and praying she would see her again. "Be careful." Her heart ached to swoop her into her arms and deliver her back to the Baum estate where she would be safe, but she knew what it felt to be caged, and she would never do that to someone else.

"I will. I've got my friends here to protect me. You go."

Lucy turned back to the battle, her magic spinning around her, eager to get back into the chaos. And into the chaos she went, doing her best to keep her vow to her brother and help end this war.

THE BATTLE RAGED ON, Fae on both sides falling at the hands of the other. The death and disorder throughout the South was more than enough to make anyone retch. The blood and viscera that covered the ground made her question more than once if it was Fae or animal.

It was likely both.

There has to be a way to stop them.

Picking up fallen swords, she blasted them into her enemies at top speed, refusing to slow. She found being in the air allowed her better sight for battle, but her magic was dimmed by the sheer numbers. Even with her magic, Sloan sent out wave after wave of soldiers, having seemingly endless numbers. Her magic had been working relentlessly, trying to do enough to stop Sloan and his army, but there were just too many and they were just too strong.

We need more Fae to stand and fight, she realized, her stomach dropping.

But who?

There was no one left.

Lucy screamed as she shoved another sword into the gut of a Northern soldier, the gurgle of blood coming from his lips making her insides putrefy at the death of more and more of her kind. She'd do anything to preserve Fae life, but her enemy called for violence, and violence is what it would get in return.

Another low rumble came from the forest, further north than before. This noise differed from the utter pandemonium that followed the woodland creatures.

No. This was like a whisper on the wind mixed with the promise of peril.

Lucy tried using her magic to stretch her sight into the far off trees, but she was spent. She could do nearly anything as an Original, but she couldn't do everything all at once.

Grunting in frustration, she pushed herself into the sky. Zooming toward the forest, she shot arrows at her adversaries down below. Arrows came shooting back at her, but she dodged them and returned fire, soaring higher, knowing it wasn't making enough of a difference.

I can sit here and aim arrows at these soldiers all damn day, but it will never be enough. There are too many of them!

When she got high enough, she threw a protection charm around her and searched the battleground for a way to win. Left and right, she squinted into the distance. The sun had set in the wake of their war and the dust and smoke made the air hazy and thick.

With another rumble, she kept her eyes on the tree line. An obscure fog covered them, but it was too far away from the battle to be smoke. It was a thick, dark mist coming from the forest. It shaded the greenery and twirled around the tree limbs as though it had a life of its own.

Like a rolling wave, more and more of it poured out of the forest, shrouded in magic.

Lucy's chest tightened in recognition. Before she could even take one moment to second guess herself, the mist shifted into a pack of shadow beasts.

At the center of them all, she saw the one thing that lit up her entire soul.

Micah, riding on the back of a shadow beast shifter, his axe raised high as he roared for the end of Sloan.

THIRTY-FIVE

MICAH

There were soldiers everywhere.

Micah wasn't sure what he had expected, but this amount of bloodshed wasn't something someone could just conjure in their mind.

Hundreds of bodies were strewn across the endless battlefield, and the clamor of war rang loudly in his ears. Swords clashed with swords, battle magic bursting from both sides. Through the hazy smoke, he saw the bodies of enormous beasts tearing each other into mangled, bloody messes.

"Get ready," Micah told Quillan as they rode into battle. Micah tried to oppose riding on the warrior's back, even in his shifted feline form, but Quillan just rolled his eyes and insisted it was the fastest way to get to where they were going, so he complied.

As they got to the first line of soldiers, Micah jumped off of the shifter's back and began slicing his axe through the air, cutting down the soldiers in blue.

Quillan and his group of shadow warriors fought in their shifted beast form, using their shadows to their advantage. Before they left, Alderic gave each of them weapons adorned with jewels imbued with alchemy to enhance their strength and endurance. Once they shifted back to their Fae bodies, they would be well prepared with weapons at hand.

At least, as prepared as war allowed.

Micah swung his axe, striking down Fae after Fae. With each fallen soldier, his resolve hardened. Death was a terrible and heavy burden to cast upon anyone, but Sloan had given them no other option.

It's for the betterment of the realms, he told himself with every kill.

And he was right, because it wasn't just the realms of Denora and Joterra they had to fight for. They also had to fight for The Elderwood, and Vytyr, and every other innocent realm who would fall during Sloan's self-righteous crusade.

Micah saw firsthand how alchemy could be wielded to hurt others when mixed with magic, and he wasn't going to stand around and let innocent Fae—and mortals, for that matter—suffer by Sloan's hand. Not if he had anything to do about it.

Wiping his bloodied axe on the lifeless body on the ground beside him, he tightened his grip just as a heavy longsword came rushing down. Micah thrust his axe high to block it, kicking his attacker to the ground with a thud. One after another, the enemy pushed on, and Micah met them swing for swing with his axe.

He sent a silent thank you to Brax for her relentless initiative to prepare him. Though he wasn't sure if it would be enough. Each time he took down one Fae, another popped up. When the Northern soldiers caught wind of his skill, they surrounded him.

Micah's eyes raged wildly as he glanced between the enemy circling him, searching for a weak point so he could escape. There was none.

With two Fae behind him and four in front, the best he could do was to attempt a roll to the side to take out the left soldier's legs. Micah took a deep breath in, preparing himself for the inevitable hurt as they each lifted their swords. With a roar, Micah brandished his axe and hung on tight. He bent his knees, ready for their onslaught, and then suddenly, they all froze around him.

Literally.

A thin sheet of ice encased each soldier, rendering them unable to move, their faces contorted and wild.

"Micah?" He heard the faint question from the lips of the one person he yearned for above all others.

He turned, facing Lucy with a breathless stare. It was as if the battle around them had ceased, because there was nothing else in existence that could have pulled him from her irresistible gaze. Micah's heart bottomed out at the sight of her. He had been so worried she would be hurt or weakened, but she looked perfect. Utterly perfect. Not a single scratch on her.

With a sigh of relief, he swung his axe to knock off the head of the two Fae behind him, dropped his hand to his side, and wrapped his arm around her waist, pulling her in close to his body. Then, he kissed her, *really* kissed her, with the passion only a liberated man could feel.

Because, after all this time, he was finally free.

Free of the confines of the Lumen property.

Free of his burden of grief that tainted his view on life.

Free to finally be the man he chose to be; creating a life on his terms, and no one else's.

His body was enraptured, his focus on her lips and her skin and her smell as the rage of battle continued on all around them. Micah was lost to Lucy, mind, body, and soul, and there was nothing stopping the free fall of relief he felt as he held her in his hands.

Lucy grasped his face with one hand, pulling away slightly to get a better look at him. Her other hand still clutched her bow tightly as she spoke, her body tense with worry. "How are you here?"

"Alderic lifted the curse," Micah told her breathlessly.

He barely had time to register the flaming arrow, heading straight for them. He shot his hand out above them, but he knew his reaction was too late. However, instead of striking them, the arrow stopped midair, a ward encompassing them and protecting them.

His eyebrows shot up, and he looked at her in question. "Was that you?"

"I couldn't kiss you while we were unguarded, could I?" Lucy replied like it was the most obvious thing in the world.

I love her so much.

There was so much on his mind, but that was the loudest thought of all. After all of this, he could finally be with her.

She looked at him carefully. "The curse is really gone?" Her words were a whispered plea over the clash of battle outside of their little bubble.

Micah lifted one side of his lips in a half-smile. As grateful as he was, there was still so much heaviness weighing on him.

"Yeah, but it's a long story. One I'd be happy to share when we win this." There was no room for *if*.

Lucy nodded and opened her mouth to speak as a barrage of arrows came crashing into their dome, sending a flicker of light over her freckles.

Green light shone from her eyes and an angry sneer spread across her face. "Hold that thought," Lucy told him. Then she dropped the protection spell and crafted a giant gust of wind to knock the surrounding Fae to the ground.

Micah's hair blew back with the onslaught as Lucy rose into the air, her green magic twisting and twirling around her menacingly.

"I should warn you," she called out to the Fae around them. "I don't take kindly to people trying to hurt those I love." She rotated in slow circles as she lifted into the air, her hair dancing around her. "And if you want to aim your fire-tipped arrows at us, well... I *love* to play with fire."

Micah looked on in awe as Lucy put her hand out before her and squeezed, summoning all the fire from the Fae's arrows. One by one, their flames went out, speeding directly into Lucy's palm. Controlling the fire, she let it roll over her fingers with a satisfied smirk.

The soldiers looked at her in horror.

Micah couldn't help but grin like an idiot in love. His badass warrior was about to rain down an inferno and they had no idea what was coming.

"Micah," she called, her ethereal voice floating over the chaos. "I will find you when I'm done here." Then she glanced at him and gave him a wink, her confidence making him want her even more.

He shook his head with a smile and ran off in the other direction, finding his Elderwood companions and joining in the throes of battle.

EACH SWING of his axe came with more and more effort, not because he was physically tired, but because mentally he could not imagine how the fight would ever end. He was bloodied and bruised, and every Fae on the battlefield looked the same. But, the Denoran military were obviously struggling more.

Micah had personally eliminated dozens of the enemy, his axe successfully cutting them down one by one, but he seemed to be the only one. The soldiers who fought by his side couldn't kill a single Northerner without teaming up, as if they were weak—which Micah knew was not the case. They were military trained Fae; the best Denora had to offer.

Maybe I just have an edge because my magic is newer, he thought to himself. *Or maybe because I hadn't been out here this whole time.*

Either way, the disparity between sides threw him. There had to be a way to win this. Sloan hadn't even made his fucking appearance yet—and whatever line of defense he had waiting in his make-shift castle was sure to be worse than all of this fucking bullshit put together.

His mind drifted to Lucy as he fought, knowing he was fighting for something important—something worthy. Here and there he would get a glimpse of her magic or hear her battle cry as she unleashed her fury on her enemies, and each time it sent a wave of pride through his chest.

If anyone could take on Sloan, it was her.

With a whimper and a growl, a massive wolf tried to limp away from a cluster of attackers.

"Hey!" Micah cried, swinging his axe in their direction to give the wolf a chance to escape. A group of three Fae shifters turned to face him, their bodies that of a man, but their faces had tusks, like a boar.

Micah gulped.

"Why don't you leave the pup alone and fight me instead?" Micah sneered as he swung his axe in his hands, sticky blood coating his fingers. Three to one wasn't ideal, but if it gave that wolf a chance to live, then it was worth it.

Luckily, his Denoran counterparts came to help, brandishing their swords with a grit Micah admired. Even with the oppressive strength of the Northern soldiers, his brothers in green never stopped pushing forward. They would do anything for their realm, and Micah was proud to fight alongside them.

With a swing of his axe, he cut the chest of one shifter, leaving a trail of blood in his wake. The Denoran soldiers swung their swords at the other tusked Fae, but nothing happened. It was as though their weapons barely made contact. Again and again, they swung and hit the shifters, but the effect was minimal, as though their blades were dull.

The distraction got the best of Micah, letting one shifter get close enough to him to slice his arm before Micah lunged away. Another powerful swing of his axe and Micah sliced the shifter's head clean off, the sickening thump more satisfying than he initially imagined.

Down to two opponents, the soldiers took one and Micah took the other. Swiping left and right, Micah met the strength of the shifter's sword hit for hit, until finally, his axe slid across his enemy's soft underbelly, gutting him and relieving him of his entrails. Micah leaned on his hands on his knees to catch his breath, but that didn't last for long.

Somehow, the other shifter was still taking on three of the Denoran soldiers.

What the fuck? How do they call themselves soldiers if they can't win a battle of one against three?

Coming up from behind, Micah lodged his axe into the back of his unsuspecting enemy. He dropped to his knees with a thud. Micah gripped his axe with two hands and put one foot on the back of the shifter as he kicked the body away, dislodging the axe.

"How were you able to penetrate him so easily?" One soldier asked Micah, barely able to catch his breath.

"The better question is, how are you guys still standing at all after pretty much having no fucking effect on these guys? Do you need better swords or something?" Micah looked at them incredulously.

"We are the head of our unit," the other soldier replied, "and that's why we are still alive." His voice was rough from battle. "These swords should slice through them like warm butter," he said, then demonstrated by taking the blade to his own hand, leaving a thin, precise cut. "There is nothing wrong with us—there is something wrong with *them*."

Micah searched the battlefield and took in exactly what the soldiers suggested. The Denoran Fae were blocking every hit they could manage, but never getting enough of a blow to take down a Northern soldier in return. It would take two or three men to just take down one, and by the way they were outnumbered, that was just not a feasible battle strategy.

So what made them different?

He picked up a sword from the tusked shifter he had slain and held it in his hand. The weight felt like a typical sword. He cut the back of the shifter's bare arm, watching as it dragged across his skin. It was a little dull, if he was being honest.

Then he rolled the brute over, getting on his knees to try to sense if there was some sort of spell making them impossible to harm. He placed his axe down and ran his hands over the shifter's jacket.

Immediately, a tremendous force repelled against him, pushing him away. It was as if he could barely make contact with him at all.

"What?" Micah murmured, putting as much force as he could to touch the shifter.

"That's the same thing that happened to us," the soldier replied. "But when you fought them, you could touch them before. What's changed?"

Micah looked at the shifter, taking in his uniform.

How could he dismantle a spell he couldn't find? Was it something in his uniform? What changed?

He picked up his axe to lean on as he stood, and all at once, the repulsion stopped.

Pausing, he looked back down at the shifter and had an idea.

"Give me your sword," he told them.

One soldier handed it to him, and Micah raised it curiously in his hands. Dropping his axe, he swung the sword at the shifter.

Nothing.

Then, picking his axe up once more, he held it in one hand and wielded the sword in the other. Swinging the sword into the enemy one last time, the blade plunged into the shifter with a brutal squelch.

"The alchemy," he whispered. Sloan had somehow made his soldiers nearly indestructible with alchemical magic.

Searching the dead soldier on the ground, he found a trail of sapphires sewn into the shirt, acting as more than just decoration.

Plucking each one off with as much speed as he could muster, he explained it to the soldiers.

"Sloan is using alchemy with his magic. It is a sort of power imbued within a stone to change the form of magic." He worked quickly, popping each stone off and collecting them in his hands. "It's why you can't breach their uniforms—it isn't your weapons, it's their defense."

"Alchemy? I've never heard of such a thing!" A soldier retorted, scoffing at the idea of a new, strange kind of magic.

"You don't need to have heard of it for it to be true," Micah said with an annoyed huff. "Listen, I've got an idea, but I need one of you to be the guinea pig."

"You want us to be a pig?" The other soldier replied with disgust.

"No," Micah said with a sigh, forgetting some phrases didn't translate to Fae. "I need one of you to be willing to try it out first. We need to see if I'm right."

"And how would you know about this, anyway?"

Micah ignored the man as he held the gems in his hand and his axe in the other. With a focused determination, he called on his power to transform the gems into a slightly different kind of alchemy. He wanted the gems to hold courage and honor, something Sloan knew nothing about.

When he felt the magic transform, the sapphires no longer looked blue. They were purple.

"How did you do that?"

Micah again ignored them, but this time he gave one of them a gem. "Swallow it."

"Excuse me?" The soldiers stood and stared at Micah with wide eyes.

"You need the gem to be touching you at all times, but you can't risk dropping it in the middle of a scuffle. It won't work to put in a pocket or a shoe, so just swallow it already."

"What if you're wrong about this?"

"Then you shit out a gem if you survive the battle."

The beady eyes of the soldier reminded him of Jasper, but really, it was just the look of fear. Maybe that's what Jasper felt all that time —fear. Sure would explain a lot. However, this soldier was nothing like Jasper, because he would do anything for the good of his realm, so he swallowed it in one forced gulp.

Micah threw him his sword, then directed him to the nearest opponent. "Now go take him down."

The soldier took a deep breath, clearly exhausted and not looking forward to the endless fight. With a curt nod, he strode over to his next opponent, refusing to let fear stop him.

Micah had to give it to them, this Denoran military was fierce. They could be on their very last breath, and they'd still swing their sword for the honor of Denora. And that's exactly what this soldier did.

Raising the sword with all of his might, he swung the blade and immediately decapitated the enemy soldier.

The other soldier gave a victorious shout, shoving his hands in the air. Then he marched toward Micah. "Give me one of those!"

Micah gave him one, then held the rest of the handful out for him to take. "Get as many of your soldiers as possible to swallow them. I'll make a couple more handfuls to try to even out this battle."

With a firm nod, the soldier ran off and Micah hurried to the other dead Northerners, optimism surging through him.

This was it. Micah couldn't believe it. This could change the tide of war. And to imagine, what if he never made it there? What if he stayed back instead?

He shuddered, not willing to consider the possibility of losing. Because losing this battle would mean losing Lucy.

Turning another Northern soldier over, the tusked shifter gasped and coughed out blood.

He wasn't dead.

Micah lurched back on his heels, clutching his axe in his hands.

"Sloan will decimate all of you," the shifter laughed, blood spurting from the sides of his mouth, trickling down his tusks. "Just wait for what he has in store for you."

Micah didn't want to hear another word. Instead, he stood, used his axe to cut off the front of the shifter's uniform jacket in order to collect the gems, and left him.

After collecting the final gemstones, he hoped he had enough for them to gain an advantage on the battlefield.

But the enemy must have realized, because as Micah passed out the final gems to the soldiers, Sloan appeared.

He walked out of his enormous castle with a crown so large it gleamed across the brutalized south. Two enormous beasts lurked behind him; creatures with feline bodies, but paws the size of polar bears. These massive cat-like creatures pawed their way from behind Sloan, trailing him wearing ornate collars.

Collars adorned with more gemstones.

More alchemy.

Shit.

At that moment, Lucy raced to meet Micah, both of them staring wide-eyed at the monster who was to blame for all of this—all the death and devastation.

Micah told her about the alchemical gemstones on the soldiers' uniforms, how he was able to give them a fighting chance. "I'm not sure it will be enough, but at least it gives them their edge back."

"We've lost so many on our side," Lucy said, bitter sadness in her voice. They looked around and saw the truth of it. Sloan's force outnumbered them to a terrifying amount.

"We need more," Micah said in agreement.

Then, at that moment, a roar filled the sky.

Not just a roar, but a terrifying screech of rage.

"What the fuck is that?" Micah asked Lucy, but from the pallor of her face, he knew she had no idea.

Lightning filled the sky, and a low rumble of thunder echoed through the airspace.

"Lightning?" Micah asked. "A storm's coming?"

"No," Lucy said, her voice hushed as the rest of the battlefield fell still, the silence jarring. "Look... that isn't lightning... It's fire."

"Fire in the sky?" Micah looked again, his eyes searching for what Lucy saw. "Then what was that thunder?"

The rumble sounded again, *whoosh, whoosh, whoosh,* like a ticking metronome, the rhythm keeping time.

Whoosh, whoosh, whoosh.

"That's not thunder," Lucy said, her eyes looking to him in complete fear.

Micah didn't know what to expect, but if it scared Lucy, then he knew it couldn't have been good. His eyes scanned for Sloan, trying to get a clue as to what they were in for, but he only ever got the back of his head as Sloan stood in front of a tent speaking to his advisors.

His eyes darted to the sky once more and a blast of fire filled the horizon.

Fae shrieked as they ducked, covering their bodies in protective charms. Some of the Northern Fae ran for cover, but Micah wouldn't move. He stood his ground, waiting to see what their next battle would be.

And then someone screamed.

"DRAGON!"

Breaching the flames, an enormous green dragon soared through the sky, roaring and blowing fire as a threat to all those below. Its scaled body the size of a semi-truck—its wingspan twice that. A glow lit up the column of the dragon's neck as another roar tumbled from its throat and the sky filled with more dragon fire.

Lucy pulled on Micah's arm in alarm, trying to get him to turn and run, but Micah held her off. "Wait." He looked around at all the Northern soldiers running for cover. His eyes flew back to Sloan, who was finally in clear view.

A smile curled over Micah's face as he looked at the unflappable Sloan, looking like he was about to piss himself.

"These dragons aren't here to support Sloan. They're here for us," Micah told Lucy, pointing to Sloan's look of utter terror.

Turning his head back to the sky, he watched as a horde of dragons entered the atmosphere above them and blasted their fire.

"You never told me you called in the dragons!" Micah hollered in celebration to Lucy.

"That's because I didn't!" Lucy replied, laughter in her voice.

When he looked over at her, she was smiling. Then she looked at Micah and pointed up to the sky.

There, riding on top of the dragon like she owned the damn thing, was Brax.

THIRTY-SIX

WES

Hiding behind an overly decorative display case of ancient weaponry was not how Wes anticipated he'd spend his time during a war, but there he was. He had been there for hours as the battle raged on, but it certainly gave him a better view of the inner workings of Sloan.

In fact, Wes started questioning Sloan's mental stability.

Sure, Sloan was of unsound mind if he truly thought he was going to kill numerous Fae and take over as king of Denora... but to have such an ornate castle made of ice in the humid south? And to have taken the time to decorate a make-shift hide out in the middle of war? It appeared he was teetering a line of diabolical genius and complete nutty insanity.

Regardless, Wes kept himself hidden as he dug for more information that could help them win. So far he had found out that Sloan had used illusion charms to distract us from their actual numbers, he had acquired an entire battalion of shifters from Kerroz, and had adorned each uniform with alchemical power.

That last one was the current topic of discussion, because Sloan was absolutely furious.

"What do you mean the stones aren't working?" Sloan had hissed at one of his military officers.

"Sir, one of the Fae fighting with the Baums figured it out and has been pulling them off the uniforms of our dead."

"What? Who is it?" The depth of his voice turned more sinister with each passing question.

"A tall Fae I've never seen before. He arrived with the shadow beasts."

Sloan's eye twitched and Wes wished he could have been present for when Sloan learned of their arrival. "The King" had been hiding in here for the entire battle so far.

I wonder if he will ever leave this ice hideout.

"I believe it is the lost Lumen, sir," his personal guard, Roger, told him.

"Lumen." The snarl from Sloan was vicious, but the pride in Wes's heart was cosmic.

Sloan roared as he stood, knocking over an ice sculpture of himself. Roger stood quietly, not even blinking at the outburst.

Damn, I wanted to knock that over myself.

Sloan shoved his hands in his hair, knocking off his ridiculous crown, and began ripping out the pale strands.

"My Lord!" One of his officers said to him, trying to stop his hysterics.

"I am your KING!" He bellowed, the maniacal rage breaking through his falsely calm demeanor.

Ah, yes. The real Sloan.

Sloan raised his hand to strike his officer when the entire castle shuddered. He lowered his hand slowly, looking at the icy roof of his castle.

"We need to get to the battle tent and discuss next steps," Sloan announced, his voice an eerie calm. He straightened his jacket, then his hair, and took the crown from Roger without another word.

Sloan had rushed out of his castle for the very first time with the murmur of their next fated plans. That's what Sloan kept calling them, "fated plans," as though the stars had anything to do with it. As though his evil was justified.

Wes would have killed him the fifth time he said the infuriating words, but the two great calynx that he had guarding him made things exceedingly more difficult. Thanks to his father's magic, the felines may not have been able to see him, nor could they hear him, but every once in a while their noses twitched with curiosity at the lingering scent they couldn't identify. He was thankful they followed Sloan, leaving Wes alone.

Without the calynx roaming around the make-shift castle, it made Wes's plans much more accommodating. He sped through the building, searching up and down for his brothers. In each cold, empty room lay nothing but darkness. There was no life in the castle at all; the grandeur was all for show. Sloan was alone with only his trusted lackey, Roger.

In no time at all, Wes finished his task and caught up to Sloan, following him across the blood-ridden terrain. Keeping his father's magic close around him, he slunk into the battle tent. Sloan's body stood rigid as he met with the lead commander of his military. Wes stayed far enough away from the calynx so that he wouldn't get in their way, yet close enough to hear each and every word.

"Sir," the lead commander spoke, greeting him. "Our numbers are dwindling."

The majority of Sloan's soldiers were on the front lines now, and with Lumen's brilliant discovery of how to counter his alchemy, it seemed the Northern soldiers were finally going down.

"We still have the might of an exceptional militaristic force at our hands," Sloan waved him off. "How many more units do we have in our barracks?"

"All units in structures one through three have been dispatched. Structure four is on standby."

"Good. Prepare them." Sloan's words bit out at the commander, then he went to stand at the front of the tent, watching the battle unfold.

Following him out, Wes stood off to the side, downwind of the calynx, but still keeping his eye on the beasts.

From his position, Wes could see Lucy and Micah find each other on the battlefield and a wave of relief surged through him. It wouldn't last long, but at least they were together, and as they stared daggers into Sloan, Wes knew they wouldn't be giving up anytime soon. He searched for his mother, not seeing her through the chaos.

Still, Wes smiled as he watched Sloan masquerade as a male of calm and dignity and not as an immature Fae who just had a temper tantrum and ripped at his hair.

Then a low rumble filled the air, and a flash of light lit across the sky. Each Fae inside and outside the tent looked around in bewilderment—even the Fae in the middle of battle paused as another round of thunder made its way across the sky.

A scream sounded in the distance and Wes followed the noise, looking into the sky at what finally made its way through... a massive horde of dragons.

His stomach dropped at the sight of such amazing creatures, but when he saw the magnificent warrior perched upon on the front dragon's shoulders, a fire lit within him.

Brax. That remarkable, breathtaking female. If I make it out of here alive... but he stopped the thought.

The outcome of his task was all that mattered. Sloan must be stopped and his family must be safe. Whatever happened beyond that didn't matter anymore.

"Are those... dragons?" the commander asked.

"Of course they're dragons," he spat. "What else could they be?"

The commander bent low, touching the floor in a low, trembling bow. "What are the plans to take the dragons down, my king?"

Wes knew Sloan had no fucking clue, and that knowledge delighted him.

"Send in the units," Sloan ordered in a rough, low voice.

"How many would you like, Sir?"

"All of them."

"But—"

The commander didn't have the chance to finish his sentence, for Sloan turned and berated him, which gave Wes the time to slink away once again. Wes had learned enough about his plans to know that they were on the right track. Besides, his favorite surprise was about to happen and he needed a nice view to enjoy the show.

He sprinted across the battlefield, thankful for the slight pause between fighting so he could make it to Lucy and Micah in time.

Finding them was easy. They were, like everyone else, staring up in the sky, watching the dragons in awe.

"Are you ready for my big reveal?" Wes whispered in Lucy's ear, making her jump.

"Where did you come from? Where have you been?" Lucy asked him, torn between anger and relief.

"Where's Mother?" Wes asked, anxiously searching for her across the crowd.

A raven landed beside him and shifted, revealing Anita. "I'm here," she said with an exhausted grin. She grabbed his arm in reassurance, calming him as much as she could.

"Did you do it?" Wes asked eagerly.

"I did," she said, nodding, tears in her eyes. "I found them."

"My brothers?" Lucy asked breathlessly, pain lacing each word. "Where are they?"

"They are on the other end of this madness," Anita said with a relieved smile. "Sloan knew we would be focused on his castle and battlefront, so he has them staged blocks from here in a small hut with just a few soldiers, but they are quite formidable."

"You didn't fight them, did you?"

"I couldn't," Anita said, with the first hint of sadness. "The shifters would have been easy to take down, but I couldn't get past whatever alchemy magic Sloan had cast upon the hut."

"Okay, that means they are safe in the meantime." Wes said, nodding his head, the next steps of his plans coming together quickly.

"Wes," Micah said to him, clasping him on the shoulder. "It's great to see you, and while I don't want to take away from the moment, you said you had a big reveal. Did you call in the dragons?"

"Absolutely," he said with a devilish grin.

"Did you set it up for her?" Anita asked, anticipation clear on her face. Their mother was ready to bring down this monster as much as the rest of them.

"What are you two talking about?" Lucy asked, getting frustrated. "I know you've been doing all of this sneaky nonsense so that I wouldn't find out and try to stop you, but I'm here now, so just tell me what in the realms you two have planned."

Anita and Wes smiled at each other—two partners in this chaotic masterpiece.

"Let's just say that fentyr-salt is used for more than just cooking, my dear," Anita told her.

"Just keep your eyes on the castle and I'll tell you in a minute." He looked up to see Brax and the other Vytyrian warriors riding the massive dragons as they got into place. Once they were in formation, Wes shot up a spark of his magic, signaling her to begin.

On his cue, Brax led the warriors and their dragons to the castle made of ice and blasted it with fire. The soldiers on the battlefield broke out into cheers, whooping and clapping each other on the shoulder as they watched the dragons attack the castle.

Wes walked behind Anita and held his hands over her ears as his grin stretched across his face. "Here it comes."

An enormous blast erupted through the castle, then another and another as the bombs he had planted triggered. They watched as the crystal ice palace went from an enormous solid structure to shards of ice in a matter of moments.

They knew the empty castle would not end the war, but it was a figurehead for everything they fought against. Besides, seeing Sloan so pissed off was just the cherry on top.

"That was amazing!" Lucy shouted, cheering with the rest of the crowd.

The wind above them whooshed all around as a dragon's enormous wings beat right above their heads, landing on the ground so close to them that Wes could smell the smoke from the dragon's mouth.

He took a step back.

Brax ran over to them and Micah pulled her into a great hug, swinging her around like a little girl. "That was so fucking badass!" He yelled, a smile stretched across his face.

Trying to fight him off, Brax did her best not to smile, but they all saw it in her eyes. She was happy, and she didn't really hate the attention from Micah. "Put me down, you roasted marshmallow."

"You know, that is the first food insult I've understood," Micah said with a laugh, planting a big slobbery kiss on her cheek as he placed her down.

She wiped it off with a sneer but greeted the others with an easy smile. Micah and Lucy just laughed as they fell into an easy embrace, watching the Fae cheering.

"So, this is what you'd rather do instead of freeing the rest of the males of the South?"

Everyone there turned to see Ruthani clad in oversized fighting leathers and holding a longsword.

"How did you get here?" Anita asked in astonishment.

"You left an entire arsenal of that traveling powder out in the open. What did you think we were going to do? Just sit around and twiddle our thumbs while we wait for your return? *If* you ever returned at all?" Ruthani spit out the words as though she was furious at them for leaving her, but the truth was just beyond that.

She was one of them. Ruthani, just like Wes, Lucy, Anita, and Micah, had been hurt by Sloan and craved revenge.

And she would get it.

"We?" Anita asked, looking behind Ruthani.

With a wave of her hand, Ruthani lifted her illusion. There behind her stood every female that was freed by Brax. "We left the children at home—war is not meant for the innocent."

"Where did you get all of this?" Wes asked, referring to the leathers and weapons.

"We went back to our homes to prepare," Ruthani said, her chin lifting in challenge. "We are going to free our families and then fight by your side."

Brax stepped forward and took Ruthani's hand in solidarity. "I would be honored to have you at my side."

Lucy took Ruthani's other hand resolutely.

Then Anita took Lucy's.

Brax lifted her lips in a devious grin and held out her hand to Anita, closing the loop.

The four females stood in a circle, embraced in a fierce determination and looking ardently into each other's eyes. Wes looked between the females curiously. They had so much in common—such ferocity behind their femininity.

"People really *do* need to stop underestimating women," Micah said to Wes quietly.

But the moment was cut short, because Sloan's furious voice echoed across the desolated battlefield.

"Will you sit by as these traitors work to hurt your king?!" He amplified his words with his magic. Northern soldiers roused as they listened to him speak. "I call upon the last of our line of defense." He roared, and the calynx roared in return. "End this today, and rejoice as we walk into a new era of Denora!"

A rumble sounded from the last structure, and soldiers began pouring out.

"Brax! Get the dragons there, now!" Wes called. "Ruthani, get to the males and free them. Anyone able to fight, send here. Anyone who needs medical attention, bring them to the estate. Mother, go with them."

Micah rushed over to give Ruthani a handful of alchemical gems to use. Then handed some to Anita, Wes, and Lucy. He gave the rest of them to Brax for her Vytyrians.

Brax ran to her dragon and jumped with such grace and speed that she was up in the air in seconds.

"Micah, I need you to fight with our soldiers. Can you do that?"

A swift nod, a fervent kiss to Lucy, and Micah was off to fight.

"Wes," Anita said quickly, trying to get a word in. "I have an idea. Let me stay."

"Mother, you have the choice to do whatever you desire," he said, looking at her curiously. "I am not in charge of you."

"No, but you are the head of this family, and I look to you."

"No. *You* are the head of this family, and we would be lost without you," Wes said, the words coming out so fast he didn't even have to think if they were true or not. Of course Anita was the head of the family—there was no other option. It didn't matter to him that she was female, she was strong and just and held the wisdom to guide them all. He shot her a half grin. "Now go do whatever diabolical plan you have in mind, and find me when you are done."

With a brightness in her eyes, she transformed and took off as a raven in the night, headed straight for Sloan.

Be careful, Mother, he pleaded.

Ruthani was off in the next moment, headed to the prisoners that were taken in the first battle that started this war.

All of this was for them.

"I'm going to Sloan," Lucy told Wes, her eyes shining a deep emerald green, her sneer trembling as her jaw clenched.

"Get lost in your magic," Wes told her, repeating the words their mother had told her.

"No," she said thoughtfully. "It is in my magic that I am found."

CHAPTER

THIRTY-SEVEN

LUCY

I am found in my magic, Lucy had told him. She had never realized the truth within that. For so long she had let the magic ravage through her, being a vessel for another, long forgotten god. She failed to stop and allow the magic to be who she *is* as much as it was what she *had*.

She closed her eyes and took a deep breath, allowing the magic to flood into every part of her body; in every blood cell, every muscle fiber, every strand of her hair. Her magic filled her until she couldn't take any more, as though it would overflow from her very being. But the reality was, she could. She could summon more and more of her magic, and continue to fill herself with the immense well of power because the magic was not something separate from her.

It *was* her.

In that moment of acceptance, her magic burst from her, creating a display of power so extraordinary it knocked over the surrounding Fae.

She rose in the air, a calmness taking over for the first time since they had arrived. Scanning the chaos below, she searched for Sloan.

774

This war could not continue without a king, and since he was finally out of hiding, it was time to take him down.

Before she could spot him, the dragons made it to the barracks. Fire rained down, trapping the soldiers inside in an enormous ball of flames. Shrieks of desperation sounded from the tower, but there was no more remorse for those who sided with Sloan. Not anymore.

The dragons worked together with fire and claw to bring the structure down to a smoldering rubble, then they turned and joined the carnage; the battle forging on.

With a satisfied grin, Lucy turned her eyes back to the swarm of bodies, searching for Sloan. Her magic did the searching for her, taking charge of soaring through the South, showing her everything in her mind. What was left of the castle was off to the right, the barracks burning to the left, and the battle tent where she saw Sloan when the dragons came lay in the middle. The only person there was a worried officer, his gaze darting left and right amidst the melee.

Her magic scanned the rest of the South. She saw as Ruthani freed the males kept captive, the female's magic overpowering Sloan's soldiers in record time.

The calynx, she thought. *Those should be easier to spot.*

Her search shot to the other side of the battle to find Sloan riding on top of one of the felines with a bow and quiver strapped to his body. However, he was not alone, for Roger and another three guards held a trio of male prisoners.

Tristan, Hugh, and Gregory.

They each had blindfolds over their eyes and gags in their mouths, their hands tied behind their backs with some magical charm.

Lucy blinked the sight away and instantly transported herself before them, refusing to waste any more time. Her magic pulsed through her body, ready to unleash utter terror on this monster, but she needed her brothers out of danger, so she contained it best she could.

The calynx snarled and came to a halt at her unexpected arrival.

Sloan's eyes widened, but only for a second. "You will let me go free or I will kill them," he roared, his words heavy with his demand. However, Lucy caught he way it wobbled at the end of his request—he was scared. With Roger at his side, he jumped down from the calynx and strode over to her, looking ruffled.

His hair was wild and the ridiculous crown sat askew atop his head. The ornate jacket he wore was ripped at the shoulder and hung off his frame.

Sloan's running, she realized with delight.

"You will let them go free or I will kill *you*," Lucy replied, the magic in her body knowing that was a promise she would die keeping.

Sloan began to laugh hysterically, the deranged smile contorting his face. "You think you can still stop me?" He took a step toward her, shucking off his jacket. "I don't need those jewels to know I can take you down. You know, I thought I loved you once," he said, the words quiet, as though he was lost deep in thought. "But I was wrong about you. Seems I was wrong about your magic as well." He got close to her and lifted his hand as though he was going to stroke her face with the gentle back of his fingers.

Her magic sent off a warning to back the fuck off and the blast knocked him back a step.

Sloan only laughed more.

Lucy looked at Roger in disbelief. "And you stand for this? You stand by his side after everything he's done?"

She wanted him to say he was wrong for following him. Lucy wanted to hear that he just got too deep into things and couldn't find a way out. Anything would have been better than what he said next.

"His only mistake was thinking he needed your family involved in his affairs." A darkness swept through Roger's features at the declaration.

Lucy sent a blast of magic straight for Roger at the same moment the three guards fell to the ground in a heap. She whipped her gaze to the side and saw why.

Wes!

He stood behind the guards with a bloodied knife in his hand. Wes used it to get the blindfolds off of his captured brothers, then he yelled for them to run.

"NO!" Sloan bellowed.

Lucy quickly created a shield and sent it over her brothers as Sloan's magic came raining down on them. She fell to her knees at the weight of his power, doing everything she could to keep her brothers safe.

Sloan screamed with rage as Roger remained unconscious on the floor next to him. Ripping a ring from his finger, he crushed it in his palm, amplifying his power over her.

Crying out, Lucy held on. She had to hold on. She would not let her brothers get hurt. She could never let Sloan take away someone she loved from her ever again.

But even as much as she wished for that to happen, his magic was just too strong. Her shields crumpled under the might of Sloan's alchemy and a blast of magic sent Lucy to the ground.

Her eyes darted to her brothers as she watched them run as fast as they possibly could, even in their weakened states. Gregory and Hugh were nearly to her, Tristan behind him with Wes pulling him along.

Lucy bit back a sob as she watched Tristan, broken and bloodied, run as swiftly as he could.

But it wasn't fast enough.

"Arrow!" Gregory choked out.

Lucy's gaze darted to Sloan, and she saw him release the arrow right for Tristan. Sloan threw his hand in the air, guiding it along with his alchemy. Lucy tried to stop it, but her magic was repelled once more.

The whizzing arrow flew straight for Tristan, and there was nothing anyone could do to stop it.

It shot through the sky and hit with a sickening thud.

Directly into Wes's back.

"No!" Lucy screamed, and her magic completely lost control. Her shadows poured out as grief overtook her like a ship lost at sea. She screamed as lightning shot from her body and flames burst from the palms of her hands.

She watched as Tristan fell to the ground and crawled back to Wes, sobbing and clinging to him, begging him to rise.

Hugh and Gregory were speaking to Lucy, but none of their words were heard. A barrage of guilt weighed heavily on her, she felt as though she was being crushed.

It was her fault another member of her family died.

It was her fault they would be in mourning.

It was her fault she accepted the vow not to sacrifice herself.

But Wes was the one to pay.

She screamed. She roared. She wailed for her family that was being ripped apart by this bastard of a Fae who cared for no one and nothing.

Then, a woodsy smell of musk and linen curled around her and a warm arm embraced her midsection, pulling her back to reality.

"Shhh, sweetheart," Micah's voice was calm, steadying her. "Come back to me."

Her shadows receded and her flames burned out as she slumped back into his chest, his arm the only thing keeping her upright.

All the while, Sloan was laughing. However, with her billowing shadows, he didn't see the other Fae that had come along with Micah.

"I've been speaking to your pets," Anita said sweetly in her entrance. "They are not very pleased with their recent treatment from you. In fact, they said they are starving and you've been with-holding food?" She was sitting on top of an actual calynx as though she was made for it.

The words were sweet and kind coming out of Anita's mouth, but Lucy knew she was setting him up for destruction. She had perfected playing pretend in front of male Fae her entire life.

"Attack!" Sloan screamed at the calynx, desperation coloring his voice. "Attack!"

"Oh, dear. They no longer respond to your commands, I'm afraid." She pet the other calynx as it came padding next to her. "You see... they've had a change of heart." Anita said, the ruthlessness coming out at last.

Bursts of magic tore from Lucy's hands, striking Sloan one after another. She wouldn't let anyone else get hurt. She would end this now.

He shielded with a clear ward and glared at her through furrowed eyebrows, the sneer on his face only making Lucy push harder.

With another blast of magic, she spoke to him in between her onslaught of power. "Why are you hiding, Laurent?"

Lucy sent a blast of magic into his shield.

"Are you finally showing everyone who you really are?"

Another blast.

"A worthless..."

Blast!

"Spineless..."

Blast!

"Weak, piece of shit."

This time she braced for his return attack, and she was ready for it.

He burst from his shield and pushed his two hands out in front of him, adorned with jewels and gems from the crown on his head and the rings on his fingers. She took stock of it all as she blocked his attack, knowing exactly what she'd be targeting next.

"You will not defeat me! I am more powerful than you! Than anyone!" Sloan shouted, the words only more of his carefully sculpted lies.

"No, Laurent," Lucy replied, sending a pulse of magic, freezing him in place. She walked up to him, her heart thundering in her chest. "You're a dick on a power trip," she smiled, taking every ring off his hands. "But that ends today."

Reaching for his crown, his magic burst through hers, throwing her backwards. He scrambled to his feet and shoved more magic at her. His alchemy being the one thing that Lucy couldn't overcome.

As Hugh, Gregory, Anita and Micah tried to come to her aid, Sloan sent more of his magic, sending them all to their knees.

"We need to get to Wes," Hugh said over the roar of magic.

They all looked at their fallen brother in desperation. He was not moving, but Tristan was still there by his side, whispering to him.

Pushing his magic into Lucy, Sloan forced her to bend as well. "You don't understand, *beloved*," he spit the word like it was poison on his tongue. "This is how this battle ends. With me on top, and you beneath me."

"I will never serve you," she rasped between clenched teeth, trying her best to stand.

He forced more magic into her, making her knees buckle. "You will kneel to me!" Then, Sloan lifted a thick sword from its sheath, and held it up, more alchemical jewels glistening in the fire of battle.

The magic in her body surged, begging to be released, but Sloan's hold on her left her powerless. Even knowing she was going to fall at the end of his sword, she refused to look away. Lucy would look directly into the eyes of her enemy and seek revenge from the void beyond. She would die with strength in her heart and no fear in her eyes. Sloan would not take that from her.

With a scowl he pulled the sword back and paused in surprise, his eyes going wide as he looked past Lucy to the forest line beyond.

A puff of hot air blew past Lucy's neck as she watched the self-proclaimed King Laurent Sloan quite literally tremble in his boots.

"I'm going to walk over to Wesley Baum," Brax said as she walked toward them. "And if you so much as make a single fucking move to one of my friends, this dragon is going to turn you to dust. Do you understand?"

Brax walked past Lucy and her family, still forced to their knees by Sloan's magic, and sprinted directly to Wes, pulling him close to her and sending her healing magic into his body.

Lucy almost sobbed in relief... but even if Wes was healed, it wouldn't stop Sloan. She wasn't sure if Sloan's powers could rival dragon fire, but it was a challenge she'd be happy to take.

"Come on now, Laurent." Lucy forced her eyes to his. "I thought you said you were the most powerful of them all," she goaded him.

She assumed one of two things would happen. Either Laurent Sloan would move to kill her as she sacrificed herself in order to give Brax the time she needed to heal Wes, or this dragon was going to fry his ass. Even if the vow she had made promised Wes she wouldn't sacrifice herself for her family, he didn't take one thing into account... Sacrificing herself for her realm was more important than anything else, and with Wes's leadership, her people could stand a fighting chance. And Sloan could never have Micah.

Wes had to live, so she would risk her death.

Sloan's eyes lit with fury and he made a move toward her at the same moment the dragon kept his promise and took a deep inhale above Lucy, blowing a jet of dragon fire directly at Sloan's head.

Sloan dropped his magic on Lucy as he shielded himself from the fire. Amazingly, the fire bounced off of his shield and Sloan exclaimed in celebration as he was safe from the bite of the flames. And while he may not have been burnt to a crisp, at least Lucy and her family were free from his power.

She tried to see Brax and Wes through the blaze, but the only thing she could do was duck down and stay out of the angry dragon's way.

Long moments passed, and her panic rose within her.

Please, please let Wes be alright.

The fiery blaze ended, and Sloan stood, a deranged smile filling his face. "I am stronger than a dragon!" He took a few steps closer to them, then paused.

Brax stood on her right, and to her left, a warm hand landed on her shoulder.

Lucy held her breath.

"There are eight of us, two calynx, and a dragon. You're really sure you're going to get away this time?" Wes's voice was rough, as though the pain still lingered.

Lucy choked down a sob of relief.

Sloan kneeled from his place on the ground and howled with laughter.

While Sloan was distracted, Micah used his magic to grip the crown from his head and smash it into the ground. Using as much force as he could, Micah crushed the metal into a heap.

"You think *wrinkling* my gems will make them not work for me?" Sloan's mirthless laugh grew.

The sound of it put Lucy on edge.

They had missed something. What did they miss?

She shifted in place, studying him, watching for the tell.

Wes moved to Micah's side and pushed his light magic into the crumpled mess of metal and gems that was once Sloan's crown. His magic changed from heat to pure light, as bright as the sun, as the metal melted.

Sloan's eyes widened for only a fraction of a second, but it was enough of a clue for Lucy.

He's afraid of the stones being destroyed, obviously... but there's something else.

Wes brightened his magic even more, causing Micah to shade his eyes as the gems burst into shards.

Sloan went quiet. He stared them down, a haze of orange coating his blue eyes.

That was it.

That was what Lucy was waiting for.

"It seems you and I were of the same mind, lost Lumen," Sloan voiced, the words like gravel. "You can't destroy something you can't find." His laughter started once again.

"You swallowed alchemical gems?" Micah asked, a growl in his voice.

"No," Lucy answered for him. "Look at his eyes." She pointed to Sloan's once ice-blue eyes to call attention to the hints of orange. "He fused the jewels into him somehow…"

"It's amazing what a bit of crushing can do to a gem. If you do it with just the right pressure, it can still hold magic." He tore the chain from his neck. "I do not need these weak gems on my body. The power is inside of me, and *you* cannot get to it."

Wes turned to Lucy, his eyes wide with a plan.

Her eyes burned with tears, but she held them back, knowing it wasn't time for an emotional reception, no matter how happy she was to see him standing next her, alive.

"Lucella," he said to her, his eyes glancing from her to Sloan, erratically. "Do you remember the gifts Father bestowed upon us?"

"Yes?" She could not understand why he brought that up. Undoubtedly his light was useful to melt the stones, but how could they melt stones they could not see? And how would her shadows help her?

Suddenly, he disappeared from the space before her.

"Where did he go?" Sloan asked, a rumble of anger breaking its way through his maniacal laughter from before.

Then a whisper filled her ear. "Father gave me his light," Wes said only to her. "And he gave you his darkness."

She tried to hold as still as possible as he whispered the words, trying not to give any hint as to where Wes was.

"We may not be able to thwart him alone, but together we can."

Lucy still didn't understand. How? How would she be able to help her family?

As though Wes could sense the tension in her body and the panic in her mind, he told her one final thing. "Protect our family, all of our people, from my light with your shadows, and let us end this once and for all. Let us get lost in the magic to find ourselves on the other side."

With a deep breath, Lucy called on all of her magic. She called on her Denoran magic that filled her veins from the moment she was born. She called on the magic from the god that resided within her, making her an Original. She called on the magic from her father that filled the void in her heart. As her breaths came quicker and quicker, she continued to call to her magic. She let it fill her, let it pour over her, let it seep from the broken crevices of her soul as she knew the endless magic would be the only thing to stop Sloan and his tirade for power.

With emerald green magic swirling around her, and black shadow magic flooding the ground around them, she thrust her hands high into the air and screamed. "Now!"

With as much force as she could, she covered each and every Fae fighting for them with her magic. Every Denoran soldier. Each Elderwood shifter and Vytyrian warrior. Every bird, deer, and wolven. Ruthani and her clan of females, along with the males they had freed. The dragons. Brax. Micah. Her family.

Everyone but Wes—because as she covered them in shadow, he became the sun. His magic kindled within him, burning brighter until Lucy was forced to cover her own eyes as well.

The power pulled at her, the light from Wes challenging her dark shadows as it tried to pry them away from the bodies she was protecting. She screamed through the effort, her body feeling as though it was being ripped into shreds. More and more heat poured over her skin as Wes bellowed through the exertion.

But none of that compared to Sloan's frantic shriek for Wes to stop. The desperate cry of pain rang through the South until there was nothing but a stunned silence filling the air. The heat subsided and Lucy released her magic, unable to hold on another moment.

She fell to a heap on the ground, too weak to hold herself up, the sound of beating wings as the dragons left the only thing filling her.

"Lucy!" Micah ran to her and scooped her up, cradling her in his arms.

"Wes," she croaked at the same time Brax screamed his name.

Lucy forced her eyes to open, searching for her brother, aching to know if his plan had worked.

Wes groaned in response, and a sob of relief left her throat, knowing her brother was alive.

Micah lifted her in his powerful arms and brought her to Wes, placing her down beside him.

Wes's skin was bright red and hot to the touch.

"What happened?" Anita asked, her voice shaking.

"Lucy protected you with Father's shadows as I used his light to burn the gems from within Sloan." Wes's voice was raspy.

"He's gone," Hugh said, shaken. "Literally, there is nothing left of him but dust."

"You cooked him?" Tristan asked.

Micah stood, slowly turning in a half circle as he looked out into the battlefield beyond. "No," he breathed. "He cooked *all* of them."

Silently, the group helped Wes and Lucy to their feet as they stared into the war zone that was once the center of Southern Denora. All that was left were charred remains, blood and gore, broken and dilapidated buildings, and... their Denoran soldiers. Wounded... but alive.

"We won."

THIRTY-EIGHT

MICAH

Micah watched as Lucy held her family. The reality was Hugh, Gregory, Tristan, and even Wes, were almost killed in battle. If she had lost them, Micah wasn't sure if she could have ever recovered... He knew firsthand how difficult grief was to overcome. He lost his mom and his grandad and it changed who he was at his core.

Lucy smiled brightly at her mother as they shed silent tears of relief, but the tears stopped as they looked around the rest of the battlefield. The war may be over, but the work was far from done.

"I will speak with our soldiers," Wes told them. "Mother, why don't you go see how Ruthani and her group are doing?"

"I'd like to go with you to speak to some of the soldiers," Tristan said softly. "Some of them were my friends on that battlefield." His voice sounded far away, as though he was stuck in a difficult memory.

"And we'd like to see how our male counterparts from the South are," Hugh said, and Gregory nodded. "We will go with Mother."

Brax turned to Micah with a half smile. There was something about the sadness in her eyes that made him pause. She must have known about the sacrifices that were made to get him here. "I will say goodbye to my Vytyrians and see the dragons off. Then I'll check in on Quillan and see how they're doing. You can find us by the forest's edge when you are ready to return."

One more nod and they were gone, leaving only Micah and Lucy alone at last.

Staring into the smoldering battle grounds, Lucy took in a deep breath, her chest rising so very slowly. Micah watched her from the corner of his eye, not knowing if she was ready to talk about it all. He shifted his weight so he was closer to her, and waited.

He wouldn't push her into talking about any of this, not after she had just watched her family almost die. Not after she had used so much of her power.

The seconds felt like hours, but then he felt it. The tiny twirl of Lucy's smallest finger wrapped around his in a silent offering, looking for nearness without demanding it.

He extended his hand to her, and she eagerly clasped it, holding as if he might be swept away if she let go. The tremble in her body could have been from exhaustion or from the terror she faced, and Micah decided it could very well be both, so he took his other arm and wrapped it around her, curling her into him.

A soft sob left her chest as she pressed against him, and he heard her gasp and hold her breath, forcing herself to stop. Micah whispered into her ear, "You don't have to pretend with me. Let it out."

Her head tilted up, and she looked at him, her eyes rimmed with red and wet with tears. "I can't let them see me cry."

"You can," he told her. "They will not judge you for that, and if they do, then they are idiots."

"They are idiots," she sniffled. "That's the problem."

"I've never seen a problem you can't fix," he said playfully, trying to lighten the mood, but all it did was cast Lucy's face to the sky.

Her eyes brightened with the pale shade of green, and she spoke the words into existence. "Rain."

Clouds rolled in and rain fell from the sky, putting out the remaining fires and cleansing the ash and soot off the faces of those all around. Lucy and Micah washed their hands and faces off in the deluge and found each other once more.

"Very clever," Micah told her. The rain would hide her tears. "But I don't understand why you won't let anyone see you cry."

"Because if I am to be treated like an equal, then I must act like a male. Male Fae do not cry, and they definitely do not weep for the loss of an enemy." The voice cracked as she spoke.

"You're crying for Sloan?" Micah asked, his chest tense.

"Absolutely not," she scoffed. "The universe is better without him... It's the rest of his soldiers. It could have been Tristan." Her mouth shook as she tried to hold in more tears. "He didn't know he was making such an error in judgment, and I would guess that many others felt the same way. Many of them were probably tricked into this, lied to about Sloan's true intentions."

Micah's lips formed a thin line, the heaviness of those words both hurtful and true. "You probably aren't wrong."

"But our soldiers will not see that. Hugh and Gregory will not see that. Too many were killed by those same enemy soldiers. I cannot weep for them." Lucy said, her voice rising as the last words sliced through the air.

"Yeah, but Tristan might be the one who needs to see it," he told her calmly. "Because he did have friends out there. He was the one almost duped into that shit show... Acknowledging those things does not make you weak, it makes you compassionate."

Lucy didn't reply to that, but wouldn't look at Micah, either. She continued to wipe the tears from her eyes; her face hardening more and more by the second.

"Come on," Micah said, taking Lucy's hand and pulling her. "Let's get out of the rain and talk... There are a few things I need to tell you."

They spent the greater part of an hour talking about the curse and Alderic's actions. Lucy's lip wobbled when Micah told her The Elderwood was closed off forever, and her green magic that had been swirling around her since the battle began settled on her shoulder as though it understood the desolate news that it would not be returning home.

"I'm so sorry I caused your family business to end," Micah said, the words coming out painfully slow. Lucy did everything she could to make her way into her that business, and it nearly cost her everything. And now it was just gone? It was possible she'd never forgive him.

"Don't apologize for someone else's actions," Lucy told him firmly. "Besides, if I were there, I would have done the same thing."

"You would have cut off ties to the portal?" Micah asked her in disbelief.

"If it meant your freedom? Of course." Lucy tilted her head as she looked at him, as though she couldn't believe he didn't understand. "Micah, you are important. You deserve to have a choice in your future. You deserve to be able to make decisions about your path, and that curse gave you no ability to do that. Alderic gave you a gift, even if it is a very hard one to bear."

She grazed her thumb on his cheek, either wiping away more ash or consoling him. He wasn't sure, but the gesture comforted him, nonetheless.

"I've got to figure out a way to get these guys back," he told her, looking out at the shadow shifters that had fought by his side. Thankfully they all survived. Being able to move between solid form and shadow helped them to combat the enemy with ease.

Lucy nodded and stood, taking his hand and walking him over to Brax, Quillan, and the other shifters.

"Need a lift, Lumen? I can call those dragons back?" Brax told him, a teasing lilt to her words.

"Yeah, I think I'll pass. That shit was terrifying."

"Leave it to males to pale at the sight of a formidable beast," Brax said, sheer joy on her lips.

"Your Vytyrian warriors sure looked badass up there," Micah chuckled. "Make sure you send our thanks."

Brax laughed and sat next to Quillan. "And you, Quill. Make sure you tell Alderic we thank him," Brax said as her gaze met with Micah's. "For everything."

Yeah, she knows.

"Don't call me Quill," Quillan replied dryly.

"I'll tell him," Micah told her, an unspoken conversation passed between them, one of appreciation and love for his best friend.

Then he looked at Lucy and every bit of his heart felt like it would shatter because he knew she wouldn't be coming with him, and he would be a selfish prick if he asked. She needed to be with her family, and he understood. But right now, he was responsible for The Elderwood warriors, and he needed to find a way to help them.

"It's time to go home," he said, looking at Lucy, and he wished she would go with him.

THIRTY-NINE

LUCY

The aftermath of war was utterly indescribable. Lucy couldn't get her mind to turn off the memories as she lay in her bedchambers in the Baum manor. All the dresses in her wardrobe somehow reminded her of Sloan, so she opted for a soft tunic and a pair of deep navy leggings. No matter how comfortable she tried to make herself, she couldn't stop seeing the devastation of war when she closed her eyes.

There was so much joy, having ended a tyrannical ruler, his control, his power... yet, there was such sorrow as well. Each of the soldiers had lost brethren on the front lines. Animals lay dead after sacrificing their lives for the lives of Fae. Even the pack of wolven was reduced to only a handful of survivors, but according to Anita, they were proud to have fought against evil and hoped this would bring more respect for their kind in the future.

The dragons were long gone. Brax had explained that she recruited Vytyrian warriors to the cause, then traveled to Kerroz. As soon as she told them the Fae needed help, they were happy to step in. Apparently they weren't always dragons, but actually shifters. They had kept their identities hidden, as is their tradition.

It all felt surreal. The oddest part of walking through the South was not the awestruck citizens bowing down to her. It was not the strange way the soldiers had considered her and her group, largely formed of females. It was that the only dead were from their side, and all of the enemy soldiers were obliterated—truly, dust in the wind.

It took days for the Fae to work together to remove the remnants of a violent war. The buildings were reformed, the bodies sent off to sea, and families were reunited.

Even her family was gifted that.

She squeezed her eyes shut tighter as she sat up, trying to shake the painful memories away. Lucy didn't know how to describe the way Anita cried as she held her three sons in her arms after they were released from captivity. Or the sound that escaped her throat as Wes stood before her, after being nearly killed with an arrow.

Even more difficult was the eerie silence on the battlefield after Wes finally killed Sloan.

Wrapping her mind around *that* fact was almost impossible. It was done. The war was over, the evil was defeated, and her people were safe... so why did everything still feel so uneasy?

A knock on her door pulled her from her troubled thoughts. "Come in," she called.

Tristan walked in, his hair longer than the last time they were in Baum manor together, but the light from his eyes was still missing. "Hey Luce," he murmured.

Lucy patted the bed next to her in invitation. They sat in companionable silence, but her mind was anything but quiet. She couldn't believe he had almost been killed.

"I almost lost you," she whispered to him, tears escaping from her hazel eyes.

He took her hand in his. "From the sound of it, we almost lost you, too."

Closing her eyes, she forced deep breaths, trying to keep her emotions down.

"Why are you locked up here, Luce?" Tristan finally asked her. "Mother said she's trying not to pry, not to push you away, but I told her this is the time to barge in. She didn't want to hear it."

"And that's why you're here? Prying?" Lucy asked, the energy gone from her usual witty remarks.

"Yes." Tristan turned to face her on the bed. "And to ask what happened with you and Lumen."

"With Micah? Nothing." She turned away from him and stood up in a hurry, walking to the other side of the room. "The battle was over and it was time for all of us to return home. I came to my home, and he went to his."

Lucy's words came out more clipped than she had intended, but avoiding that part of the battle aftermath had been the hardest.

"It's time to go home," Micah had told her. Then he took his Elderwood warriors and left with them, saying he needed to see if he could figure out how to get them back to their realm.

She wasn't sure why she thought he'd come home with her... Denora wasn't his home. And Joterra wasn't hers... so who were they kidding, really?

"Ah, so that's what it is," Tristan said, a small smile making its way over his face as he glanced at her from across the room.

"What *what* is?" Lucy snapped, turning to face him from her spot near the door.

"Why all the arguing?" Wes said, stepping into her bedchambers.

"No one invited you in here," Lucy told him, frustrated by the brothers who couldn't seem to stay out of her personal life.

"Luce is upset because Micah went home and didn't invite her." Tristan's curt response made Lucy cast magic to the flower vase on the side table, knocking it into his lap and spilling water all over his trousers.

He only laughed.

"Lucy, since when do you need an invitation of any kind to do what you want?" Wes asked, a twinkle in his eye.

She crossed her arms in front of her. "What do you expect me to do? Leave my family after we are finally together again? All to chase after some male?"

Tristan stood from the bed and walked up to her. "That's all he is, huh?"

Lucy turned her face away from him, but Wes was there by her side, gently taking her chin in his hand. The look in his eye was so much like their father's and all she felt at that moment was grief.

She pushed his hand away and turned from them both.

"The threat to us is gone, Lucy," Wes said. "The boys will come back from Lord Klimek in a fortnight, and they are absolutely oblivious to the danger we faced. Hugh and Gregory are here, spending time with Mother before they must get back, and Hugh will soon be with Lisette. That beautiful baby that will be born any day now and bring even more joy to our family. Mother is fine," he said, breaking out into a chuckle. "I mean, really, did you see her out there?"

He tried to get her to respond. To laugh, to smile, anything—but Lucy refused. Because even if everyone was safe, how long would it last? How long would it be until something else tried to tear their family apart?

"Luce," Tristan said. "Look at me. I'm fine."

Her eyes shot to his, and she refused to pretend she wasn't mad. "But you weren't fine. And you didn't tell us until it was too fucking late. Until you did some boneheaded thing and left our family without a second thought."

"Well, it seems like bonehead, split-second decisions run in the family then," Tristan teased, not letting her words hurt him.

He was talking about her decision to leave Denora to go to The Elderwood on her own to prove to her family she was worthy of more than being shipped off to an arranged marriage. It truly felt like a lifetime ago, and in a way, it was. Lucy was not the same person she was when all of this started. She changed more and more with each passing day.

"Yes, we can all agree you two are the boneheads of the family,"

Wes said, slinging an arm around each of their necks, bringing them in close. "But can we also agree that life here needs to change?"

Lucy stilled under his words. Pulling away, she turned to him, looking into his eyes. "What do you mean?"

He smiled and jerked his head toward the door. "Come on," he said, letting them go and walking out of the room. "We've got a meeting we can't miss."

WALKING INTO THE STUDY, Lucy wasn't entirely sure what to expect. However, when she saw a formal meeting underway, she felt oddly underdressed.

Anita stood to the side silently, respectfully greeting their guests, looking as beautiful as ever in a deep violet dress.

The chairs were arranged for an official assembly, and when she saw who was in attendance, her heart thrummed wildly in her chest. King Tralont sat in the study, Duke Renfro by his side. Across from them sat... Ruthani? And to her shock, it was Brax beside her.

There was another seat in the row, and Lucy stayed back, waiting for Wes to sit, but instead, he remained standing.

"Go sit," Lucy whispered to him eagerly, not wanting to offend the King.

"The seat is yours, Lucella," her mother said. Then she walked over to her father's old desk and sat as head of the house.

Lucy's mouth went dry. Was her mother purposefully disrespecting King Tralont?

Wes simply took her hand and led her to the seat, then stood back with a wink as she stared on in awe.

What the fuck is happening?

"Miss Lucella," Duke Renfro spoke at last.

"Duke Renfro, King Tralont," she said with a bow of her head in return.

"It appears we have some business to discuss," King Tralont said, boredom in his tone as though he would rather be anywhere else. His gaze kept trailing to Anita as she sat at the large desk.

"I have informed our king of the transgressions of Lord Sloan," Duke Renfro shared. "He has been stripped of all titles and has forfeited the right to the Northern Territory."

"Well, that's good, since he's dead and can no longer claim it," Brax said sarcastically.

Lucy was all for putting people in their place, but the *king*? She almost choked on her tongue.

"Quite," was all Tralont replied.

Duke Renfro continued on. "I have also shared with King Tralont your valor during battle. Without your courage and bravery, our realm would have suffered greatly. We'd also like to thank the mortal that joined you in battle, but we did not think traveling to Joterra was the best decision at this time."

"He is not *only* mortal," Lucy said before she realized she had said it.

"Lucy is right," Wes continued. "He is Alderic Lumen's ancestor, and a great and powerful Fae."

"He is... both Fae *and* mortal?" Tralont asked, curiously. "I have never heard such a thing."

"Perhaps if you would have listened to my son the first time then you would be more privy to the happenings of your people," Anita said sharply.

Oh my stars, Lucy panicked. *The king is going to sentence all of us to death for our disrespect.*

"Perhaps you're right," he replied.

Lucy nearly fell out of her chair.

Ruthani was the only other person in the room looking as surprised as Lucy felt.

Brax sat back lazily without a care. Tristan and Wes stood with secretive smiles on their faces. And Anita sat like a queen, fearing nothing and no one.

"As I said, there is business to attend to," Tralont continued, "if we can get on with it without any more outbursts?"

Lucy just nodded her head as Anita stared on, stone faced.

"Ahem," the king went on. "To begin with, Duke Renfro will relinquish his command of the military immediately."

Lucy felt a pit in her stomach.

He is going to punish him because he helped us?

"You can't do that," Wes said, standing up for him.

The king shot him a glare that would have brought Corvus Baum to his knees. "You will let me finish speaking. I will let you know when I am in need of your input."

Wes's lips formed a tight line as he took a step back, obeying his king.

"Renfro will relinquish his command and take on the position of Lord of the Northern Territory."

Duke Renfro's jaw dropped slightly. "My King? Are you sure?"

"Why are there still people speaking?" The king complained as he looked to the ceiling, his hand on his head. "Master Wesley Baum will take over Renfro's position as the leader of our Denoran military."

It was Wes's turn to stare slack jawed at the king.

"Do either of you have objections?"

They shook their heads "no" in reply, and the king broke his first small smile.

"As for the females of the room," the king said, uncertainty in his voice. "It is unheard of for a group of females, such as yourselves, to have created such a powerful force. If I am not mistaken, it was you four at the front lines of this battle? Freeing our prisoners from the South? Using almighty power to stop Sloan? Speaking with the wolven to fight on our side. And..." he looked at each of them sitting there, Ruthani, Lucy, Anita, and then stopped on Brax. "Riding on dragons?"

"You're damn right," Brax said with a devilish grin on her face.

King Tralont broke into a hearty chuckle.

Lucy assumed this was the most Tralont showed amusement.

"Well, it seems as though we owe you our gratitude," the king said.

"You owe us more than that," Anita spoke.

Lucy wondered when her heart would stop pounding so loudly in her ears so that she could hear people speak. Because there was no way in all the realms that her mother just said what she thought she said.

"Excuse me?" Tralont replied, taken aback.

"The reason Lord Sloan had so many followers is because Denoran traditions are horridly out of date," Anita said, then she stood from her seat and stepped in front of the desk. "Sloan offered freedoms to females so that they may become equal to their male counterparts. He considered more support to the needy so that the poverty lines between us may not be so steep. He was a tyrannical maniac, but he had original ideas that we should not ignore."

Something within Lucy loosened in that moment. She had been so convinced that she was so blind to have followed Sloan for so long that she really doubted how it started. Knowing her mother also thought that his preliminary views of Denora were meaningful gave such relief to Lucy.

"How dare you share in your support of the male who tried to overthrow the crown!" Tralont stood, fully offended by Anita's response.

Lucy got up and stood next to her mother, then Brax and Ruthani followed suit. Wes and Tristan stayed back, allowing them to speak for themselves. They didn't need any males rushing in to save the day.

"We are not looking to overthrow you, King Tralont," Lucy said carefully. "We are looking for a seat at the table."

"Why? Denoran tradition has not changed for a millennia!"

"Exactly. Which means it's out of date and needs to catch up with the rest of existence," Brax snapped.

"We are not looking for more than others. We are looking for our equal share." Anita's shoulders straightened as she spoke, her regal posture making her every bit of a leader Lucy would be proud to follow.

"We want to pick our own jobs," Lucy said. "And not just in typical female positions."

"We want to pick our own partners," Ruthani shared. "No more arranged marriages."

"And we want to elect our own heads of house," Wes said, finally. "Anita Baum is the most qualified person for this position in our home, and I guarantee other houses feel the same about their female leadership."

"And you must provide to those who have less than others," Brax said, pointing to Tralont. "No more of this nonsense where the poor Fae have to suffer in silence as the rich Fae stuff their faces with gray poupon."

"What in the realms is gray poupon?" Tristan asked Wes under his breath, but all Wes could do was laugh.

Duke Renfro stood, trying to calm people to their chairs again. Once everyone sat, he spoke. "Correct me if I am wrong, but what I am hearing is that you are insistent that we improve our rights for females and that we need to provide a better quality of life for the most needy of our population?"

All four females replied at once. "Yes."

Renfro shot a small smile to each of them, then he turned back to the king. "King Tralont? These seem like reasonable requests, do they not?"

The king let out a gruff, noncommittal noise.

"I'm sure if these formidable Fae could stand against any enemy to the throne and fight for the people of Denora, then they only have the best intentions in mind, do they not?"

The king let out another gruff noise, but it seemed more like assent.

"Very well," Duke Renfro said, turning away from the king and smiling at the Fae in the room. "We will get that started and look forward to updating you on our progress."

He gave them a quiet wink, then led the king to the door, leaving the Baum estate.

Lucy stood frozen in place as the room erupted in celebration. She couldn't believe any of what just transpired had actually occurred. Did her mother really talk back to the King of Denora? Did Wes really just get the position of commander of their military?

"What's wrong, Baum?" Brax said to her, punching her shoulder to break her of her shock.

"I can't believe that just happened."

"Personally, I can't believe you're still here."

"And where should I be?"

"Lucella Baum," Anita said over the celebration. "If you don't get your behind to Micah Lumen this instant, I'm going to ask Brax to feed you to a dragon." She smiled and laughed with pure joy.

"You want me to leave?" Lucy asked, unsure how to decipher her words.

The cheering stopped and Anita walked over to her daughter. Cupping her face gently, Anita looked deeply into Lucy's eyes. "I want you to follow your heart. And there's only one place you can find it."

"But this is my home," Lucy replied, her panic growing once again.

"Home isn't a place," Brax told her, and Anita dropped her hands. "It's so much more than that. It's where you find solace after a long, hard day. It's where you feel safe when everything else feels too hard. It's where your heart resides."

Each of her brothers gave her an encouraging nod, and Ruthani just smiled.

Brax grinned at her. "Go home, Lucy."

Home.

FORTY

MICAH

The warriors from The Elderwood had no interest in staying in Micah's cabin, so they worked together to cut down a few trees and build temporary homes in the center of the wooded property. They told Micah they preferred to be among the trees and valued their privacy.

Micah couldn't blame them. He made for shit company as he moped around the cabin, missing Lucy. Alderic traveled between the cabin and the camp where the warriors lived, giving Quillan and his shifters more attention. As much as he wanted to connect with Alderic, they needed Alderic more. Whereas Micah had gained more than he could have ever imagined, the warriors had only lost.

Micah wasn't sure what to do.

Should he go home and visit his dad?

Should he wait around and see if Brax was going to come back and check on him?

Would Lucy ever return?

And who was he now that he wasn't the Guardian? It had taken him so much time to finally come to terms with who he was in that role, and now it was just gone? Another path ripped away from him?

He played these same thoughts over and over in his head and never came up with an answer. His desire to see his dad surpassed all else, but he couldn't take the risk of venturing beyond the property and potentially losing the opportunity to connect with either Brax or Lucy.

So, instead, he stayed. He told himself that after a month or two, if nothing changed, he would give the cabin over to the warriors and take up his dad's offer to go live with him and Lori. They had an overly rambunctious dog named Zero, but otherwise, they were good people. People who loved him. Although he couldn't say they really knew him anymore.

He had been pacing around his bedroom in the cabin, unwilling to go back downstairs and face reality. He was tired of looking out the window and not seeing the visitors he craved. He was tired of looking at his phone and knowing he should pick it up and fucking call his dad. He was tired of laying in bed, staring at the ceiling doing jack shit.

It felt insane to go from fighting in a full-blown war to coming home to peace and quiet. It was too damn jarring.

His gaze caught on a glinting red jewel in the corner of his room. He cringed when he saw the axe that saved dozens unceremoniously shoved away.

A weapon that special shouldn't be mixed in with my dirty socks, he thought to himself. Then an idea came to him.

He stormed downstairs, grabbed a can of nails and some pieces of wood and put his mind to work, doing what he did best and pushing the pain away.

BY THE TIME he was done, he had created a beautiful two-piece wall anchor to display his axe. The wood needed to be prepped and stained, but so far, he was pretty happy with how it turned out.

"Since when are you the woodworker?"

Micah spun to find Lucy sitting on a cut down tree trunk next to the fire pit. His heart raced as he took her in. She wore a light, comfortable shirt and tight navy leggings, accentuating her curves even more. Her hair was loose, and she was playing with the ends as if she was contemplating putting it back into its customary braid. A shy smile played on her lips.

"Well, I figured I had all this wood around to put to good use," he replied.

They just looked at one another, smiling until Micah couldn't take it anymore.

"Is this visit for business or pleasure?" He asked, knowing one of those answers could cleave his heart in two.

"Perhaps both," she teased as she stood up. Slowly, they walked toward one another.

Micah sighed as he took her in. There was pain and hurt there in her eyes, but she was the one who needed to let him in. He couldn't force himself into her life again if that wasn't what she wanted or needed.

She paused a few steps away from him, her freckles on her perfect face dancing in shadows from the canopy of leaves above them.

"If you are here for a social visit, does that mean you are here to see me?" Micah asked, realizing he sounded juvenile but not giving one fuck. He was done playing games, and he just needed to know where they stood.

She nodded.

"Is this you saying goodbye to me again?" He asked, his throat bobbing at the terrifying possibility.

She shook her head no.

"Do you plan on staying for a while?" He asked, his mouth dry.

Lucy shook her head once more.

His heart fell, his mind raced, his soul shattered.

I should have known this was coming.

He closed his eyes and dropped his head, trying to think of what to say next. She placed her hand on his and he wasn't sure if it felt like ecstasy or torture.

"I don't think a while will be long enough," she whispered.

Micah's gaze darted to hers, his eyes wide in wait.

"I was thinking more along the lines of *forever*, if that was okay with you."

Before she could finish her last word, Micah pulled her to him, his lips finding hers in a wild rush of kisses.

Forever?

His hands cradled her face as he kissed every freckle, the tip of her nose, the curve of her lip, the line of her jaw down her neck.

She giggled as her hands gripped his shirt and pulled him closer to her. "Hold on," she whispered, and then they were in his room.

He pulled off her shirt and began kissing every inch of her body that he could reach. Behind her ear. The divot in her neck, then across her clavicle. He went lower, cupping her breasts and taking each pink tip between his lips, listening to her moan his name. He got halfway down her body before he paused, resting his forehead on her stomach.

Holding her close, his fingers pressed down on her soft curves. "You mean it?"

"Promise me forever, Micah." Her words were breathless and full of burning devotion.

Her hazel eyes searing into his was his complete undoing.

Bringing his lips to hers, they were a clash of lips and tongue and heated desire. She pulled his shirt over his head and he tore at her leggings, destroying them so he could feast on every bit of her flesh, and he did. Her hips bucked, his tongue wandered, and she screamed his name like he was the only thing she would ever need again.

When she was warm and ready, he kissed her once more and sank down into her, making her gasp. Their desperate pace slowed as they stared at one another, and Micah committed the moment to memory.

"I promise."

~

GIGGLING AND FEEDING each other bits of cheese, Micah and Lucy sat head to head at the corner of the kitchen table. She pulled on a pair of leggings she had stored in his drawers months ago, and one of his clean shirts. He loved the way she looked in that shirt in his kitchen, so happy and carefree. Leaning in, he kissed her again, never wanting it to end.

"Sorry to interrupt," Alderic said from the doorway. Chuckling, he made his way across the kitchen to the fridge as Lucy pulled away, blushing. "You two lovebirds have been busy today and I've tried to leave the house to you, but an old Fae gets hungry sometimes."

"I'm sorry," Lucy said, blushing. "I never meant to keep anyone away." She stood, flattened her shirt and walked over to Alderic, smiling. "It is so great to see you again."

"Same to you, Lucy," he said sincerely. "I knew you'd be back," he said, then shot an *I told you so* look to Micah. "What took you so long?"

"It's a long story," she said sheepishly. "I wanted to say thank you, and I'm sorry." Lucy wrapped her arms around her midsection. "I know your sacrifice was immense, but I thank you for freeing Micah." Lucy placed her hand out, landing on his arm—but when her skin connected with his, she jumped back with a yelp.

"What's wrong? Are you okay?" Both Alderic and Micah ran to her, thrown by the strange outburst.

Her eyes widened, and she nodded vigorously. "Yes. Yes, I'm fine." Then she shot her gaze to Alderic, asking, "Where are your soldiers? Call them over to the portal immediately."

"What?" Alderic asked. "I don't understand. The portal is gone, Lucy. There is nothing left there for us."

"Trust me," she said with a smile that reached ear to ear.

Alderic merely nodded and left the room, his eyes furrowed in confusion.

"What's going on, Lu?" Micah asked her.

"Come on, I'll show you," she said, pulling him out the door.

Lucy marched outside directly to the tree stump where the portal once stood. The fallen tree was still on the ground, too large to remove on his own. Micah didn't have it in him to ask the warriors to move it so soon.

A rustle of tree leaves and hurried footsteps followed in their wake, Alderic gathering his brethren as quickly as possible.

"Miss Lucy," Quillan said to her.

"First, let me say thank you to each of you," Lucy said seriously. "Your sacrifice gave my people the upper hand in the war, and if it weren't for you, I truly believe we would have lost many more Fae lives. You all fought valiantly, and you will be honored for many years to come."

Each warrior picked up their staff and slammed it to the ground in unison—their typical way of communication.

"Thank you," Quillan said, stepping forward. "But why are we gathered around the broken portal? There is nothing left for us here."

"You're right," she replied with a crooked smile. "There is nothing left here for you, but there was something left for *me*."

She picked up her right hand and held it out to them, showing her palm glowing a bright green light.

"What?" Micah asked, shocked. Then his eyes darted to the tree, and there at the middle of the fallen tree trunk, the same symbol began to glow, first green, then white.

He looked back at Lucy's hand and watched as the emerald green mist soared from her palm and wound around her body, then the felled tree.

"It's time for you to go home," Lucy said with a grateful smile.

"Can that even be possible?" One of the warriors asked.

"Anything seems to be possible with this one," Alderic said in awe.

"Will we be able to go visit them?" Micah asked her, hope lifting in his chest.

She shook her head. "I'm not sure, but I don't think so. This feels like a one-way trip." Her magic poured out of her in earnest, a green shimmering mist twirling like a tornado. "But I would hurry if I were you, because someone here is awfully excited."

Micah looked at Alderic and Quillan, words not coming to him. He wasn't ready to say goodbye—they barely had time together.

As if Alderic could read his mind, he nodded and clasped Micah on the shoulder. "I will stay if you ask me to." His voice was quiet and full of love.

Micah considered it. Having Alderic would bridge that gap between his life and his mom's. It would help him understand his magic. It would mean everything.

But this was not Alderic's home, and there were so many others who relied on him that needed him more.

"You have done so much for me. I just ask if you find a way back, come visit." Micah said, taking in a deep breath of air. "Until then... Thank you."

They met in a warm embrace and Micah knew it would be the last time he ever saw anyone from The Elderwood ever again.

"Goodbye," Alderic told him. "You have made the Lumen legacy something to be proud of."

Quillan smiled and clasped him on the shoulder. "You are a worthy man to know."

Then, the warriors and Alderic stood before the broken tree, and Lucy's magic came out in a rush, surrounding them. The immensity of its light grew and grew until it became too bright. Micah covered his eyes with his hand, trying to see, until suddenly, a flash of light so bright forced Micah onto the ground.

When he opened his eyes and stood, the men were gone and Lucy's green mist had vanished.

"What happened? Did it work?" Micah asked.

Lucy smiled and nodded. "They are gone, back to The Elder-wood." Then she lifted her hand and looked down at her right palm. It was clear, no sign of the sigil anywhere. "My magic is gone, too."

Micah's smile dropped. "What do you mean? Are you okay?" He

held her hand in his and looked it over, analyzing her face, trying to ensure she was safe.

"Yes," she laughed. "I don't feel it anymore inside of me, but I can tell..." she closed her eyes. "It's happy. It's home." Then she took his face in her hands and kissed him gently. "And so am I."

EPILOGUE

ANITA

Anita sat at the desk that was now hers. The entire study belonged to her now, in fact, as head of house. She sat in the same wingback chair her husband once sat in, and looked around the room. While there were things she was excited to change, like more windows for better light, and she was definitely going to burn Jasper's desk, there were other things she was excited to keep, like the oversized fireplace that really had no place in a room this size or the comfortable couches her family now sat in when they gathered.

That in of itself was the biggest change through this entire ordeal... Her family was once so separated by linear expectations. Tradition always expected the eldest sons to take over the family business. Then, the eldest daughter was promised to a formidable Fae. Over time, the youngest children would follow in the elder's footsteps... There was really no room for true conversation. There wasn't time to talk about wants and desires, and there was certainly no space for talking over fears.

But now that had all changed.

Her family sat in this room countless times, working together and listening to one another.

The only thing that could have made it perfect was if Corvus was there to see it all.

Over the past months, she liked to think he was around, watching her, sending his love from the great beyond. But more than anything, she missed talking to him. She had taken to writing him notes; it made her feel that he was closer. And every time she felt overwhelming joy or pain, or if it was just a slow, rainy day, she did just that.

Dearest Corvus,

Life has a funny way of leading you to be exactly where you are meant to be... While I wish it were you here by my side, I know that you live on through our children. I see it in their shining eyes when they are up to something devious. I see it in their smiles when they are overcome with joy. I see it in their immense power that you have shared with them, creating some of the toughest Fae to ever walk the realm.

It has been quite interesting to see the landscape of Denora change—in both our connections to one another and the way our government is run.

Lord Renfro has expanded his reach from the North to the rest of Denora, uniting us as one strong realm once again. He has also opened the gates to our business as we oversee the mining of ore from the North. We are using it to improve our weaponry as we no longer have access to The Elderwood.

Hugh and Gregory are working hard in the South. They work closely with me and assist me here in Central Denora when I am needed in the North. Hugh and Lisette are doing wonderfully and our grandchild is a magnificent delight.

Wes has taken a liking to his new position as commander of the military. The king offered him the title of Duke Baum, but he respectfully declined, saying he'd rather be hands-on with his soldiers. Your gifts to him have helped him find who he really is and what he truly wants in this life. I have never seen him happier. Although, I suspect his additional time with that hilarious Brax has something to do with it. Can you believe she called him a moldy corn cob last week?

Tristan has been here at the house with me much more lately. He spends so much time with Henry and Simon, it really is a blessing. Tristan has taken a liking to art and has been seeing a counselor for his trauma during the war. It has been a hard road for him, and we are so proud of his progress.

Henry and Simon have found an interest in farming and have been taking their lessons straight to the fields, though their tutors seem to despise it.

To be quite frank, my favorite part of this "changed Denora" are these new roles the king has allowed Denorans. So many Fae are following their heart, and there is much joy in the kingdom.

Lucy has followed her heart, as well. You were right about her all along. She is so much more—our warrior of light.

You know, I laughed when you gave Wes your light and Lucy your shadows. Initially, I thought your magic had made a mistake. I thought the light would go to Lucy for her namesake and the shadows to Wes for his never ending brooding, but I see now that you made no errors. You gave Lucy the shadows to show her not to be afraid of the dark sides of her and light to Wesley to allow him to shine brighter than the sun.

You have always guided our family, and I know you will continue to do so. In the meantime, I will lead our family with the love and compassion you've always shared with me, with as much of your stubbornness as I can muster. Our love has always been a choice, and I would choose it again and again.

Thank you for giving our love wings to fly and to follow our family across the realms. You are always with us and will forever have my heart. There is no force that can ever separate us, and you will be mine for all time.

Your dearest love,

Anita

"Are you almost ready, Madame?" Bernard asked her from the

doorway. He gave her a polite smile as he straightened his ornate uniform he only ever took out for formal occasions.

"Absolutely," Anita said. "Just one more moment."

P.S.

Lucy picked violet flowers for her wedding in remembrance of you. They are stunning, just like her. You would be so proud. I'm sorry the two of you didn't have more time together, but we feel you with us today on her wedding day. Send a butterfly her way.

And with that, Anita Baum sealed her letter to her deceased husband, straightened her magnificent flowing gown, and walked to the garden where Lucy was to marry Micah, and they would live side by side in an equal partnership because their love was a choice, too. And in those choices, they would always choose to try to understand, they would always choose to forgive, and they would always choose to love.

EPILOGUE
LUCY

Pull. Slide. Sand.

The same movements that once brought her peace in a time of turmoil now gave her peace in a time of complete and utter joy. She sat under the great shade of the trees in their yard as she looked back on the past decade of her life. Her father would be gone for ten years that week and it was causing many difficult memories to reappear.

Memories of her father's death.

Flashbacks to the icy male who tried to take everything away from her.

But also the reassuring comfort of the male who gave her life once again.

"Abe! Get back over here!" Micah yelled from the line of trees, chasing after a barefoot little boy in overalls.

Abe cackled as he sped away from his father, sprinting directly to the tree house Micah made him on his 3rd birthday. "You can't get me, dad!" His sweet voice called out.

Lucy laughed as Micah tripped over a branch and caught himself at the last minute. "Man, is it me or has he gotten faster?"

"It's those Fae genetics." Lucy winked at her husband, and he reached down and gave her a kiss. She would never get tired of those kisses.

"I'm trying to get his shoes on," Micah said, holding up a pair of gym shoes and a pair of socks. "I swear, hanging out with Brax and he's become more feral than ever."

"Abe!" Lucy called to him in singsong. "Mommy wants to hear another story!"

Micah gave her a look that said *that's not going to work*, but Lucy just raised her eyebrows and waited him out. She knew exactly what Abe loved most, and it was telling anyone within earshot his favorite stories.

Slowly, little footsteps made their way to Lucy, and when she turned she saw Abe, all of six years old, holding up a stick and brandishing it like a sword.

"Daddy and Uncle Wes once battled alongside a dragon, Mommy! Did you know that?"

She feigned shock. "I did not! Why don't you sit down and tell me all about it." She patted the seat next to her on the long wooden bench.

"Yeah! Auntie Brax came in on a DRAGON and then it was all like *rooooarrrr*!!! Then Daddy fought with his axe like *swing swing*, and then Uncle Wes used his flashlight powers and melted the bad guys brains!" As he told the story, Lucy casually put on his socks and laced his shoes, tying them tight.

"And I was just there to cheer them on, huh?" Lucy said, jokingly. She always loved listening to her child, a perfect little mesh of Fae and mortal upbringing. He believed in magic, but only saw bits and pieces in their lives. Abe traveled with them back and forth between realms and they were waiting to see if his mortal or Fae genetics were stronger before they decided to follow any educational pathways.

Lucy was perfectly happy if Abe wound up with no magic. She

loved him more than words could describe, and she was proud of the life she and Micah had built.

"No, Mommy," Abe said, like she was crazy. "You were there as their protector. That's what you do, Momma. You keep us all safe." He smiled and his toothless grin made her smile in return.

"And where did you hear that story?" Lucy asked, surprise filling her.

"That's the story Daddy and Uncle Wes tell me all the time!" Abe proclaimed. "You should see when we get Uncle Tristan to play, too. He always picks to play you and he grabs the blankets to make the shadows." Abe jumped off the bench and zoomed around the yard with his arms outstretched, pretending to carry a blanket over his shoulders.

She bit her bottom lip, and her eyebrows furrowed, trying to keep in the tears.

Micah sat down next to her. "I always invite you to play, you know." He nudged her shoulder with his.

"That's what you tell him?" She looked at her husband with tears brimming in her eyes.

"You can cry around me," he said, wiping away a tear that escaped. "And yes, that is how the story goes. I think Hugh was the one to tell it first, and it's been his favorite story ever since."

"Well you don't need to exaggerate," Lucy said with a huff of laughter, wiping the wetness from her cheeks.

Micah grabbed her chin and turned it toward him slowly. "There is no exaggeration, Lu. You are our protector. You always will be." Then he kissed her softly, only to be interrupted by Abe jumping into their lap to separate them, pulling on Micah's hand and demanding more play time.

Micah gave her a quick peck and followed Abe into the forest, talking of dragons, and shadow shifters, and the most beautiful place they could ever travel.

The leaves overhead ruffled in the breeze and the sun shone brightly as they danced. Lucy closed her eyes as she listened to the joyous laughter from her son and gratitude filled her from head to toe.

Tonight is a full moon, she thought to herself with a giggle.

So many years ago she was stranded in Joterra, waiting for a full moon so she could recharge her amulet and rush back to her home. She never thought her life would be filled with so much love, all thanks to a dying amulet, a quarter moon, and the man who stole her heart.

Acknowledgments

We made it.

It has been a little over two years, and the end is finally here. We dove right into The Lumen Legacy and have experienced it all together. Well, all of us, and Lucy, of course.

We've traveled to Joterra, to fawn over our broody and reliable Micah. We've journeyed through to The Elderwood and fell in love with the most beautiful landscape. We've explored all over Denora, from the cold icy North to the exhilarating South. We've battled at the Baum estate and have come out on top. We've met Fae and mortals. We've flown on dragons and rode on shadow shifters. We've solved mysteries and gained alchemy. We've done it all... together.

It's mind blowing to know that I came up with an idea on a whim, and what was supposed to be a free short story has turned into a complete trilogy with a spin-off short story. (If you haven't read <u>The Bowyer's Baker</u> yet, check out my website!)

Through it all, I have had the most amazing support system imaginable. My husband has always cheered me on, encouraging me to follow my dreams, and helping with the logistics to make it happen. He even named the first book! Hubby, I wouldn't be where I am today without you and your love, and it means more to me than I could ever put into words.

Mom, you've been my number one proofreader and supporter, making sure I tie it all up with a nice little bow, and I appreciate all of your time and dedication you've given to me and my series over the years. Not to mention always being my biggest fan and helping me land amazing experiences because of it!

Kids. I am finally done, and yes, I will play jungle animals with you now.

To my friends... You have all pushed me to keep going and I love you for it. From my coworkers asking me why they still see me at work, or friends asking me when the next book is ready, I appreciate your constant support. You've made me feel seen throughout this entire journey, and that is a wild thing. When people introduce me to others and say "and she's an author!" it never fails to make my heart swell with pride.

My writing friends—there are so many of you! Elayna, you've never wavered on your support. Lisa, you always encourage me to keep going. Jess, you read my whole series in a week simply because I needed another set of eyes, I will NEVER forget that! Becca, I love connecting over this journey. Nisha, Daniela, Lisette, Cassandra— The list can truly go on forever, because this industry is a group of amazing individuals who lift each other up. I will forever be grateful for the amazing community I've found in all of you.

To my readers: We made it! Sometimes it felt like the finish line would never come, yet here we are. I hope you are proud of Lucy and the growth she's made. I hope you found a part of yourself somewhere in this book. We all get lost sometimes, but that doesn't mean we stop trying. I hope you see throughout all of these characters: Lucy, Micah, Wes, Anita, Brax—even Ruthani and Tristan—it is okay to be lost sometimes. In relationships, occupations, friendships, families... The world is big and scary, but you don't need to do it alone. Remember to lean on those who love you.

And when you're feeling spicy, call someone a moldy vegetable and see if that helps.

XO SA

About the Author

S.A. Heiden has always lived in her own fictitious world with her nose in a book. She thrives off of coffee, fantasy, and wine and indulged in all three as she wrote her first of many books for you!

When she isn't writing, she's hanging with her family and her dog, Penny.

Keep an eye out for more books to come! Make sure to stay in touch on her website www.saheiden.com, join her newsletter, and follow her on Facebook, Instagram, and Goodreads!

9 7 9 8 9 8 8 2 7 0 9 7 3